MIDDLE SCHOOL
MISADVENTURES

MIDDLE SCHOOL
MISADVENTURES

JASON PLATT

LITTLE, BROWN AND COMPANY
NEW YORK BOSTON

ABOUT THIS BOOK

The illustrations for this book were done in Corel Painter on the Wacom Cintiq companion and colored in Adobe Photoshop. This book was edited by Russ Busse and designed by Christina Quintero. The production was supervised by Erika Schwartz, and the production editor was Annie McDonnell. The text was set in MisterAndMeBook, and the display type is MisterAndMe.

Little, Brown and Company
Hachette Book Group
1290 Avenue of the Americas, New York, NY 10104
Visit us at LBYR.com

First Edition: April 2019

Little, Brown and Company is a division of Hachette Book Group, Inc.
The Little, Brown name and logo are trademarks of Hachette Book Group, Inc.

The publisher is not responsible for websites (or their content) that are not owned by the publisher.

Library of Congress Cataloging-in-Publication Data
Names: Platt, Jason, author, illustrator.
Title: Middle school misadventures / by Jason Platt.
Description: First edition. | New York; Boston : Little, Brown and Company, 2019. | Summary: "In order to avoid extra work, middle schooler Newell agrees to participate in a school-wide talent show—without a talent"— Provided by publisher.
Identifiers: LCCN 2018033369| ISBN 9780316416863 (hardcover) | ISBN 9780316416887 (trade pbk.) | ISBN 9780316416870 (ebook) | ISBN 9780316528832 (library ebk. edition)
Subjects: LCSH: Graphic novels. | CYAC: Graphic novels. | Middle schools—Fiction. | Schools—Fiction. | Talent shows—Fiction. | Fathers and sons—Fiction.
Classification: LCC PZ7.7.P55 Mid 2019 | DDC 741.5/973—dc23
LC record available at https://lccn.loc.gov/2018033369

ISBNs: 978-0-316-41686-3 (hardcover), 978-0-316-41688-7 (pbk.), 978-0-316-41687-0 (ebook), 978-0-316-52967-9 (ebook), 978-0-316-53033-0 (ebook)

Printed in China

1010

Hardcover: 10 9 8 7 6 5 4 3 2 1
Paperback: 10 9 8 7 6 5 4 3 2 1

TO MY MOM, WHO ALWAYS MADE SURE I HAD
PAPER TO DRAW ON,

TO MY WIFE, WHO TOLD ME TO NEVER GIVE UP,

AND, ESPECIALLY TO MY SON—
WITHOUT HIM AND OUR ADVENTURES
THIS BOOK WOULD NOT BE IN YOUR HANDS.

* * *

I'M THE LUCKIEST GUY IN THE WORLD.

CHAPTER ONE
I SWEAR THAT THIS IS A TRUE STORY

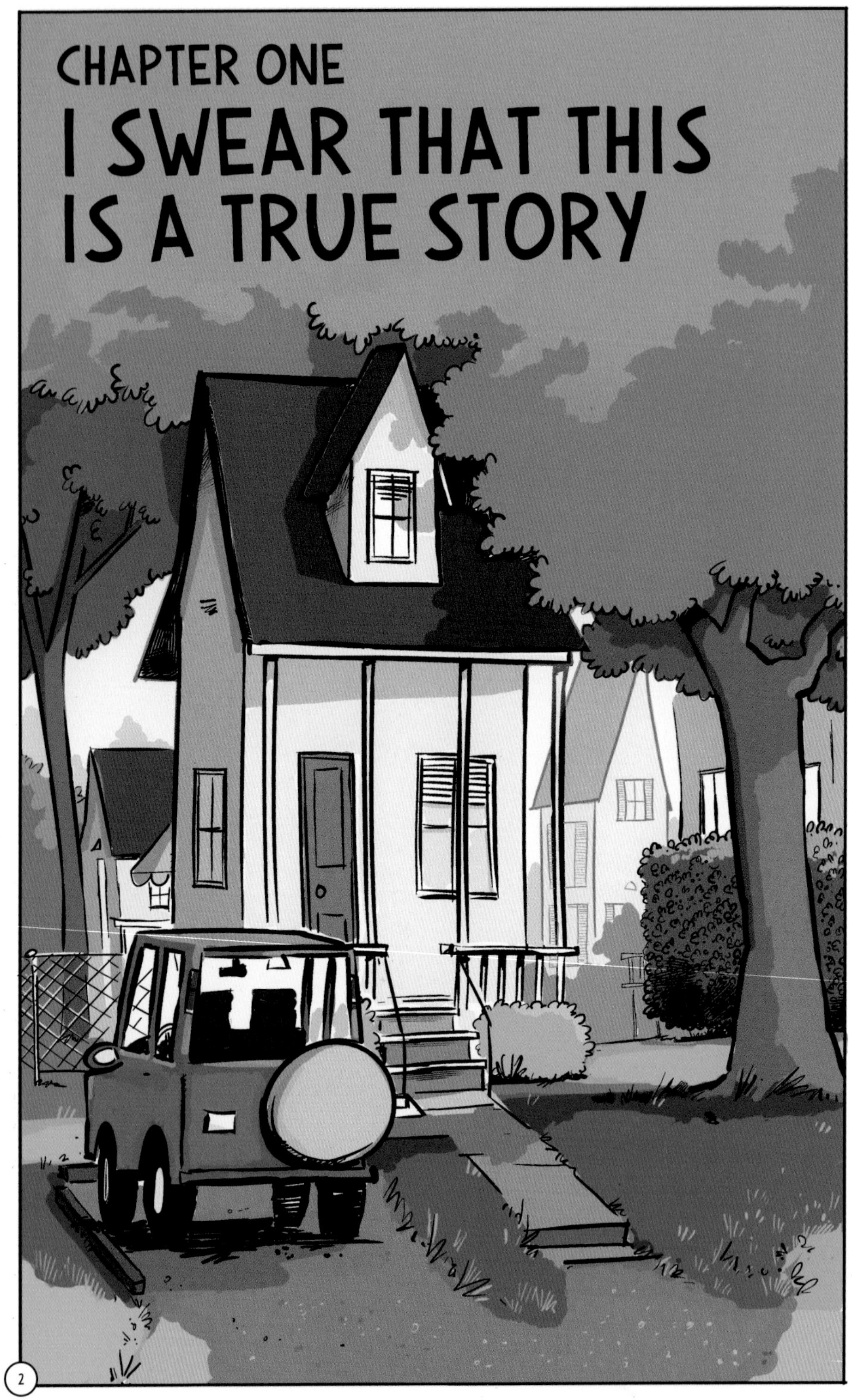

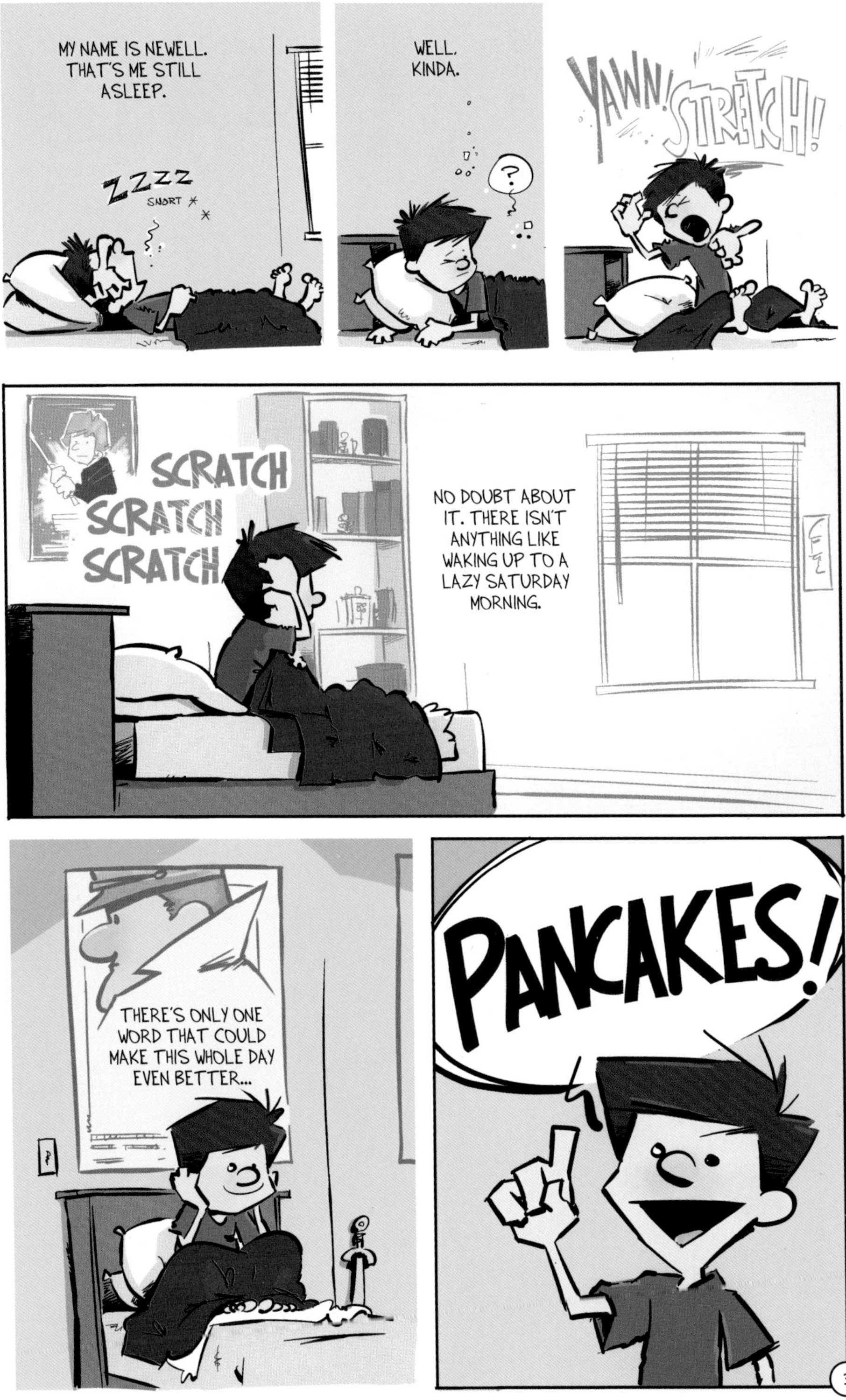
MY NAME IS NEWELL. THAT'S ME STILL ASLEEP.
ZZZZ
SNORT
WELL, KINDA.
?
YAWN! STRETCH!
SCRATCH
SCRATCH
SCRATCH
NO DOUBT ABOUT IT. THERE ISN'T ANYTHING LIKE WAKING UP TO A LAZY SATURDAY MORNING.
THERE'S ONLY ONE WORD THAT COULD MAKE THIS WHOLE DAY EVEN BETTER...
PANCAKES!

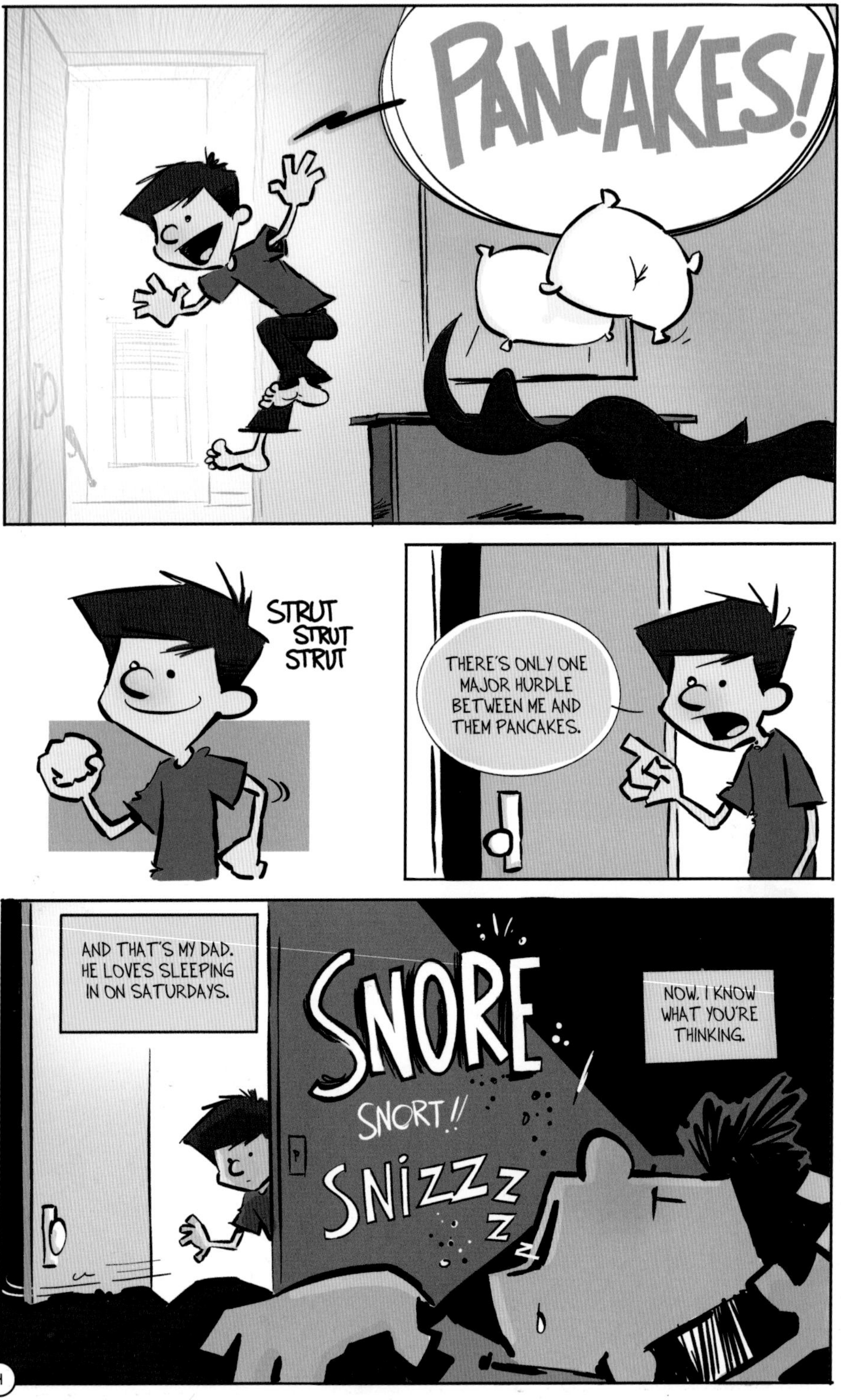
PANCAKES!
STRUT
STRUT
STRUT
THERE'S ONLY ONE MAJOR HURDLE BETWEEN ME AND THEM PANCAKES.
AND THAT'S MY DAD. HE LOVES SLEEPING IN ON SATURDAYS.
SNORE
SNORT!!
SNIZZZ
NOW, I KNOW WHAT YOU'RE THINKING.

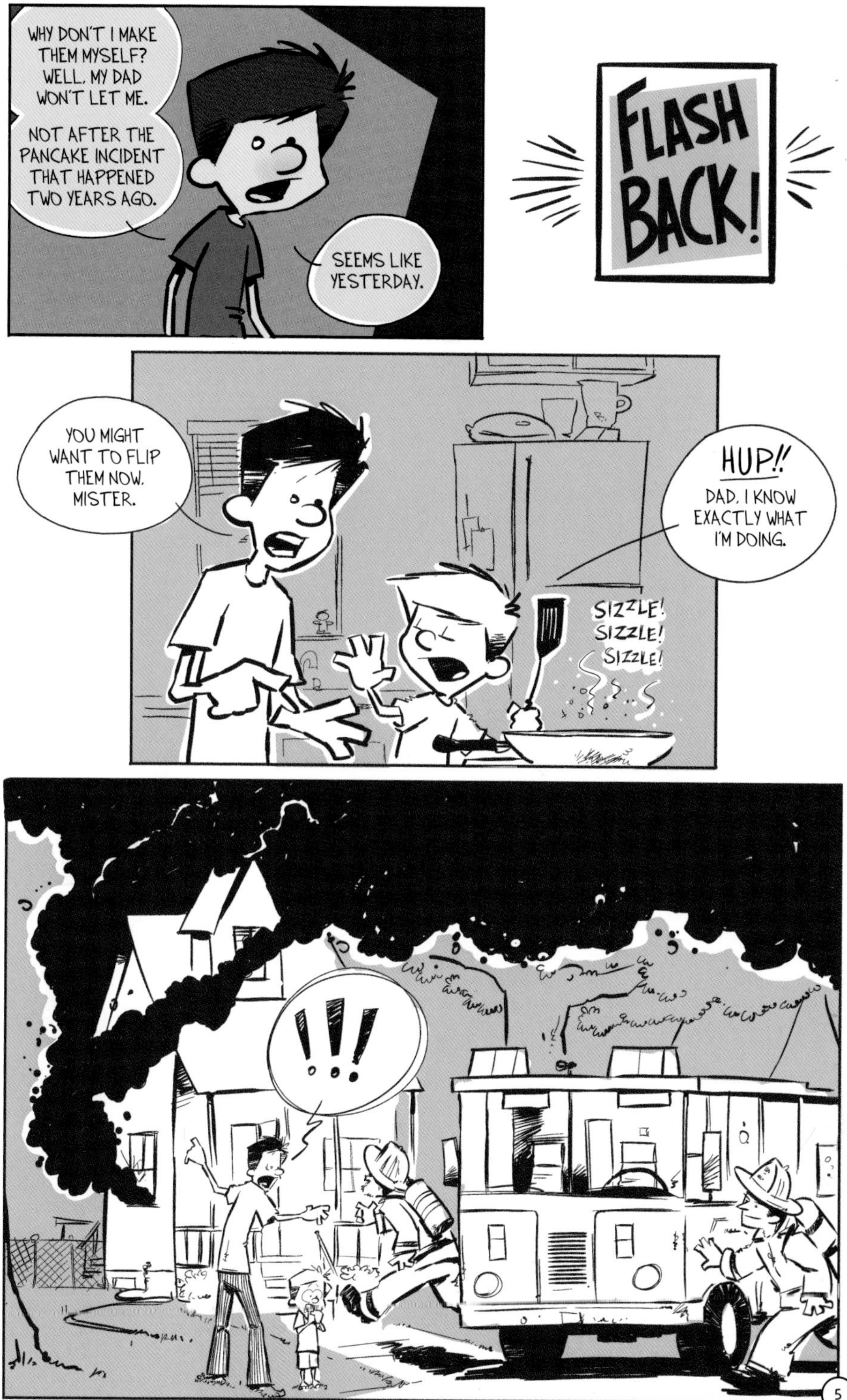
WHY DON'T I MAKE THEM MYSELF? WELL, MY DAD WON'T LET ME.
NOT AFTER THE PANCAKE INCIDENT THAT HAPPENED TWO YEARS AGO.
SEEMS LIKE YESTERDAY.
FLASH BACK!
YOU MIGHT WANT TO FLIP THEM NOW, MISTER.
HUP!!
DAD, I KNOW EXACTLY WHAT I'M DOING.
SIZZLE! SIZZLE! SIZZLE!
!!!

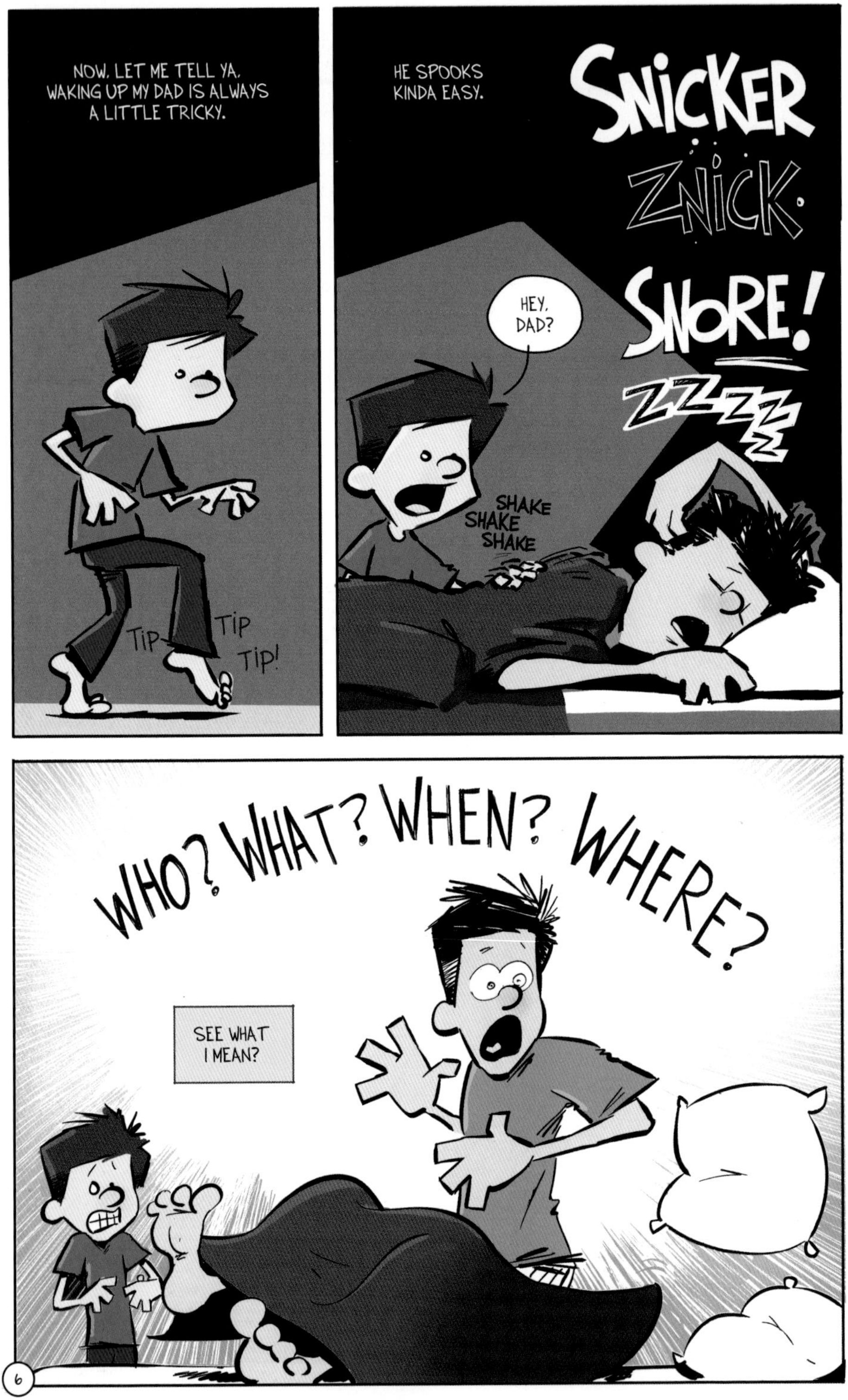
NOW, LET ME TELL YA, WAKING UP MY DAD IS ALWAYS A LITTLE TRICKY.
TIP
TIP
TIP!
HE SPOOKS KINDA EASY.
SNICKER
ZNICK
SNORE!
ZZZZZ
HEY, DAD?
SHAKE SHAKE SHAKE
WHO? WHAT? WHEN? WHERE?
SEE WHAT I MEAN?

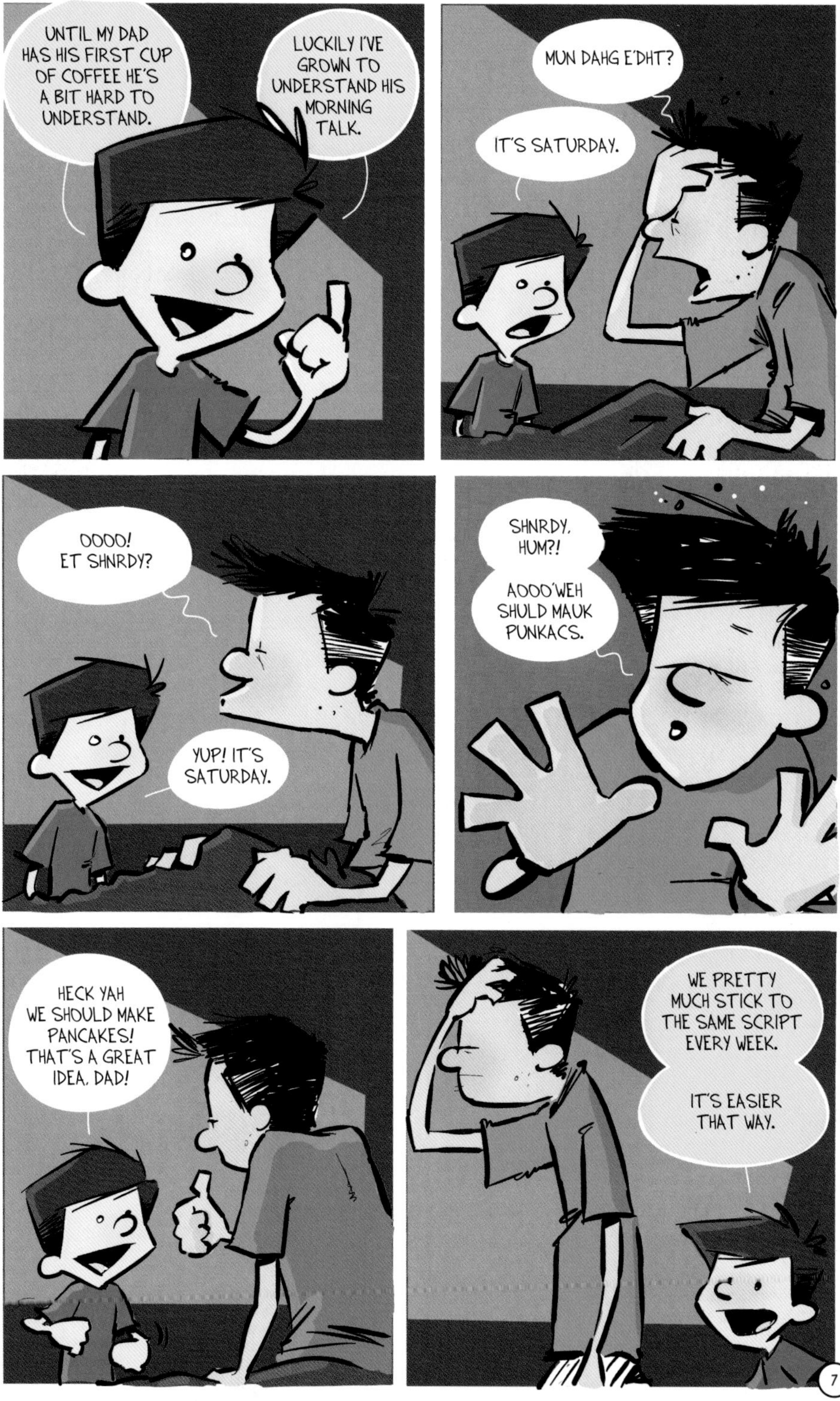
UNTIL MY DAD HAS HIS FIRST CUP OF COFFEE HE'S A BIT HARD TO UNDERSTAND.
LUCKILY I'VE GROWN TO UNDERSTAND HIS MORNING TALK.
MUN DAHG E'DHT?
IT'S SATURDAY.
OOOO! ET SHNRDY?
YUP! IT'S SATURDAY.
SHNRDY, HUM?!
AOOO'WEH SHULD MAUK PUNKACS.
HECK YAH WE SHOULD MAKE PANCAKES! THAT'S A GREAT IDEA, DAD!
WE PRETTY MUCH STICK TO THE SAME SCRIPT EVERY WEEK.
IT'S EASIER THAT WAY.

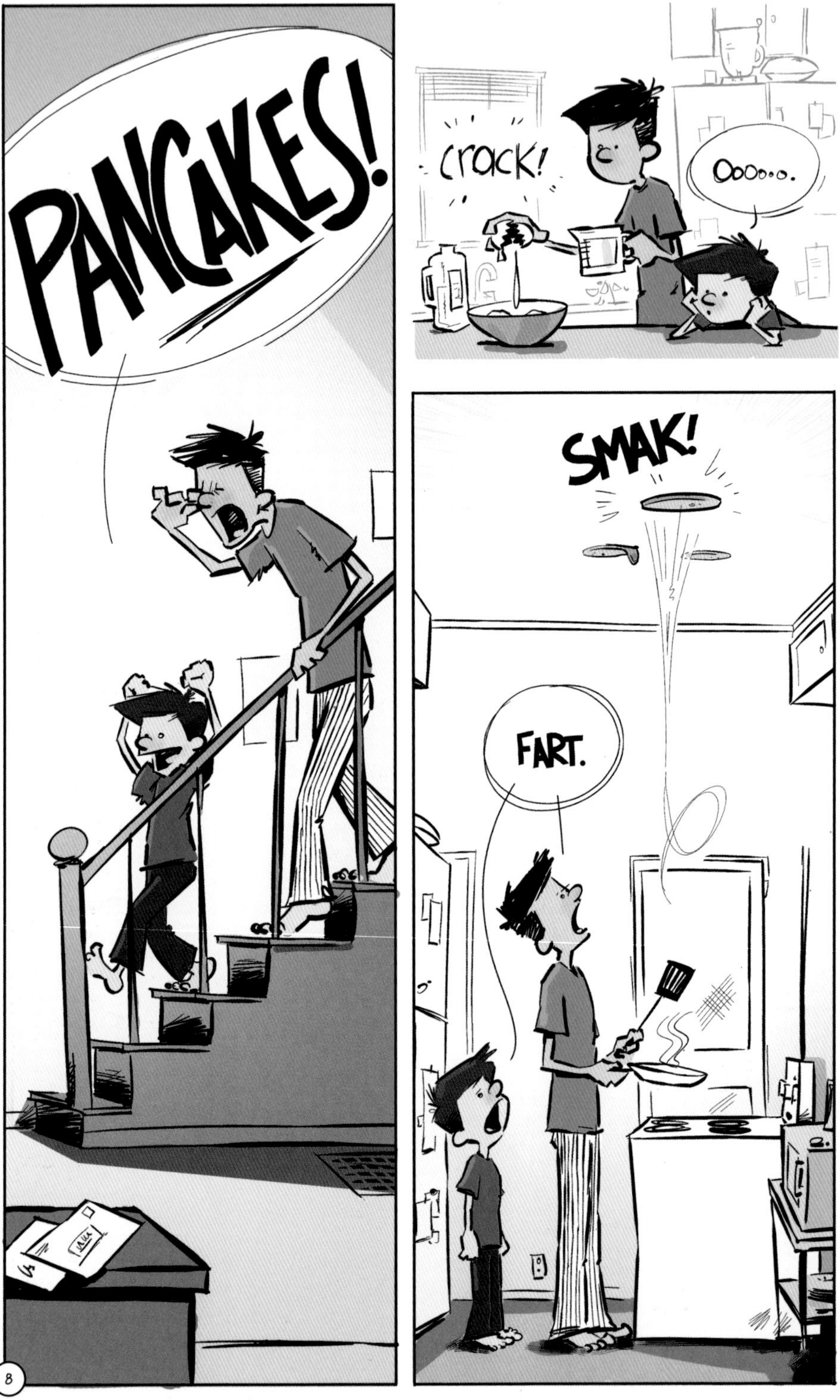
PANCAKES!
Crack!
Oooo.o.
SMAK!
FART.

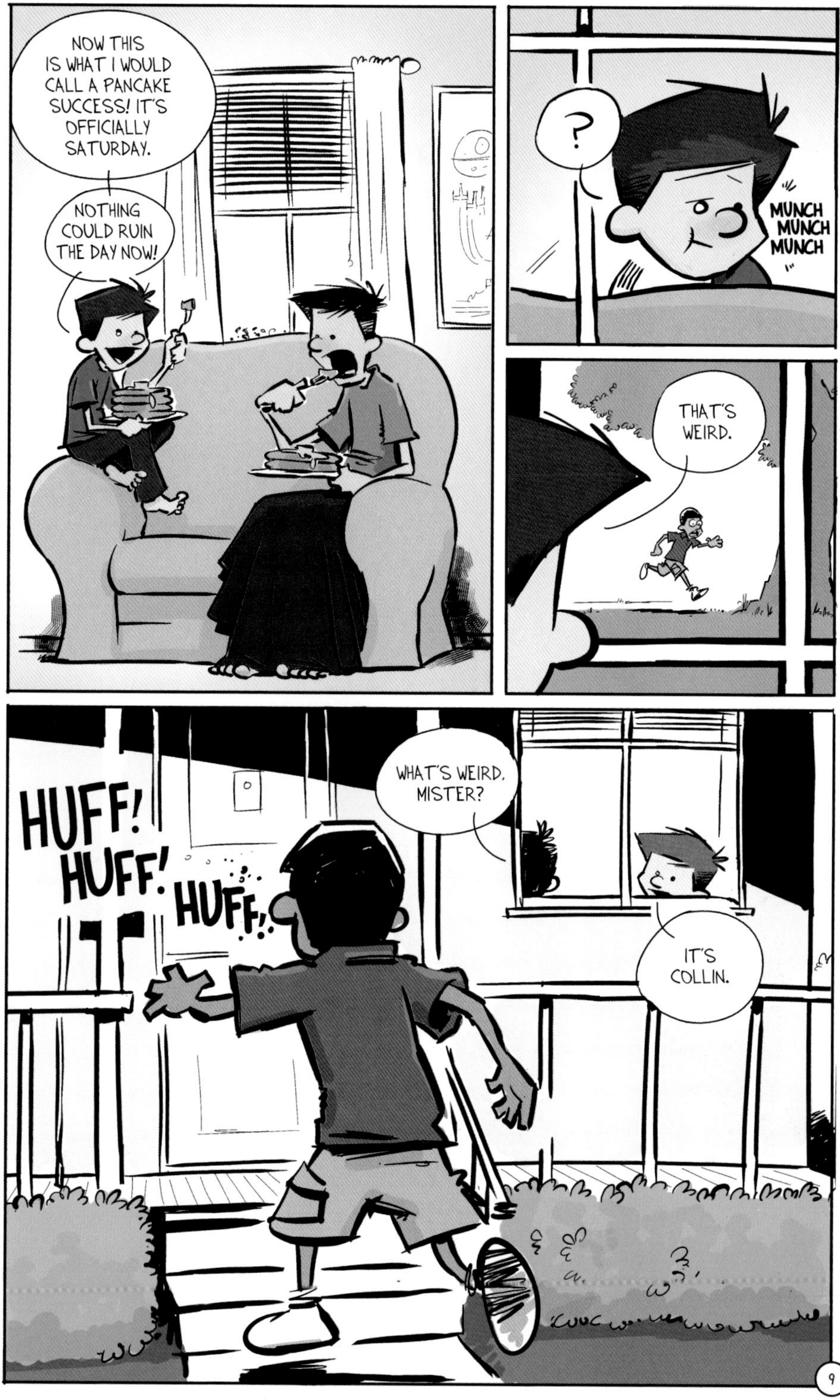
NOW THIS IS WHAT I WOULD CALL A PANCAKE SUCCESS! IT'S OFFICIALLY SATURDAY.
NOTHING COULD RUIN THE DAY NOW!
?
MUNCH MUNCH MUNCH
THAT'S WEIRD.
HUFF! HUFF! HUFF!
WHAT'S WEIRD, MISTER?
IT'S COLLIN.

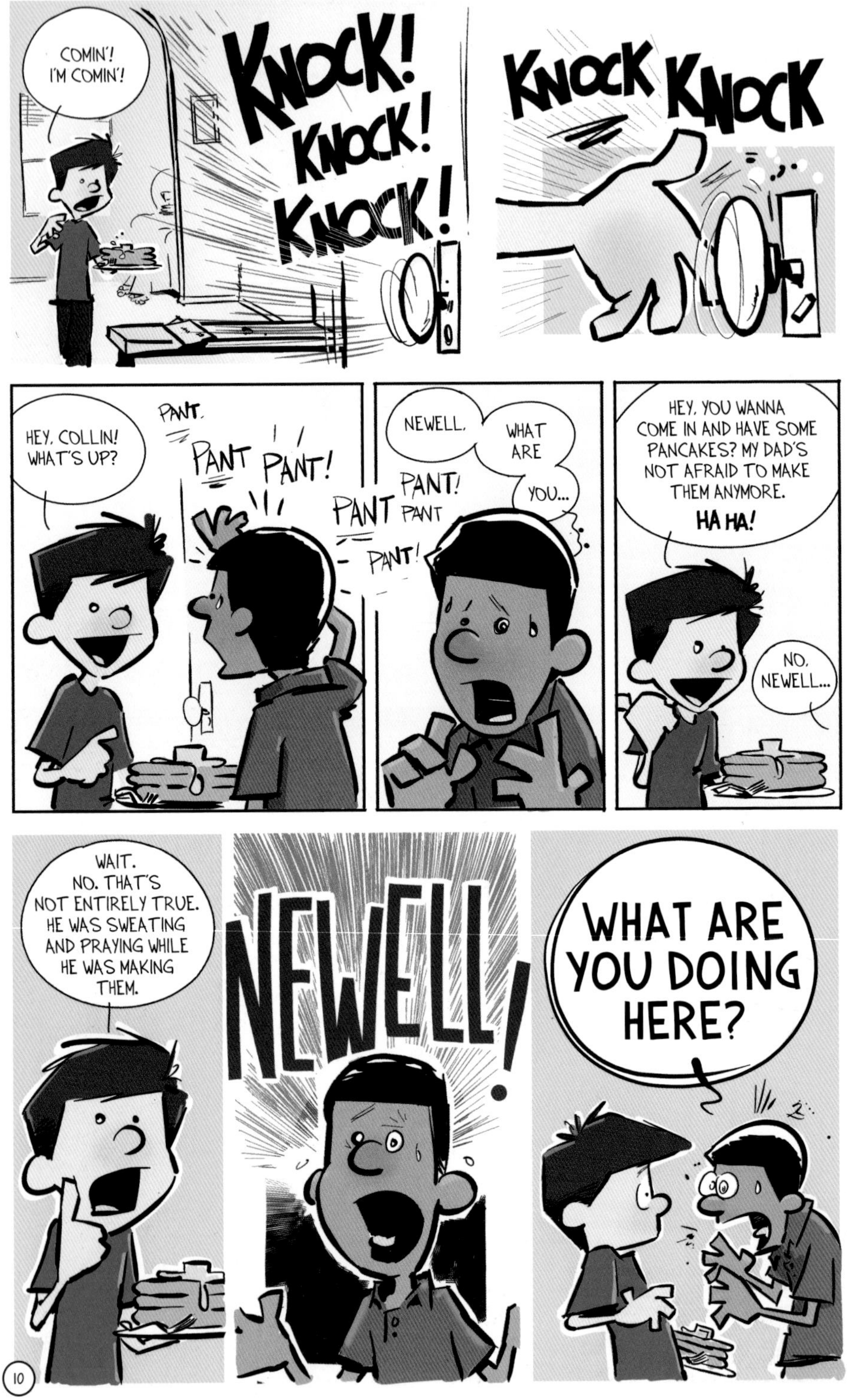
COMIN'! I'M COMIN'!
KNOCK! KNOCK! KNOCK!
KNOCK KNOCK
HEY, COLLIN! WHAT'S UP?
PANT. PANT PANT!
PANT PANT! PANT PANT PANT!
NEWELL,
WHAT ARE
YOU...
HEY, YOU WANNA COME IN AND HAVE SOME PANCAKES? MY DAD'S NOT AFRAID TO MAKE THEM ANYMORE.
HA HA!
NO, NEWELL...
WAIT. NO. THAT'S NOT ENTIRELY TRUE. HE WAS SWEATING AND PRAYING WHILE HE WAS MAKING THEM.
NEWELL!
WHAT ARE YOU DOING HERE?

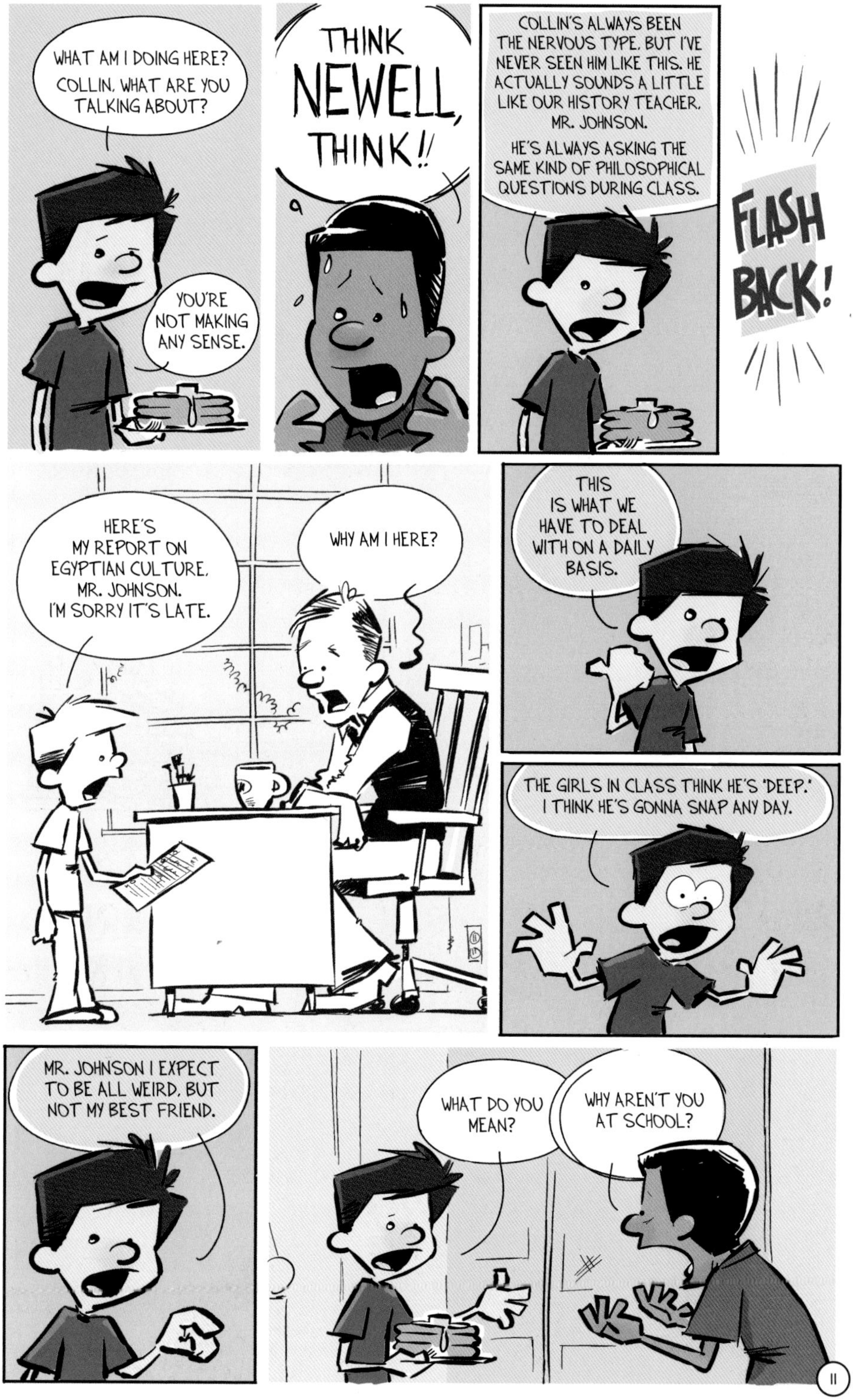
WHAT AM I DOING HERE?
COLLIN, WHAT ARE YOU TALKING ABOUT?
YOU'RE NOT MAKING ANY SENSE.
THINK NEWELL, THINK!!
COLLIN'S ALWAYS BEEN THE NERVOUS TYPE, BUT I'VE NEVER SEEN HIM LIKE THIS. HE ACTUALLY SOUNDS A LITTLE LIKE OUR HISTORY TEACHER, MR. JOHNSON.
HE'S ALWAYS ASKING THE SAME KIND OF PHILOSOPHICAL QUESTIONS DURING CLASS.
FLASH BACK!
HERE'S MY REPORT ON EGYPTIAN CULTURE, MR. JOHNSON. I'M SORRY IT'S LATE.
WHY AM I HERE?
THIS IS WHAT WE HAVE TO DEAL WITH ON A DAILY BASIS.
THE GIRLS IN CLASS THINK HE'S "DEEP." I THINK HE'S GONNA SNAP ANY DAY.
MR. JOHNSON I EXPECT TO BE ALL WEIRD, BUT NOT MY BEST FRIEND.
WHAT DO YOU MEAN?
WHY AREN'T YOU AT SCHOOL?

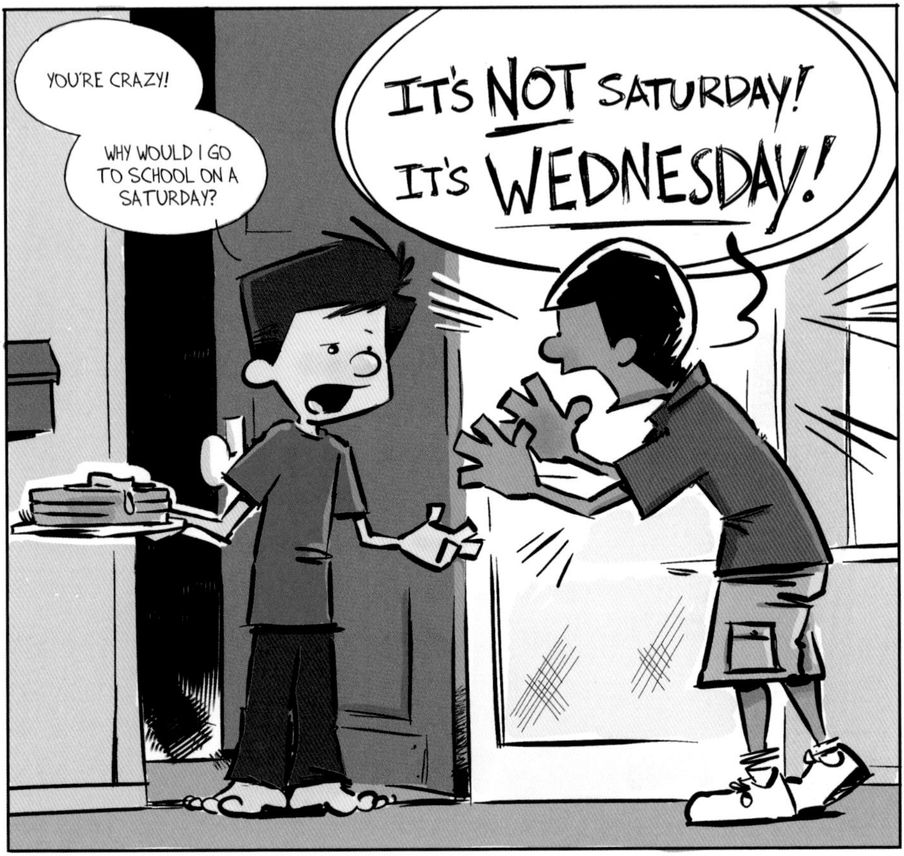
YOU'RE CRAZY!
WHY WOULD I GO TO SCHOOL ON A SATURDAY?
IT'S NOT SATURDAY! IT'S WEDNESDAY!

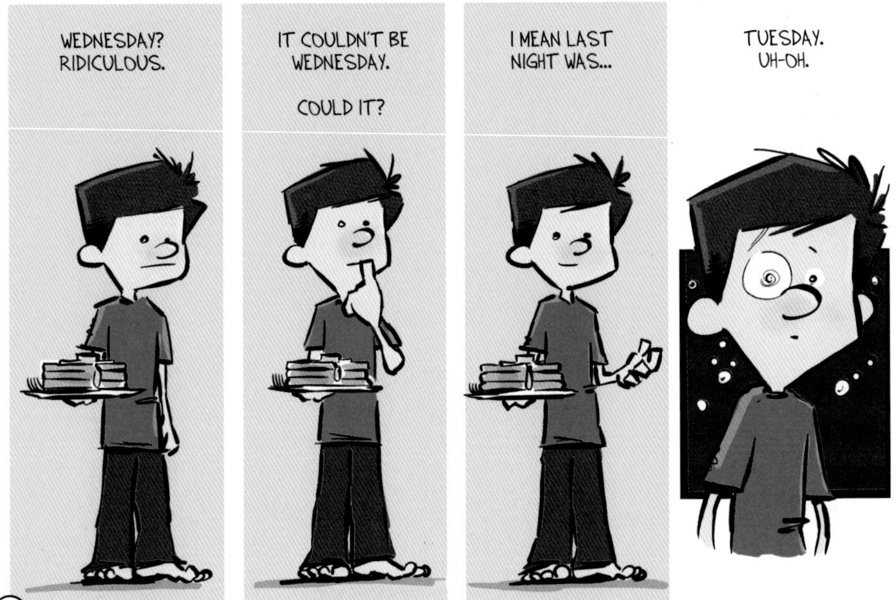
WEDNESDAY? RIDICULOUS.
IT COULDN'T BE WEDNESDAY.
COULD IT?
I MEAN LAST NIGHT WAS...
TUESDAY. UH-OH.

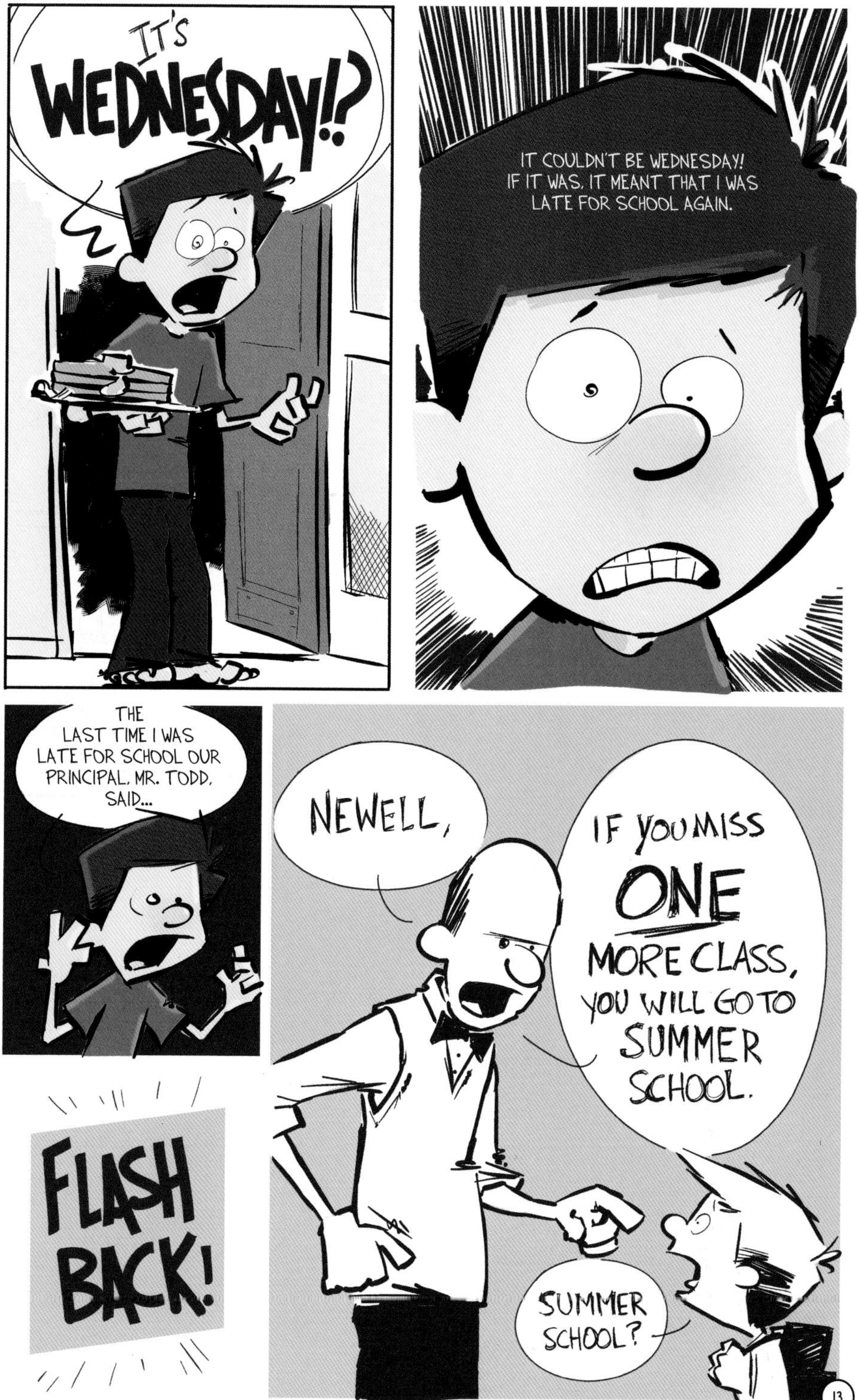
IT'S WEDNESDAY!?
IT COULDN'T BE WEDNESDAY! IF IT WAS, IT MEANT THAT I WAS LATE FOR SCHOOL AGAIN.
THE LAST TIME I WAS LATE FOR SCHOOL OUR PRINCIPAL, MR. TODD, SAID...
FLASH BACK!
NEWELL,
IF YOU MISS ONE MORE CLASS, YOU WILL GO TO SUMMER SCHOOL.
SUMMER SCHOOL?

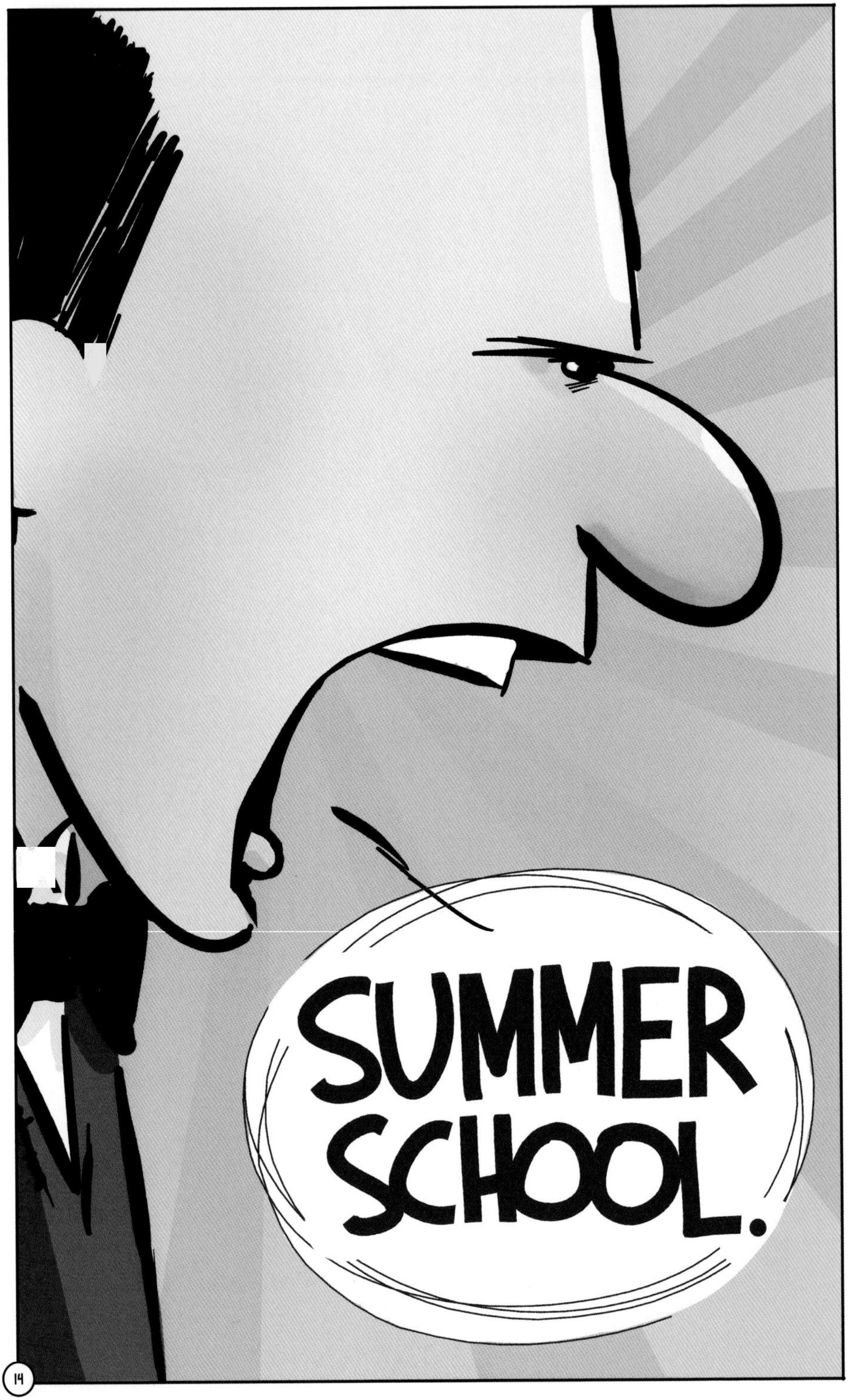
SUMMER SCHOOL.

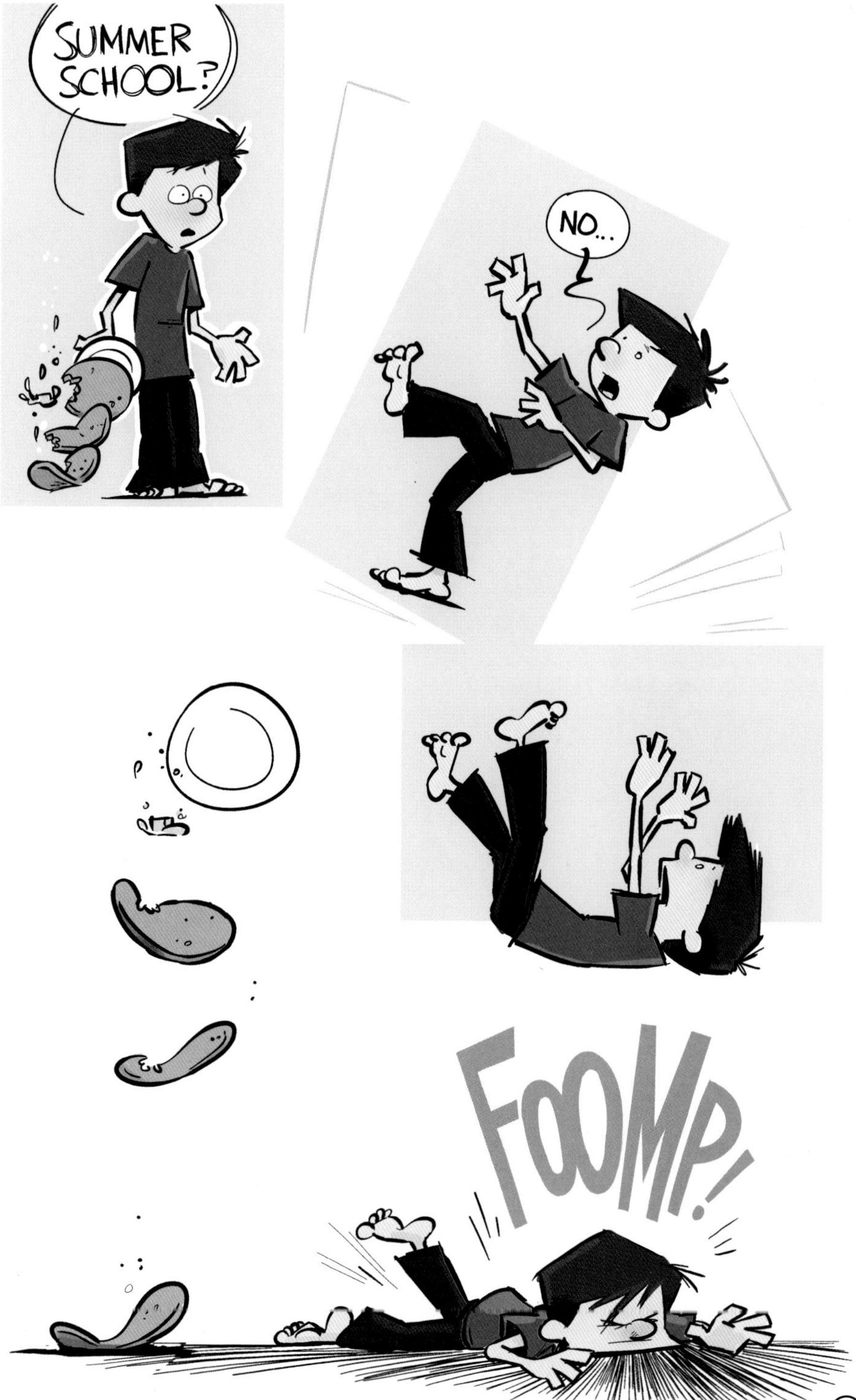
SUMMER SCHOOL?
NO...
FOOMP!

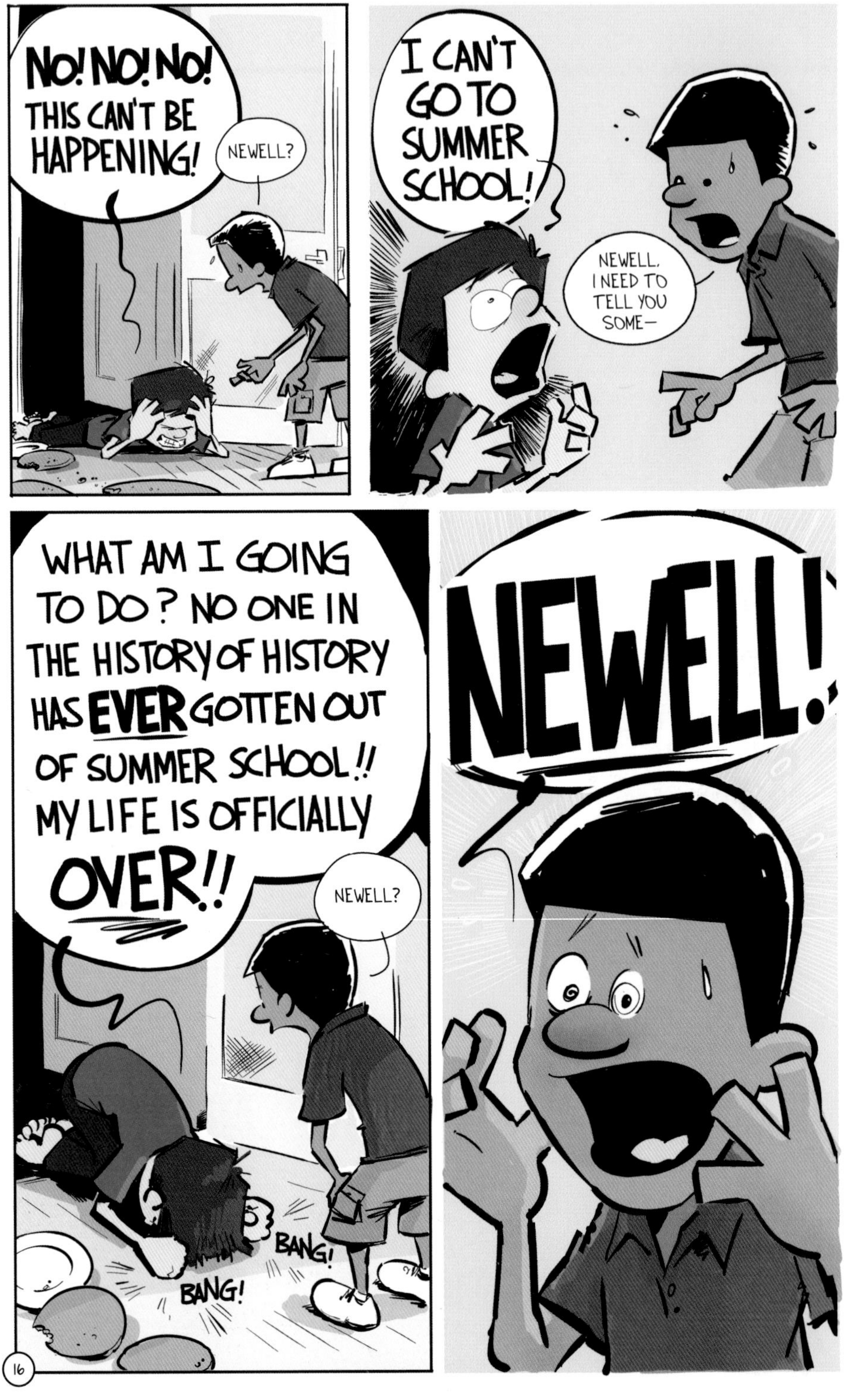
NO! NO! NO! THIS CAN'T BE HAPPENING!
NEWELL?
I CAN'T GO TO SUMMER SCHOOL!
NEWELL, I NEED TO TELL YOU SOME—
WHAT AM I GOING TO DO? NO ONE IN THE HISTORY OF HISTORY HAS EVER GOTTEN OUT OF SUMMER SCHOOL!! MY LIFE IS OFFICIALLY OVER!!
NEWELL?
BANG!
BANG!
NEWELL!

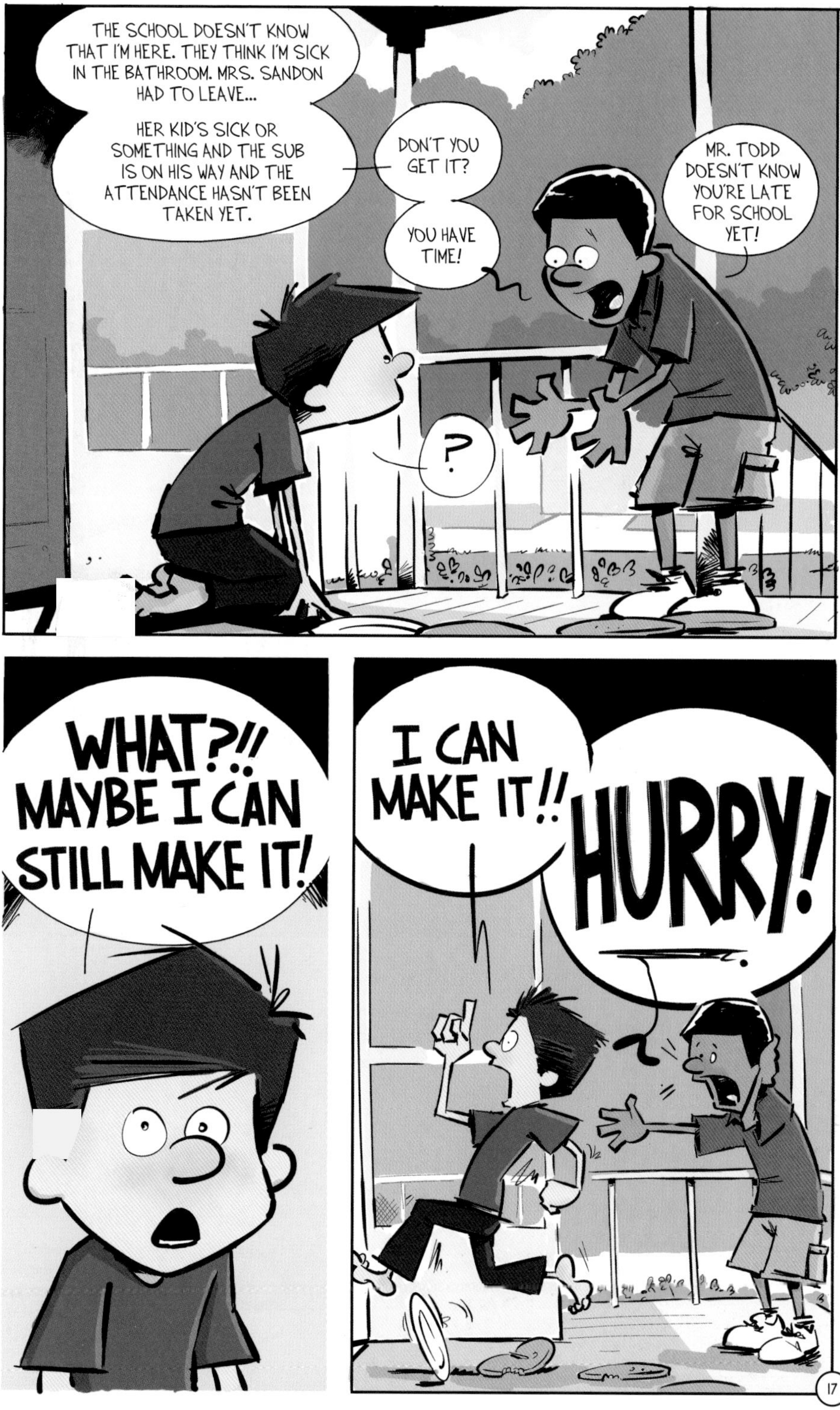
THE SCHOOL DOESN'T KNOW THAT I'M HERE. THEY THINK I'M SICK IN THE BATHROOM. MRS. SANDON HAD TO LEAVE...
HER KID'S SICK OR SOMETHING AND THE SUB IS ON HIS WAY AND THE ATTENDANCE HASN'T BEEN TAKEN YET.
DON'T YOU GET IT?
YOU HAVE TIME!
MR. TODD DOESN'T KNOW YOU'RE LATE FOR SCHOOL YET!
?
WHAT?!! MAYBE I CAN STILL MAKE IT!
I CAN MAKE IT!!
HURRY!

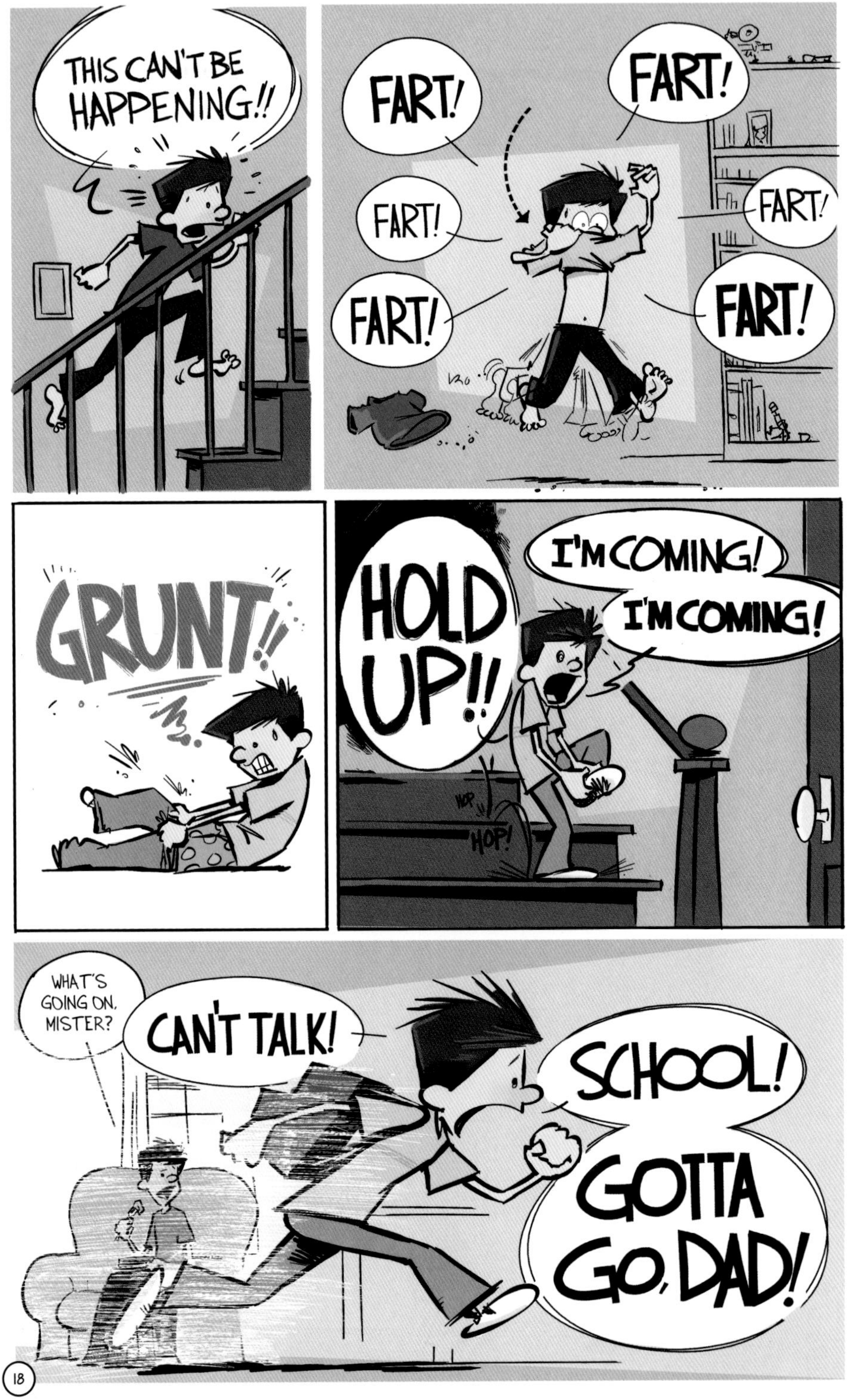
THIS CAN'T BE HAPPENING!!
FART!
FART!
FART!
FART!
FART!
FART!
GRUNT!!
HOLD UP!!
I'M COMING!
I'M COMING!
HOP
HOP!
WHAT'S GOING ON, MISTER?
CAN'T TALK!
SCHOOL!
GOTTA GO, DAD!

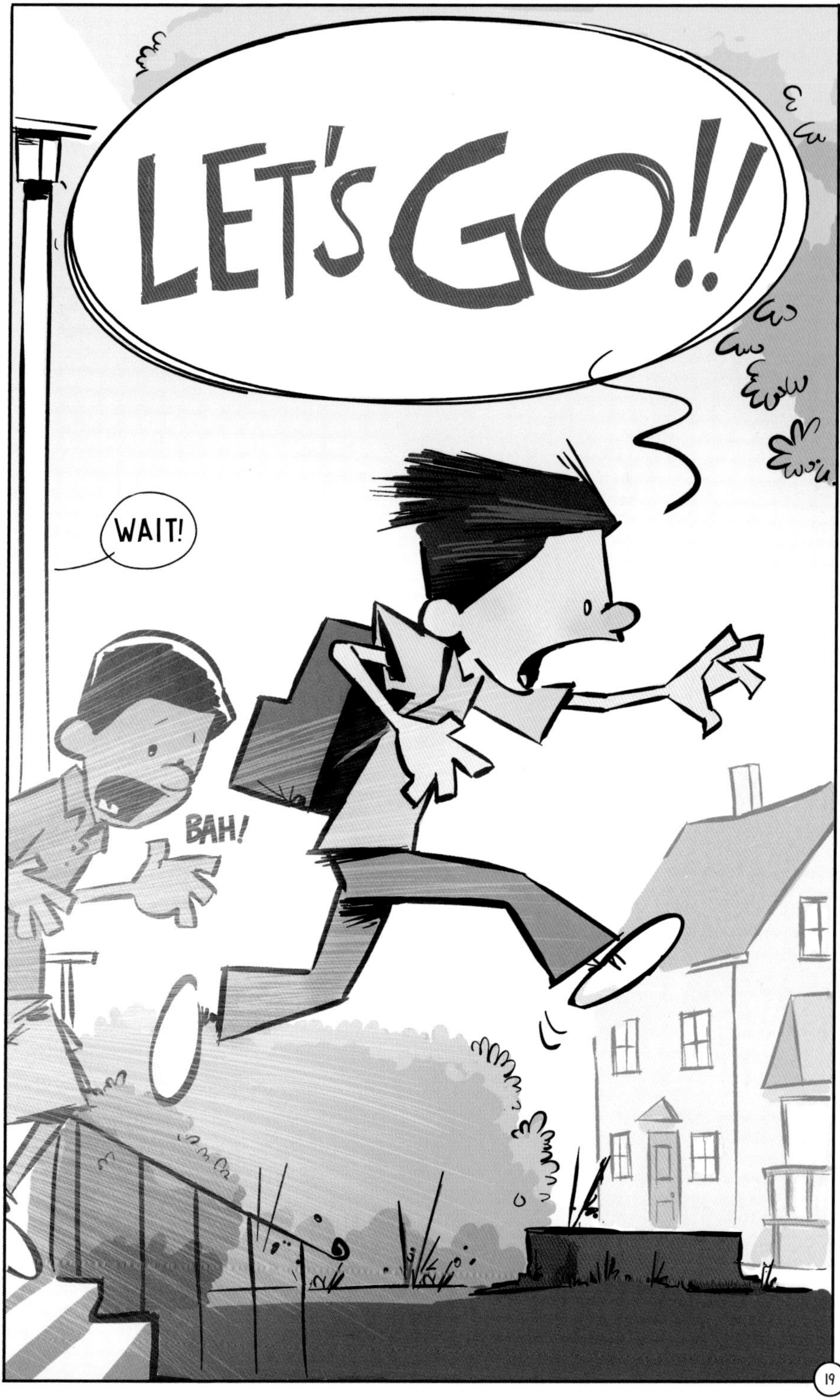
LET'S GO!!
WAIT!
BAH!

CHAPTER TWO
GETTING TO SCHOOL IS HARDER THAN I THOUGHT

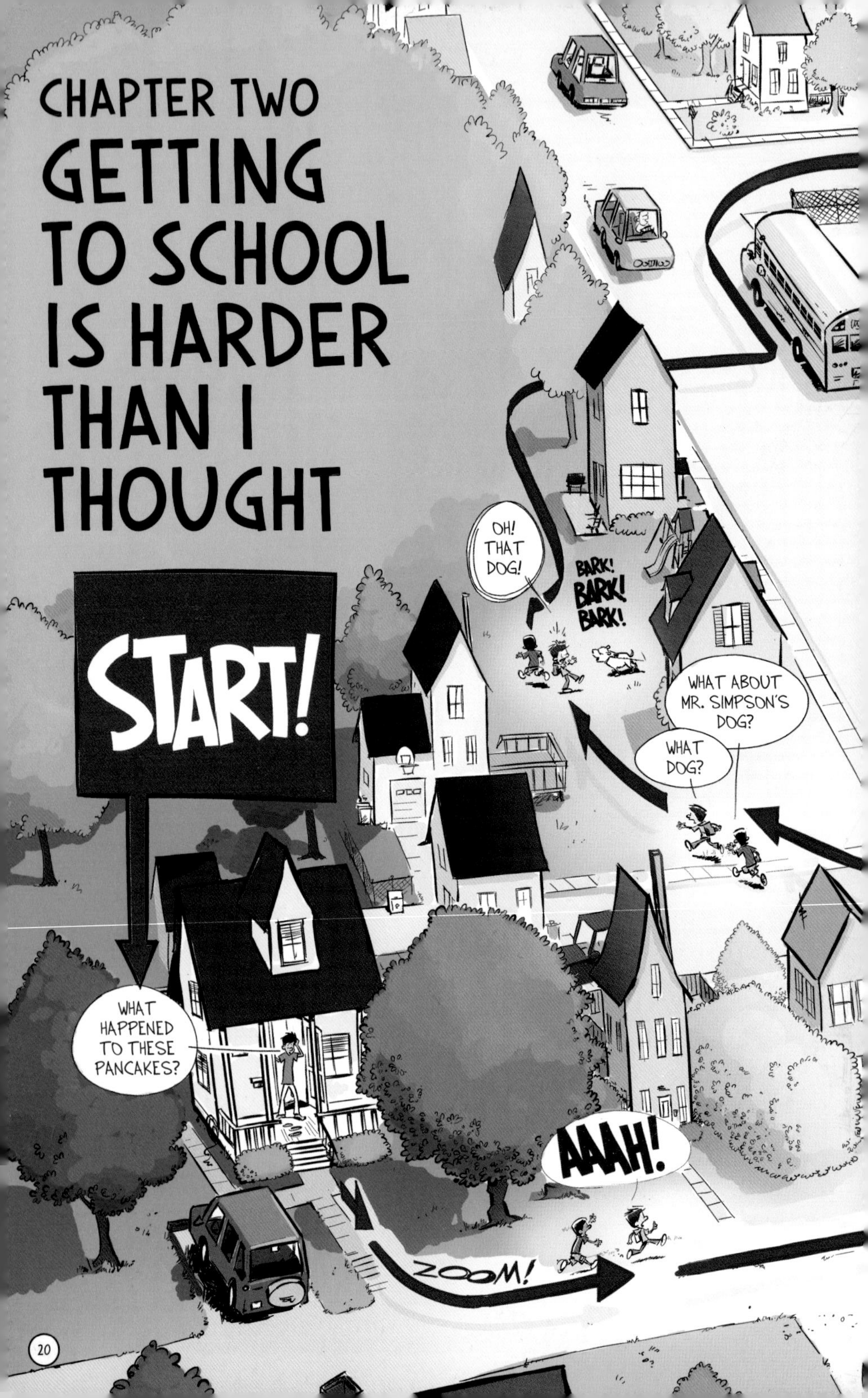
START!
WHAT HAPPENED TO THESE PANCAKES?
ZOOM!
AAAH!
WHAT ABOUT MR. SIMPSON'S DOG?
WHAT DOG?
OH! THAT DOG!
BARK! BARK! BARK!

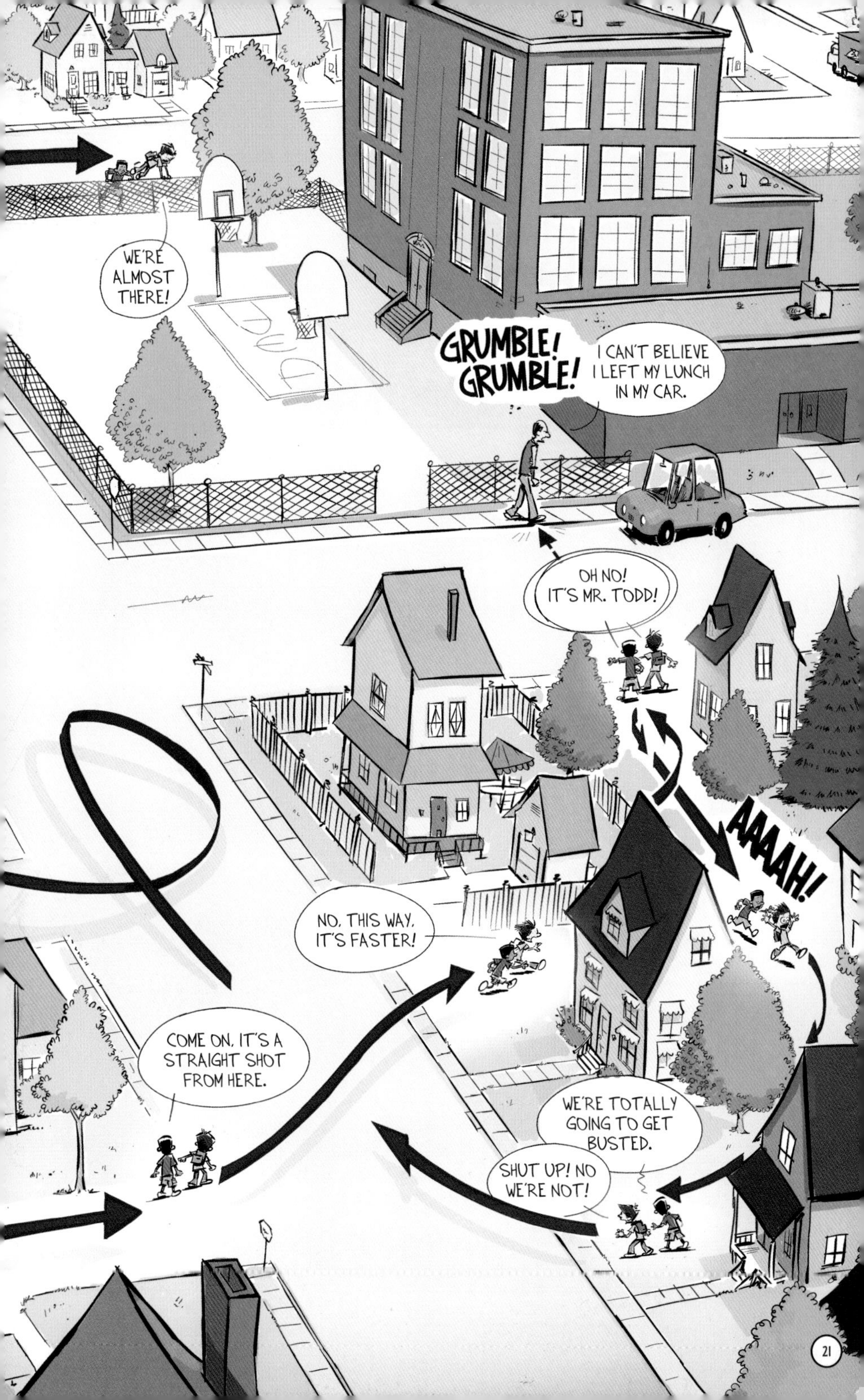
WE'RE ALMOST THERE!
GRUMBLE! GRUMBLE!
I CAN'T BELIEVE I LEFT MY LUNCH IN MY CAR.
OH NO! IT'S MR. TODD!
AAAAH!
NO, THIS WAY, IT'S FASTER!
COME ON, IT'S A STRAIGHT SHOT FROM HERE.
WE'RE TOTALLY GOING TO GET BUSTED.
SHUT UP! NO WE'RE NOT!

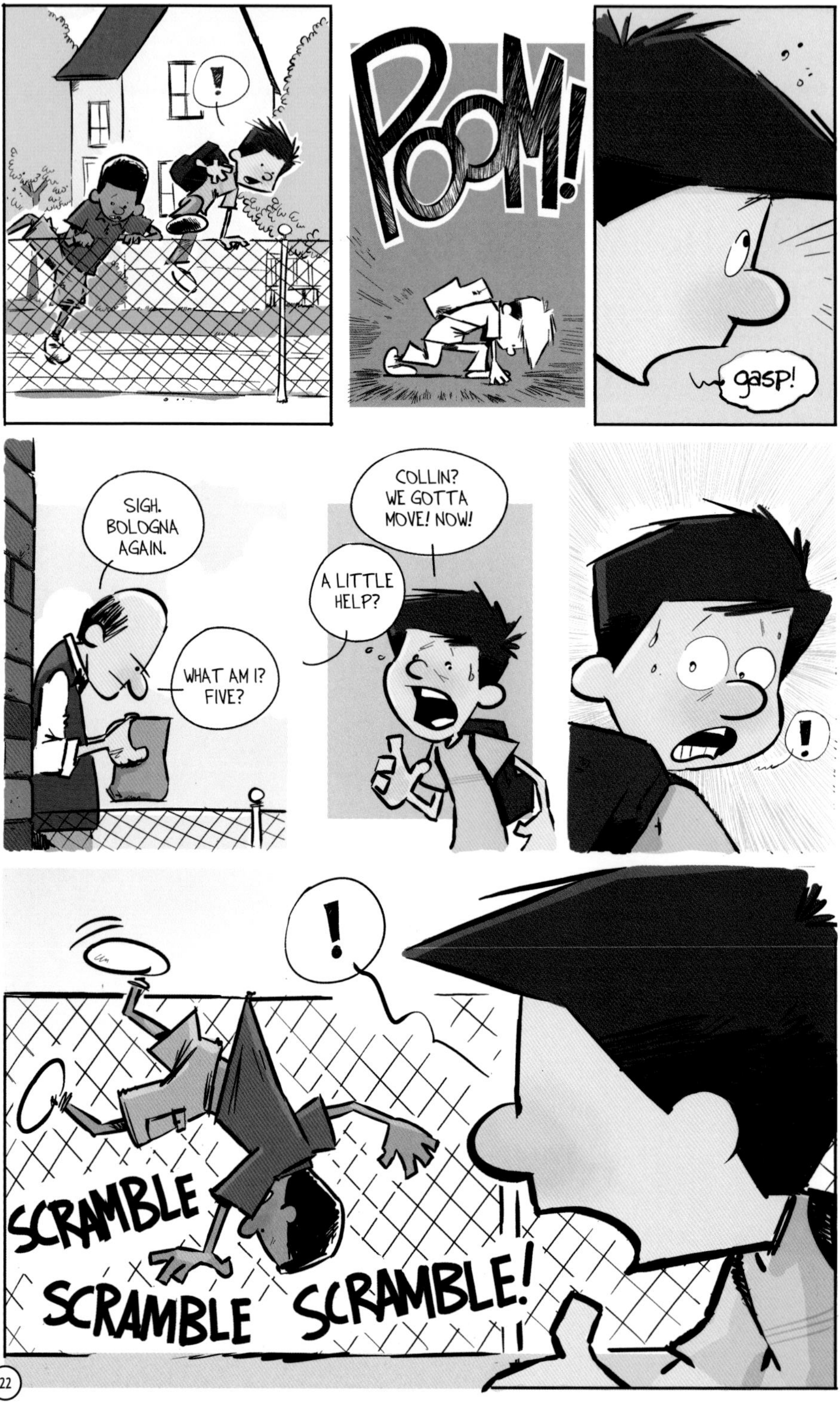
!
POOM!
gasp!
SIGH. BOLOGNA AGAIN.
WHAT AM I? FIVE?
COLLIN? WE GOTTA MOVE! NOW!
A LITTLE HELP?
!
!
SCRAMBLE
SCRAMBLE
SCRAMBLE!

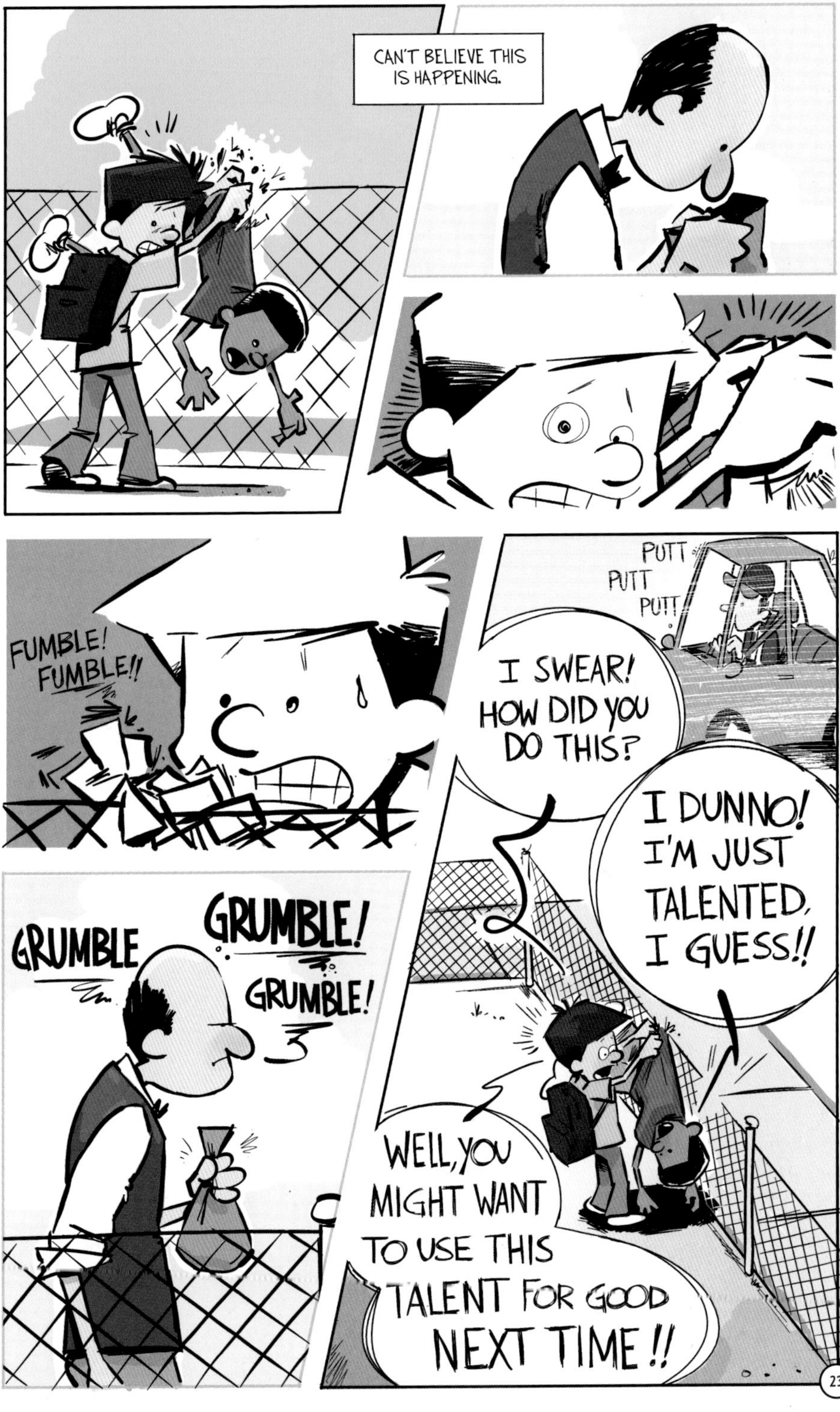
CAN'T BELIEVE THIS IS HAPPENING.
FUMBLE! FUMBLE!!
PUTT PUTT PUTT
I SWEAR! HOW DID YOU DO THIS?
I DUNNO! I'M JUST TALENTED, I GUESS!!
GRUMBLE
GRUMBLE!
GRUMBLE!
WELL, YOU MIGHT WANT TO USE THIS TALENT FOR GOOD NEXT TIME!!

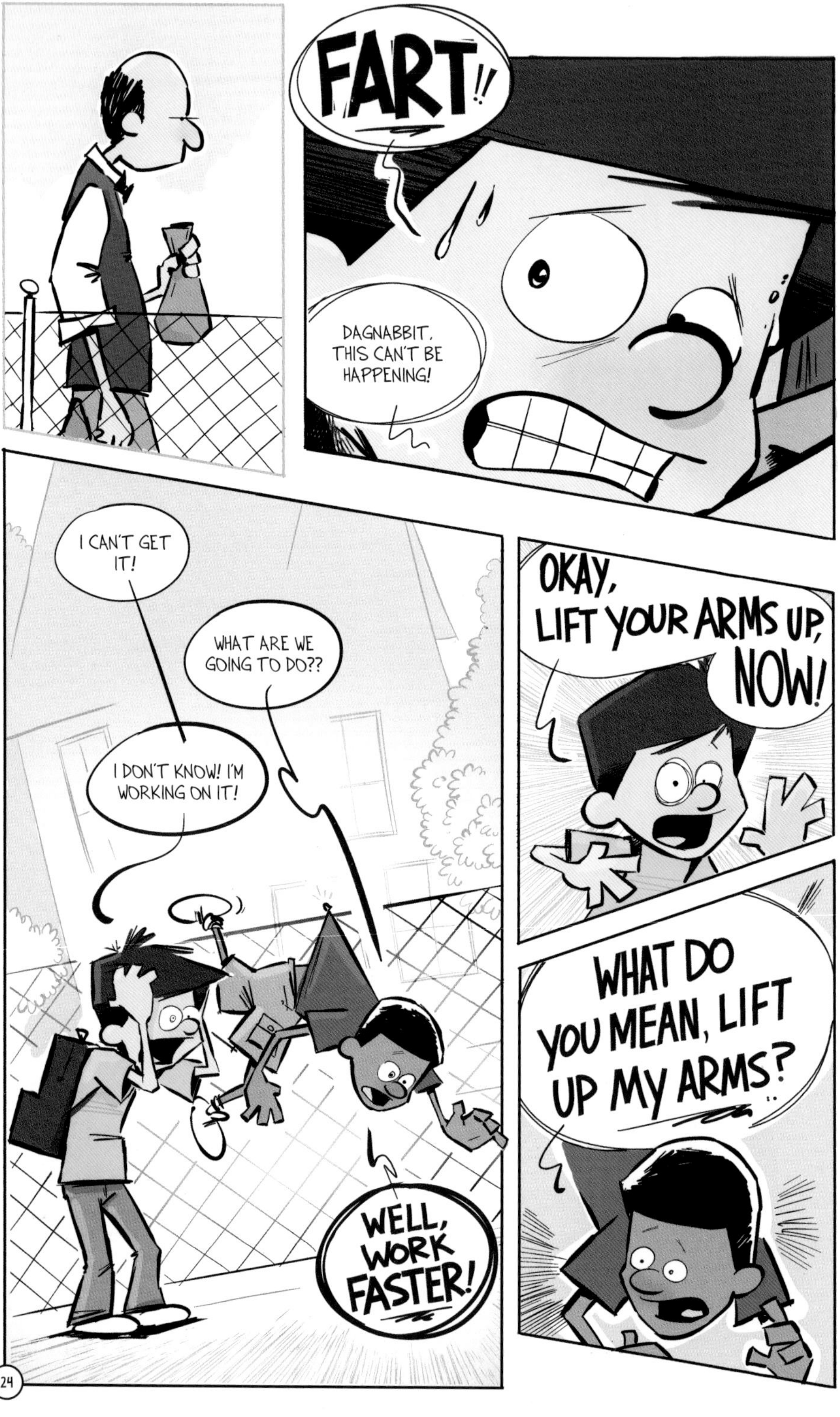
FART!!
DAGNABBIT, THIS CAN'T BE HAPPENING!
I CAN'T GET IT!
WHAT ARE WE GOING TO DO??
I DON'T KNOW! I'M WORKING ON IT!
WELL, WORK FASTER!
OKAY, LIFT YOUR ARMS UP, NOW!
WHAT DO YOU MEAN, LIFT UP MY ARMS?

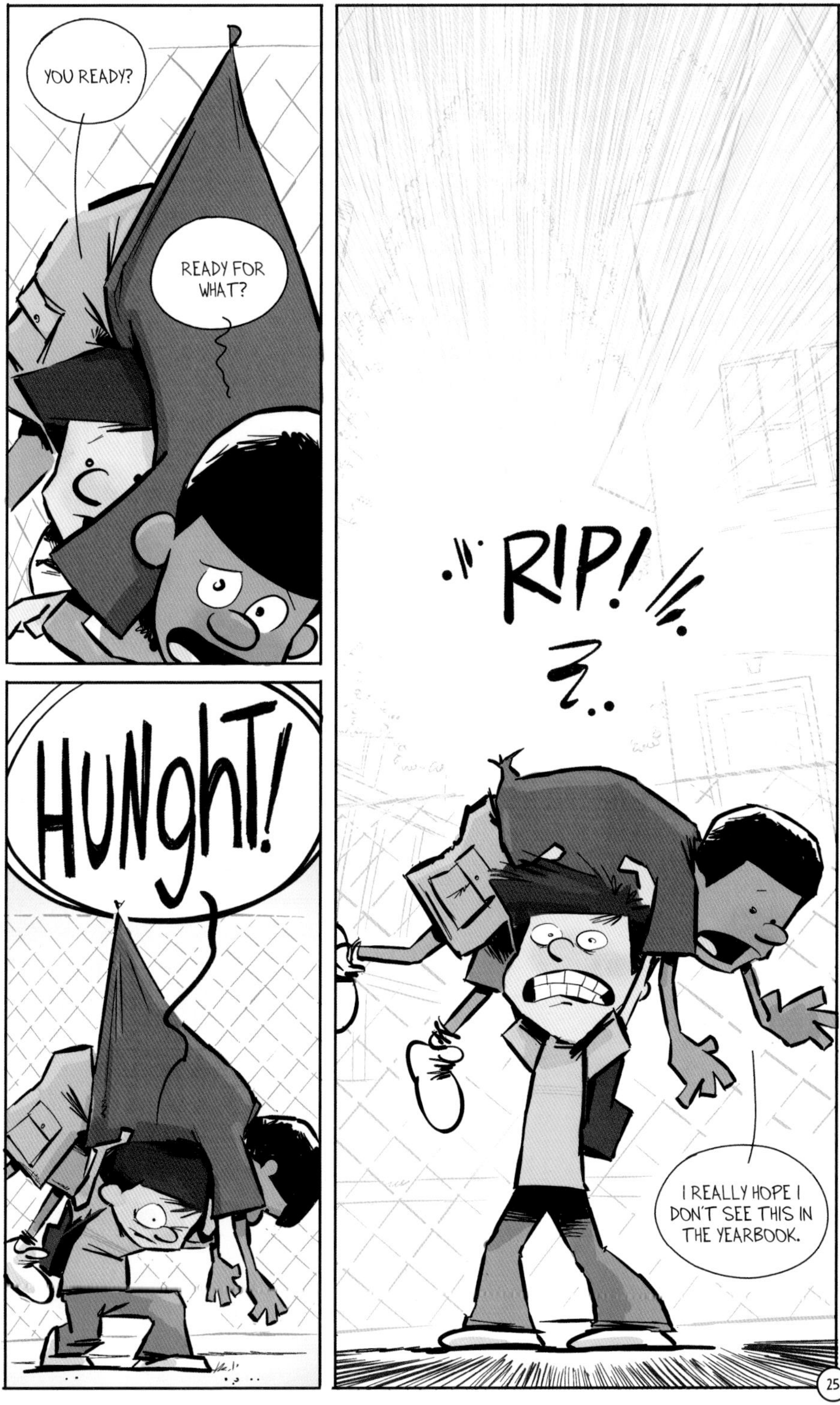

YOU READY?
READY FOR WHAT?
HUNghT!
RIP!
I REALLY HOPE I DON'T SEE THIS IN THE YEARBOOK.

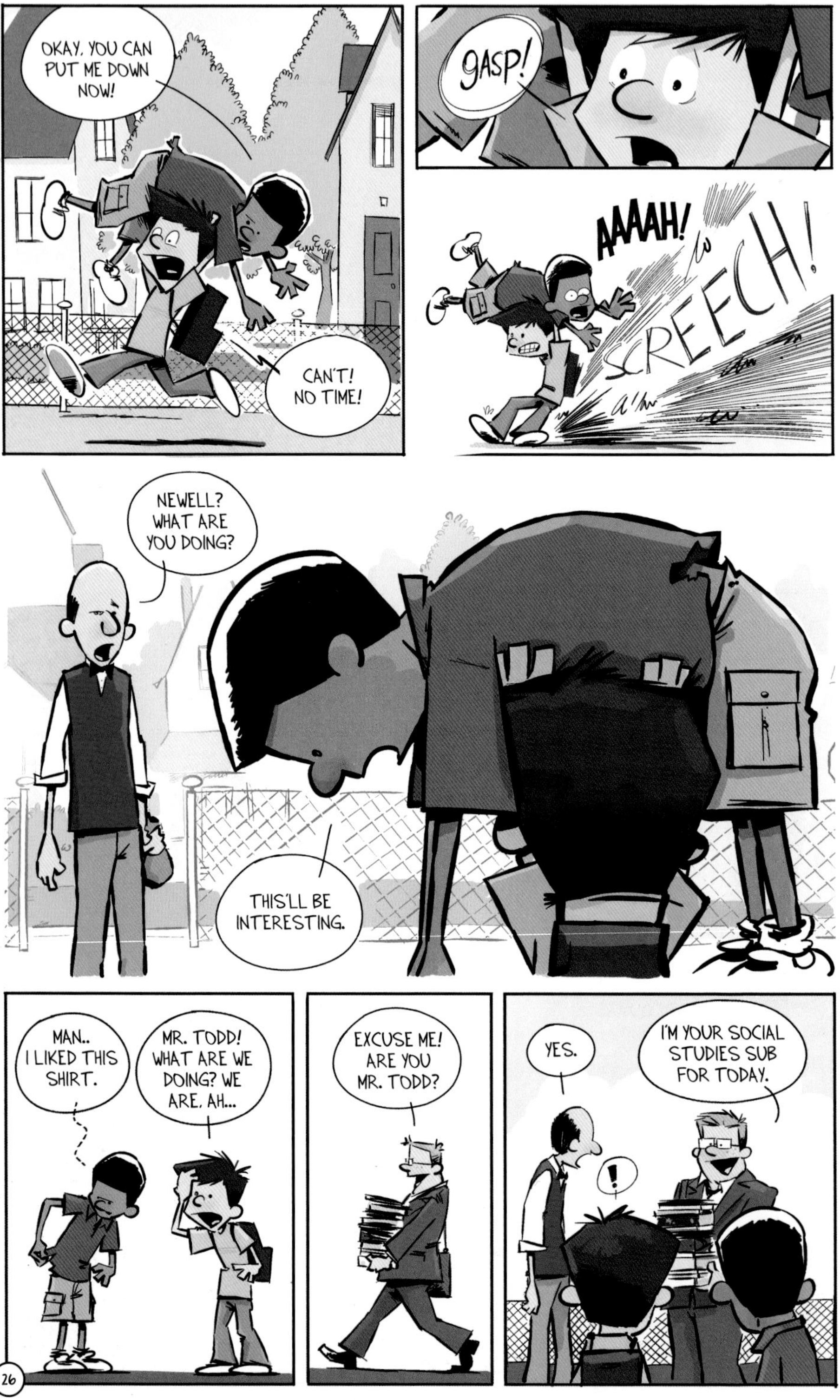
OKAY, YOU CAN PUT ME DOWN NOW!
CAN'T! NO TIME!
GASP!
AAAAH!
SCREECH!
NEWELL? WHAT ARE YOU DOING?
THIS'LL BE INTERESTING.
MAN.. I LIKED THIS SHIRT.
MR. TODD! WHAT ARE WE DOING? WE ARE, AH...
EXCUSE ME! ARE YOU MR. TODD?
YES.
I'M YOUR SOCIAL STUDIES SUB FOR TODAY.
!

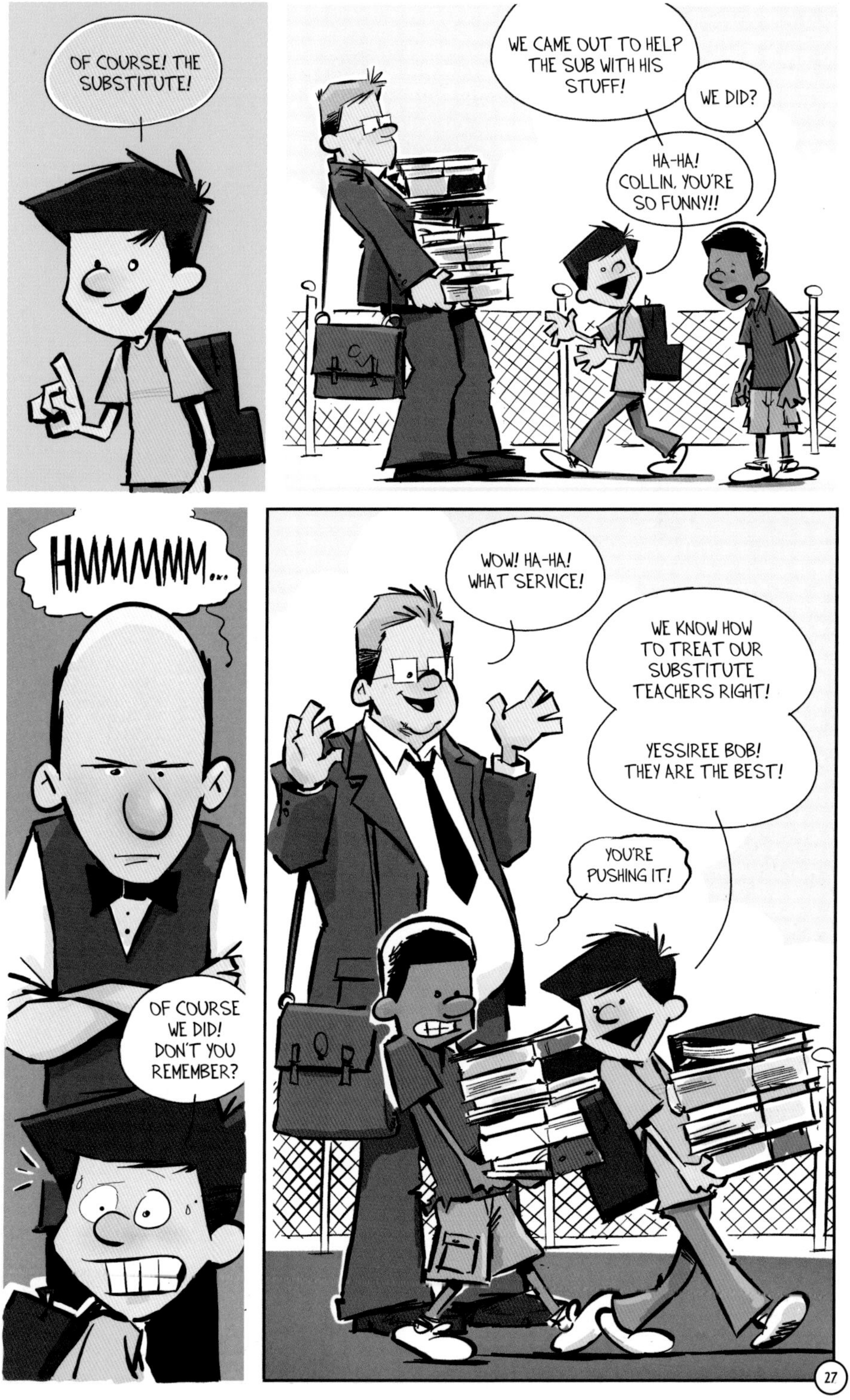
OF COURSE! THE SUBSTITUTE!
WE CAME OUT TO HELP THE SUB WITH HIS STUFF!
WE DID?
HA-HA! COLLIN, YOU'RE SO FUNNY!!
HMMMMM...
OF COURSE WE DID! DON'T YOU REMEMBER?
WOW! HA-HA! WHAT SERVICE!
WE KNOW HOW TO TREAT OUR SUBSTITUTE TEACHERS RIGHT!
YESSIREE BOB! THEY ARE THE BEST!
YOU'RE PUSHING IT!

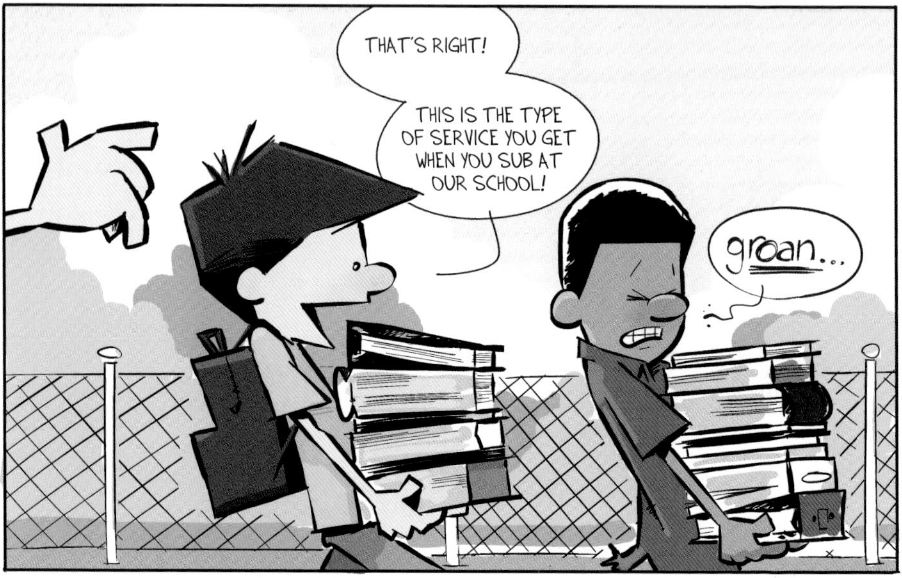
THAT'S RIGHT!
THIS IS THE TYPE OF SERVICE YOU GET WHEN YOU SUB AT OUR SCHOOL!
groan...

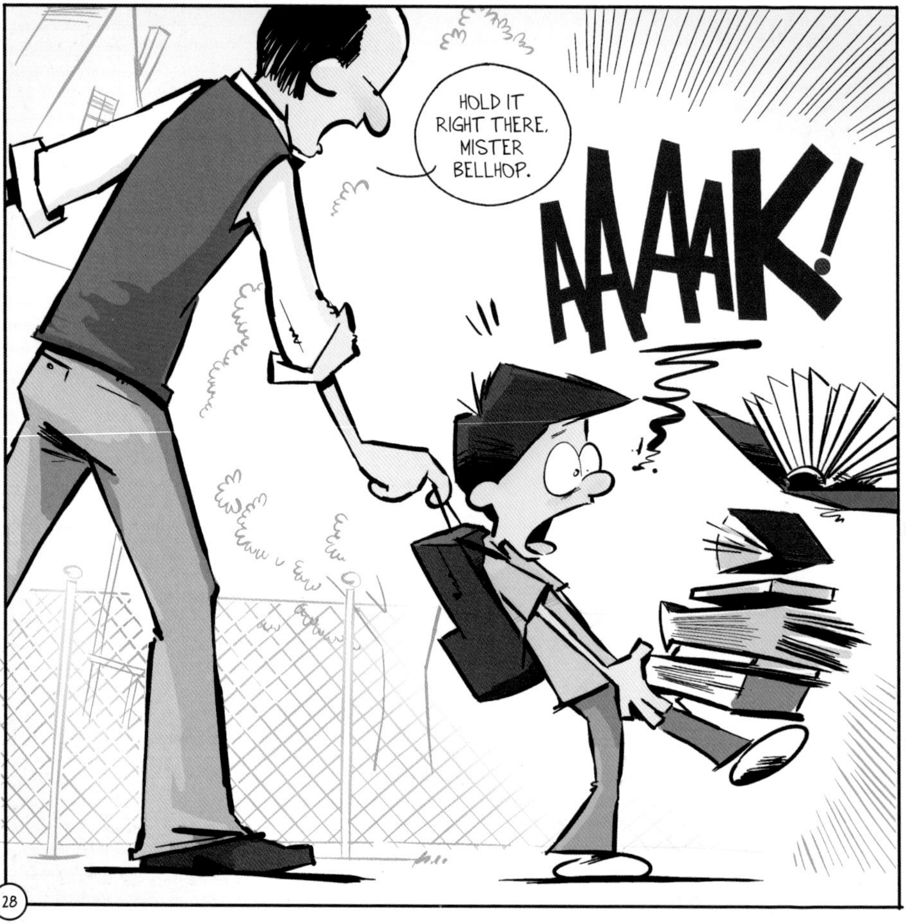
HOLD IT RIGHT THERE, MISTER BELLHOP.
AAAAK!

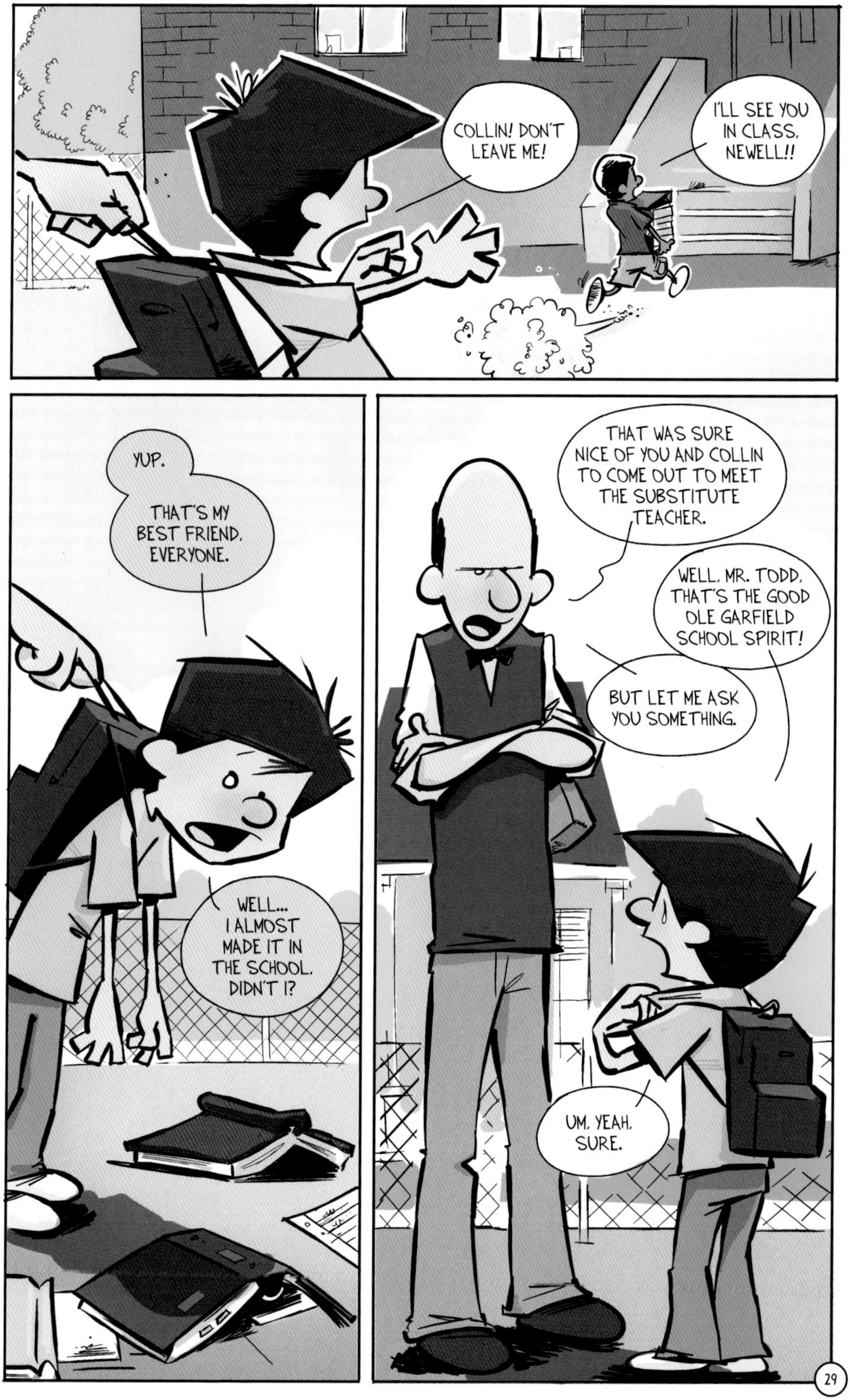
COLLIN! DON'T LEAVE ME!
I'LL SEE YOU IN CLASS, NEWELL!!
YUP.
THAT'S MY BEST FRIEND, EVERYONE.
WELL... I ALMOST MADE IT IN THE SCHOOL, DIDN'T I?
THAT WAS SURE NICE OF YOU AND COLLIN TO COME OUT TO MEET THE SUBSTITUTE TEACHER.
WELL, MR. TODD, THAT'S THE GOOD OLE GARFIELD SCHOOL SPIRIT!
BUT LET ME ASK YOU SOMETHING.
UM, YEAH, SURE.

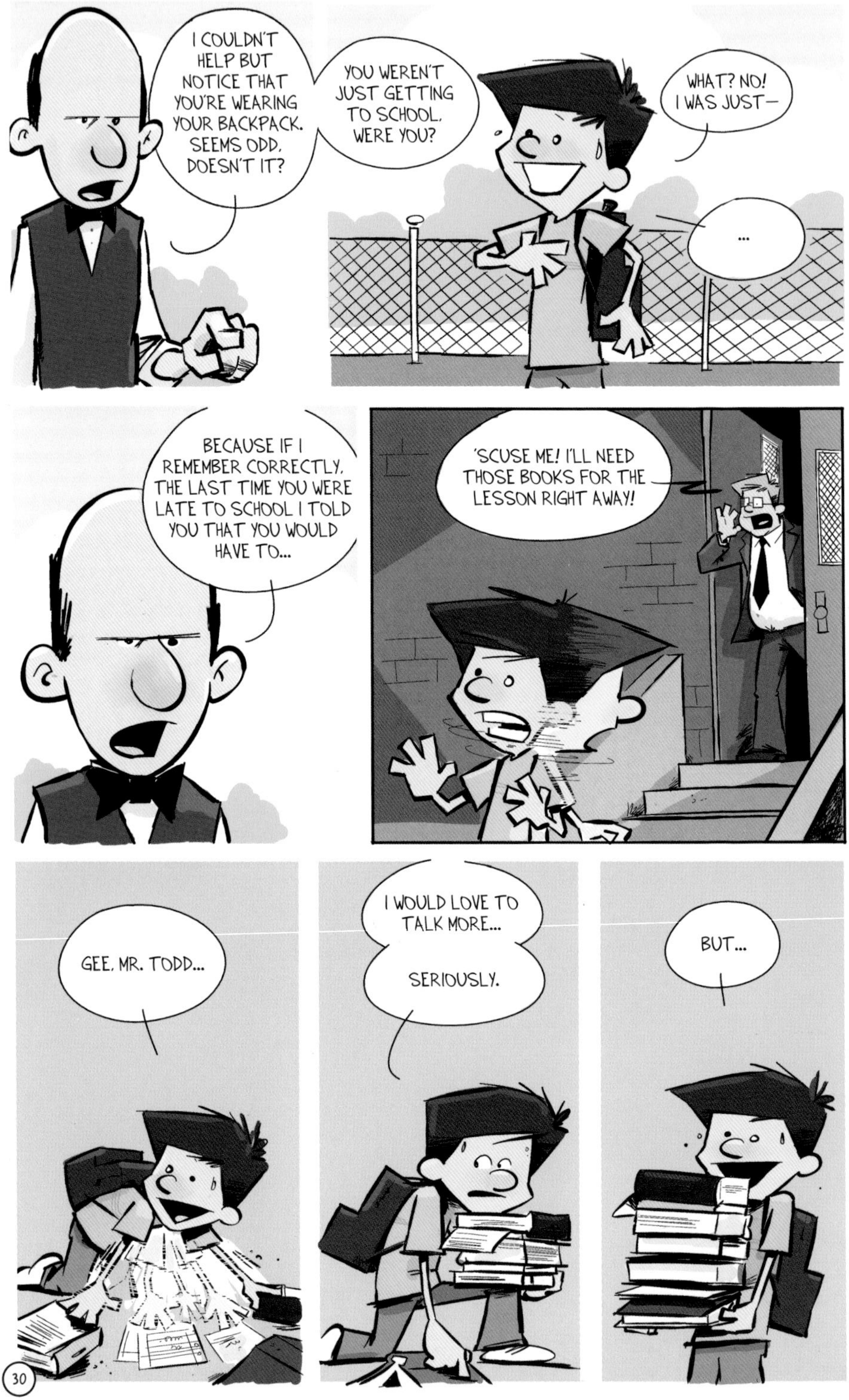
I COULDN'T HELP BUT NOTICE THAT YOU'RE WEARING YOUR BACKPACK. SEEMS ODD, DOESN'T IT?
YOU WEREN'T JUST GETTING TO SCHOOL, WERE YOU?
WHAT? NO! I WAS JUST—
...
BECAUSE IF I REMEMBER CORRECTLY, THE LAST TIME YOU WERE LATE TO SCHOOL I TOLD YOU THAT YOU WOULD HAVE TO...
'SCUSE ME! I'LL NEED THOSE BOOKS FOR THE LESSON RIGHT AWAY!
GEE, MR. TODD...
I WOULD LOVE TO TALK MORE...
SERIOUSLY.
BUT...

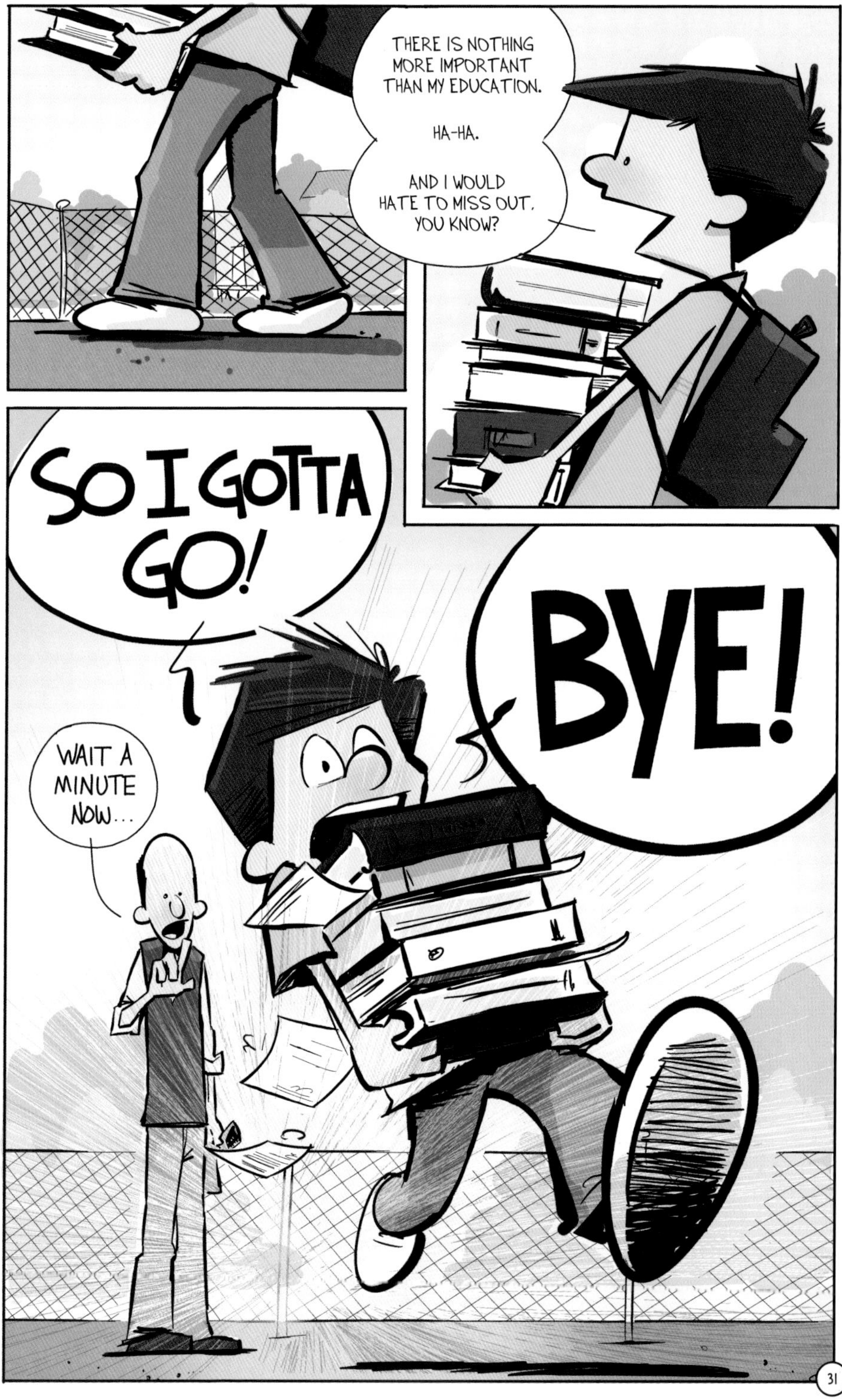
THERE IS NOTHING MORE IMPORTANT THAN MY EDUCATION.
HA-HA.
AND I WOULD HATE TO MISS OUT, YOU KNOW?
SO I GOTTA GO!
BYE!
WAIT A MINUTE NOW...

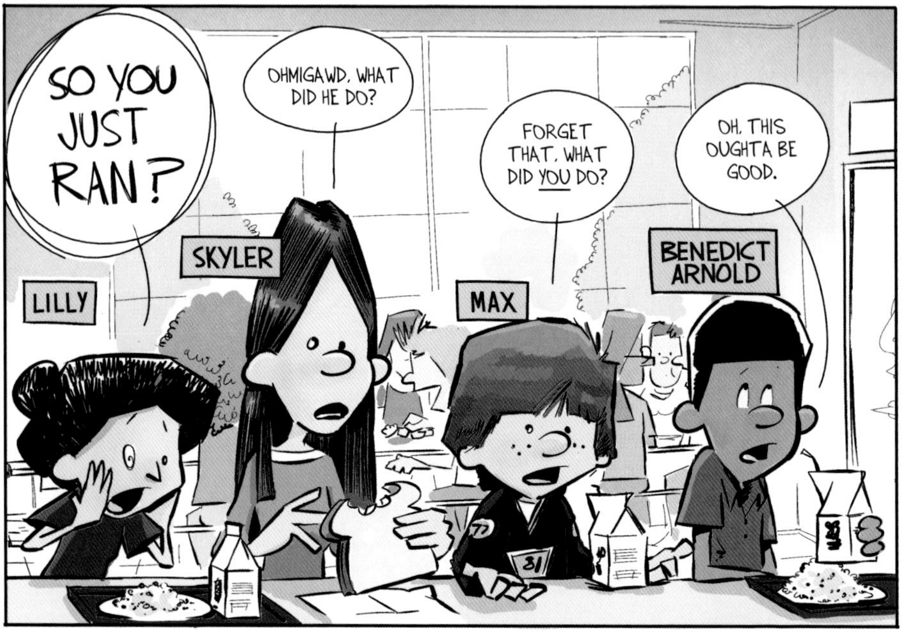
SO YOU JUST RAN?
OHMIGAWD, WHAT DID HE DO?
FORGET THAT, WHAT DID YOU DO?
OH, THIS OUGHTA BE GOOD.
LILLY
SKYLER
MAX
BENEDICT ARNOLD

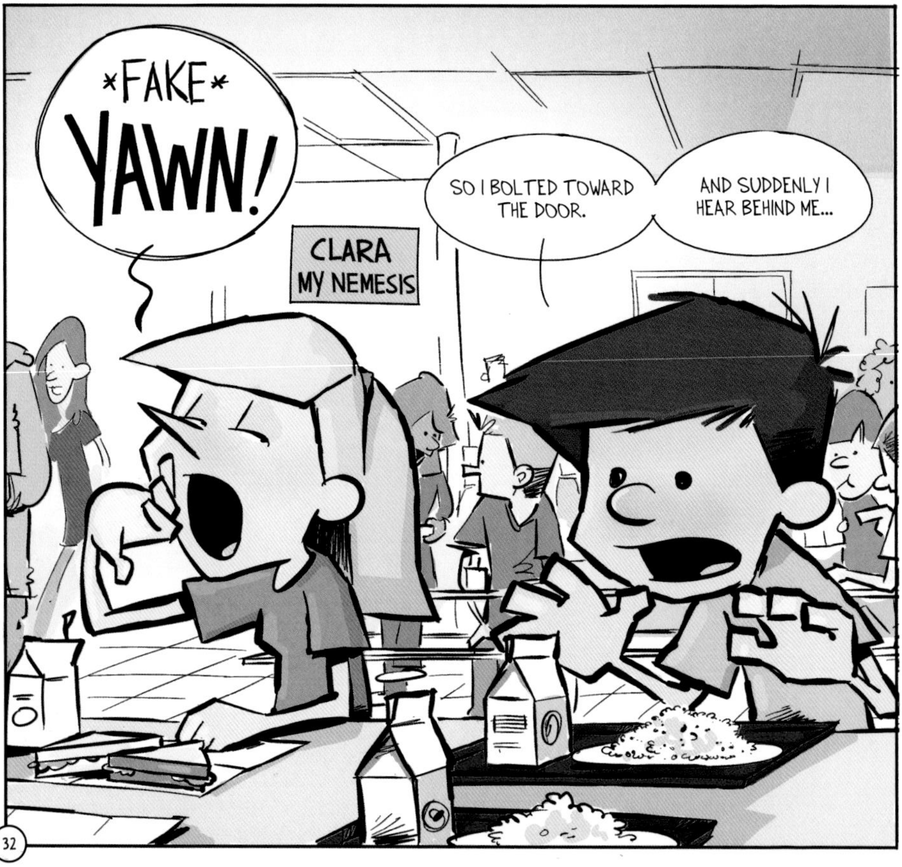
FAKE YAWN!
SO I BOLTED TOWARD THE DOOR.
AND SUDDENLY I HEAR BEHIND ME...
CLARA MY NEMESIS

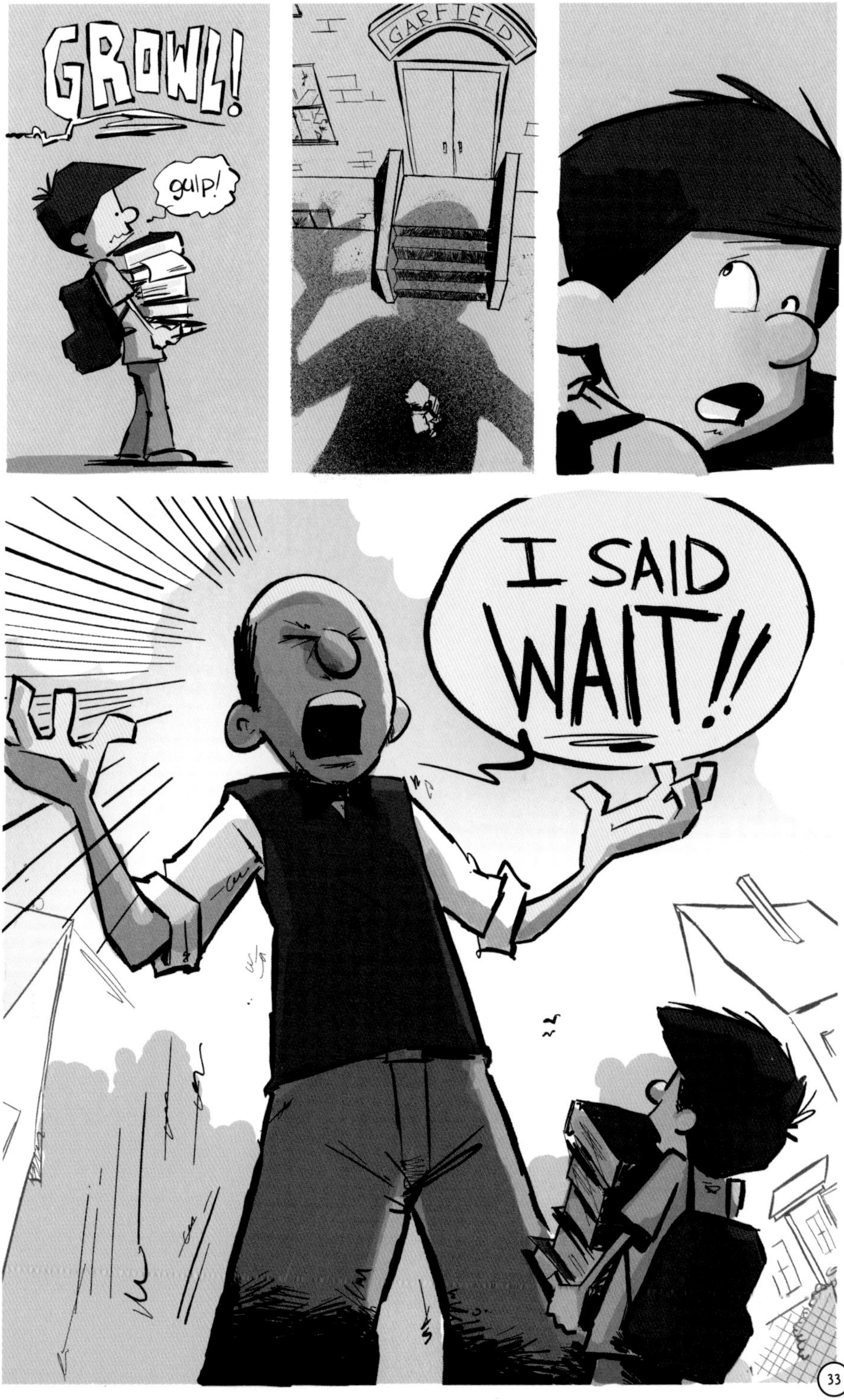
GROWL!
gulp!
GARFIELD
I SAID WAIT!!

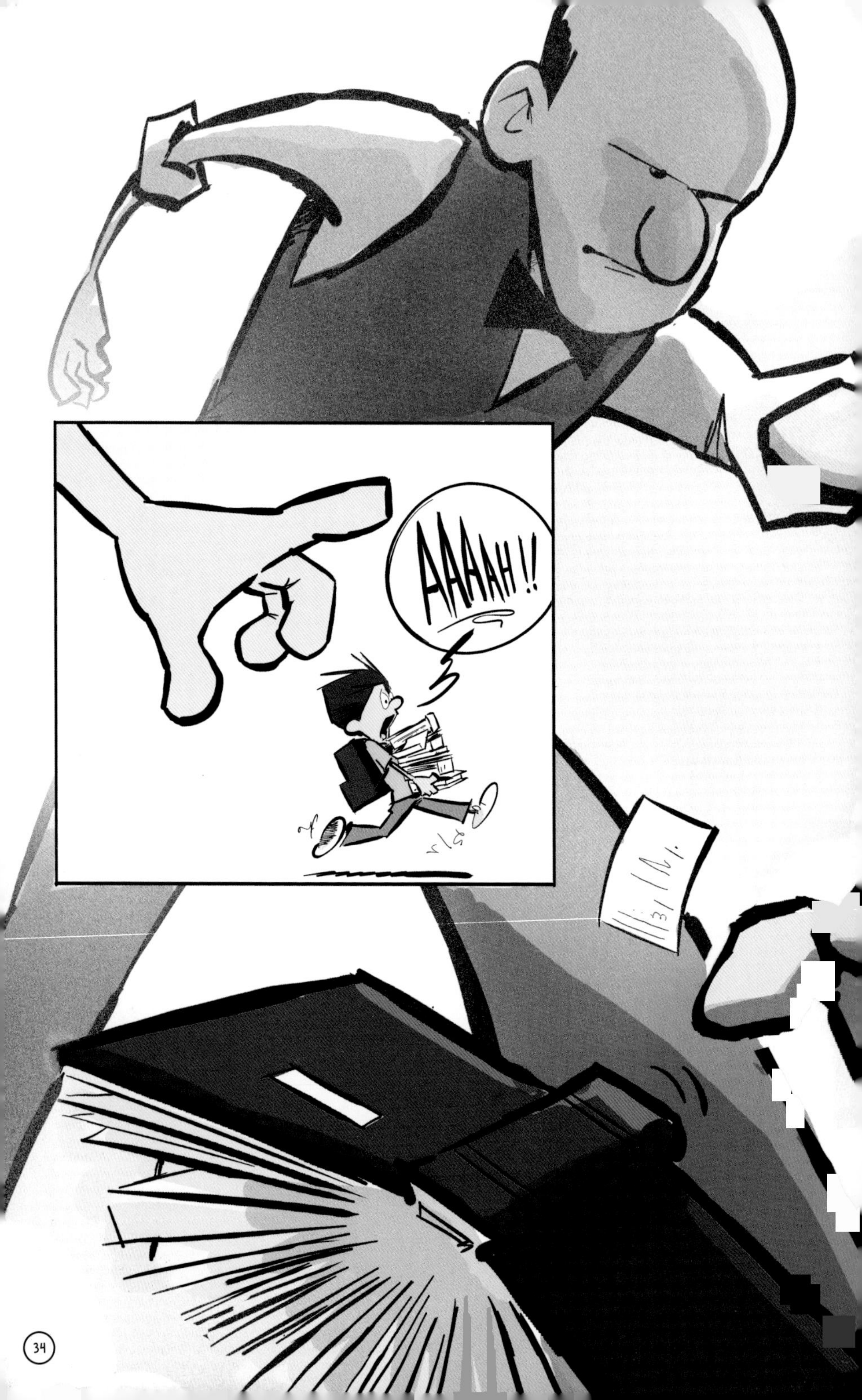
AAAAH!!

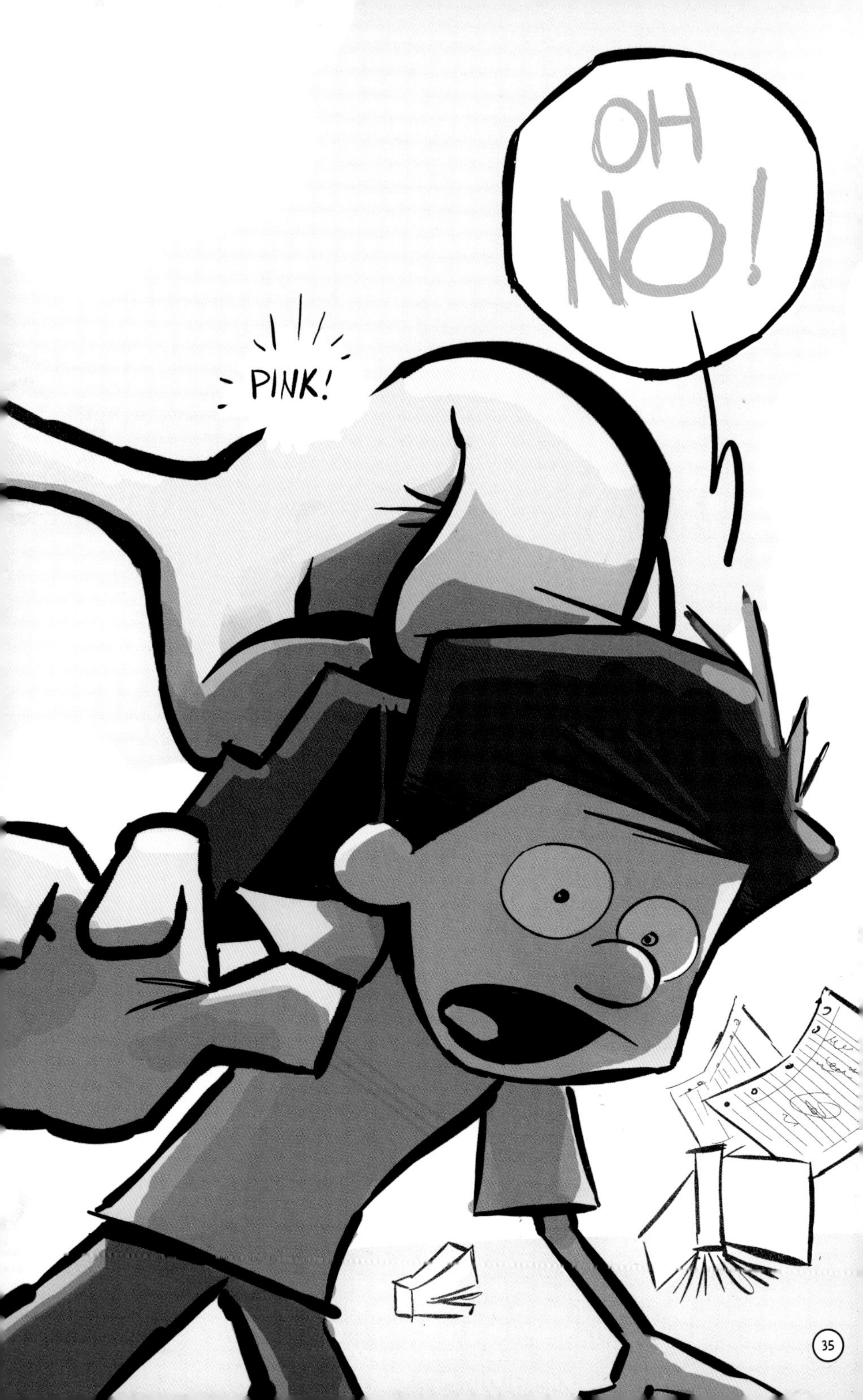
PINK!
OH NO!

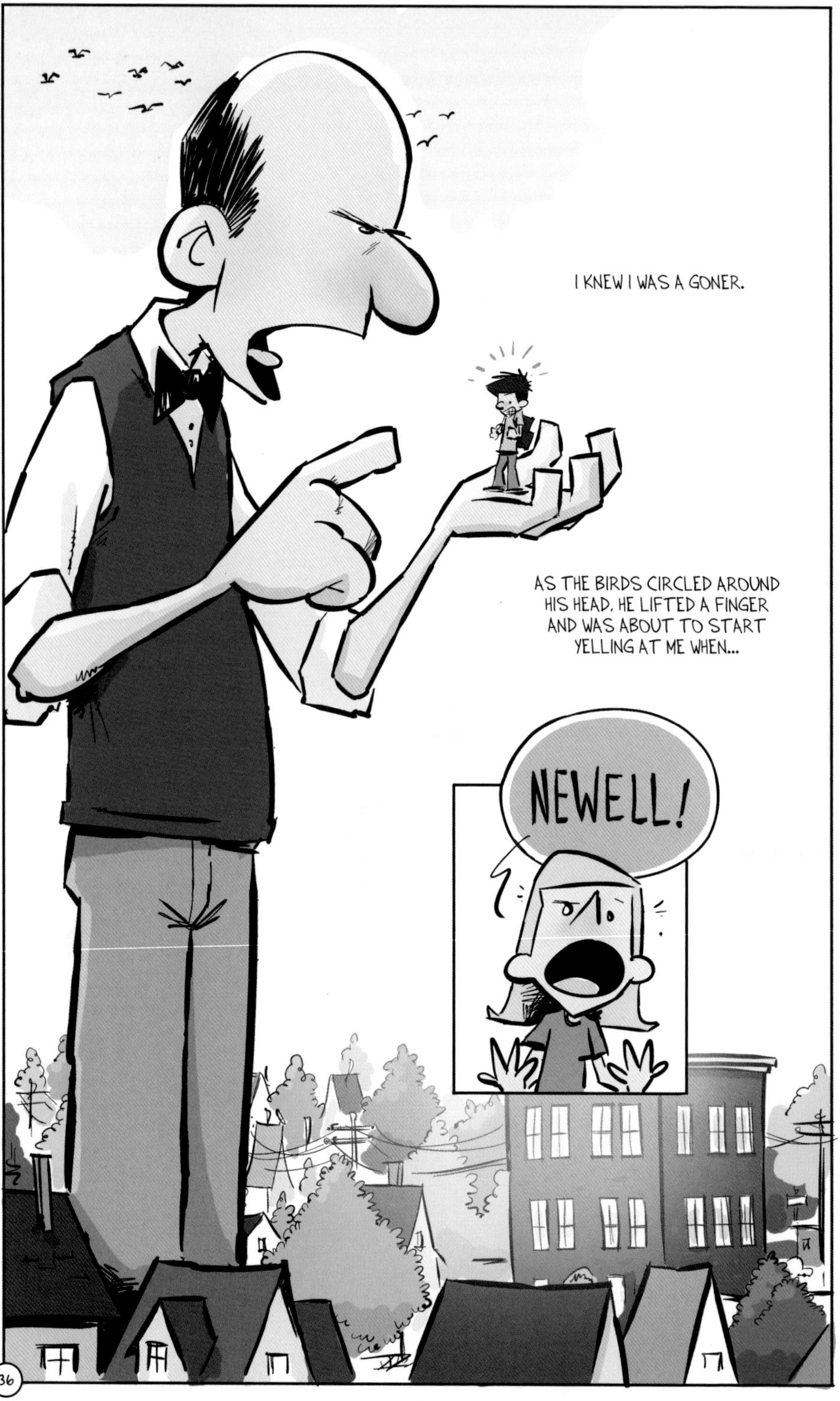
I KNEW I WAS A GONER.
AS THE BIRDS CIRCLED AROUND HIS HEAD, HE LIFTED A FINGER AND WAS ABOUT TO START YELLING AT ME WHEN...
NEWELL!

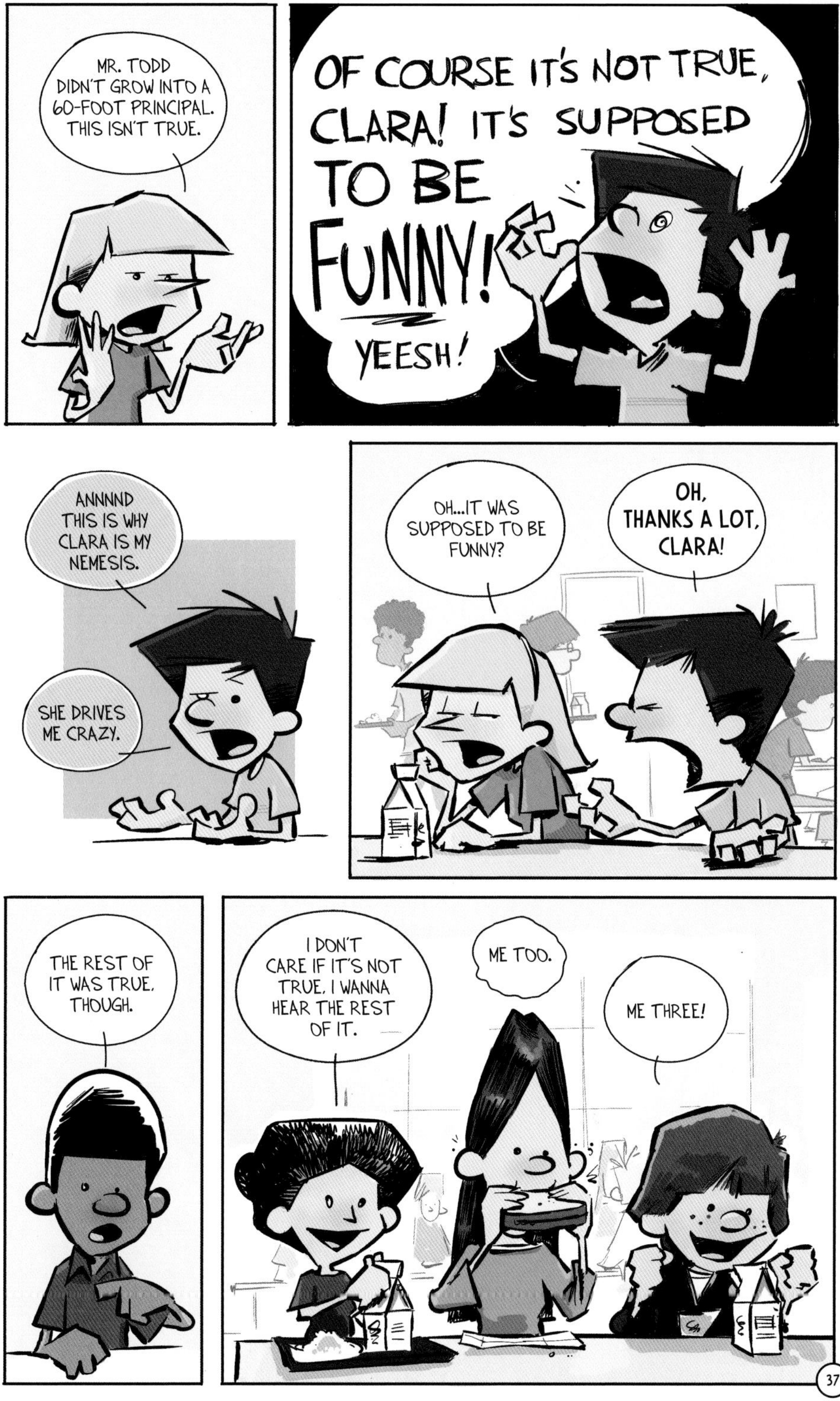
MR. TODD DIDN'T GROW INTO A 60-FOOT PRINCIPAL. THIS ISN'T TRUE.
OF COURSE IT'S NOT TRUE, CLARA! IT'S SUPPOSED TO BE FUNNY!
YEESH!
ANNNND THIS IS WHY CLARA IS MY NEMESIS.
SHE DRIVES ME CRAZY.
OH...IT WAS SUPPOSED TO BE FUNNY?
OH, THANKS A LOT, CLARA!
THE REST OF IT WAS TRUE, THOUGH.
I DON'T CARE IF IT'S NOT TRUE, I WANNA HEAR THE REST OF IT.
ME TOO.
ME THREE!

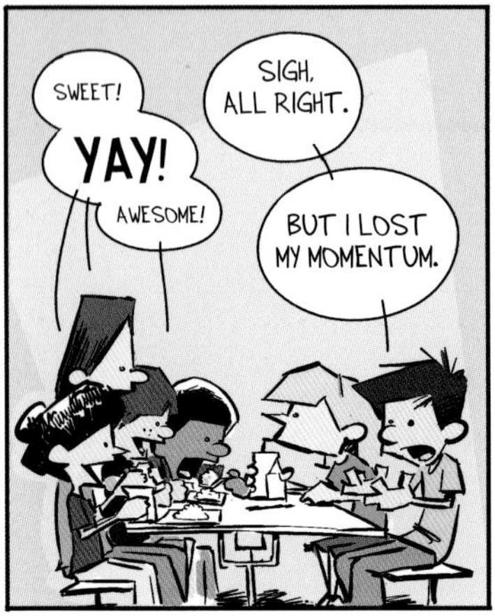
SWEET!
YAY!
AWESOME!
SIGH, ALL RIGHT.
BUT I LOST MY MOMENTUM.

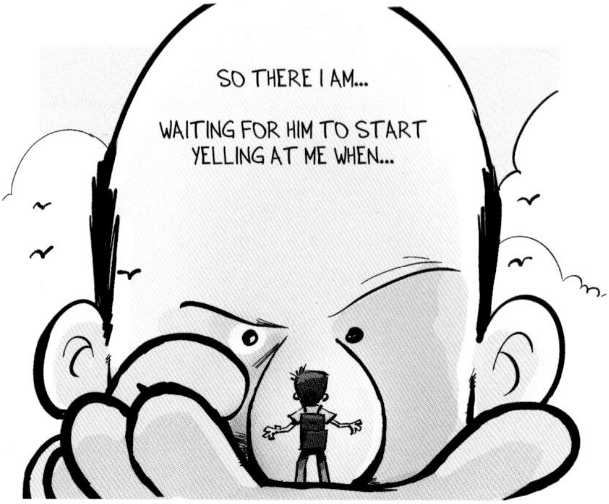
SO THERE I AM...
WAITING FOR HIM TO START YELLING AT ME WHEN...

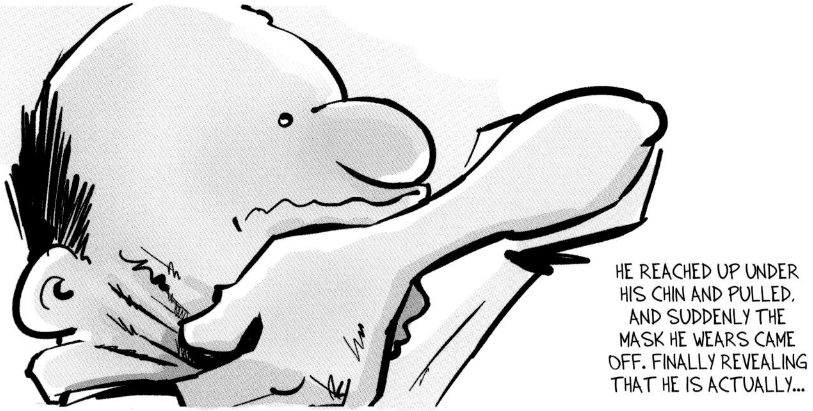
HE REACHED UP UNDER HIS CHIN AND PULLED, AND SUDDENLY THE MASK HE WEARS CAME OFF. FINALLY REVEALING THAT HE IS ACTUALLY...

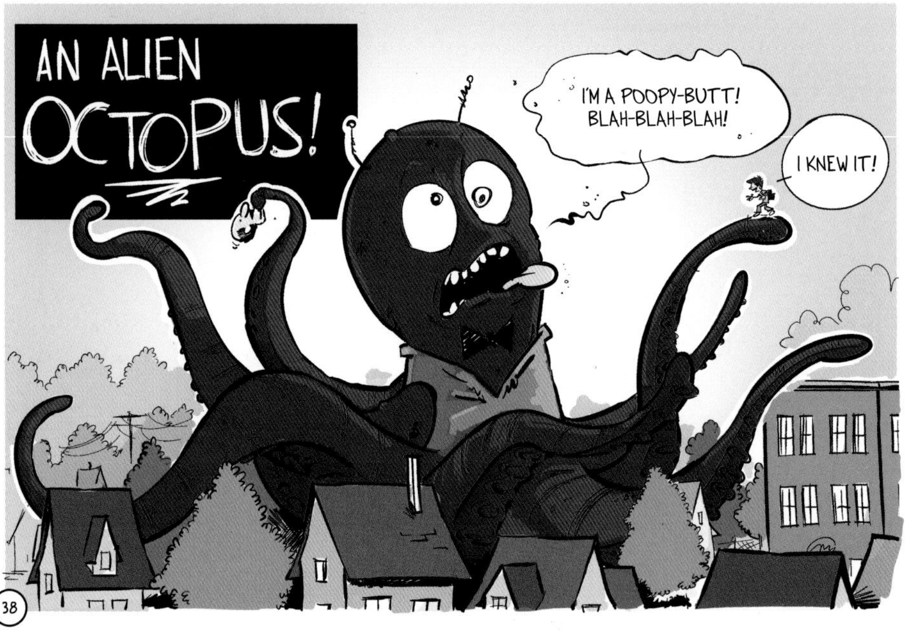
AN ALIEN OCTOPUS!
I'M A POOPY-BUTT! BLAH-BLAH-BLAH!
I KNEW IT!

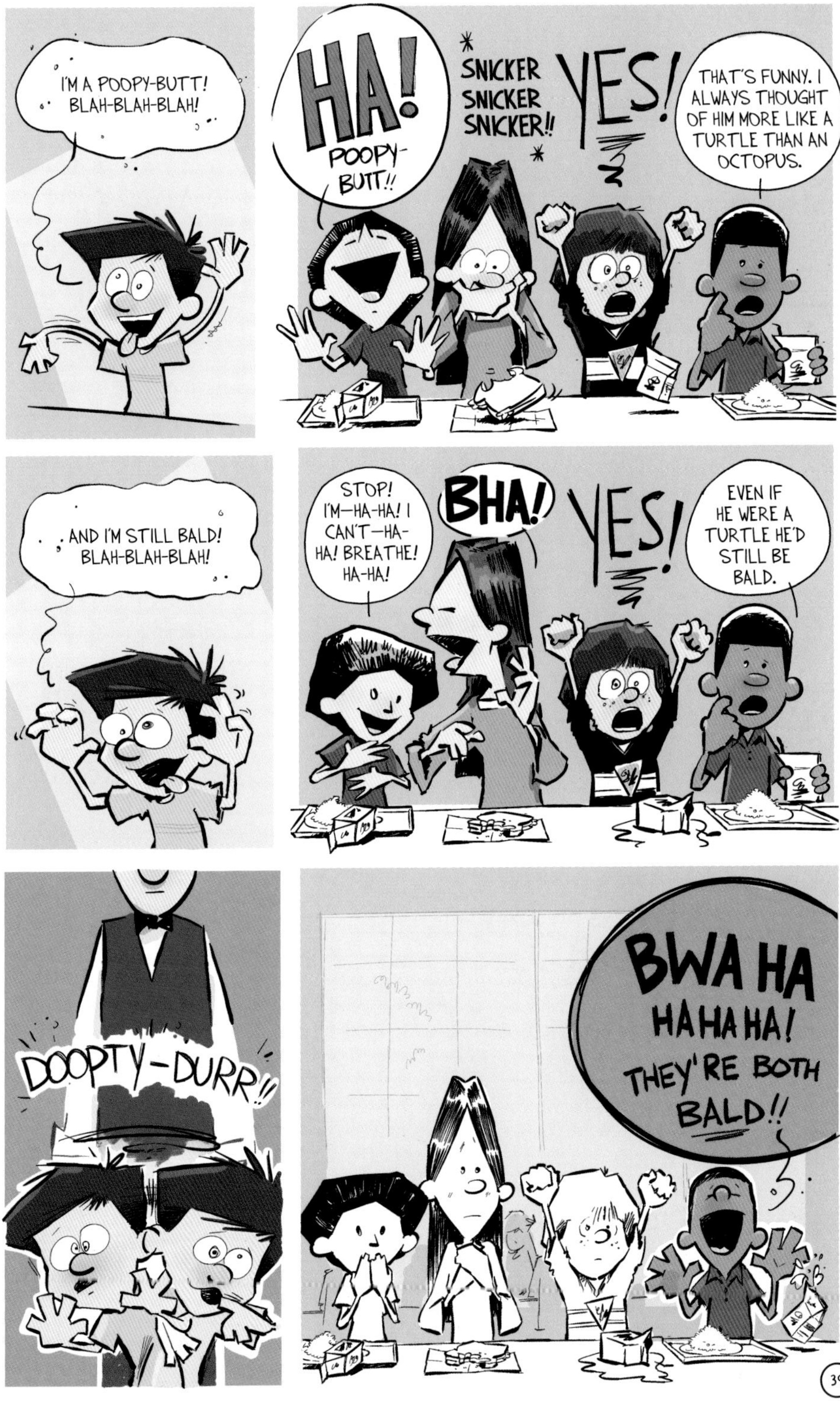
I'M A POOPY-BUTT! BLAH-BLAH-BLAH!
HA! POOPY-BUTT!!
SNICKER SNICKER SNICKER!!
YES!
THAT'S FUNNY. I ALWAYS THOUGHT OF HIM MORE LIKE A TURTLE THAN AN OCTOPUS.
...AND I'M STILL BALD! BLAH-BLAH-BLAH!
STOP! I'M—HA-HA! I CAN'T—HA-HA! BREATHE! HA-HA!
BHA!
YES!
EVEN IF HE WERE A TURTLE HE'D STILL BE BALD.
DOOPTY-DURR!!
BWA HA HA HA HA! THEY'RE BOTH BALD!!

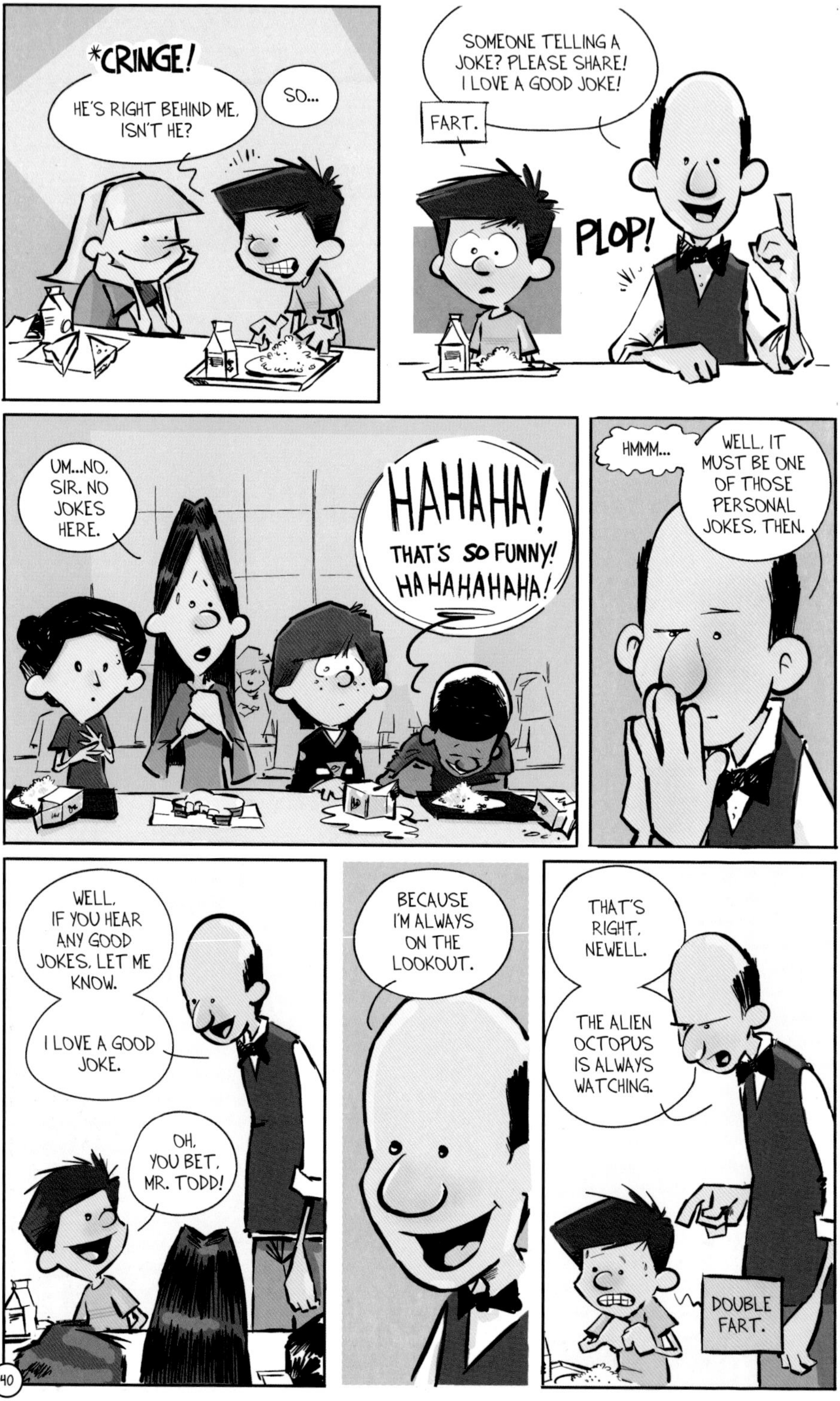
*CRINGE!
HE'S RIGHT BEHIND ME, ISN'T HE?
SO...
SOMEONE TELLING A JOKE? PLEASE SHARE! I LOVE A GOOD JOKE!
FART.
PLOP!
UM...NO, SIR. NO JOKES HERE.
HAHAHA!
THAT'S SO FUNNY! HAHAHAHAHA!
HMMM...
WELL, IT MUST BE ONE OF THOSE PERSONAL JOKES, THEN.
WELL, IF YOU HEAR ANY GOOD JOKES, LET ME KNOW.
I LOVE A GOOD JOKE.
OH, YOU BET, MR. TODD!
BECAUSE I'M ALWAYS ON THE LOOKOUT.
THAT'S RIGHT, NEWELL.
THE ALIEN OCTOPUS IS ALWAYS WATCHING.
DOUBLE FART.

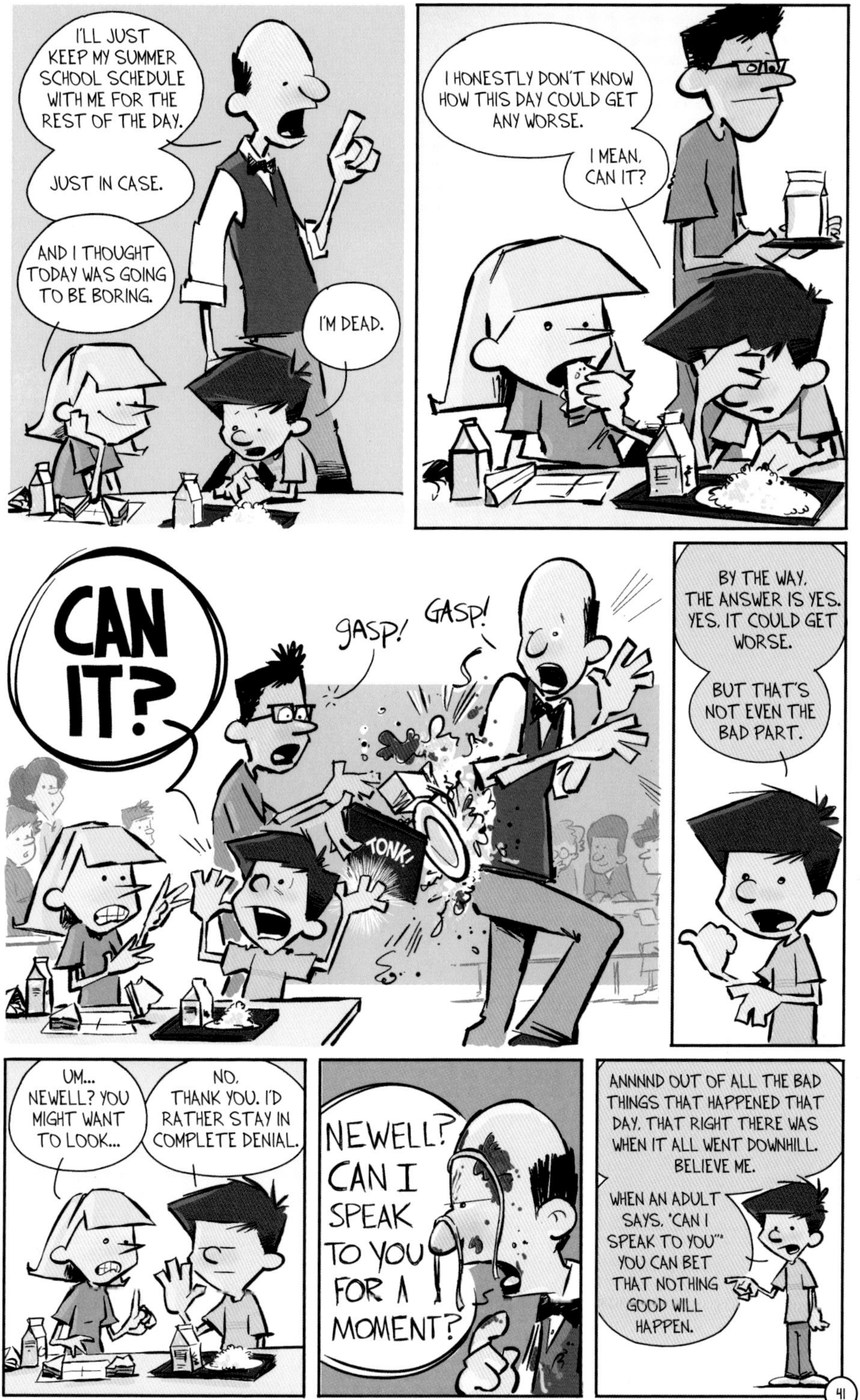
I'LL JUST KEEP MY SUMMER SCHOOL SCHEDULE WITH ME FOR THE REST OF THE DAY.
JUST IN CASE.
AND I THOUGHT TODAY WAS GOING TO BE BORING.
I'M DEAD.
I HONESTLY DON'T KNOW HOW THIS DAY COULD GET ANY WORSE.
I MEAN, CAN IT?
CAN IT?
GASP!
GASP!
TONK!
BY THE WAY, THE ANSWER IS YES. YES, IT COULD GET WORSE.
BUT THAT'S NOT EVEN THE BAD PART.
UM... NEWELL? YOU MIGHT WANT TO LOOK...
NO, THANK YOU. I'D RATHER STAY IN COMPLETE DENIAL.
NEWELL? CAN I SPEAK TO YOU FOR A MOMENT?
ANNNND OUT OF ALL THE BAD THINGS THAT HAPPENED THAT DAY, THAT RIGHT THERE WAS WHEN IT ALL WENT DOWNHILL. BELIEVE ME.
WHEN AN ADULT SAYS, 'CAN I SPEAK TO YOU'* YOU CAN BET THAT NOTHING GOOD WILL HAPPEN.

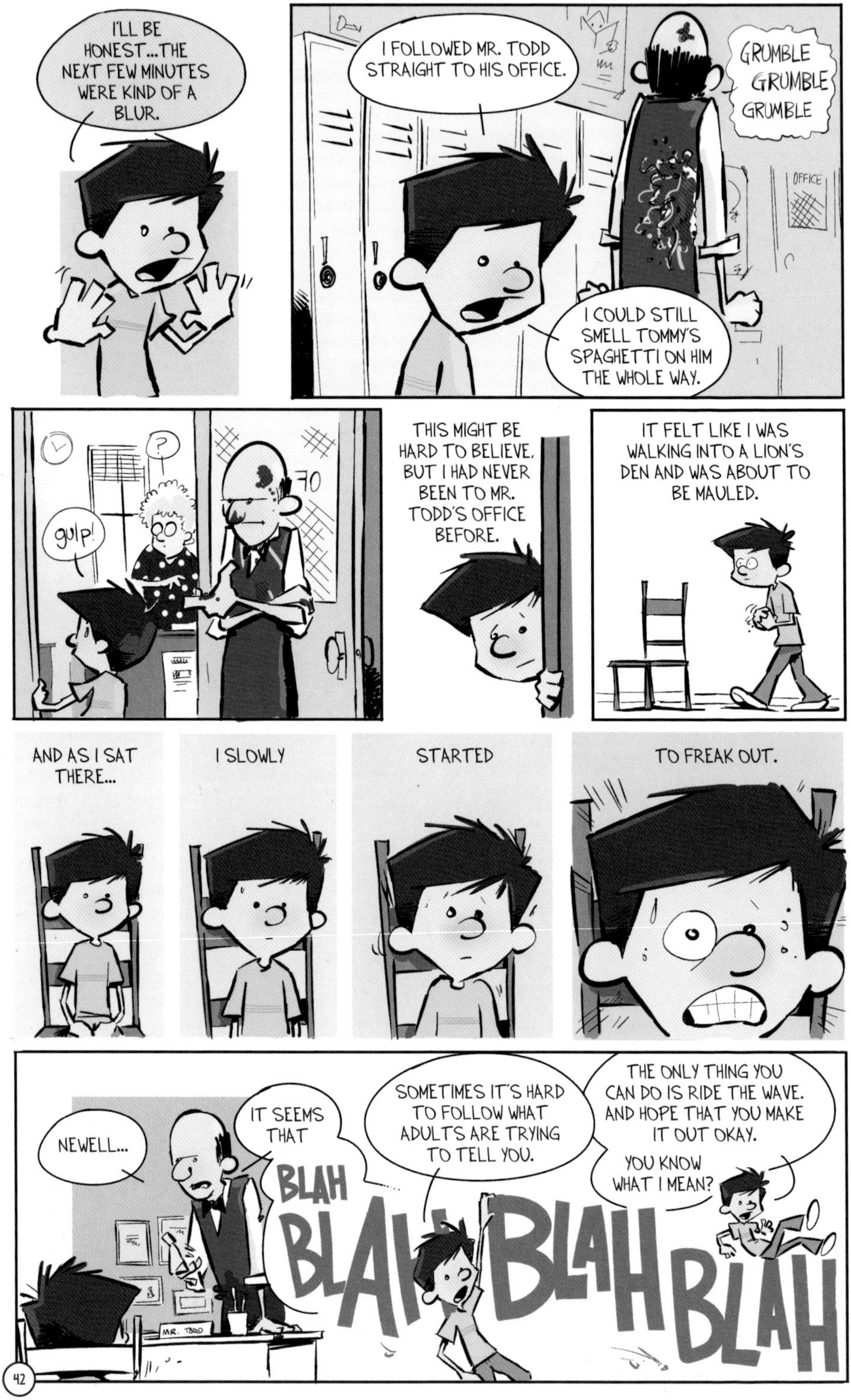
I'LL BE HONEST...THE NEXT FEW MINUTES WERE KIND OF A BLUR.
I FOLLOWED MR. TODD STRAIGHT TO HIS OFFICE.
GRUMBLE GRUMBLE GRUMBLE
OFFICE
I COULD STILL SMELL TOMMY'S SPAGHETTI ON HIM THE WHOLE WAY.
gulp!
?
70
THIS MIGHT BE HARD TO BELIEVE, BUT I HAD NEVER BEEN TO MR. TODD'S OFFICE BEFORE.
IT FELT LIKE I WAS WALKING INTO A LION'S DEN AND WAS ABOUT TO BE MAULED.
AND AS I SAT THERE...
I SLOWLY
STARTED
TO FREAK OUT.
NEWELL...
IT SEEMS THAT
SOMETIMES IT'S HARD TO FOLLOW WHAT ADULTS ARE TRYING TO TELL YOU.
THE ONLY THING YOU CAN DO IS RIDE THE WAVE. AND HOPE THAT YOU MAKE IT OUT OKAY.
YOU KNOW WHAT I MEAN?
BLAH
BLAH
BLAH
BLAH
MR. TODD

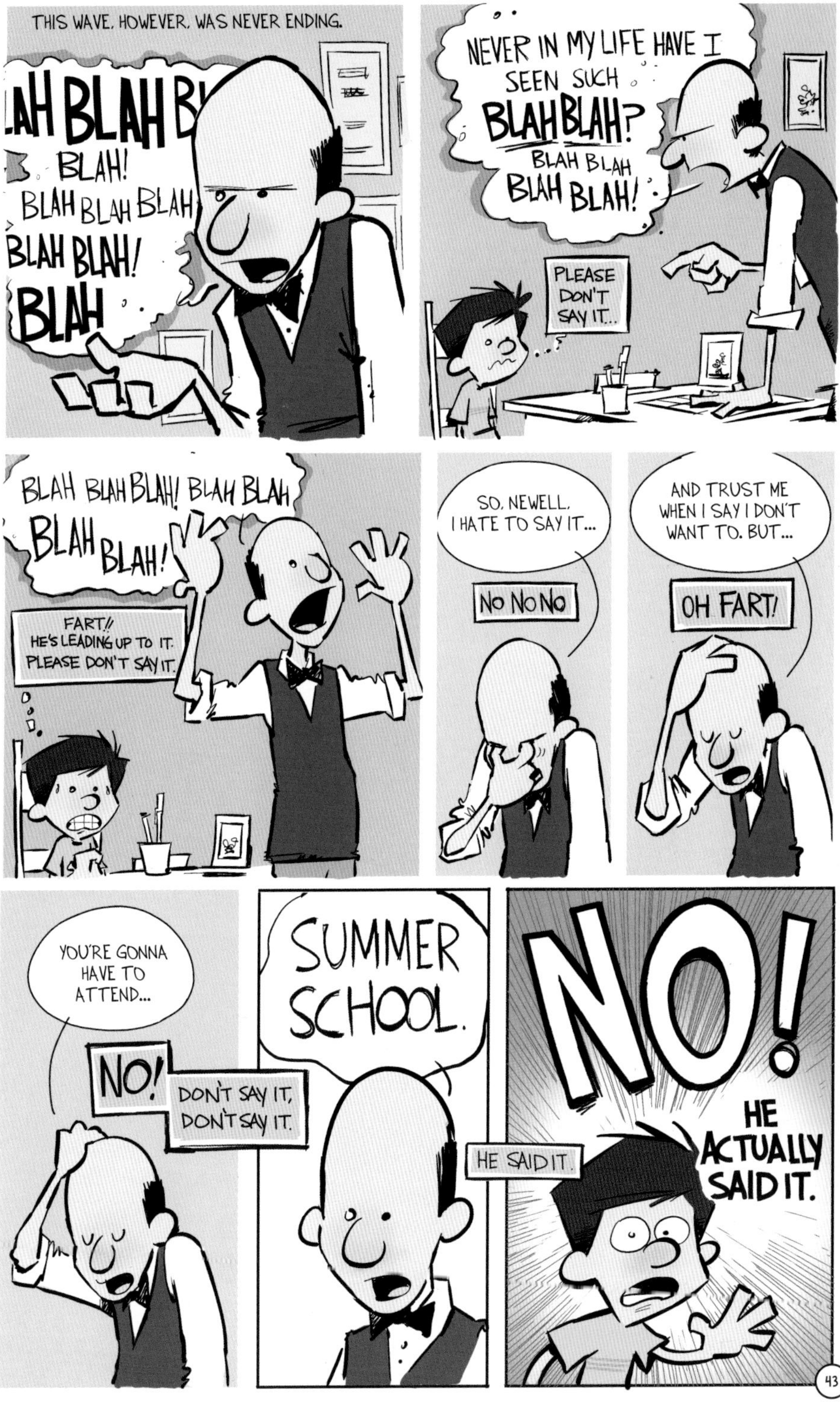
THIS WAVE, HOWEVER, WAS NEVER ENDING.
BLAH BLAH
BLAH!
BLAH BLAH BLAH
BLAH BLAH!
BLAH
NEVER IN MY LIFE HAVE I SEEN SUCH BLAH BLAH? BLAH BLAH BLAH BLAH!
PLEASE DON'T SAY IT...
BLAH BLAH BLAH! BLAH BLAH BLAH BLAH!
FART!! HE'S LEADING UP TO IT. PLEASE DON'T SAY IT.
SO, NEWELL, I HATE TO SAY IT...
NO NO NO
AND TRUST ME WHEN I SAY I DON'T WANT TO. BUT...
OH FART!
YOU'RE GONNA HAVE TO ATTEND...
NO!
DON'T SAY IT, DON'T SAY IT.
SUMMER SCHOOL.
HE SAID IT.
NO!
HE ACTUALLY SAID IT.

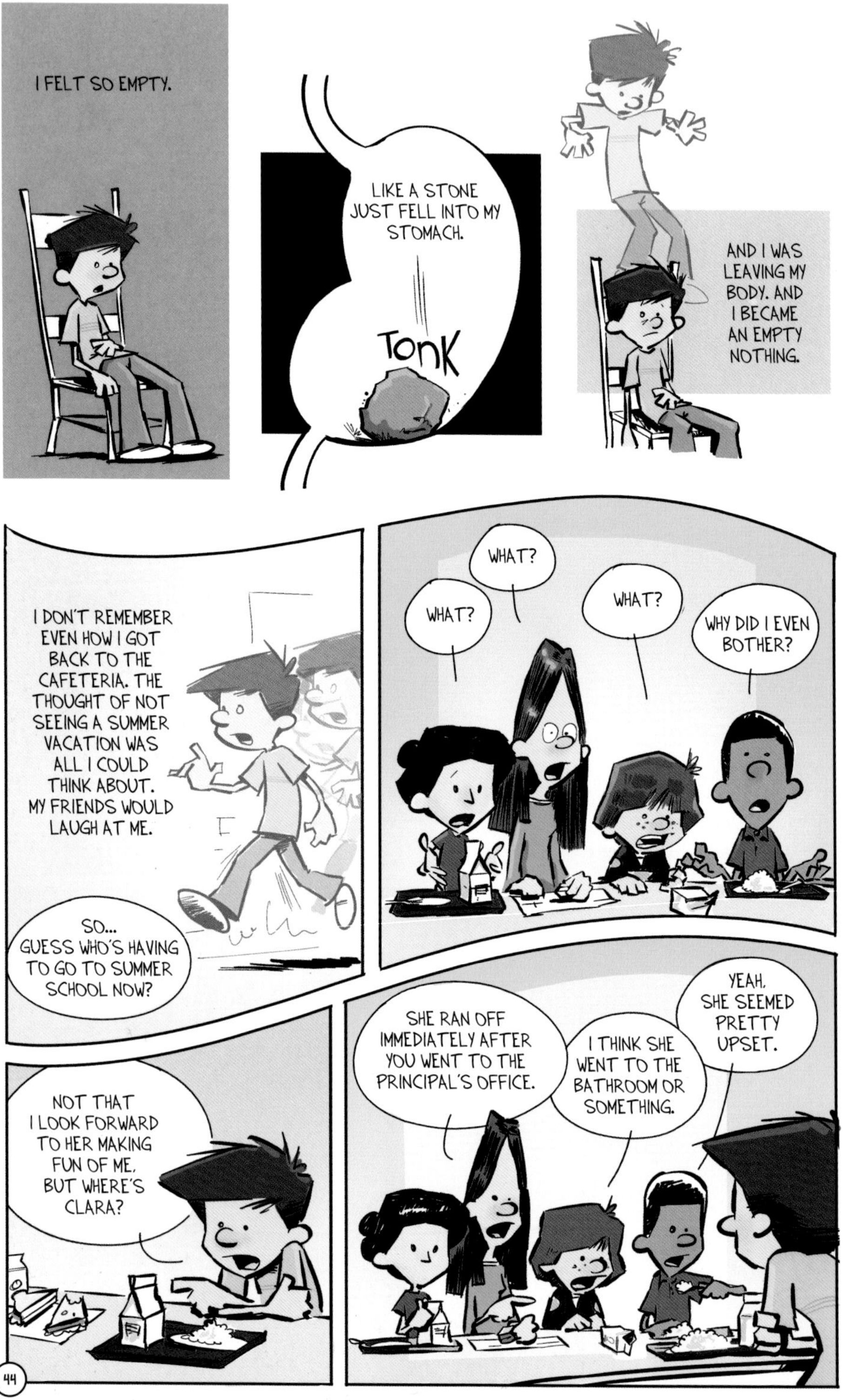

I FELT SO EMPTY.
LIKE A STONE JUST FELL INTO MY STOMACH.
TONK
AND I WAS LEAVING MY BODY. AND I BECAME AN EMPTY NOTHING.
I DON'T REMEMBER EVEN HOW I GOT BACK TO THE CAFETERIA. THE THOUGHT OF NOT SEEING A SUMMER VACATION WAS ALL I COULD THINK ABOUT. MY FRIENDS WOULD LAUGH AT ME.
SO... GUESS WHO'S HAVING TO GO TO SUMMER SCHOOL NOW?
WHAT?
WHAT?
WHAT?
WHY DID I EVEN BOTHER?
NOT THAT I LOOK FORWARD TO HER MAKING FUN OF ME, BUT WHERE'S CLARA?
SHE RAN OFF IMMEDIATELY AFTER YOU WENT TO THE PRINCIPAL'S OFFICE.
I THINK SHE WENT TO THE BATHROOM OR SOMETHING.
YEAH, SHE SEEMED PRETTY UPSET.

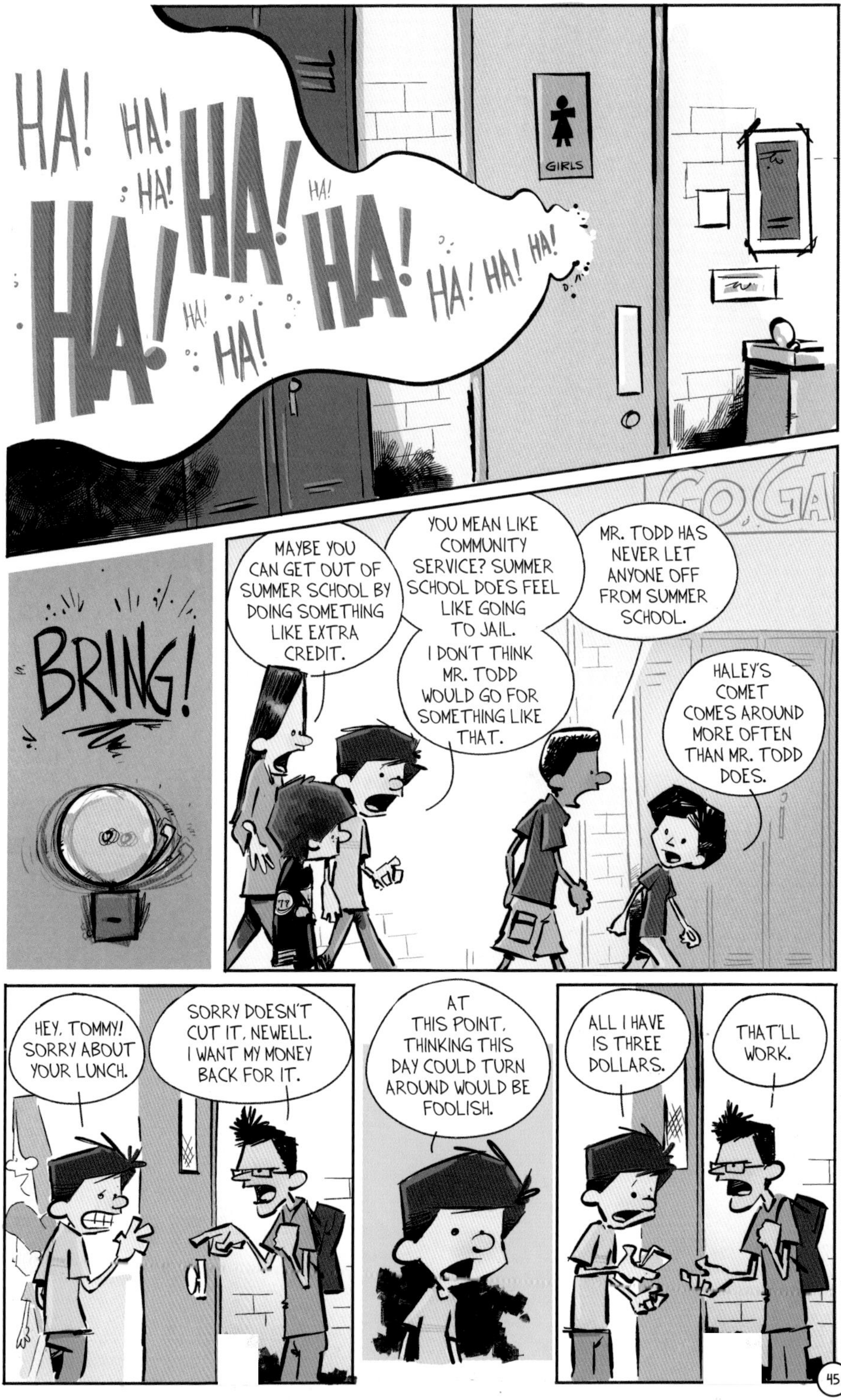
HA! HA! HA! HA! HA! HA! HA! HA! HA! HA! HA! HA! HA!
GIRLS
BRING!
MAYBE YOU CAN GET OUT OF SUMMER SCHOOL BY DOING SOMETHING LIKE EXTRA CREDIT.
YOU MEAN LIKE COMMUNITY SERVICE? SUMMER SCHOOL DOES FEEL LIKE GOING TO JAIL.
I DON'T THINK MR. TODD WOULD GO FOR SOMETHING LIKE THAT.
MR. TODD HAS NEVER LET ANYONE OFF FROM SUMMER SCHOOL.
HALEY'S COMET COMES AROUND MORE OFTEN THAN MR. TODD DOES.
HEY, TOMMY! SORRY ABOUT YOUR LUNCH.
SORRY DOESN'T CUT IT, NEWELL. I WANT MY MONEY BACK FOR IT.
AT THIS POINT, THINKING THIS DAY COULD TURN AROUND WOULD BE FOOLISH.
ALL I HAVE IS THREE DOLLARS.
THAT'LL WORK.

CHAPTER THREE

THE FUN DOESN'T STOP THERE

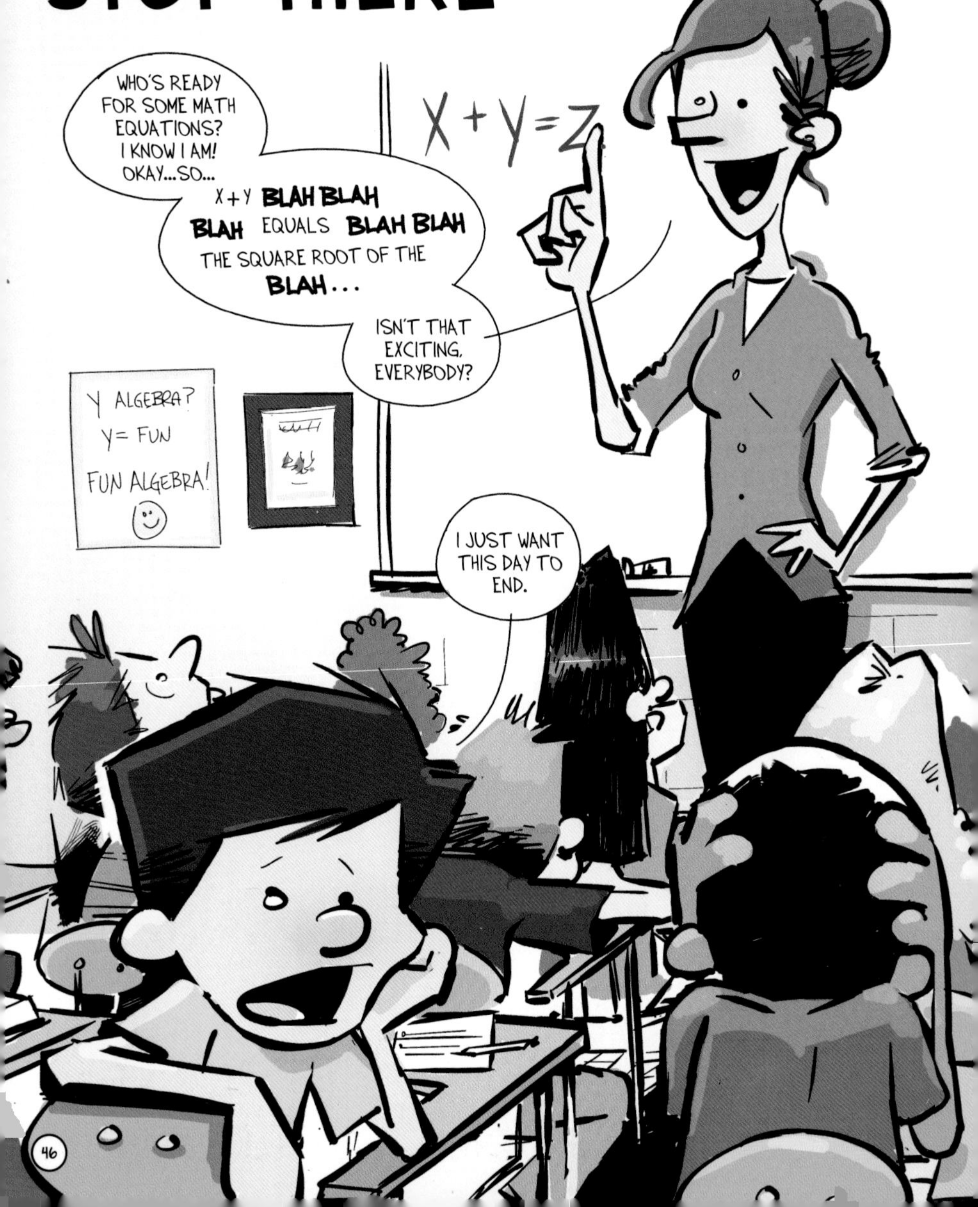

WHO'S READY FOR SOME MATH EQUATIONS? I KNOW I AM! OKAY...SO...
X + Y BLAH BLAH BLAH EQUALS BLAH BLAH THE SQUARE ROOT OF THE BLAH...
ISN'T THAT EXCITING, EVERYBODY?
X + Y = Z
Y ALGEBRA?
Y= FUN
FUN ALGEBRA!
I JUST WANT THIS DAY TO END.

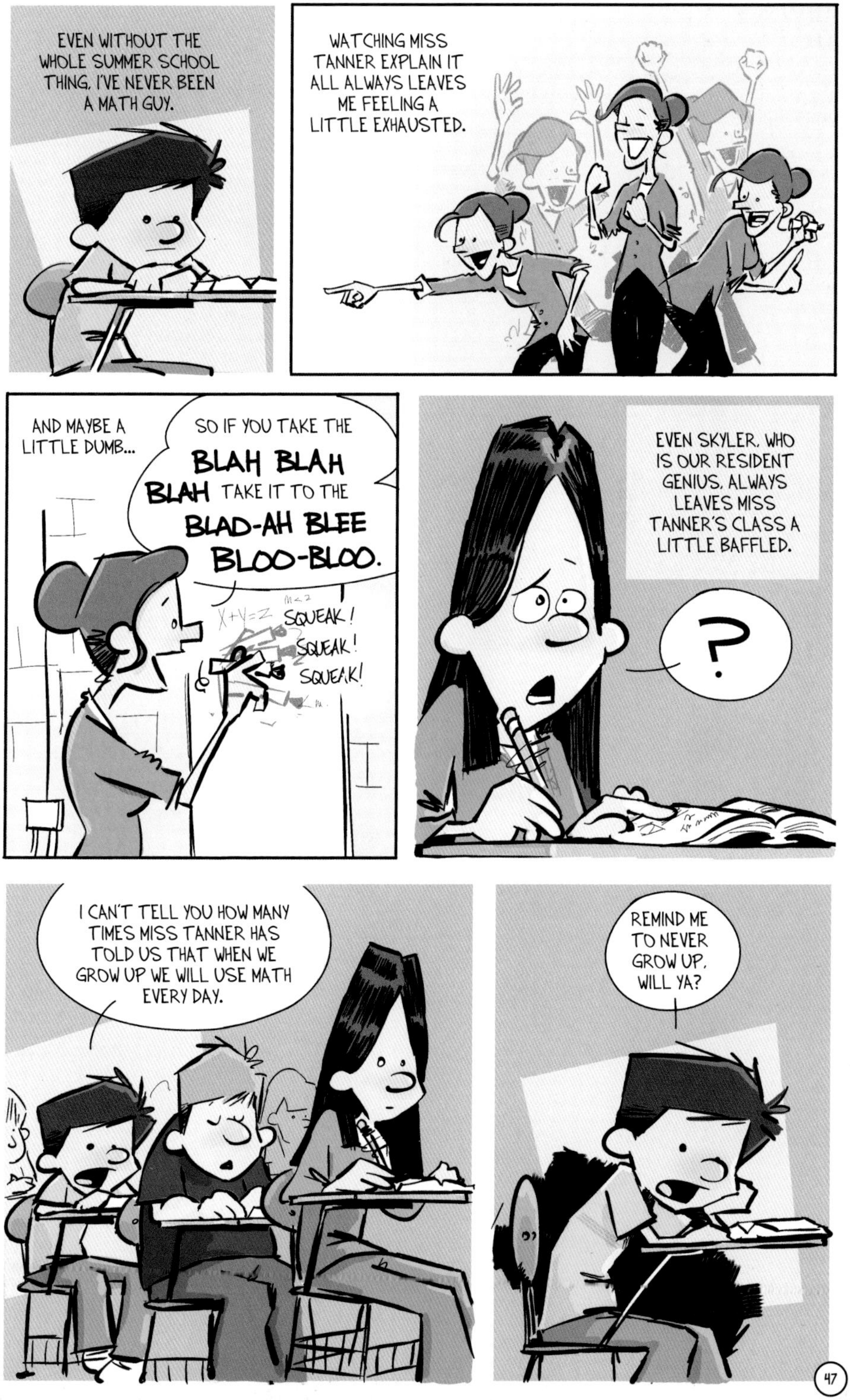
EVEN WITHOUT THE WHOLE SUMMER SCHOOL THING, I'VE NEVER BEEN A MATH GUY.
WATCHING MISS TANNER EXPLAIN IT ALL ALWAYS LEAVES ME FEELING A LITTLE EXHAUSTED.
AND MAYBE A LITTLE DUMB...
SO IF YOU TAKE THE BLAH BLAH BLAH TAKE IT TO THE BLAD-AH BLEE BLOO-BLOO.
X+Y=Z
SQUEAK!
SQUEAK!
SQUEAK!
EVEN SKYLER, WHO IS OUR RESIDENT GENIUS, ALWAYS LEAVES MISS TANNER'S CLASS A LITTLE BAFFLED.
?
I CAN'T TELL YOU HOW MANY TIMES MISS TANNER HAS TOLD US THAT WHEN WE GROW UP WE WILL USE MATH EVERY DAY.
REMIND ME TO NEVER GROW UP, WILL YA?

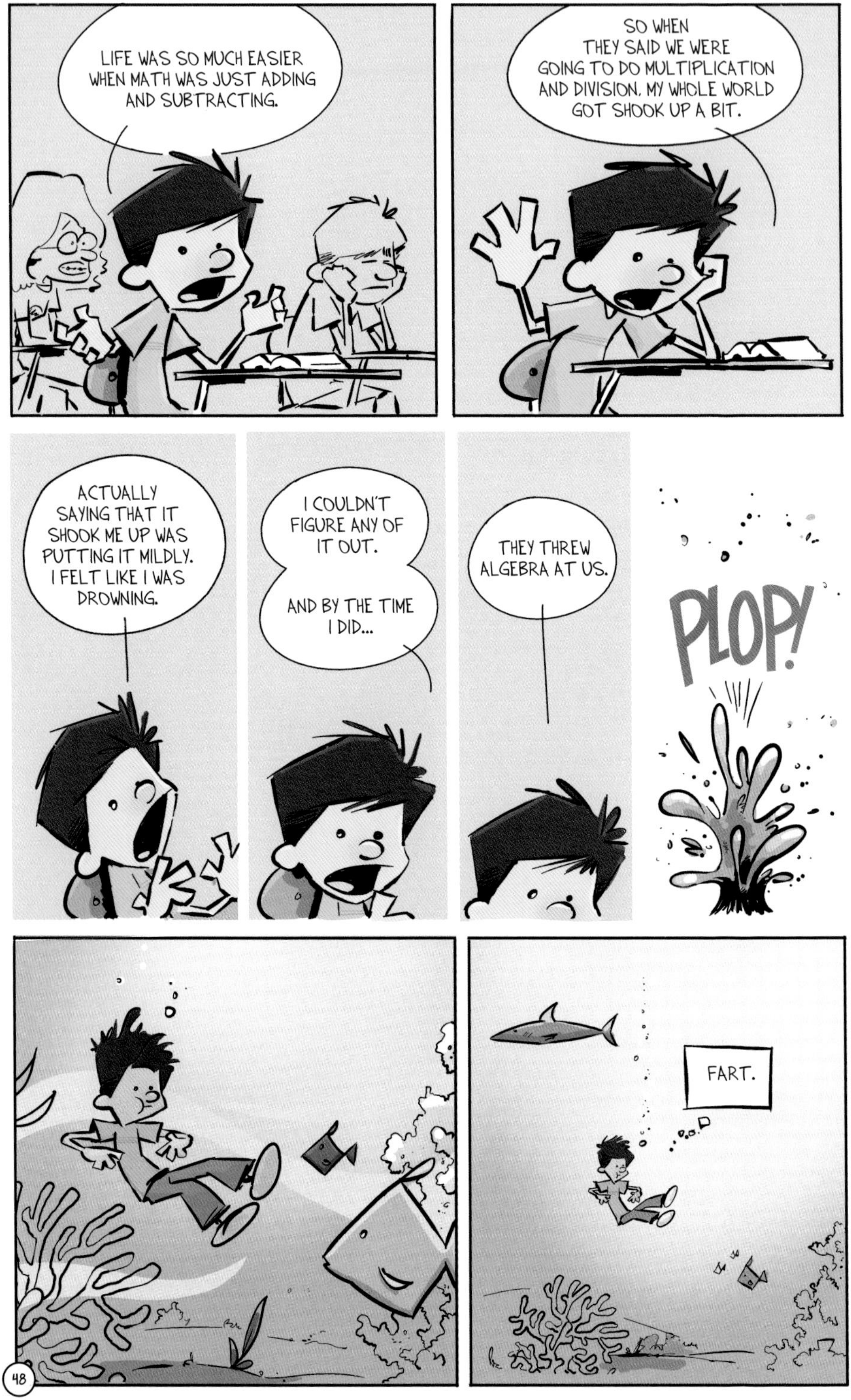
LIFE WAS SO MUCH EASIER WHEN MATH WAS JUST ADDING AND SUBTRACTING.
SO WHEN THEY SAID WE WERE GOING TO DO MULTIPLICATION AND DIVISION, MY WHOLE WORLD GOT SHOOK UP A BIT.
ACTUALLY SAYING THAT IT SHOOK ME UP WAS PUTTING IT MILDLY. I FELT LIKE I WAS DROWNING.
I COULDN'T FIGURE ANY OF IT OUT.
AND BY THE TIME I DID...
THEY THREW ALGEBRA AT US.
PLOP!
FART.

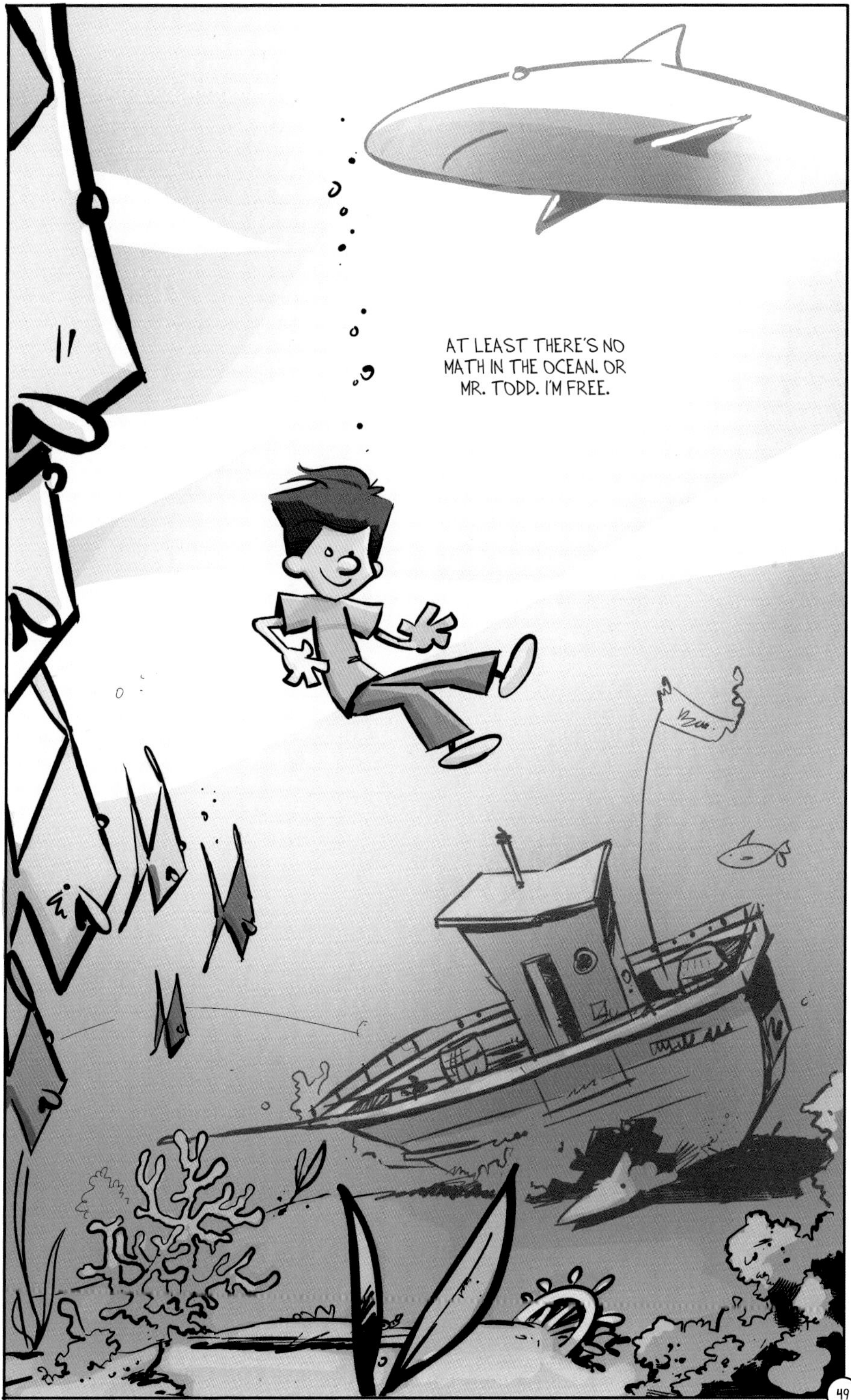
AT LEAST THERE'S NO
MATH IN THE OCEAN. OR
MR. TODD. I'M FREE.

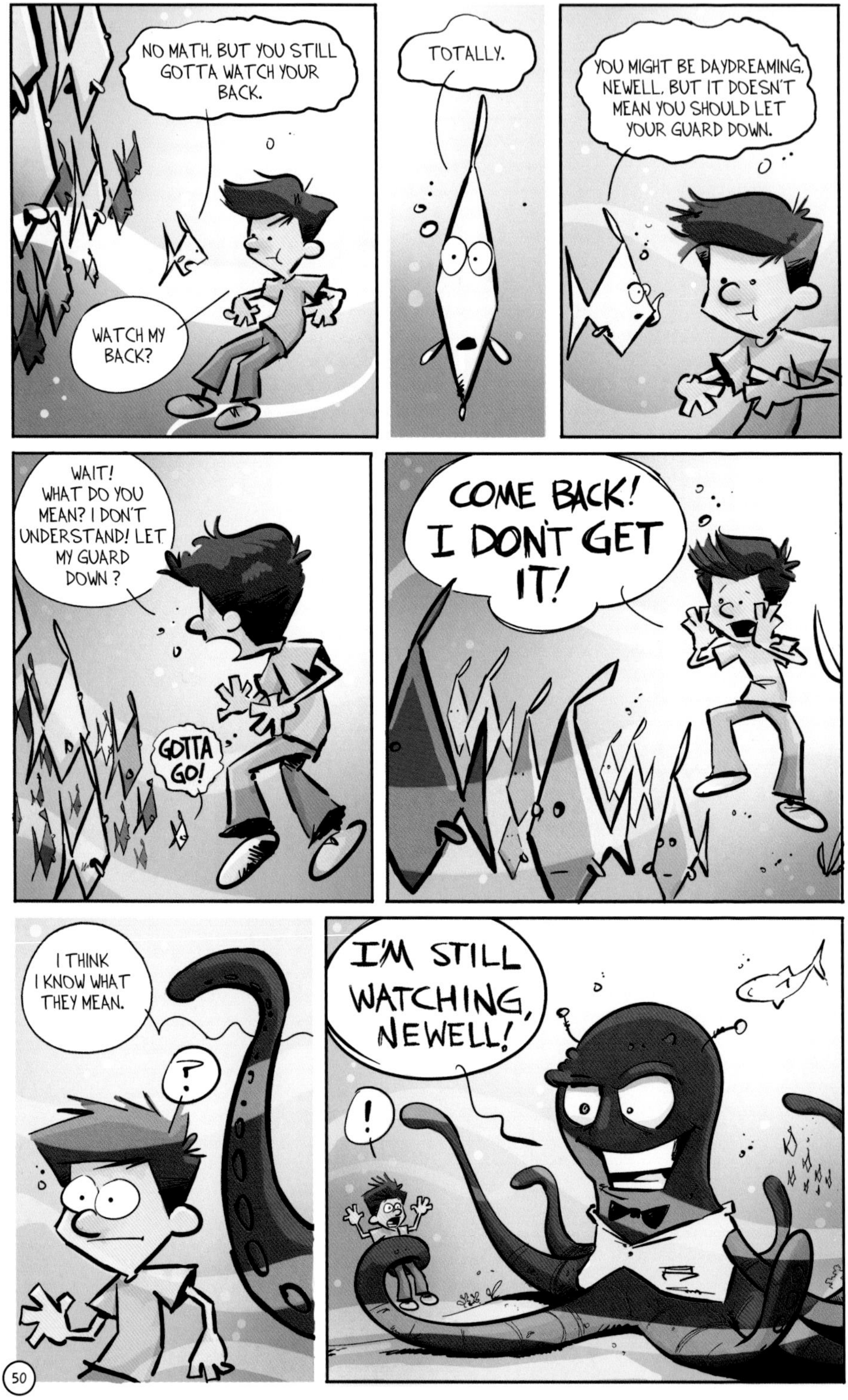
NO MATH, BUT YOU STILL GOTTA WATCH YOUR BACK.
WATCH MY BACK?
TOTALLY.
YOU MIGHT BE DAYDREAMING, NEWELL, BUT IT DOESN'T MEAN YOU SHOULD LET YOUR GUARD DOWN.
WAIT! WHAT DO YOU MEAN? I DON'T UNDERSTAND! LET MY GUARD DOWN?
GOTTA GO!
COME BACK! I DON'T GET IT!
I THINK I KNOW WHAT THEY MEAN.
?
I'M STILL WATCHING, NEWELL!
!

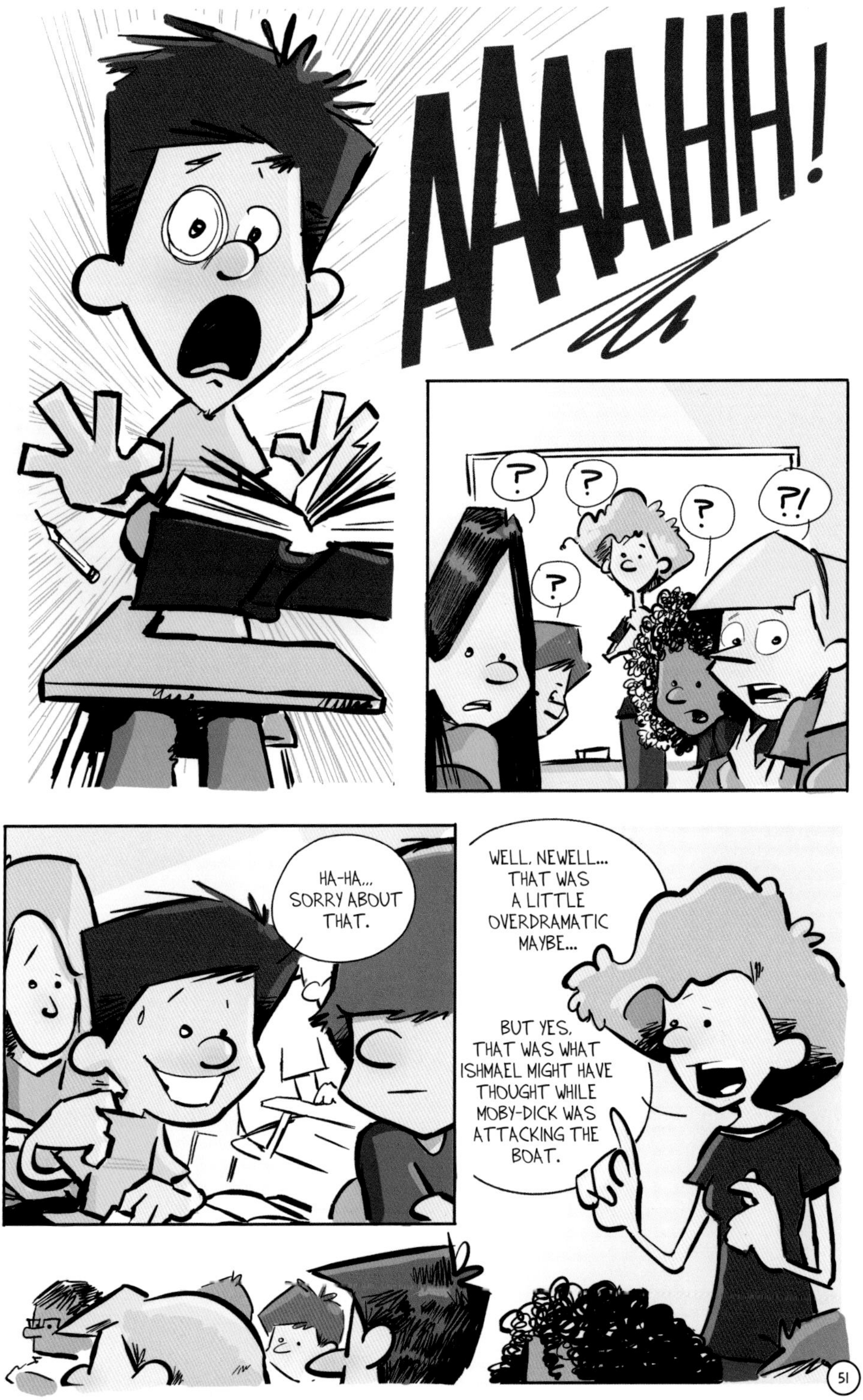
AAAAHH!
?
?
?
?
?!
HA-HA... SORRY ABOUT THAT.
WELL, NEWELL... THAT WAS A LITTLE OVERDRAMATIC MAYBE...
BUT YES, THAT WAS WHAT ISHMAEL MIGHT HAVE THOUGHT WHILE MOBY-DICK WAS ATTACKING THE BOAT.

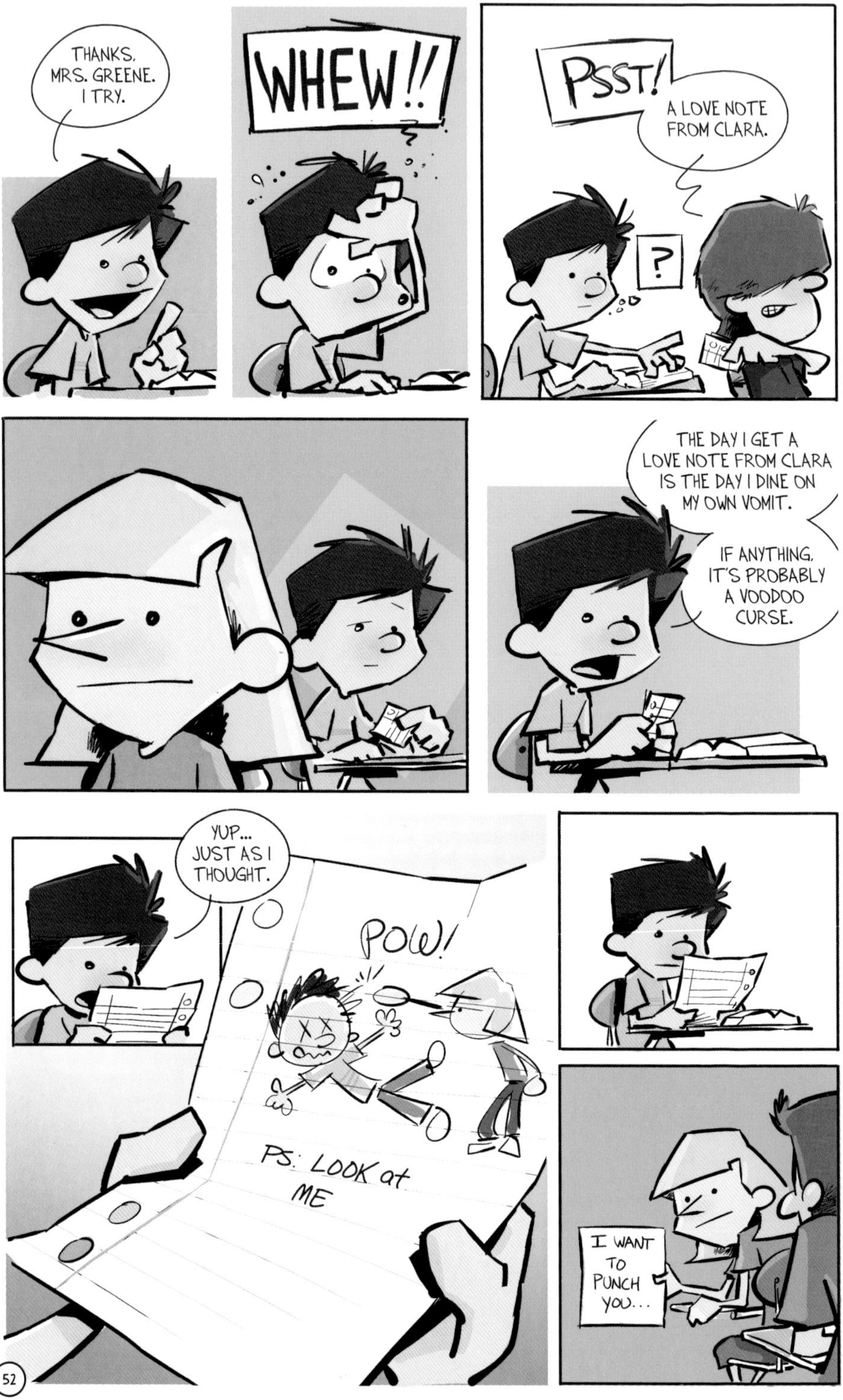
THANKS, MRS. GREENE. I TRY.
WHEW!!
PSST!
A LOVE NOTE FROM CLARA.
?
THE DAY I GET A LOVE NOTE FROM CLARA IS THE DAY I DINE ON MY OWN VOMIT.
IF ANYTHING, IT'S PROBABLY A VOODOO CURSE.
YUP... JUST AS I THOUGHT.
POW!
PS: LOOK at ME
I WANT TO PUNCH YOU...

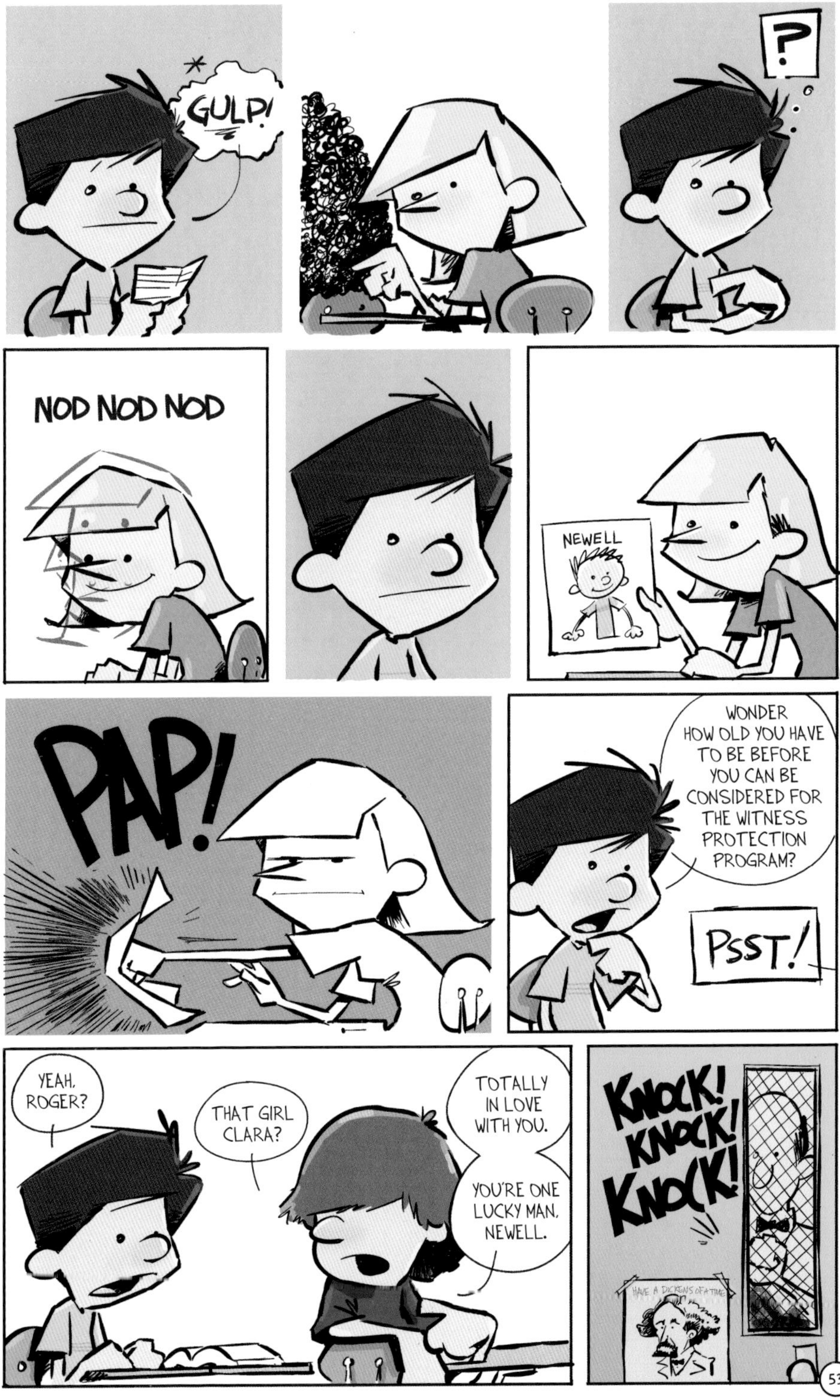
GULP!
?
NOD NOD NOD
NEWELL
PAP!
WONDER HOW OLD YOU HAVE TO BE BEFORE YOU CAN BE CONSIDERED FOR THE WITNESS PROTECTION PROGRAM?
PSST!
YEAH, ROGER?
THAT GIRL CLARA?
TOTALLY IN LOVE WITH YOU.
YOU'RE ONE LUCKY MAN, NEWELL.
KNOCK! KNOCK! KNOCK!
HAVE A DICKENS OF A TIME

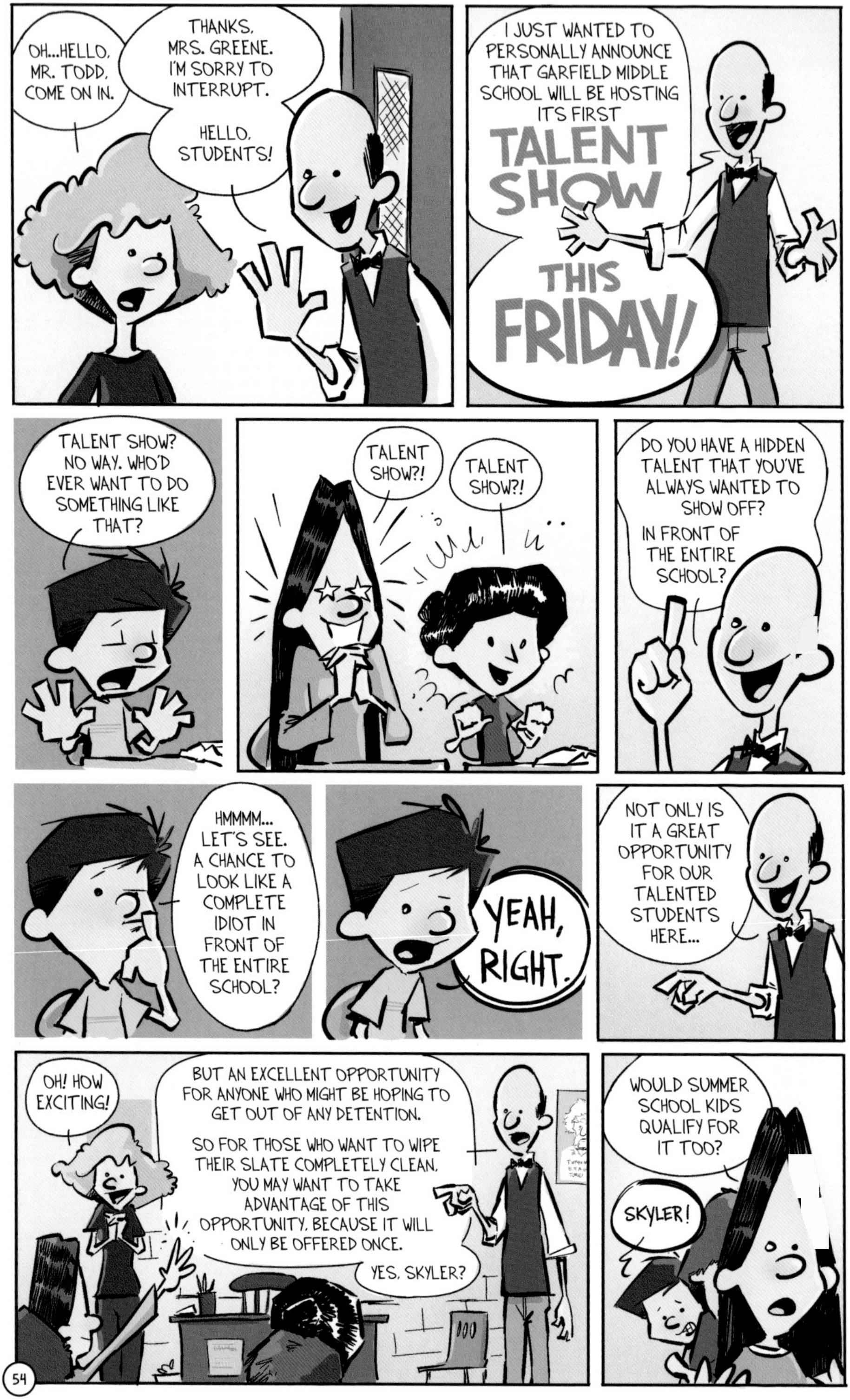
OH...HELLO, MR. TODD. COME ON IN.
THANKS, MRS. GREENE. I'M SORRY TO INTERRUPT.
HELLO, STUDENTS!
I JUST WANTED TO PERSONALLY ANNOUNCE THAT GARFIELD MIDDLE SCHOOL WILL BE HOSTING ITS FIRST TALENT SHOW THIS FRIDAY!
TALENT SHOW? NO WAY. WHO'D EVER WANT TO DO SOMETHING LIKE THAT?
TALENT SHOW?!
TALENT SHOW?!
DO YOU HAVE A HIDDEN TALENT THAT YOU'VE ALWAYS WANTED TO SHOW OFF?
IN FRONT OF THE ENTIRE SCHOOL?
HMMMM... LET'S SEE. A CHANCE TO LOOK LIKE A COMPLETE IDIOT IN FRONT OF THE ENTIRE SCHOOL?
YEAH, RIGHT.
NOT ONLY IS IT A GREAT OPPORTUNITY FOR OUR TALENTED STUDENTS HERE...
OH! HOW EXCITING!
BUT AN EXCELLENT OPPORTUNITY FOR ANYONE WHO MIGHT BE HOPING TO GET OUT OF ANY DETENTION.
SO FOR THOSE WHO WANT TO WIPE THEIR SLATE COMPLETELY CLEAN, YOU MAY WANT TO TAKE ADVANTAGE OF THIS OPPORTUNITY, BECAUSE IT WILL ONLY BE OFFERED ONCE.
YES, SKYLER?
WOULD SUMMER SCHOOL KIDS QUALIFY FOR IT TOO?
SKYLER!

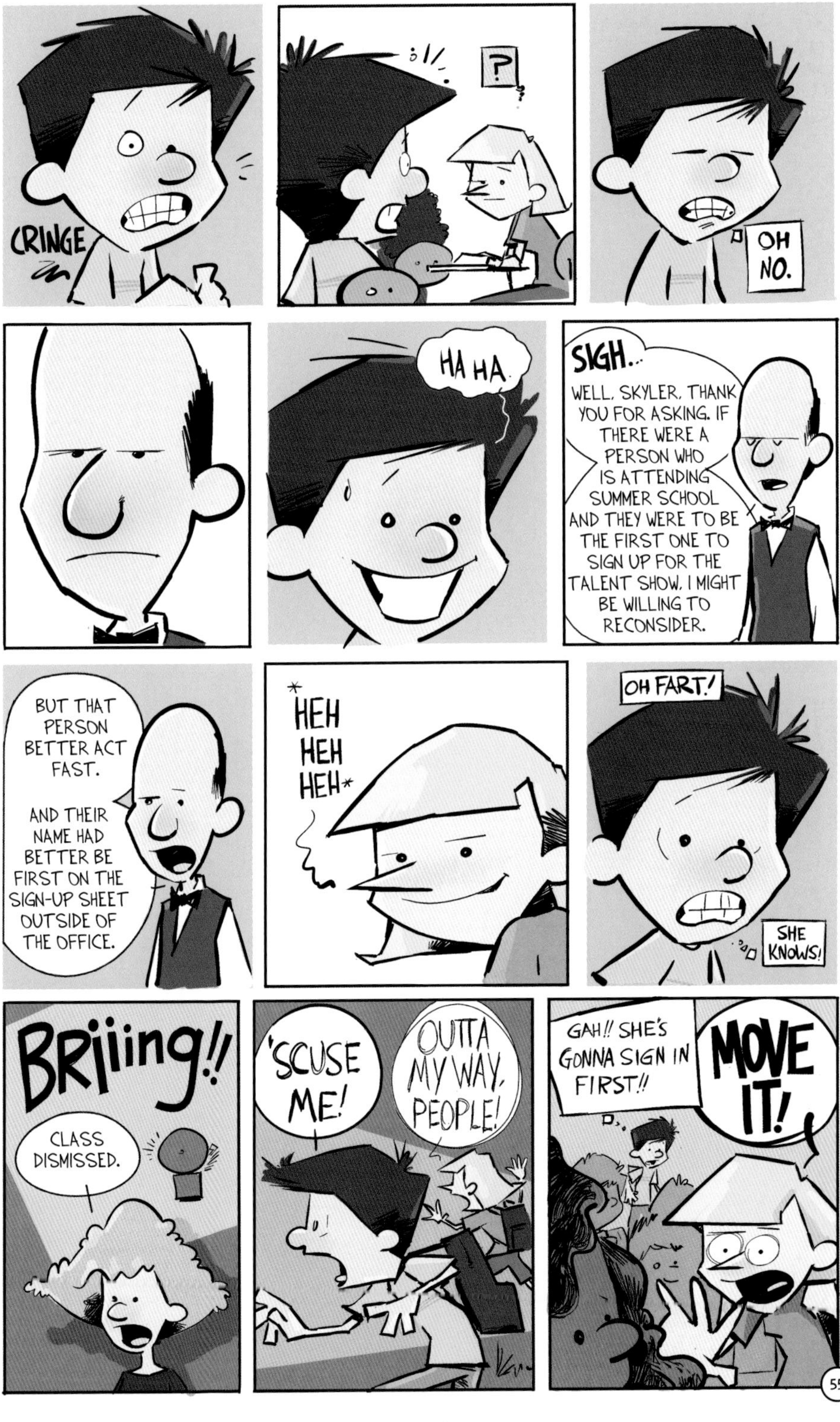
CRINGE
?
OH NO.
HA HA.
SIGH...
WELL, SKYLER, THANK YOU FOR ASKING. IF THERE WERE A PERSON WHO IS ATTENDING SUMMER SCHOOL AND THEY WERE TO BE THE FIRST ONE TO SIGN UP FOR THE TALENT SHOW, I MIGHT BE WILLING TO RECONSIDER.
BUT THAT PERSON BETTER ACT FAST.
AND THEIR NAME HAD BETTER BE FIRST ON THE SIGN-UP SHEET OUTSIDE OF THE OFFICE.
HEH HEH HEH
OH FART!
SHE KNOWS!
Briiing!!
CLASS DISMISSED.
'SCUSE ME!
OUTTA MY WAY, PEOPLE!
GAH!! SHE'S GONNA SIGN IN FIRST!!
MOVE IT!

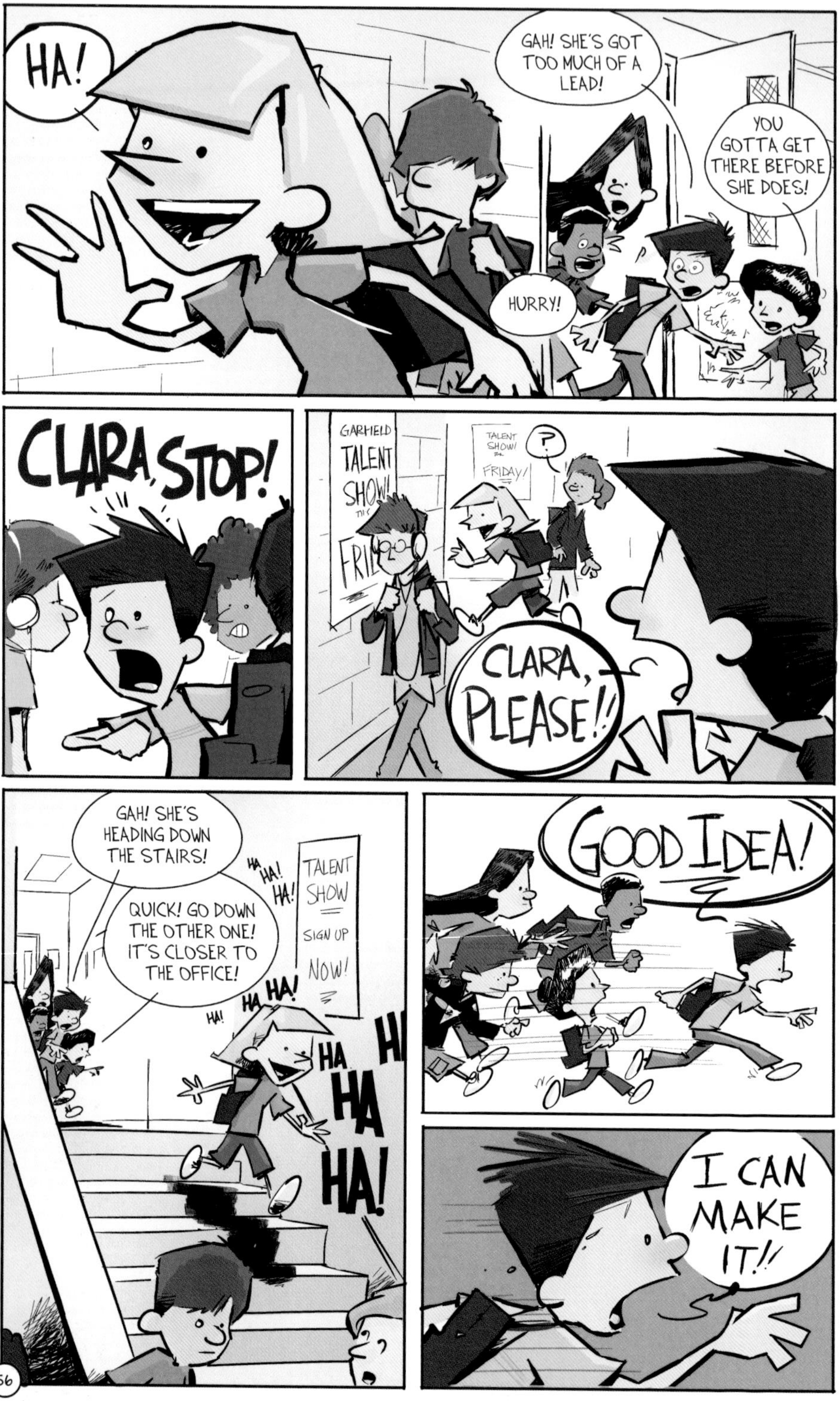
HA!
GAH! SHE'S GOT TOO MUCH OF A LEAD!
YOU GOTTA GET THERE BEFORE SHE DOES!
HURRY!
CLARA, STOP!
GARFIELD TALENT SHOW! THIS FRI
TALENT SHOW! FRIDAY!
?
CLARA, PLEASE!!
GAH! SHE'S HEADING DOWN THE STAIRS!
HA HA! HA!
TALENT SHOW SIGN UP NOW!
QUICK! GO DOWN THE OTHER ONE! IT'S CLOSER TO THE OFFICE!
HA! HA HA!
HA HA HA!
GOOD IDEA!
I CAN MAKE IT!!

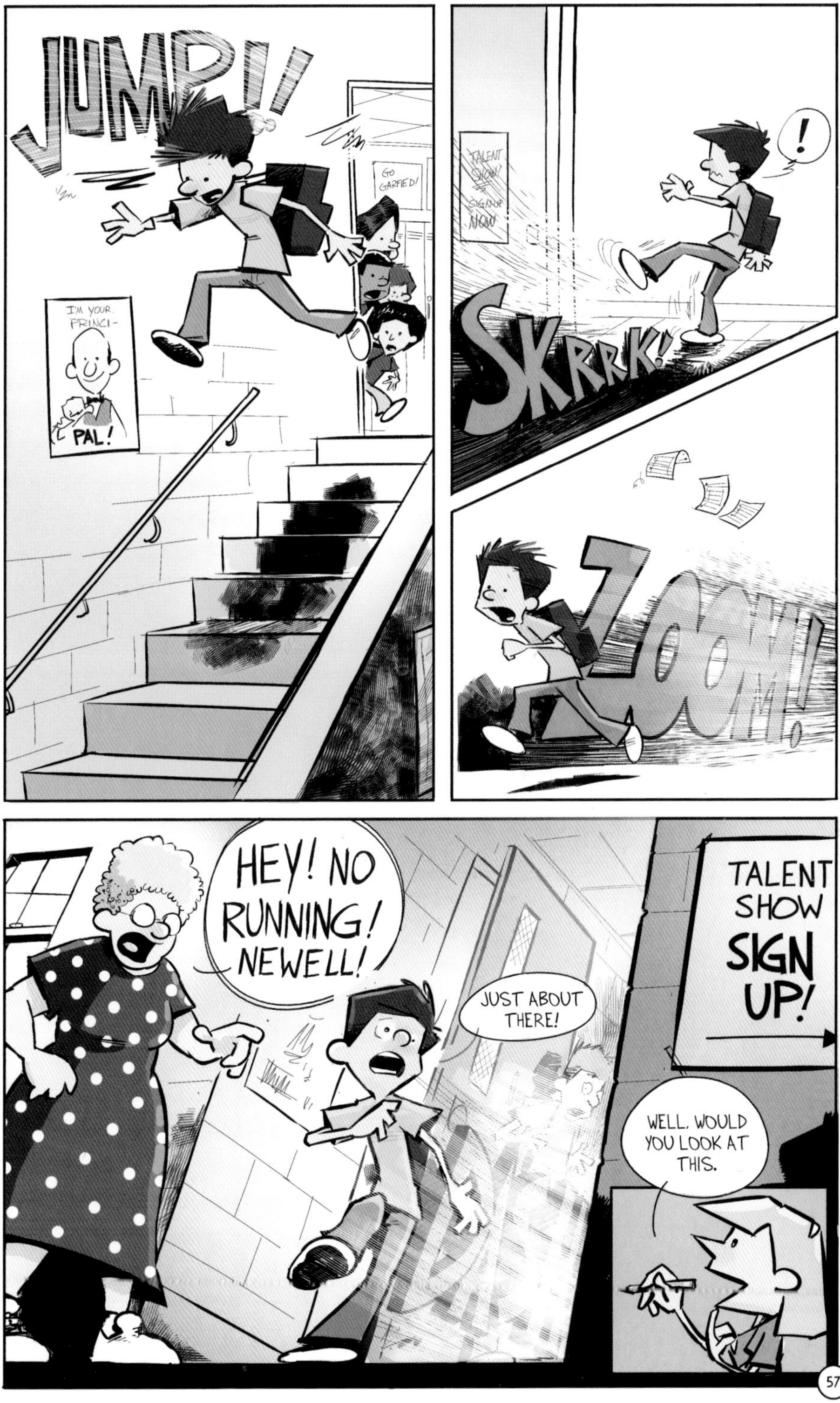
JUMP!!
GO GARFIELD!
I'M YOUR PRINCI-PAL!
TALENT SHOW! SIGN UP NOW
!
SKRRK!
ZOOM!
HEY! NO RUNNING! NEWELL!
JUST ABOUT THERE!
TALENT SHOW SIGN UP!
WELL, WOULD YOU LOOK AT THIS.

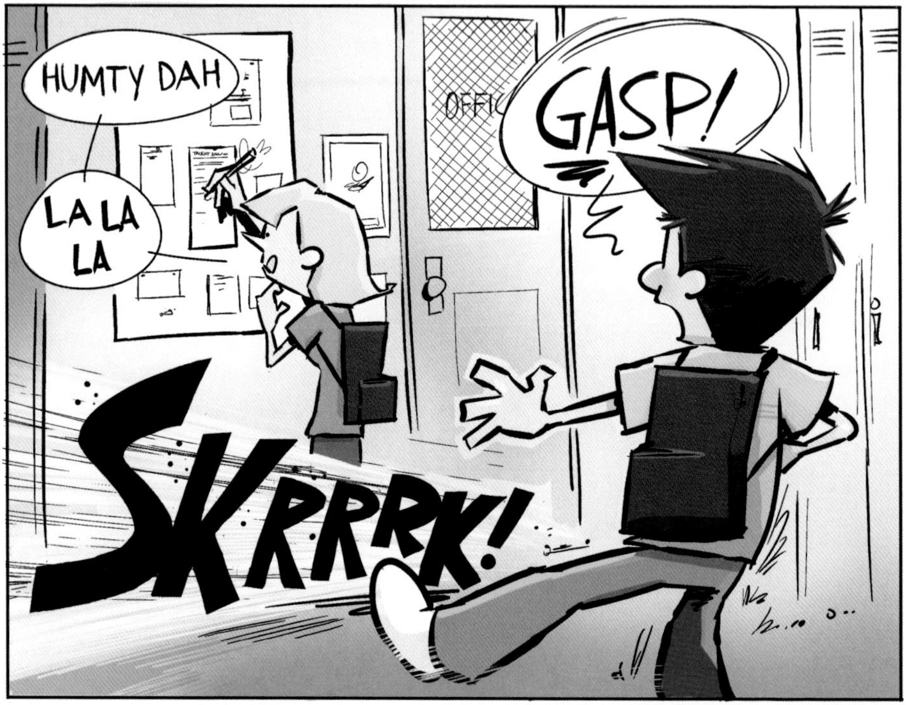
HUMTY DAH
LA LA LA
GASP!
SKRRRK!

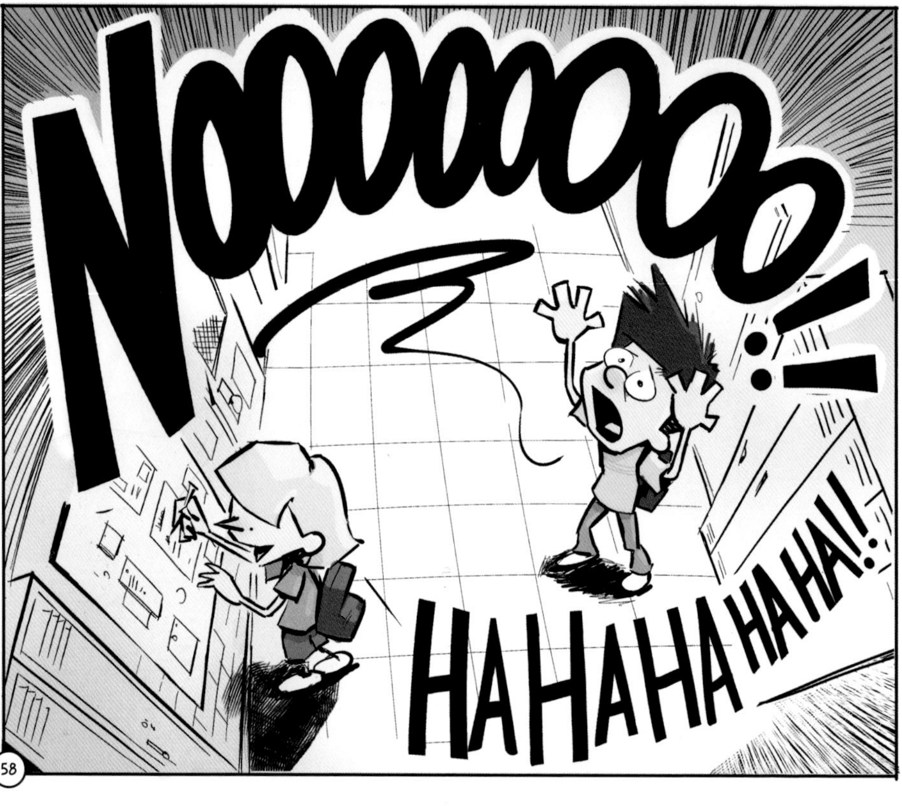
NOOOOOOO!!
HAHAHAHAHAHA!

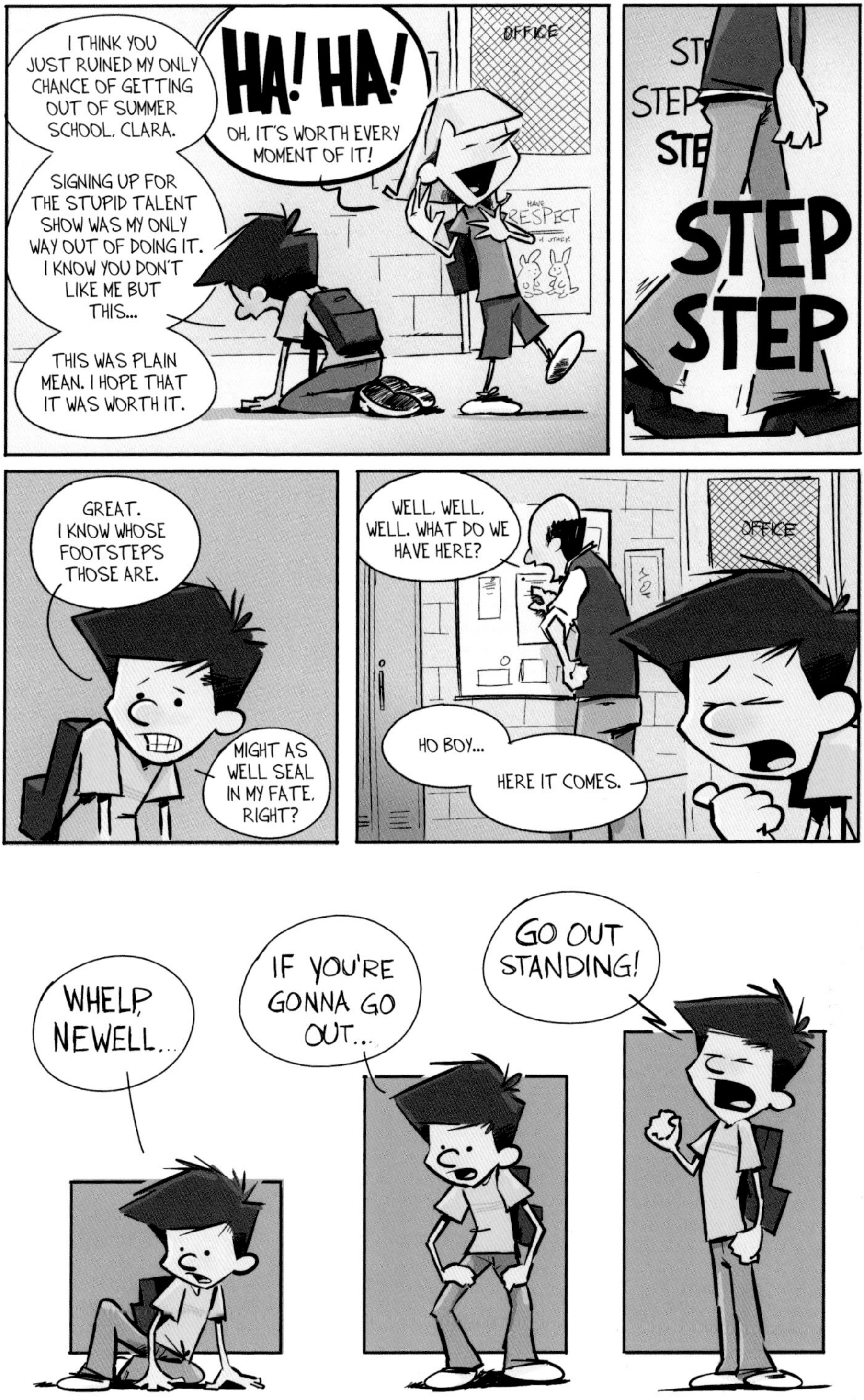
I THINK YOU JUST RUINED MY ONLY CHANCE OF GETTING OUT OF SUMMER SCHOOL, CLARA.
SIGNING UP FOR THE STUPID TALENT SHOW WAS MY ONLY WAY OUT OF DOING IT. I KNOW YOU DON'T LIKE ME BUT THIS...
THIS WAS PLAIN MEAN. I HOPE THAT IT WAS WORTH IT.
HA! HA!
OH, IT'S WORTH EVERY MOMENT OF IT!
OFFICE
HAVE RESPECT
STEP
STEP
STEP
STEP
STEP
GREAT. I KNOW WHOSE FOOTSTEPS THOSE ARE.
MIGHT AS WELL SEAL IN MY FATE, RIGHT?
WELL, WELL, WELL. WHAT DO WE HAVE HERE?
OFFICE
HO BOY...
HERE IT COMES.
WHELP, NEWELL...
IF YOU'RE GONNA GO OUT...
GO OUT STANDING!

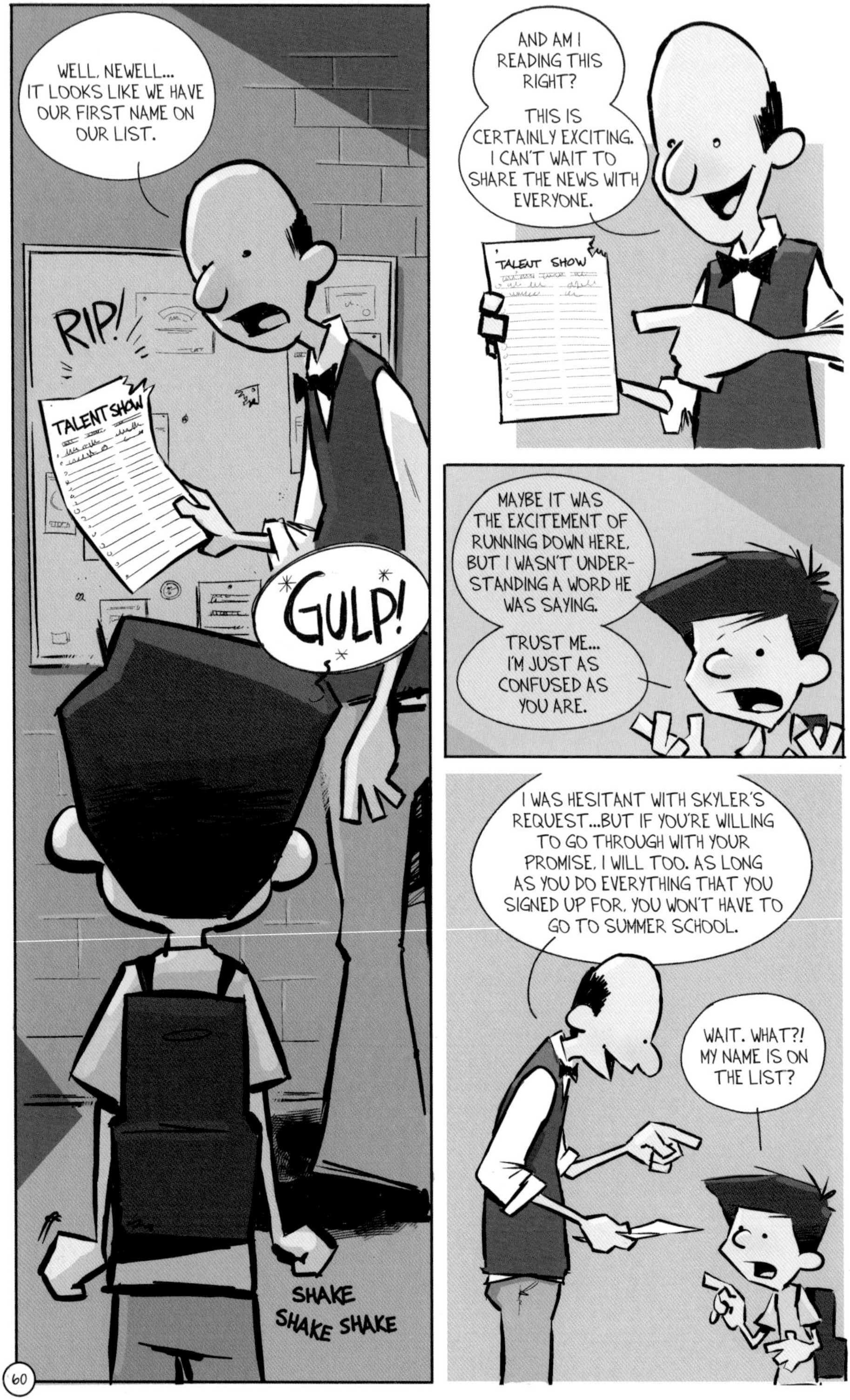
WELL, NEWELL... IT LOOKS LIKE WE HAVE OUR FIRST NAME ON OUR LIST.
RIP!
TALENT SHOW
GULP!
SHAKE SHAKE SHAKE
AND AM I READING THIS RIGHT?
THIS IS CERTAINLY EXCITING. I CAN'T WAIT TO SHARE THE NEWS WITH EVERYONE.
TALENT SHOW
MAYBE IT WAS THE EXCITEMENT OF RUNNING DOWN HERE, BUT I WASN'T UNDER-STANDING A WORD HE WAS SAYING.
TRUST ME... I'M JUST AS CONFUSED AS YOU ARE.
I WAS HESITANT WITH SKYLER'S REQUEST...BUT IF YOU'RE WILLING TO GO THROUGH WITH YOUR PROMISE, I WILL TOO. AS LONG AS YOU DO EVERYTHING THAT YOU SIGNED UP FOR, YOU WON'T HAVE TO GO TO SUMMER SCHOOL.
WAIT. WHAT?! MY NAME IS ON THE LIST?

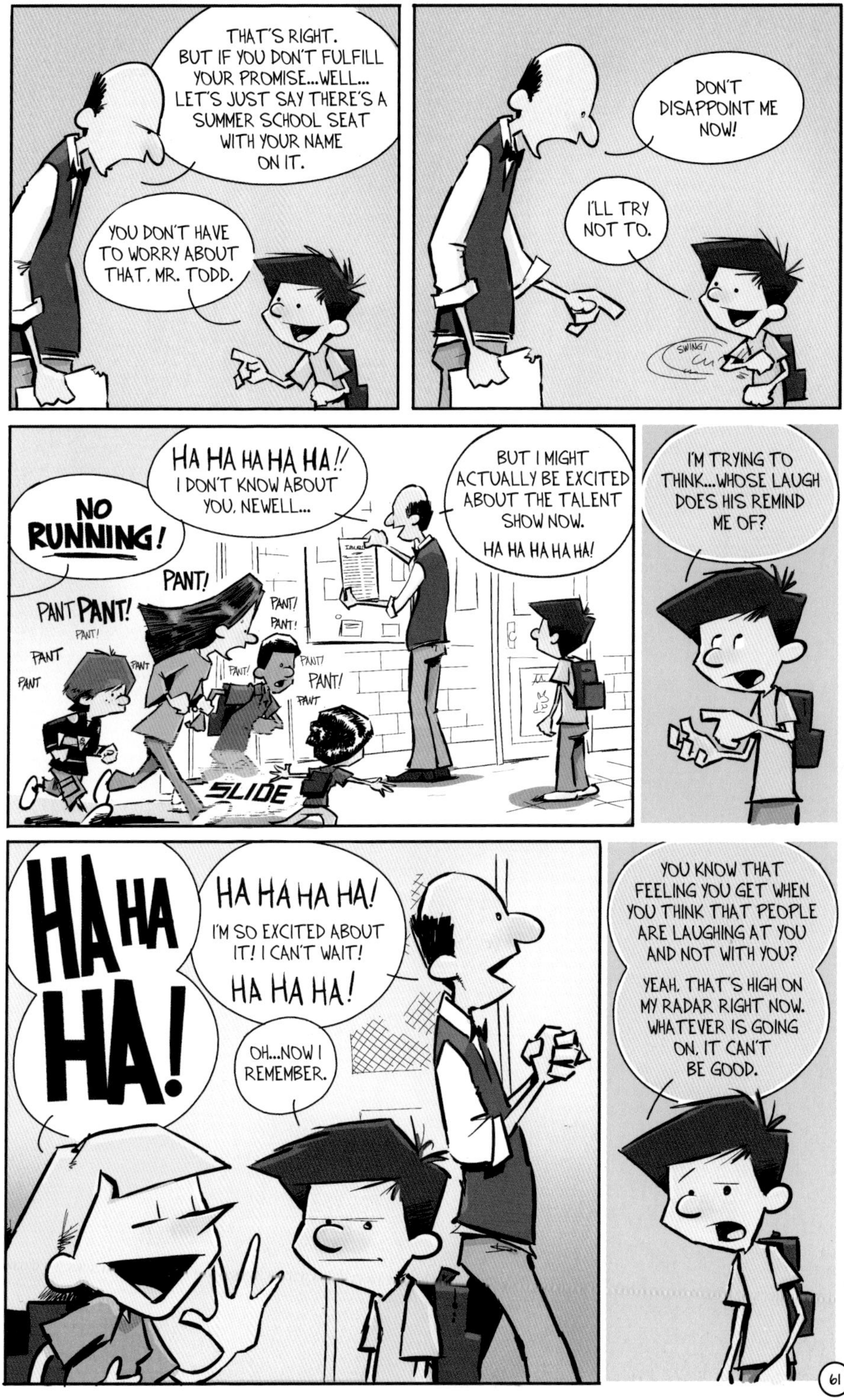
THAT'S RIGHT. BUT IF YOU DON'T FULFILL YOUR PROMISE...WELL... LET'S JUST SAY THERE'S A SUMMER SCHOOL SEAT WITH YOUR NAME ON IT.
YOU DON'T HAVE TO WORRY ABOUT THAT, MR. TODD.
DON'T DISAPPOINT ME NOW!
I'LL TRY NOT TO.
SWING!
NO RUNNING!
HA HA HA HA HA!! I DON'T KNOW ABOUT YOU, NEWELL...
BUT I MIGHT ACTUALLY BE EXCITED ABOUT THE TALENT SHOW NOW.
HA HA HA HA HA!
PANT! PANT PANT! PANT! PANT PANT PANT PANT! PANT! PANT! PANT! PANT! PANT!
SLIDE
I'M TRYING TO THINK...WHOSE LAUGH DOES HIS REMIND ME OF?
HA HA HA!
HA HA HA HA!
I'M SO EXCITED ABOUT IT! I CAN'T WAIT!
HA HA HA!
OH...NOW I REMEMBER.
YOU KNOW THAT FEELING YOU GET WHEN YOU THINK THAT PEOPLE ARE LAUGHING AT YOU AND NOT WITH YOU?
YEAH, THAT'S HIGH ON MY RADAR RIGHT NOW. WHATEVER IS GOING ON, IT CAN'T BE GOOD.

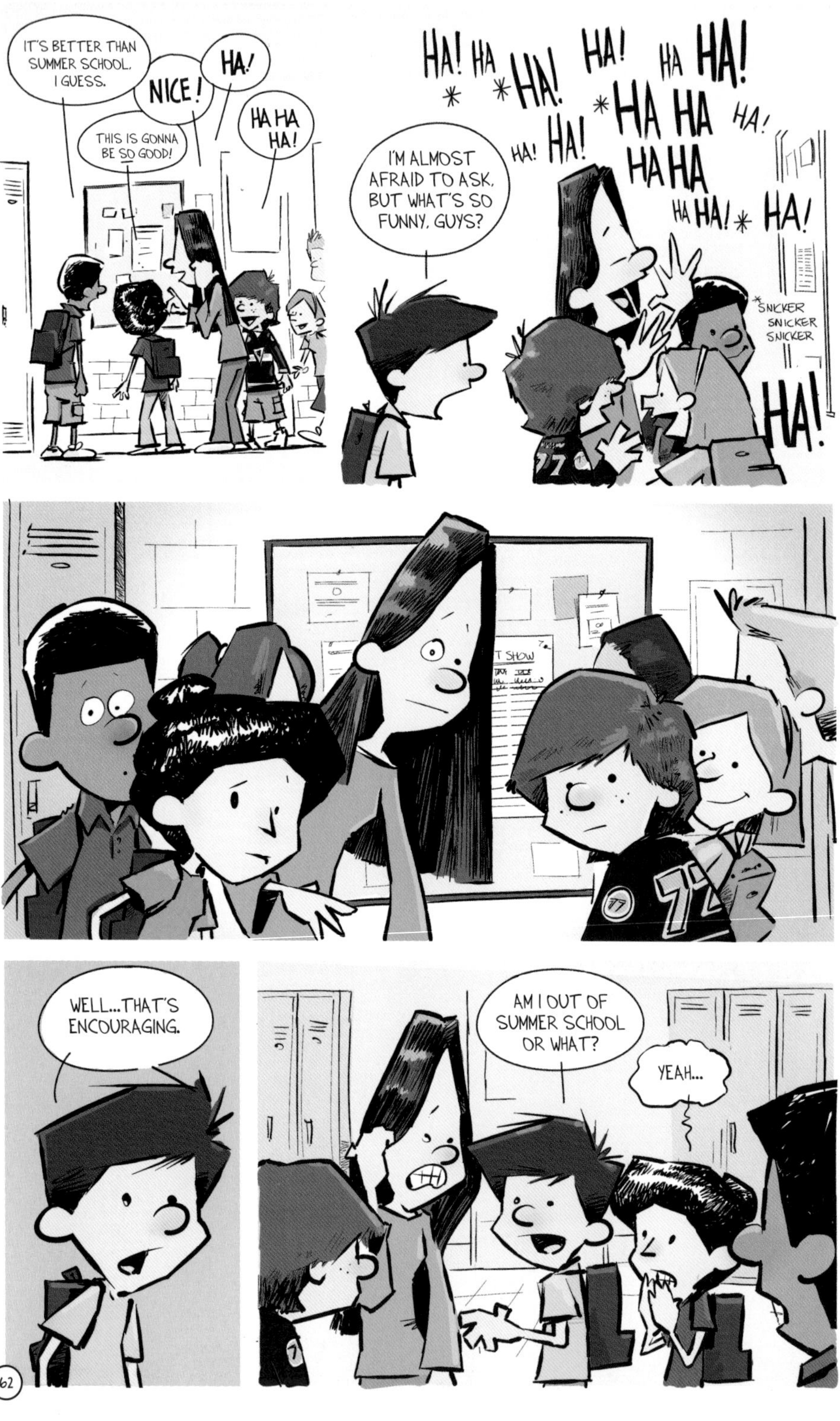
IT'S BETTER THAN SUMMER SCHOOL, I GUESS.
NICE!
HA!
THIS IS GONNA BE SO GOOD!
HA HA HA!
I'M ALMOST AFRAID TO ASK, BUT WHAT'S SO FUNNY, GUYS?
HA! HA HA! HA! HA HA! HA HA HA HA! HA! HA HA HA HA! HA!
SNICKER SNICKER SNICKER
HA!
WELL...THAT'S ENCOURAGING.
AM I OUT OF SUMMER SCHOOL OR WHAT?
YEAH...

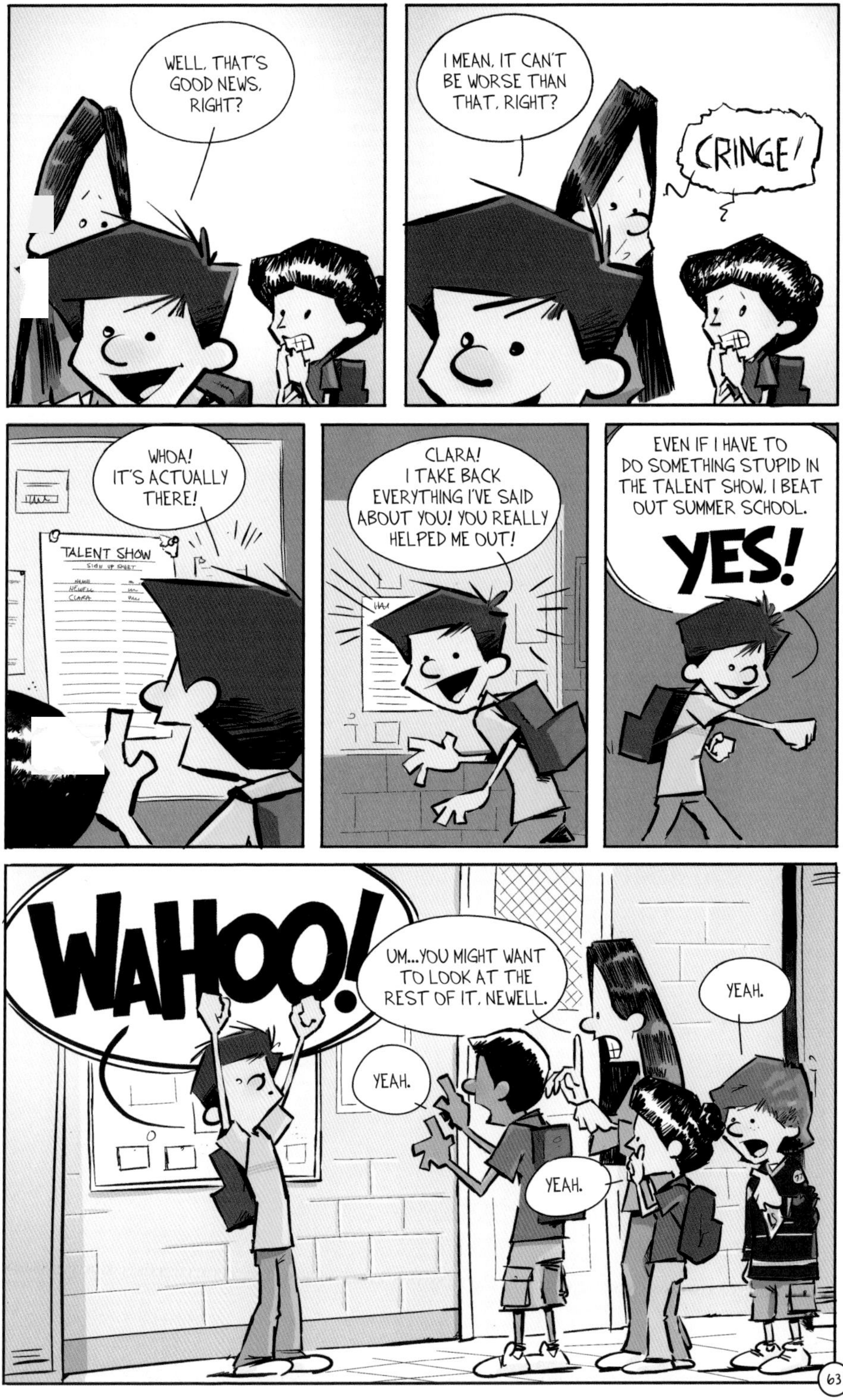
WELL, THAT'S GOOD NEWS, RIGHT?
I MEAN, IT CAN'T BE WORSE THAN THAT, RIGHT?
CRINGE!
WHOA! IT'S ACTUALLY THERE!
TALENT SHOW
CLARA! I TAKE BACK EVERYTHING I'VE SAID ABOUT YOU! YOU REALLY HELPED ME OUT!
EVEN IF I HAVE TO DO SOMETHING STUPID IN THE TALENT SHOW, I BEAT OUT SUMMER SCHOOL.
YES!
WAHOO!
UM...YOU MIGHT WANT TO LOOK AT THE REST OF IT, NEWELL.
YEAH.
YEAH.
YEAH.

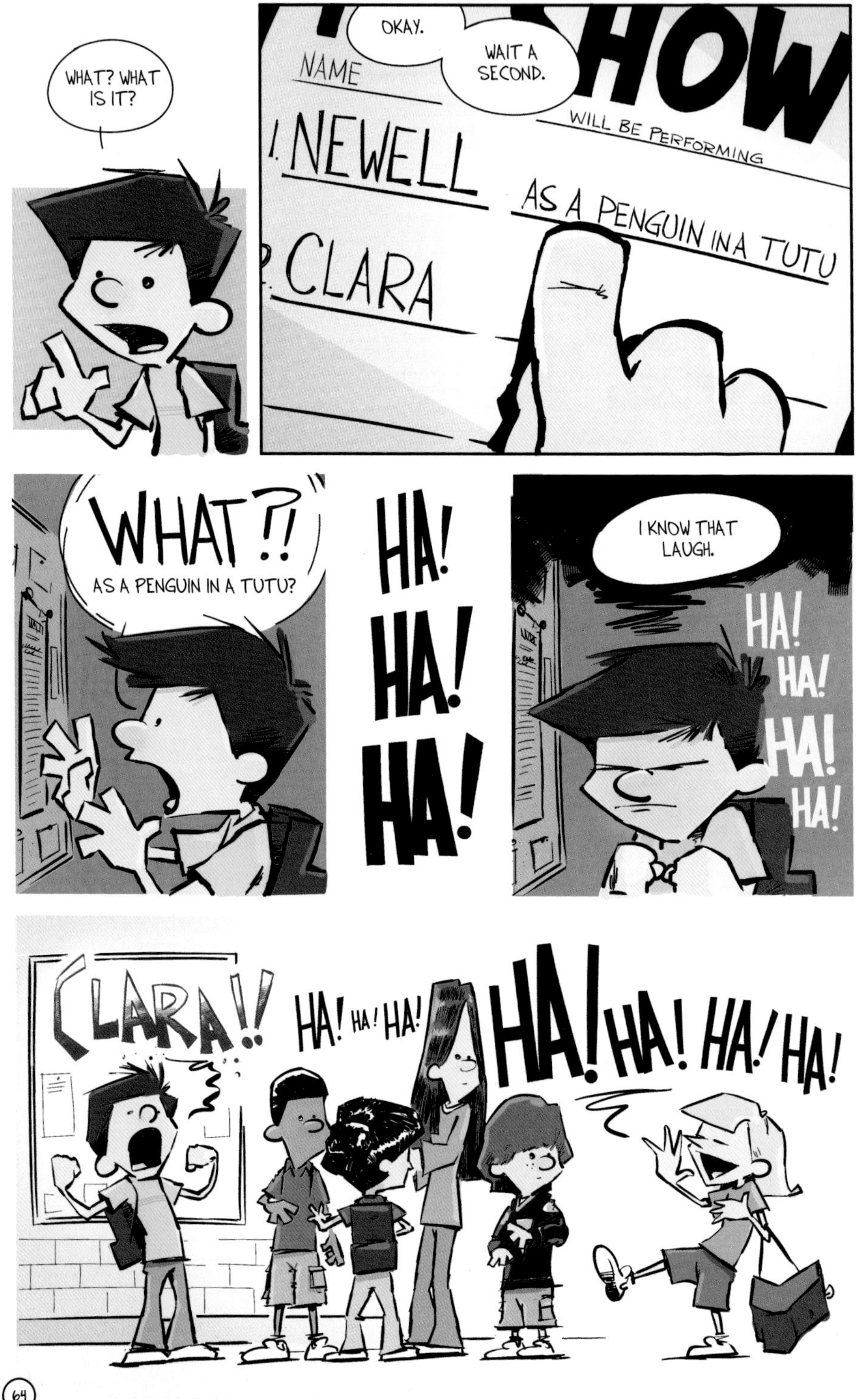
WHAT? WHAT IS IT?
OKAY.
WAIT A SECOND.
NAME
SHOW
WILL BE PERFORMING
1. NEWELL
AS A PENGUIN IN A TUTU
2. CLARA
WHAT?!
AS A PENGUIN IN A TUTU?
HA! HA! HA!
I KNOW THAT LAUGH.
HA! HA! HA! HA!
CLARA!!
HA! HA! HA! HA! HA! HA! HA!

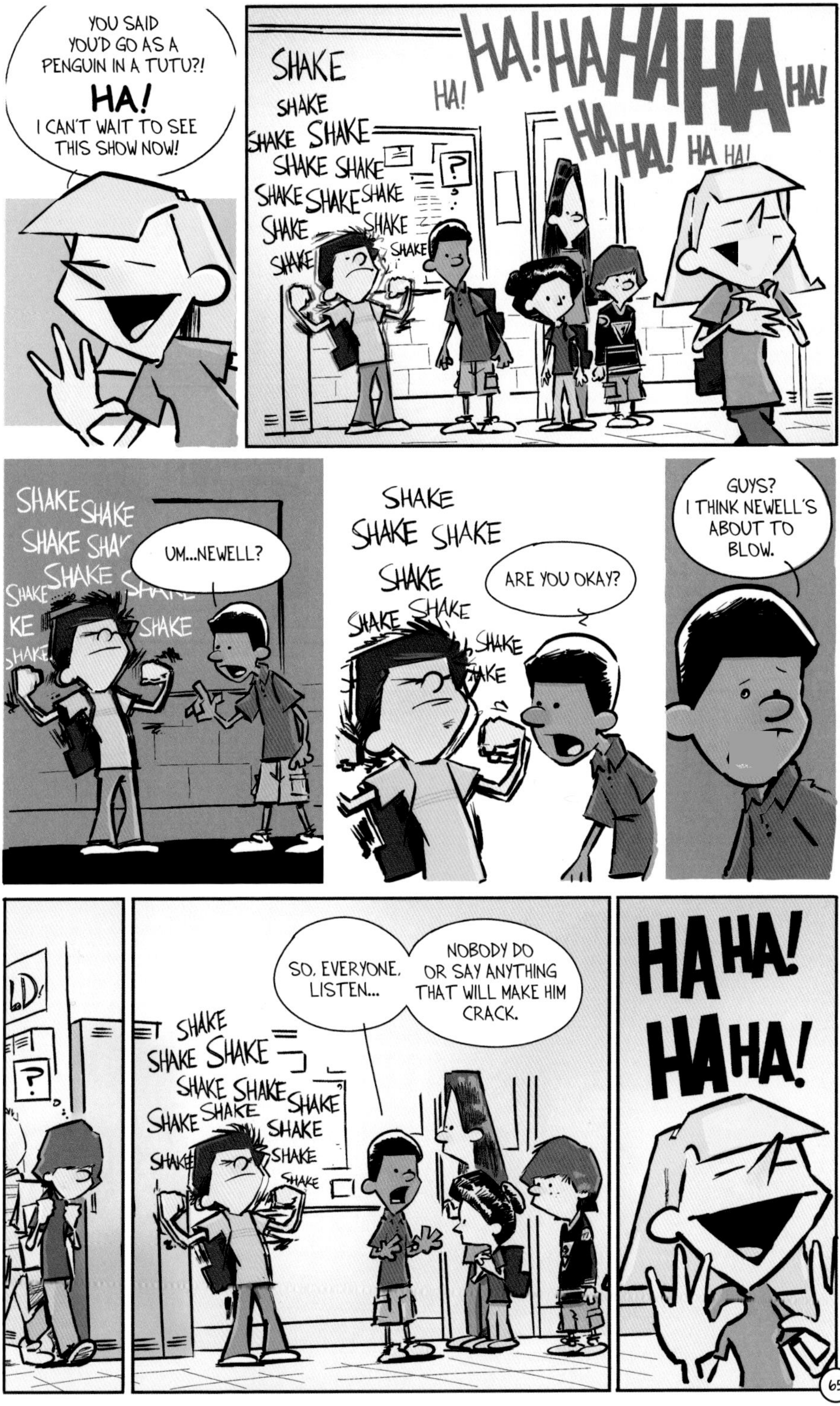
YOU SAID YOU'D GO AS A PENGUIN IN A TUTU?! HA! I CAN'T WAIT TO SEE THIS SHOW NOW!
SHAKE SHAKE SHAKE SHAKE SHAKE SHAKE SHAKE SHAKE SHAKE SHAKE SHAKE SHAKE SHAKE
HA! HA! HA HA HA HA HA! HA HA! HA HA!
UM...NEWELL?
SHAKE SHAKE SHAKE SHAKE SHAKE SHAKE
ARE YOU OKAY?
GUYS? I THINK NEWELL'S ABOUT TO BLOW.
SO, EVERYONE, LISTEN...
NOBODY DO OR SAY ANYTHING THAT WILL MAKE HIM CRACK.
SHAKE SHAKE SHAKE SHAKE SHAKE SHAKE SHAKE SHAKE SHAKE SHAKE SHAKE
HAHA! HAHA!

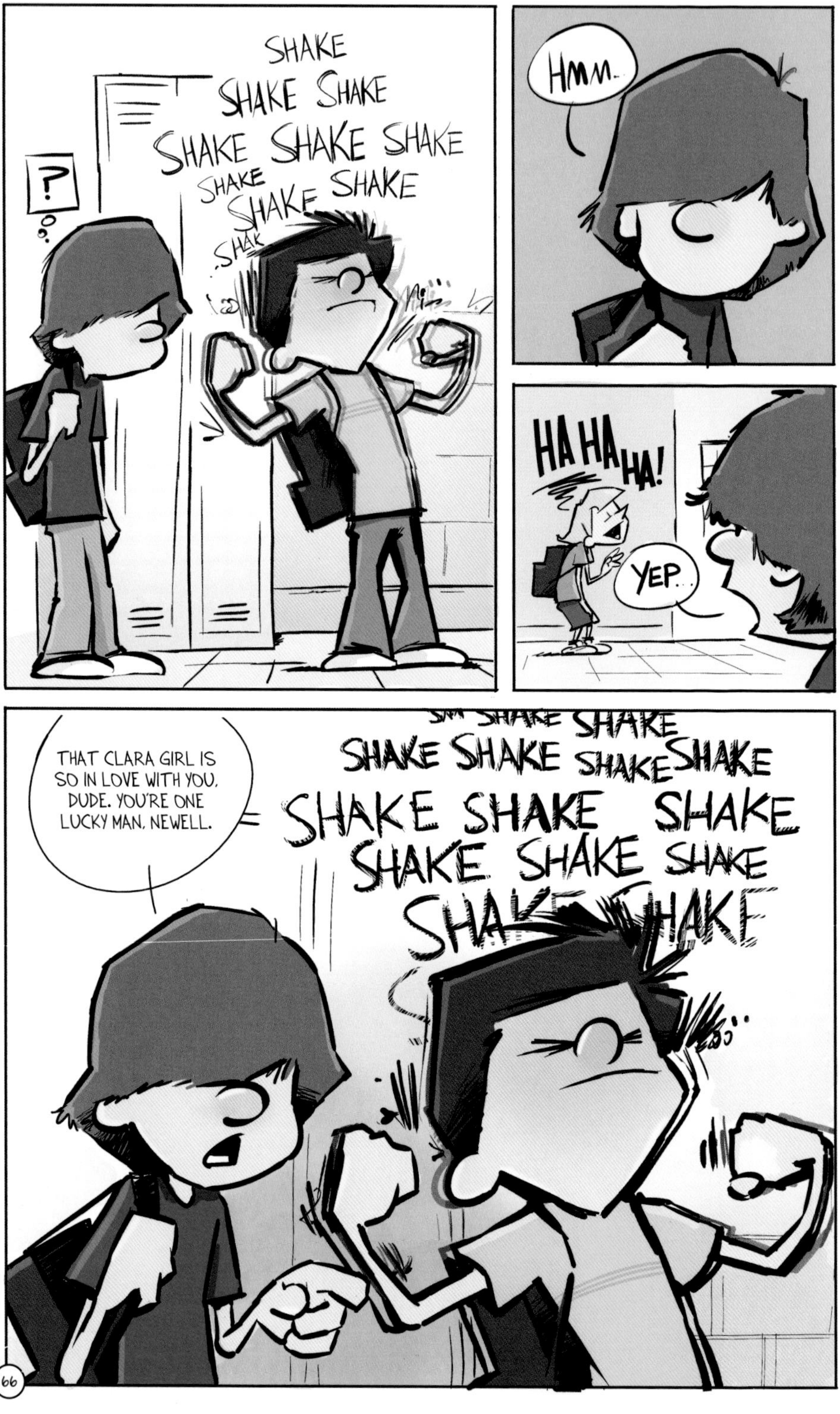
SHAKE
SHAKE SHAKE
SHAKE SHAKE SHAKE
SHAKE SHAKE
?
HMM..
HA HA HA!
YEP...
THAT CLARA GIRL IS SO IN LOVE WITH YOU, DUDE. YOU'RE ONE LUCKY MAN, NEWELL.
SHAKE SHAKE SHAKE SHAKE
SHAKE SHAKE SHAKE
SHAKE SHAKE SHAKE

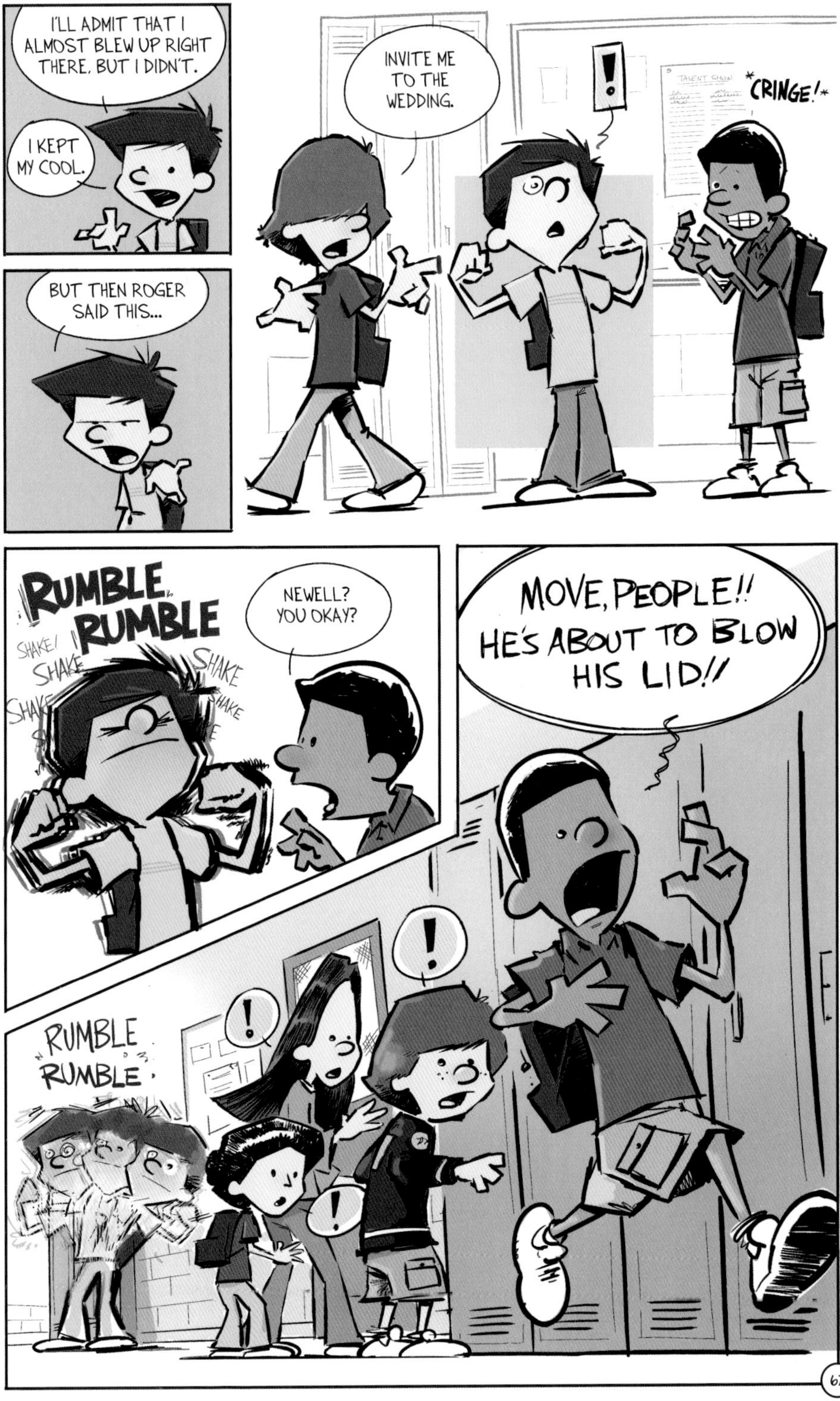
I'LL ADMIT THAT I ALMOST BLEW UP RIGHT THERE, BUT I DIDN'T.
I KEPT MY COOL.
BUT THEN ROGER SAID THIS...
INVITE ME TO THE WEDDING.
!
CRINGE!
RUMBLE RUMBLE
SHAKE! SHAKE SHAKE SHAKE SHAKE
NEWELL? YOU OKAY?
MOVE, PEOPLE!! HE'S ABOUT TO BLOW HIS LID!!
!
!
!
RUMBLE RUMBLE

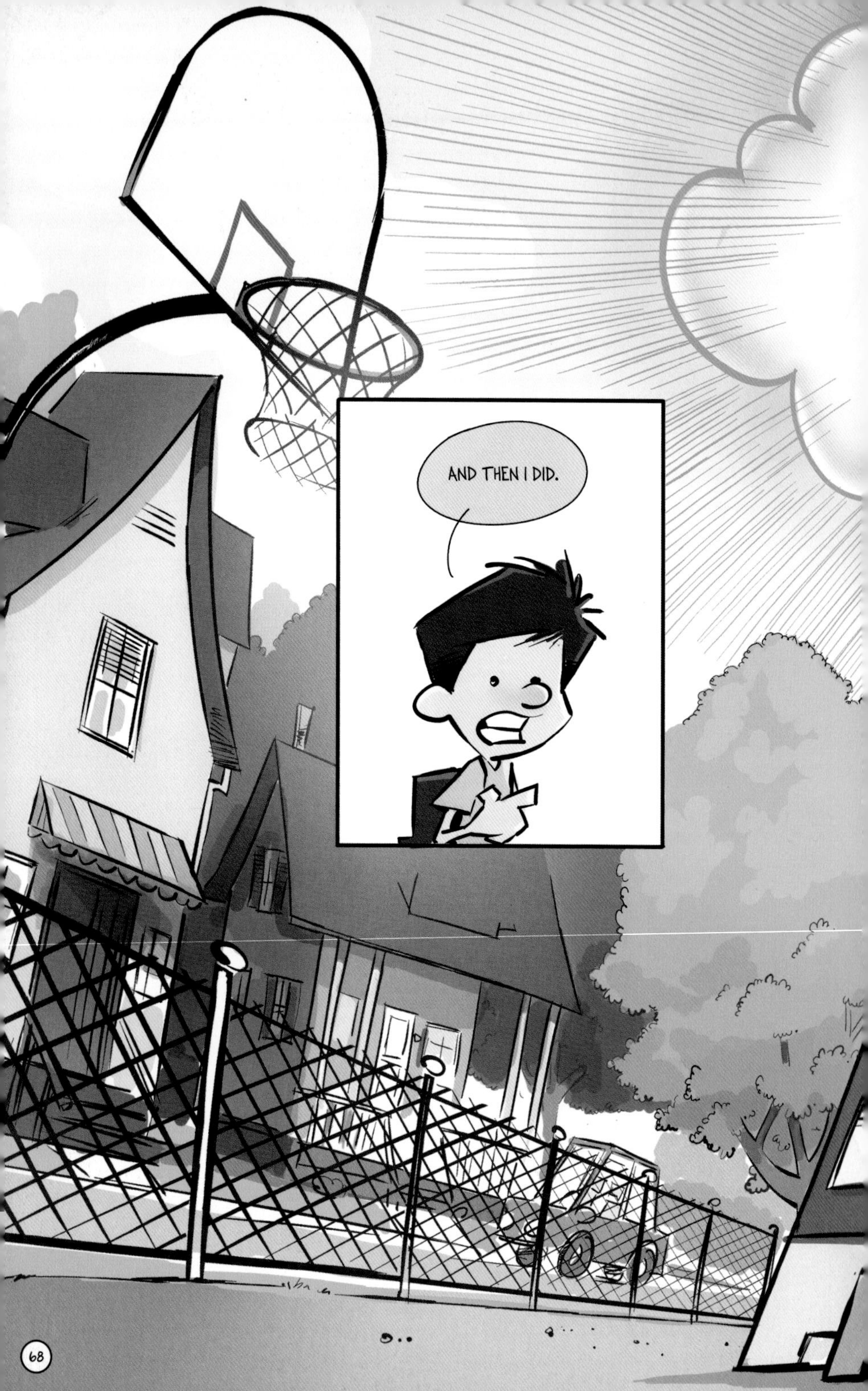
AND THEN I DID.

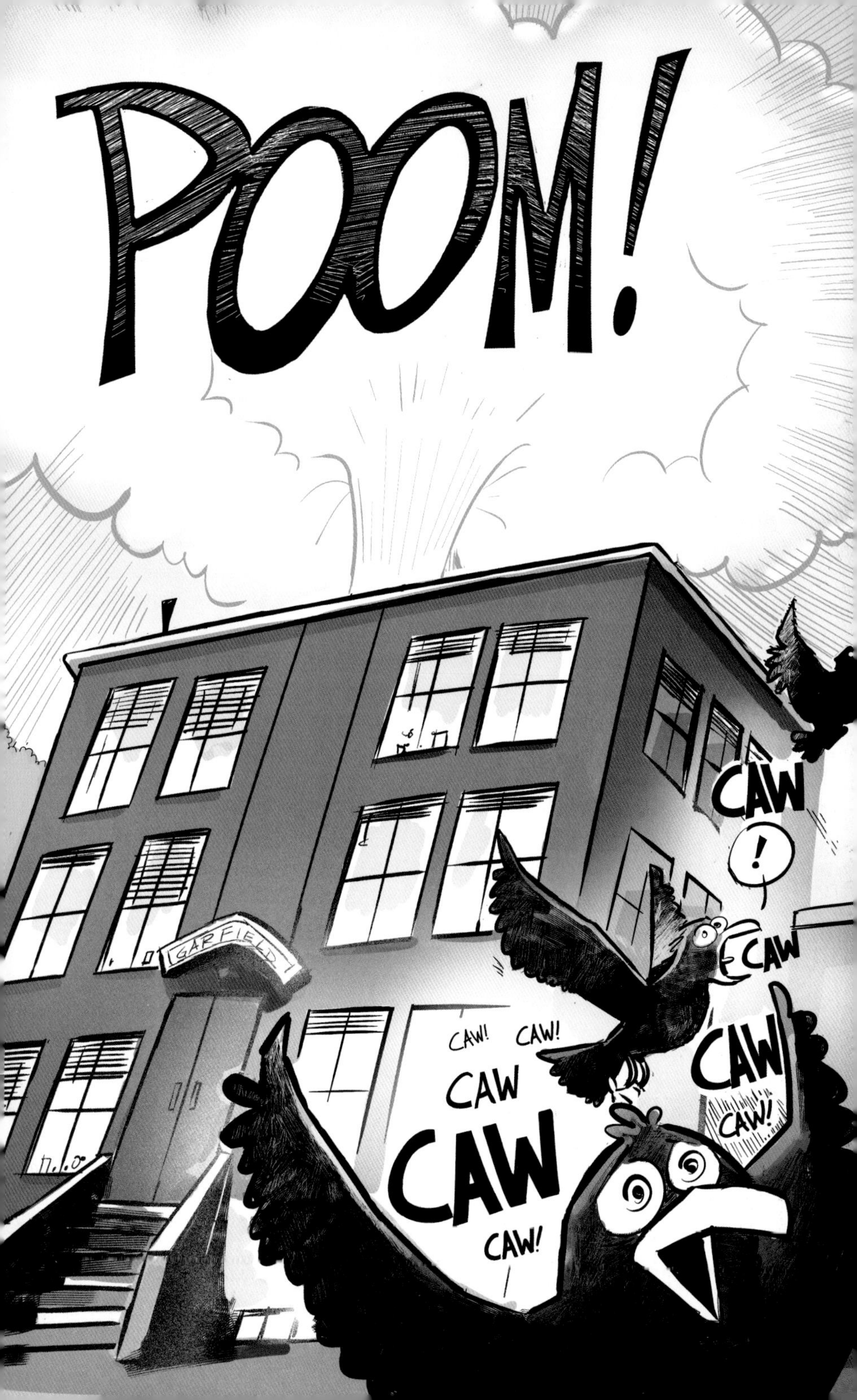
POOM!
GARFIELD
CAW
!
CAW
CAW! CAW!
CAW
CAW
CAW!
CAW
CAW!

CHAPTER FOUR
GRUMBLE

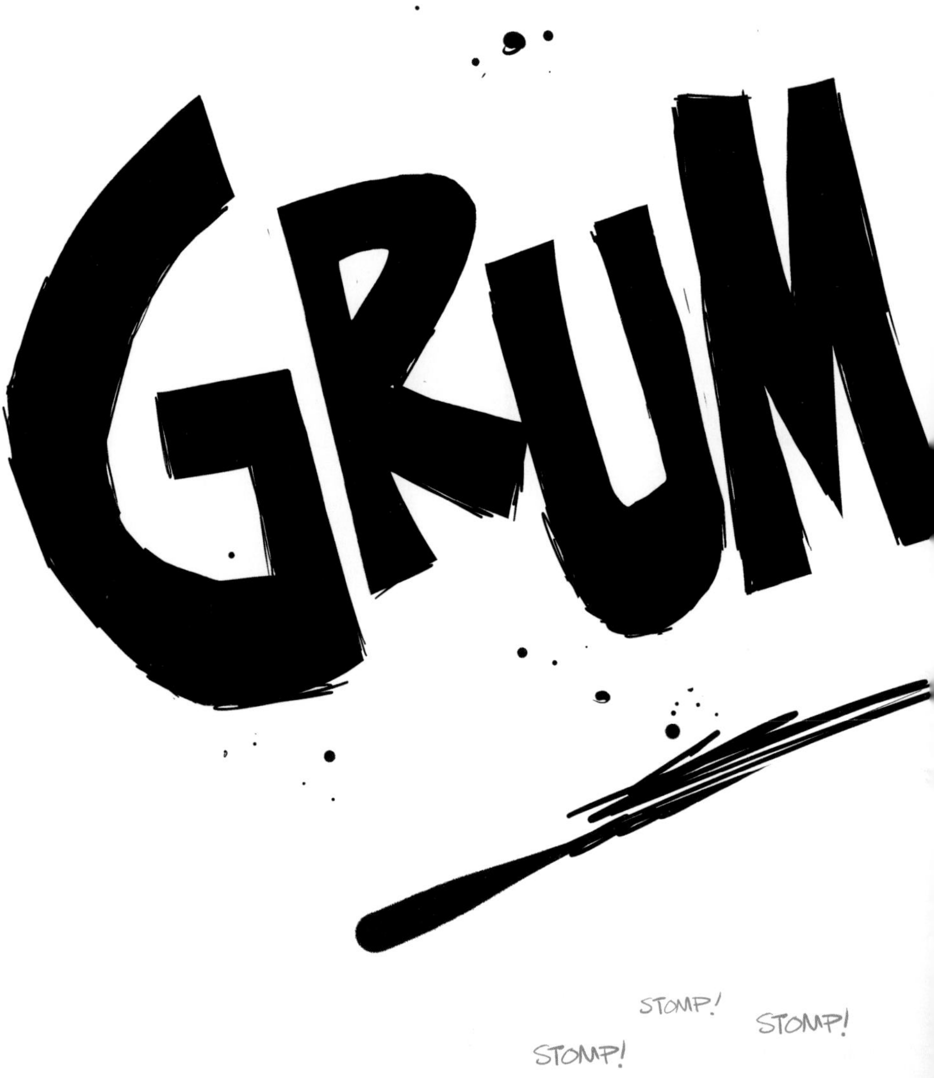
GRUM
STOMP!
STOMP!
STOMP!

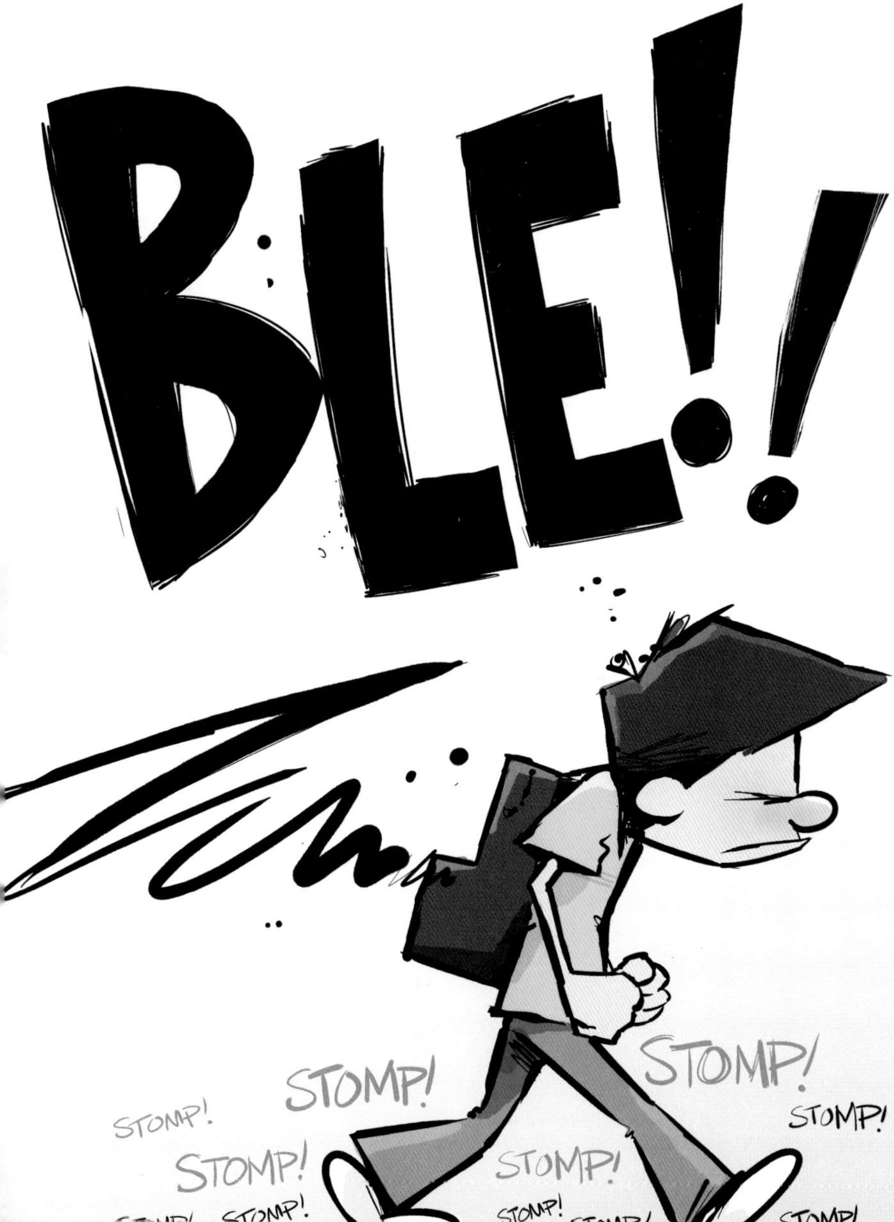
BLE!!
STOMP!
STOMP!
STOMP!
STOMP!
STOMP!
STOMP!
STOMP!
STOMP!
STOMP!
STOMP!
STOMP!

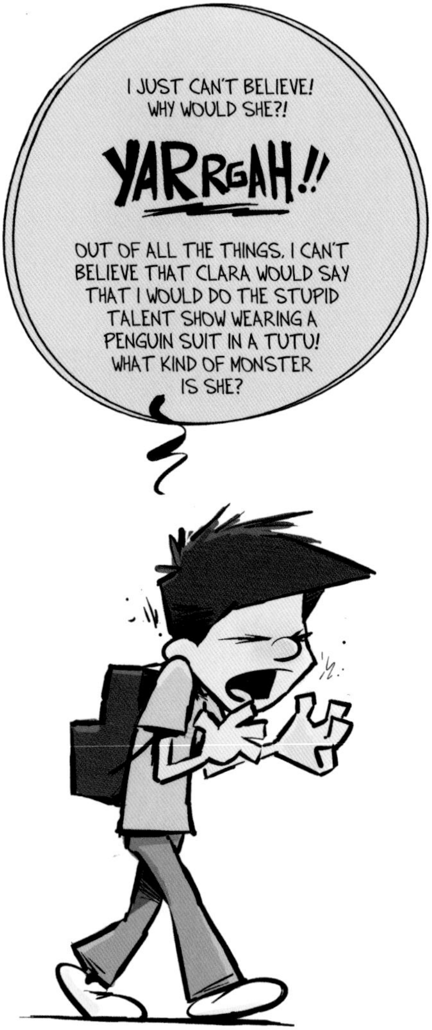
I JUST CAN'T BELIEVE! WHY WOULD SHE?!
YARRGAH!!
OUT OF ALL THE THINGS, I CAN'T BELIEVE THAT CLARA WOULD SAY THAT I WOULD DO THE STUPID TALENT SHOW WEARING A PENGUIN SUIT IN A TUTU! WHAT KIND OF MONSTER IS SHE?

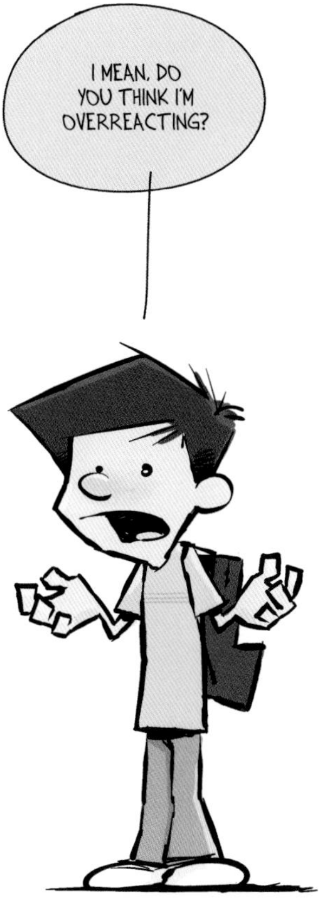
I MEAN, DO YOU THINK I'M OVERREACTING?

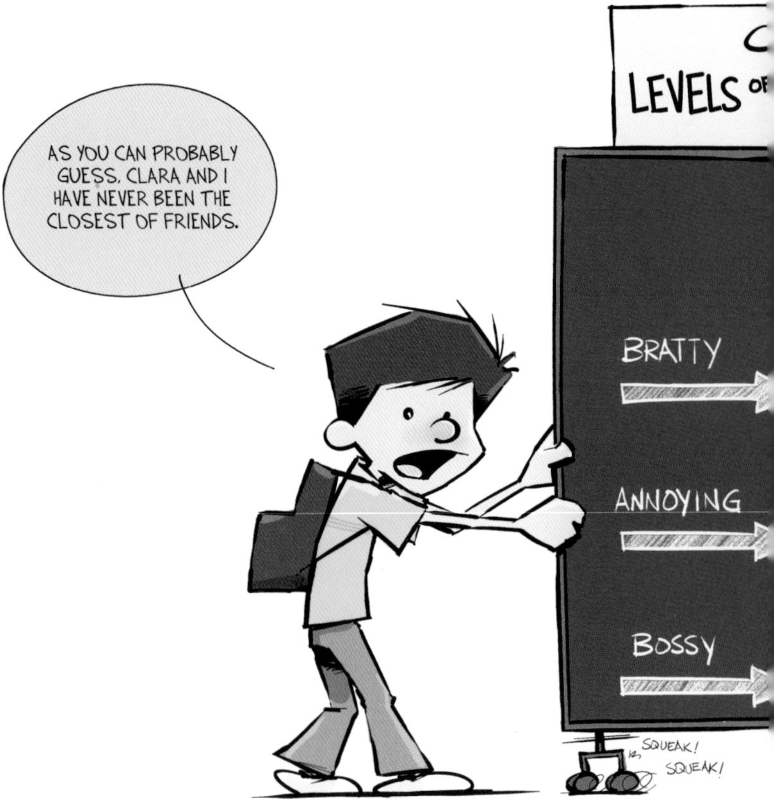
AS YOU CAN PROBABLY GUESS, CLARA AND I HAVE NEVER BEEN THE CLOSEST OF FRIENDS.
LEVELS OF
BRATTY
ANNOYING
BOSSY
SQUEAK!
SQUEAK!

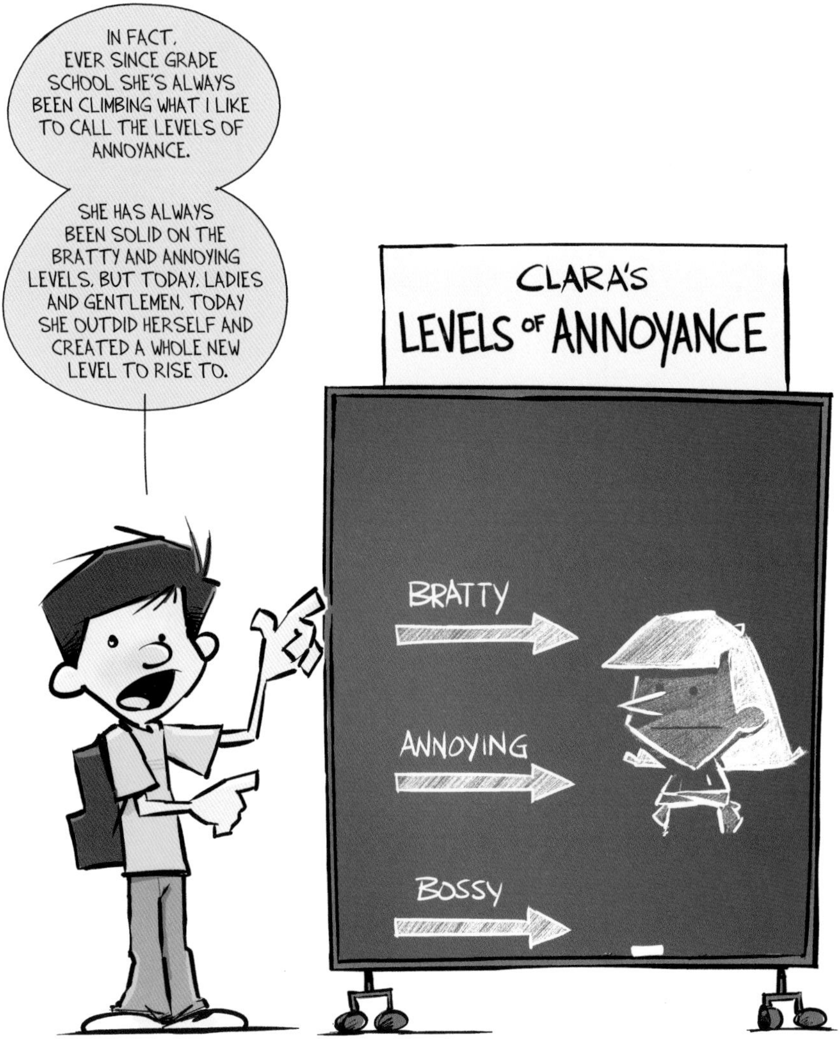
IN FACT, EVER SINCE GRADE SCHOOL SHE'S ALWAYS BEEN CLIMBING WHAT I LIKE TO CALL THE LEVELS OF ANNOYANCE.
SHE HAS ALWAYS BEEN SOLID ON THE BRATTY AND ANNOYING LEVELS, BUT TODAY, LADIES AND GENTLEMEN, TODAY SHE OUTDID HERSELF AND CREATED A WHOLE NEW LEVEL TO RISE TO.
CLARA'S LEVELS OF ANNOYANCE
BRATTY
ANNOYING
BOSSY

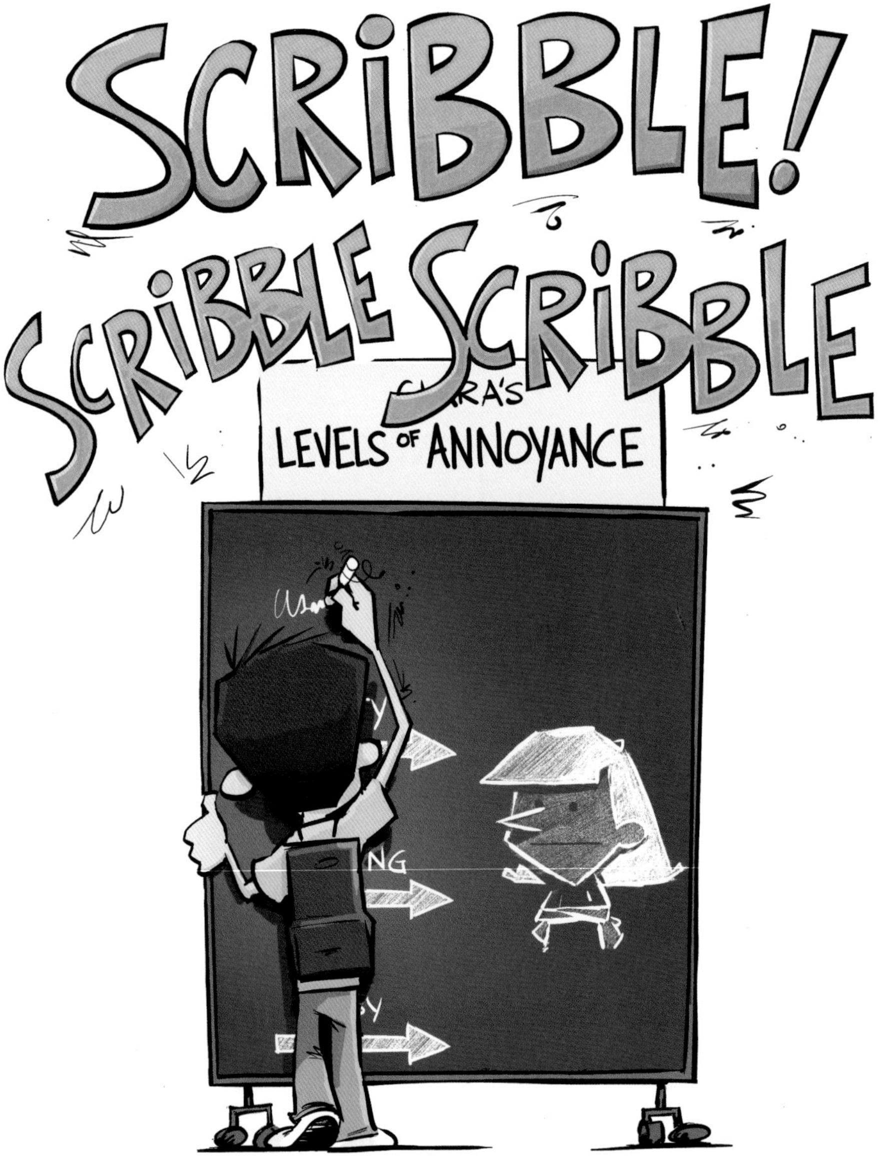
SCRIBBLE!
SCRIBBLE SCRIBBLE SCRIBBLE
LEVELS OF ANNOYANCE

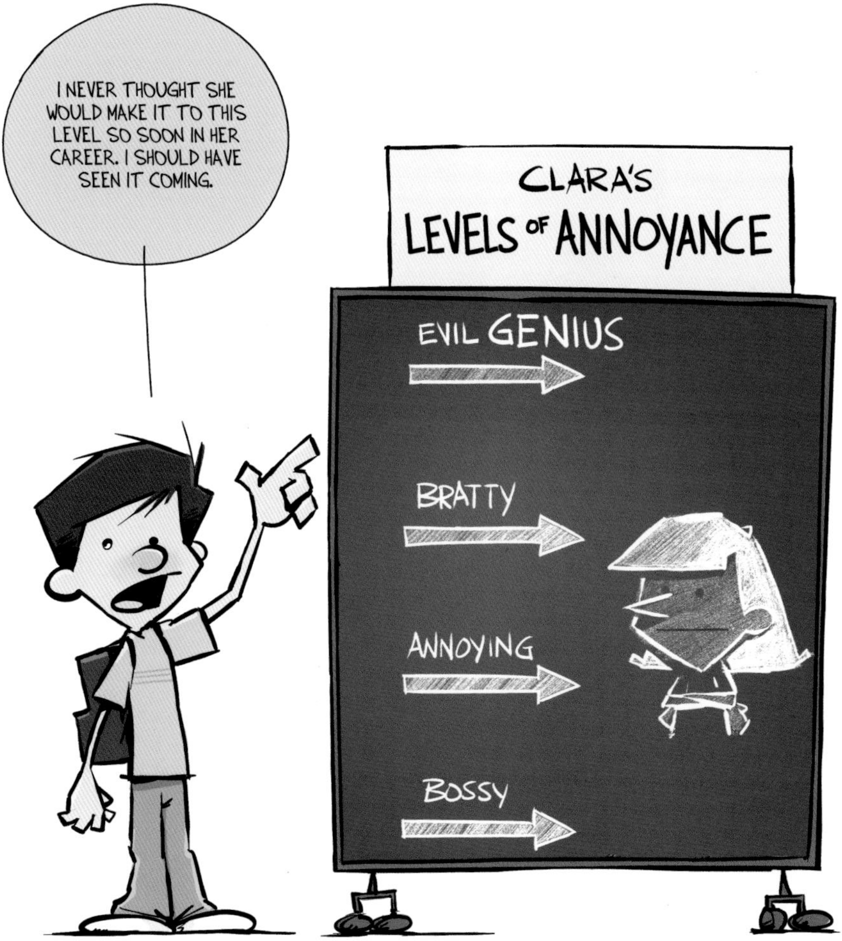
I NEVER THOUGHT SHE WOULD MAKE IT TO THIS LEVEL SO SOON IN HER CAREER. I SHOULD HAVE SEEN IT COMING.
CLARA'S LEVELS OF ANNOYANCE
EVIL GENIUS
BRATTY
ANNOYING
BOSSY

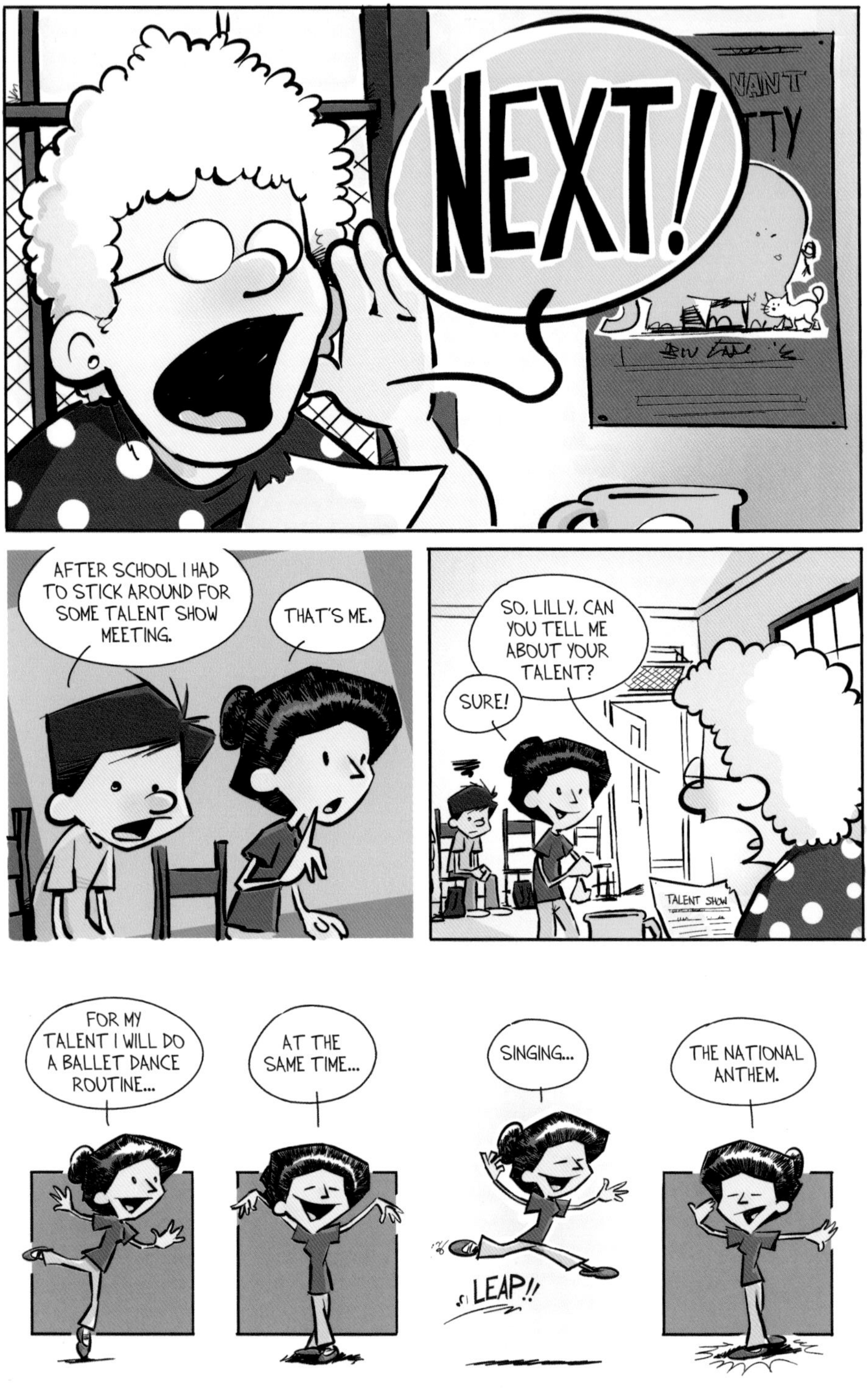
NEXT!
AFTER SCHOOL I HAD TO STICK AROUND FOR SOME TALENT SHOW MEETING.
THAT'S ME.
SO, LILLY, CAN YOU TELL ME ABOUT YOUR TALENT?
SURE!
TALENT SHOW
FOR MY TALENT I WILL DO A BALLET DANCE ROUTINE...
AT THE SAME TIME...
SINGING...
LEAP!!
THE NATIONAL ANTHEM.

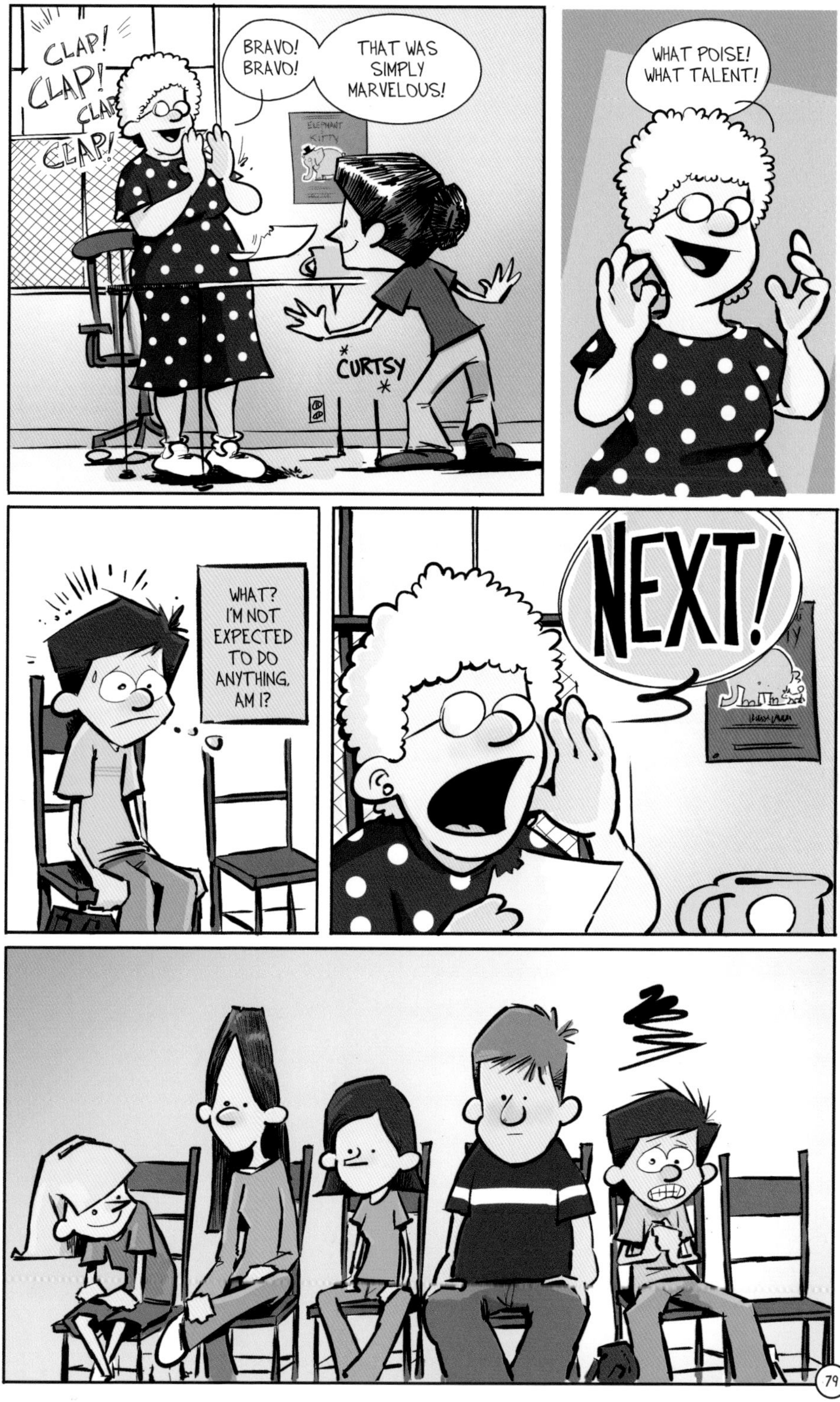
CLAP! CLAP! CLAP! CLAP!
BRAVO! BRAVO!
THAT WAS SIMPLY MARVELOUS!
* CURTSY *
WHAT POISE! WHAT TALENT!
WHAT? I'M NOT EXPECTED TO DO ANYTHING, AM I?
NEXT!

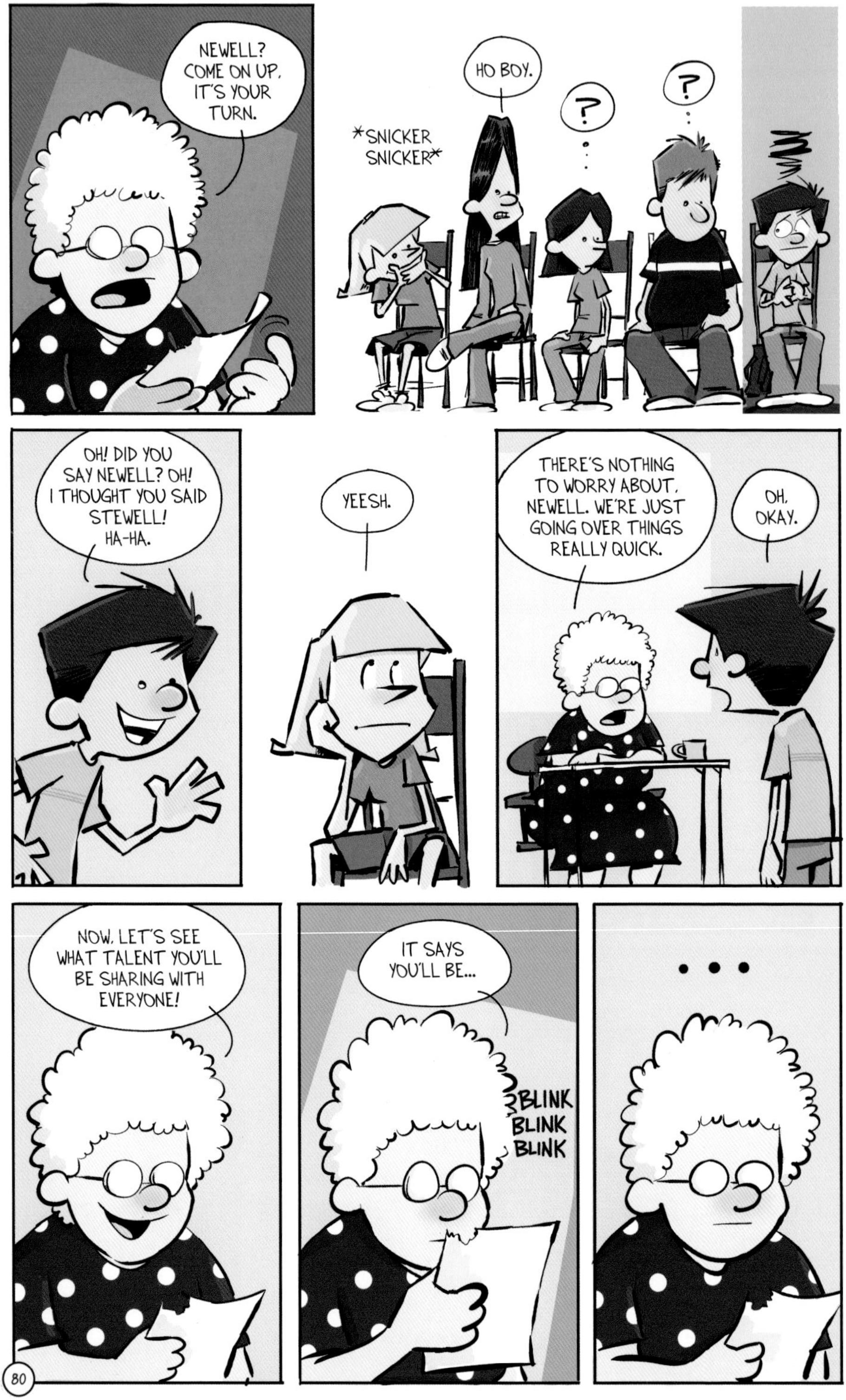
NEWELL? COME ON UP. IT'S YOUR TURN.
SNICKER SNICKER
HO BOY.
?
?
OH! DID YOU SAY NEWELL? OH! I THOUGHT YOU SAID STEWELL! HA-HA.
YEESH.
THERE'S NOTHING TO WORRY ABOUT, NEWELL. WE'RE JUST GOING OVER THINGS REALLY QUICK.
OH. OKAY.
NOW, LET'S SEE WHAT TALENT YOU'LL BE SHARING WITH EVERYONE!
IT SAYS YOU'LL BE...
BLINK BLINK BLINK
• • •

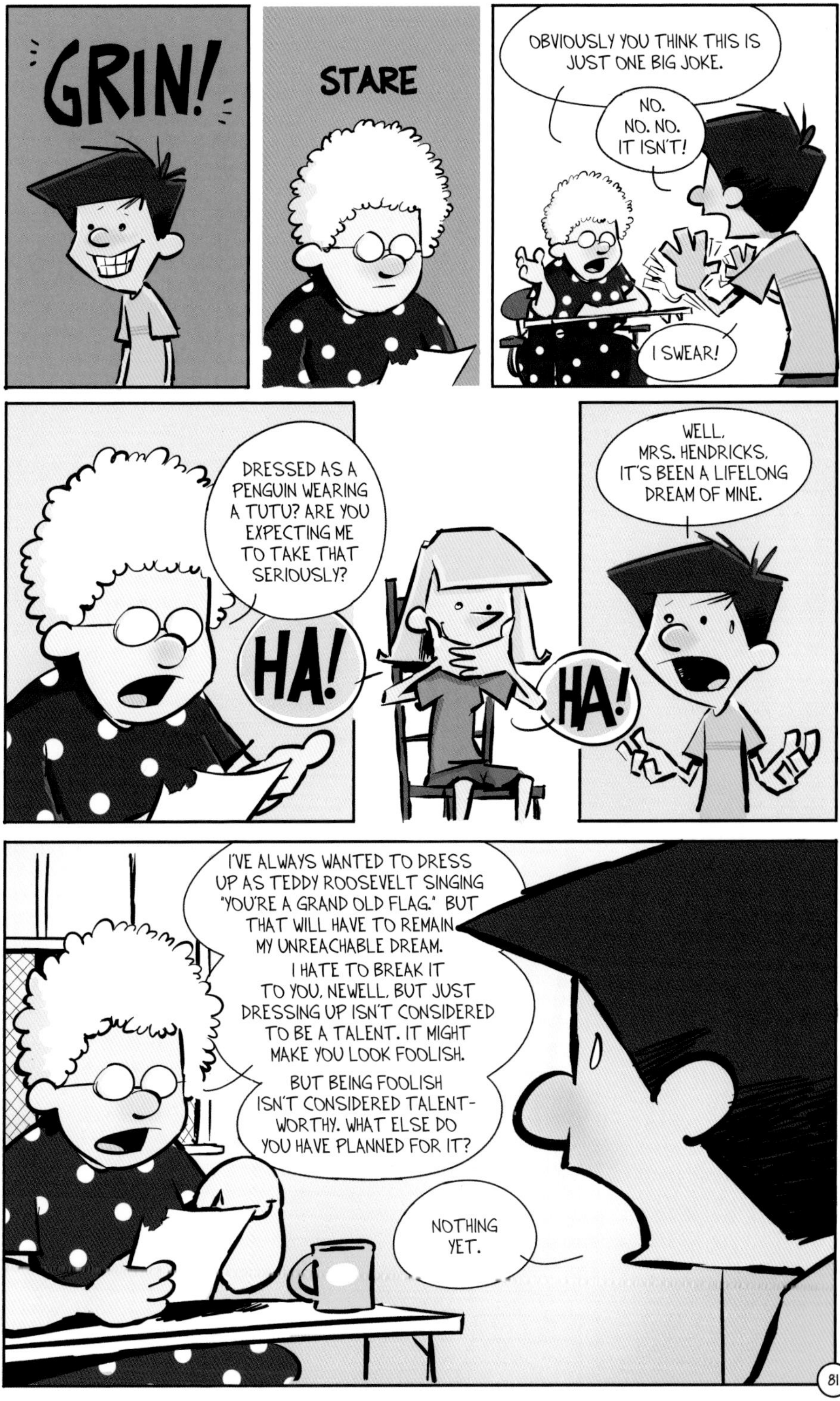

GRIN!
STARE
OBVIOUSLY YOU THINK THIS IS JUST ONE BIG JOKE.
NO. NO. NO. IT ISN'T!
I SWEAR!
DRESSED AS A PENGUIN WEARING A TUTU? ARE YOU EXPECTING ME TO TAKE THAT SERIOUSLY?
HA!
HA!
WELL, MRS. HENDRICKS, IT'S BEEN A LIFELONG DREAM OF MINE.
I'VE ALWAYS WANTED TO DRESS UP AS TEDDY ROOSEVELT SINGING "YOU'RE A GRAND OLD FLAG." BUT THAT WILL HAVE TO REMAIN MY UNREACHABLE DREAM.
I HATE TO BREAK IT TO YOU, NEWELL, BUT JUST DRESSING UP ISN'T CONSIDERED TO BE A TALENT. IT MIGHT MAKE YOU LOOK FOOLISH.
BUT BEING FOOLISH ISN'T CONSIDERED TALENT-WORTHY. WHAT ELSE DO YOU HAVE PLANNED FOR IT?
NOTHING YET.

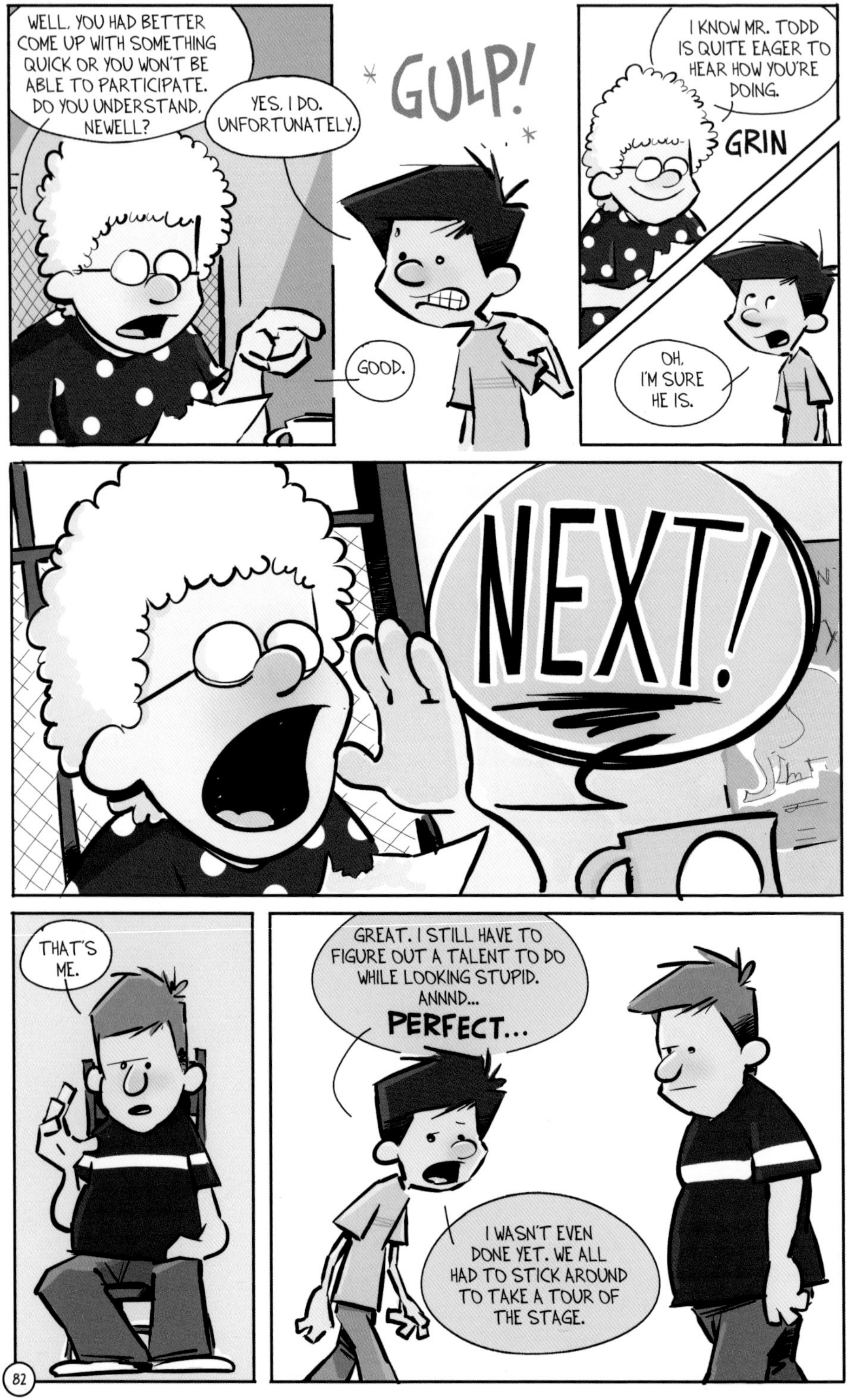
WELL, YOU HAD BETTER COME UP WITH SOMETHING QUICK OR YOU WON'T BE ABLE TO PARTICIPATE. DO YOU UNDERSTAND, NEWELL?
YES, I DO. UNFORTUNATELY.
GULP!
GOOD.
I KNOW MR. TODD IS QUITE EAGER TO HEAR HOW YOU'RE DOING.
GRIN
OH, I'M SURE HE IS.
NEXT!
THAT'S ME.
GREAT. I STILL HAVE TO FIGURE OUT A TALENT TO DO WHILE LOOKING STUPID. ANNND... PERFECT...
I WASN'T EVEN DONE YET. WE ALL HAD TO STICK AROUND TO TAKE A TOUR OF THE STAGE.

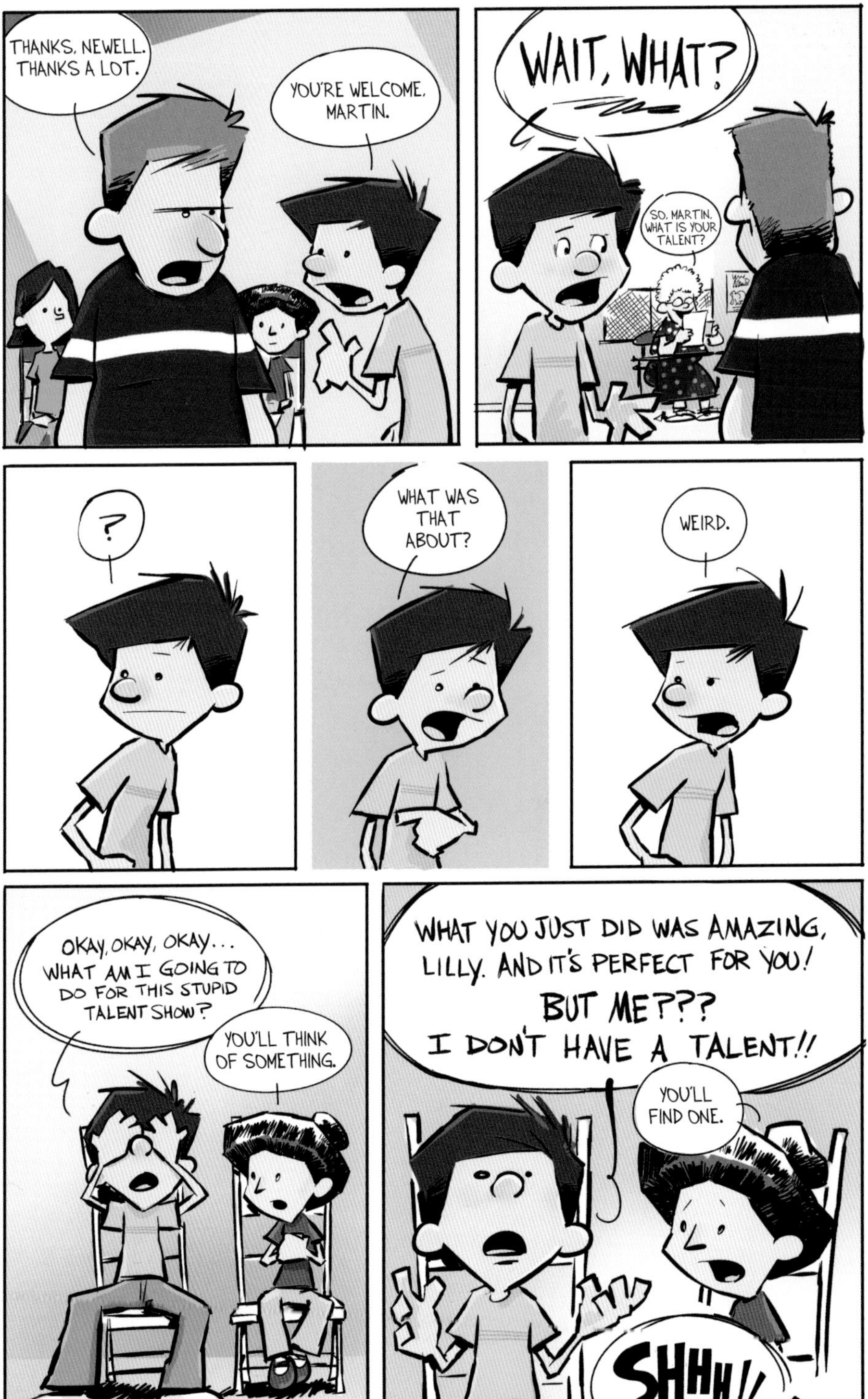
THANKS, NEWELL. THANKS A LOT.
YOU'RE WELCOME, MARTIN.
WAIT, WHAT?
SO, MARTIN, WHAT IS YOUR TALENT?
?
WHAT WAS THAT ABOUT?
WEIRD.
OKAY, OKAY, OKAY... WHAT AM I GOING TO DO FOR THIS STUPID TALENT SHOW?
YOU'LL THINK OF SOMETHING.
WHAT YOU JUST DID WAS AMAZING, LILLY. AND IT'S PERFECT FOR YOU! BUT ME??? I DON'T HAVE A TALENT!!
YOU'LL FIND ONE.
SHHH!!

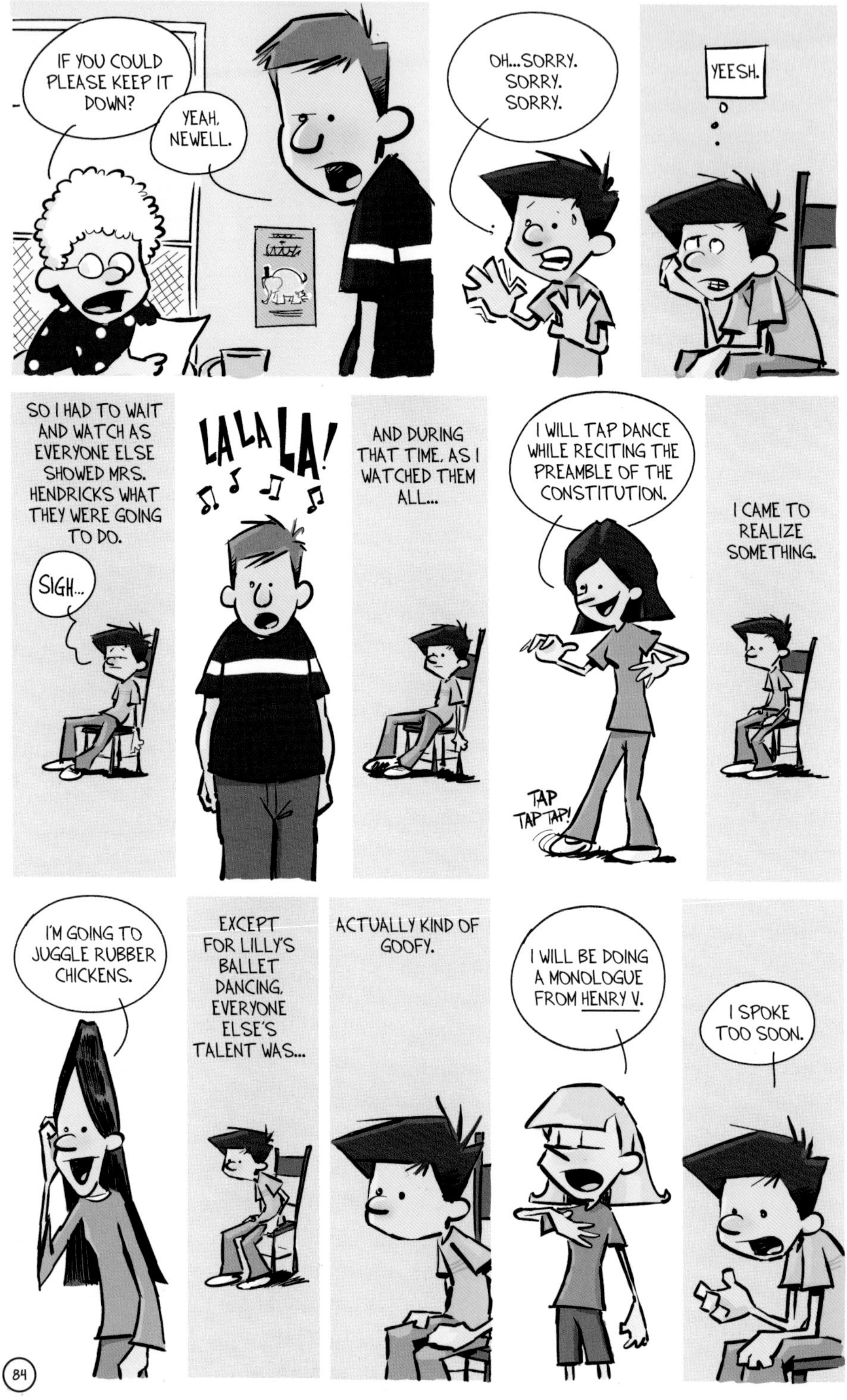

IF YOU COULD PLEASE KEEP IT DOWN?
YEAH, NEWELL.
OH...SORRY. SORRY. SORRY.
YEESH.
SO I HAD TO WAIT AND WATCH AS EVERYONE ELSE SHOWED MRS. HENDRICKS WHAT THEY WERE GOING TO DO.
SIGH...
LA LA LA!
AND DURING THAT TIME, AS I WATCHED THEM ALL...
I WILL TAP DANCE WHILE RECITING THE PREAMBLE OF THE CONSTITUTION.
TAP TAP TAP!
I CAME TO REALIZE SOMETHING.
I'M GOING TO JUGGLE RUBBER CHICKENS.
EXCEPT FOR LILLY'S BALLET DANCING, EVERYONE ELSE'S TALENT WAS...
ACTUALLY KIND OF GOOFY.
I WILL BE DOING A MONOLOGUE FROM HENRY V.
I SPOKE TOO SOON.

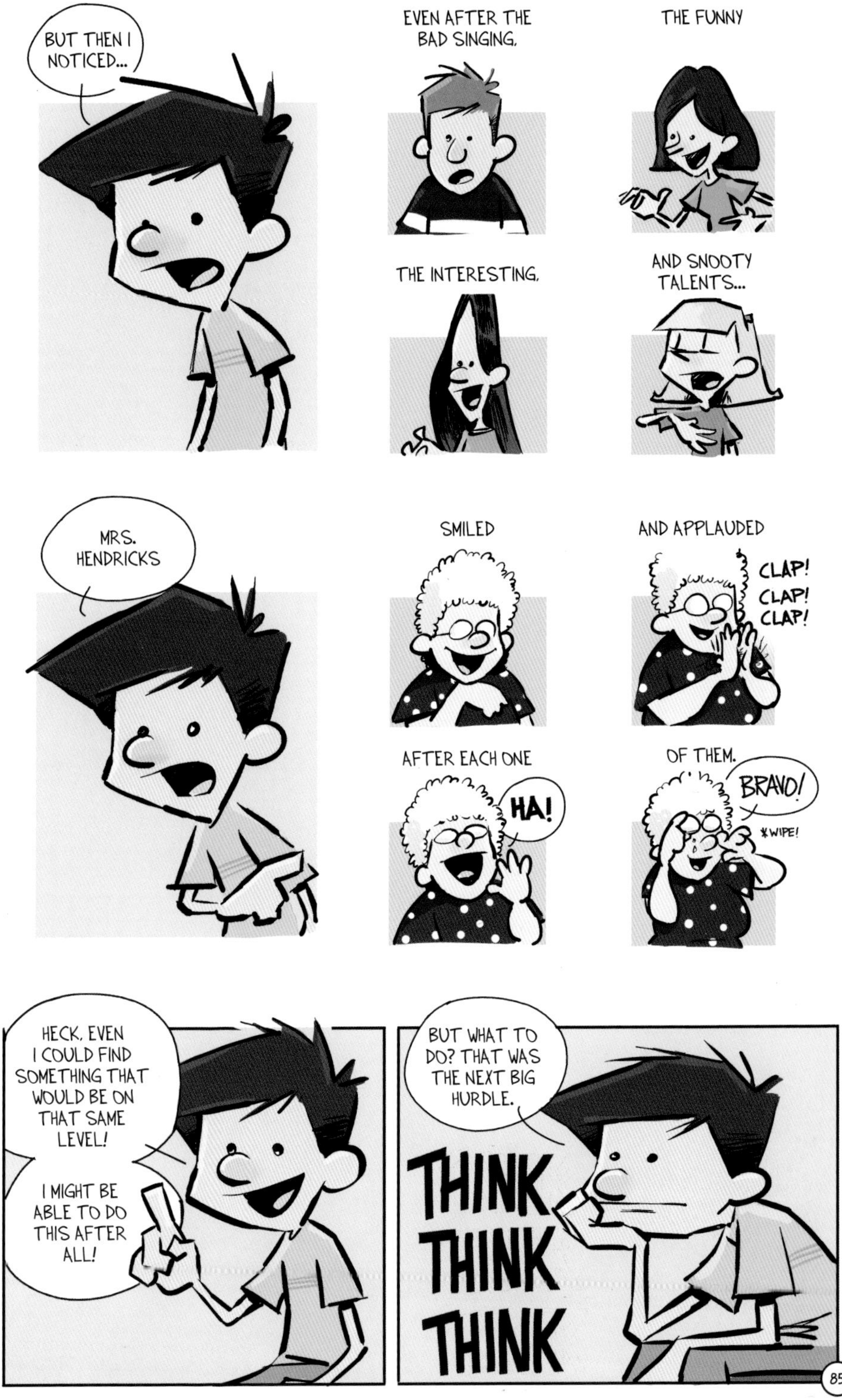

BUT THEN I NOTICED...
EVEN AFTER THE BAD SINGING,
THE FUNNY
THE INTERESTING,
AND SNOOTY TALENTS...
MRS. HENDRICKS
SMILED
AND APPLAUDED
CLAP! CLAP! CLAP!
AFTER EACH ONE
HA!
OF THEM.
BRAVO!
*WIPE!
HECK, EVEN I COULD FIND SOMETHING THAT WOULD BE ON THAT SAME LEVEL!
I MIGHT BE ABLE TO DO THIS AFTER ALL!
BUT WHAT TO DO? THAT WAS THE NEXT BIG HURDLE.
THINK
THINK
THINK

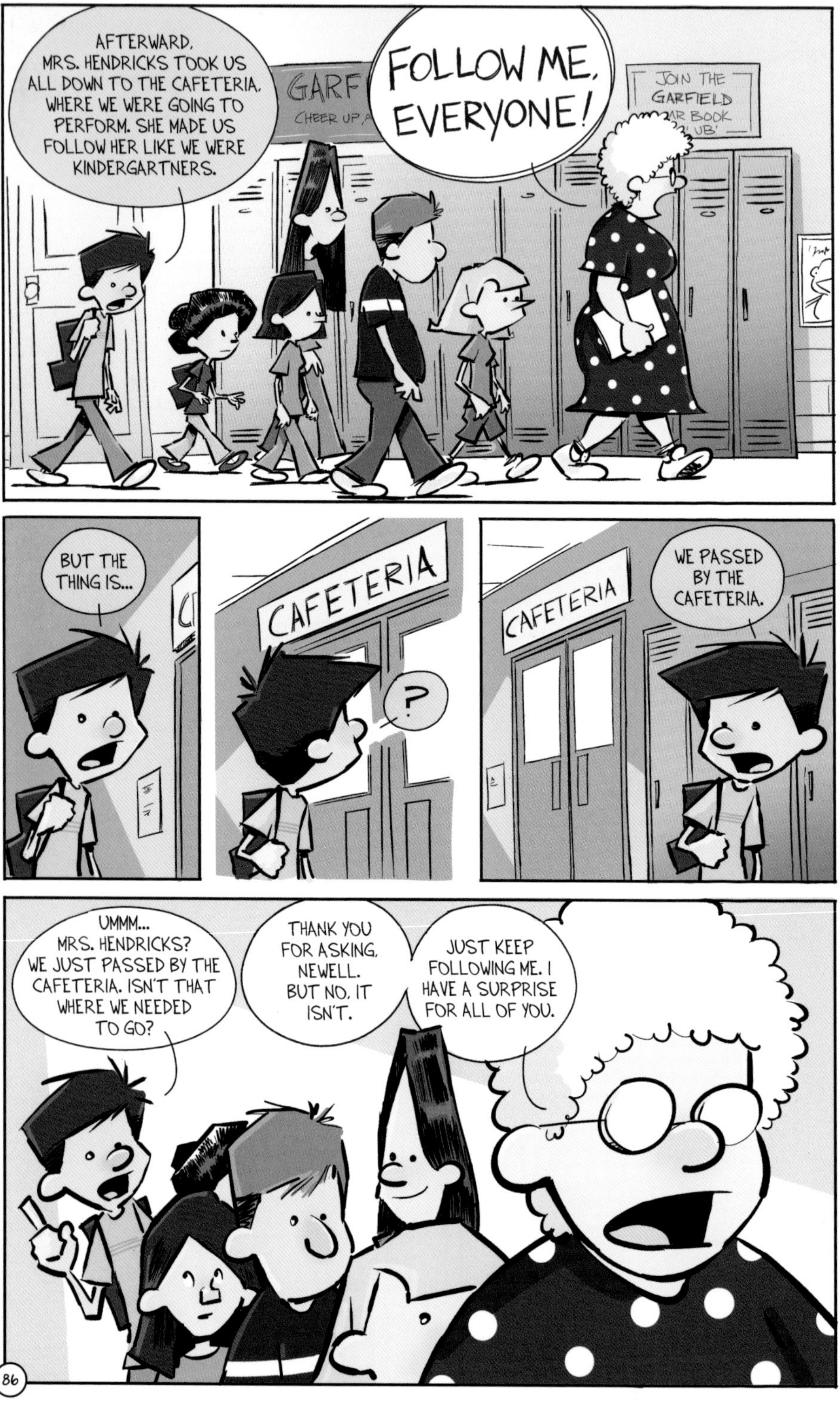
AFTERWARD, MRS. HENDRICKS TOOK US ALL DOWN TO THE CAFETERIA, WHERE WE WERE GOING TO PERFORM. SHE MADE US FOLLOW HER LIKE WE WERE KINDERGARTNERS.
FOLLOW ME, EVERYONE!
CHEER UP,
JOIN THE GARFIELD
BUT THE THING IS...
CAFETERIA
?
CAFETERIA
WE PASSED BY THE CAFETERIA.
UMMM... MRS. HENDRICKS? WE JUST PASSED BY THE CAFETERIA. ISN'T THAT WHERE WE NEEDED TO GO?
THANK YOU FOR ASKING, NEWELL. BUT NO, IT ISN'T.
JUST KEEP FOLLOWING ME. I HAVE A SURPRISE FOR ALL OF YOU.

A SURPRISE? WHY DOES THAT WORRY ME?

SHE'S PROBABLY TAKING ALL OF US TO A MEDIEVAL TORTURE CHAMBER.

UM. GUYS?

GUYS?

YOU MIGHT NOT BE TOO FAR OFF.

AHEM!

ARE YOU FOUR GOING TO JOIN US?

HISS
HISS HISS
HISS
HISS HISS
HISS HISS HISS
HISS

WHY IS SHE...

UM...

GOING...

DOWN...

THE STAIRWELL?!?!

CHAPTER FIVE
THE STAIRWELL

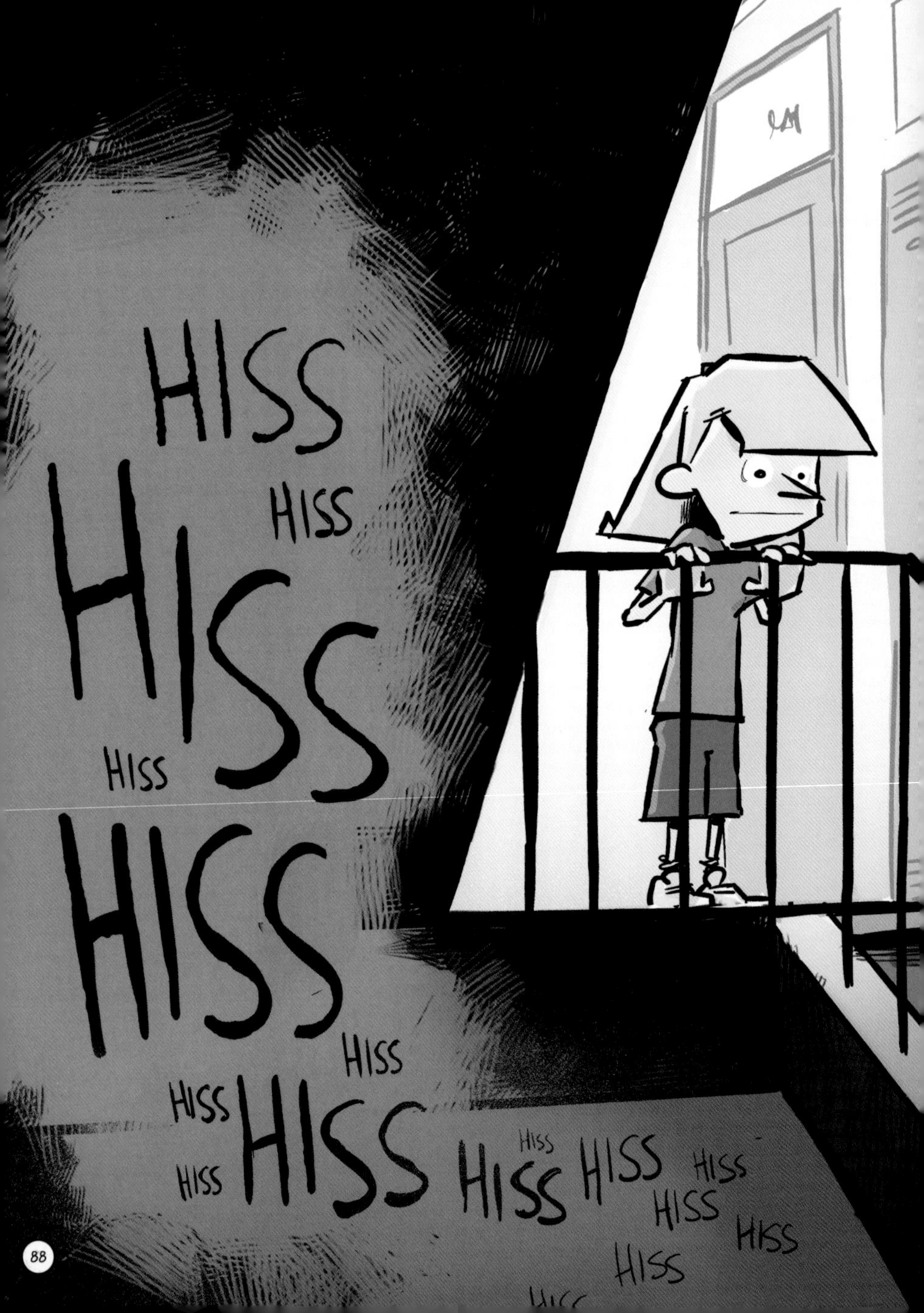

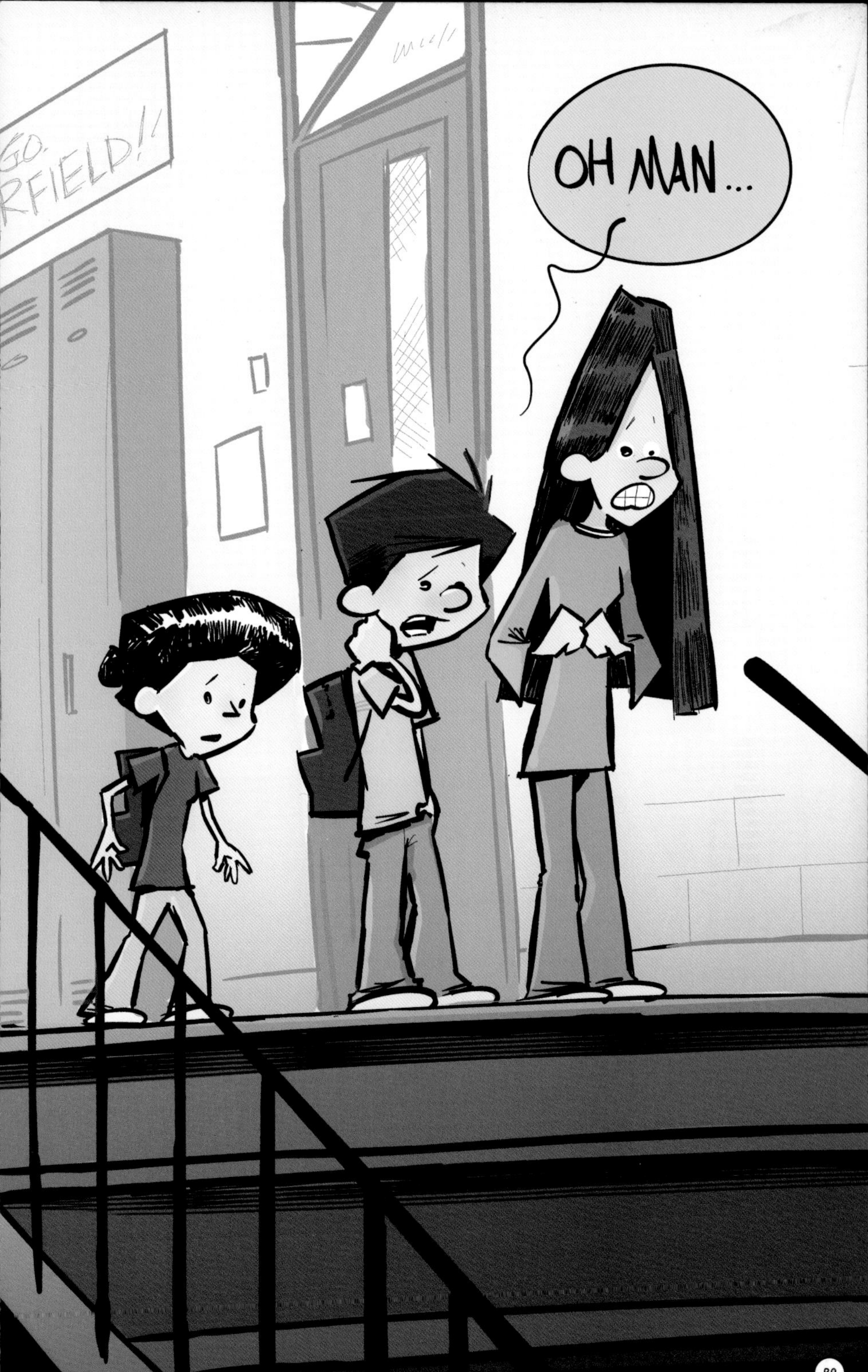
GO.
RFIELD!!
OH MAN...

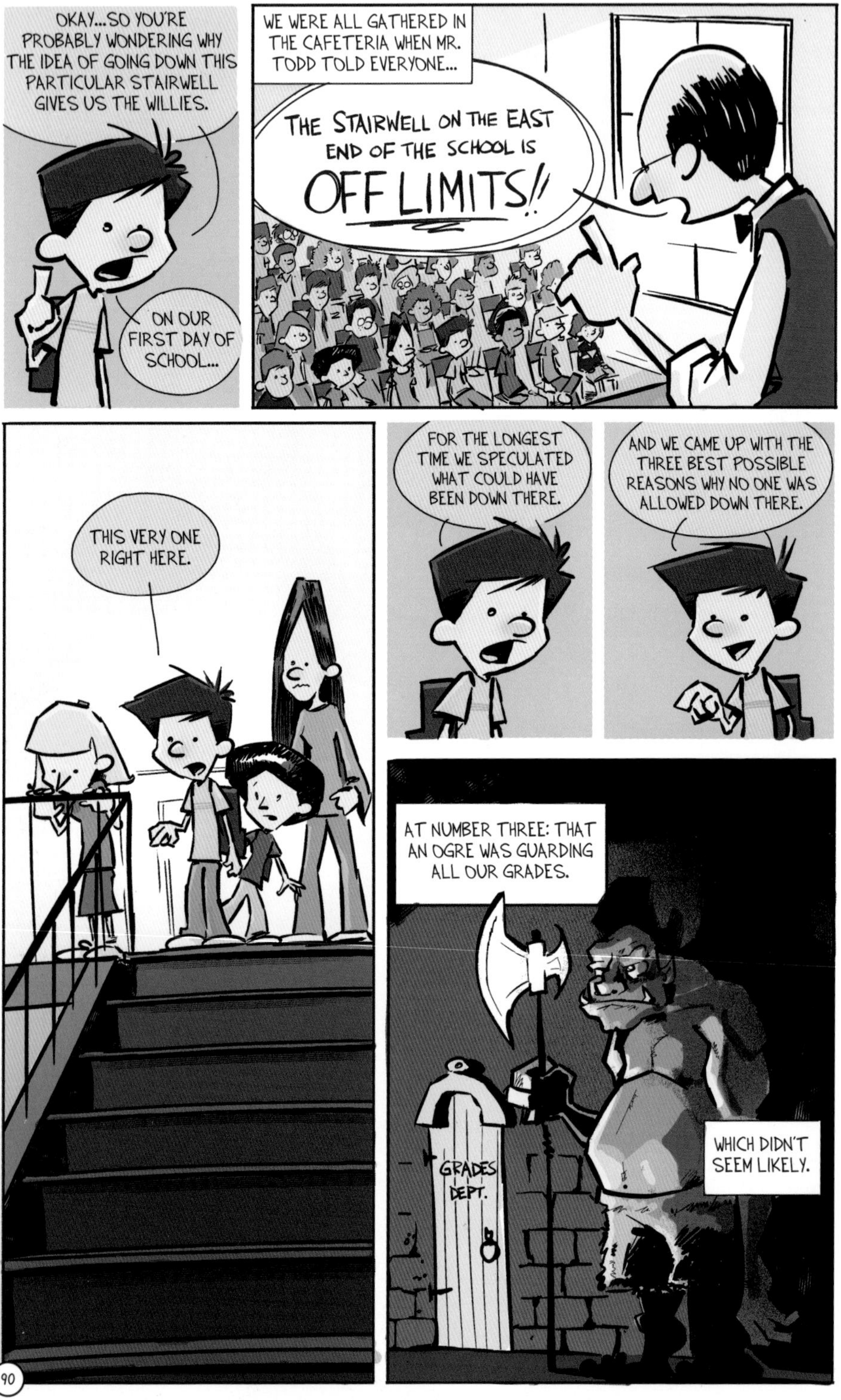
OKAY...SO YOU'RE PROBABLY WONDERING WHY THE IDEA OF GOING DOWN THIS PARTICULAR STAIRWELL GIVES US THE WILLIES.
ON OUR FIRST DAY OF SCHOOL...
WE WERE ALL GATHERED IN THE CAFETERIA WHEN MR. TODD TOLD EVERYONE...
THE STAIRWELL ON THE EAST END OF THE SCHOOL IS OFF LIMITS!!
THIS VERY ONE RIGHT HERE.
FOR THE LONGEST TIME WE SPECULATED WHAT COULD HAVE BEEN DOWN THERE.
AND WE CAME UP WITH THE THREE BEST POSSIBLE REASONS WHY NO ONE WAS ALLOWED DOWN THERE.
AT NUMBER THREE: THAT AN OGRE WAS GUARDING ALL OUR GRADES.
GRADES DEPT.
WHICH DIDN'T SEEM LIKELY.

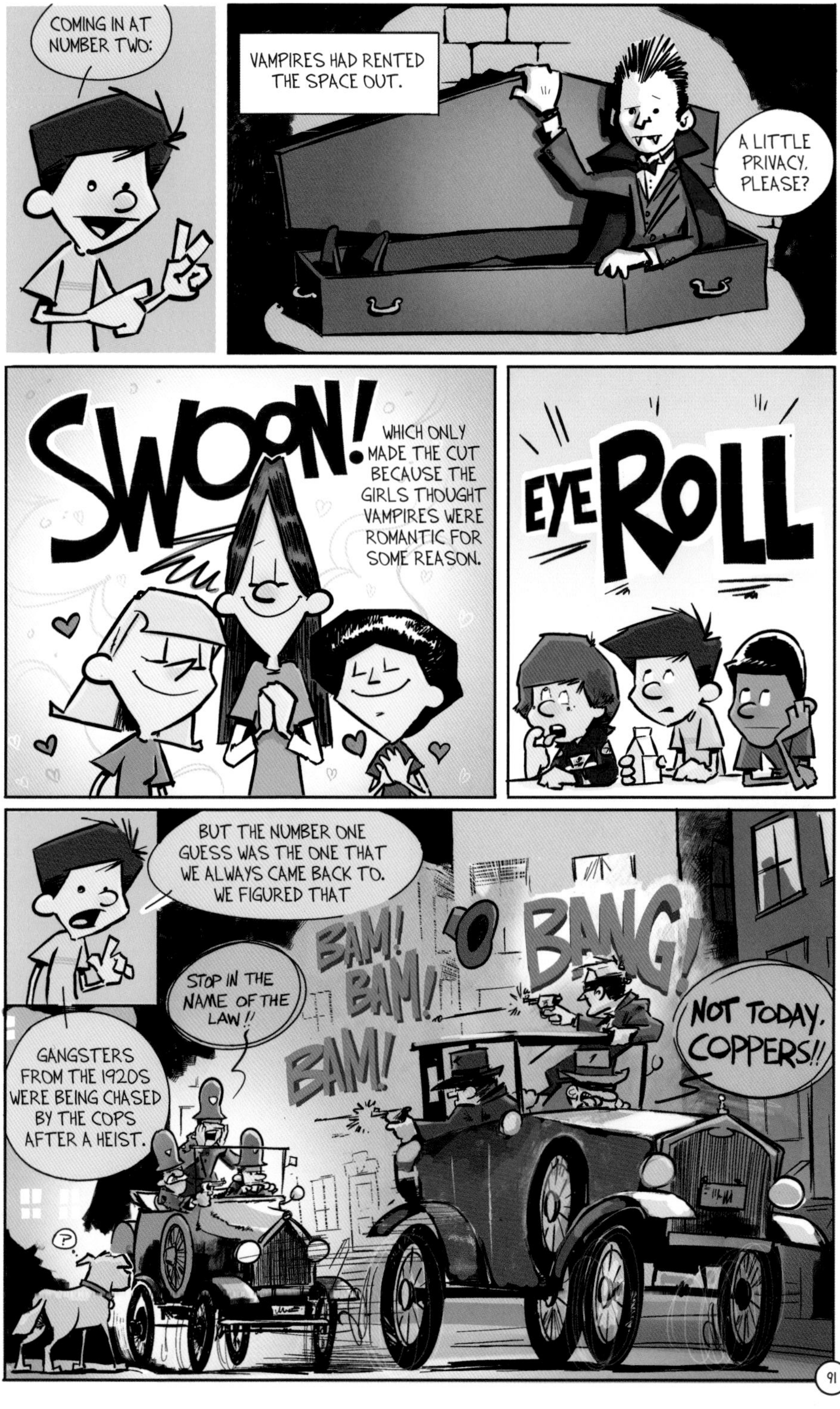
COMING IN AT NUMBER TWO:
VAMPIRES HAD RENTED THE SPACE OUT.
A LITTLE PRIVACY, PLEASE?
SWOON!
WHICH ONLY MADE THE CUT BECAUSE THE GIRLS THOUGHT VAMPIRES WERE ROMANTIC FOR SOME REASON.
EYE ROLL
BUT THE NUMBER ONE GUESS WAS THE ONE THAT WE ALWAYS CAME BACK TO. WE FIGURED THAT
GANGSTERS FROM THE 1920S WERE BEING CHASED BY THE COPS AFTER A HEIST.
STOP IN THE NAME OF THE LAW!!
BAM! BAM! BAM!
BANG!
NOT TODAY, COPPERS!!

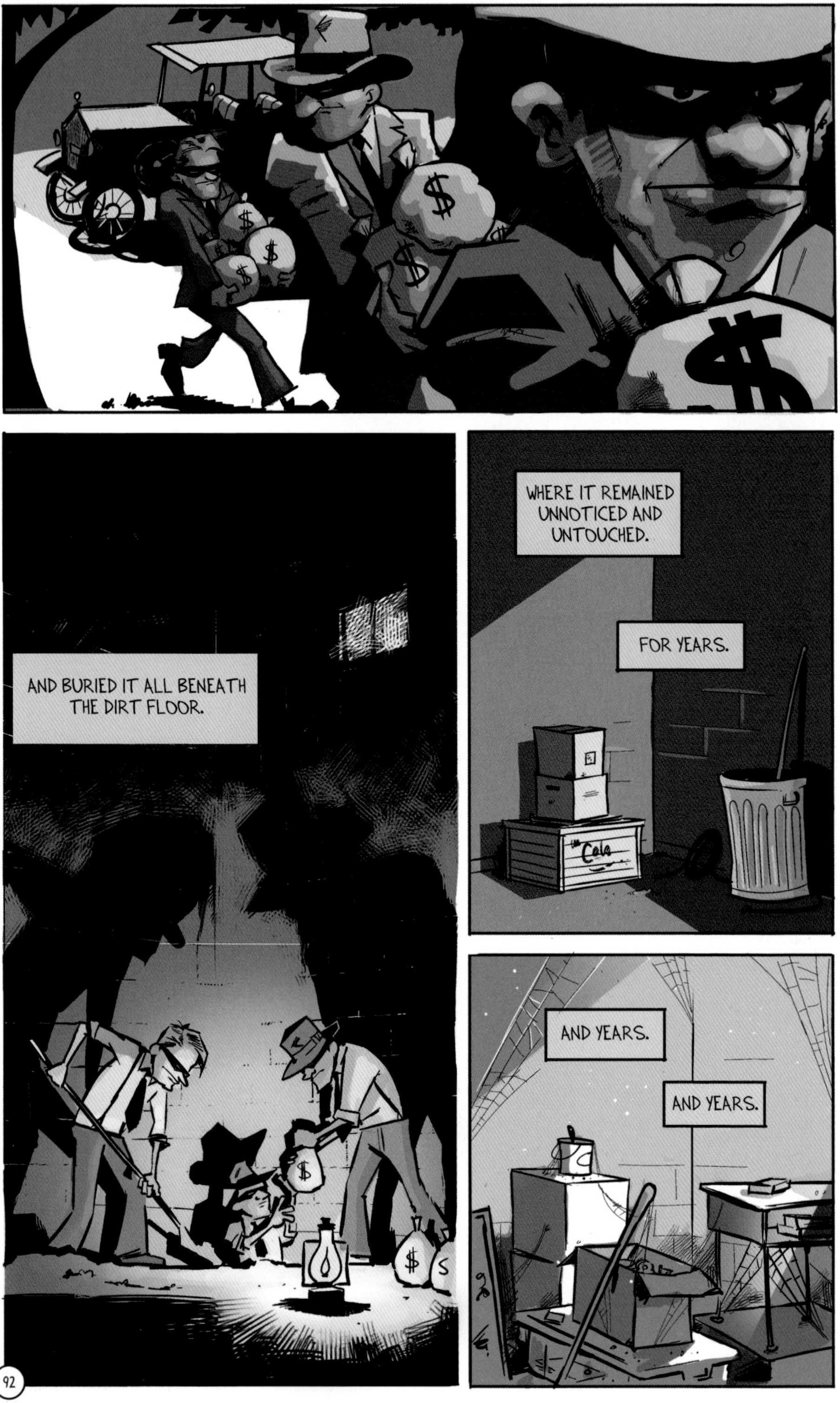
AND BURIED IT ALL BENEATH THE DIRT FLOOR.
WHERE IT REMAINED UNNOTICED AND UNTOUCHED.
FOR YEARS.
AND YEARS.
AND YEARS.

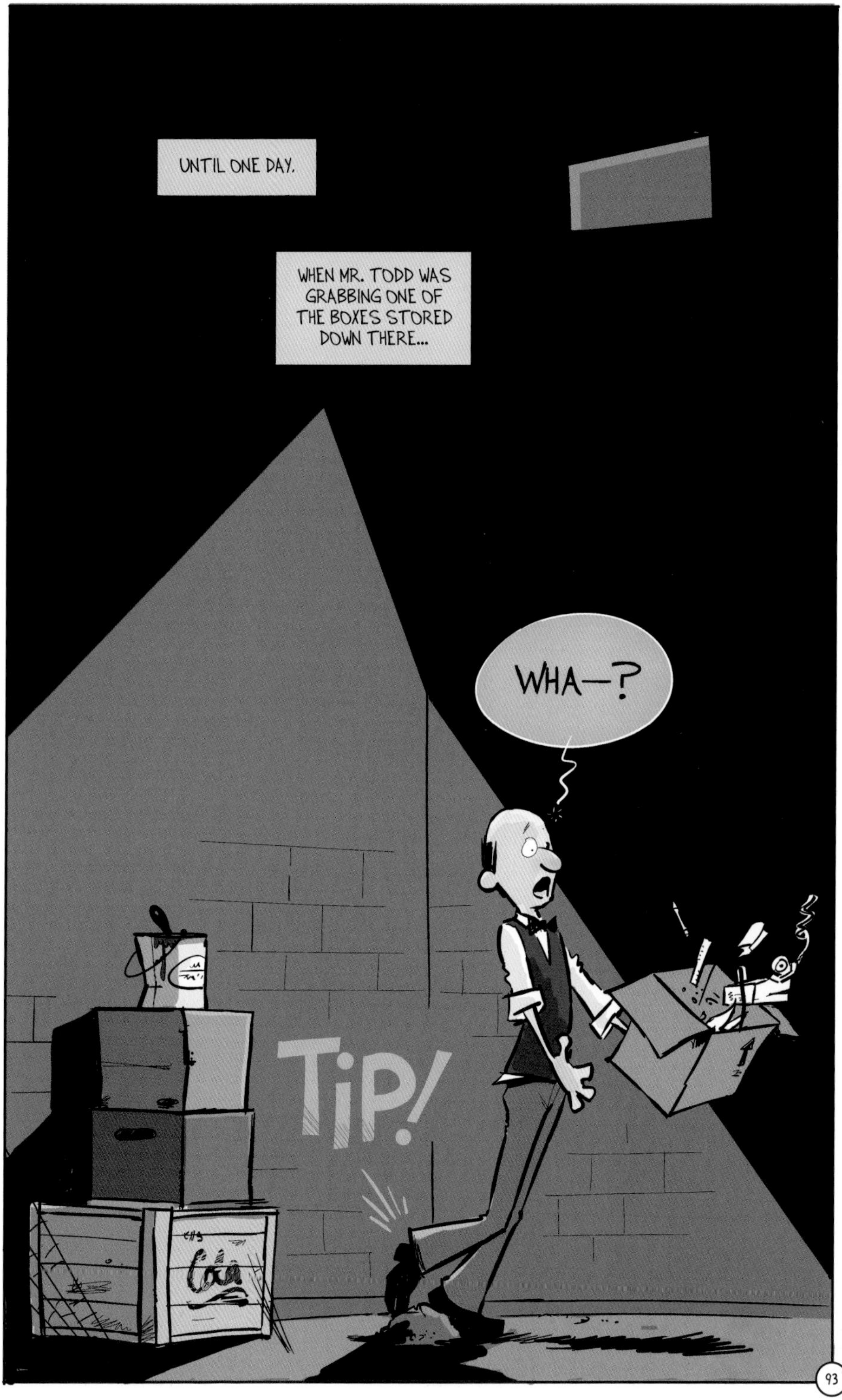
UNTIL ONE DAY.
WHEN MR. TODD WAS GRABBING ONE OF THE BOXES STORED DOWN THERE...
WHA—?
TIP!

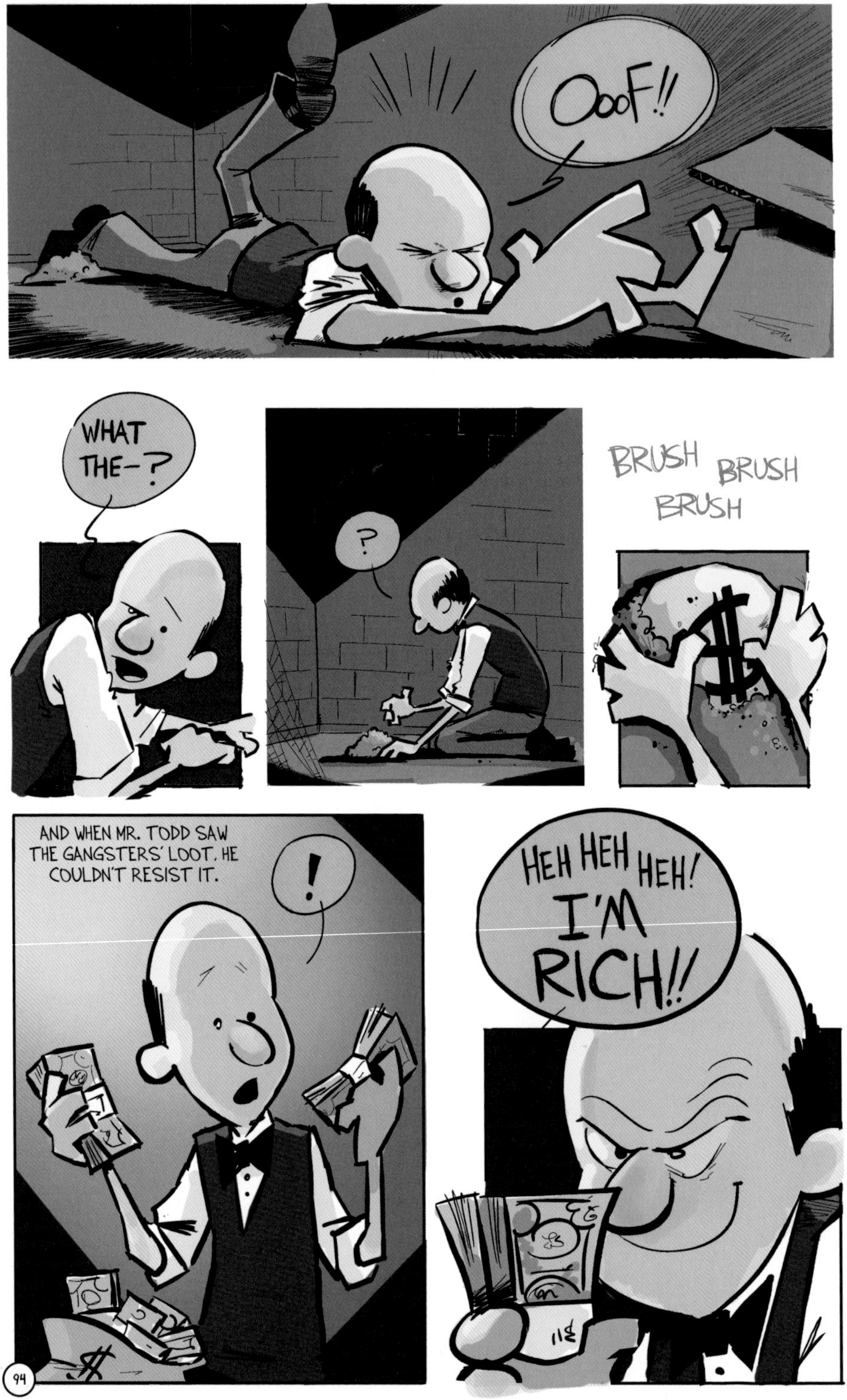
OooF!!
WHAT THE–?
?
BRUSH BRUSH BRUSH
AND WHEN MR. TODD SAW THE GANGSTERS' LOOT, HE COULDN'T RESIST IT.
!
HEH HEH HEH! I'M RICH!!

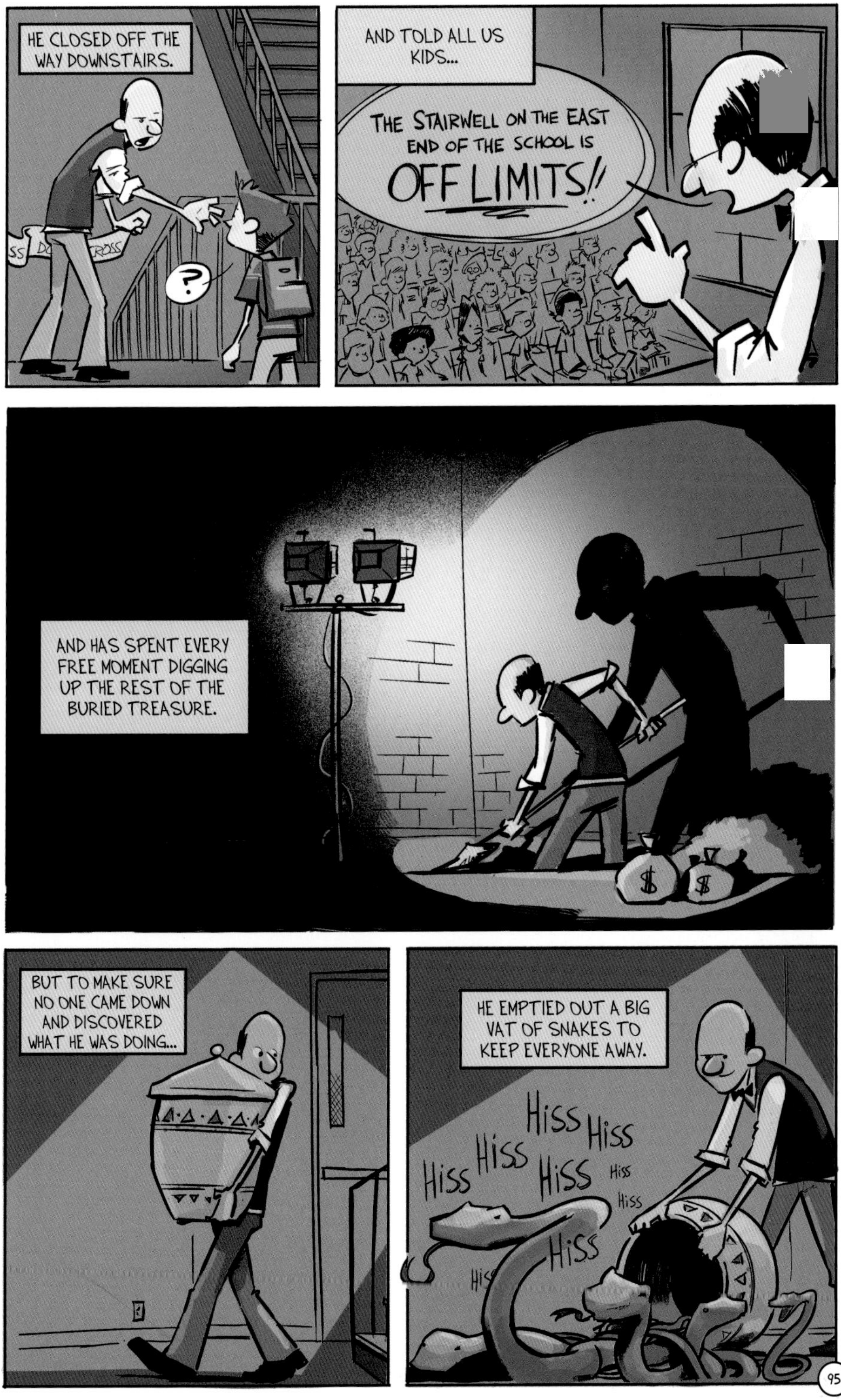
HE CLOSED OFF THE WAY DOWNSTAIRS.
?
AND TOLD ALL US KIDS...
THE STAIRWELL ON THE EAST END OF THE SCHOOL IS OFF LIMITS!!
AND HAS SPENT EVERY FREE MOMENT DIGGING UP THE REST OF THE BURIED TREASURE.
$
$
BUT TO MAKE SURE NO ONE CAME DOWN AND DISCOVERED WHAT HE WAS DOING...
HE EMPTIED OUT A BIG VAT OF SNAKES TO KEEP EVERYONE AWAY.
Hiss Hiss Hiss Hiss Hiss Hiss Hiss Hiss

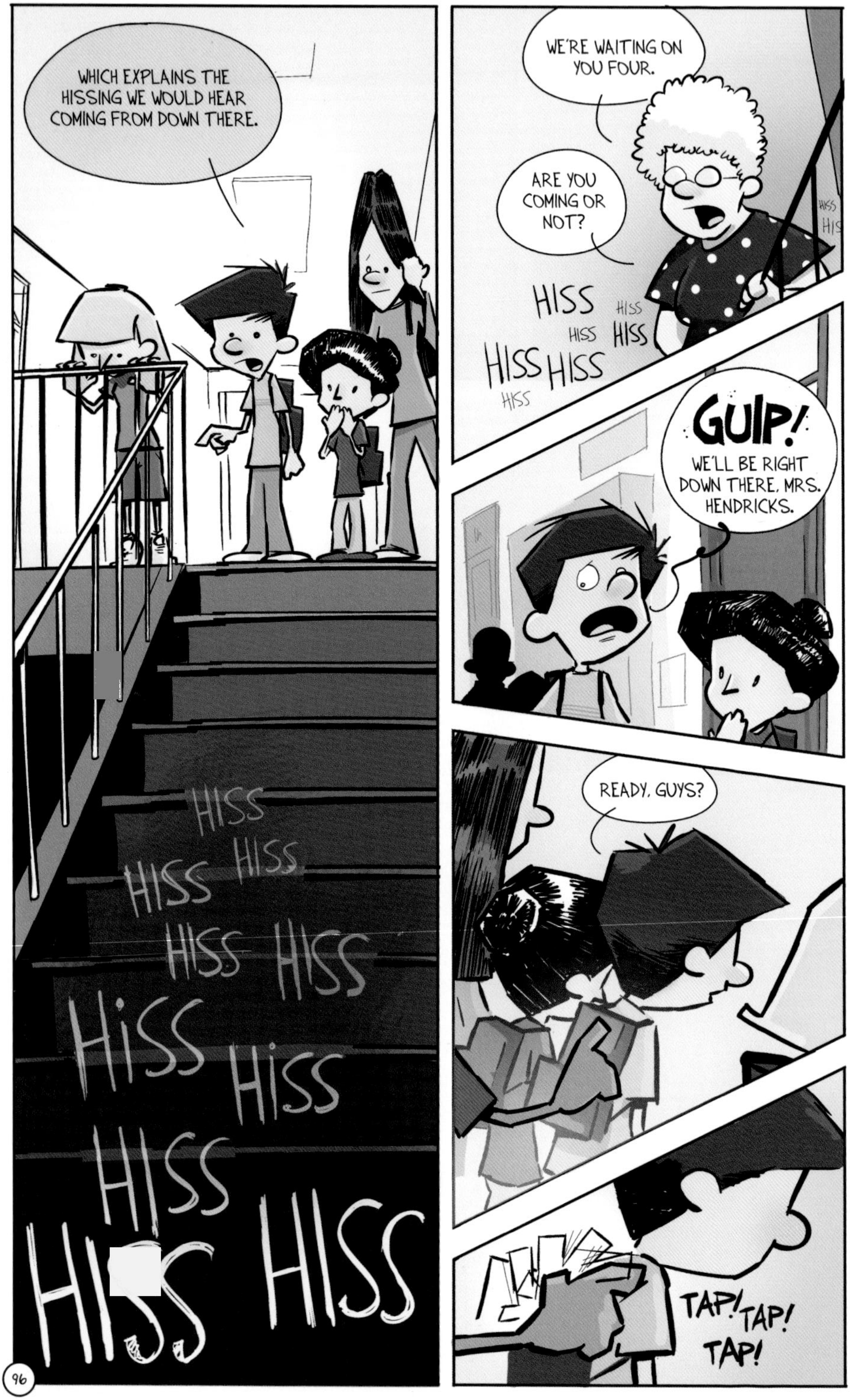
WHICH EXPLAINS THE HISSING WE WOULD HEAR COMING FROM DOWN THERE.
HISS HISS HISS HISS HISS HISS HISS HISS HISS HISS
WE'RE WAITING ON YOU FOUR.
ARE YOU COMING OR NOT?
HISS HISS HISS HISS HISS HISS HISS
GULP!
WE'LL BE RIGHT DOWN THERE, MRS. HENDRICKS.
READY, GUYS?
TAP! TAP! TAP!

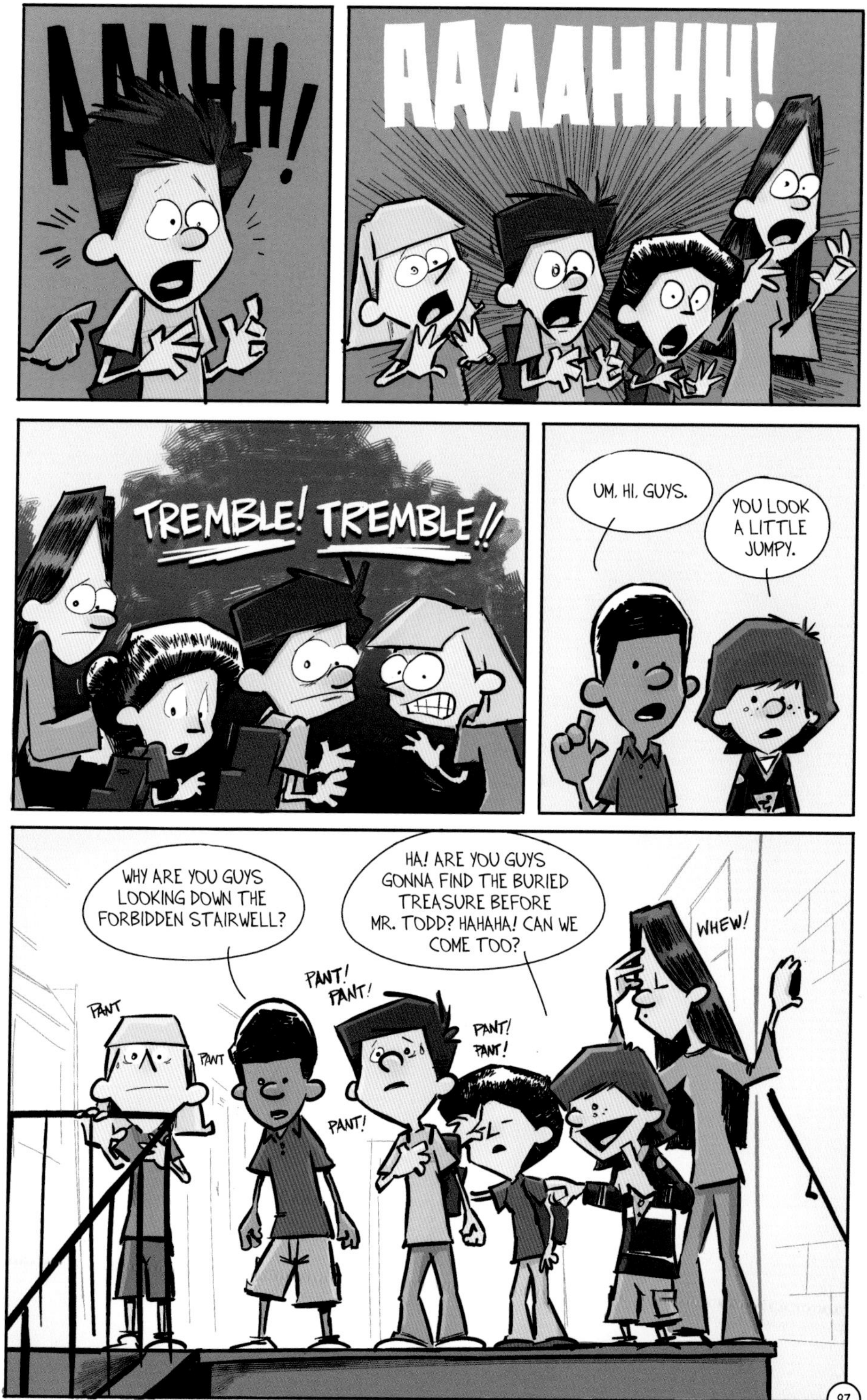
AAAHH!
AAAAHHH!
TREMBLE! TREMBLE!!
UM, HI, GUYS.
YOU LOOK A LITTLE JUMPY.
WHY ARE YOU GUYS LOOKING DOWN THE FORBIDDEN STAIRWELL?
HA! ARE YOU GUYS GONNA FIND THE BURIED TREASURE BEFORE MR. TODD? HAHAHA! CAN WE COME TOO?
WHEW!
PANT
PANT
PANT! PANT!
PANT!
PANT! PANT!

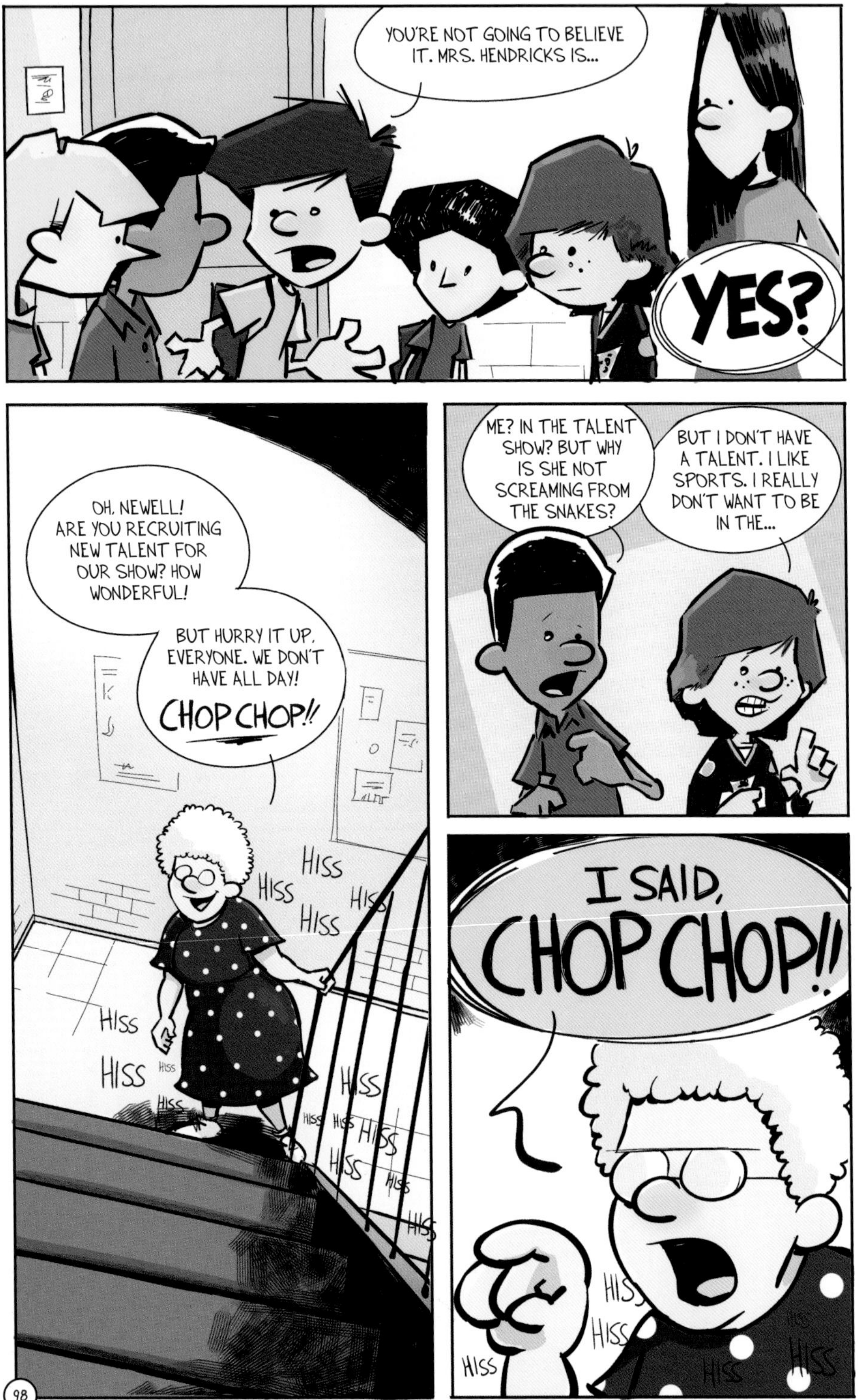
YOU'RE NOT GOING TO BELIEVE IT. MRS. HENDRICKS IS...
YES?
OH, NEWELL! ARE YOU RECRUITING NEW TALENT FOR OUR SHOW? HOW WONDERFUL!
BUT HURRY IT UP, EVERYONE. WE DON'T HAVE ALL DAY!
CHOP CHOP!!
HISS HISS HISS HISS
HISS HISS HISS HISS
HISS HISS HISS HISS HISS HISS HISS
ME? IN THE TALENT SHOW? BUT WHY IS SHE NOT SCREAMING FROM THE SNAKES?
BUT I DON'T HAVE A TALENT. I LIKE SPORTS. I REALLY DON'T WANT TO BE IN THE...
I SAID, CHOP CHOP!!
HISS HISS HISS HISS HISS HISS

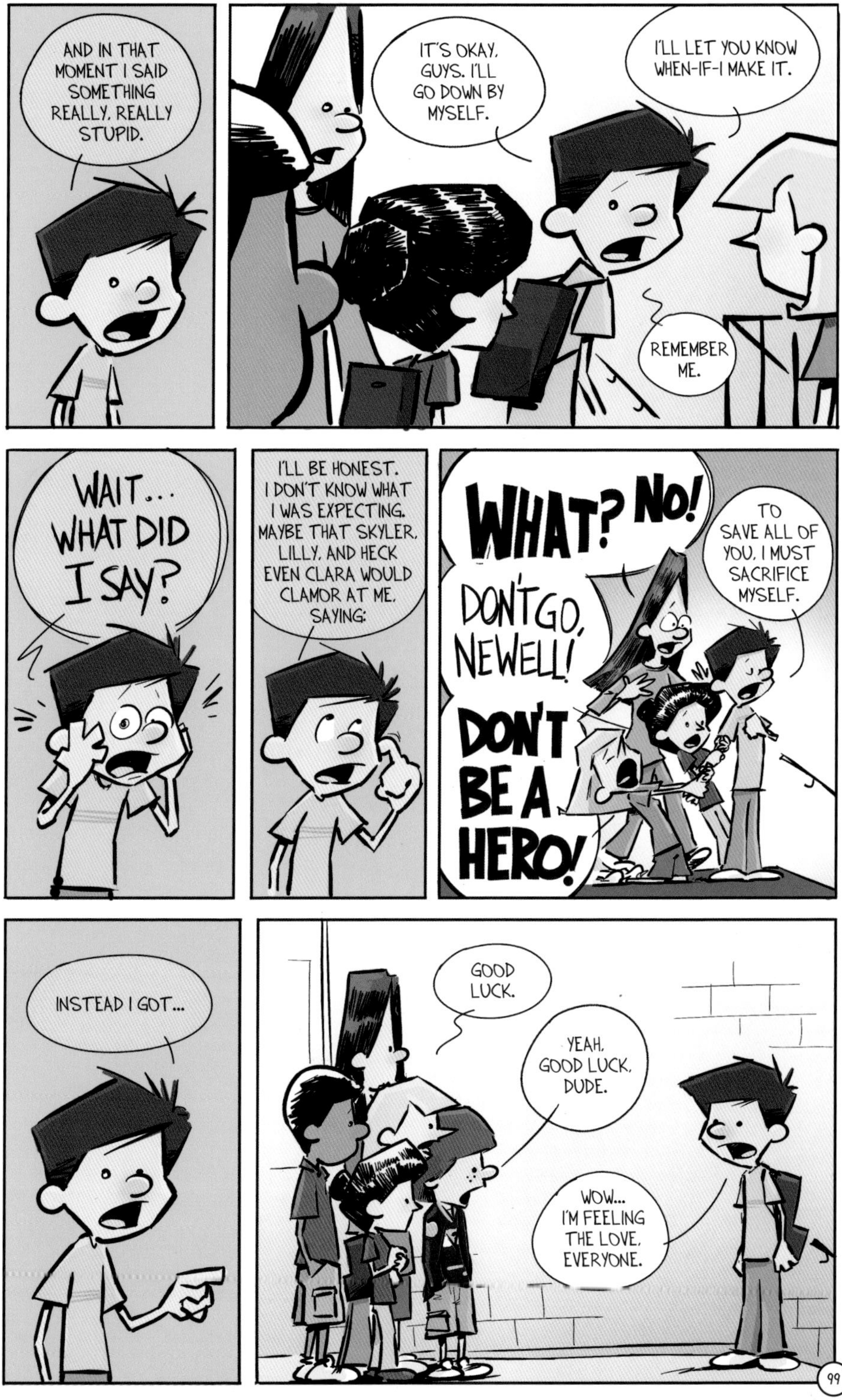
AND IN THAT MOMENT I SAID SOMETHING REALLY, REALLY STUPID.
IT'S OKAY, GUYS. I'LL GO DOWN BY MYSELF.
I'LL LET YOU KNOW WHEN-IF-I MAKE IT.
REMEMBER ME.
WAIT... WHAT DID I SAY?
I'LL BE HONEST. I DON'T KNOW WHAT I WAS EXPECTING. MAYBE THAT SKYLER, LILLY, AND HECK EVEN CLARA WOULD CLAMOR AT ME, SAYING:
WHAT? NO!
DON'T GO, NEWELL!
DON'T BE A HERO!
TO SAVE ALL OF YOU, I MUST SACRIFICE MYSELF.
INSTEAD I GOT...
GOOD LUCK.
YEAH, GOOD LUCK, DUDE.
WOW... I'M FEELING THE LOVE, EVERYONE.

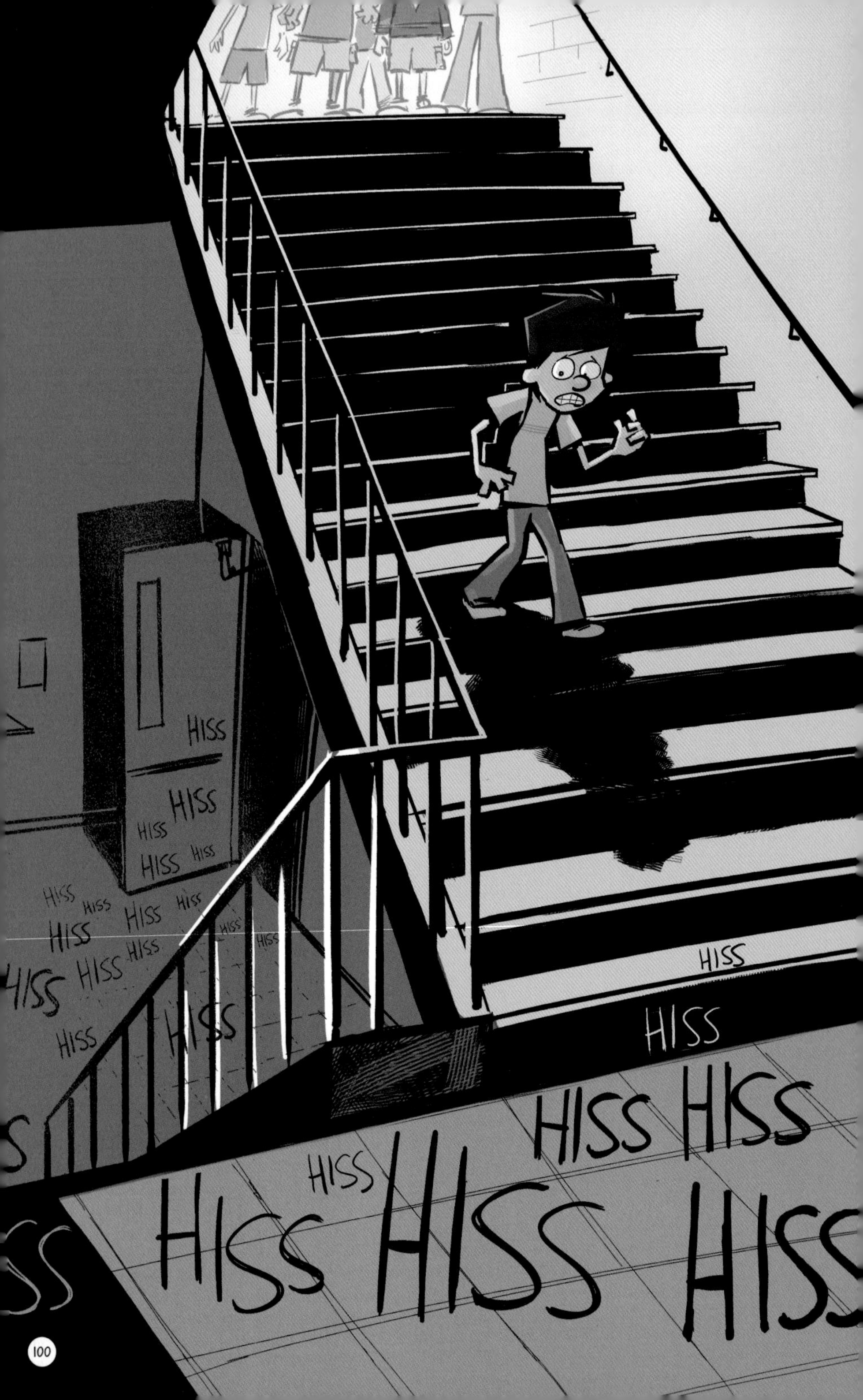
HISS
HISS
HISS
HISS
HISS
HISS
HISS
HISS
HISS
HISS
HISS
HISS
HISS
HISS
HISS
HISS
HISS
HISS HISS
HISS
HISS HISS

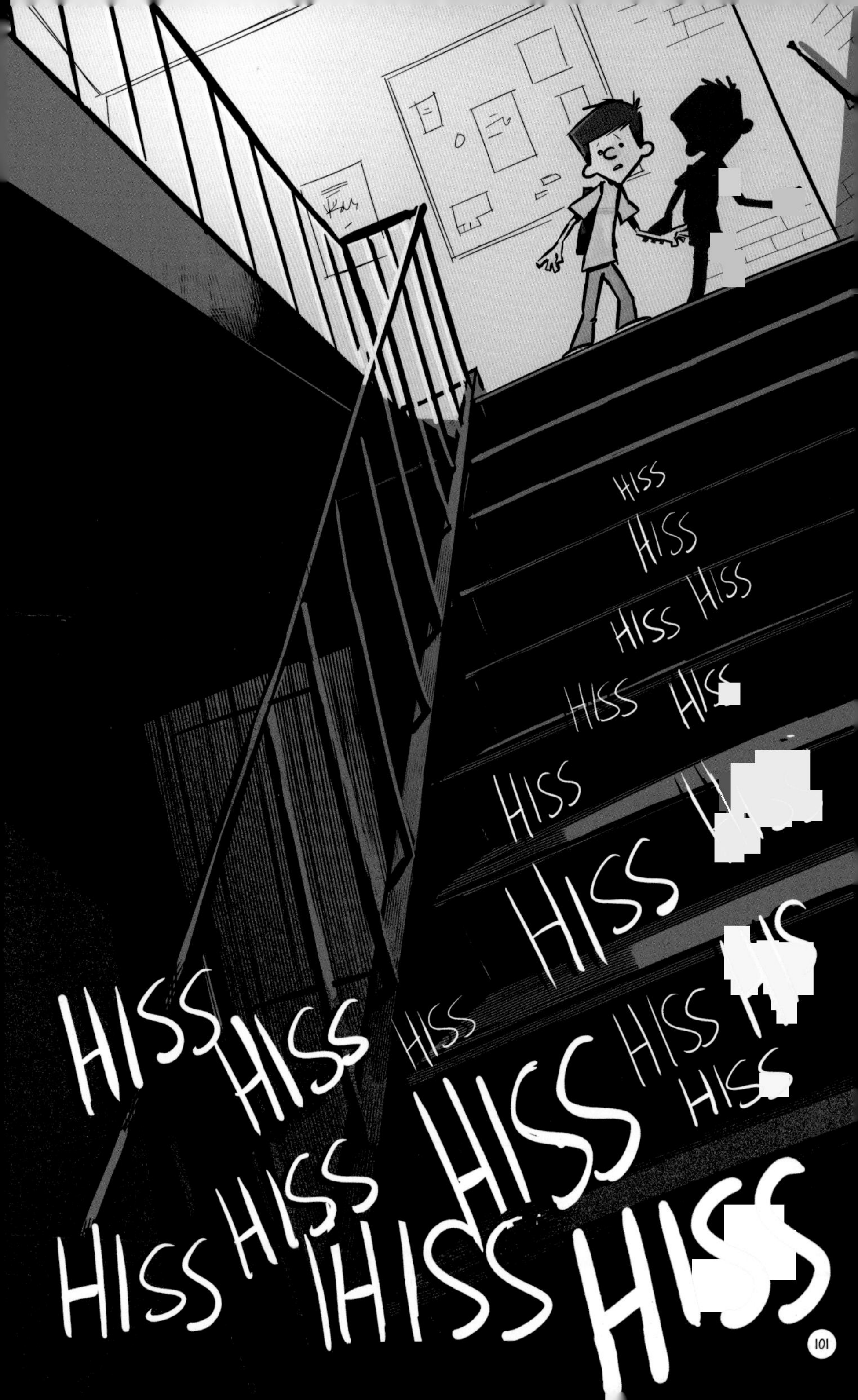
HISS
HISS
HISS HISS
HISS
HISS
HISS
HISS HISS HISS
HISS
HISS HISS
HISS
HISS HISS HISS

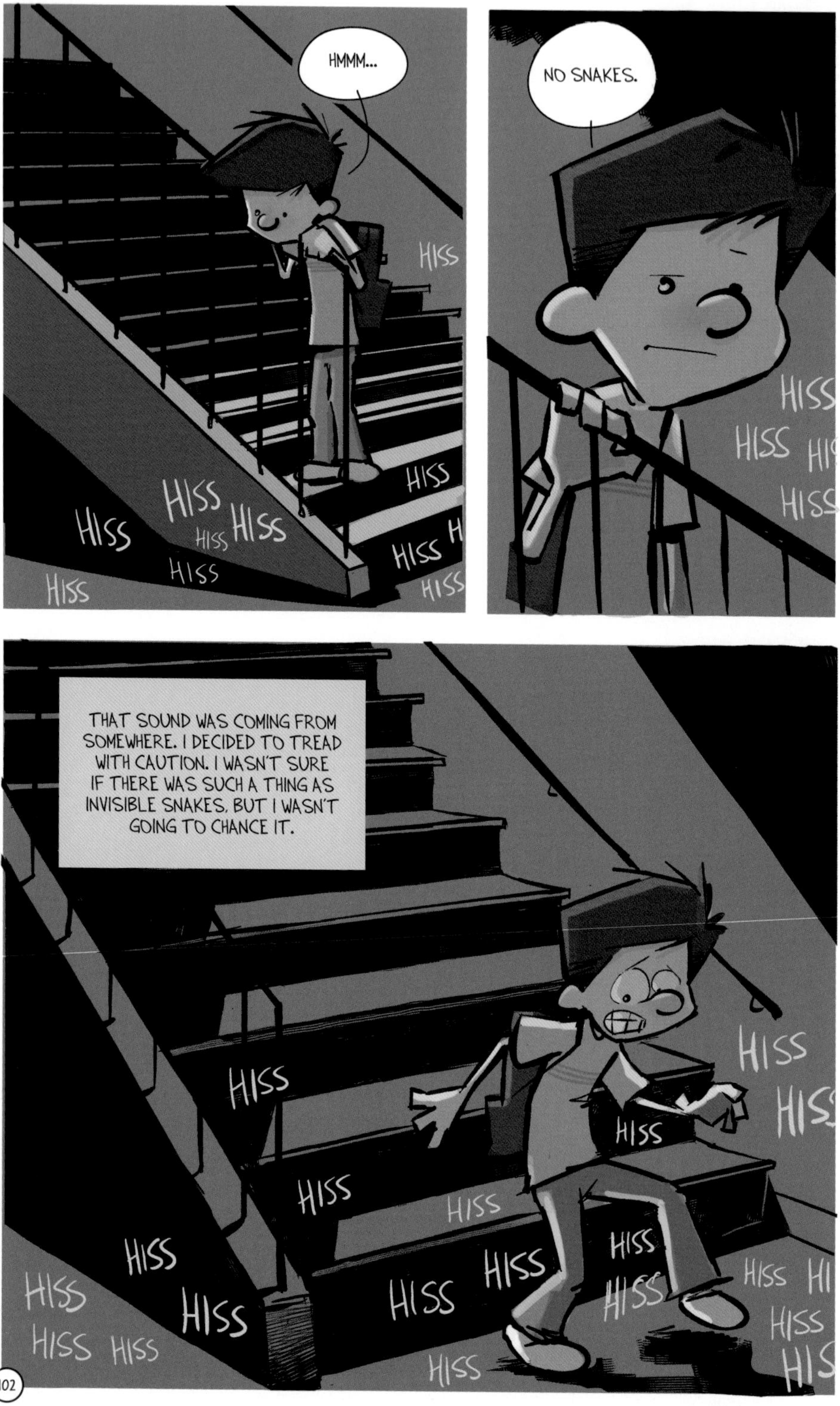
HMMM...
HISS
HISS
HISS
HISS
HISS
HISS
HISS
HISS
HISS
NO SNAKES.
HISS
HISS
HISS
THAT SOUND WAS COMING FROM SOMEWHERE. I DECIDED TO TREAD WITH CAUTION. I WASN'T SURE IF THERE WAS SUCH A THING AS INVISIBLE SNAKES, BUT I WASN'T GOING TO CHANCE IT.
HISS
HISS
HISS
HISS
HISS
HISS
HISS
HISS
HISS
HISS
HISS
HISS
HISS
HISS
HISS
HISS
HISS

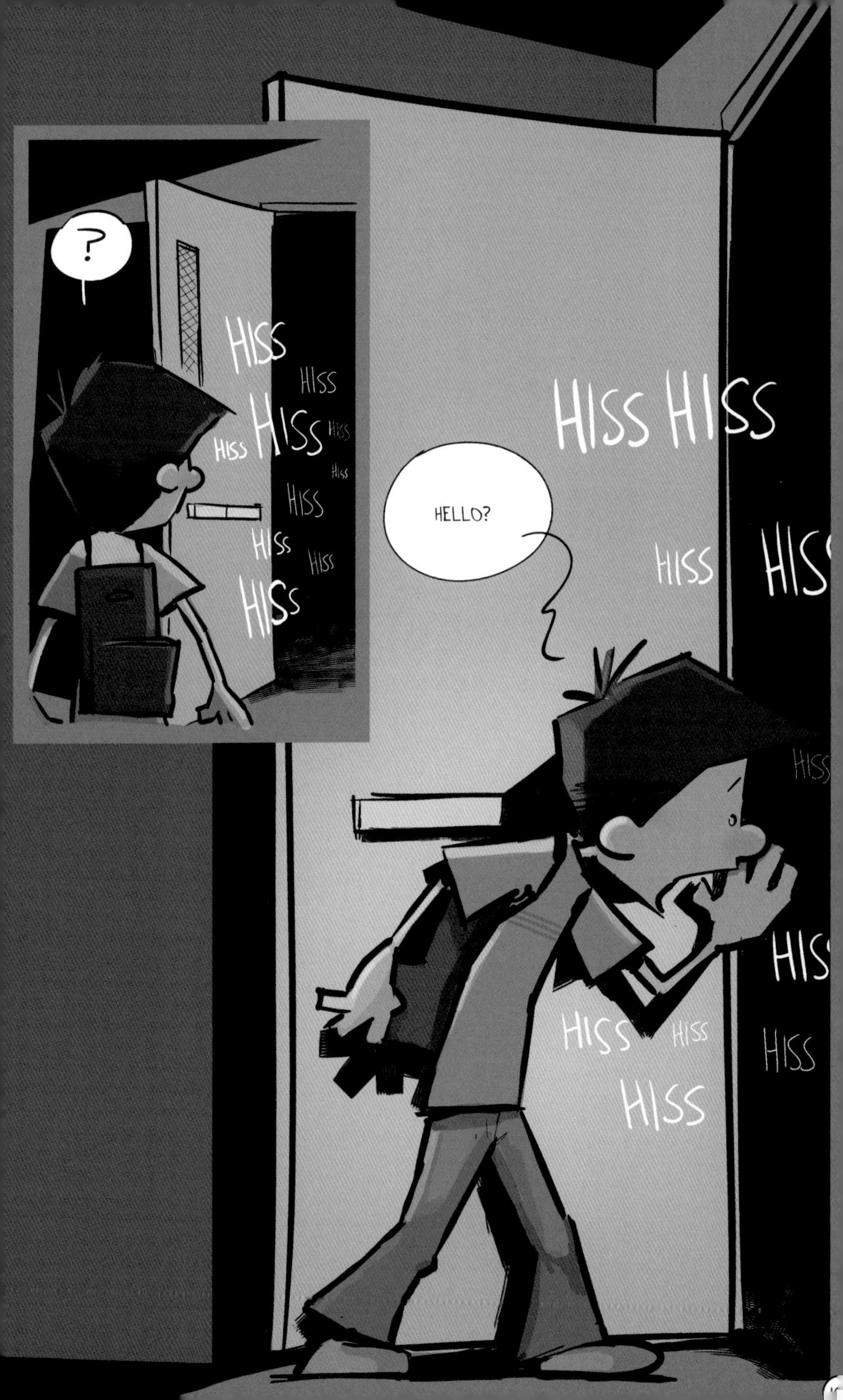
?
HISS
HISS
HISS HISS HISS
HISS
HISS
HISS
HISS
HISS
HISS HISS
HELLO?
HISS HISS
HISS
HISS
HISS
HISS HISS
HISS
HISS

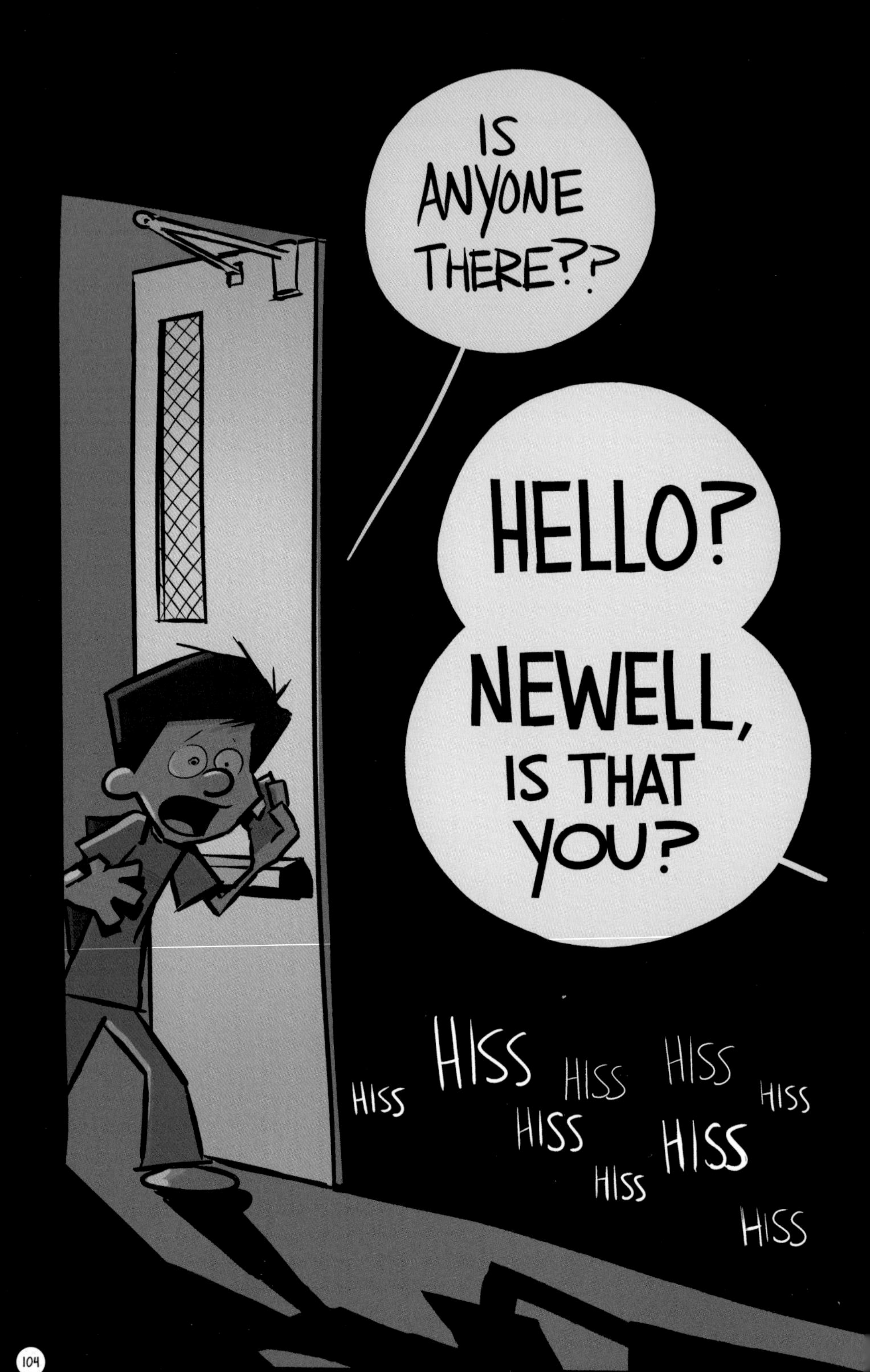
IS ANYONE THERE??
HELLO?
NEWELL, IS THAT YOU?
HISS HISS HISS HISS HISS HISS HISS HISS HISS

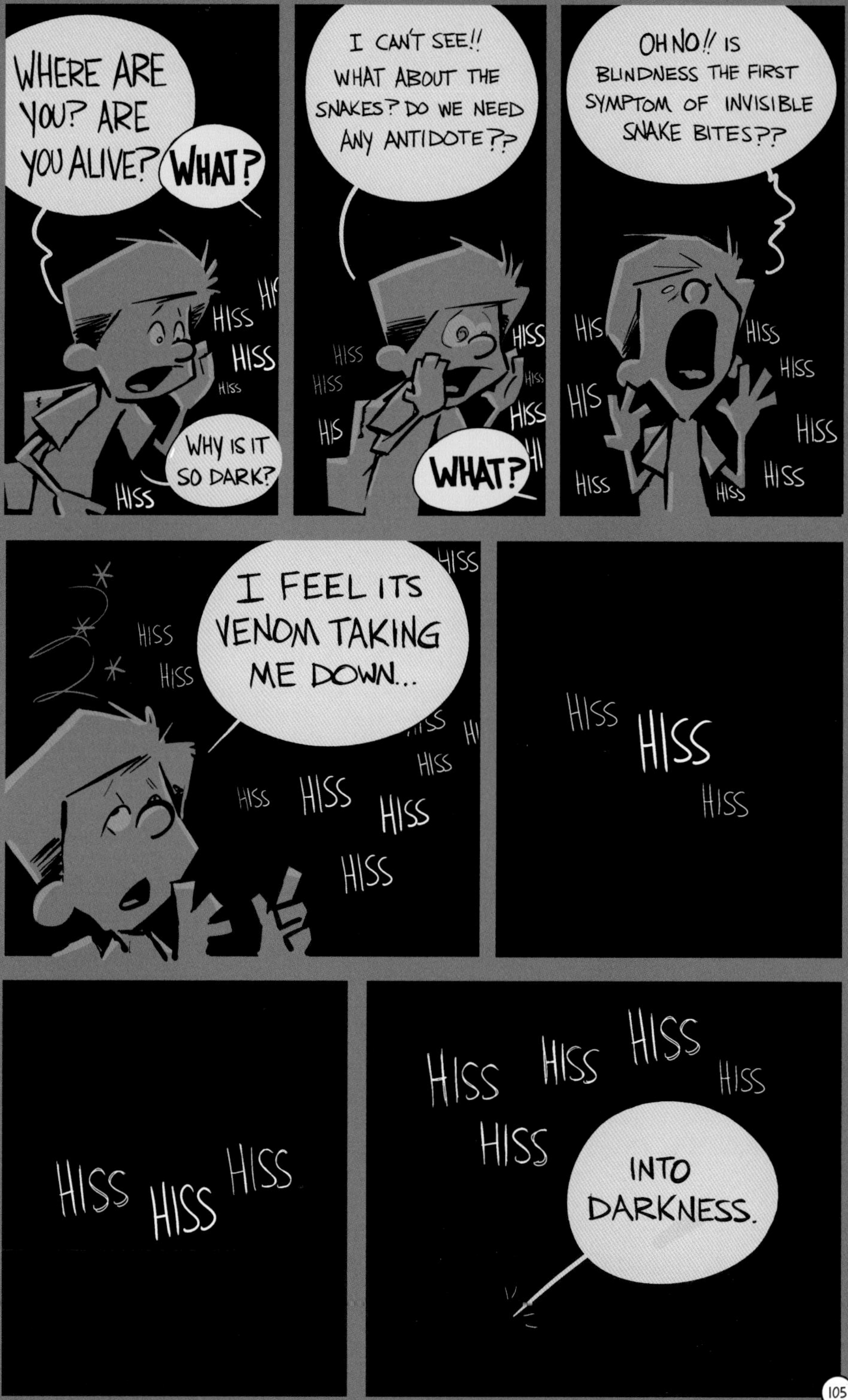
WHERE ARE YOU? ARE YOU ALIVE?
WHAT?
HISS
HISS
HISS
WHY IS IT SO DARK?
HISS
I CAN'T SEE!! WHAT ABOUT THE SNAKES? DO WE NEED ANY ANTIDOTE??
HISS
HISS
HIS
HISS
HISS
WHAT?
OH NO!! IS BLINDNESS THE FIRST SYMPTOM OF INVISIBLE SNAKE BITES??
HIS
HISS
HISS
HIS
HISS
HISS
HISS
HISS
HISS
I FEEL ITS VENOM TAKING ME DOWN...
HISS
HISS
HISS
HISS
HISS
HISS
HISS
HISS
HISS
HISS
HISS
HISS
HISS
HISS
HISS
HISS
HISS
HISS
HISS
INTO DARKNESS.

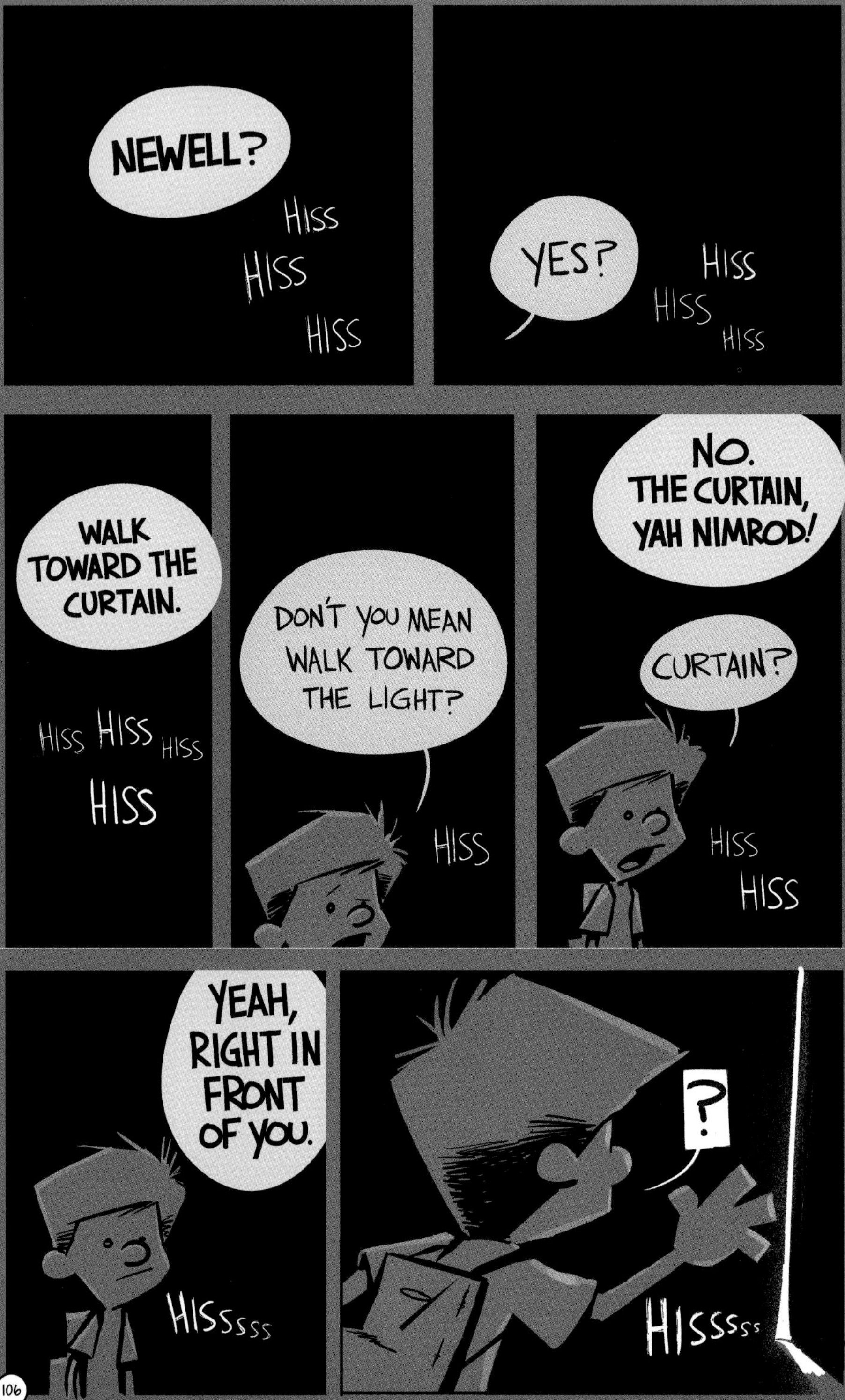

NEWELL?
HISS
HISS
HISS
YES?
HISS
HISS
HISS
WALK TOWARD THE CURTAIN.
HISS HISS HISS
HISS
DON'T YOU MEAN WALK TOWARD THE LIGHT?
HISS
NO. THE CURTAIN, YAH NIMROD!
CURTAIN?
HISS
HISS
YEAH, RIGHT IN FRONT OF YOU.
HISSsss
?
HISSSss

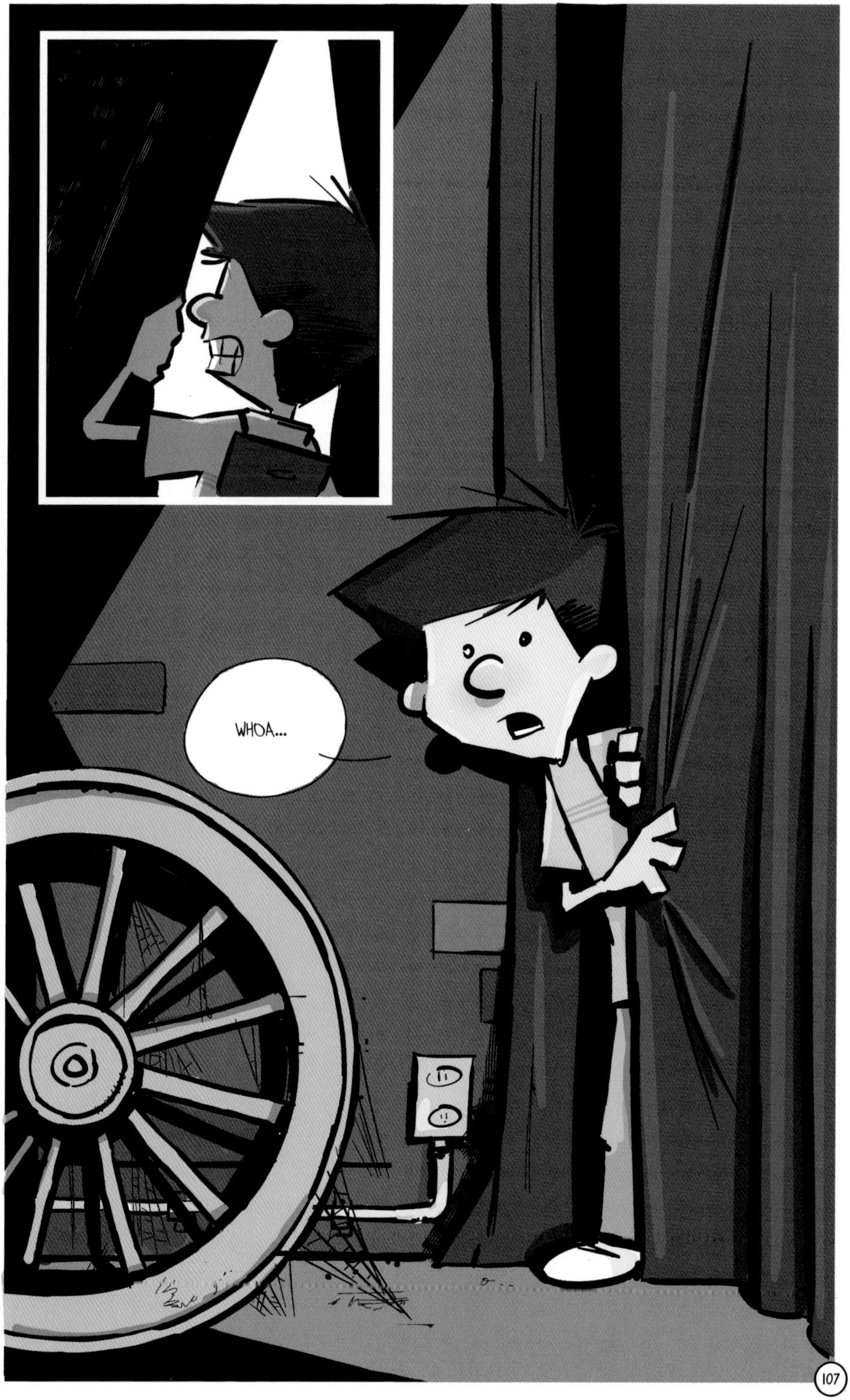
WHOA...

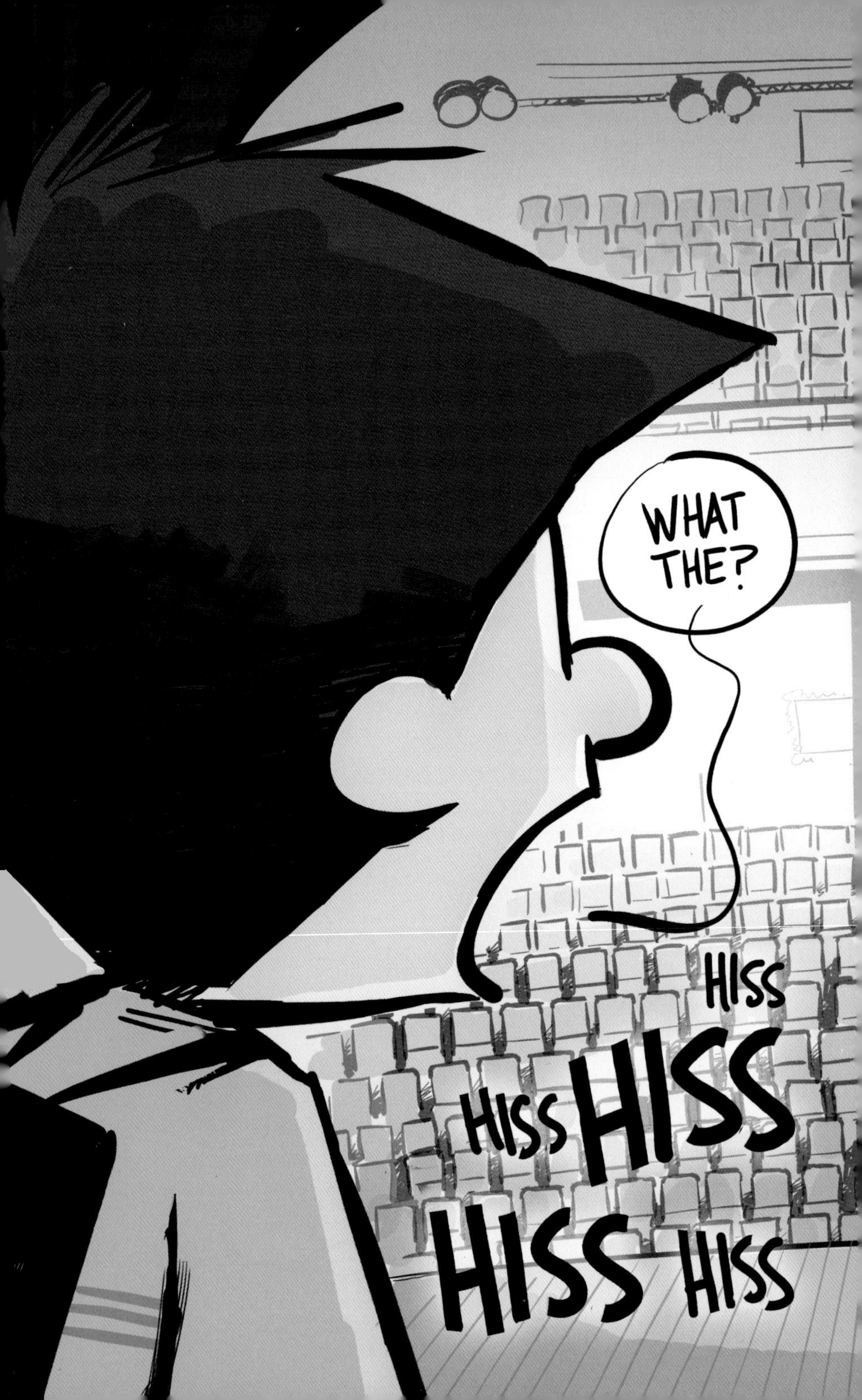
WHAT THE?
HISS
HISS HISS
HISS HISS

CHAPTER SIX
THIS ISN'T THE CAFETERIA

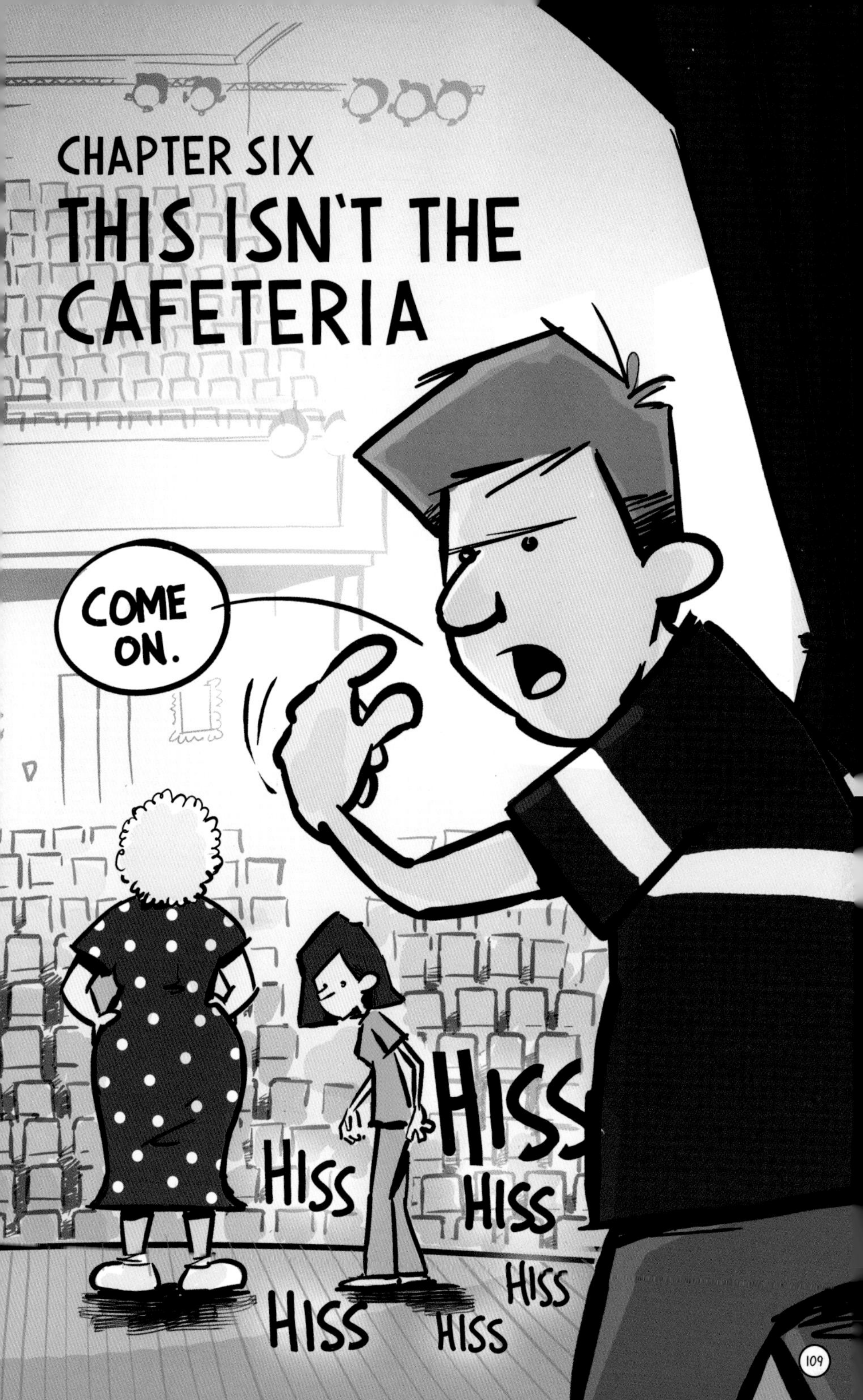
COME ON.
HISS
HISS
HISS
HISS
HISS
HISS

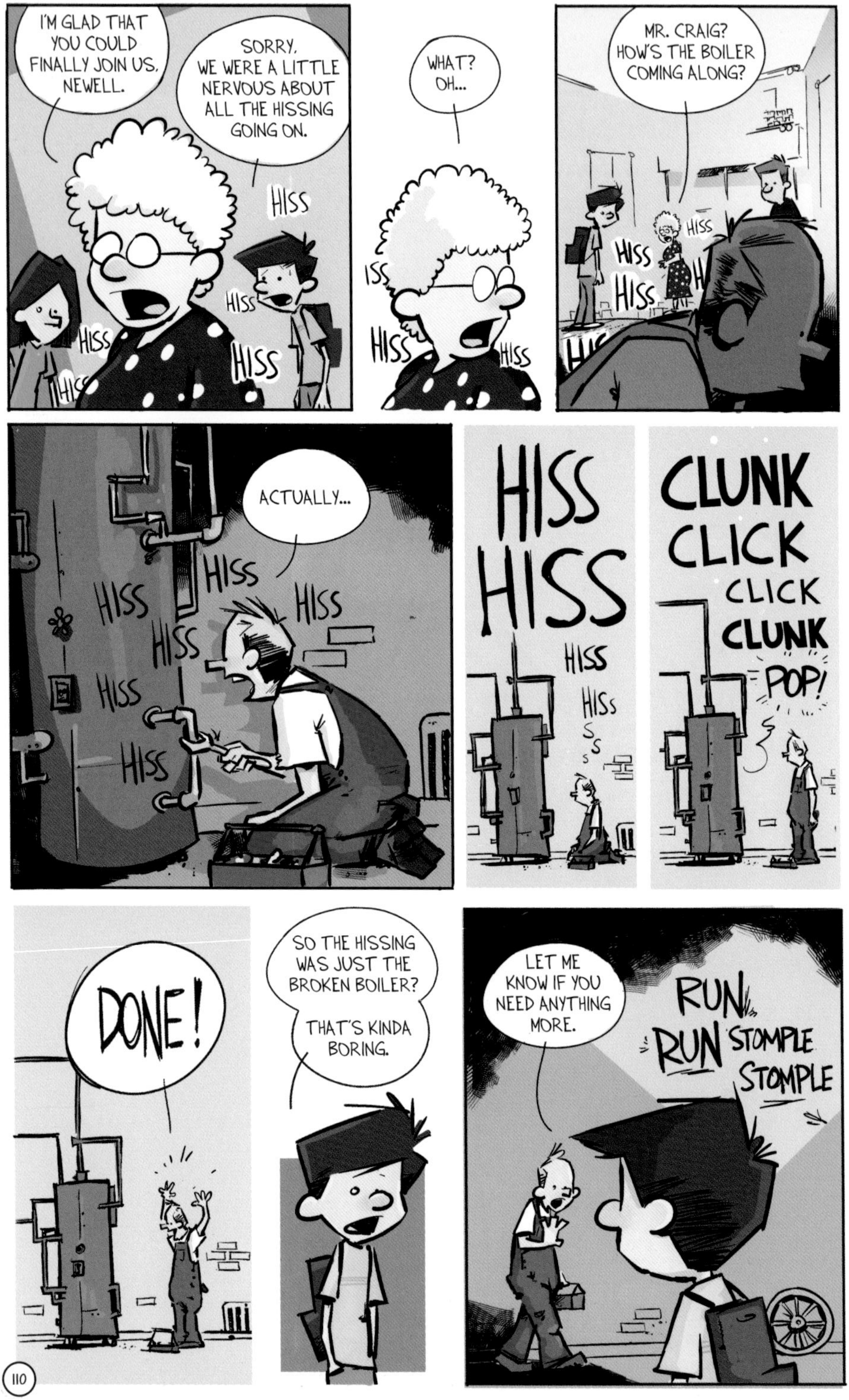
I'M GLAD THAT YOU COULD FINALLY JOIN US, NEWELL.
SORRY, WE WERE A LITTLE NERVOUS ABOUT ALL THE HISSING GOING ON.
HISS
HISS
HISS
HISS
WHAT? OH...
HISS
HISS
MR. CRAIG? HOW'S THE BOILER COMING ALONG?
HISS
HISS
HISS
ACTUALLY...
HISS
HISS
HISS
HISS
HISS
HISS
HISS
HISS
HISS
HISS
CLUNK
CLICK
CLICK
CLUNK
POP!
DONE!
SO THE HISSING WAS JUST THE BROKEN BOILER?
THAT'S KINDA BORING.
LET ME KNOW IF YOU NEED ANYTHING MORE.
RUN
RUN
STOMPLE
STOMPLE

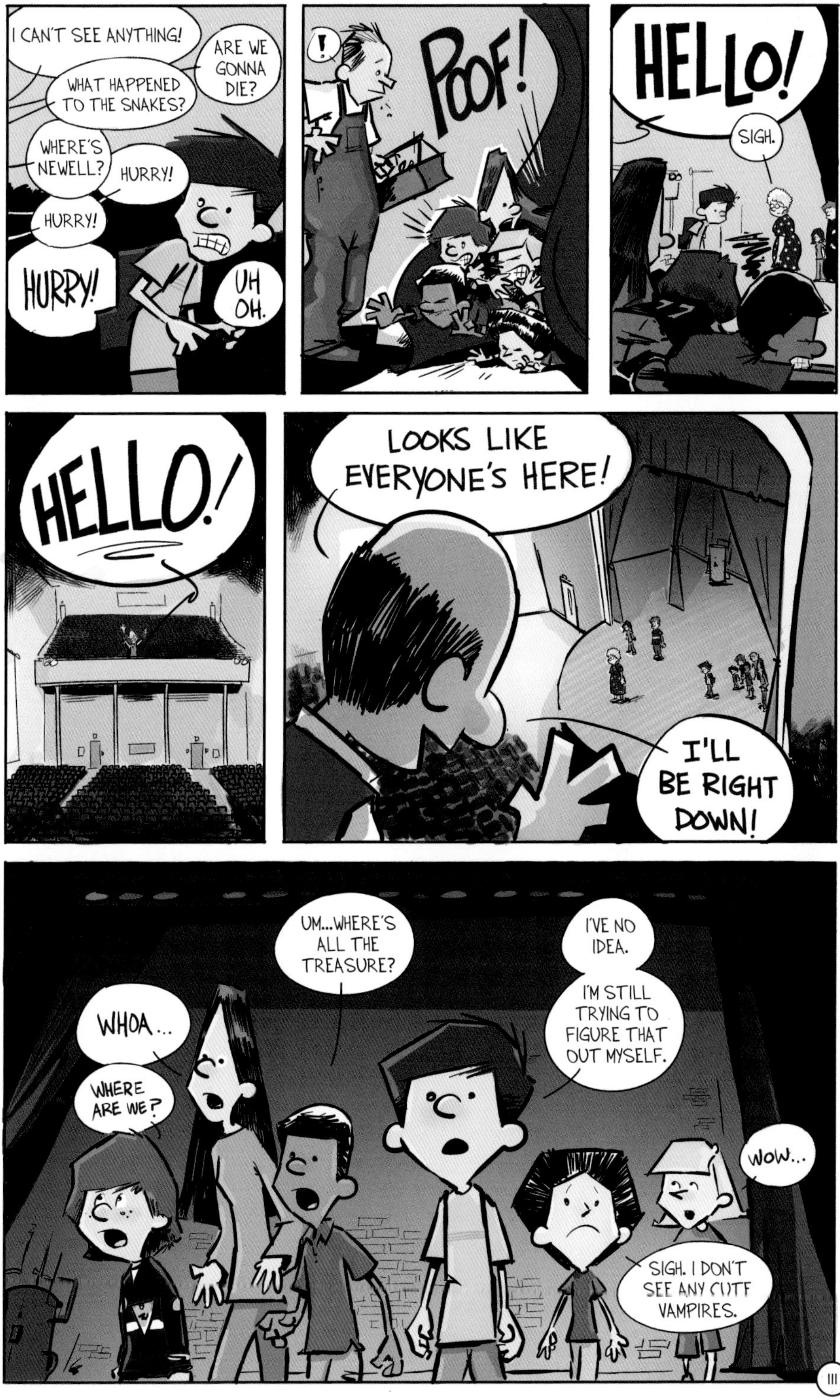
I CAN'T SEE ANYTHING!
ARE WE GONNA DIE?
WHAT HAPPENED TO THE SNAKES?
WHERE'S NEWELL?
HURRY!
HURRY!
HURRY!
UH OH.
!
POOF!
HELLO!
SIGH.
HELLO!
LOOKS LIKE EVERYONE'S HERE!
I'LL BE RIGHT DOWN!
WHOA...
WHERE ARE WE?
UM...WHERE'S ALL THE TREASURE?
I'VE NO IDEA.
I'M STILL TRYING TO FIGURE THAT OUT MYSELF.
WOW...
SIGH. I DON'T SEE ANY CUTE VAMPIRES.

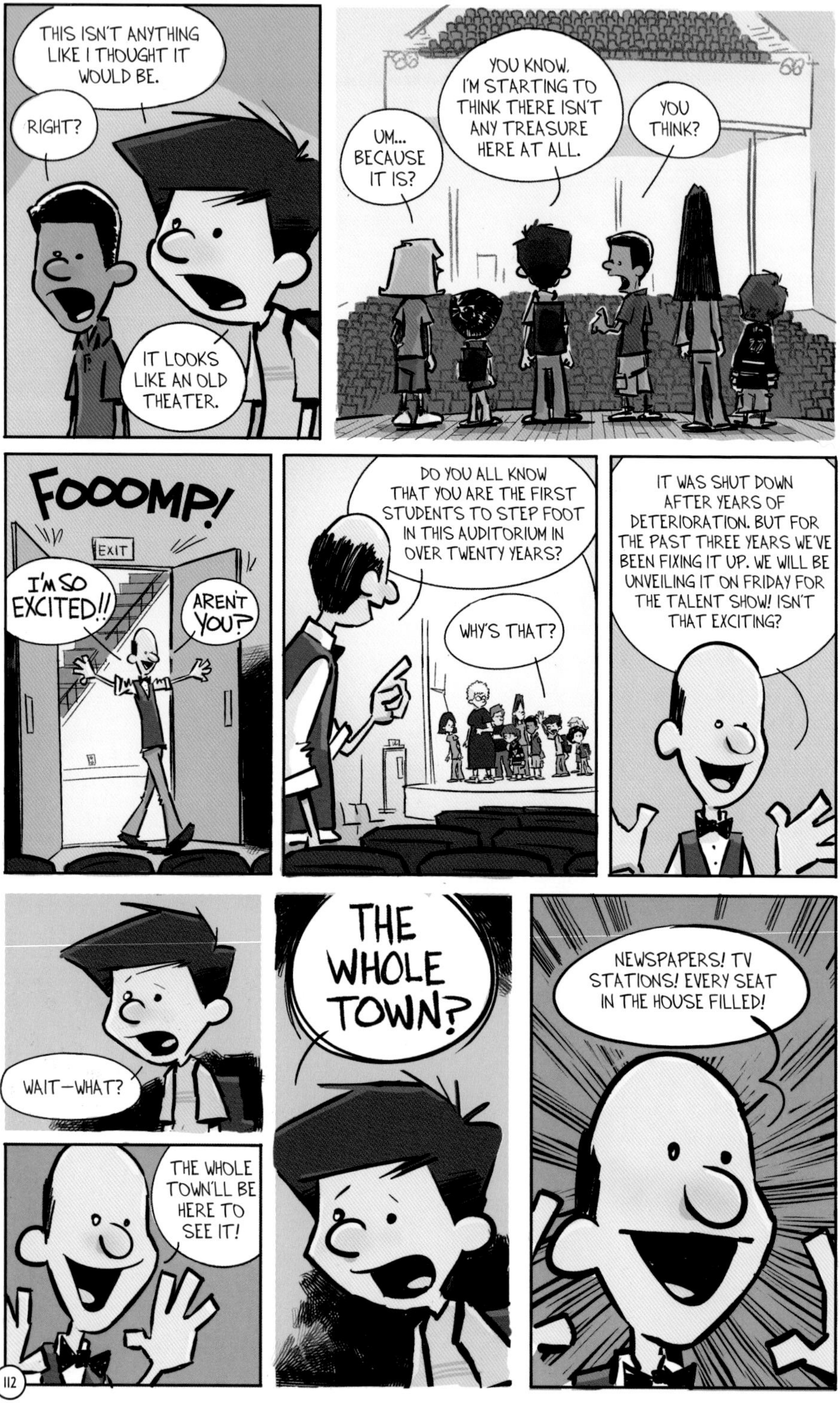

THIS ISN'T ANYTHING LIKE I THOUGHT IT WOULD BE.
RIGHT?
IT LOOKS LIKE AN OLD THEATER.
UM... BECAUSE IT IS?
YOU KNOW, I'M STARTING TO THINK THERE ISN'T ANY TREASURE HERE AT ALL.
YOU THINK?
FOOOMP!
EXIT
I'M SO EXCITED!!
AREN'T YOU?
DO YOU ALL KNOW THAT YOU ARE THE FIRST STUDENTS TO STEP FOOT IN THIS AUDITORIUM IN OVER TWENTY YEARS?
WHY'S THAT?
IT WAS SHUT DOWN AFTER YEARS OF DETERIORATION. BUT FOR THE PAST THREE YEARS WE'VE BEEN FIXING IT UP. WE WILL BE UNVEILING IT ON FRIDAY FOR THE TALENT SHOW! ISN'T THAT EXCITING?
WAIT—WHAT?
THE WHOLE TOWN'LL BE HERE TO SEE IT!
THE WHOLE TOWN?
NEWSPAPERS! TV STATIONS! EVERY SEAT IN THE HOUSE FILLED!

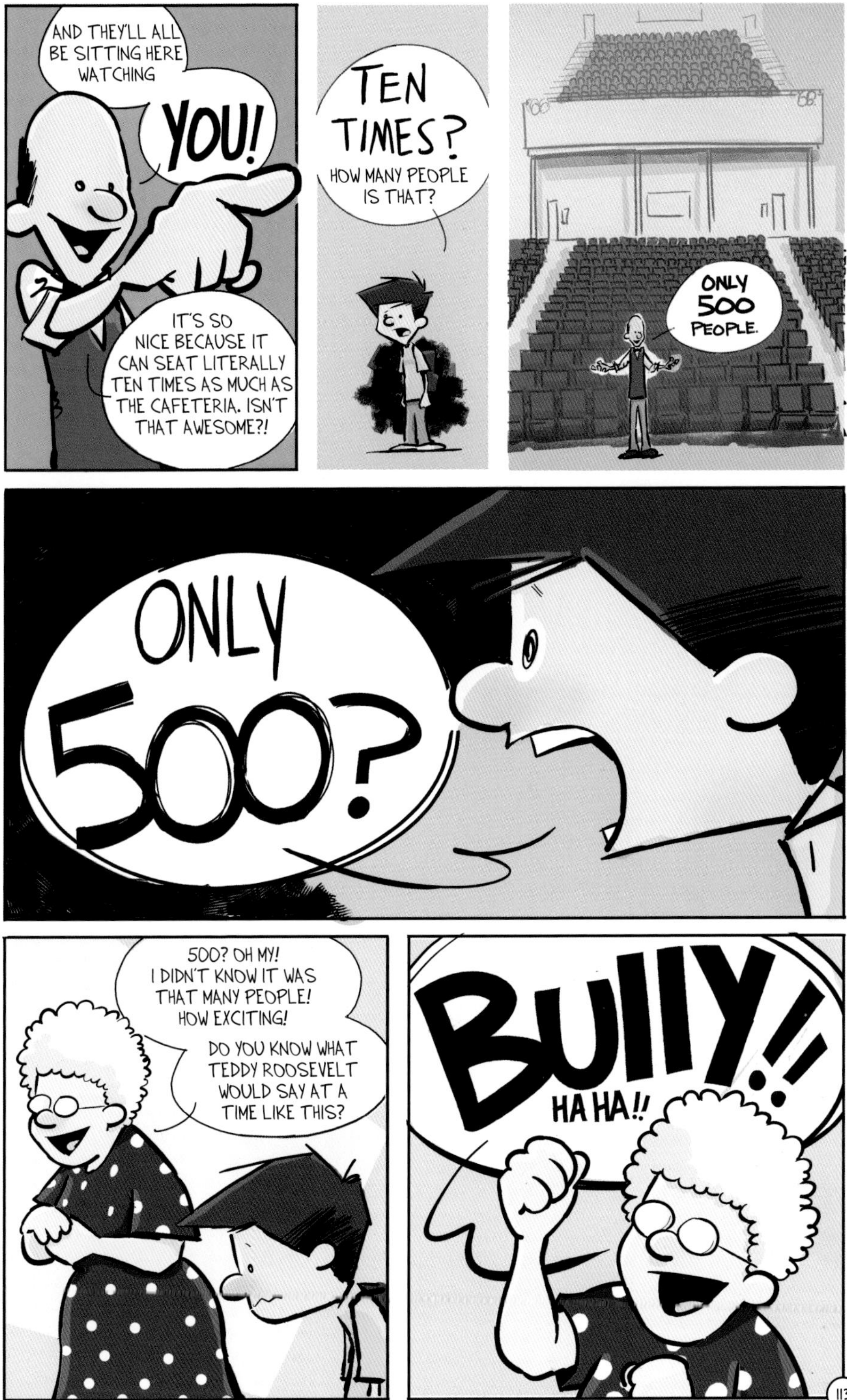
AND THEY'LL ALL BE SITTING HERE WATCHING
YOU!
IT'S SO NICE BECAUSE IT CAN SEAT LITERALLY TEN TIMES AS MUCH AS THE CAFETERIA. ISN'T THAT AWESOME?!
TEN TIMES?
HOW MANY PEOPLE IS THAT?
ONLY 500 PEOPLE.
ONLY 500?
500? OH MY! I DIDN'T KNOW IT WAS THAT MANY PEOPLE! HOW EXCITING!
DO YOU KNOW WHAT TEDDY ROOSEVELT WOULD SAY AT A TIME LIKE THIS?
BULLY!!
HA HA!!

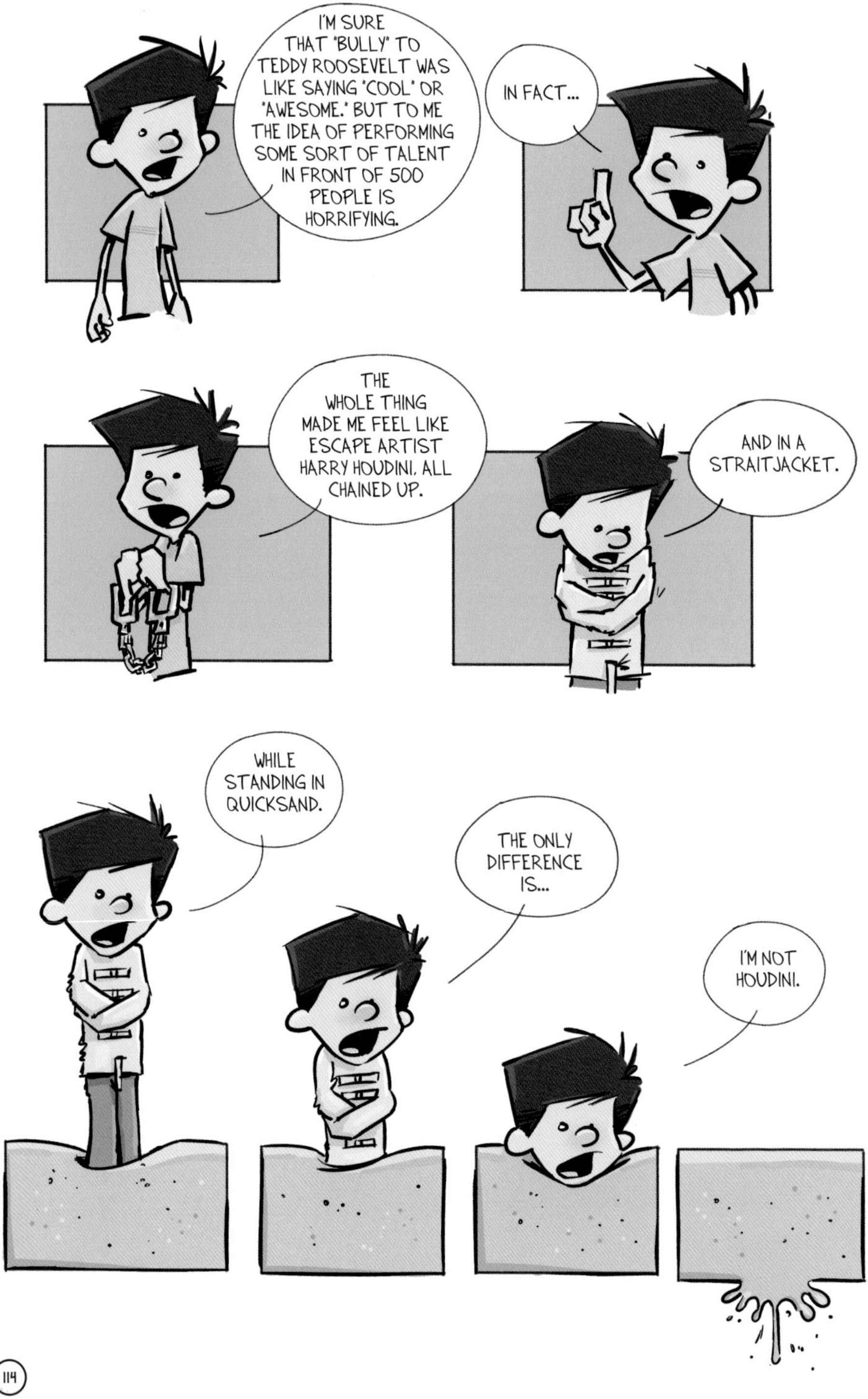
I'M SURE THAT "BULLY" TO TEDDY ROOSEVELT WAS LIKE SAYING "COOL" OR "AWESOME." BUT TO ME THE IDEA OF PERFORMING SOME SORT OF TALENT IN FRONT OF 500 PEOPLE IS HORRIFYING.
IN FACT...
THE WHOLE THING MADE ME FEEL LIKE ESCAPE ARTIST HARRY HOUDINI, ALL CHAINED UP.
AND IN A STRAITJACKET.
WHILE STANDING IN QUICKSAND.
THE ONLY DIFFERENCE IS...
I'M NOT HOUDINI.

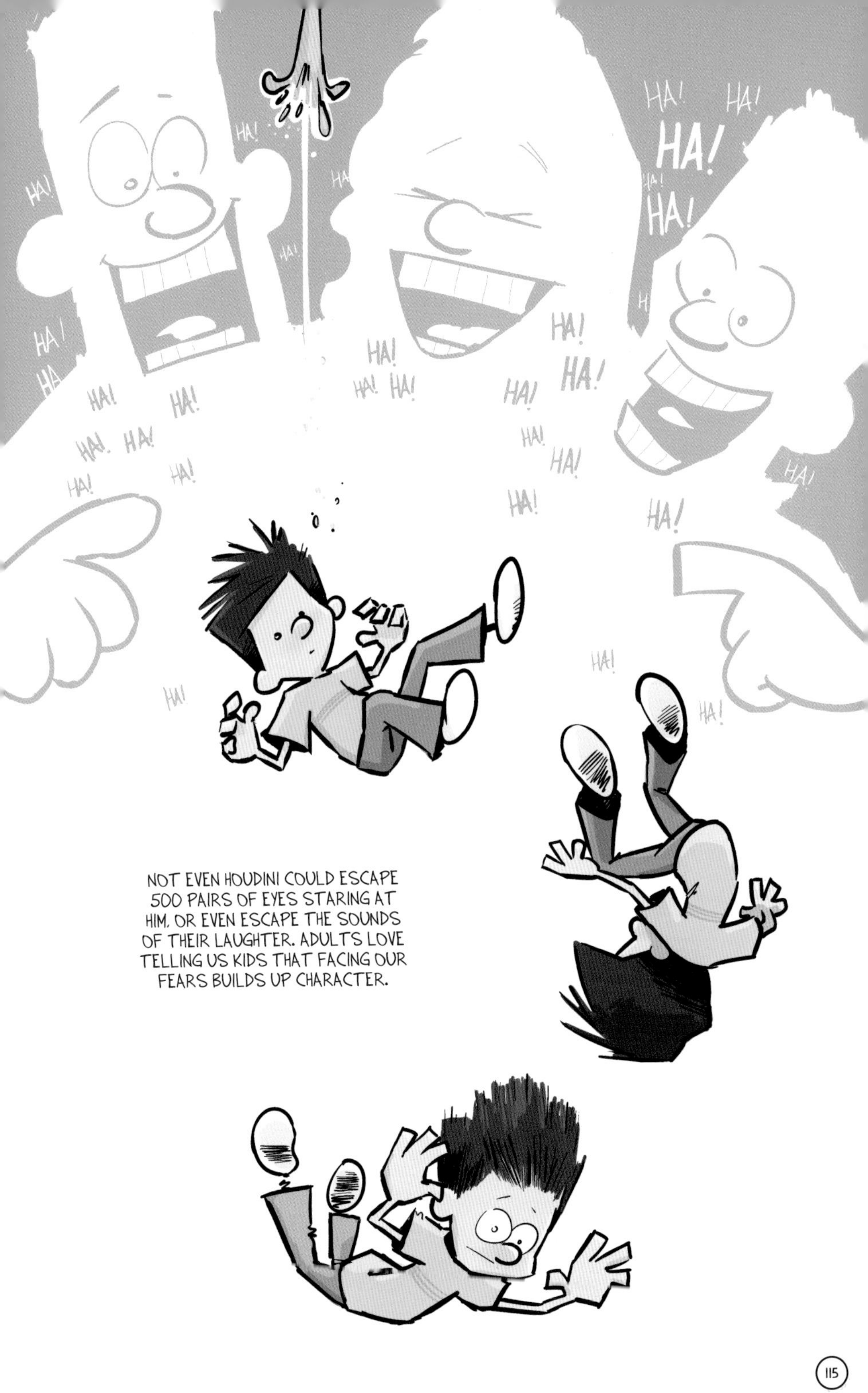
HA! HA!
HA!
HA!
HA!
HA!
HA!
HA!
HA!
HA! HA!
HA!
HA! HA!
HA!
HA!
HA!
HA!
NOT EVEN HOUDINI COULD ESCAPE 500 PAIRS OF EYES STARING AT HIM, OR EVEN ESCAPE THE SOUNDS OF THEIR LAUGHTER. ADULTS LOVE TELLING US KIDS THAT FACING OUR FEARS BUILDS UP CHARACTER.

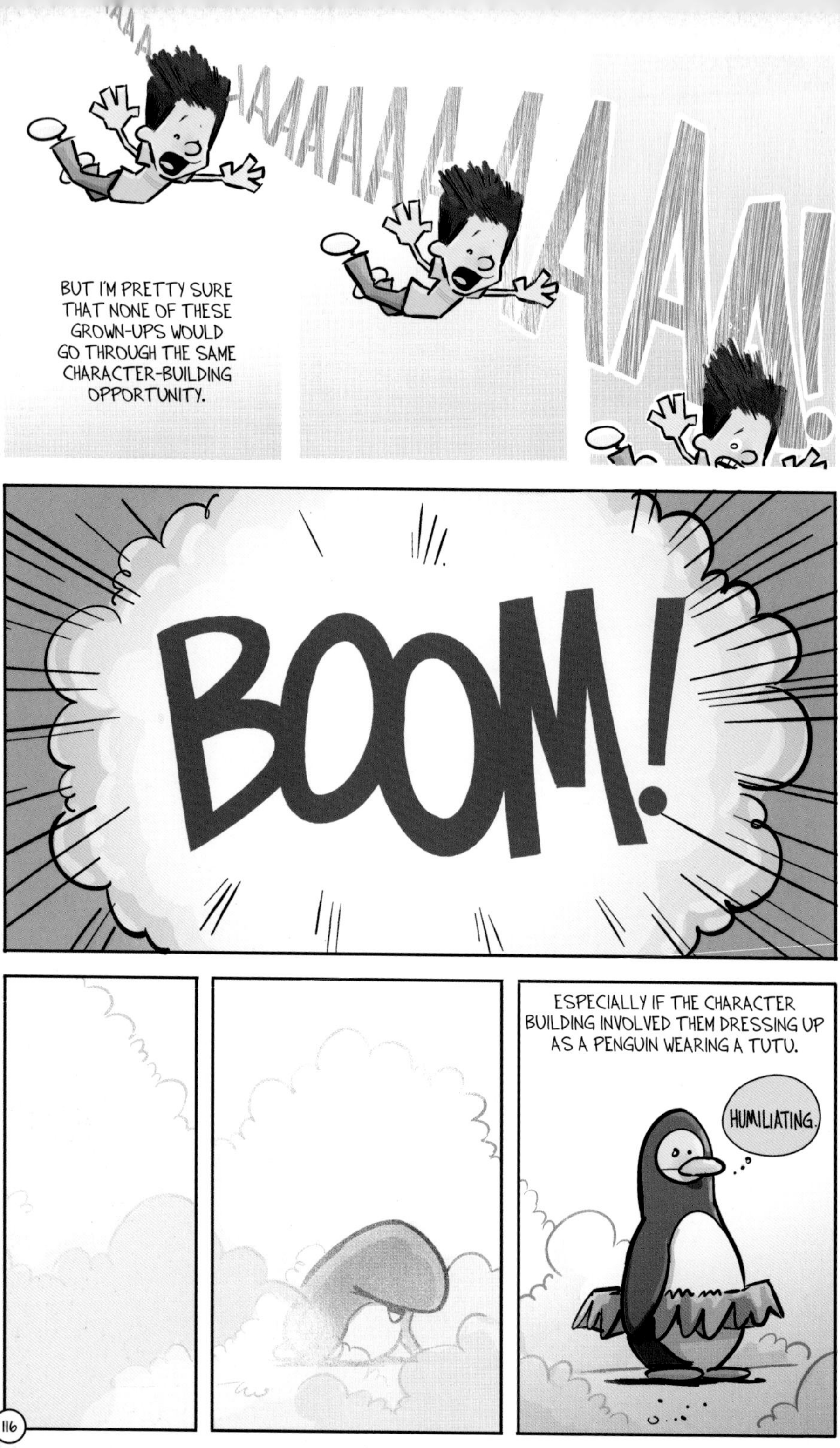
AAAAAAAAAAAAAAAAAAA!
BUT I'M PRETTY SURE THAT NONE OF THESE GROWN-UPS WOULD GO THROUGH THE SAME CHARACTER-BUILDING OPPORTUNITY.
BOOM!
ESPECIALLY IF THE CHARACTER BUILDING INVOLVED THEM DRESSING UP AS A PENGUIN WEARING A TUTU.
HUMILIATING.

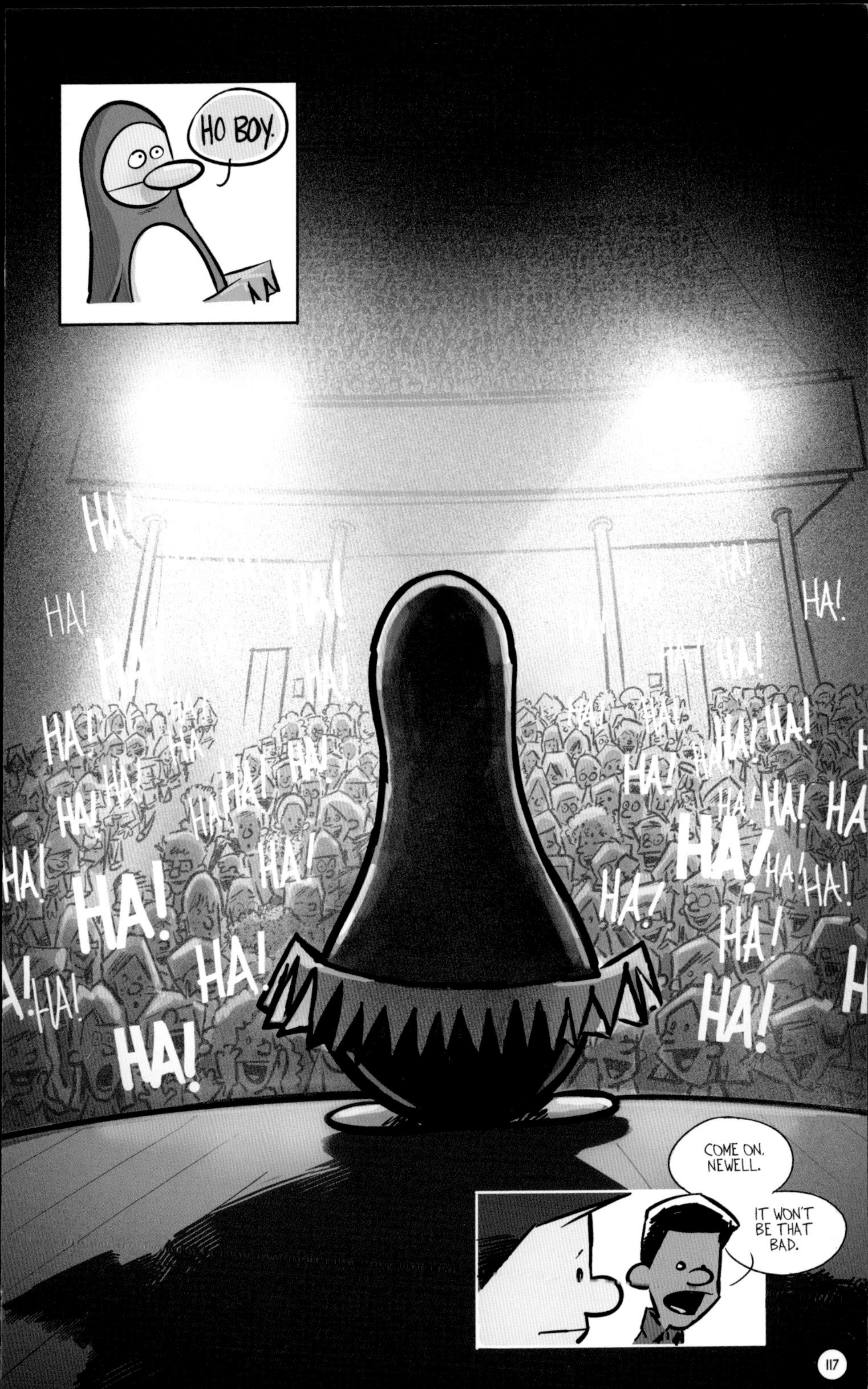
HO BOY.
HA! HA! HA! HA! HA! HA! HA! HA! HA!
COME ON, NEWELL.
IT WON'T BE THAT BAD.

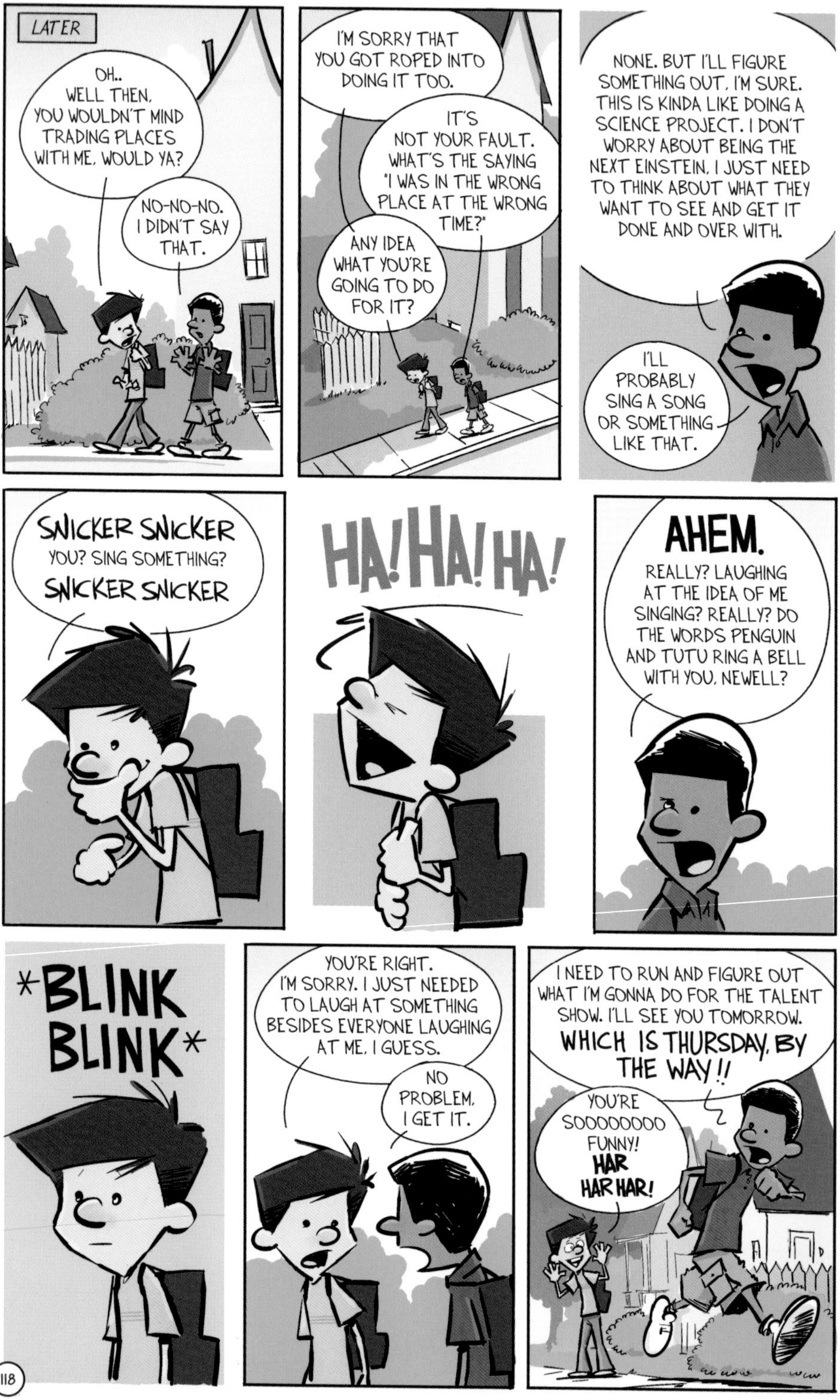
LATER
OH.. WELL THEN, YOU WOULDN'T MIND TRADING PLACES WITH ME, WOULD YA?
NO-NO-NO. I DIDN'T SAY THAT.
I'M SORRY THAT YOU GOT ROPED INTO DOING IT TOO.
IT'S NOT YOUR FAULT. WHAT'S THE SAYING "I WAS IN THE WRONG PLACE AT THE WRONG TIME?"
ANY IDEA WHAT YOU'RE GOING TO DO FOR IT?
NONE. BUT I'LL FIGURE SOMETHING OUT, I'M SURE. THIS IS KINDA LIKE DOING A SCIENCE PROJECT. I DON'T WORRY ABOUT BEING THE NEXT EINSTEIN, I JUST NEED TO THINK ABOUT WHAT THEY WANT TO SEE AND GET IT DONE AND OVER WITH.
I'LL PROBABLY SING A SONG OR SOMETHING LIKE THAT.
SNICKER SNICKER YOU? SING SOMETHING? SNICKER SNICKER
HA! HA! HA!
AHEM. REALLY? LAUGHING AT THE IDEA OF ME SINGING? REALLY? DO THE WORDS PENGUIN AND TUTU RING A BELL WITH YOU, NEWELL?
BLINK BLINK
YOU'RE RIGHT. I'M SORRY. I JUST NEEDED TO LAUGH AT SOMETHING BESIDES EVERYONE LAUGHING AT ME, I GUESS.
NO PROBLEM, I GET IT.
I NEED TO RUN AND FIGURE OUT WHAT I'M GONNA DO FOR THE TALENT SHOW. I'LL SEE YOU TOMORROW. WHICH IS THURSDAY, BY THE WAY!!
YOU'RE SOOOOOOOO FUNNY! HAR HAR HAR!

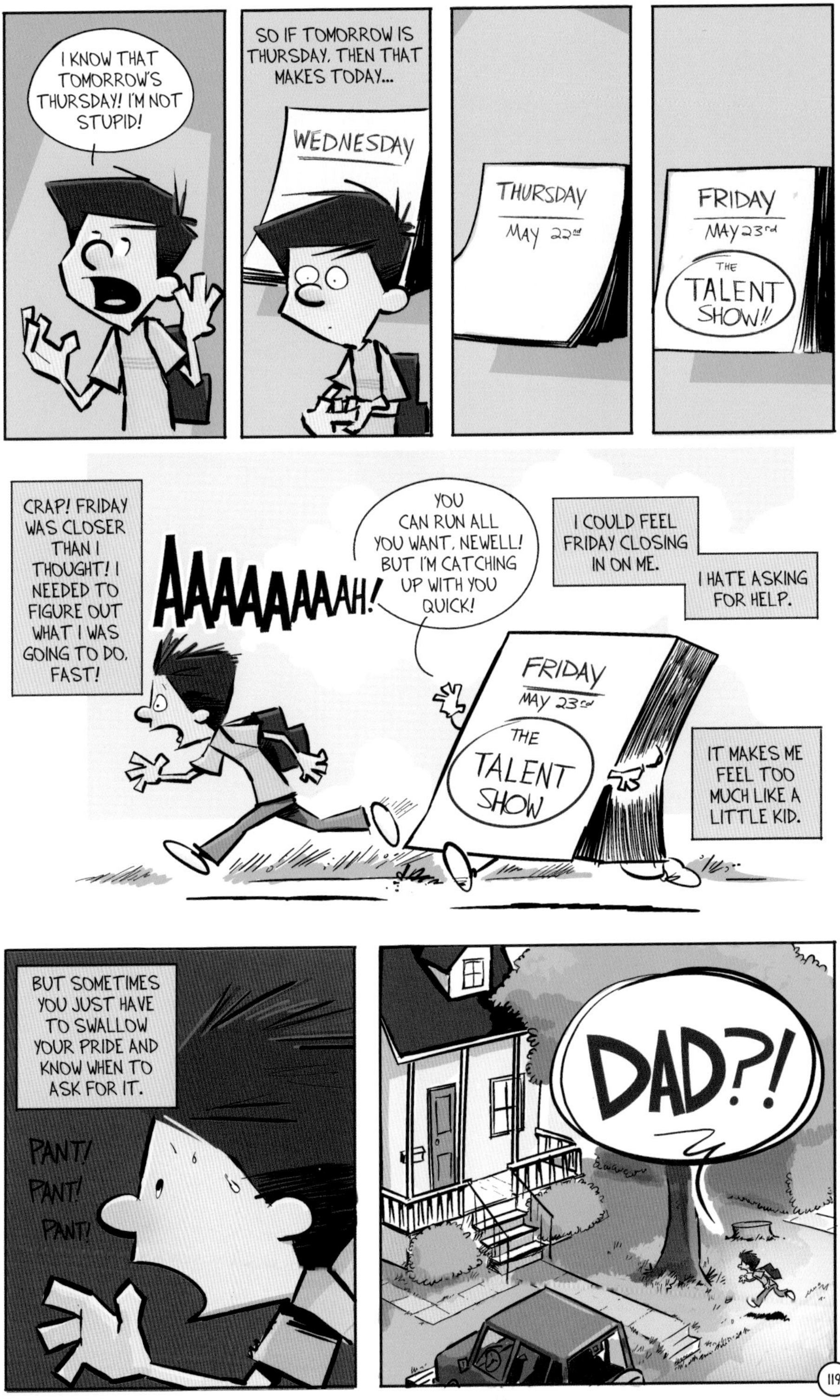
I KNOW THAT TOMORROW'S THURSDAY! I'M NOT STUPID!
SO IF TOMORROW IS THURSDAY, THEN THAT MAKES TODAY...
WEDNESDAY
THURSDAY
MAY 22nd
FRIDAY
MAY 23rd
THE TALENT SHOW!!
CRAP! FRIDAY WAS CLOSER THAN I THOUGHT! I NEEDED TO FIGURE OUT WHAT I WAS GOING TO DO, FAST!
AAAAAAAAAH!
YOU CAN RUN ALL YOU WANT, NEWELL! BUT I'M CATCHING UP WITH YOU QUICK!
I COULD FEEL FRIDAY CLOSING IN ON ME.
I HATE ASKING FOR HELP.
FRIDAY
MAY 23rd
THE TALENT SHOW
IT MAKES ME FEEL TOO MUCH LIKE A LITTLE KID.
BUT SOMETIMES YOU JUST HAVE TO SWALLOW YOUR PRIDE AND KNOW WHEN TO ASK FOR IT.
PANT! PANT! PANT!
DAD?!

CHAPTER SEVEN
WHAT DO I DO?

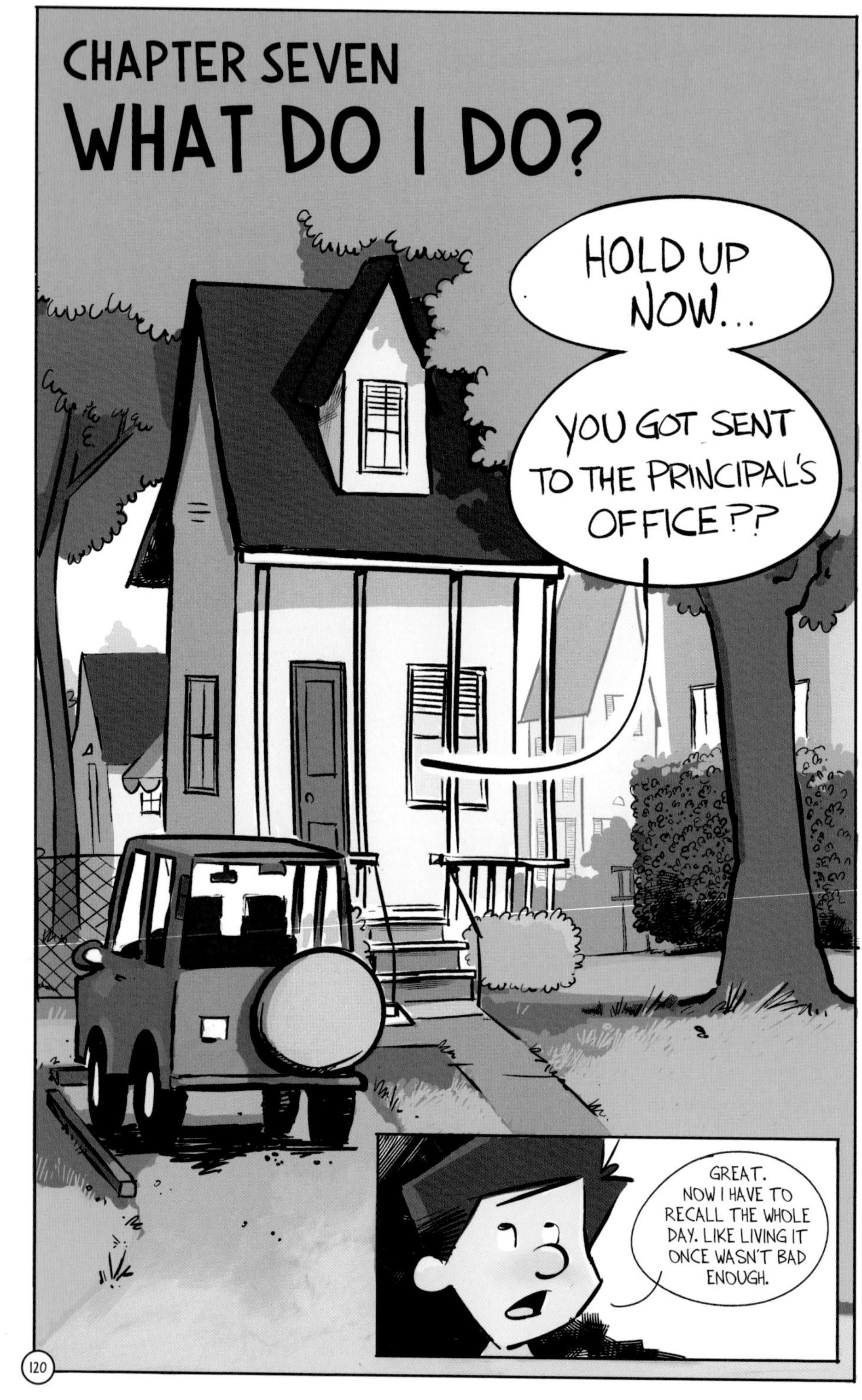
HOLD UP NOW...
YOU GOT SENT TO THE PRINCIPAL'S OFFICE??
GREAT. NOW I HAVE TO RECALL THE WHOLE DAY. LIKE LIVING IT ONCE WASN'T BAD ENOUGH.

WELL?

WELL... IT'S AH... I'M KINDA OF, AH

SPIT IT OUT.

SO I DID.

I TOLD HIM THE WHOLE STORY.

ABOUT COLLIN AND ME RUNNING TO SCHOOL.

MAKING FUN OF MR. TODD... AND GETTING CAUGHT.

DOOPTY DURR

ABOUT HAVING TO ATTEND SUMMER SCHOOL. WHICH HE DIDN'T EVEN BLINK AT. AND THE HALLWAY CHASE WITH CLARA.

!

THE WHOLE TIME MY DAD'S ARMS WERE CROSSED AND HIS LEFT FOOT KEPT TAPPING. A SURE SIGN THAT HE WASN'T HAPPY.

SO...

TAP! TAP! TAP!

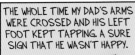
HAVE TO PERFORM IN THE SCHOOL'S TALENT SHOW THIS FRIDAY.

THE TALENT SHOW, HUH?

OH MAN... HERE IT COMES.

SIGH...
NEWELL, I DON'T KNOW WHAT TO SAY, EXCEPT...

THAT'S **AWESOME!!**

yeesh...

I KNEW HE'D BE EXCITED ABOUT IT. THAT'S EXACTLY WHY I WAS HESITANT IN TELLING HIM ABOUT THIS WHOLE MESS.

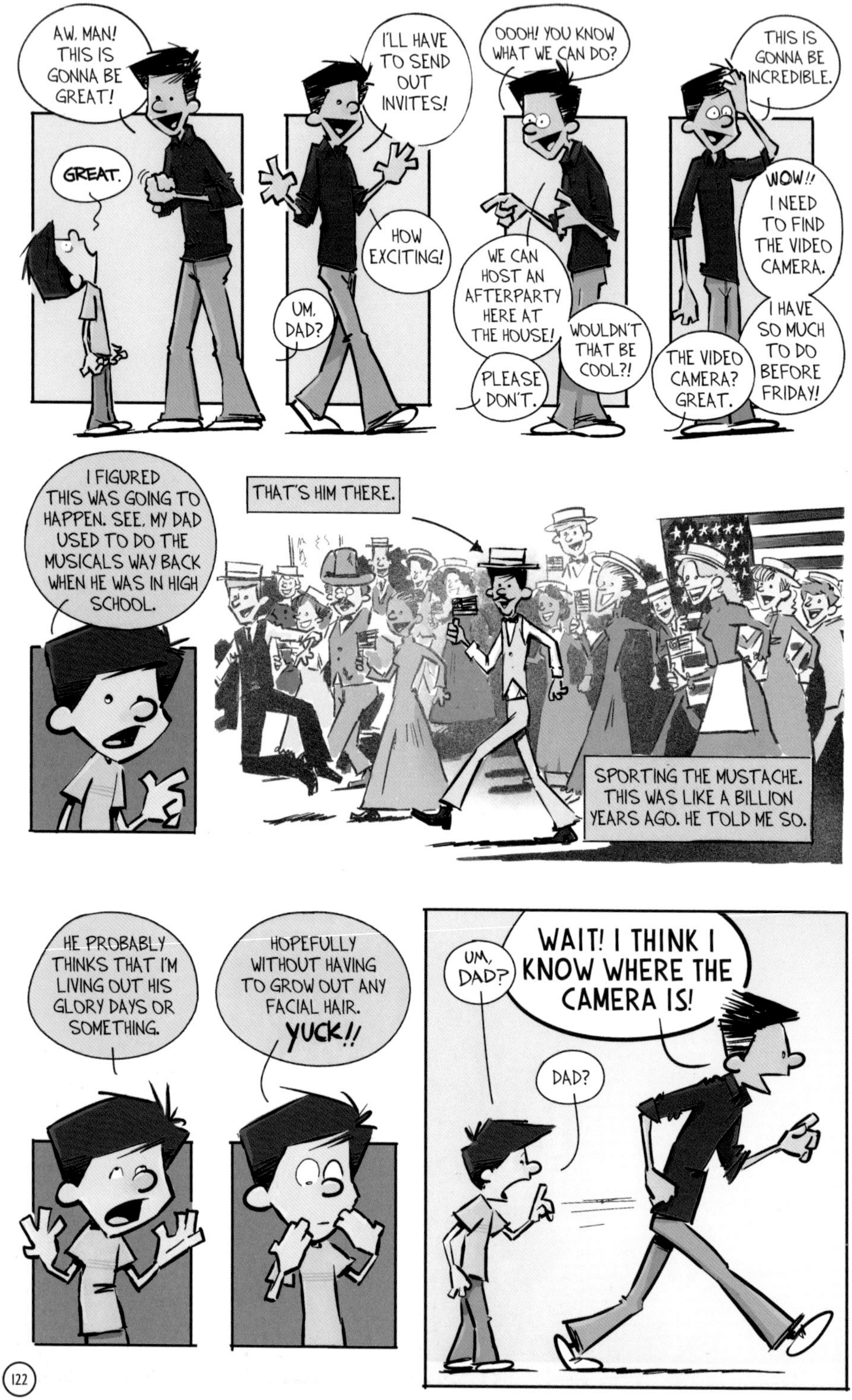
AW, MAN! THIS IS GONNA BE GREAT!
GREAT.
I'LL HAVE TO SEND OUT INVITES!
HOW EXCITING!
UM, DAD?
OOOH! YOU KNOW WHAT WE CAN DO?
WE CAN HOST AN AFTERPARTY HERE AT THE HOUSE!
WOULDN'T THAT BE COOL?!
PLEASE DON'T.
THIS IS GONNA BE INCREDIBLE.
WOW!! I NEED TO FIND THE VIDEO CAMERA.
I HAVE SO MUCH TO DO BEFORE FRIDAY!
THE VIDEO CAMERA? GREAT.
I FIGURED THIS WAS GOING TO HAPPEN. SEE, MY DAD USED TO DO THE MUSICALS WAY BACK WHEN HE WAS IN HIGH SCHOOL.
THAT'S HIM THERE.
SPORTING THE MUSTACHE. THIS WAS LIKE A BILLION YEARS AGO. HE TOLD ME SO.
HE PROBABLY THINKS THAT I'M LIVING OUT HIS GLORY DAYS OR SOMETHING.
HOPEFULLY WITHOUT HAVING TO GROW OUT ANY FACIAL HAIR. YUCK!!
UM, DAD?
WAIT! I THINK I KNOW WHERE THE CAMERA IS!
DAD?

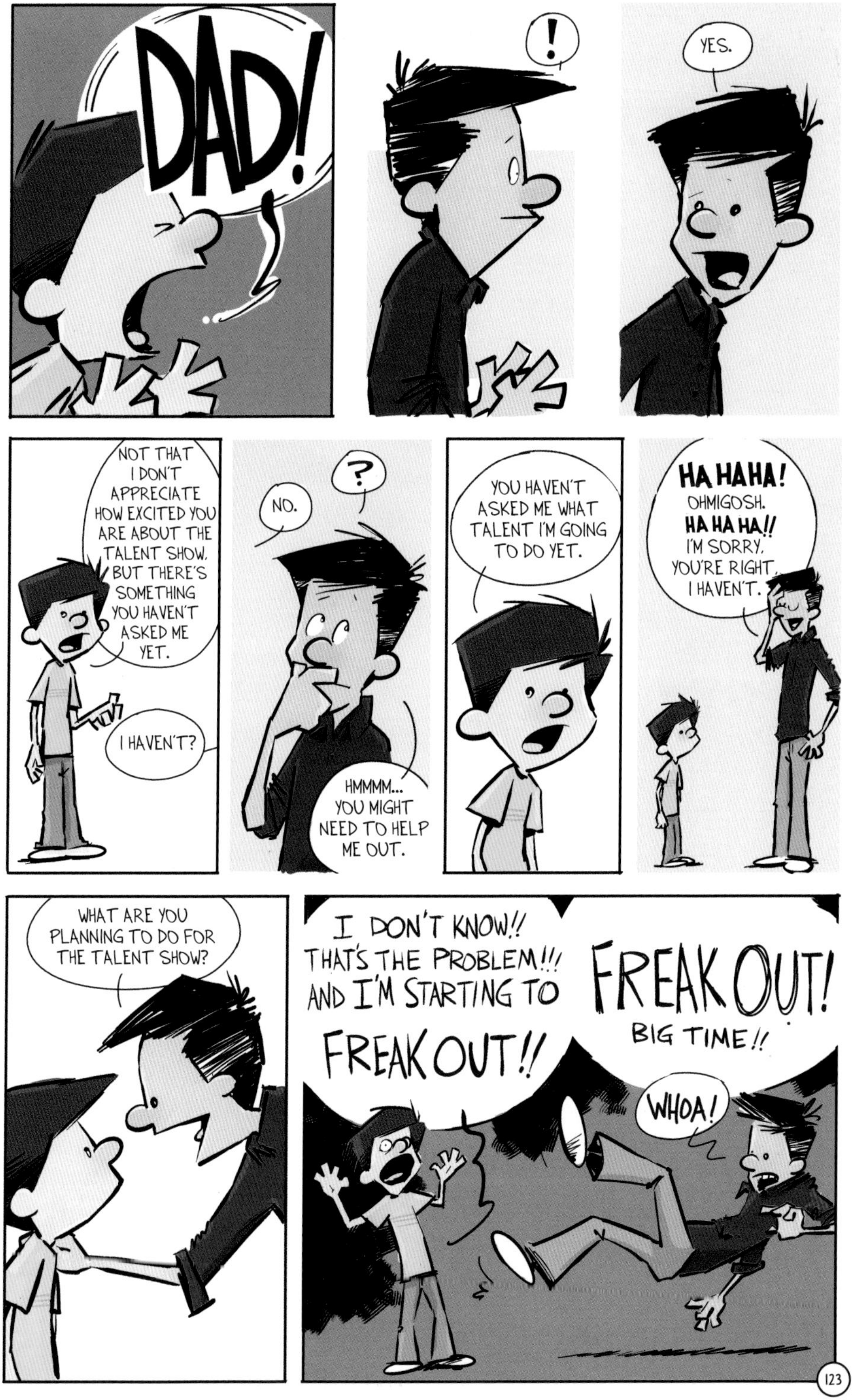
DAD!
!
YES.
NOT THAT I DON'T APPRECIATE HOW EXCITED YOU ARE ABOUT THE TALENT SHOW, BUT THERE'S SOMETHING YOU HAVEN'T ASKED ME YET.
I HAVEN'T?
?
NO.
HMMMM... YOU MIGHT NEED TO HELP ME OUT.
YOU HAVEN'T ASKED ME WHAT TALENT I'M GOING TO DO YET.
HA HA HA! OHMIGOSH. HA HA HA!! I'M SORRY, YOU'RE RIGHT, I HAVEN'T.
WHAT ARE YOU PLANNING TO DO FOR THE TALENT SHOW?
I DON'T KNOW!! THAT'S THE PROBLEM!!! AND I'M STARTING TO FREAK OUT!!
FREAK OUT! BIG TIME!!
WHOA!

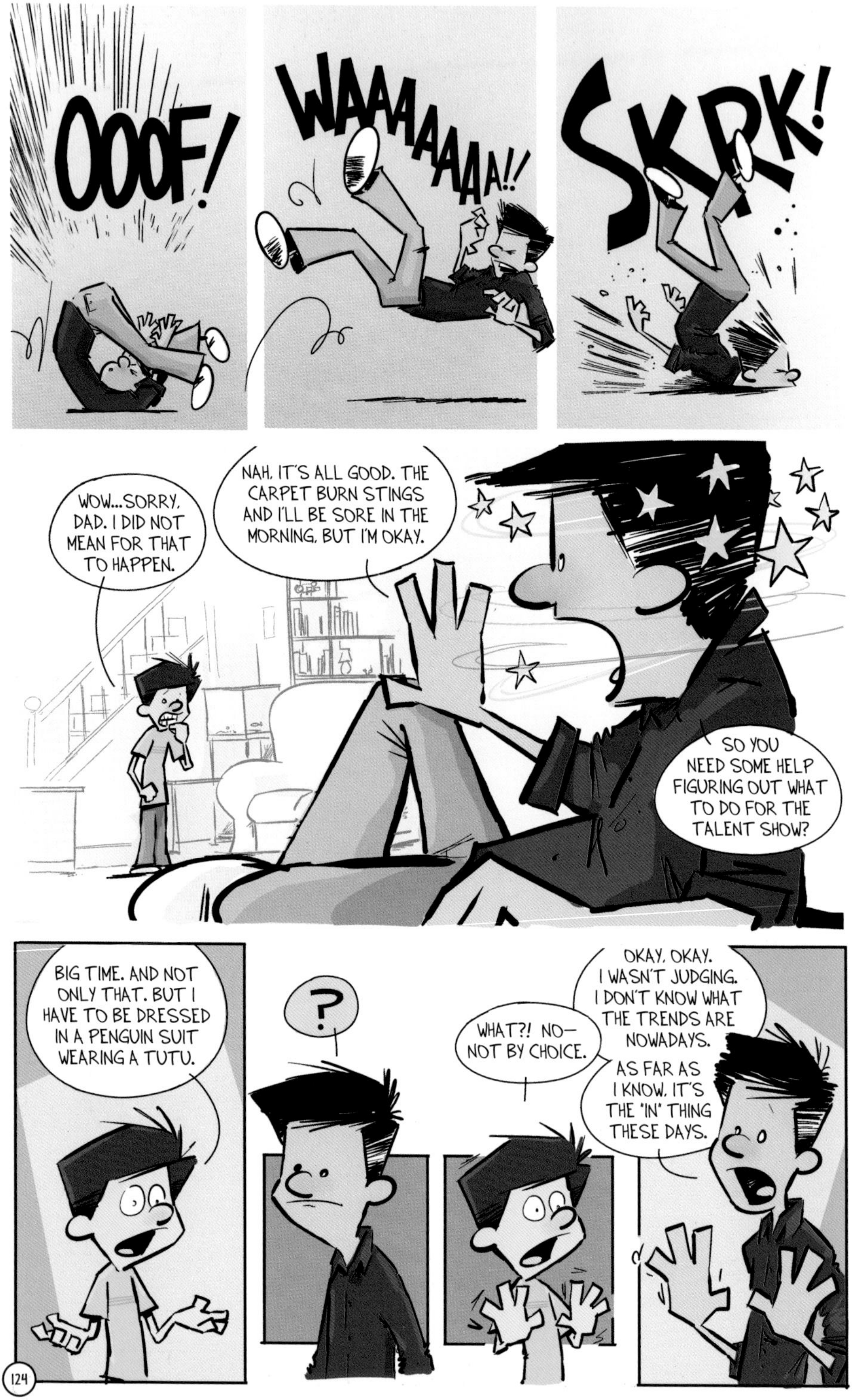
OOOF!
WAAAAAAAA!!
SKRK!
WOW...SORRY, DAD. I DID NOT MEAN FOR THAT TO HAPPEN.
NAH, IT'S ALL GOOD. THE CARPET BURN STINGS AND I'LL BE SORE IN THE MORNING, BUT I'M OKAY.
SO YOU NEED SOME HELP FIGURING OUT WHAT TO DO FOR THE TALENT SHOW?
BIG TIME. AND NOT ONLY THAT. BUT I HAVE TO BE DRESSED IN A PENGUIN SUIT WEARING A TUTU.
?
WHAT?! NO— NOT BY CHOICE.
OKAY, OKAY. I WASN'T JUDGING. I DON'T KNOW WHAT THE TRENDS ARE NOWADAYS.
AS FAR AS I KNOW, IT'S THE "IN" THING THESE DAYS.

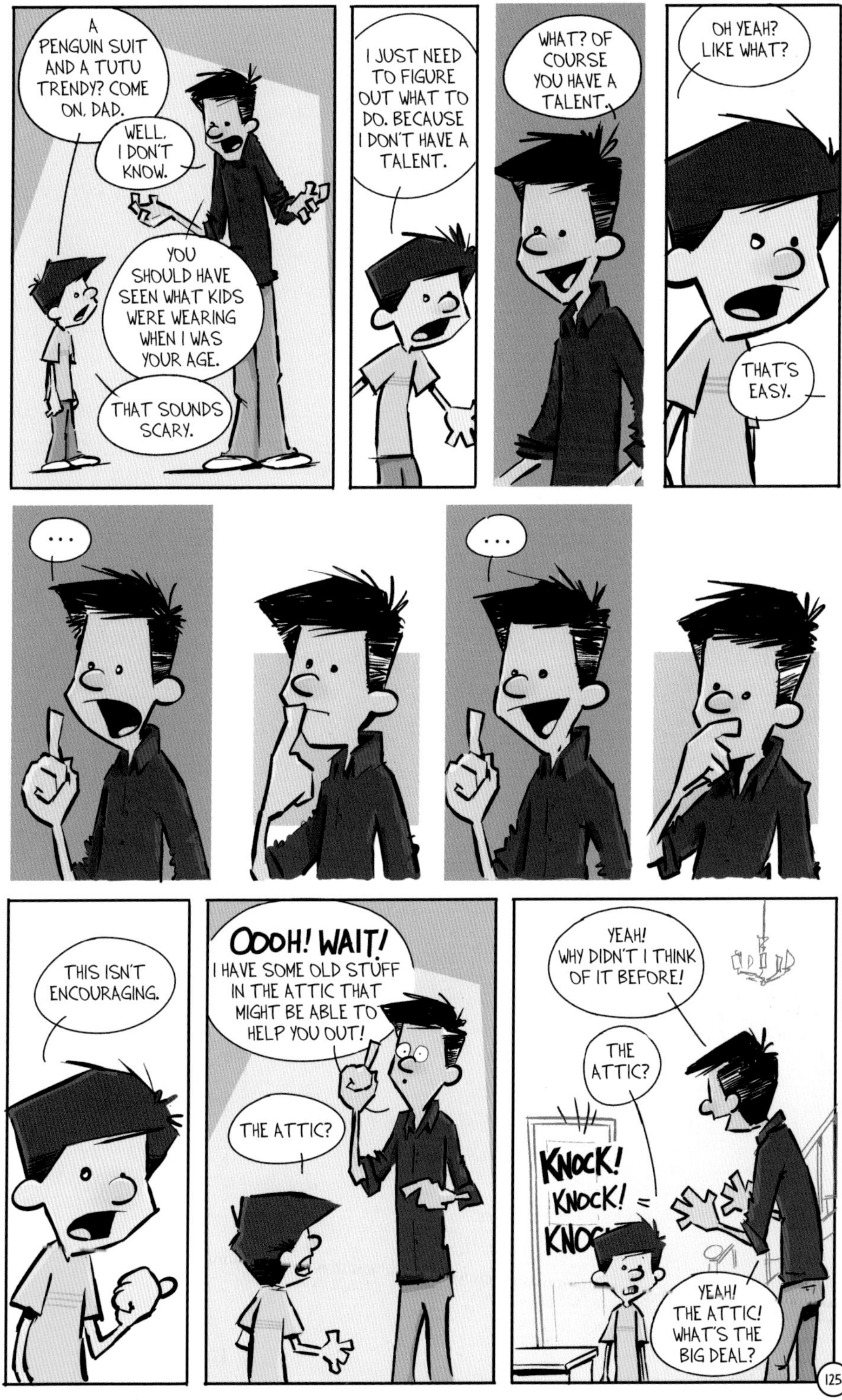

A PENGUIN SUIT AND A TUTU TRENDY? COME ON, DAD.
WELL, I DON'T KNOW.
YOU SHOULD HAVE SEEN WHAT KIDS WERE WEARING WHEN I WAS YOUR AGE.
THAT SOUNDS SCARY.
I JUST NEED TO FIGURE OUT WHAT TO DO. BECAUSE I DON'T HAVE A TALENT.
WHAT? OF COURSE YOU HAVE A TALENT.
OH YEAH? LIKE WHAT?
THAT'S EASY.
...
...
THIS ISN'T ENCOURAGING.
OOOH! WAIT!
I HAVE SOME OLD STUFF IN THE ATTIC THAT MIGHT BE ABLE TO HELP YOU OUT!
THE ATTIC?
YEAH! WHY DIDN'T I THINK OF IT BEFORE!
THE ATTIC?
KNOCK! KNOCK!
YEAH! THE ATTIC! WHAT'S THE BIG DEAL?

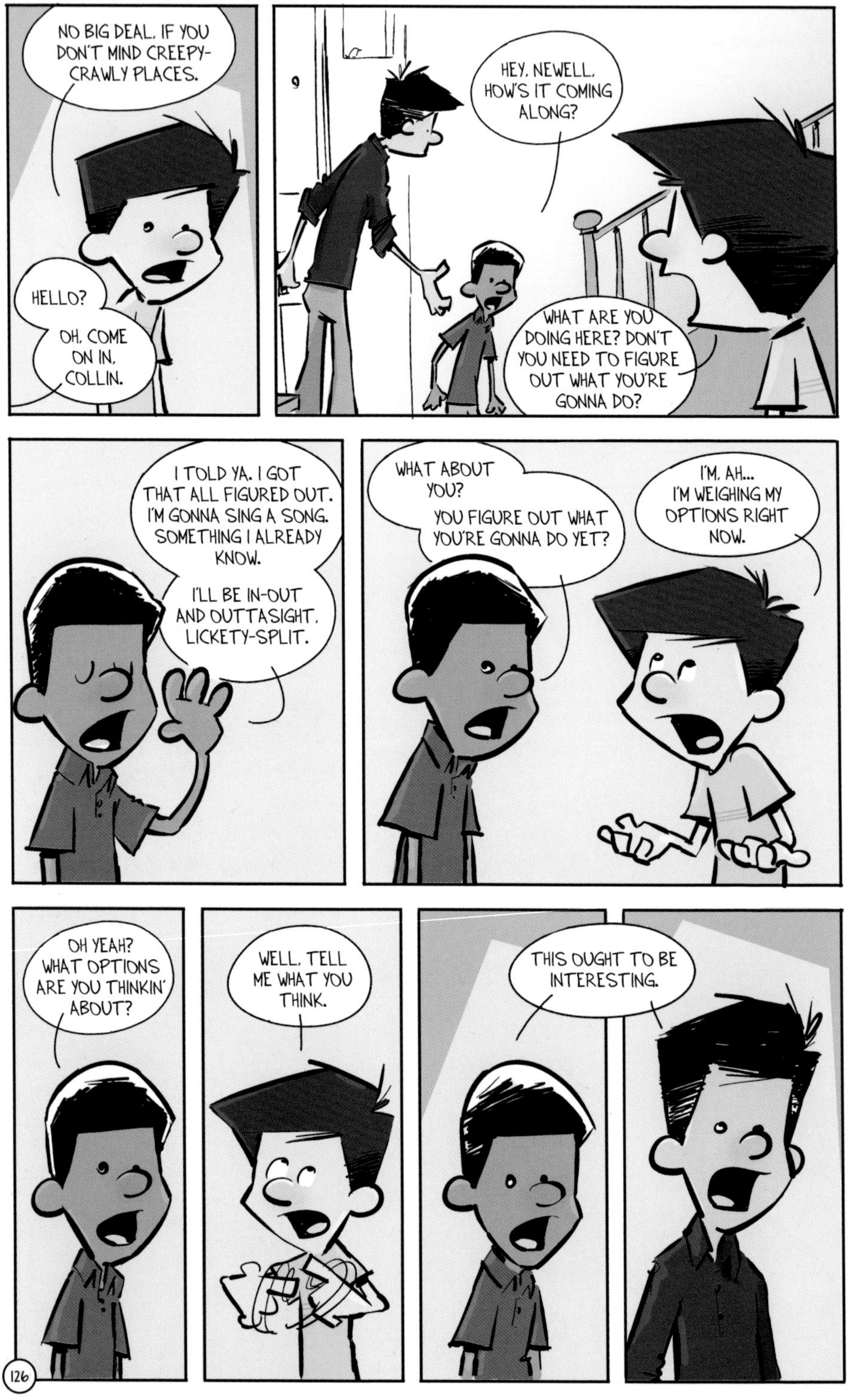
NO BIG DEAL, IF YOU DON'T MIND CREEPY-CRAWLY PLACES.
HELLO?
OH, COME ON IN, COLLIN.
HEY, NEWELL, HOW'S IT COMING ALONG?
WHAT ARE YOU DOING HERE? DON'T YOU NEED TO FIGURE OUT WHAT YOU'RE GONNA DO?
I TOLD YA. I GOT THAT ALL FIGURED OUT. I'M GONNA SING A SONG. SOMETHING I ALREADY KNOW.
I'LL BE IN-OUT AND OUTTASIGHT, LICKETY-SPLIT.
WHAT ABOUT YOU?
YOU FIGURE OUT WHAT YOU'RE GONNA DO YET?
I'M, AH... I'M WEIGHING MY OPTIONS RIGHT NOW.
OH YEAH? WHAT OPTIONS ARE YOU THINKIN' ABOUT?
WELL, TELL ME WHAT YOU THINK.
THIS OUGHT TO BE INTERESTING.

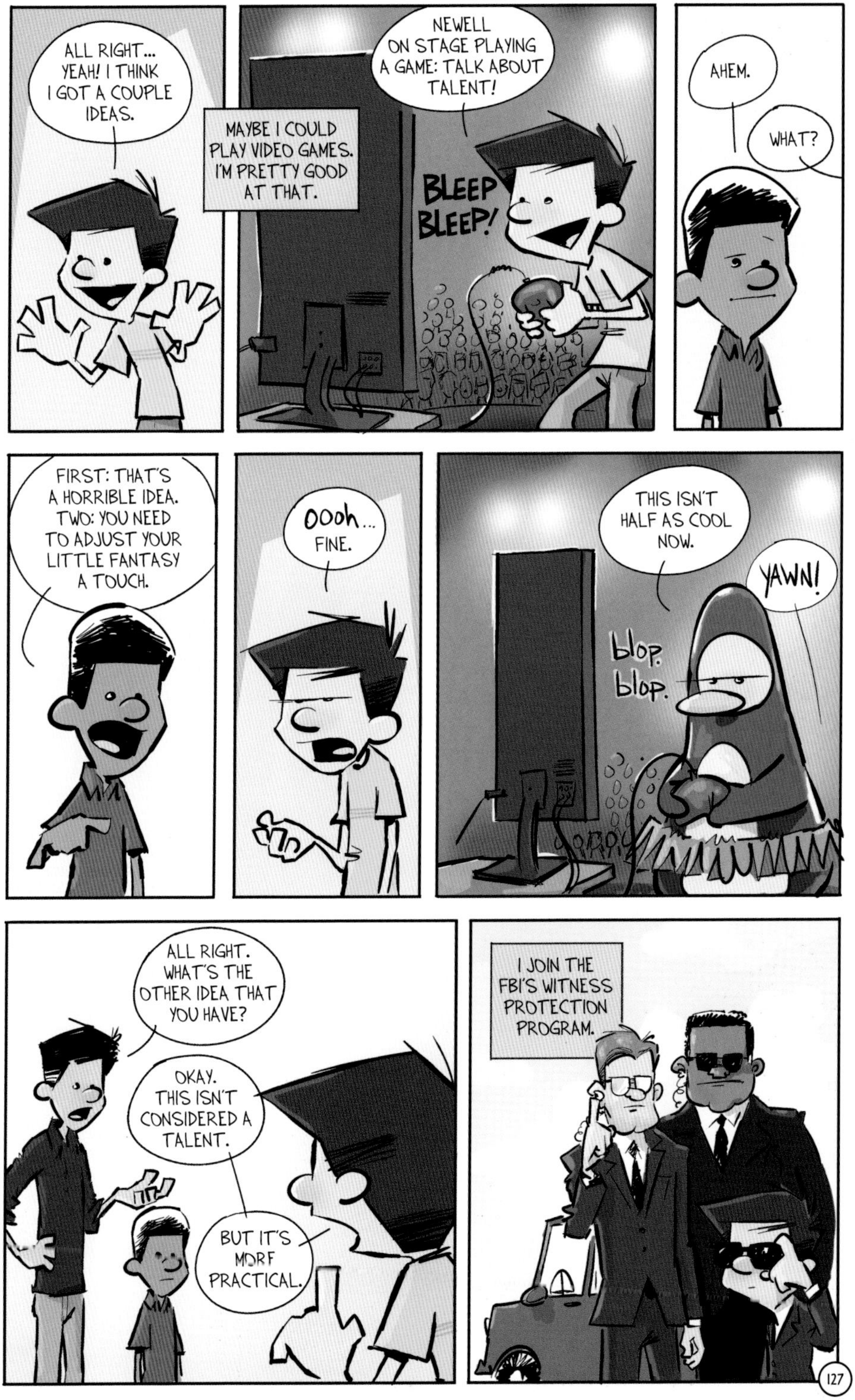
ALL RIGHT... YEAH! I THINK I GOT A COUPLE IDEAS.
MAYBE I COULD PLAY VIDEO GAMES. I'M PRETTY GOOD AT THAT.
NEWELL ON STAGE PLAYING A GAME: TALK ABOUT TALENT!
BLEEP BLEEP!
AHEM.
WHAT?
FIRST: THAT'S A HORRIBLE IDEA. TWO: YOU NEED TO ADJUST YOUR LITTLE FANTASY A TOUCH.
OOOh... FINE.
THIS ISN'T HALF AS COOL NOW.
YAWN!
blop. blop.
ALL RIGHT. WHAT'S THE OTHER IDEA THAT YOU HAVE?
OKAY. THIS ISN'T CONSIDERED A TALENT.
BUT IT'S MORE PRACTICAL.
I JOIN THE FBI'S WITNESS PROTECTION PROGRAM.

AND THEY FLY ME TO SOME REMOTE ISLAND OUT IN THE PACIFIC.
ZOOM!
FBI

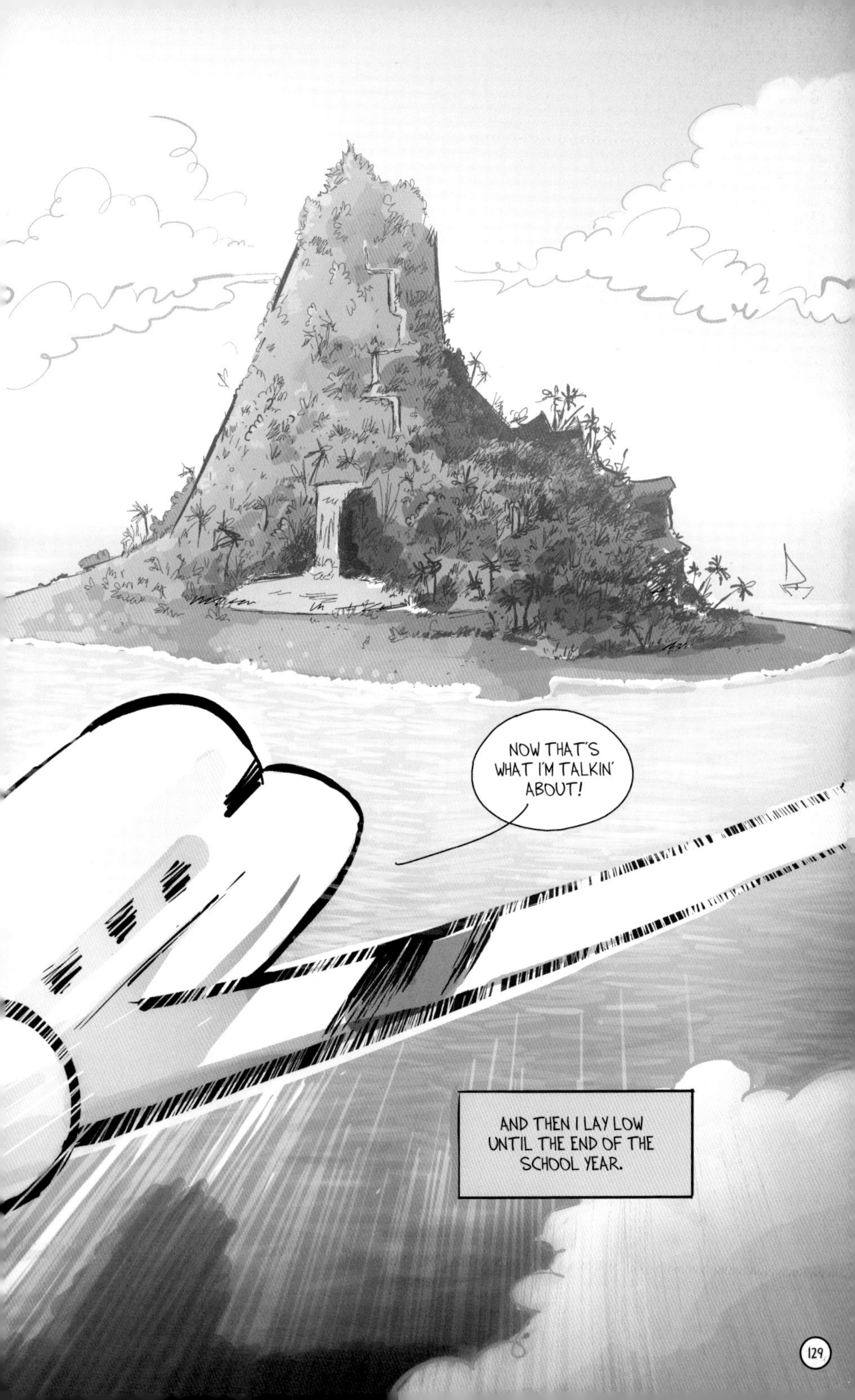
NOW THAT'S WHAT I'M TALKIN' ABOUT!
AND THEN I LAY LOW UNTIL THE END OF THE SCHOOL YEAR.

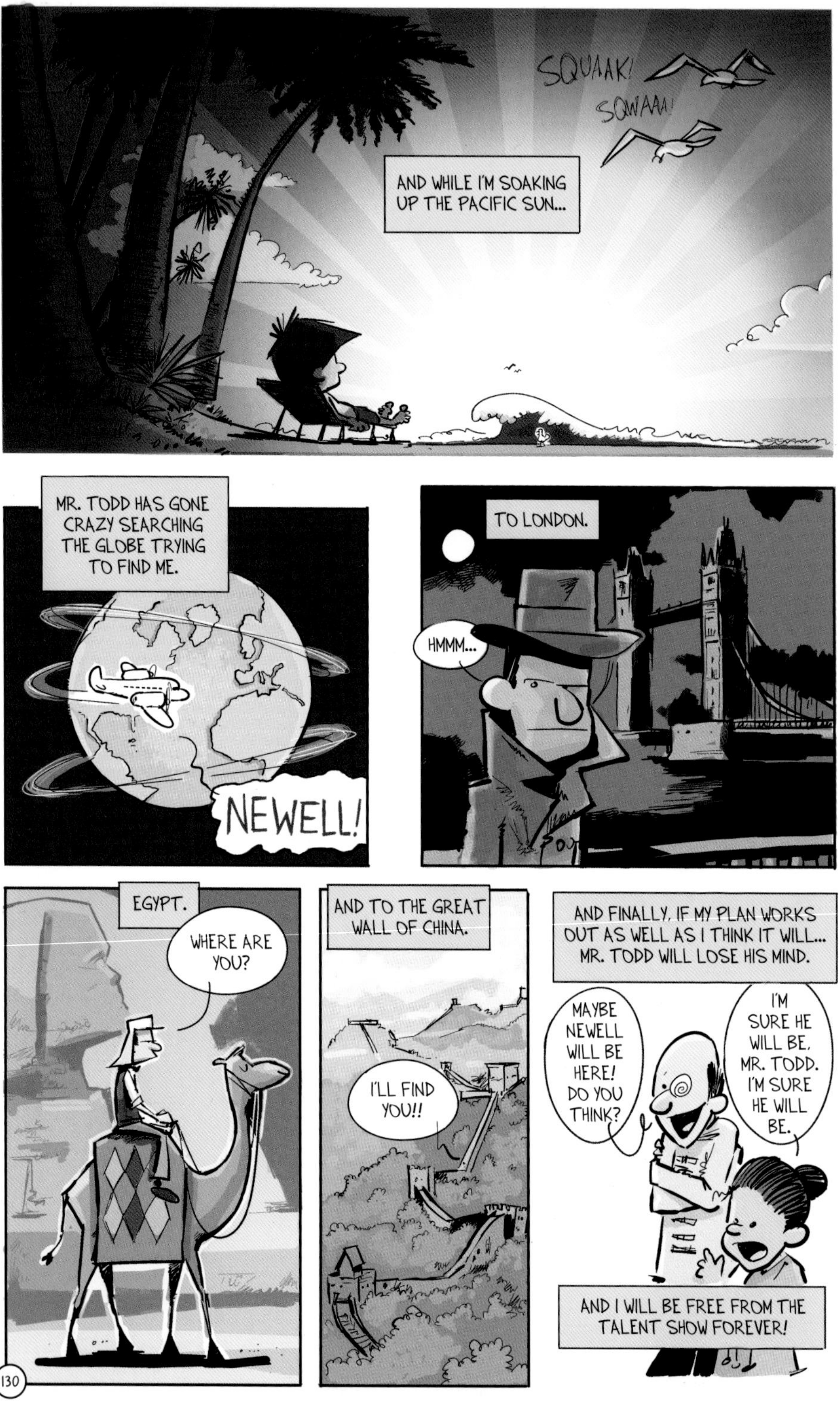
SQUAAK!
SQWAAA!
AND WHILE I'M SOAKING UP THE PACIFIC SUN...
MR. TODD HAS GONE CRAZY SEARCHING THE GLOBE TRYING TO FIND ME.
NEWELL!
TO LONDON.
HMMM...
EGYPT.
WHERE ARE YOU?
AND TO THE GREAT WALL OF CHINA.
I'LL FIND YOU!!
AND FINALLY, IF MY PLAN WORKS OUT AS WELL AS I THINK IT WILL... MR. TODD WILL LOSE HIS MIND.
MAYBE NEWELL WILL BE HERE! DO YOU THINK?
I'M SURE HE WILL BE, MR. TODD. I'M SURE HE WILL BE.
AND I WILL BE FREE FROM THE TALENT SHOW FOREVER!

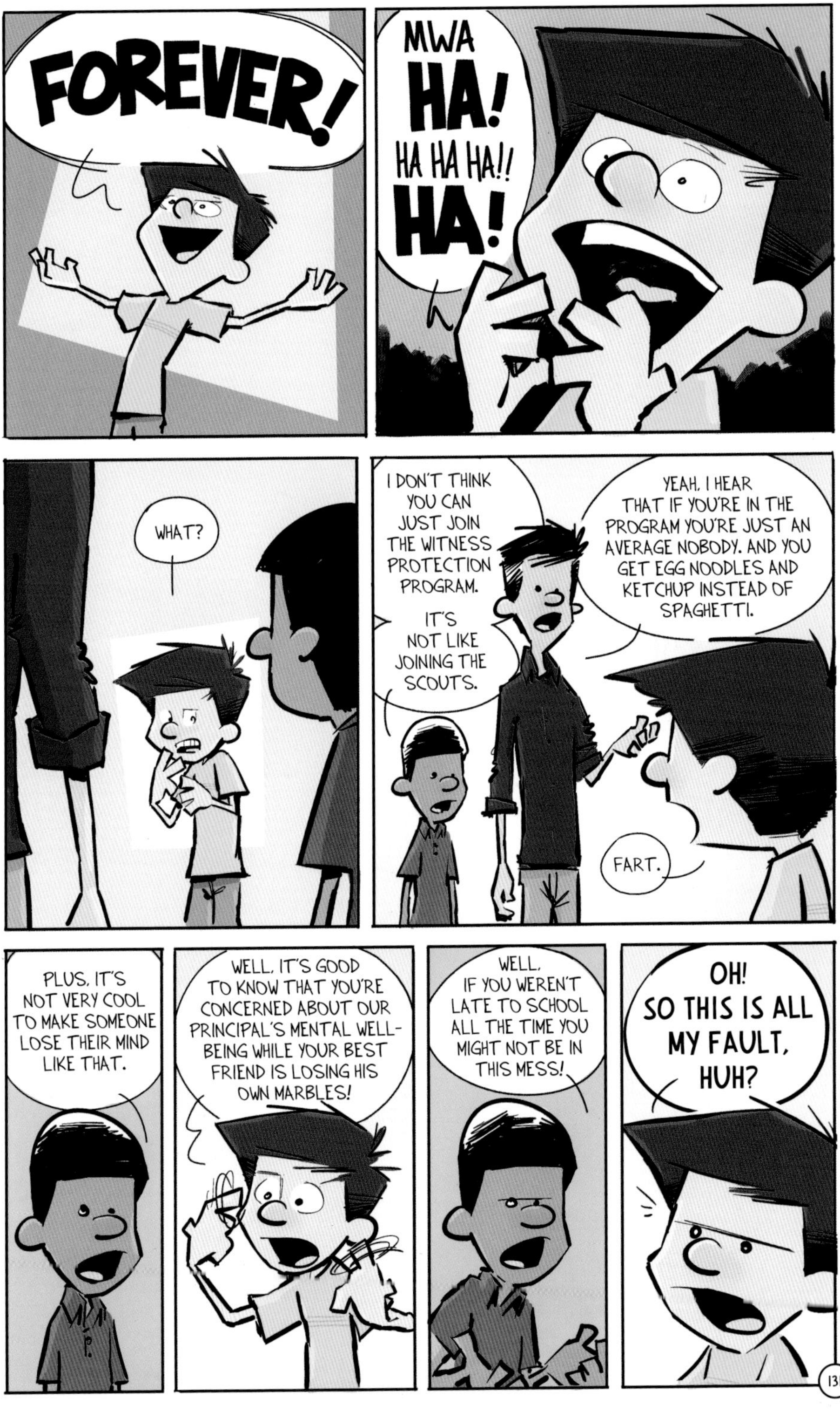
FOREVER!
MWA HA! HA HA HA!! HA!
WHAT?
I DON'T THINK YOU CAN JUST JOIN THE WITNESS PROTECTION PROGRAM.
IT'S NOT LIKE JOINING THE SCOUTS.
YEAH, I HEAR THAT IF YOU'RE IN THE PROGRAM YOU'RE JUST AN AVERAGE NOBODY. AND YOU GET EGG NOODLES AND KETCHUP INSTEAD OF SPAGHETTI.
FART.
PLUS, IT'S NOT VERY COOL TO MAKE SOMEONE LOSE THEIR MIND LIKE THAT.
WELL, IT'S GOOD TO KNOW THAT YOU'RE CONCERNED ABOUT OUR PRINCIPAL'S MENTAL WELL-BEING WHILE YOUR BEST FRIEND IS LOSING HIS OWN MARBLES!
WELL, IF YOU WEREN'T LATE TO SCHOOL ALL THE TIME YOU MIGHT NOT BE IN THIS MESS!
OH! SO THIS IS ALL MY FAULT, HUH?

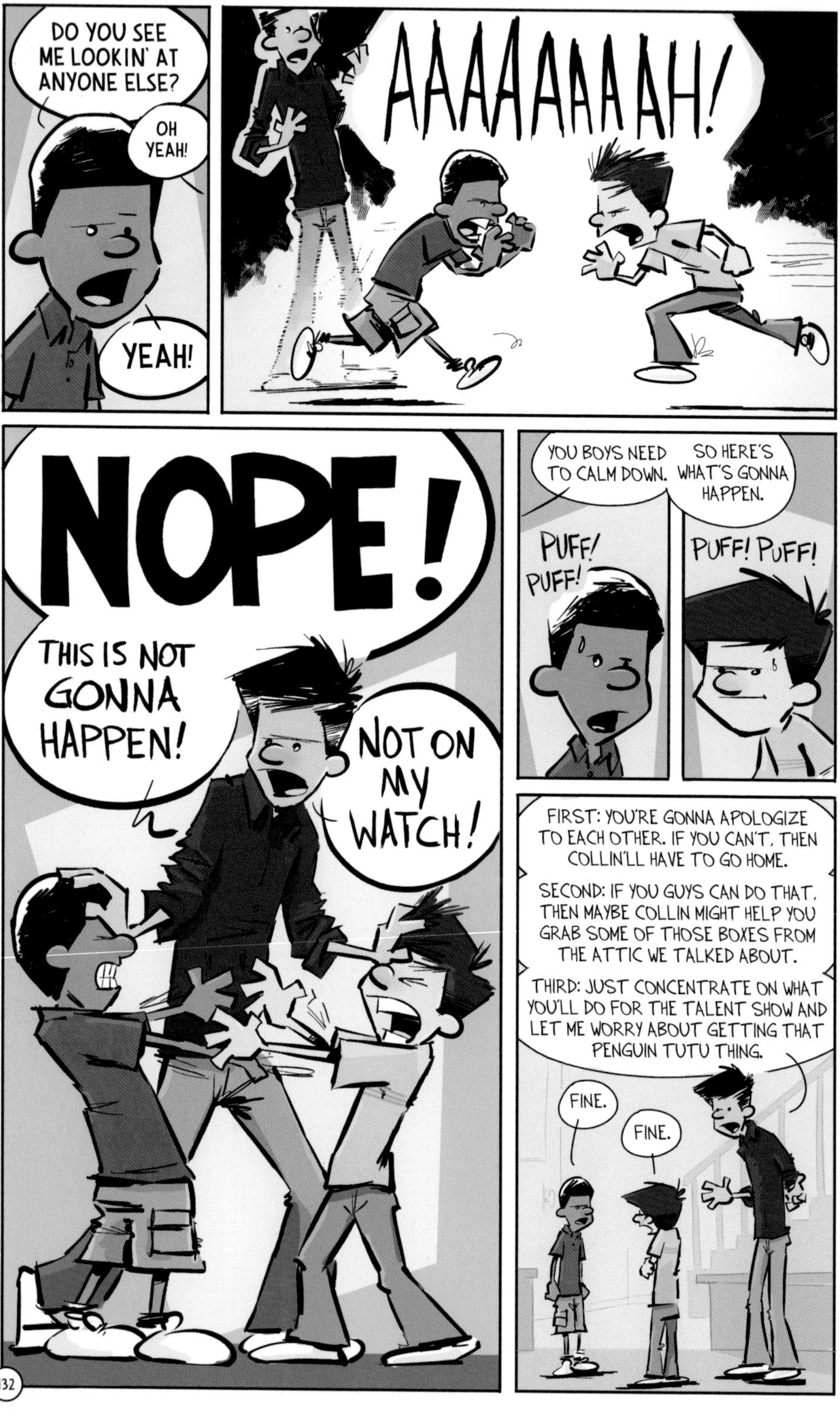
DO YOU SEE ME LOOKIN' AT ANYONE ELSE?
OH YEAH!
YEAH!
AAAAAAAAH!
NOPE!
THIS IS NOT GONNA HAPPEN!
NOT ON MY WATCH!
YOU BOYS NEED TO CALM DOWN.
SO HERE'S WHAT'S GONNA HAPPEN.
PUFF! PUFF!
PUFF! PUFF!
FIRST: YOU'RE GONNA APOLOGIZE TO EACH OTHER. IF YOU CAN'T, THEN COLLIN'LL HAVE TO GO HOME.
SECOND: IF YOU GUYS CAN DO THAT, THEN MAYBE COLLIN MIGHT HELP YOU GRAB SOME OF THOSE BOXES FROM THE ATTIC WE TALKED ABOUT.
THIRD: JUST CONCENTRATE ON WHAT YOU'LL DO FOR THE TALENT SHOW AND LET ME WORRY ABOUT GETTING THAT PENGUIN TUTU THING.
FINE.
FINE.

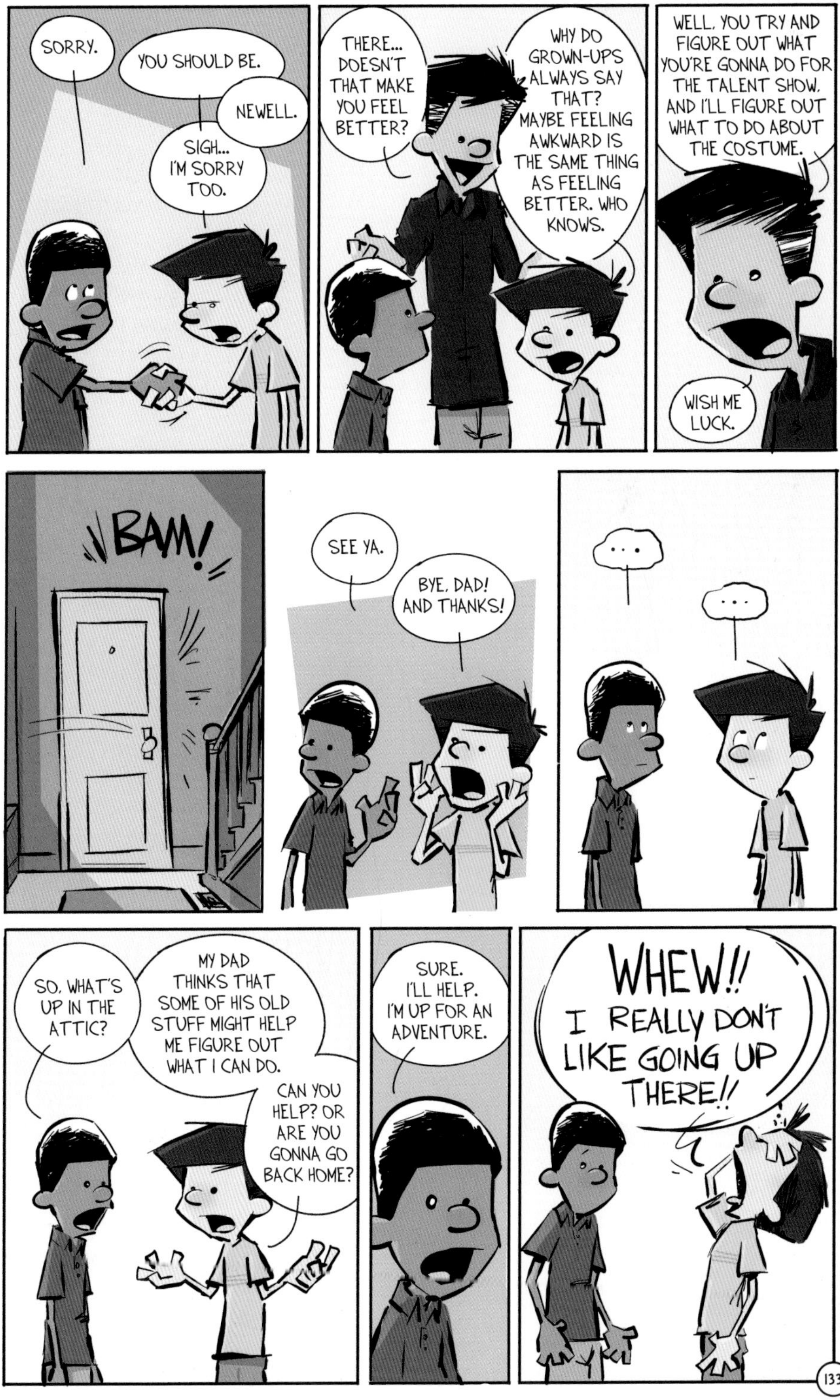
SORRY.
YOU SHOULD BE.
NEWELL.
SIGH... I'M SORRY TOO.
THERE... DOESN'T THAT MAKE YOU FEEL BETTER?
WHY DO GROWN-UPS ALWAYS SAY THAT? MAYBE FEELING AWKWARD IS THE SAME THING AS FEELING BETTER. WHO KNOWS.
WELL, YOU TRY AND FIGURE OUT WHAT YOU'RE GONNA DO FOR THE TALENT SHOW, AND I'LL FIGURE OUT WHAT TO DO ABOUT THE COSTUME.
WISH ME LUCK.
BAM!
SEE YA.
BYE, DAD! AND THANKS!
...
...
SO, WHAT'S UP IN THE ATTIC?
MY DAD THINKS THAT SOME OF HIS OLD STUFF MIGHT HELP ME FIGURE OUT WHAT I CAN DO.
CAN YOU HELP? OR ARE YOU GONNA GO BACK HOME?
SURE. I'LL HELP. I'M UP FOR AN ADVENTURE.
WHEW!!
I REALLY DON'T LIKE GOING UP THERE!!

SO, COME ON. WHAT'S IT ABOUT THE ATTIC THAT YOU DON'T LIKE?

IF I WERE A WEREWOLF I'D PROBABLY FIND IT COMFY.

WELL... TO BE HONEST, I'VE NEVER BEEN IN IT BEFORE. BUT EVERY TIME MY DAD'S GONE UP THERE IT'S ALL DARK AND STUFF. AND I HEAR ALL THESE WEIRD CREAKING SOUNDS.

I'M NOT LOOKING FORWARD TO THIS, I CAN TELL YOU THAT.

IT MUST BE A RITE OF PASSAGE OR SOMETHING. LET'S HOPE I CAN REACH THE CORD.

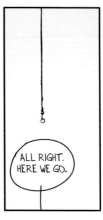

ALL RIGHT, HERE WE GO.

FUMBLE! FUMBLE!

YOU ALMOST GOT IT.

YEAH, I'LL GET IT THIS TIME.

BOING!

DING!

HUZZAH! I GOT IT!

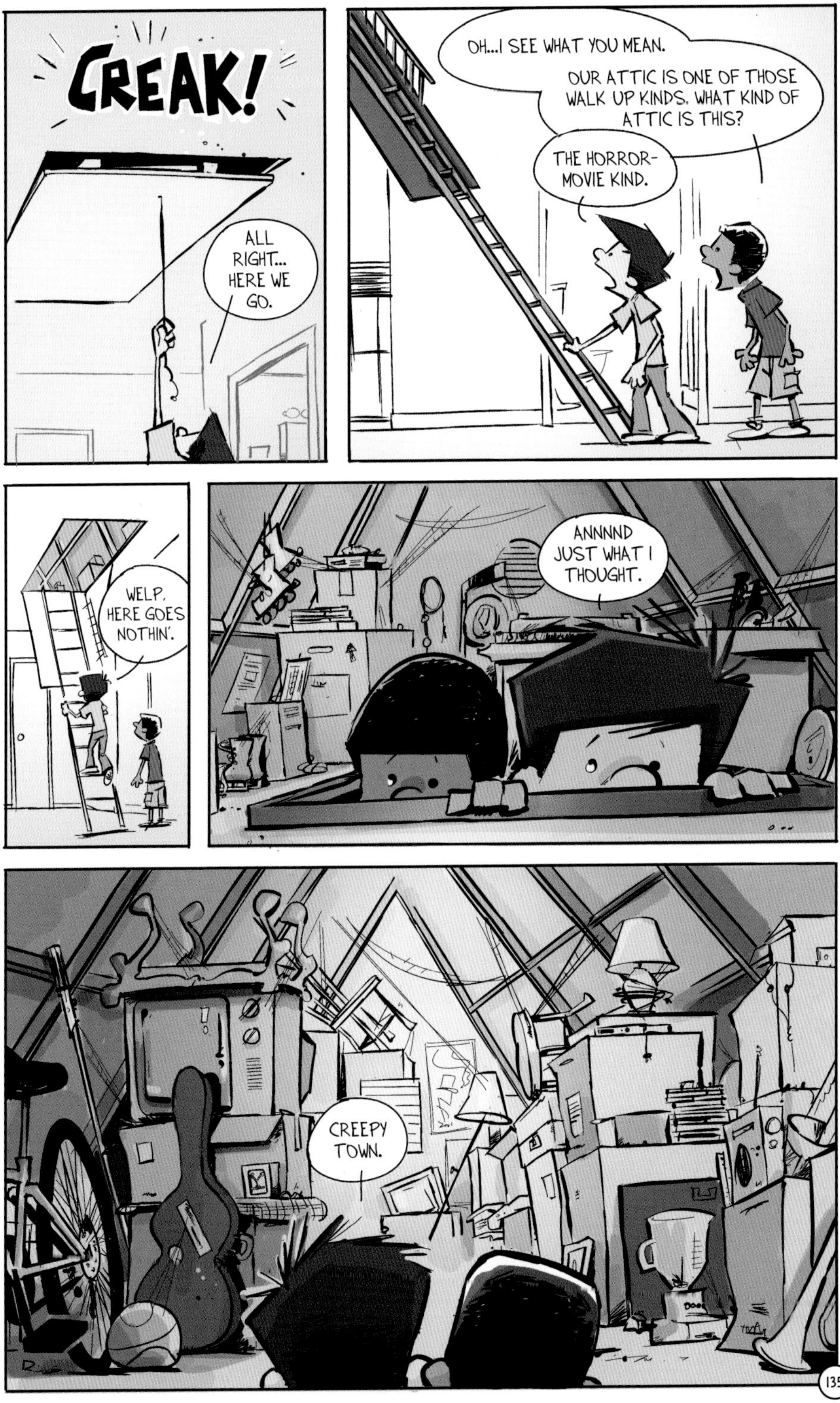
CREAK!
ALL RIGHT... HERE WE GO.
OH...I SEE WHAT YOU MEAN.
OUR ATTIC IS ONE OF THOSE WALK UP KINDS. WHAT KIND OF ATTIC IS THIS?
THE HORROR-MOVIE KIND.
WELP. HERE GOES NOTHIN'.
ANNNND JUST WHAT I THOUGHT.
CREEPY TOWN.

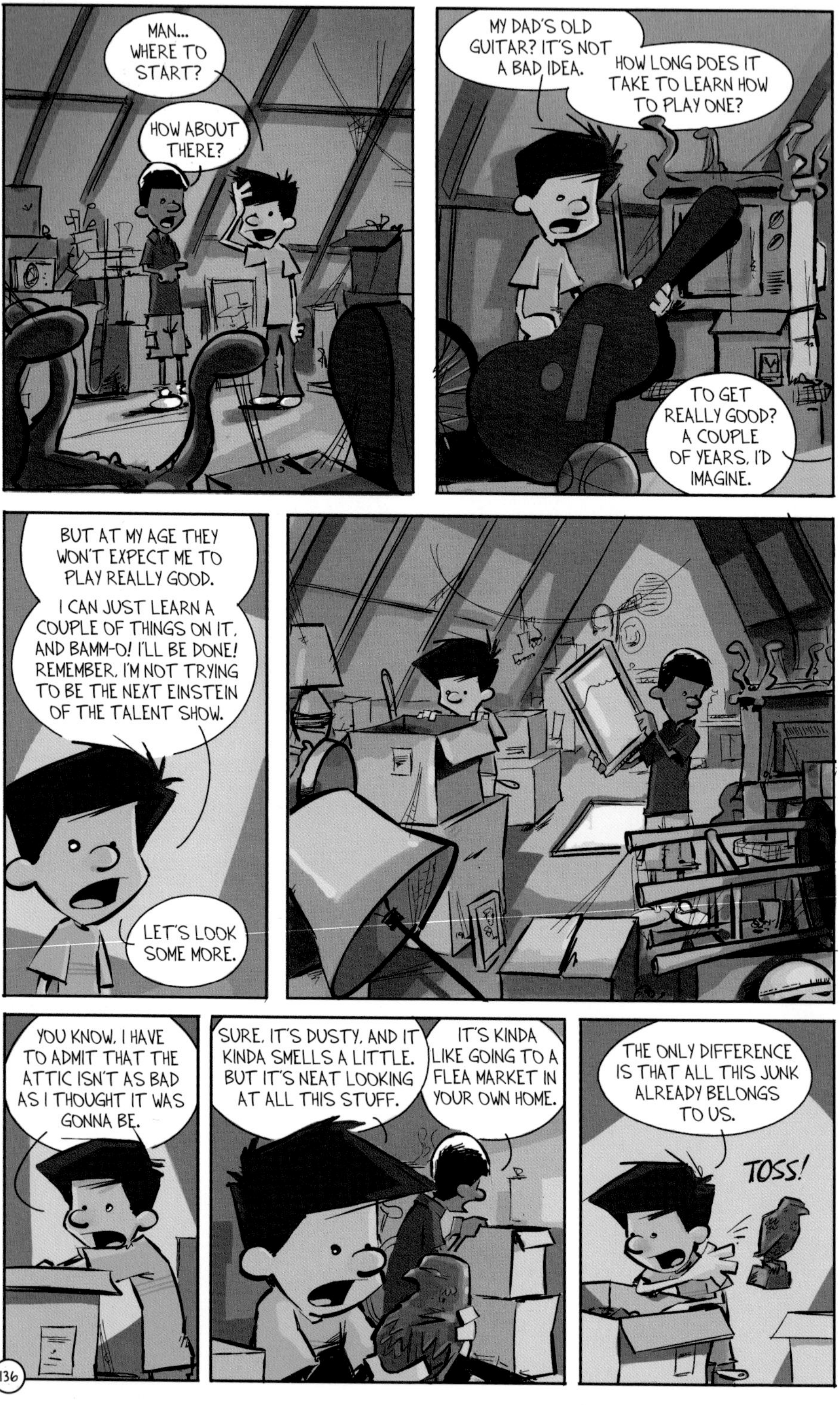

MAN... WHERE TO START?
HOW ABOUT THERE?
MY DAD'S OLD GUITAR? IT'S NOT A BAD IDEA.
HOW LONG DOES IT TAKE TO LEARN HOW TO PLAY ONE?
TO GET REALLY GOOD? A COUPLE OF YEARS, I'D IMAGINE.
BUT AT MY AGE THEY WON'T EXPECT ME TO PLAY REALLY GOOD.
I CAN JUST LEARN A COUPLE OF THINGS ON IT, AND BAMM-O! I'LL BE DONE! REMEMBER, I'M NOT TRYING TO BE THE NEXT EINSTEIN OF THE TALENT SHOW.
LET'S LOOK SOME MORE.
YOU KNOW, I HAVE TO ADMIT THAT THE ATTIC ISN'T AS BAD AS I THOUGHT IT WAS GONNA BE.
SURE, IT'S DUSTY, AND IT KINDA SMELLS A LITTLE. BUT IT'S NEAT LOOKING AT ALL THIS STUFF.
IT'S KINDA LIKE GOING TO A FLEA MARKET IN YOUR OWN HOME.
THE ONLY DIFFERENCE IS THAT ALL THIS JUNK ALREADY BELONGS TO US.
TOSS!

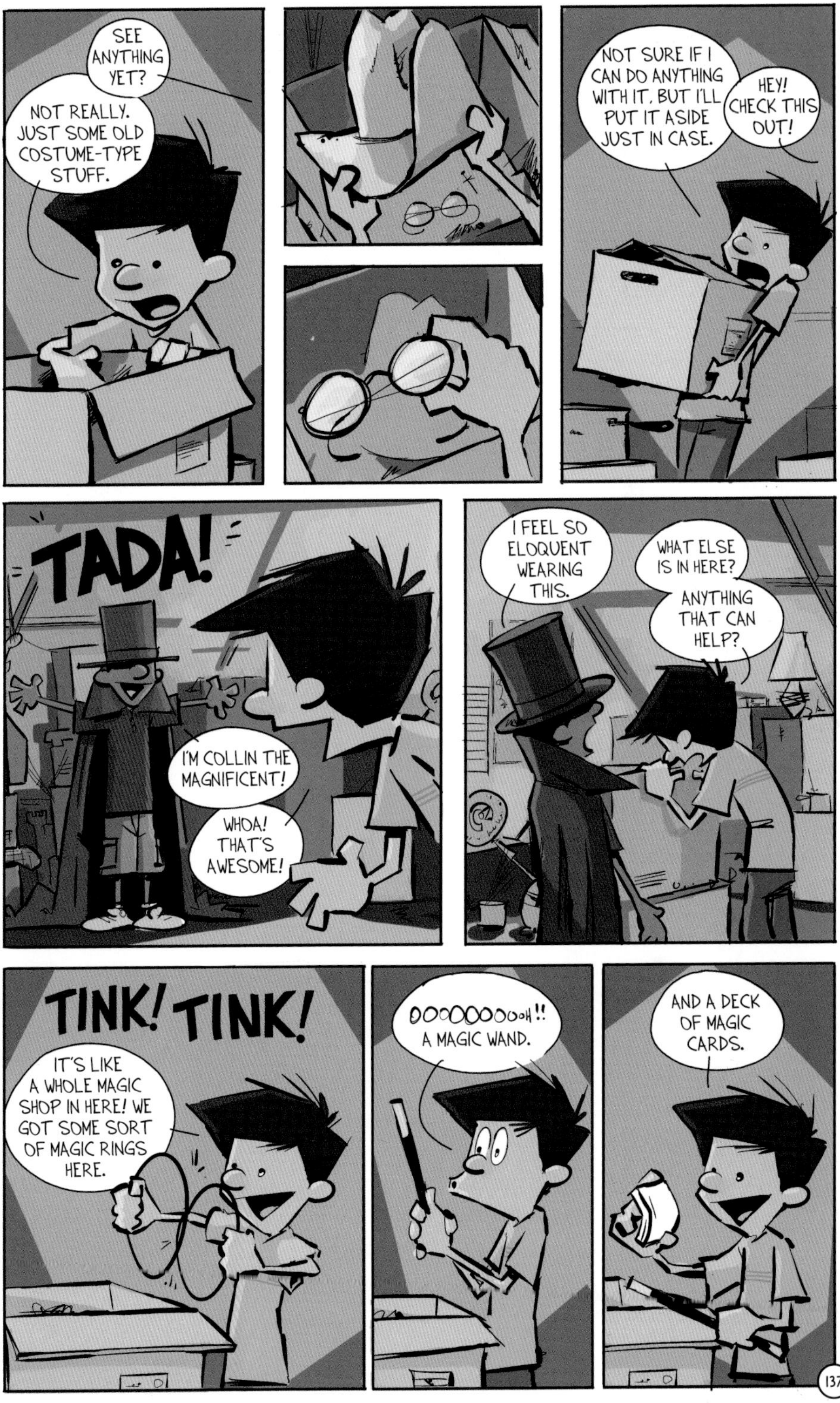
SEE ANYTHING YET?
NOT REALLY. JUST SOME OLD COSTUME-TYPE STUFF.
NOT SURE IF I CAN DO ANYTHING WITH IT, BUT I'LL PUT IT ASIDE JUST IN CASE.
HEY! CHECK THIS OUT!
TADA!
I'M COLLIN THE MAGNIFICENT!
WHOA! THAT'S AWESOME!
I FEEL SO ELOQUENT WEARING THIS.
WHAT ELSE IS IN HERE?
ANYTHING THAT CAN HELP?
TINK! TINK!
IT'S LIKE A WHOLE MAGIC SHOP IN HERE! WE GOT SOME SORT OF MAGIC RINGS HERE.
OOOOOOOOOOH!! A MAGIC WAND.
AND A DECK OF MAGIC CARDS.

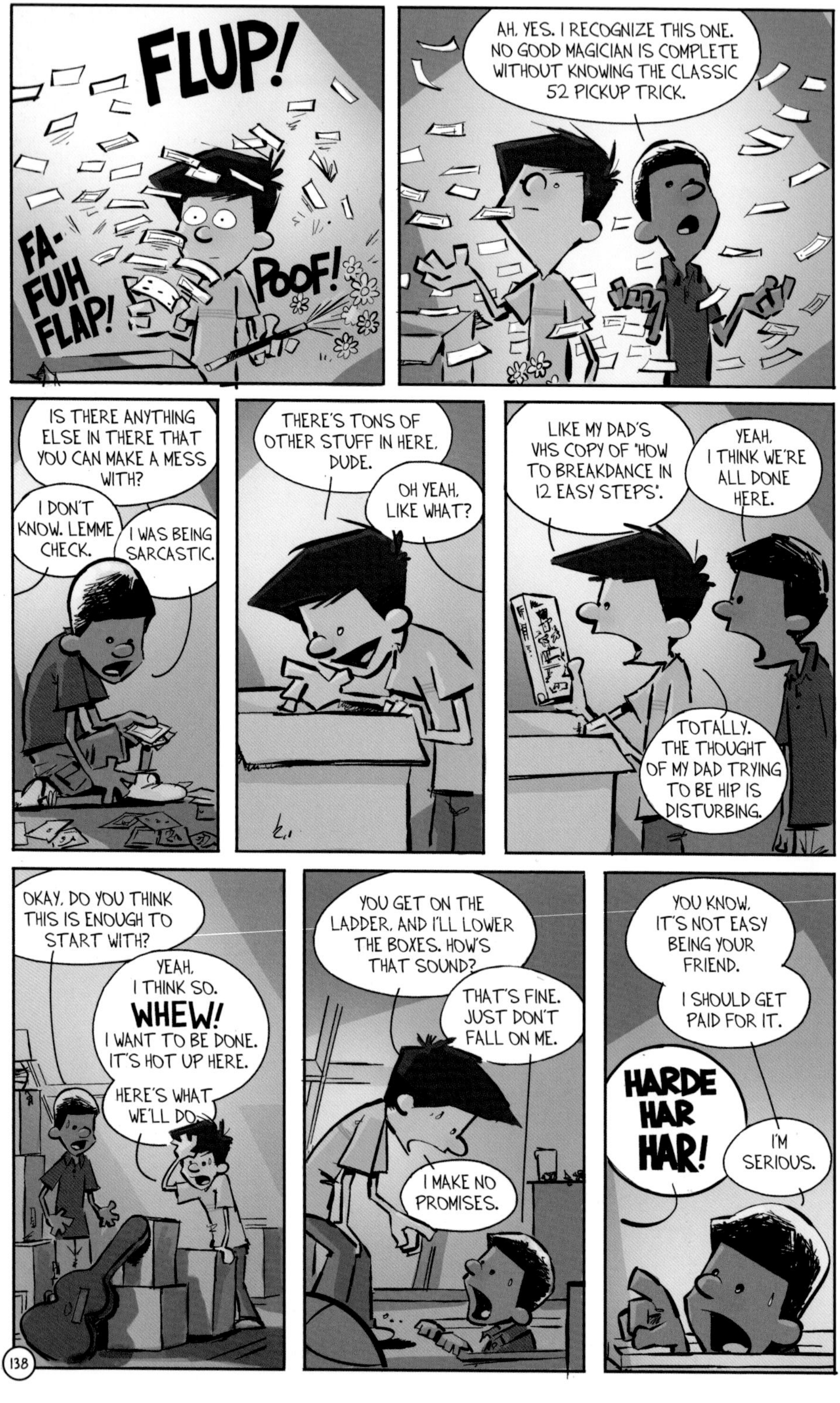
FLUP!
FA-FUH FLAP!
POOF!
AH, YES. I RECOGNIZE THIS ONE. NO GOOD MAGICIAN IS COMPLETE WITHOUT KNOWING THE CLASSIC 52 PICKUP TRICK.
IS THERE ANYTHING ELSE IN THERE THAT YOU CAN MAKE A MESS WITH?
I DON'T KNOW. LEMME CHECK.
I WAS BEING SARCASTIC.
THERE'S TONS OF OTHER STUFF IN HERE, DUDE.
OH YEAH, LIKE WHAT?
LIKE MY DAD'S VHS COPY OF "HOW TO BREAKDANCE IN 12 EASY STEPS".
YEAH, I THINK WE'RE ALL DONE HERE.
TOTALLY. THE THOUGHT OF MY DAD TRYING TO BE HIP IS DISTURBING.
OKAY, DO YOU THINK THIS IS ENOUGH TO START WITH?
YEAH, I THINK SO. WHEW! I WANT TO BE DONE. IT'S HOT UP HERE.
HERE'S WHAT WE'LL DO.
YOU GET ON THE LADDER, AND I'LL LOWER THE BOXES. HOW'S THAT SOUND?
THAT'S FINE. JUST DON'T FALL ON ME.
I MAKE NO PROMISES.
YOU KNOW, IT'S NOT EASY BEING YOUR FRIEND.
I SHOULD GET PAID FOR IT.
HARDE HAR HAR!
I'M SERIOUS.

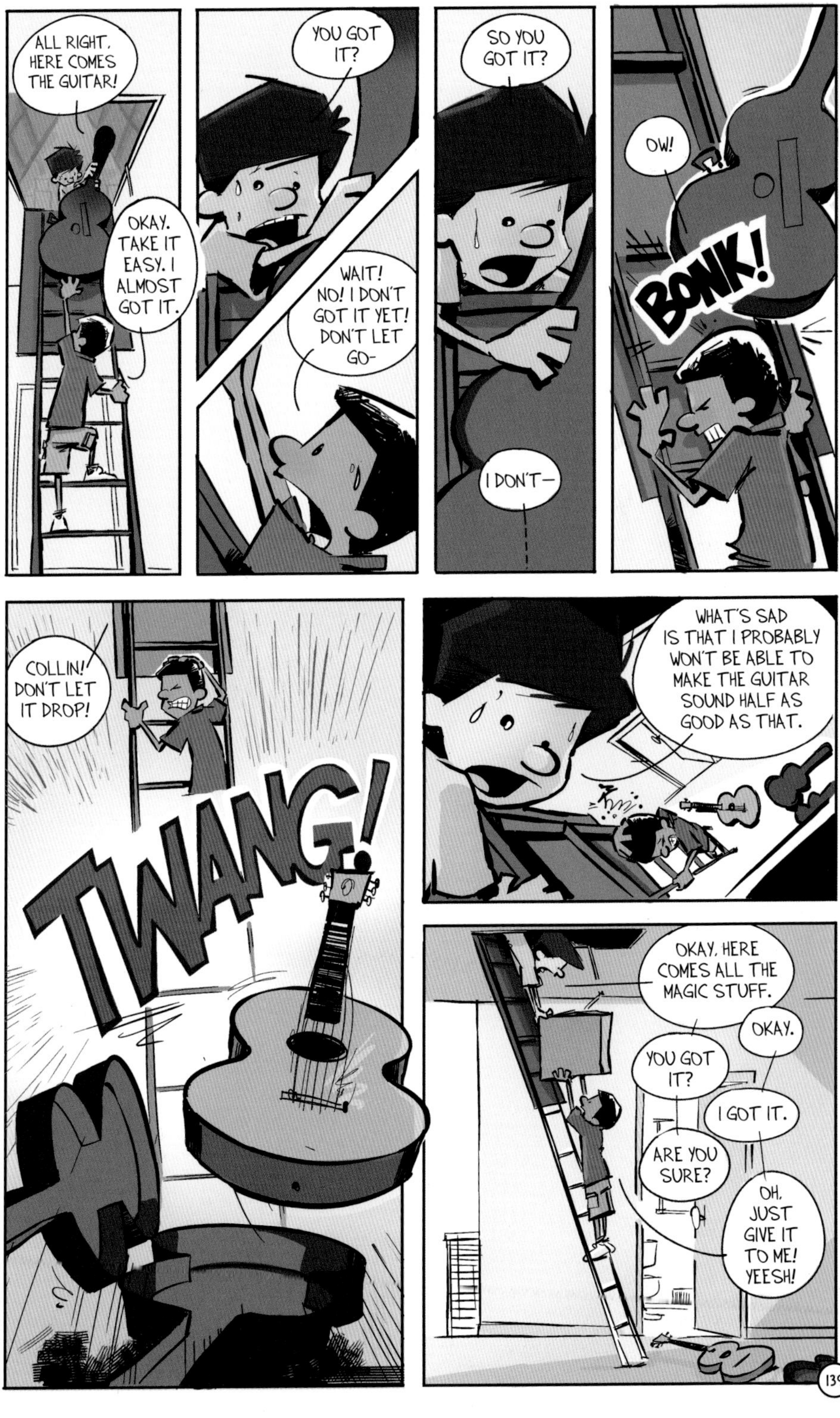

ALL RIGHT, HERE COMES THE GUITAR!
OKAY. TAKE IT EASY. I ALMOST GOT IT.
YOU GOT IT?
WAIT! NO! I DON'T GOT IT YET! DON'T LET GO-
SO YOU GOT IT?
I DON'T—
OW!
BONK!
COLLIN! DON'T LET IT DROP!
TWANG!
WHAT'S SAD IS THAT I PROBABLY WON'T BE ABLE TO MAKE THE GUITAR SOUND HALF AS GOOD AS THAT.
OKAY, HERE COMES ALL THE MAGIC STUFF.
OKAY.
YOU GOT IT?
I GOT IT.
ARE YOU SURE?
OH, JUST GIVE IT TO ME! YEESH!

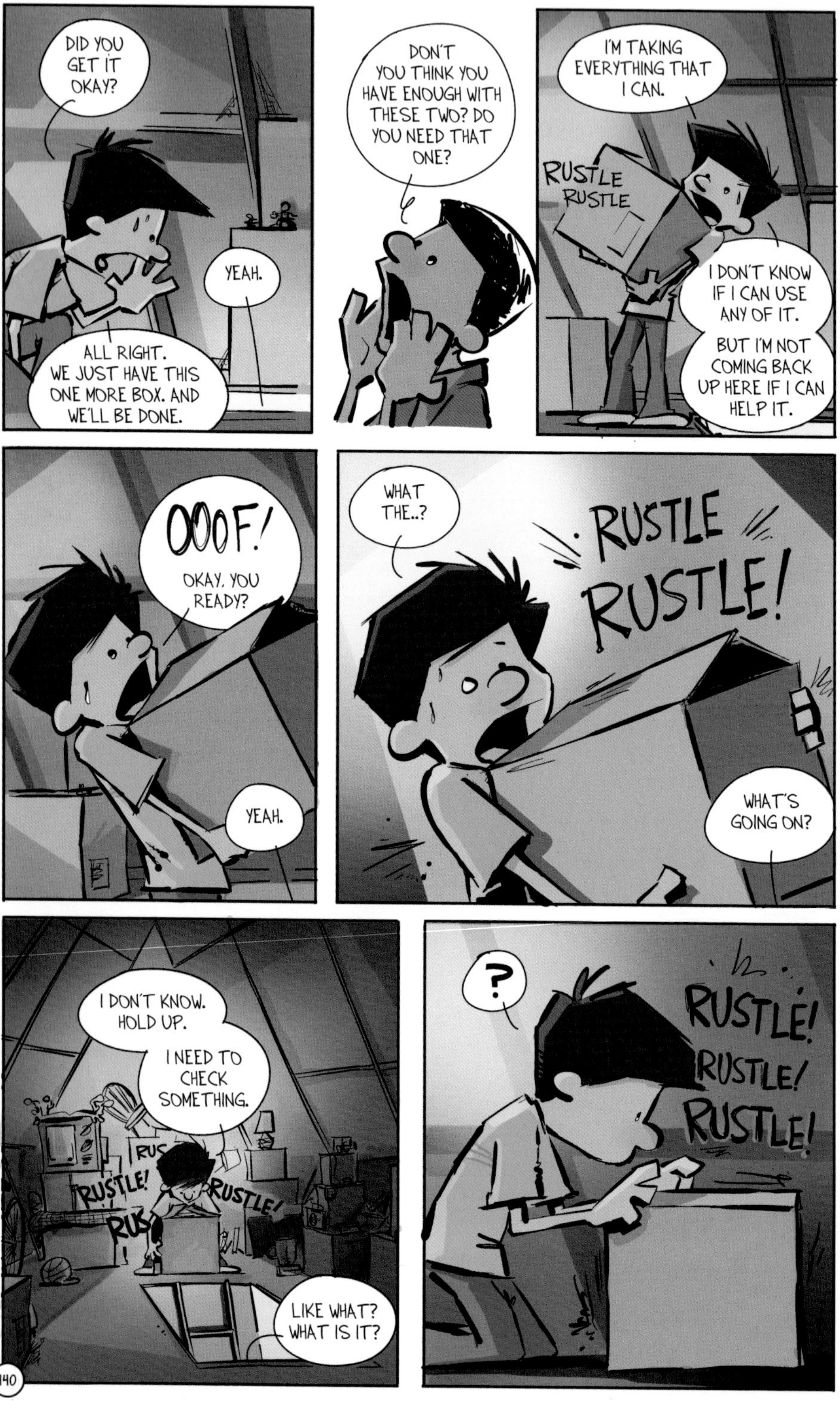
DID YOU GET IT OKAY?
ALL RIGHT. WE JUST HAVE THIS ONE MORE BOX. AND WE'LL BE DONE.
YEAH.
DON'T YOU THINK YOU HAVE ENOUGH WITH THESE TWO? DO YOU NEED THAT ONE?
I'M TAKING EVERYTHING THAT I CAN.
RUSTLE RUSTLE
I DON'T KNOW IF I CAN USE ANY OF IT.
BUT I'M NOT COMING BACK UP HERE IF I CAN HELP IT.
OOOF!
OKAY, YOU READY?
YEAH.
WHAT THE..?
RUSTLE RUSTLE!
WHAT'S GOING ON?
I DON'T KNOW. HOLD UP.
I NEED TO CHECK SOMETHING.
RUS RUSTLE! RUSTLE! RUS
LIKE WHAT? WHAT IS IT?
?
RUSTLE! RUSTLE! RUSTLE!

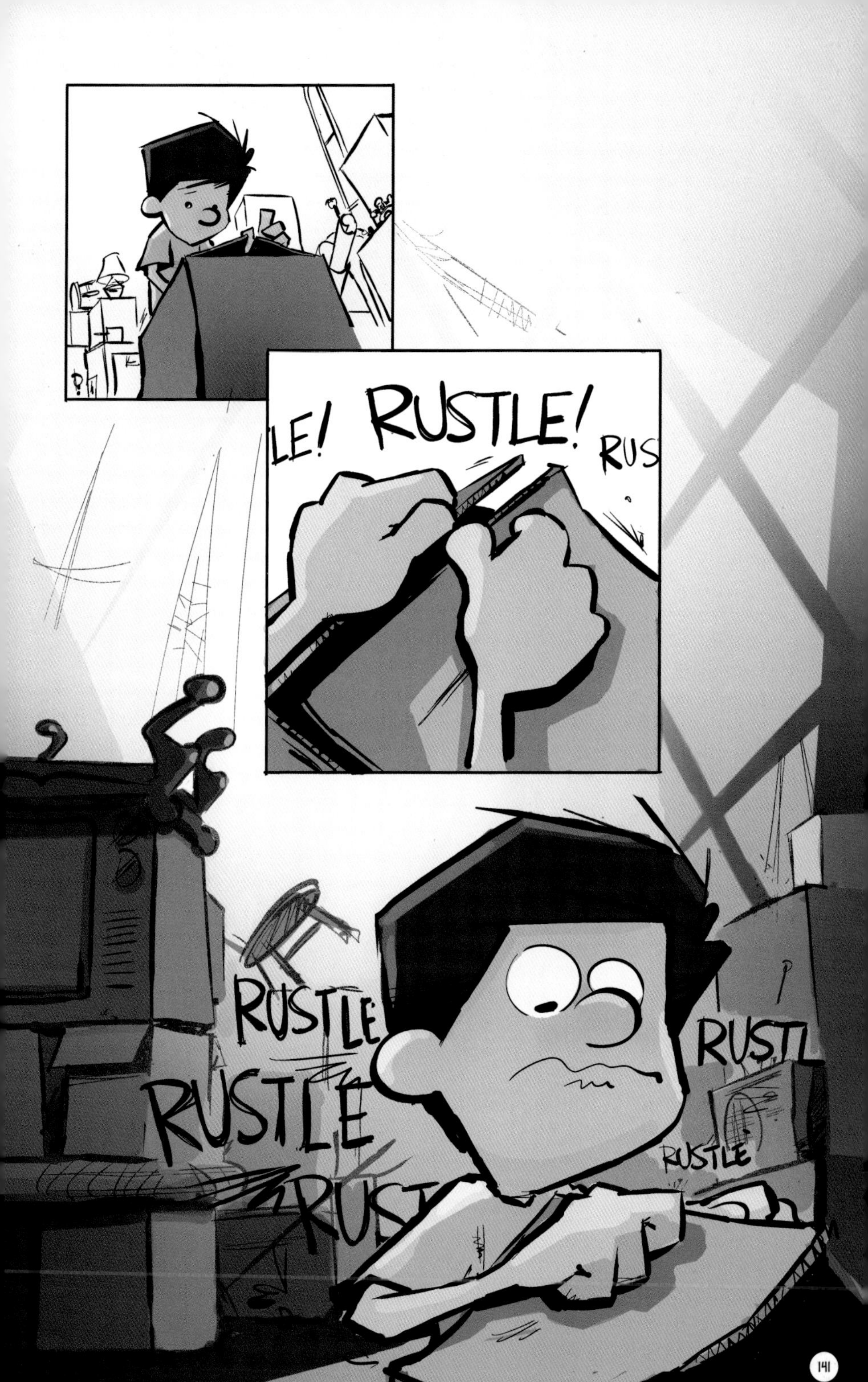

LE! RUSTLE! RUS
RUSTLE
RUSTLE
RUST
RUSTL
RUSTLE

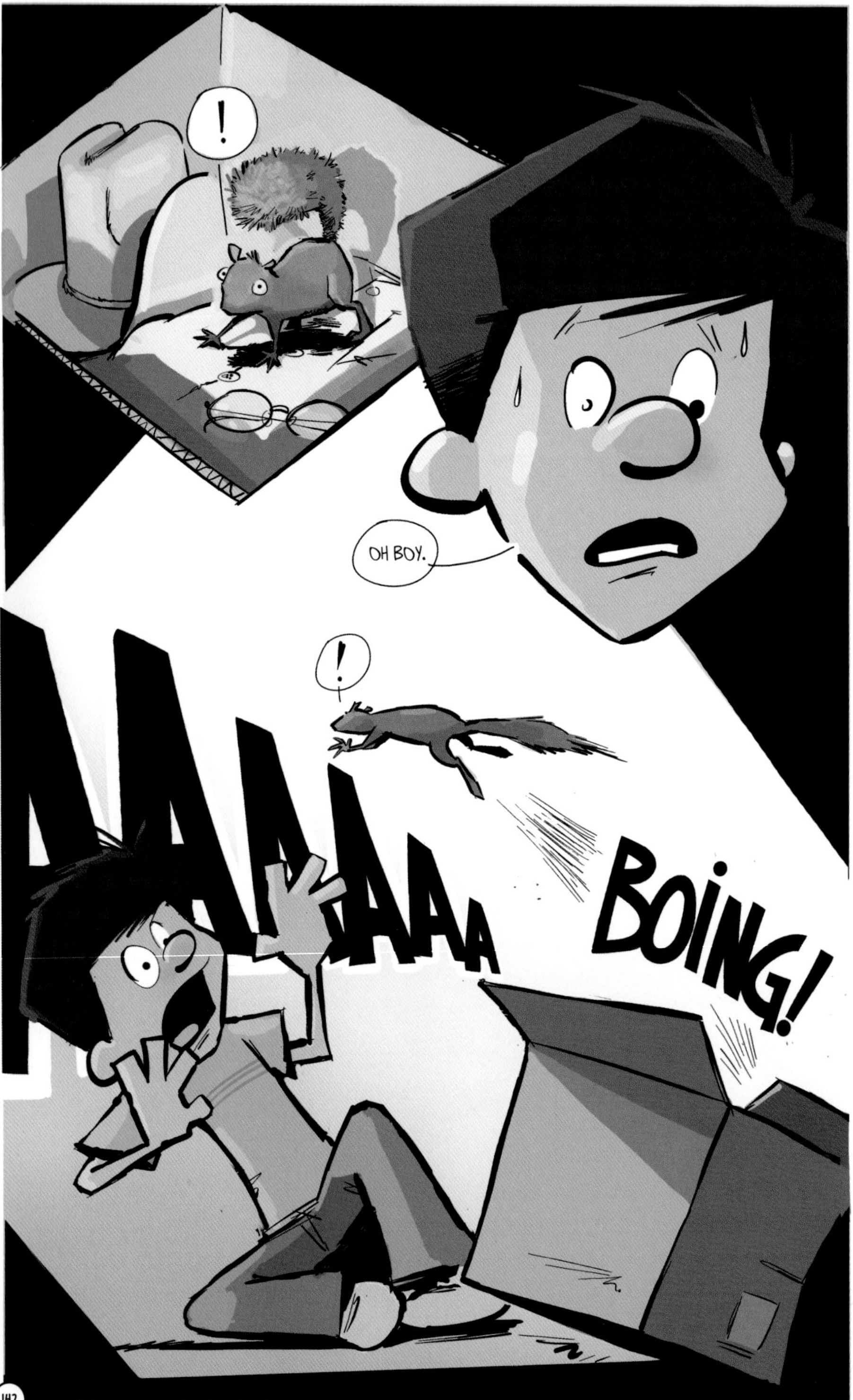
!
OH BOY.
!
AAAAAAAA
BOING!

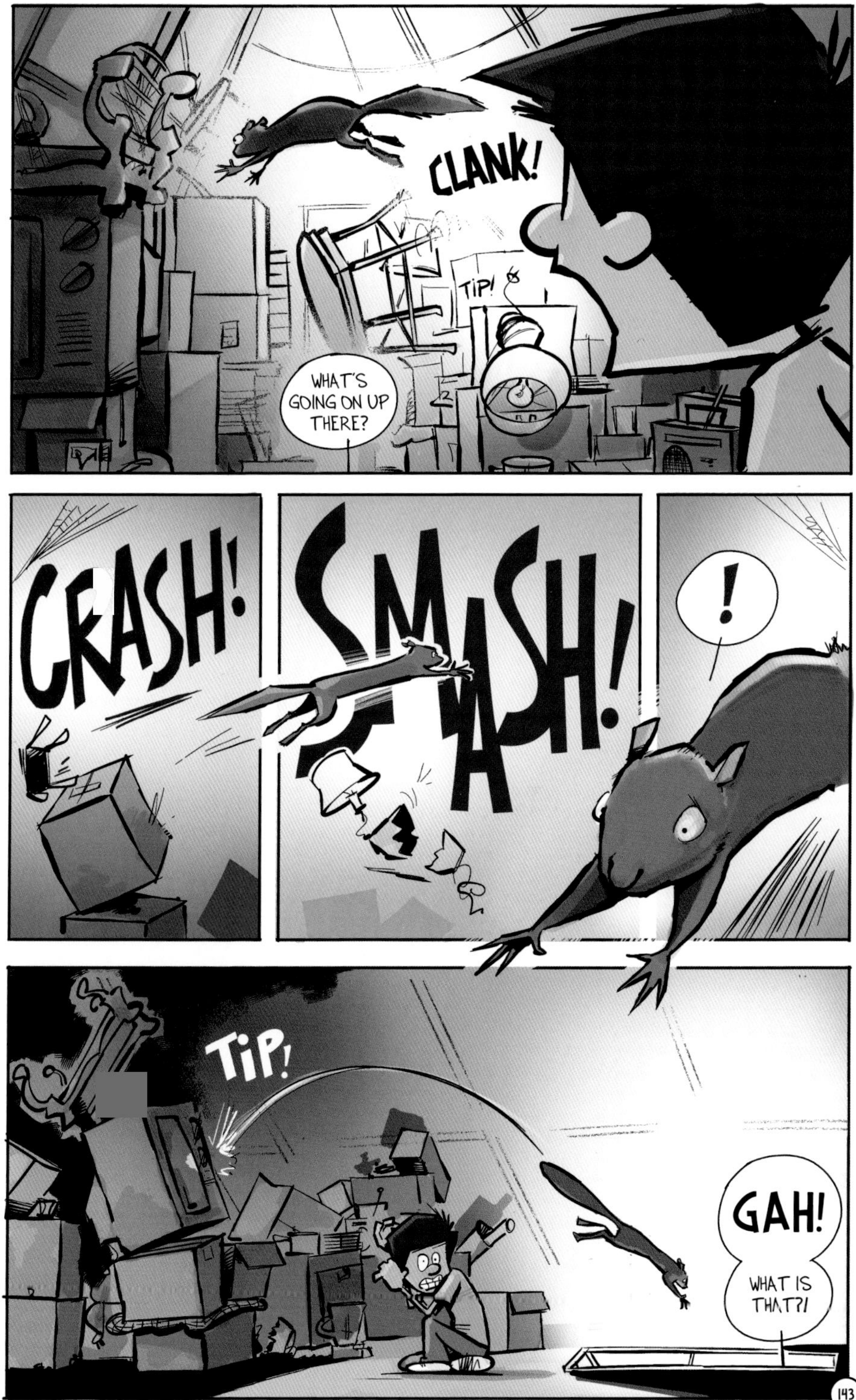
CLANK!
TIP!
WHAT'S GOING ON UP THERE?
CRASH!
SMASH!
!
TIP!
GAH!
WHAT IS THAT?!

CHAPTER EIGHT
YOU DON'T KNOW UNLESS YOU TRY

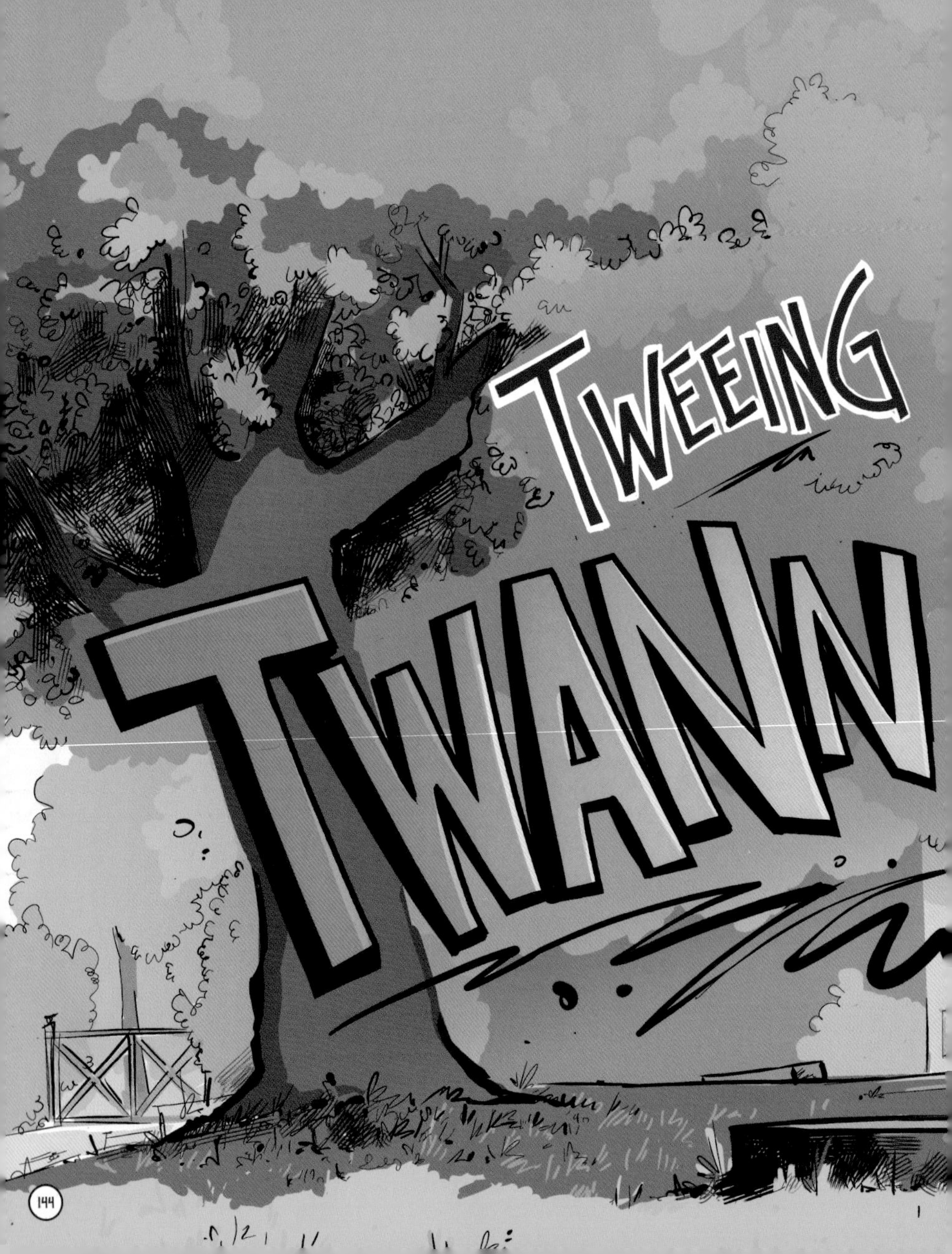
TWEEING
TWANW

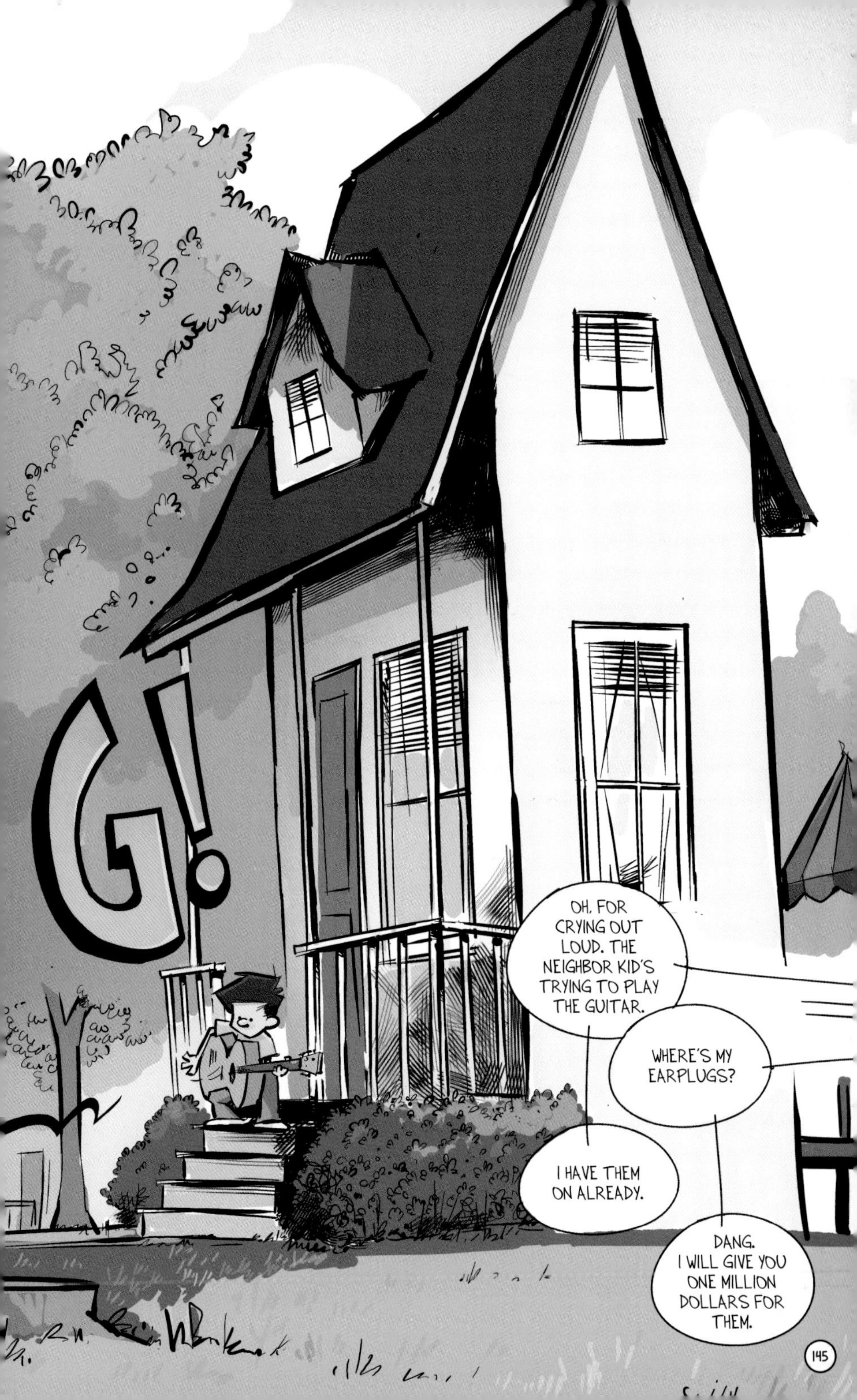
G!
OH, FOR CRYING OUT LOUD. THE NEIGHBOR KID'S TRYING TO PLAY THE GUITAR.
WHERE'S MY EARPLUGS?
I HAVE THEM ON ALREADY.
DANG. I WILL GIVE YOU ONE MILLION DOLLARS FOR THEM.

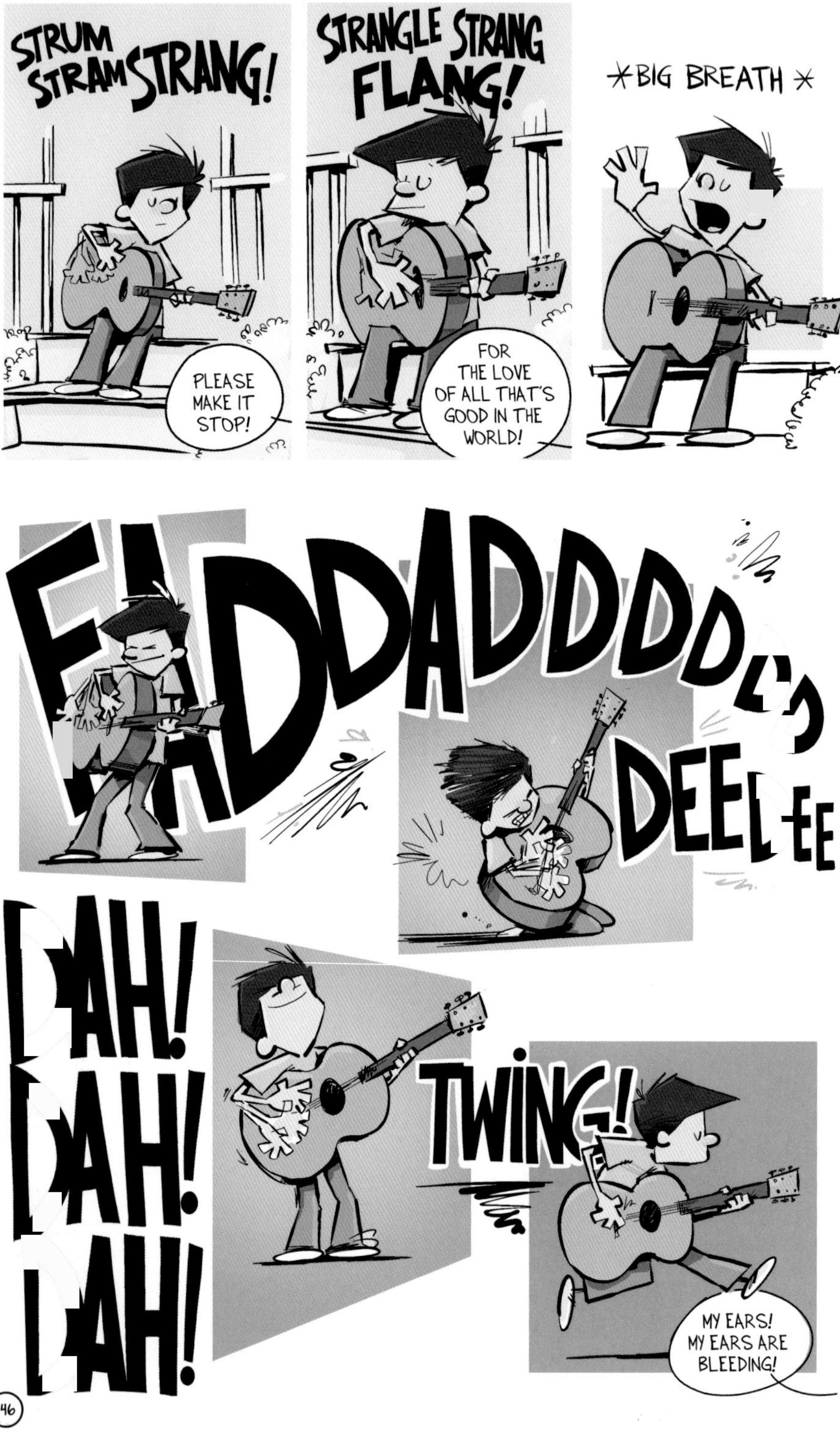
STRUM STRAM STRANG!
PLEASE MAKE IT STOP!
STRANGLE STRANG FLANG!
FOR THE LOVE OF ALL THAT'S GOOD IN THE WORLD!
BIG BREATH
DEE-EE
DAH! DAH! DAH!
TWING!
MY EARS! MY EARS ARE BLEEDING!

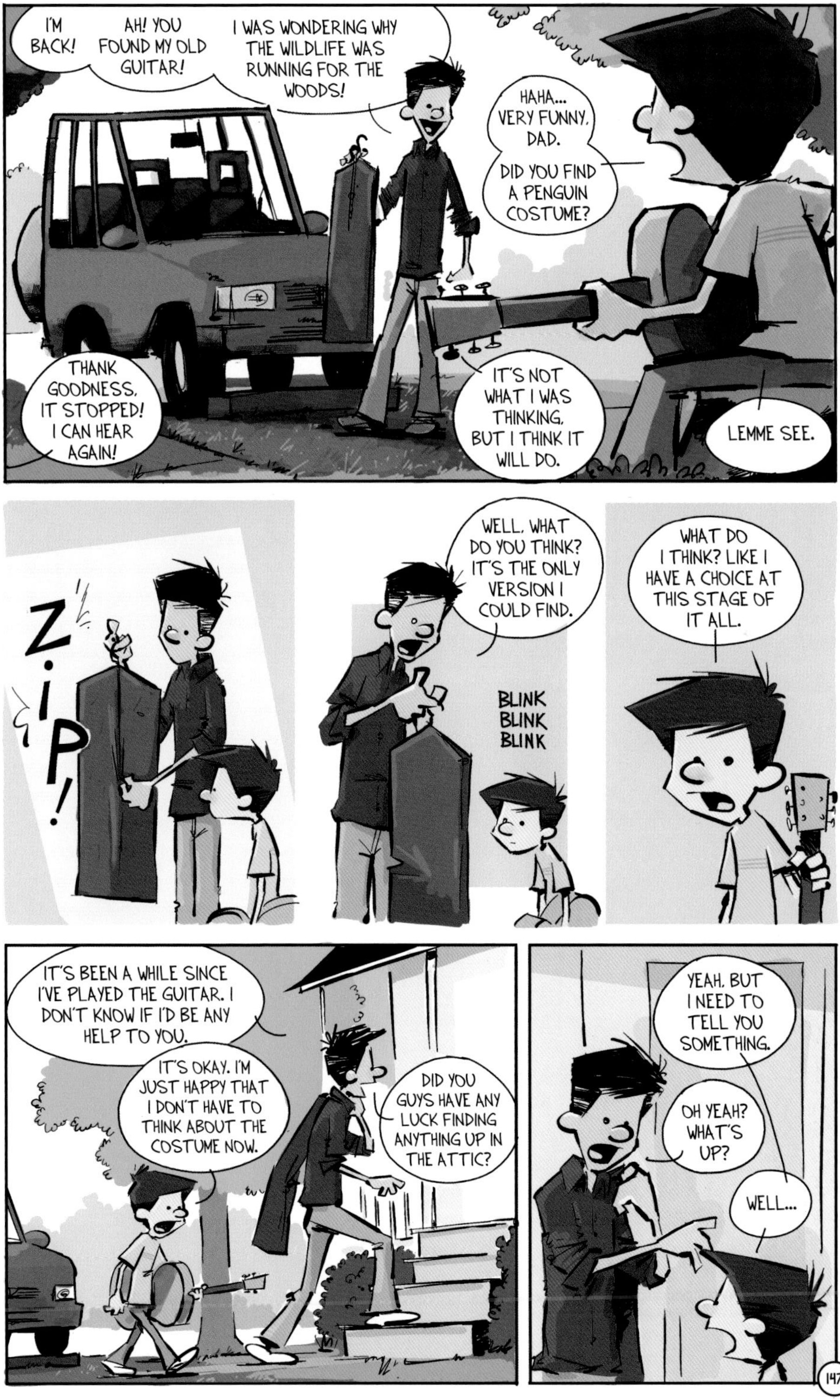
I'M BACK!
AH! YOU FOUND MY OLD GUITAR!
I WAS WONDERING WHY THE WILDLIFE WAS RUNNING FOR THE WOODS!
HAHA... VERY FUNNY, DAD.
DID YOU FIND A PENGUIN COSTUME?
THANK GOODNESS, IT STOPPED! I CAN HEAR AGAIN!
IT'S NOT WHAT I WAS THINKING, BUT I THINK IT WILL DO.
LEMME SEE.
ZIP!
WELL, WHAT DO YOU THINK? IT'S THE ONLY VERSION I COULD FIND.
BLINK BLINK BLINK
WHAT DO I THINK? LIKE I HAVE A CHOICE AT THIS STAGE OF IT ALL.
IT'S BEEN A WHILE SINCE I'VE PLAYED THE GUITAR. I DON'T KNOW IF I'D BE ANY HELP TO YOU.
IT'S OKAY. I'M JUST HAPPY THAT I DON'T HAVE TO THINK ABOUT THE COSTUME NOW.
DID YOU GUYS HAVE ANY LUCK FINDING ANYTHING UP IN THE ATTIC?
YEAH, BUT I NEED TO TELL YOU SOMETHING.
OH YEAH? WHAT'S UP?
WELL...

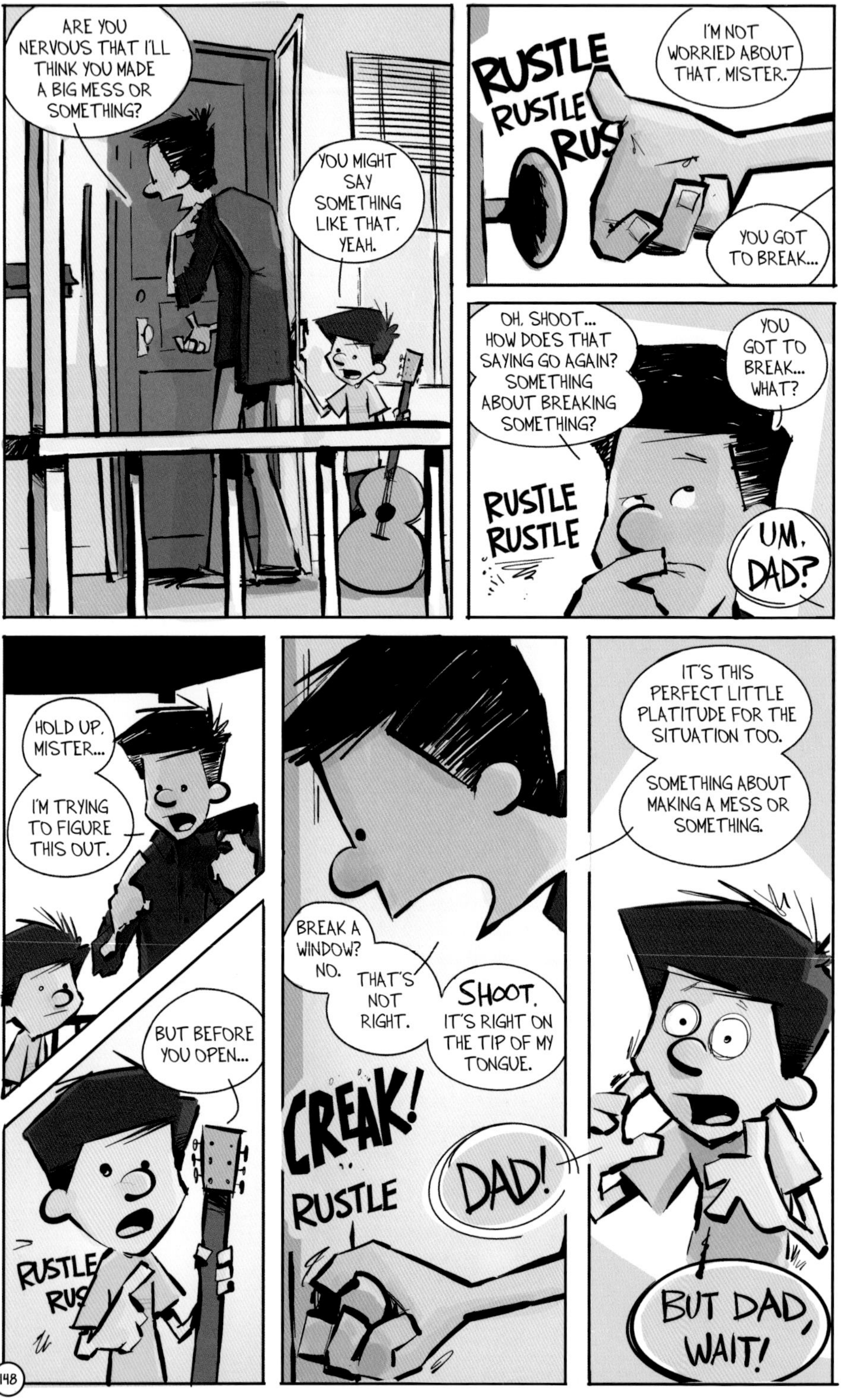

ARE YOU NERVOUS THAT I'LL THINK YOU MADE A BIG MESS OR SOMETHING?
YOU MIGHT SAY SOMETHING LIKE THAT, YEAH.
RUSTLE
RUSTLE
RUS
I'M NOT WORRIED ABOUT THAT, MISTER.
YOU GOT TO BREAK...
OH, SHOOT... HOW DOES THAT SAYING GO AGAIN? SOMETHING ABOUT BREAKING SOMETHING?
YOU GOT TO BREAK... WHAT?
RUSTLE RUSTLE
UM, DAD?
HOLD UP, MISTER...
I'M TRYING TO FIGURE THIS OUT.
BUT BEFORE YOU OPEN...
RUSTLE
RUS
BREAK A WINDOW? NO.
THAT'S NOT RIGHT.
SHOOT. IT'S RIGHT ON THE TIP OF MY TONGUE.
CREAK!
RUSTLE
DAD!
IT'S THIS PERFECT LITTLE PLATITUDE FOR THE SITUATION TOO.
SOMETHING ABOUT MAKING A MESS OR SOMETHING.
BUT DAD, WAIT!

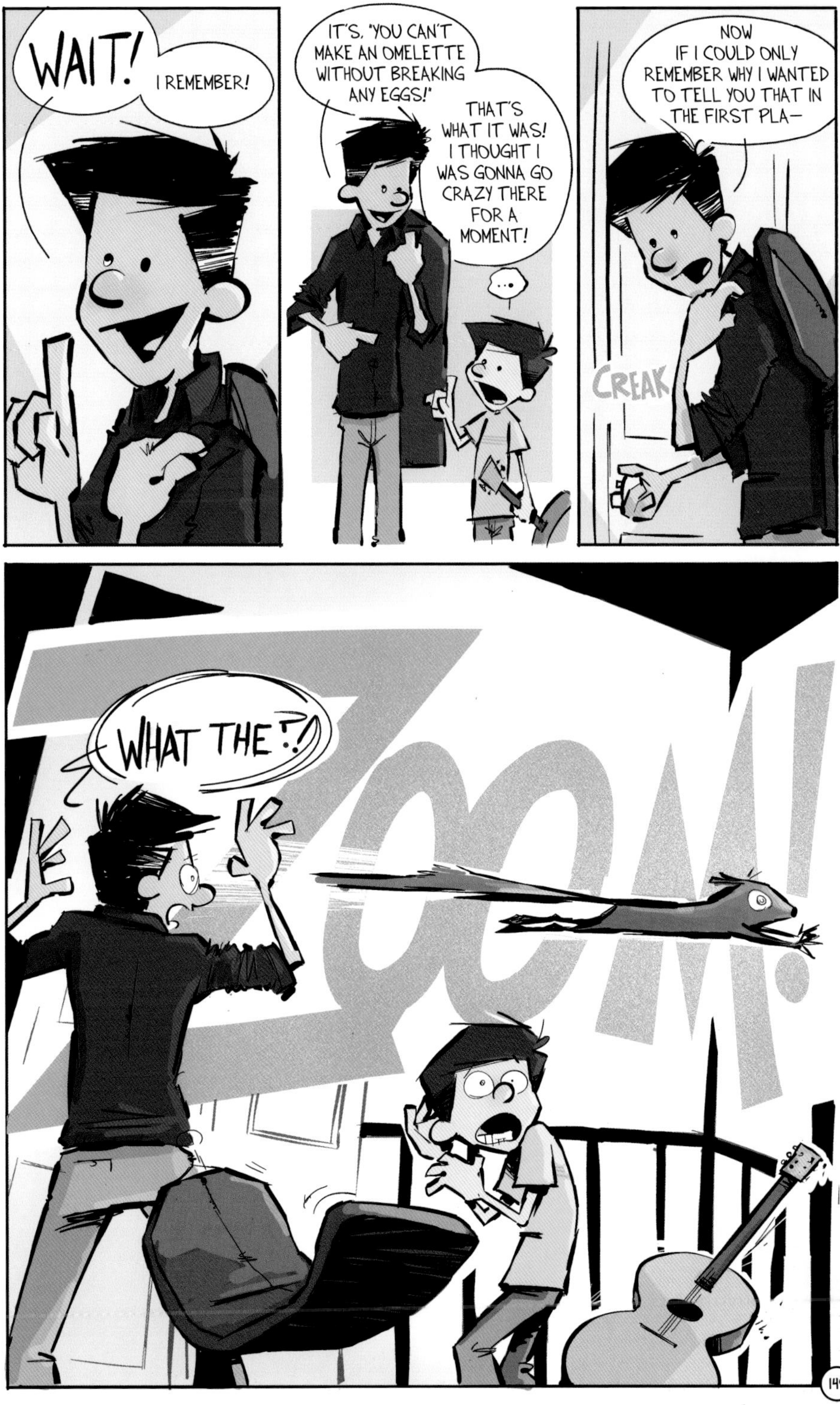

WAIT!
I REMEMBER!
IT'S, "YOU CAN'T MAKE AN OMELETTE WITHOUT BREAKING ANY EGGS!"
THAT'S WHAT IT WAS! I THOUGHT I WAS GONNA GO CRAZY THERE FOR A MOMENT!
...
NOW IF I COULD ONLY REMEMBER WHY I WANTED TO TELL YOU THAT IN THE FIRST PLA—
CREAK
WHAT THE ?!
ZOOM!

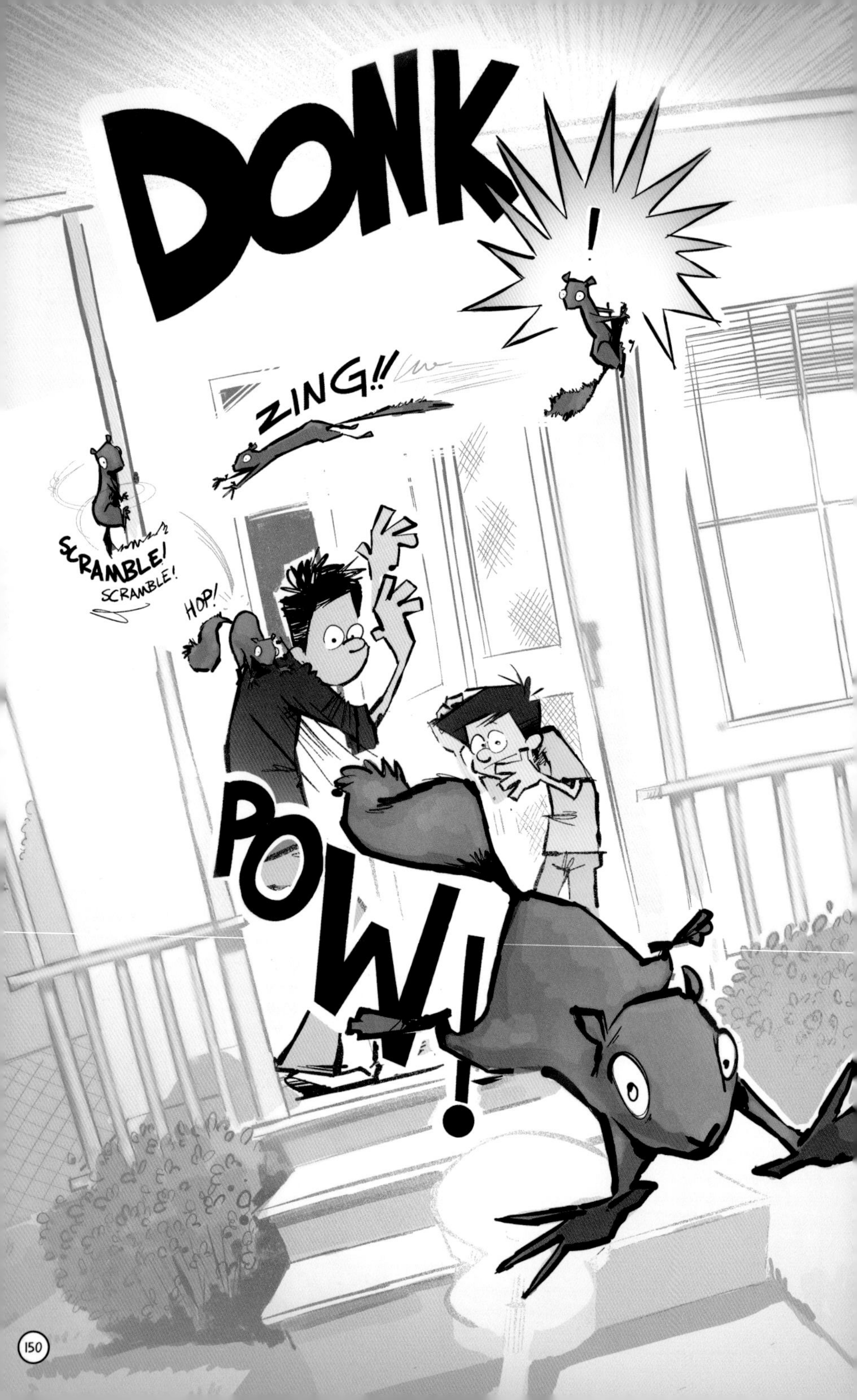
DONK!
ZING!!
SCRAMBLE!
SCRAMBLE!
HOP!
POW!

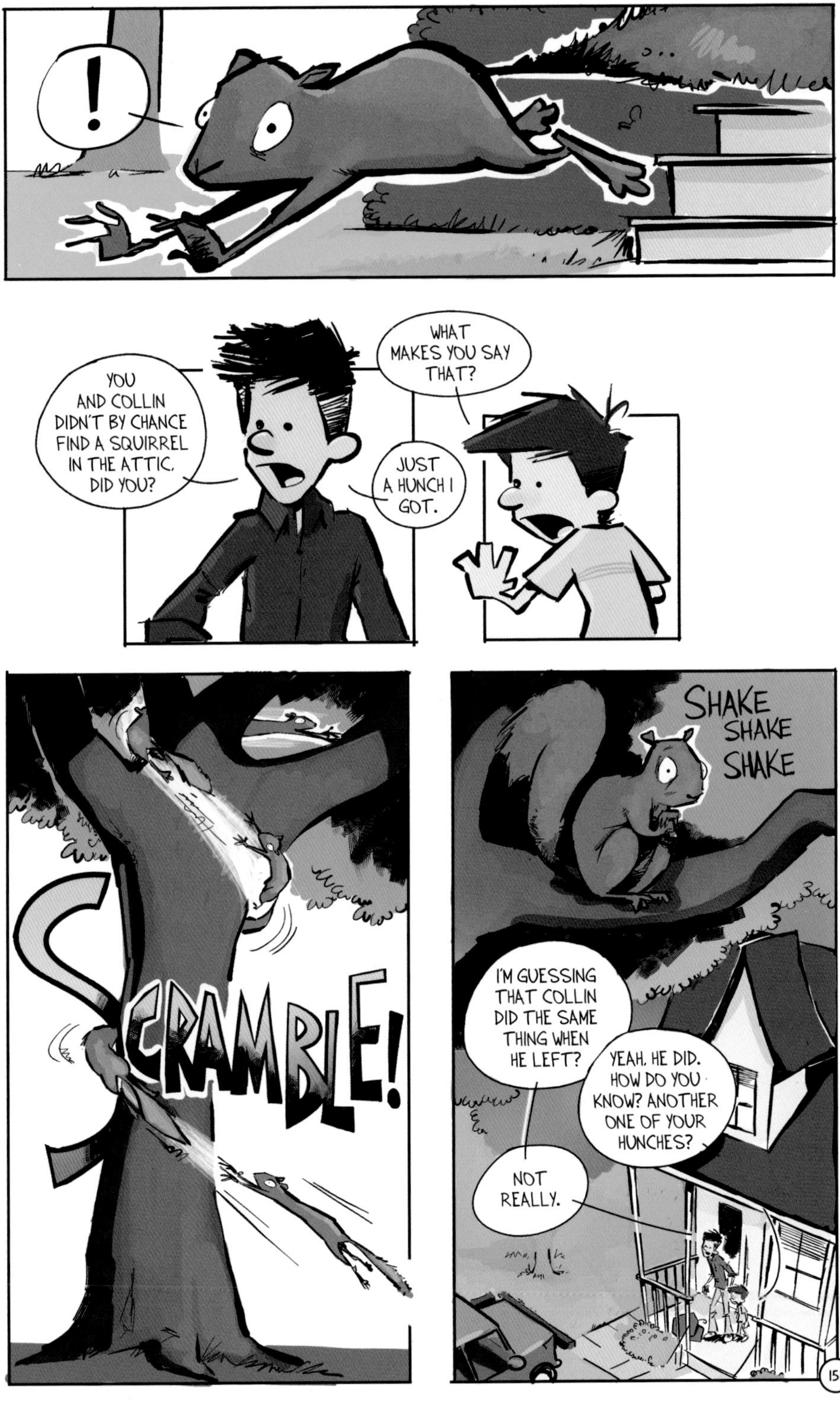
!
YOU AND COLLIN DIDN'T BY CHANCE FIND A SQUIRREL IN THE ATTIC, DID YOU?
WHAT MAKES YOU SAY THAT?
JUST A HUNCH I GOT.
SCRAMBLE!
SHAKE
SHAKE
SHAKE
I'M GUESSING THAT COLLIN DID THE SAME THING WHEN HE LEFT?
YEAH, HE DID. HOW DO YOU KNOW? ANOTHER ONE OF YOUR HUNCHES?
NOT REALLY.

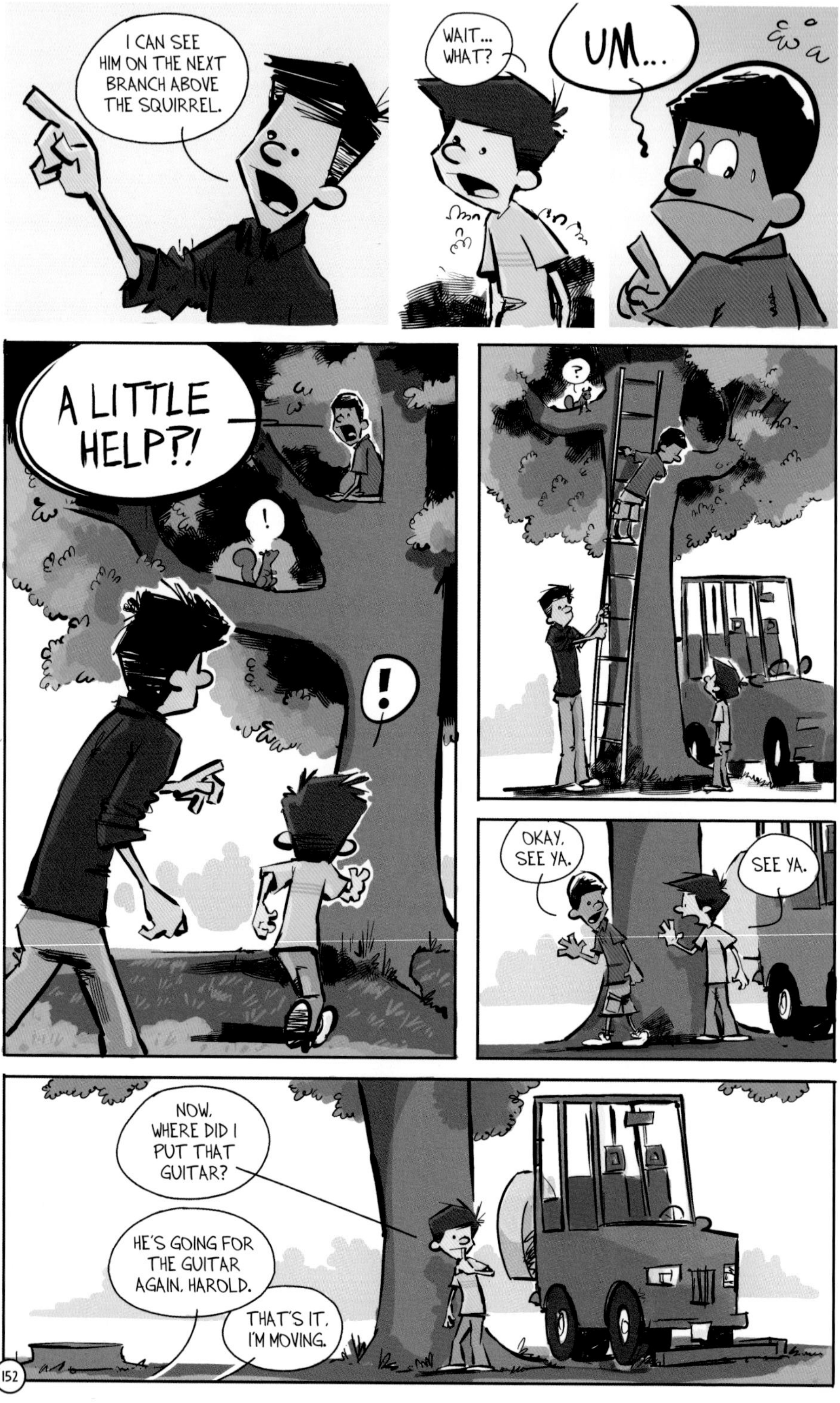
I CAN SEE HIM ON THE NEXT BRANCH ABOVE THE SQUIRREL.
WAIT... WHAT?
UM...
A LITTLE HELP?!
!
!
?
OKAY, SEE YA.
SEE YA.
NOW, WHERE DID I PUT THAT GUITAR?
HE'S GOING FOR THE GUITAR AGAIN, HAROLD.
THAT'S IT, I'M MOVING.

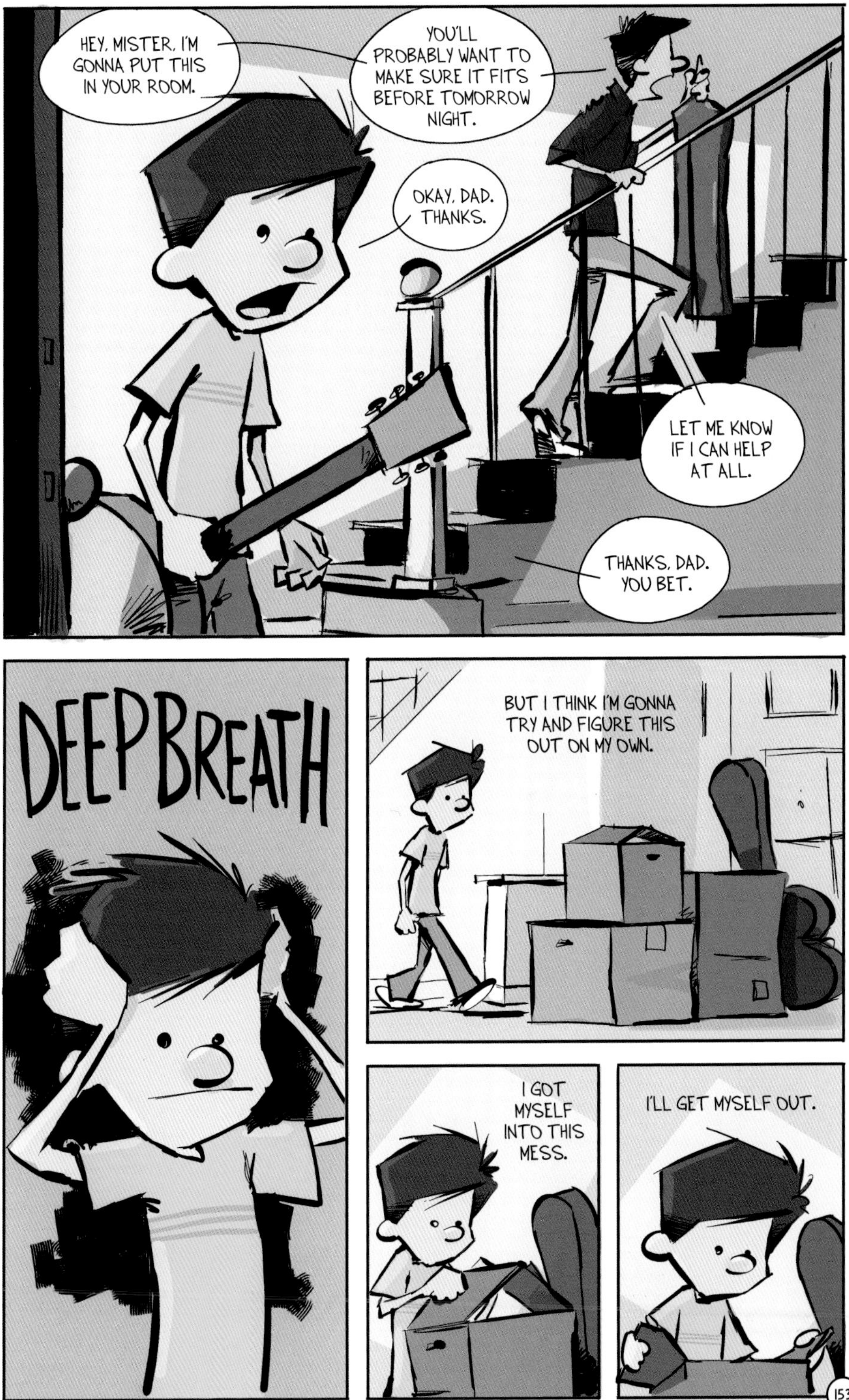
HEY, MISTER, I'M GONNA PUT THIS IN YOUR ROOM.
YOU'LL PROBABLY WANT TO MAKE SURE IT FITS BEFORE TOMORROW NIGHT.
OKAY, DAD. THANKS.
LET ME KNOW IF I CAN HELP AT ALL.
THANKS, DAD.
YOU BET.
DEEP BREATH
BUT I THINK I'M GONNA TRY AND FIGURE THIS OUT ON MY OWN.
I GOT MYSELF INTO THIS MESS.
I'LL GET MYSELF OUT.

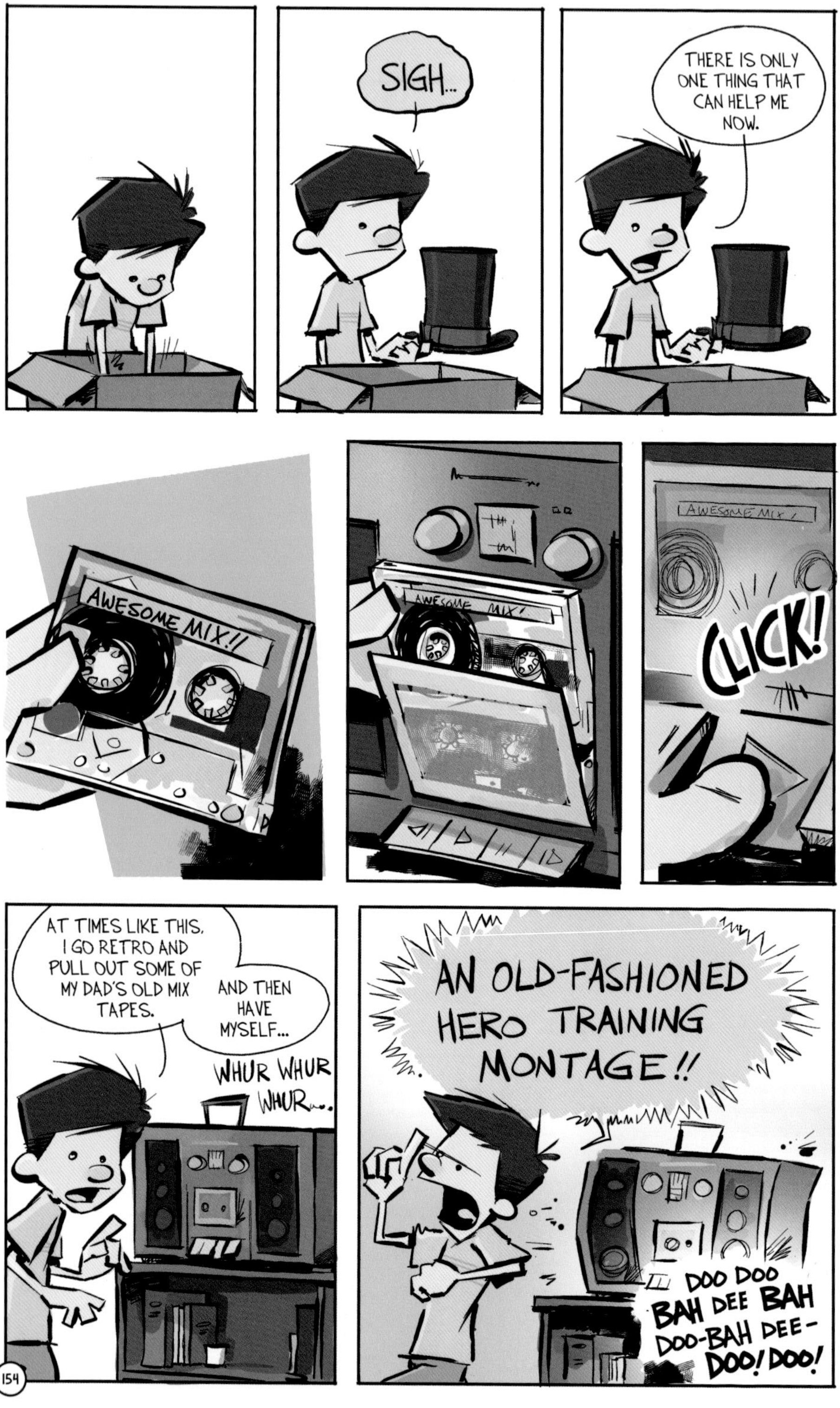
SIGH...
THERE IS ONLY ONE THING THAT CAN HELP ME NOW.
AWESOME MIX!!
AWESOME MIX!
AWESOME MIX!
CLICK!
AT TIMES LIKE THIS, I GO RETRO AND PULL OUT SOME OF MY DAD'S OLD MIX TAPES.
AND THEN HAVE MYSELF...
WHUR WHUR WHUR...
AN OLD-FASHIONED HERO TRAINING MONTAGE!!
DOO DOO BAH DEE BAH DOO-BAH DEE-DOO! DOO!

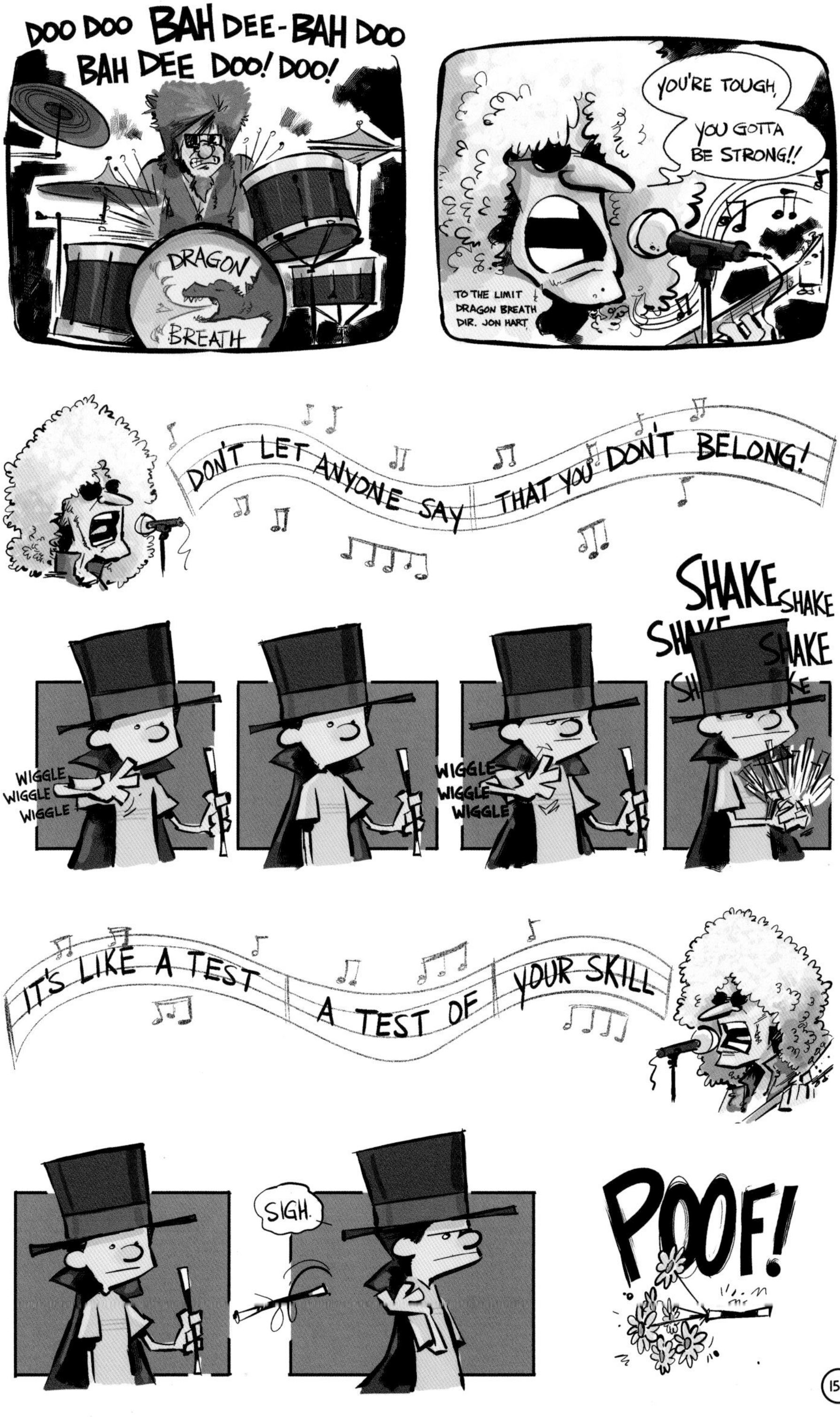

DOO DOO BAH DEE-BAH DOO BAH DEE DOO! DOO!
DRAGON BREATH
YOU'RE TOUGH, YOU GOTTA BE STRONG!!
TO THE LIMIT
DRAGON BREATH
DIR. JON HART
DON'T LET ANYONE SAY THAT YOU DON'T BELONG!
WIGGLE WIGGLE WIGGLE
WIGGLE WIGGLE WIGGLE
SHAKE SHAKE SHAKE SHAKE
IT'S LIKE A TEST A TEST OF YOUR SKILL
SIGH.
POOF!

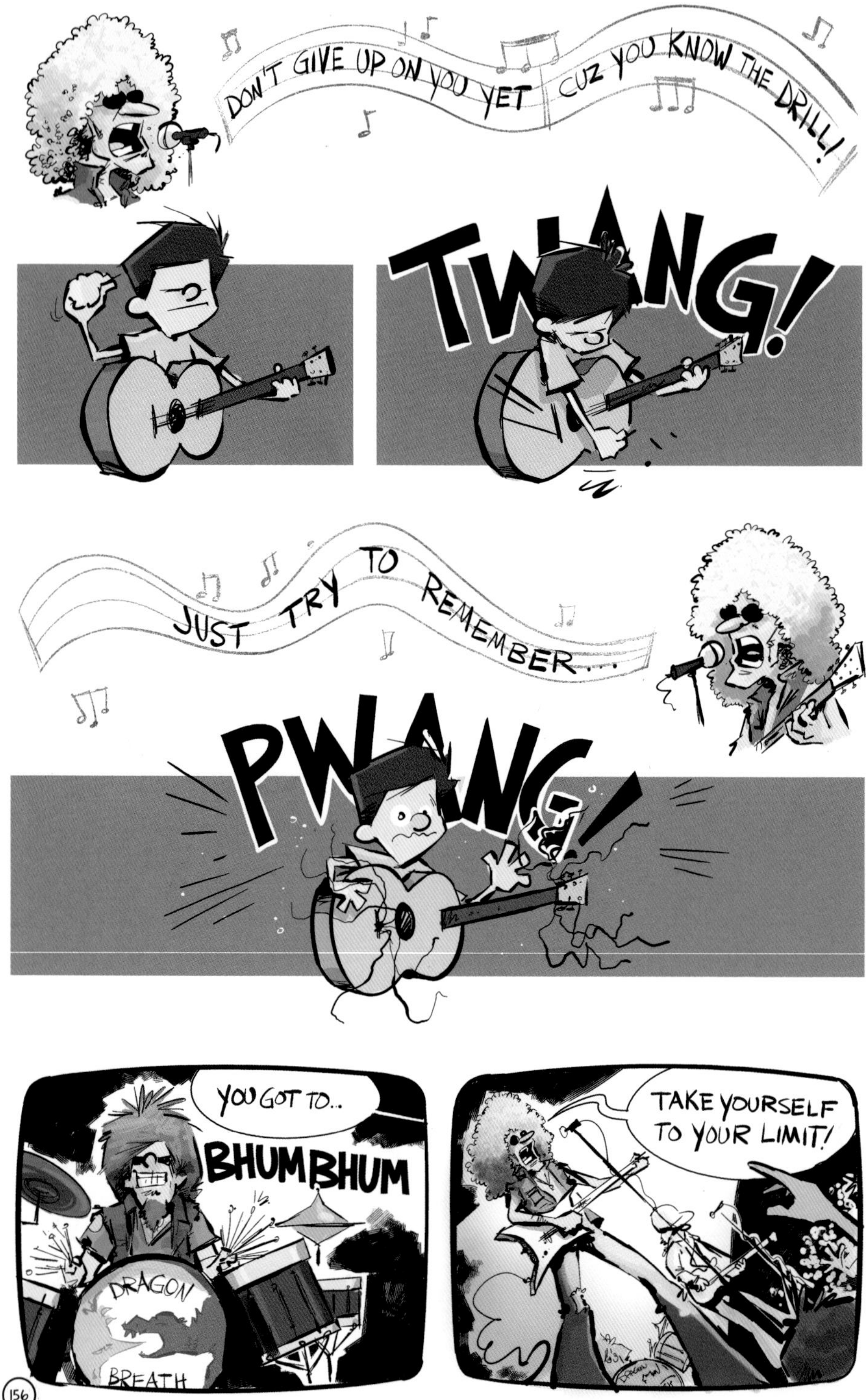
DON'T GIVE UP ON YOU YET
CUZ YOU KNOW THE DRILL!
TWANG!
JUST TRY TO REMEMBER...
PWANG!
YOU GOT TO..
BHUMBHUM
DRAGON BREATH
TAKE YOURSELF TO YOUR LIMIT!

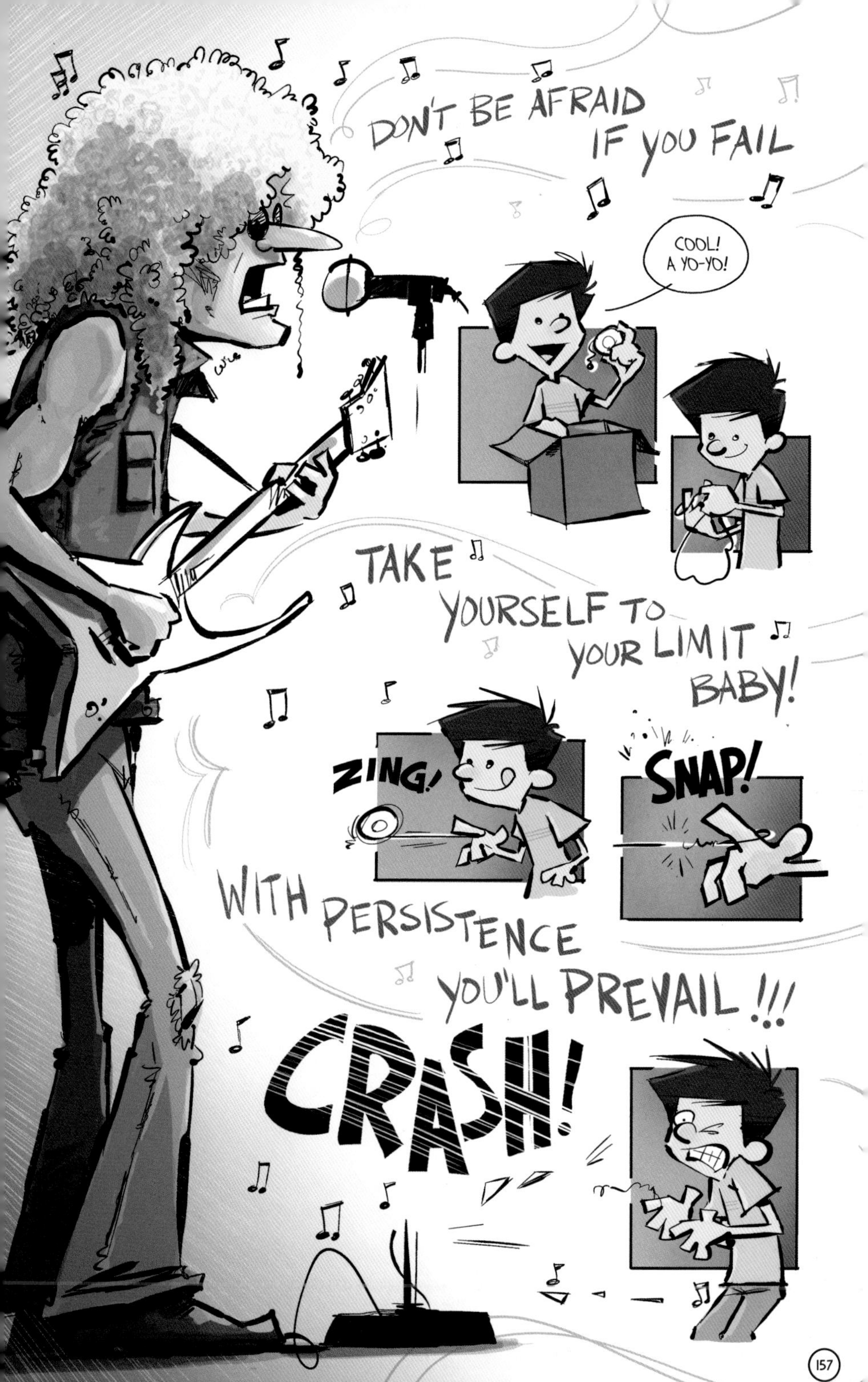
DON'T BE AFRAID IF YOU FAIL
COOL! A YO-YO!
TAKE YOURSELF TO YOUR LIMIT BABY!
ZING!
SNAP!
WITH PERSISTENCE YOU'LL PREVAIL !!!
CRASH!

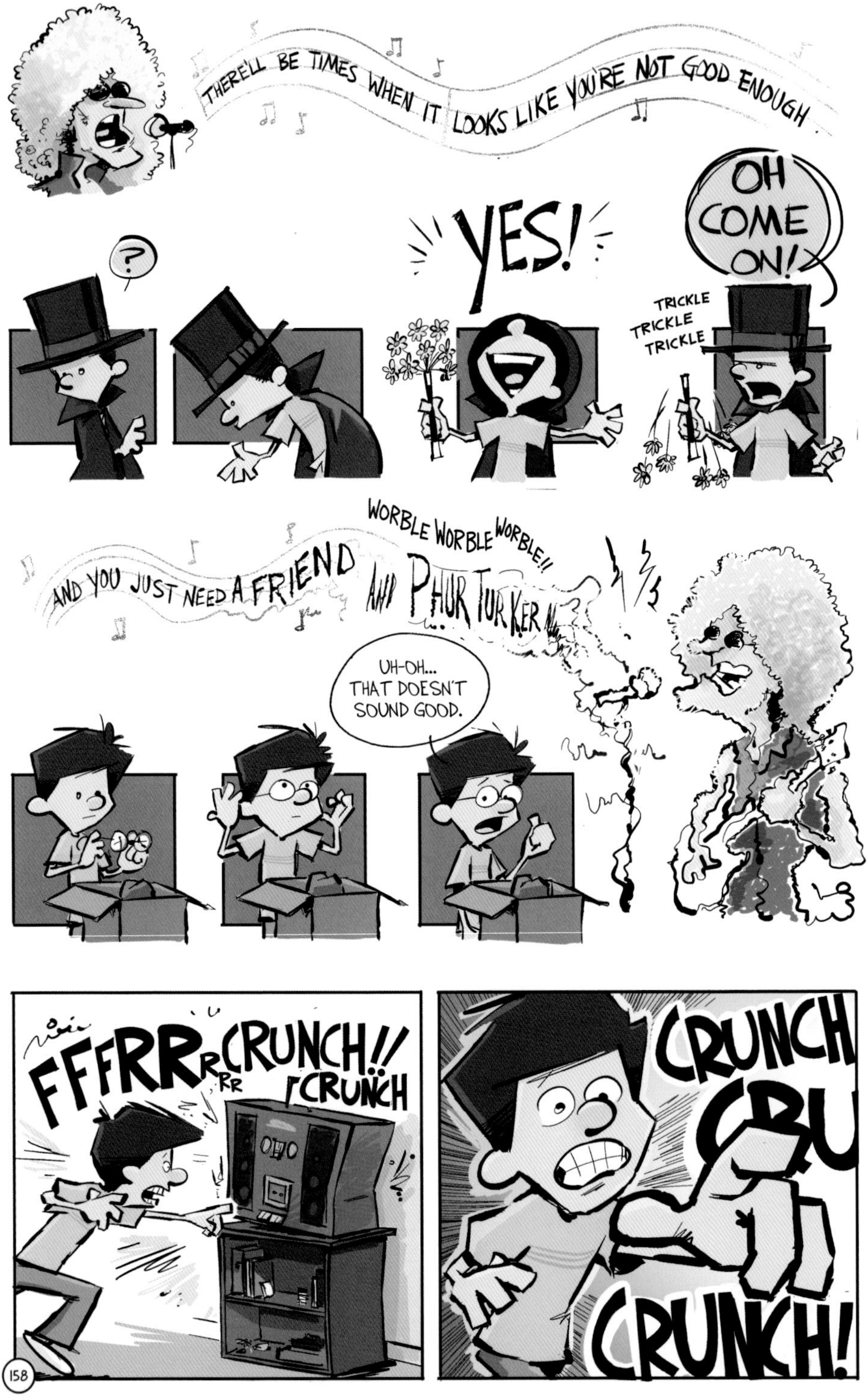
THERE'LL BE TIMES WHEN IT LOOKS LIKE YOU'RE NOT GOOD ENOUGH
?
YES!
OH COME ON!
TRICKLE
TRICKLE
TRICKLE
AND YOU JUST NEED A FRIEND
WORBLE WORBLE WORBLE!!
UH-OH... THAT DOESN'T SOUND GOOD.
FFFRRrrr CRUNCH!!
CRUNCH
CRUNCH
CRUNCH!

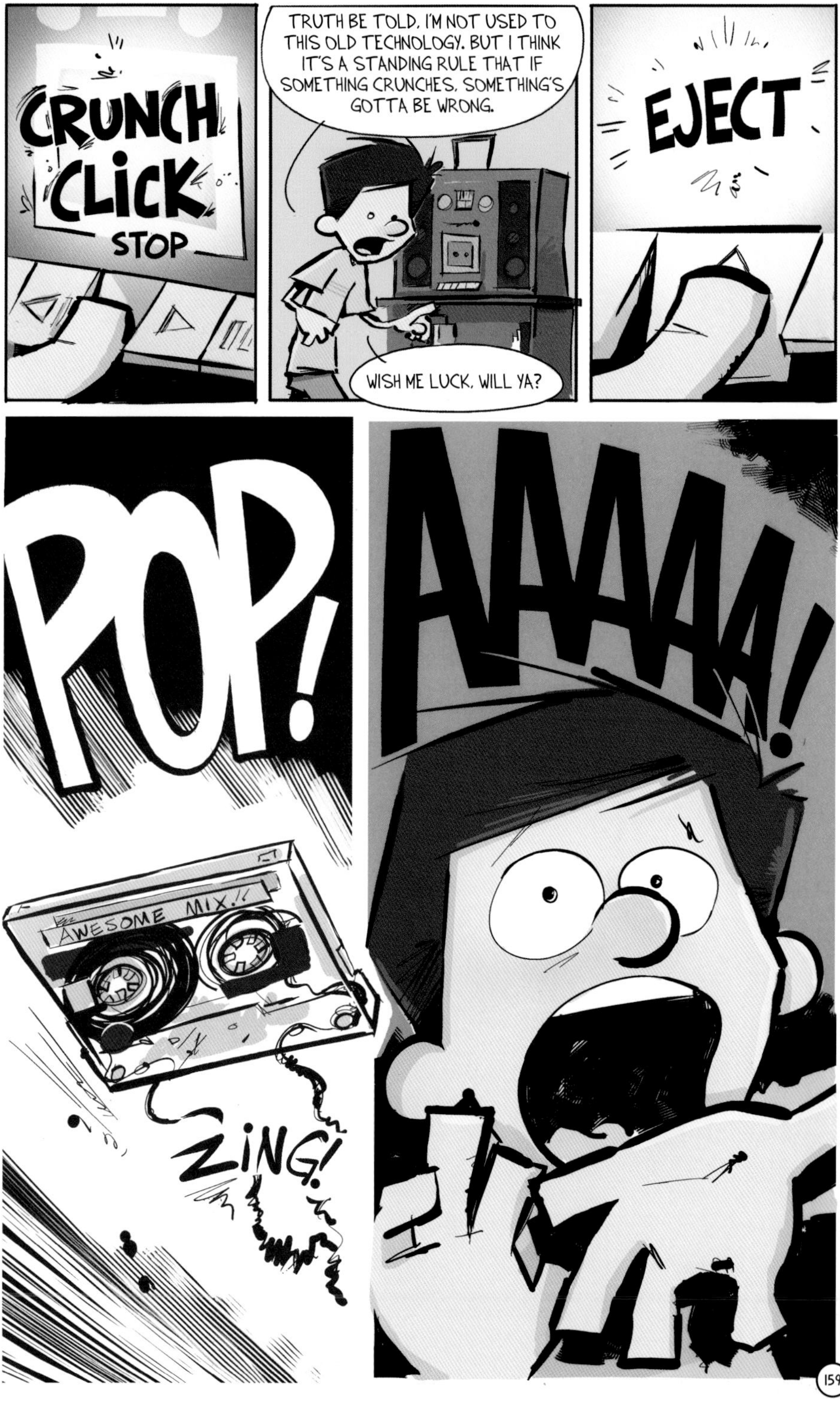
CRUNCH
CLICK
STOP
TRUTH BE TOLD, I'M NOT USED TO THIS OLD TECHNOLOGY. BUT I THINK IT'S A STANDING RULE THAT IF SOMETHING CRUNCHES, SOMETHING'S GOTTA BE WRONG.
WISH ME LUCK, WILL YA?
EJECT
POP!
AAAAA!
AWESOME MIX!!
ZING!

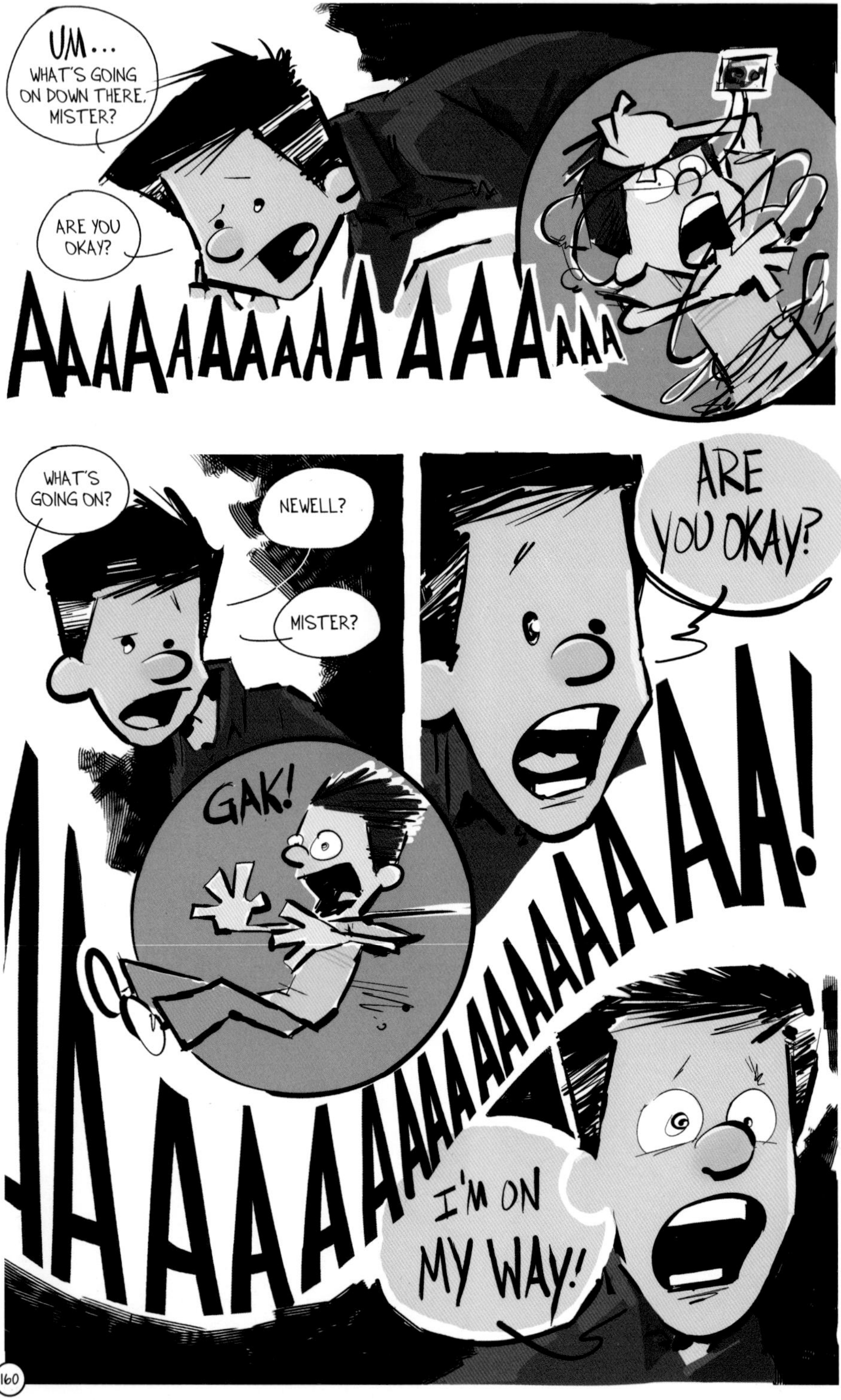
UM...
WHAT'S GOING ON DOWN THERE, MISTER?
ARE YOU OKAY?
AAAAAAAAAA AAAAAA
WHAT'S GOING ON?
NEWELL?
MISTER?
ARE YOU OKAY?
GAK!
AAAAAAAAAAAAAAAAAAA!
I'M ON MY WAY!

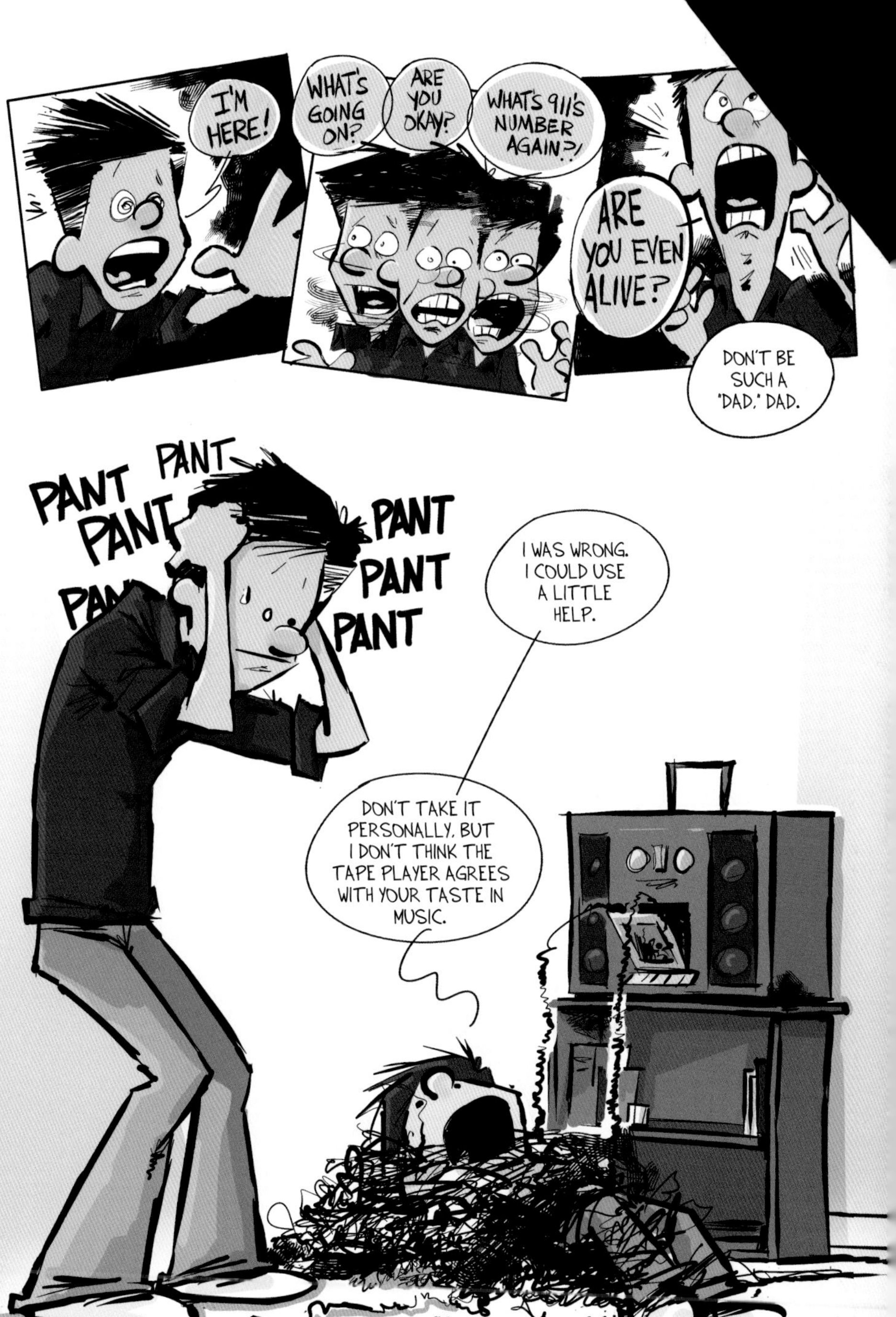
I'M HERE!
WHAT'S GOING ON?
ARE YOU OKAY?
WHAT'S 911'S NUMBER AGAIN?!
ARE YOU EVEN ALIVE?
DON'T BE SUCH A "DAD," DAD.
PANT PANT PANT PANT PANT PANT PANT PANT
I WAS WRONG. I COULD USE A LITTLE HELP.
DON'T TAKE IT PERSONALLY, BUT I DON'T THINK THE TAPE PLAYER AGREES WITH YOUR TASTE IN MUSIC.

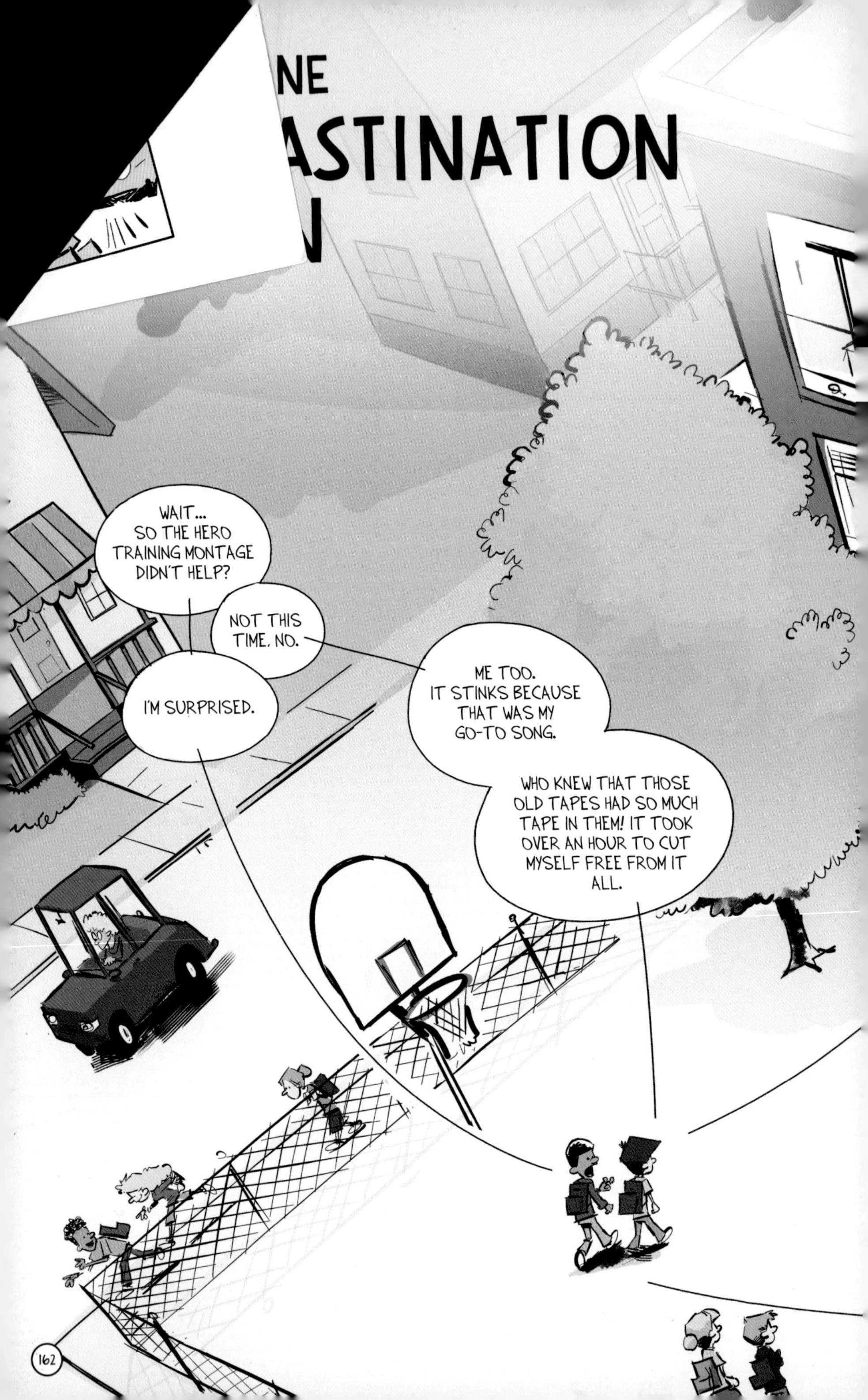
NE
ASTINATION
N
WAIT... SO THE HERO TRAINING MONTAGE DIDN'T HELP?
NOT THIS TIME, NO.
I'M SURPRISED.
ME TOO. IT STINKS BECAUSE THAT WAS MY GO-TO SONG.
WHO KNEW THAT THOSE OLD TAPES HAD SO MUCH TAPE IN THEM! IT TOOK OVER AN HOUR TO CUT MYSELF FREE FROM IT ALL.

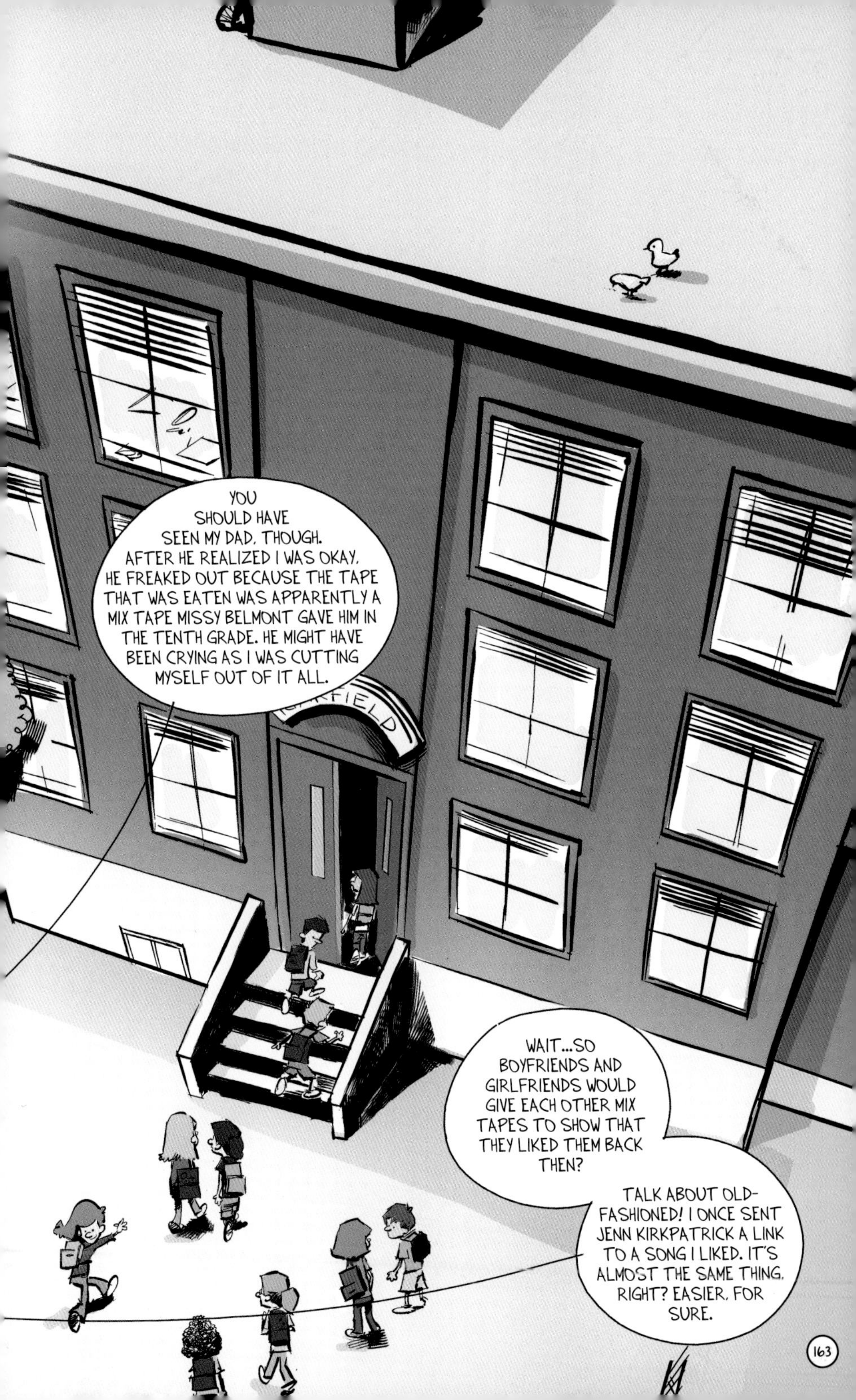
YOU SHOULD HAVE SEEN MY DAD, THOUGH. AFTER HE REALIZED I WAS OKAY, HE FREAKED OUT BECAUSE THE TAPE THAT WAS EATEN WAS APPARENTLY A MIX TAPE MISSY BELMONT GAVE HIM IN THE TENTH GRADE. HE MIGHT HAVE BEEN CRYING AS I WAS CUTTING MYSELF OUT OF IT ALL.
WAIT...SO BOYFRIENDS AND GIRLFRIENDS WOULD GIVE EACH OTHER MIX TAPES TO SHOW THAT THEY LIKED THEM BACK THEN?
TALK ABOUT OLD-FASHIONED! I ONCE SENT JENN KIRKPATRICK A LINK TO A SONG I LIKED. IT'S ALMOST THE SAME THING, RIGHT? EASIER, FOR SURE.

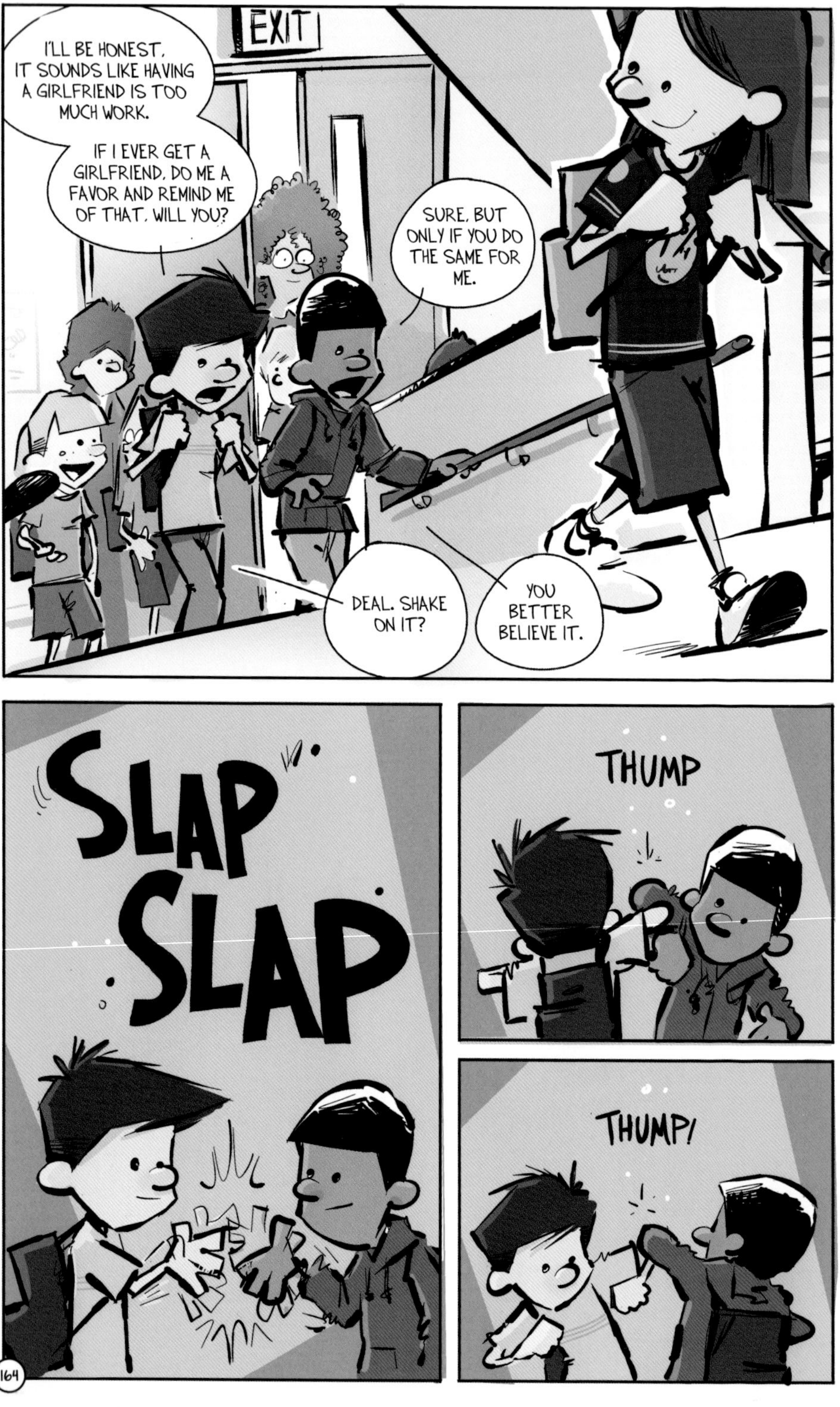
EXIT
I'LL BE HONEST, IT SOUNDS LIKE HAVING A GIRLFRIEND IS TOO MUCH WORK.
IF I EVER GET A GIRLFRIEND, DO ME A FAVOR AND REMIND ME OF THAT, WILL YOU?
SURE, BUT ONLY IF YOU DO THE SAME FOR ME.
DEAL. SHAKE ON IT?
YOU BETTER BELIEVE IT.
SLAP SLAP
THUMP
THUMP!

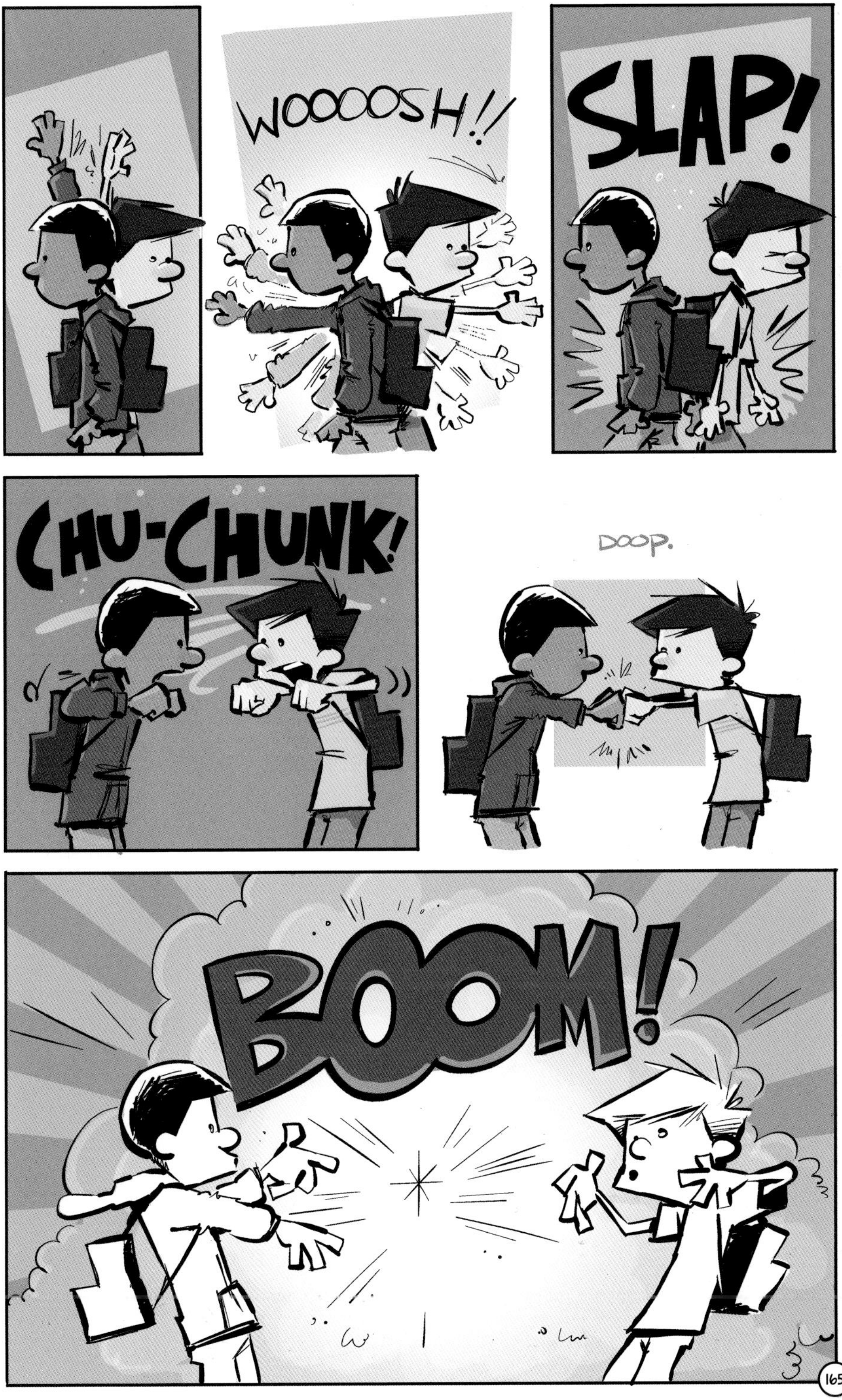
WOOOOSH!!
SLAP!
CHU-CHUNK!
DOOP.
BOOM!

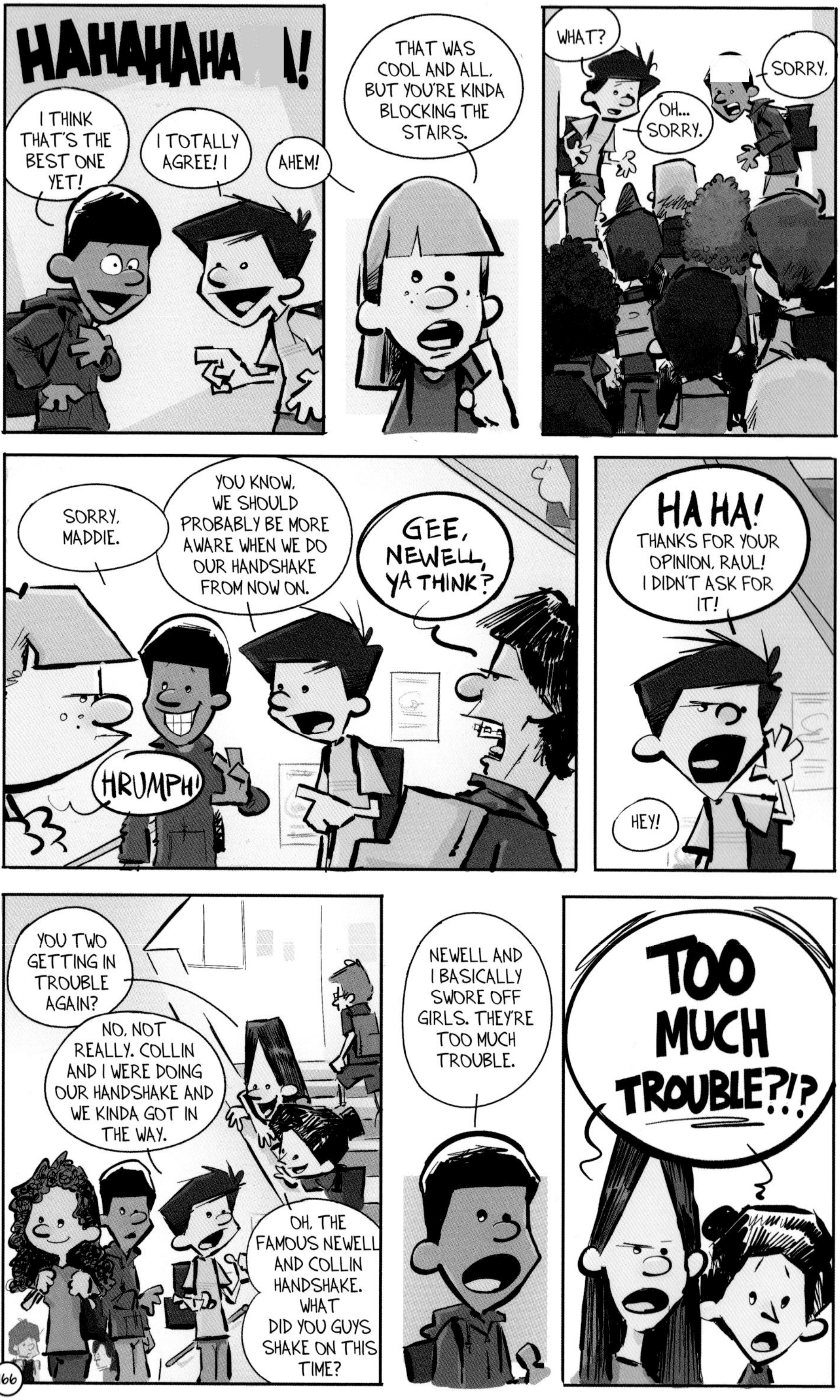

HAHAHAHA!
I THINK THAT'S THE BEST ONE YET!
I TOTALLY AGREE! I
AHEM!
THAT WAS COOL AND ALL, BUT YOU'RE KINDA BLOCKING THE STAIRS.
WHAT?
OH... SORRY.
SORRY.
SORRY, MADDIE.
YOU KNOW, WE SHOULD PROBABLY BE MORE AWARE WHEN WE DO OUR HANDSHAKE FROM NOW ON.
GEE, NEWELL, YA THINK?
HRUMPH!
HA HA! THANKS FOR YOUR OPINION, RAUL! I DIDN'T ASK FOR IT!
HEY!
YOU TWO GETTING IN TROUBLE AGAIN?
NO, NOT REALLY. COLLIN AND I WERE DOING OUR HANDSHAKE AND WE KINDA GOT IN THE WAY.
OH, THE FAMOUS NEWELL AND COLLIN HANDSHAKE. WHAT DID YOU GUYS SHAKE ON THIS TIME?
NEWELL AND I BASICALLY SWORE OFF GIRLS. THEY'RE TOO MUCH TROUBLE.
TOO MUCH TROUBLE?!?

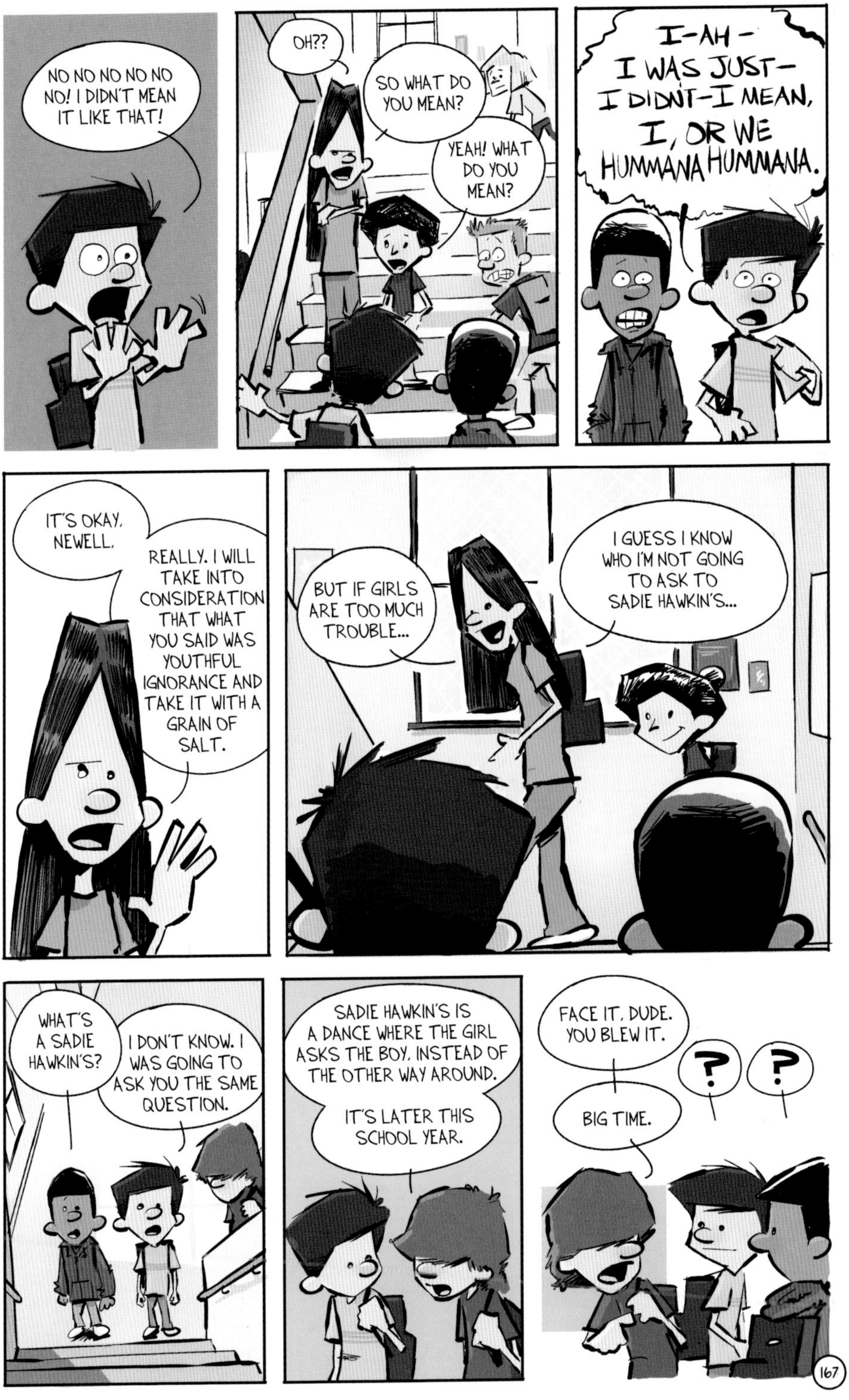
NO NO NO NO NO NO! I DIDN'T MEAN IT LIKE THAT!
OH??
SO WHAT DO YOU MEAN?
YEAH! WHAT DO YOU MEAN?
I-AH - I WAS JUST- I DIDN'T-I MEAN, I, OR WE HUMMANA HUMMANA.
IT'S OKAY, NEWELL.
REALLY. I WILL TAKE INTO CONSIDERATION THAT WHAT YOU SAID WAS YOUTHFUL IGNORANCE AND TAKE IT WITH A GRAIN OF SALT.
BUT IF GIRLS ARE TOO MUCH TROUBLE...
I GUESS I KNOW WHO I'M NOT GOING TO ASK TO SADIE HAWKIN'S...
WHAT'S A SADIE HAWKIN'S?
I DON'T KNOW. I WAS GOING TO ASK YOU THE SAME QUESTION.
SADIE HAWKIN'S IS A DANCE WHERE THE GIRL ASKS THE BOY, INSTEAD OF THE OTHER WAY AROUND.
IT'S LATER THIS SCHOOL YEAR.
FACE IT, DUDE. YOU BLEW IT.
BIG TIME.
?
?

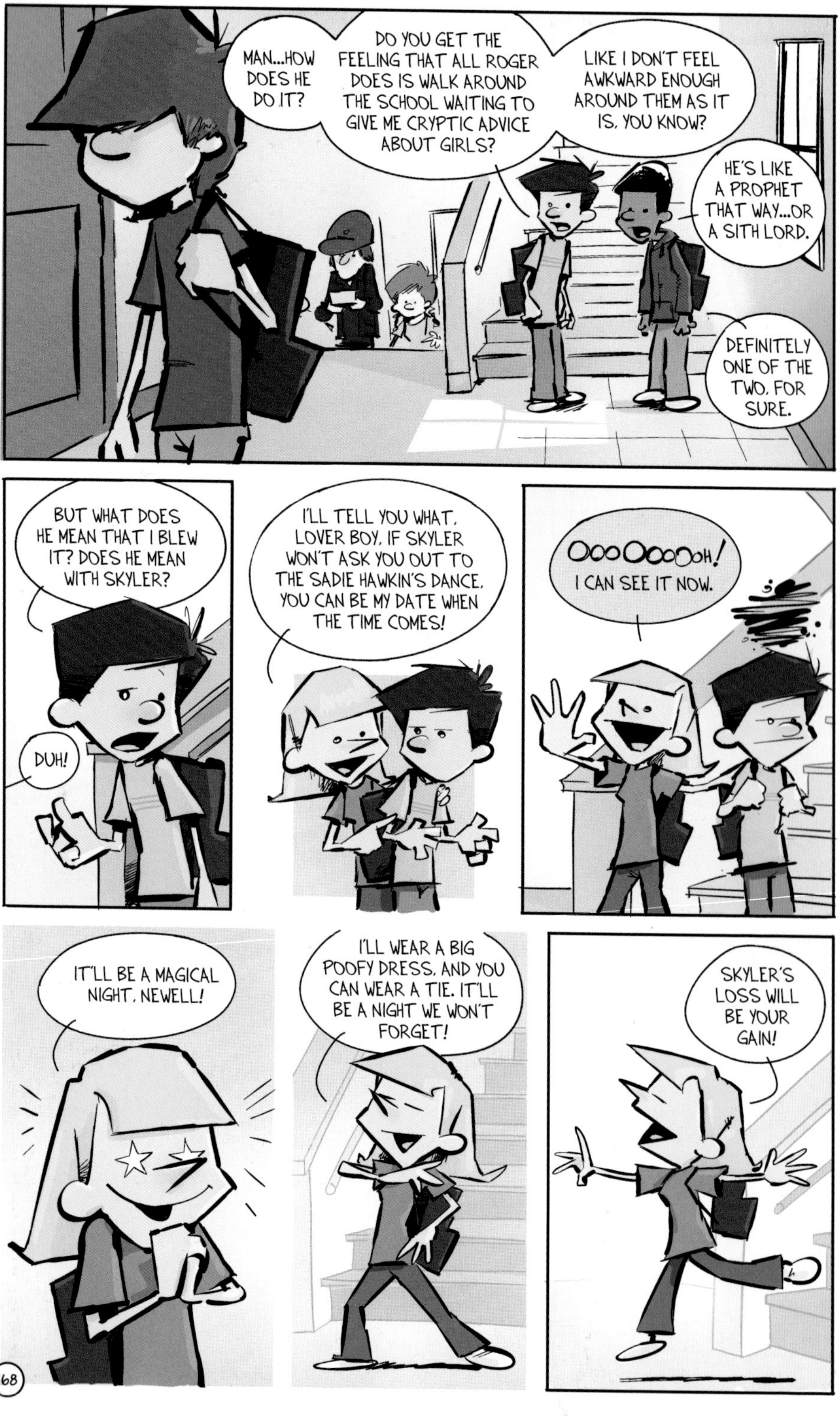
MAN...HOW DOES HE DO IT?
DO YOU GET THE FEELING THAT ALL ROGER DOES IS WALK AROUND THE SCHOOL WAITING TO GIVE ME CRYPTIC ADVICE ABOUT GIRLS?
LIKE I DON'T FEEL AWKWARD ENOUGH AROUND THEM AS IT IS, YOU KNOW?
HE'S LIKE A PROPHET THAT WAY...OR A SITH LORD.
DEFINITELY ONE OF THE TWO, FOR SURE.
BUT WHAT DOES HE MEAN THAT I BLEW IT? DOES HE MEAN WITH SKYLER?
DUH!
I'LL TELL YOU WHAT, LOVER BOY, IF SKYLER WON'T ASK YOU OUT TO THE SADIE HAWKIN'S DANCE, YOU CAN BE MY DATE WHEN THE TIME COMES!
OOOOOOOOH! I CAN SEE IT NOW.
IT'LL BE A MAGICAL NIGHT, NEWELL!
I'LL WEAR A BIG POOFY DRESS, AND YOU CAN WEAR A TIE. IT'LL BE A NIGHT WE WON'T FORGET!
SKYLER'S LOSS WILL BE YOUR GAIN!

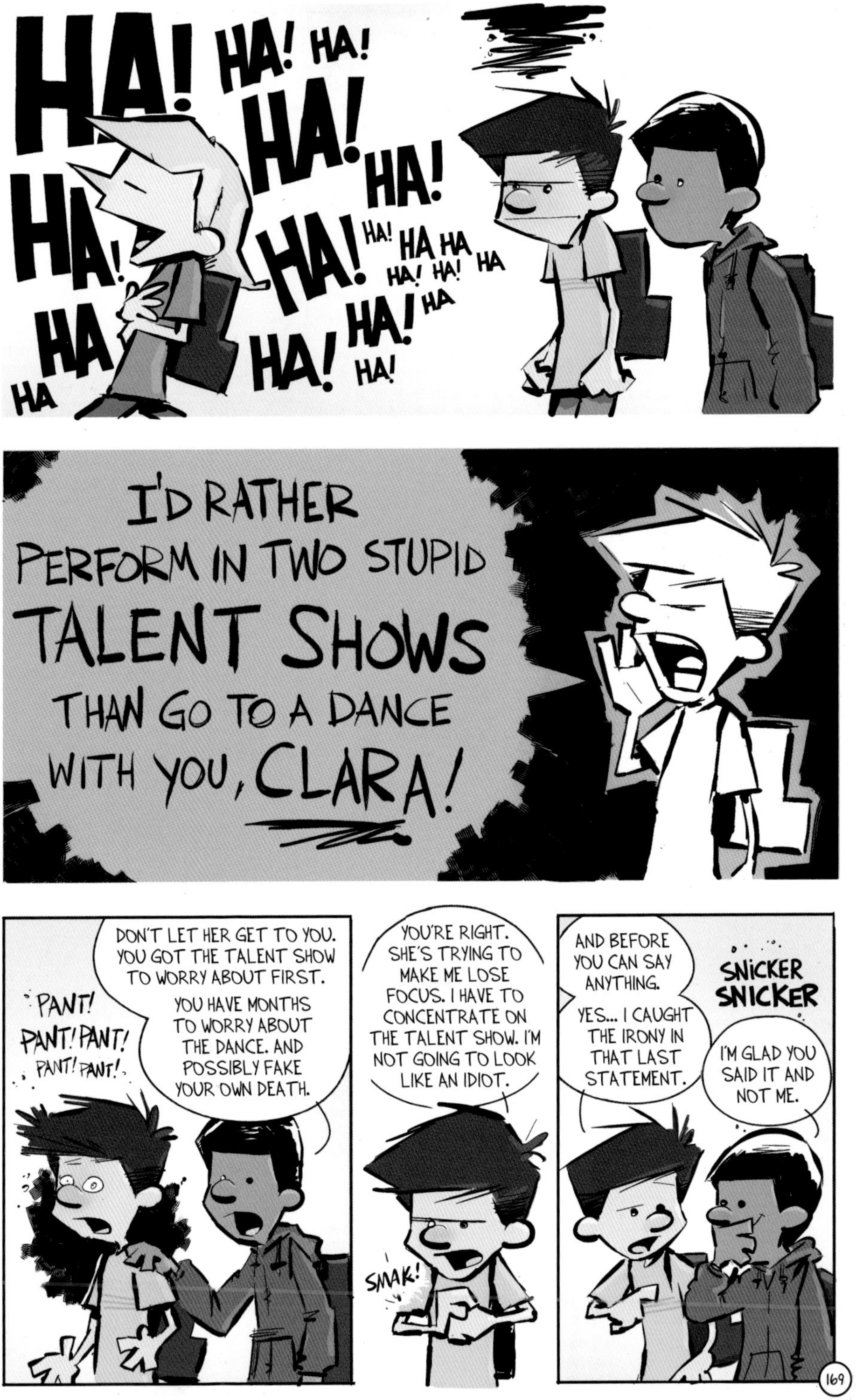
HA! HA! HA!
HA!
HA!
HA!
HA!
HA!
HA! HA HA HA! HA! HA
HA HA
HA! HA! HA HA!
HA
I'D RATHER PERFORM IN TWO STUPID TALENT SHOWS THAN GO TO A DANCE WITH YOU, CLARA!
DON'T LET HER GET TO YOU. YOU GOT THE TALENT SHOW TO WORRY ABOUT FIRST.
PANT! PANT! PANT! PANT! PANT!
YOU HAVE MONTHS TO WORRY ABOUT THE DANCE. AND POSSIBLY FAKE YOUR OWN DEATH.
YOU'RE RIGHT. SHE'S TRYING TO MAKE ME LOSE FOCUS. I HAVE TO CONCENTRATE ON THE TALENT SHOW. I'M NOT GOING TO LOOK LIKE AN IDIOT.
SMAK!
AND BEFORE YOU CAN SAY ANYTHING.
YES... I CAUGHT THE IRONY IN THAT LAST STATEMENT.
SNICKER SNICKER
I'M GLAD YOU SAID IT AND NOT ME.

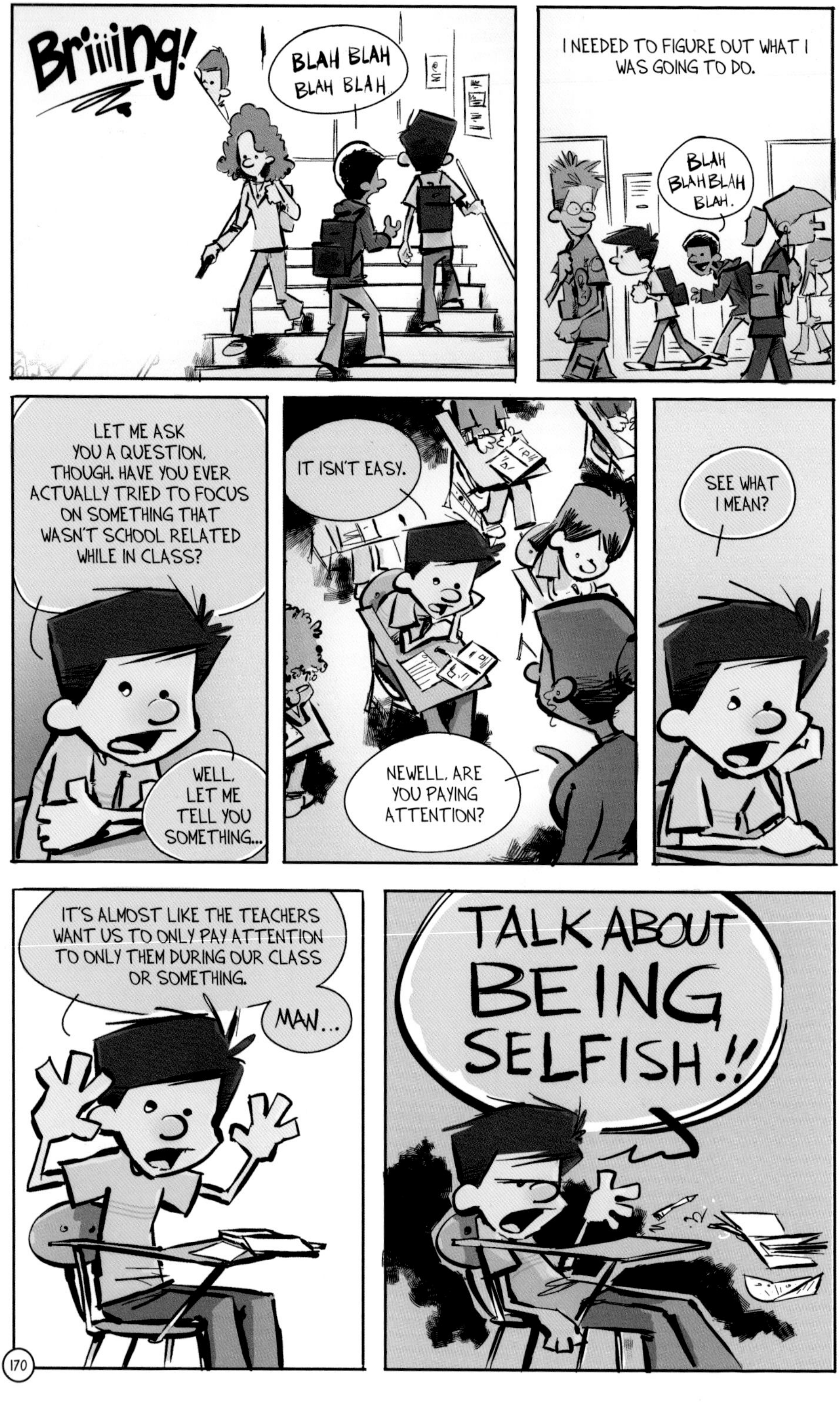
Briiiing!
BLAH BLAH BLAH BLAH
I NEEDED TO FIGURE OUT WHAT I WAS GOING TO DO.
BLAH BLAH BLAH BLAH.
LET ME ASK YOU A QUESTION, THOUGH. HAVE YOU EVER ACTUALLY TRIED TO FOCUS ON SOMETHING THAT WASN'T SCHOOL RELATED WHILE IN CLASS?
WELL, LET ME TELL YOU SOMETHING...
IT ISN'T EASY.
NEWELL, ARE YOU PAYING ATTENTION?
SEE WHAT I MEAN?
IT'S ALMOST LIKE THE TEACHERS WANT US TO ONLY PAY ATTENTION TO ONLY THEM DURING OUR CLASS OR SOMETHING.
MAN...
TALK ABOUT BEING SELFISH!!

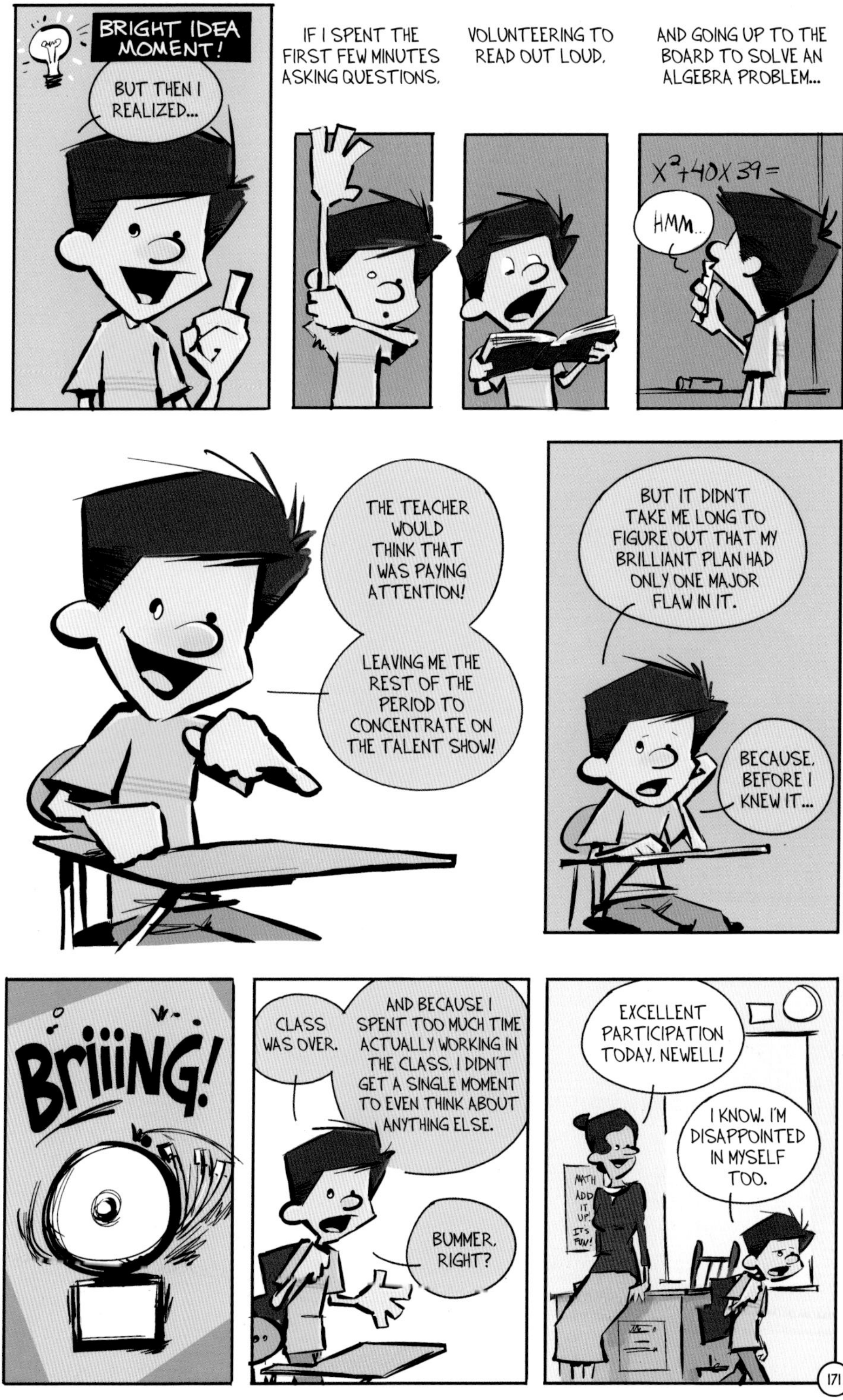

BRIGHT IDEA MOMENT!
BUT THEN I REALIZED...
IF I SPENT THE FIRST FEW MINUTES ASKING QUESTIONS,
VOLUNTEERING TO READ OUT LOUD,
AND GOING UP TO THE BOARD TO SOLVE AN ALGEBRA PROBLEM...
X²+40X 39=
HMM...
THE TEACHER WOULD THINK THAT I WAS PAYING ATTENTION!
LEAVING ME THE REST OF THE PERIOD TO CONCENTRATE ON THE TALENT SHOW!
BUT IT DIDN'T TAKE ME LONG TO FIGURE OUT THAT MY BRILLIANT PLAN HAD ONLY ONE MAJOR FLAW IN IT.
BECAUSE, BEFORE I KNEW IT...
BriiiNG!
CLASS WAS OVER.
AND BECAUSE I SPENT TOO MUCH TIME ACTUALLY WORKING IN THE CLASS, I DIDN'T GET A SINGLE MOMENT TO EVEN THINK ABOUT ANYTHING ELSE.
BUMMER, RIGHT?
EXCELLENT PARTICIPATION TODAY, NEWELL!
MATH ADD IT UP! IT'S FUN!
I KNOW. I'M DISAPPOINTED IN MYSELF TOO.

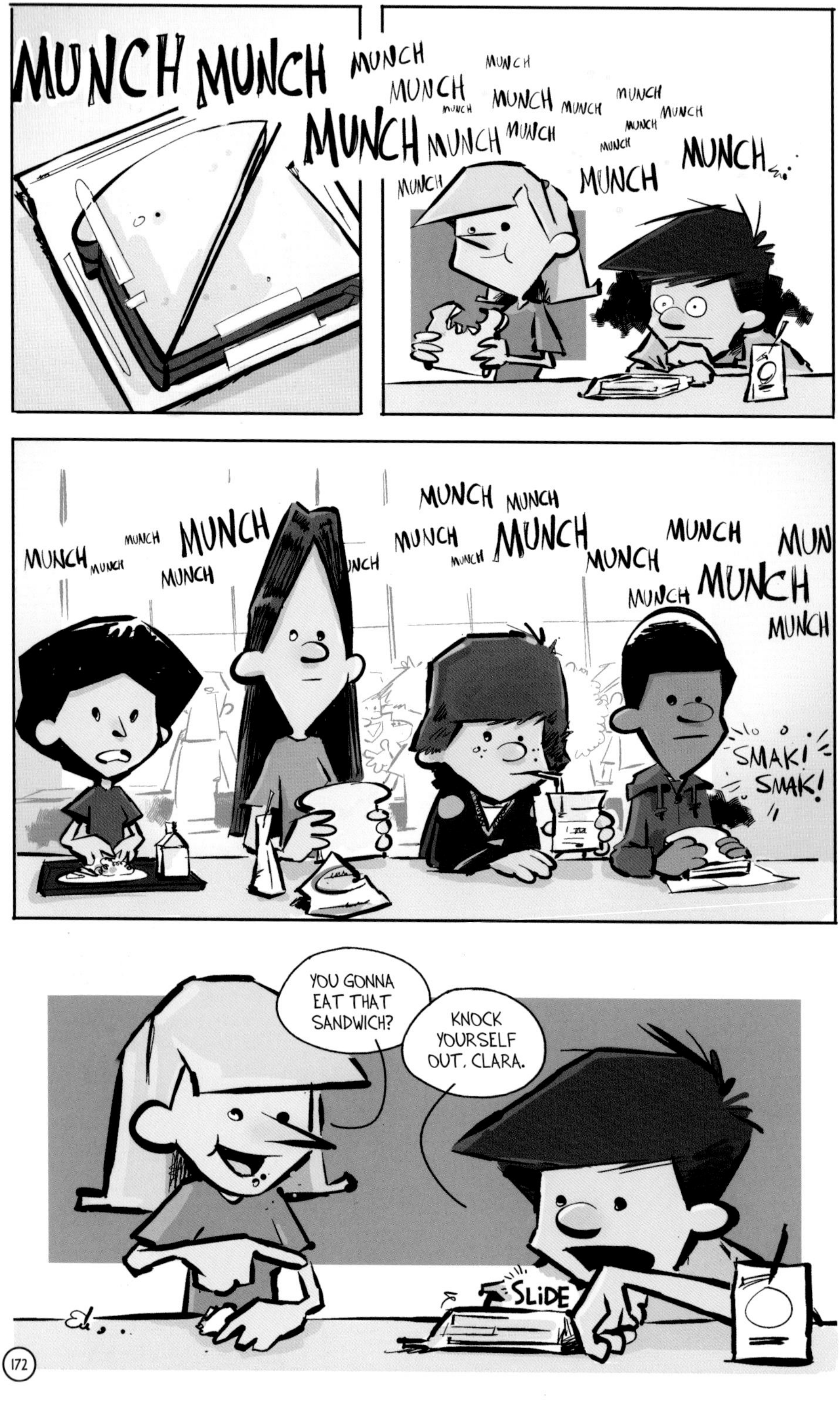
MUNCH MUNCH MUNCH
MUNCH
MUNCH
MUNCH
MUNCH MUNCH
MUNCH
MUNCH
MUNCH
MUNCH MUNCH MUNCH
MUNCH
MUNCH
MUNCH
MUNCH
MUNCH MUNCH
MUNCH
MUNCH
MUNCH
MUNCH
MUNCH
MUNCH
MUNCH
MUNCH
MUNCH
MUNCH
MUNCH
MUNCH
MUNCH
MUNCH
MUNCH
SMAK!
SMAK!
YOU GONNA EAT THAT SANDWICH?
KNOCK YOURSELF OUT, CLARA.
SLIDE

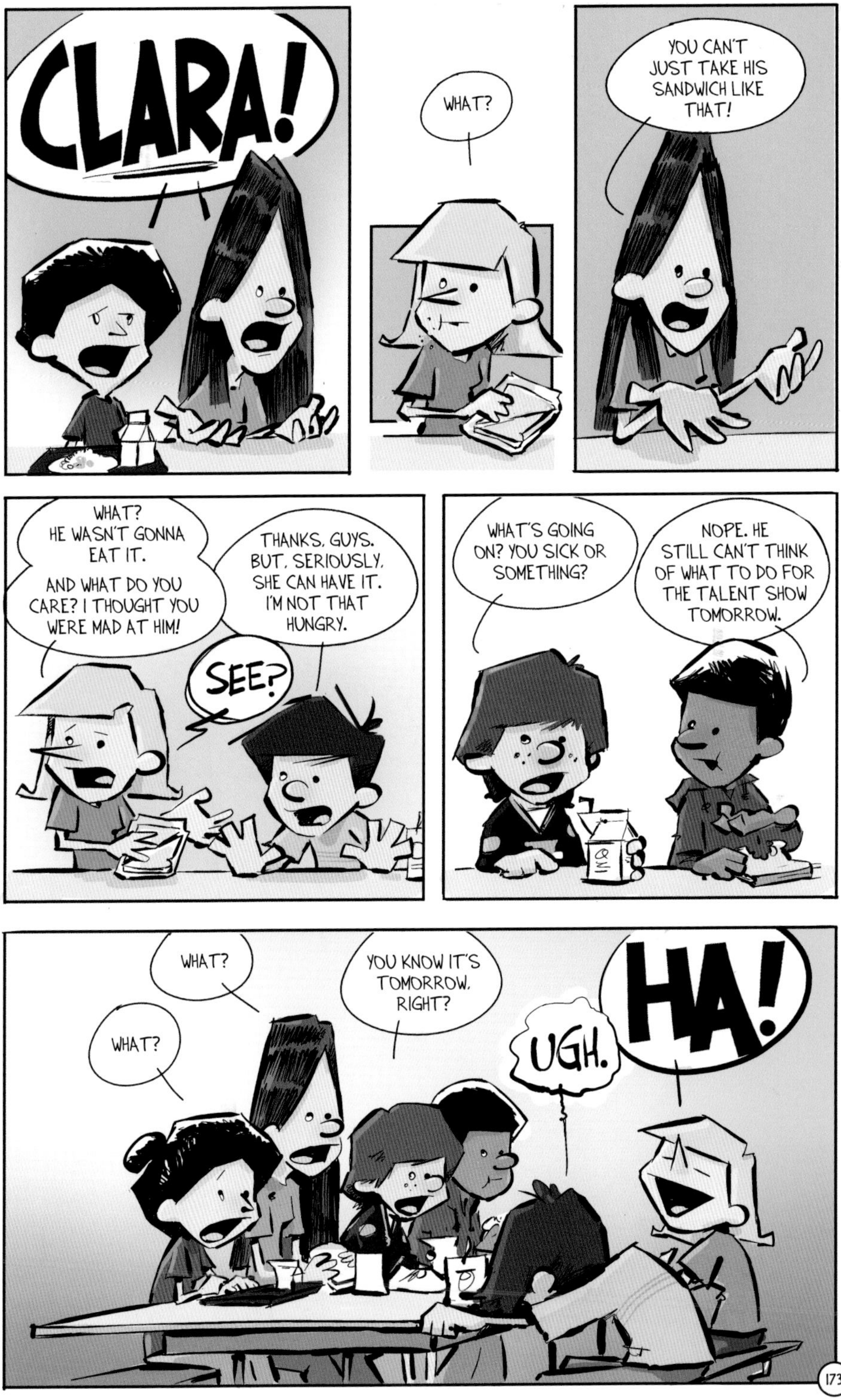
CLARA!
WHAT?
YOU CAN'T JUST TAKE HIS SANDWICH LIKE THAT!
WHAT? HE WASN'T GONNA EAT IT.
AND WHAT DO YOU CARE? I THOUGHT YOU WERE MAD AT HIM!
SEE?
THANKS, GUYS. BUT, SERIOUSLY, SHE CAN HAVE IT. I'M NOT THAT HUNGRY.
WHAT'S GOING ON? YOU SICK OR SOMETHING?
NOPE. HE STILL CAN'T THINK OF WHAT TO DO FOR THE TALENT SHOW TOMORROW.
WHAT?
WHAT?
YOU KNOW IT'S TOMORROW, RIGHT?
UGH.
HA!

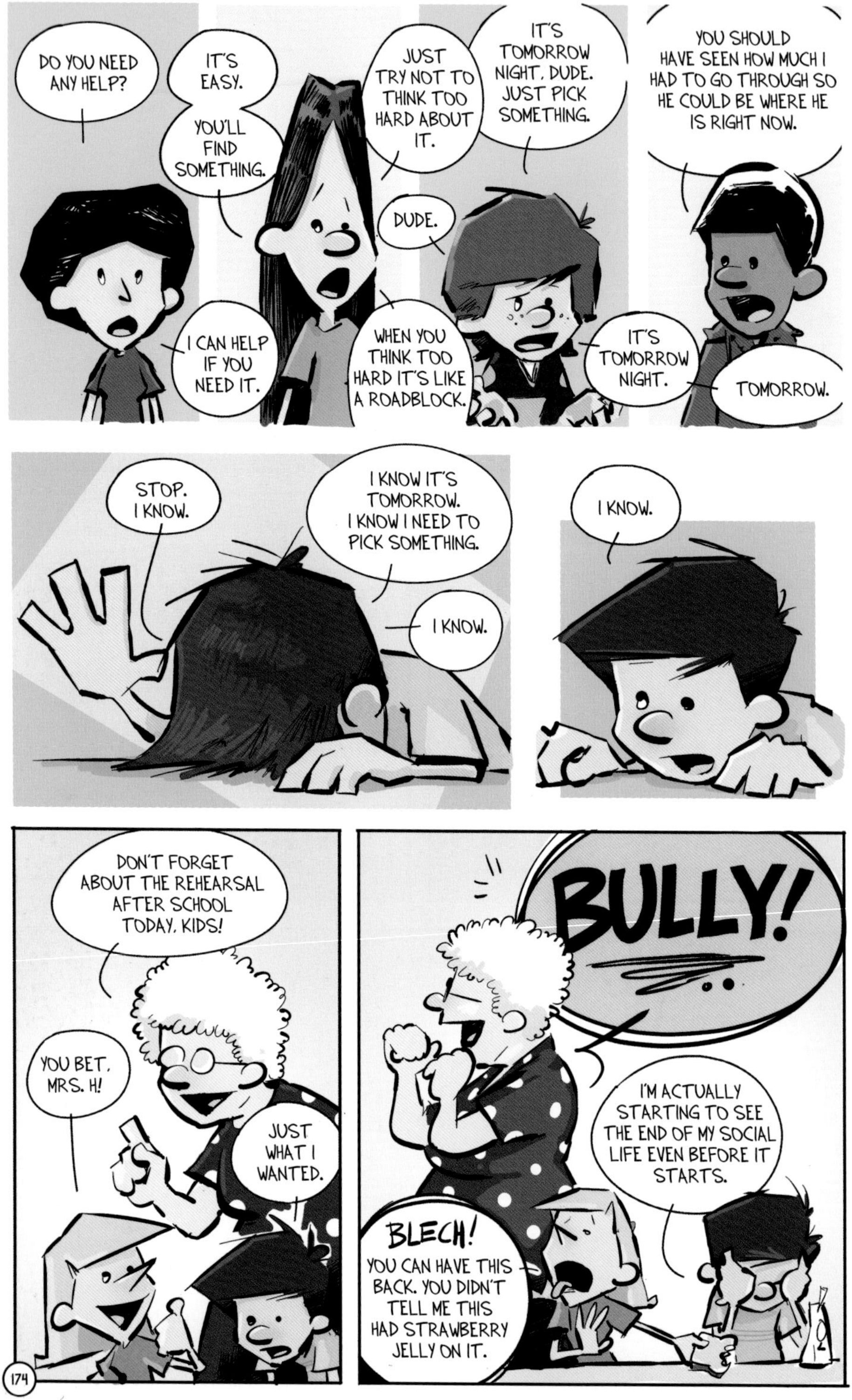
DO YOU NEED ANY HELP?
IT'S EASY.
YOU'LL FIND SOMETHING.
I CAN HELP IF YOU NEED IT.
JUST TRY NOT TO THINK TOO HARD ABOUT IT.
DUDE.
WHEN YOU THINK TOO HARD IT'S LIKE A ROADBLOCK.
IT'S TOMORROW NIGHT, DUDE. JUST PICK SOMETHING.
IT'S TOMORROW NIGHT.
YOU SHOULD HAVE SEEN HOW MUCH I HAD TO GO THROUGH SO HE COULD BE WHERE HE IS RIGHT NOW.
TOMORROW.
STOP. I KNOW.
I KNOW IT'S TOMORROW. I KNOW I NEED TO PICK SOMETHING.
I KNOW.
I KNOW.
DON'T FORGET ABOUT THE REHEARSAL AFTER SCHOOL TODAY, KIDS!
YOU BET, MRS. H!
JUST WHAT I WANTED.
BULLY!
I'M ACTUALLY STARTING TO SEE THE END OF MY SOCIAL LIFE EVEN BEFORE IT STARTS.
BLECH!
YOU CAN HAVE THIS BACK. YOU DIDN'T TELL ME THIS HAD STRAWBERRY JELLY ON IT.

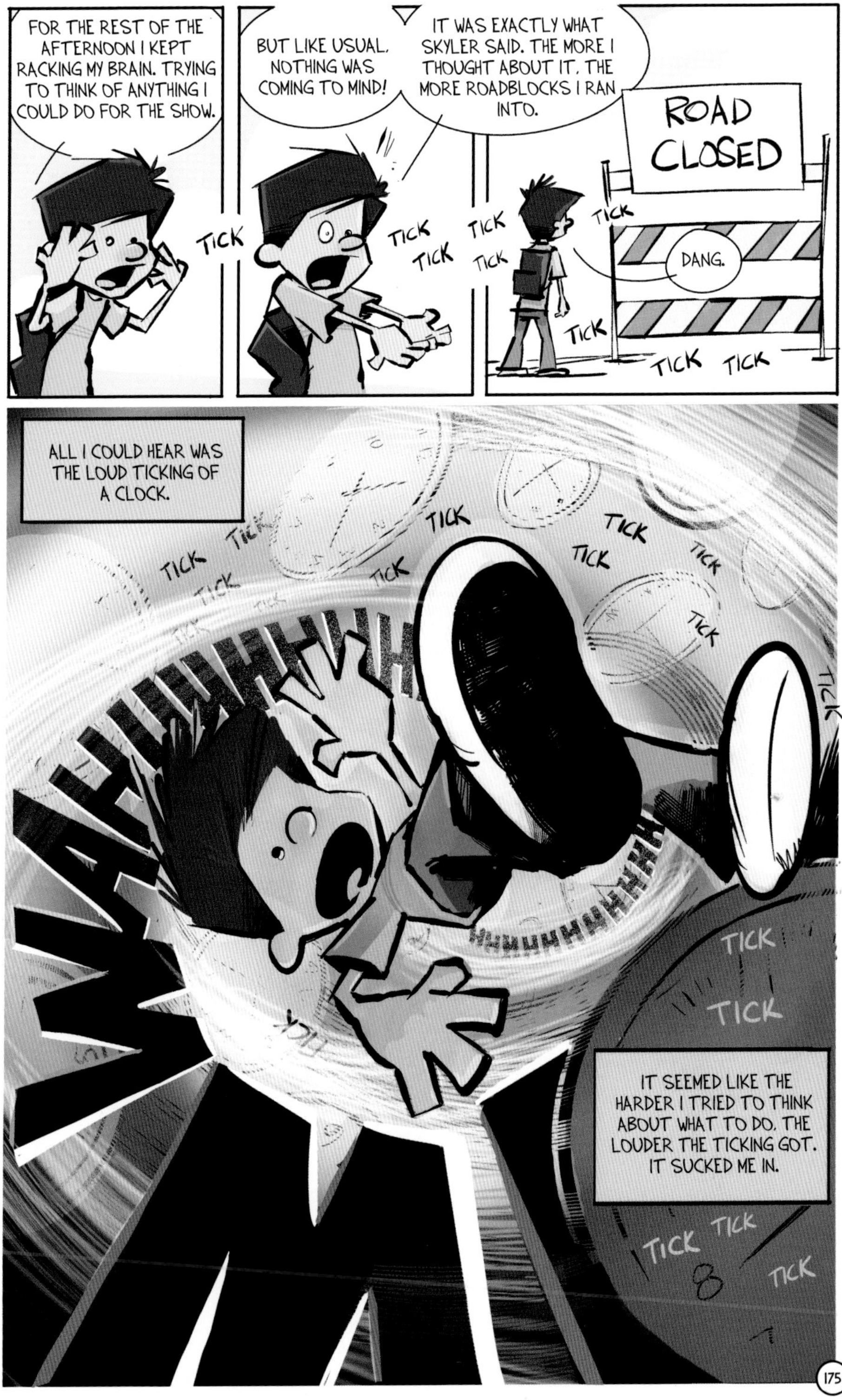
FOR THE REST OF THE AFTERNOON I KEPT RACKING MY BRAIN. TRYING TO THINK OF ANYTHING I COULD DO FOR THE SHOW.
TICK
BUT LIKE USUAL, NOTHING WAS COMING TO MIND!
IT WAS EXACTLY WHAT SKYLER SAID. THE MORE I THOUGHT ABOUT IT, THE MORE ROADBLOCKS I RAN INTO.
TICK
TICK
TICK
TICK
TICK
ROAD CLOSED
DANG.
TICK
TICK
TICK
ALL I COULD HEAR WAS THE LOUD TICKING OF A CLOCK.
WAHHHHHHHHHHHHHHHHHHHHHHH
TICK
TICK
TICK
TICK
TICK
TICK
TICK
TICK
IT SEEMED LIKE THE HARDER I TRIED TO THINK ABOUT WHAT TO DO, THE LOUDER THE TICKING GOT. IT SUCKED ME IN.
TICK
TICK
TICK

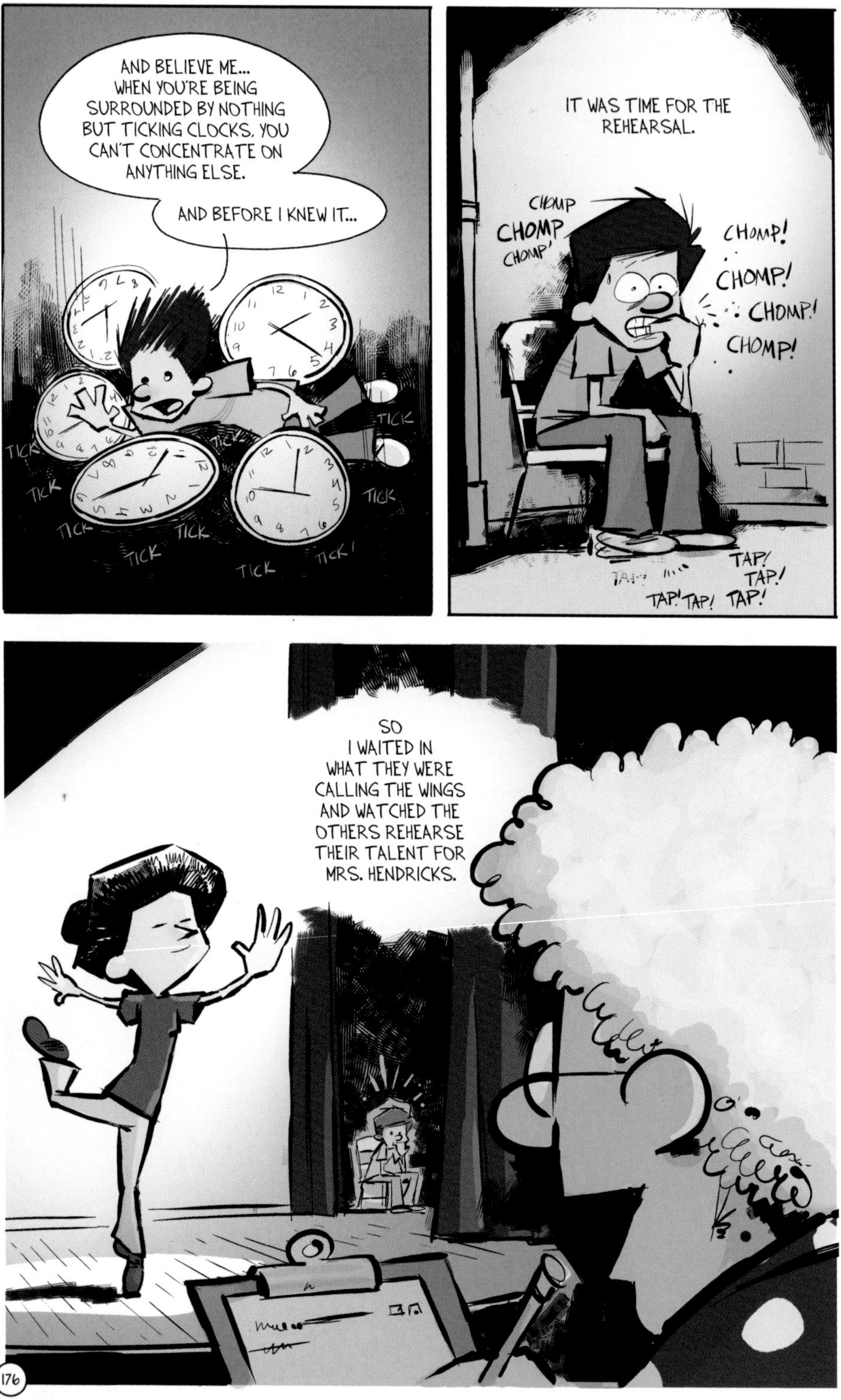
AND BELIEVE ME... WHEN YOU'RE BEING SURROUNDED BY NOTHING BUT TICKING CLOCKS, YOU CAN'T CONCENTRATE ON ANYTHING ELSE.
AND BEFORE I KNEW IT...
TICK
TICK
TICK
TICK
TICK
TICK
TICK
TICK
TICK!
IT WAS TIME FOR THE REHEARSAL.
CHOMP
CHOMP
CHOMP'
CHOMP!
CHOMP!
CHOMP!
CHOMP!
TAP!
TAP!
TAP! TAP! TAP!
SO I WAITED IN WHAT THEY WERE CALLING THE WINGS AND WATCHED THE OTHERS REHEARSE THEIR TALENT FOR MRS. HENDRICKS.

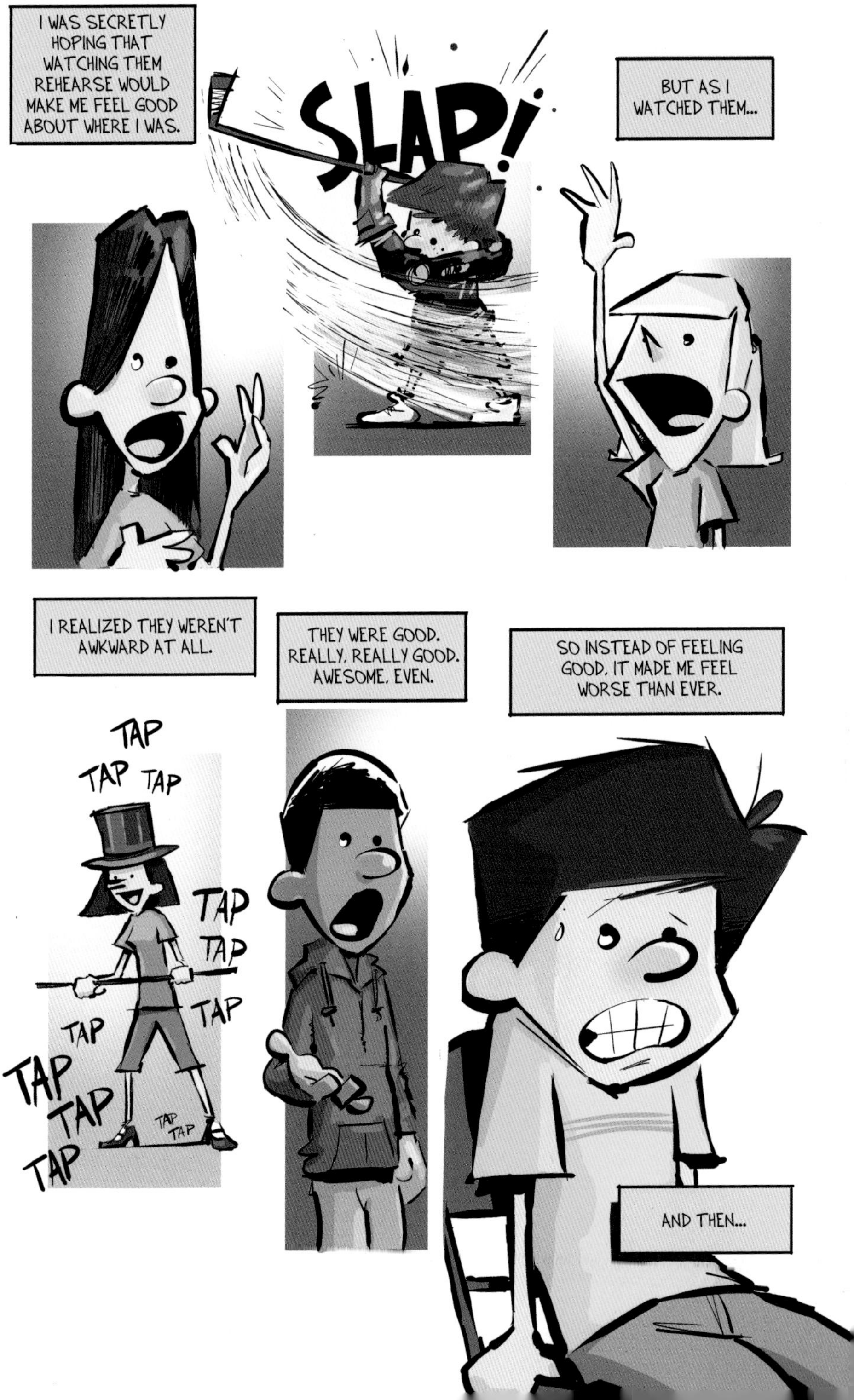
I WAS SECRETLY HOPING THAT WATCHING THEM REHEARSE WOULD MAKE ME FEEL GOOD ABOUT WHERE I WAS.
SLAP!
BUT AS I WATCHED THEM...
I REALIZED THEY WEREN'T AWKWARD AT ALL.
THEY WERE GOOD. REALLY, REALLY GOOD. AWESOME, EVEN.
SO INSTEAD OF FEELING GOOD, IT MADE ME FEEL WORSE THAN EVER.
TAP TAP TAP
TAP TAP TAP
TAP TAP TAP TAP
TAP TAP
AND THEN...

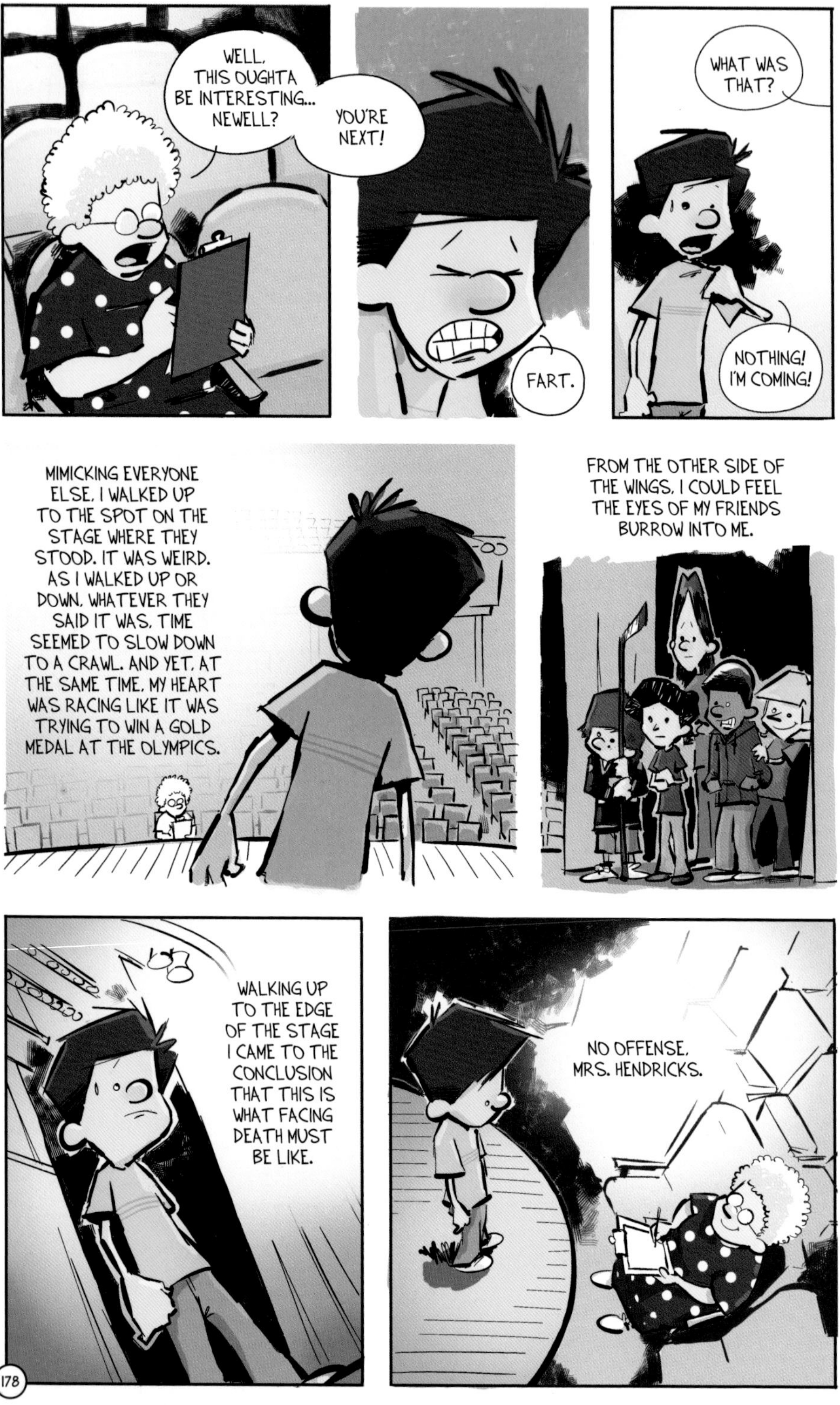
WELL, THIS OUGHTA BE INTERESTING... NEWELL?
YOU'RE NEXT!
FART.
WHAT WAS THAT?
NOTHING! I'M COMING!
MIMICKING EVERYONE ELSE, I WALKED UP TO THE SPOT ON THE STAGE WHERE THEY STOOD. IT WAS WEIRD. AS I WALKED UP OR DOWN, WHATEVER THEY SAID IT WAS, TIME SEEMED TO SLOW DOWN TO A CRAWL. AND YET, AT THE SAME TIME, MY HEART WAS RACING LIKE IT WAS TRYING TO WIN A GOLD MEDAL AT THE OLYMPICS.
FROM THE OTHER SIDE OF THE WINGS, I COULD FEEL THE EYES OF MY FRIENDS BURROW INTO ME.
WALKING UP TO THE EDGE OF THE STAGE I CAME TO THE CONCLUSION THAT THIS IS WHAT FACING DEATH MUST BE LIKE.
NO OFFENSE, MRS. HENDRICKS.

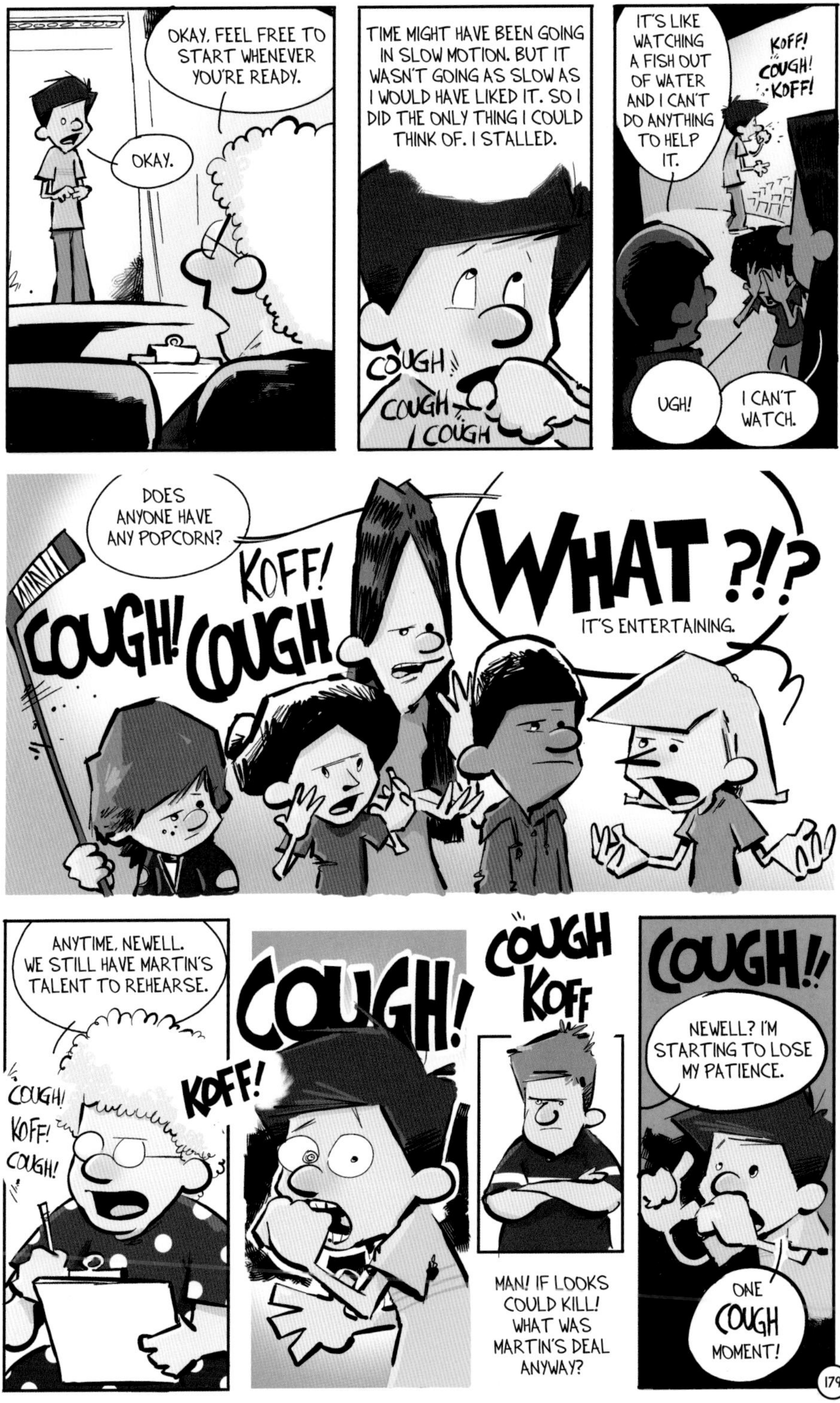
OKAY. FEEL FREE TO START WHENEVER YOU'RE READY.
OKAY.
TIME MIGHT HAVE BEEN GOING IN SLOW MOTION. BUT IT WASN'T GOING AS SLOW AS I WOULD HAVE LIKED IT. SO I DID THE ONLY THING I COULD THINK OF. I STALLED.
COUGH
COUGH
COUGH
IT'S LIKE WATCHING A FISH OUT OF WATER AND I CAN'T DO ANYTHING TO HELP IT.
KOFF! COUGH! KOFF!
UGH!
I CAN'T WATCH.
DOES ANYONE HAVE ANY POPCORN?
COUGH! KOFF! COUGH
WHAT?!?
IT'S ENTERTAINING.
ANYTIME, NEWELL. WE STILL HAVE MARTIN'S TALENT TO REHEARSE.
COUGH! KOFF! COUGH!
KOFF!
COUGH!
COUGH KOFF
MAN! IF LOOKS COULD KILL! WHAT WAS MARTIN'S DEAL ANYWAY?
COUGH!!
NEWELL? I'M STARTING TO LOSE MY PATIENCE.
ONE COUGH MOMENT!

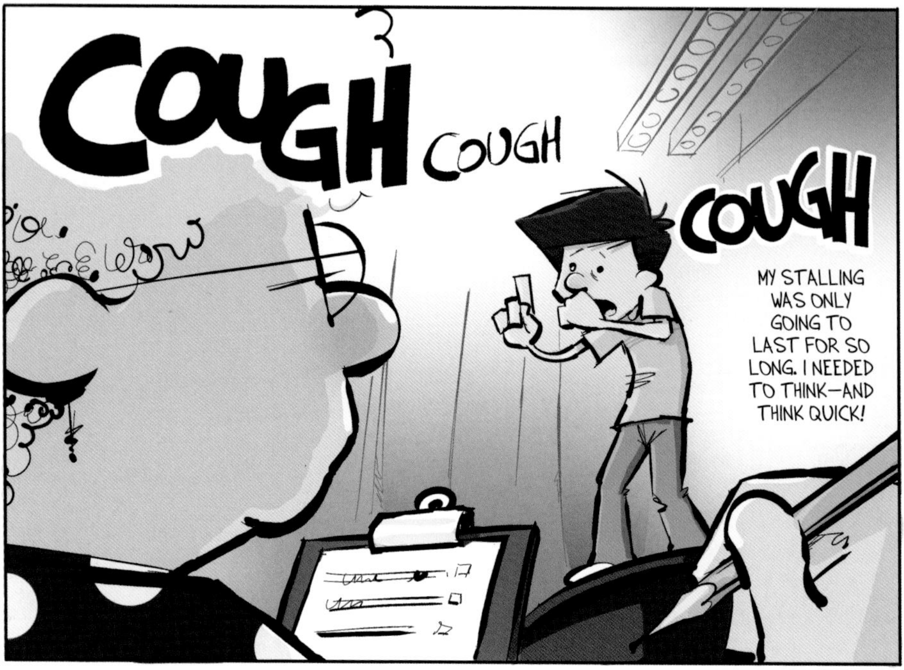
COUGH
COUGH
COUGH
MY STALLING WAS ONLY GOING TO LAST FOR SO LONG. I NEEDED TO THINK—AND THINK QUICK!

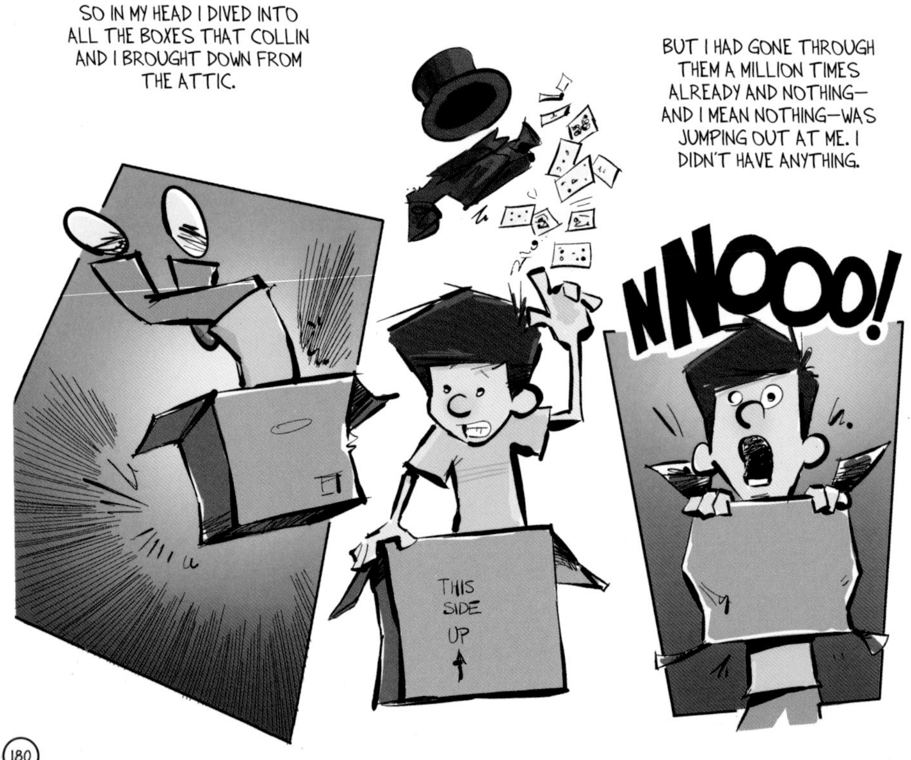
SO IN MY HEAD I DIVED INTO ALL THE BOXES THAT COLLIN AND I BROUGHT DOWN FROM THE ATTIC.
BUT I HAD GONE THROUGH THEM A MILLION TIMES ALREADY AND NOTHING—AND I MEAN NOTHING—WAS JUMPING OUT AT ME. I DIDN'T HAVE ANYTHING.
THIS SIDE UP
NNOOO!

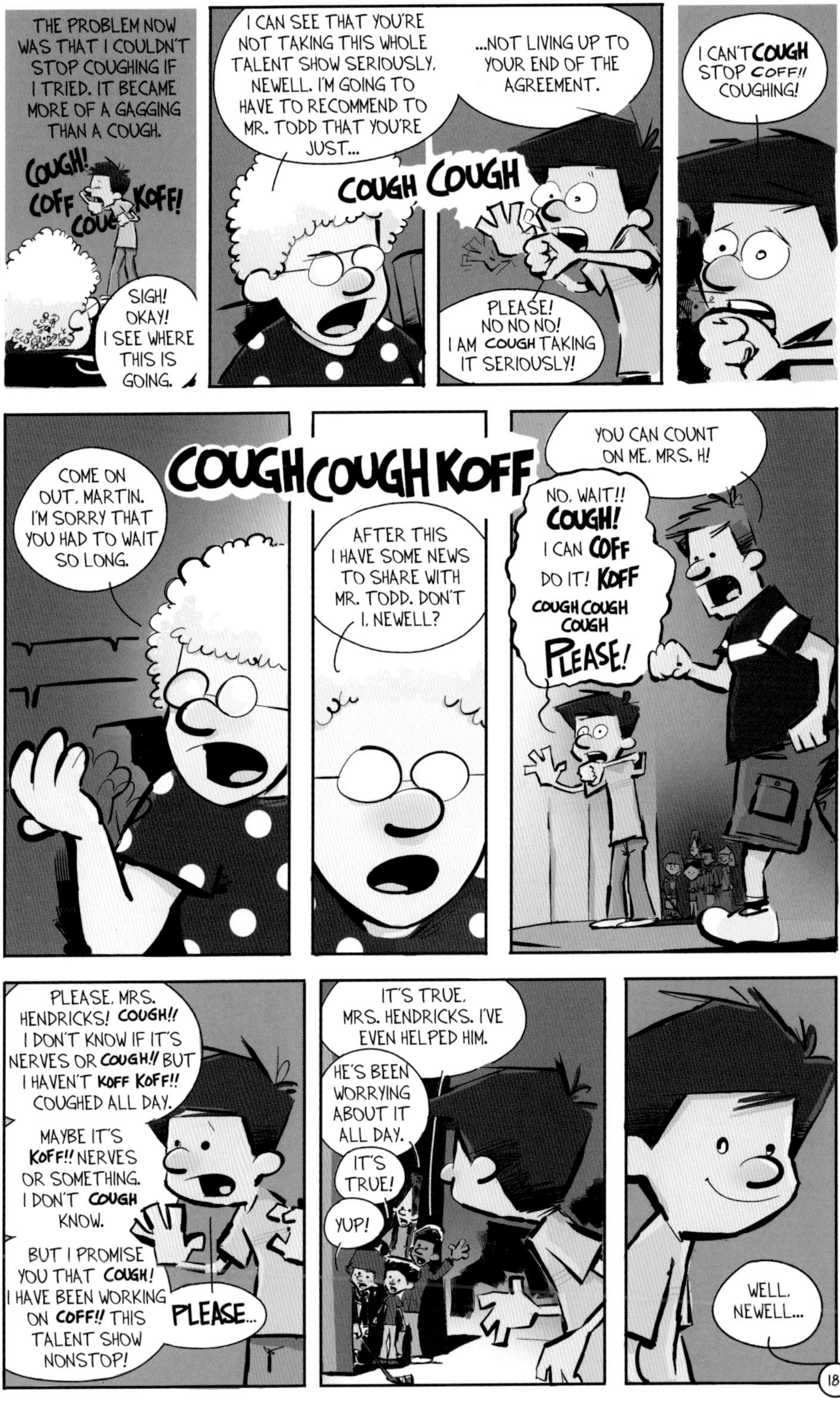
THE PROBLEM NOW WAS THAT I COULDN'T STOP COUGHING IF I TRIED. IT BECAME MORE OF A GAGGING THAN A COUGH.
COUGH!
COFF
KOFF!
SIGH! OKAY! I SEE WHERE THIS IS GOING.
I CAN SEE THAT YOU'RE NOT TAKING THIS WHOLE TALENT SHOW SERIOUSLY, NEWELL. I'M GOING TO HAVE TO RECOMMEND TO MR. TODD THAT YOU'RE JUST...
...NOT LIVING UP TO YOUR END OF THE AGREEMENT.
COUGH COUGH
PLEASE! NO NO NO! I AM COUGH TAKING IT SERIOUSLY!
I CAN'T COUGH STOP COFF!! COUGHING!
COUGH COUGH KOFF
COME ON OUT, MARTIN. I'M SORRY THAT YOU HAD TO WAIT SO LONG.
AFTER THIS I HAVE SOME NEWS TO SHARE WITH MR. TODD. DON'T I, NEWELL?
YOU CAN COUNT ON ME, MRS. H!
NO, WAIT!! COUGH! I CAN COFF DO IT! KOFF COUGH COUGH COUGH PLEASE!
PLEASE, MRS. HENDRICKS! COUGH!! I DON'T KNOW IF IT'S NERVES OR COUGH!! BUT I HAVEN'T KOFF KOFF!! COUGHED ALL DAY.
MAYBE IT'S KOFF!! NERVES OR SOMETHING. I DON'T COUGH KNOW.
BUT I PROMISE YOU THAT COUGH! I HAVE BEEN WORKING ON COFF!! THIS TALENT SHOW NONSTOP!
PLEASE...
IT'S TRUE, MRS. HENDRICKS. I'VE EVEN HELPED HIM.
HE'S BEEN WORRYING ABOUT IT ALL DAY.
IT'S TRUE!
YUP!
WELL, NEWELL...

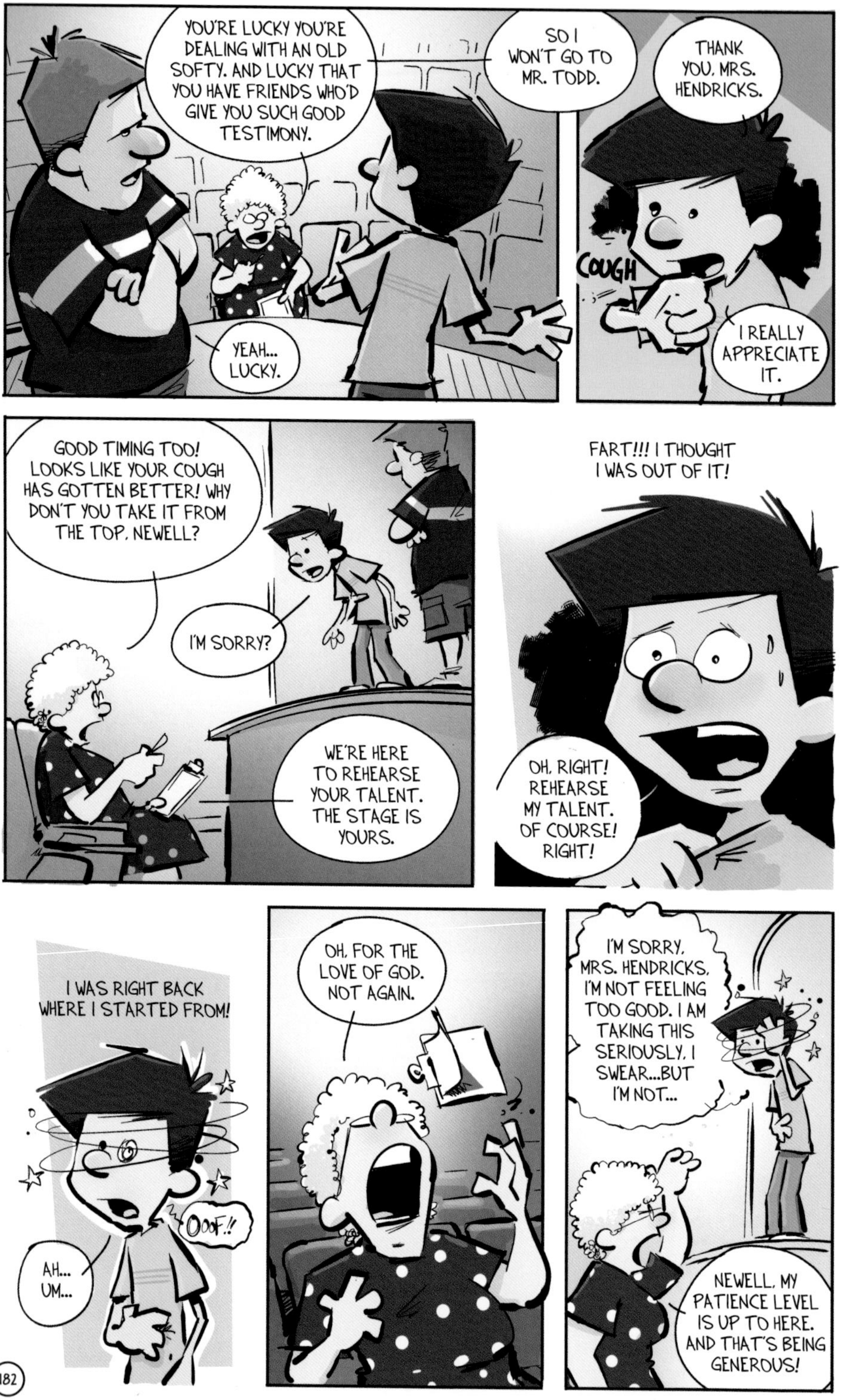
YOU'RE LUCKY YOU'RE DEALING WITH AN OLD SOFTY. AND LUCKY THAT YOU HAVE FRIENDS WHO'D GIVE YOU SUCH GOOD TESTIMONY.
SO I WON'T GO TO MR. TODD.
YEAH... LUCKY.
THANK YOU, MRS. HENDRICKS.
COUGH
I REALLY APPRECIATE IT.
GOOD TIMING TOO! LOOKS LIKE YOUR COUGH HAS GOTTEN BETTER! WHY DON'T YOU TAKE IT FROM THE TOP, NEWELL?
I'M SORRY?
WE'RE HERE TO REHEARSE YOUR TALENT. THE STAGE IS YOURS.
FART!!! I THOUGHT I WAS OUT OF IT!
OH, RIGHT! REHEARSE MY TALENT. OF COURSE! RIGHT!
I WAS RIGHT BACK WHERE I STARTED FROM!
OOOF!!
AH... UM...
OH, FOR THE LOVE OF GOD. NOT AGAIN.
I'M SORRY, MRS. HENDRICKS, I'M NOT FEELING TOO GOOD. I AM TAKING THIS SERIOUSLY, I SWEAR...BUT I'M NOT...
NEWELL, MY PATIENCE LEVEL IS UP TO HERE. AND THAT'S BEING GENEROUS!

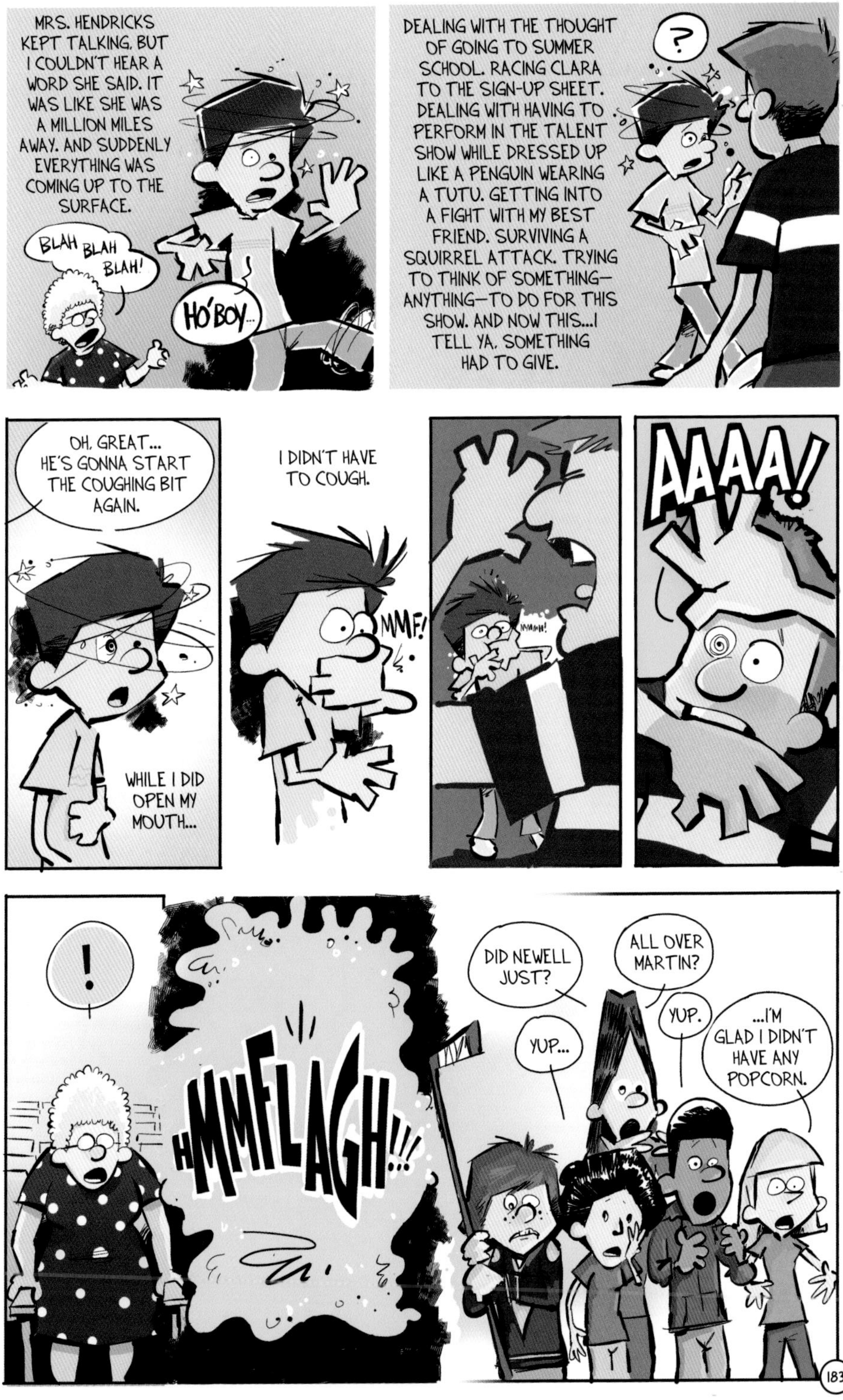
MRS. HENDRICKS KEPT TALKING, BUT I COULDN'T HEAR A WORD SHE SAID. IT WAS LIKE SHE WAS A MILLION MILES AWAY. AND SUDDENLY EVERYTHING WAS COMING UP TO THE SURFACE.
BLAH BLAH BLAH!
HO'BOY...
DEALING WITH THE THOUGHT OF GOING TO SUMMER SCHOOL. RACING CLARA TO THE SIGN-UP SHEET. DEALING WITH HAVING TO PERFORM IN THE TALENT SHOW WHILE DRESSED UP LIKE A PENGUIN WEARING A TUTU. GETTING INTO A FIGHT WITH MY BEST FRIEND. SURVIVING A SQUIRREL ATTACK. TRYING TO THINK OF SOMETHING—ANYTHING—TO DO FOR THIS SHOW. AND NOW THIS...I TELL YA, SOMETHING HAD TO GIVE.
?
OH, GREAT... HE'S GONNA START THE COUGHING BIT AGAIN.
WHILE I DID OPEN MY MOUTH...
I DIDN'T HAVE TO COUGH.
MMF!
AAAA!
!
HMMFLAGH!!!
DID NEWELL JUST?
ALL OVER MARTIN?
YUP...
YUP.
...I'M GLAD I DIDN'T HAVE ANY POPCORN.

CHAPTER TEN
ICY METAPHORS

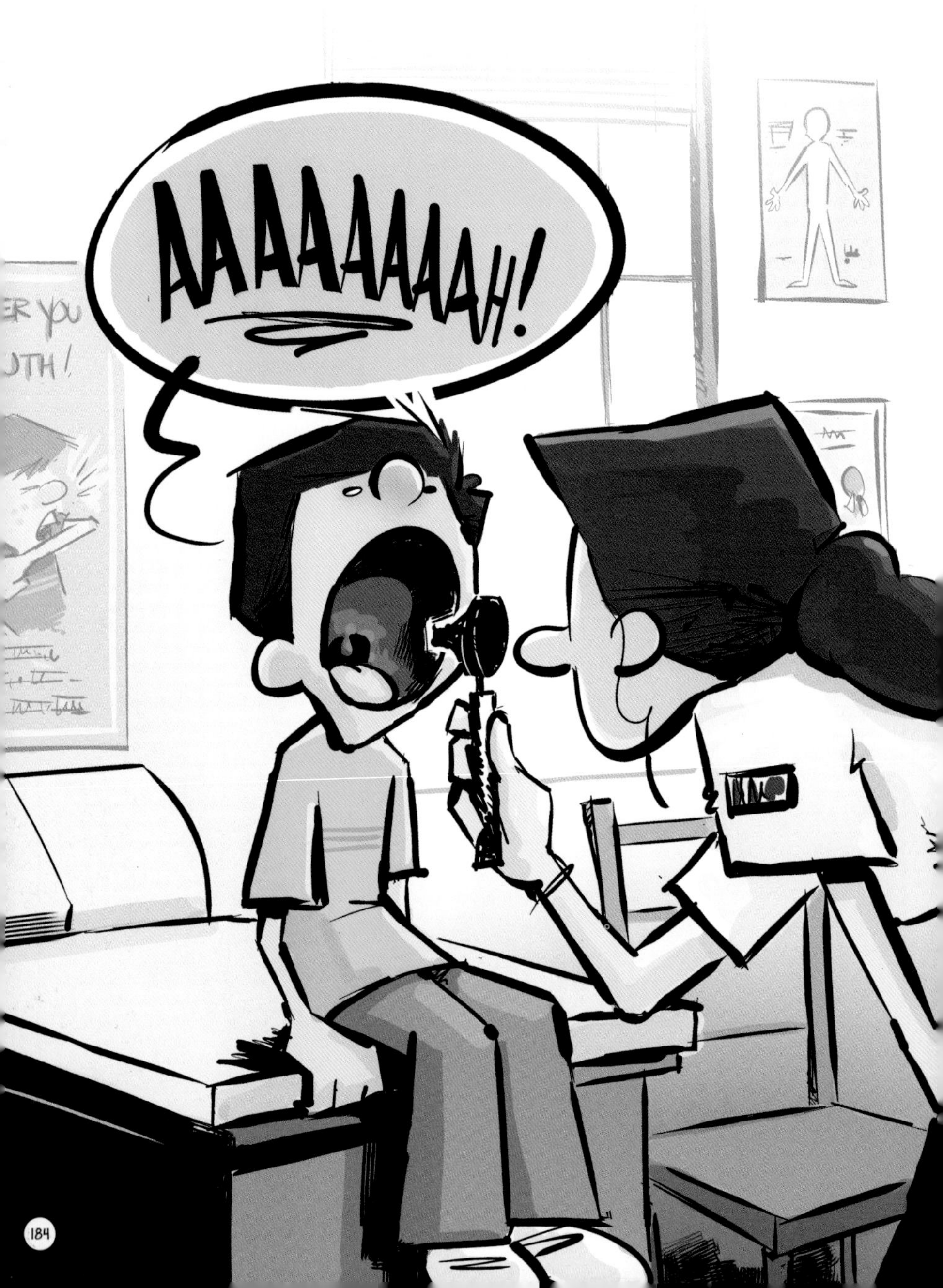
AAAAAAAAH!

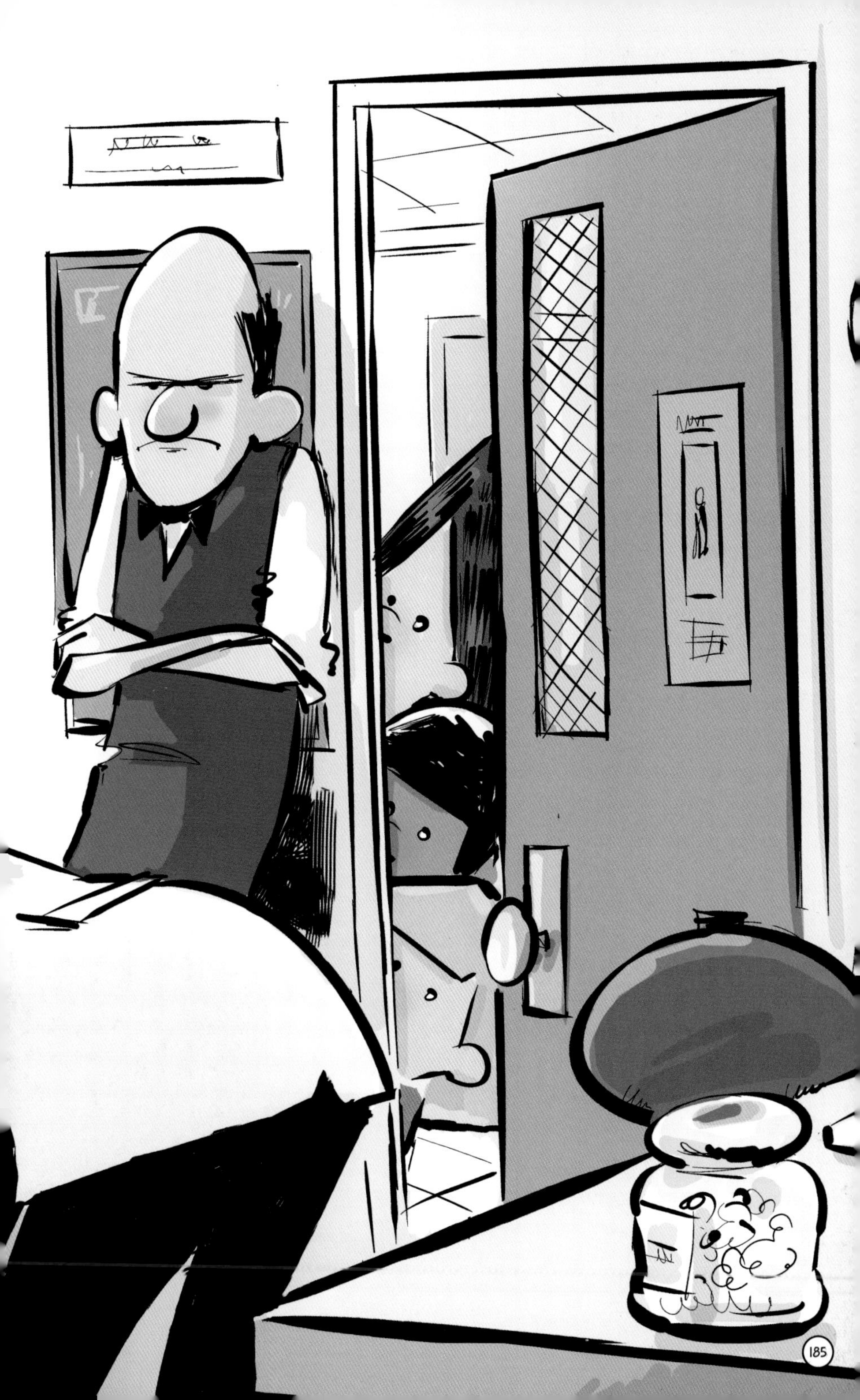

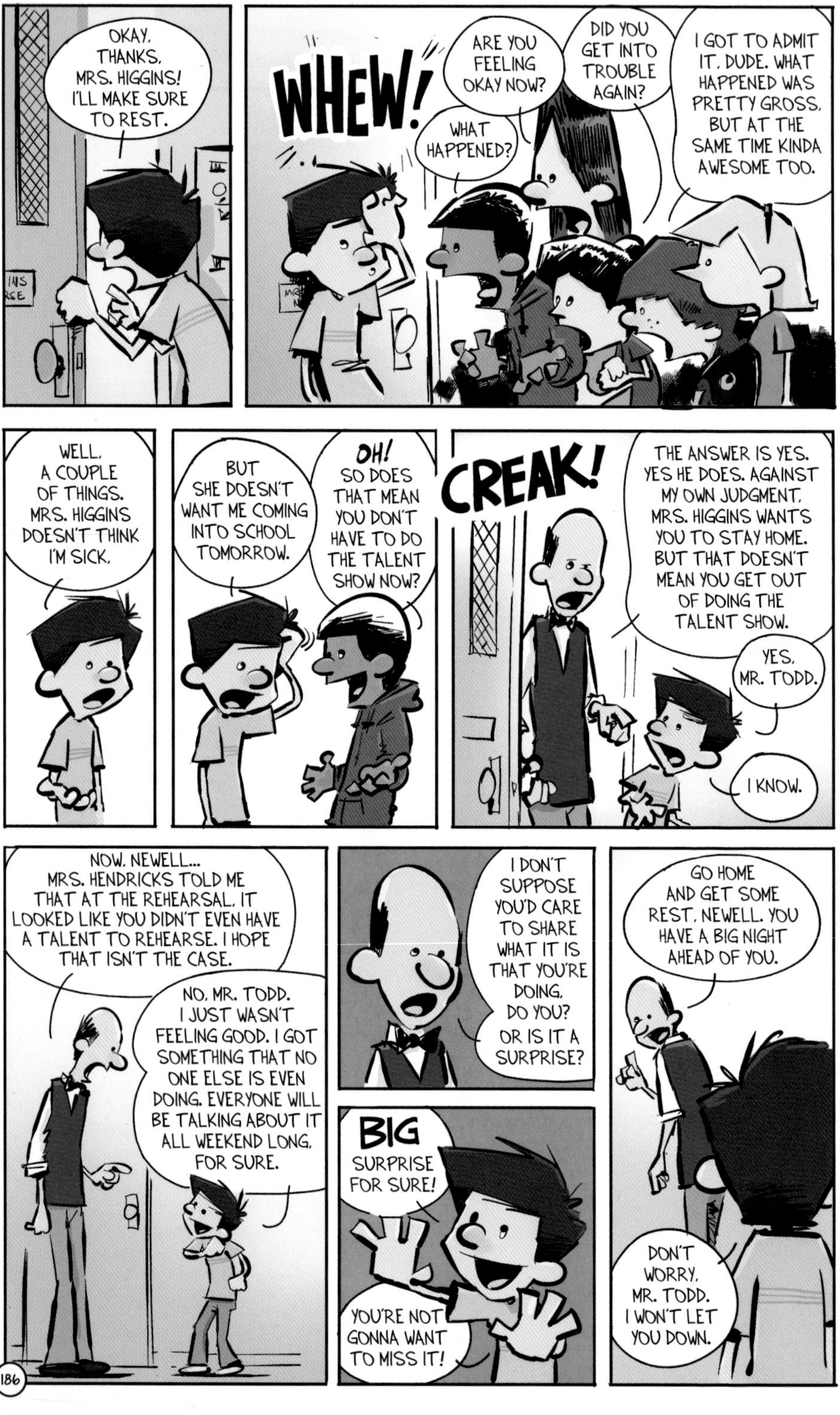
OKAY, THANKS, MRS. HIGGINS! I'LL MAKE SURE TO REST.
WHEW!
ARE YOU FEELING OKAY NOW?
WHAT HAPPENED?
DID YOU GET INTO TROUBLE AGAIN?
I GOT TO ADMIT IT, DUDE. WHAT HAPPENED WAS PRETTY GROSS, BUT AT THE SAME TIME KINDA AWESOME TOO.
WELL, A COUPLE OF THINGS. MRS. HIGGINS DOESN'T THINK I'M SICK,
BUT SHE DOESN'T WANT ME COMING INTO SCHOOL TOMORROW.
OH! SO DOES THAT MEAN YOU DON'T HAVE TO DO THE TALENT SHOW NOW?
CREAK!
THE ANSWER IS YES. YES HE DOES. AGAINST MY OWN JUDGMENT, MRS. HIGGINS WANTS YOU TO STAY HOME. BUT THAT DOESN'T MEAN YOU GET OUT OF DOING THE TALENT SHOW.
YES, MR. TODD.
I KNOW.
NOW, NEWELL... MRS. HENDRICKS TOLD ME THAT AT THE REHEARSAL, IT LOOKED LIKE YOU DIDN'T EVEN HAVE A TALENT TO REHEARSE. I HOPE THAT ISN'T THE CASE.
NO, MR. TODD. I JUST WASN'T FEELING GOOD. I GOT SOMETHING THAT NO ONE ELSE IS EVEN DOING. EVERYONE WILL BE TALKING ABOUT IT ALL WEEKEND LONG, FOR SURE.
I DON'T SUPPOSE YOU'D CARE TO SHARE WHAT IT IS THAT YOU'RE DOING, DO YOU?
OR IS IT A SURPRISE?
BIG SURPRISE FOR SURE!
YOU'RE NOT GONNA WANT TO MISS IT!
GO HOME AND GET SOME REST, NEWELL. YOU HAVE A BIG NIGHT AHEAD OF YOU.
DON'T WORRY, MR. TODD. I WON'T LET YOU DOWN.

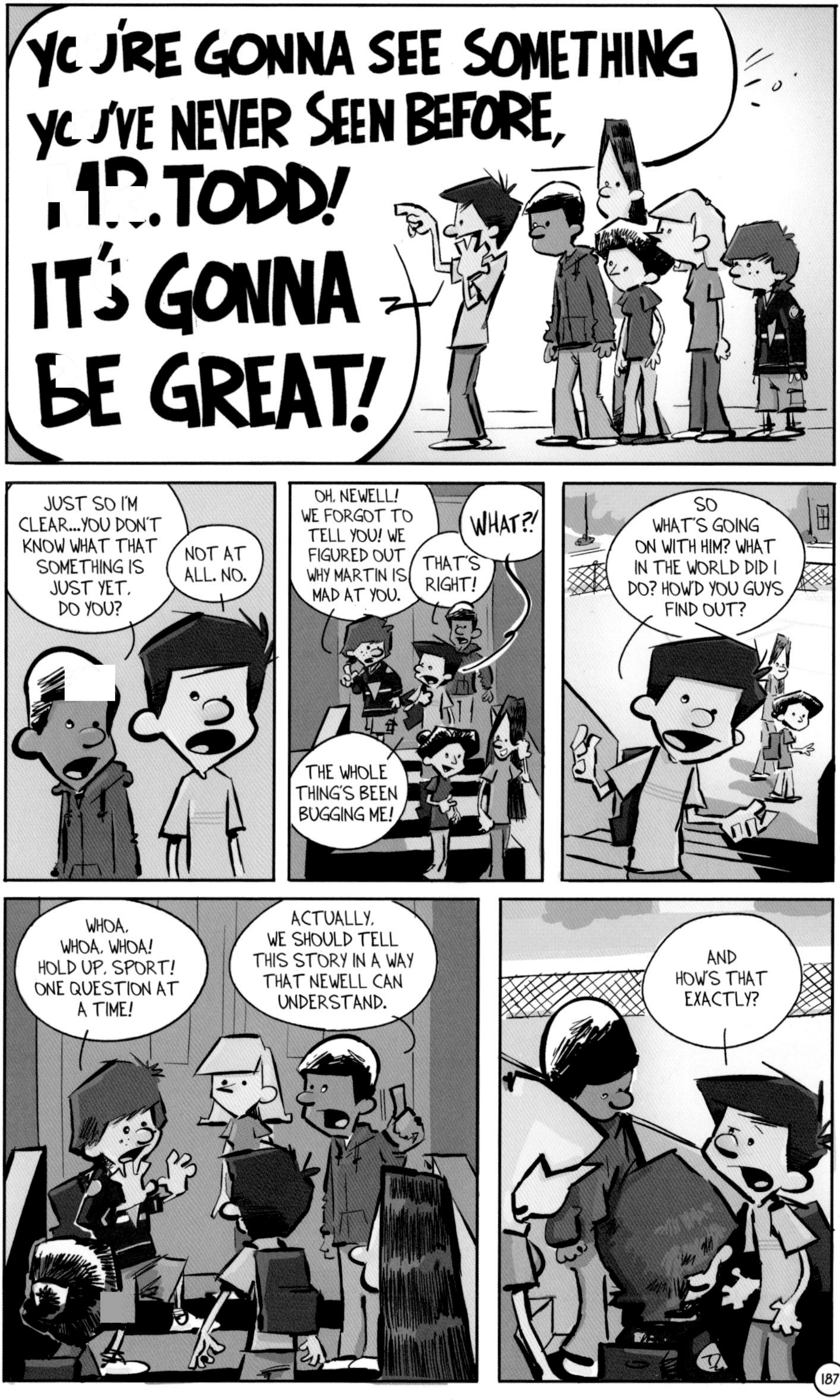
YOU'RE GONNA SEE SOMETHING YOU'VE NEVER SEEN BEFORE, TODD! IT'S GONNA BE GREAT!
JUST SO I'M CLEAR...YOU DON'T KNOW WHAT THAT SOMETHING IS JUST YET, DO YOU?
NOT AT ALL. NO.
OH, NEWELL! WE FORGOT TO TELL YOU! WE FIGURED OUT WHY MARTIN IS MAD AT YOU.
THAT'S RIGHT!
WHAT?!
THE WHOLE THING'S BEEN BUGGING ME!
SO WHAT'S GOING ON WITH HIM? WHAT IN THE WORLD DID I DO? HOW'D YOU GUYS FIND OUT?
WHOA, WHOA, WHOA! HOLD UP, SPORT! ONE QUESTION AT A TIME!
ACTUALLY, WE SHOULD TELL THIS STORY IN A WAY THAT NEWELL CAN UNDERSTAND.
AND HOW'S THAT EXACTLY?

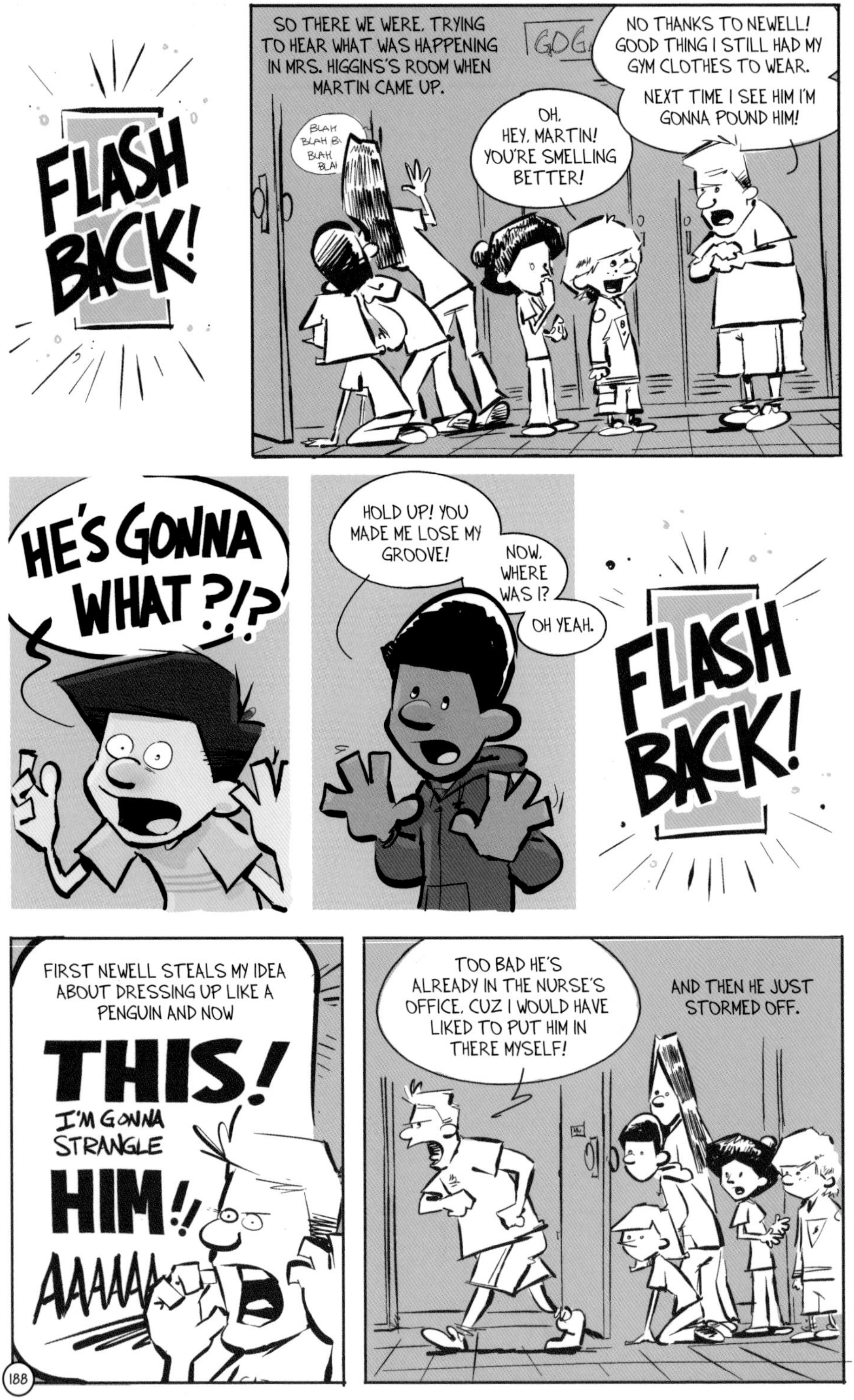
FLASH BACK!
SO THERE WE WERE, TRYING TO HEAR WHAT WAS HAPPENING IN MRS. HIGGINS'S ROOM WHEN MARTIN CAME UP.
BLAH BLAH BLAH BLAH
NO THANKS TO NEWELL! GOOD THING I STILL HAD MY GYM CLOTHES TO WEAR.
NEXT TIME I SEE HIM I'M GONNA POUND HIM!
OH, HEY, MARTIN! YOU'RE SMELLING BETTER!
HE'S GONNA WHAT?!?
HOLD UP! YOU MADE ME LOSE MY GROOVE!
NOW, WHERE WAS I?
OH YEAH.
FLASH BACK!
FIRST NEWELL STEALS MY IDEA ABOUT DRESSING UP LIKE A PENGUIN AND NOW
THIS!
I'M GONNA STRANGLE
HIM!!
AAAAAA
TOO BAD HE'S ALREADY IN THE NURSE'S OFFICE, CUZ I WOULD HAVE LIKED TO PUT HIM IN THERE MYSELF!
AND THEN HE JUST STORMED OFF.

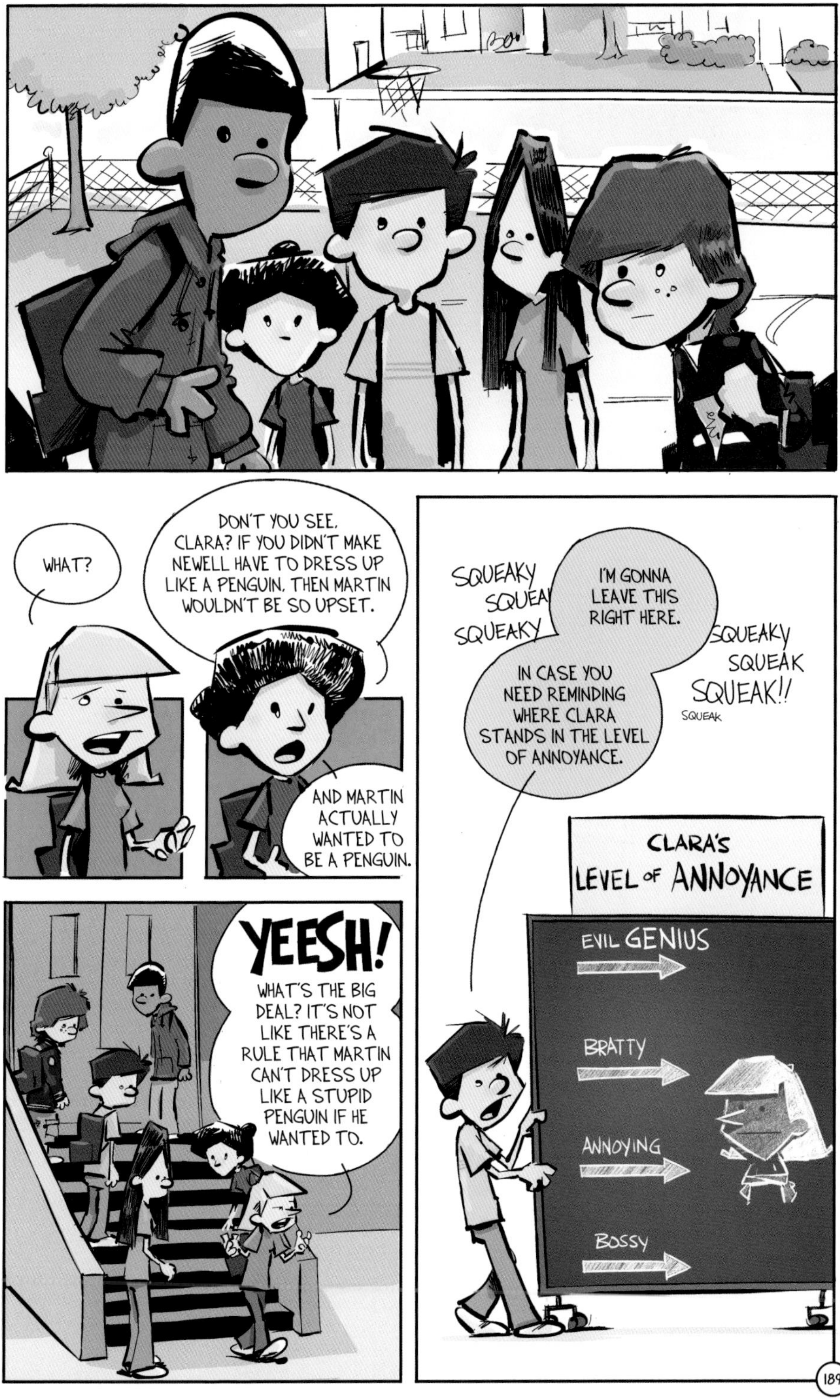
WHAT?
DON'T YOU SEE, CLARA? IF YOU DIDN'T MAKE NEWELL HAVE TO DRESS UP LIKE A PENGUIN, THEN MARTIN WOULDN'T BE SO UPSET.
AND MARTIN ACTUALLY WANTED TO BE A PENGUIN.
YEESH!
WHAT'S THE BIG DEAL? IT'S NOT LIKE THERE'S A RULE THAT MARTIN CAN'T DRESS UP LIKE A STUPID PENGUIN IF HE WANTED TO.
SQUEAKY
SQUEAK
SQUEAKY
I'M GONNA LEAVE THIS RIGHT HERE.
SQUEAKY
SQUEAK
SQUEAK!!
SQUEAK
IN CASE YOU NEED REMINDING WHERE CLARA STANDS IN THE LEVEL OF ANNOYANCE.
CLARA'S LEVEL OF ANNOYANCE
EVIL GENIUS
BRATTY
ANNOYING
BOSSY

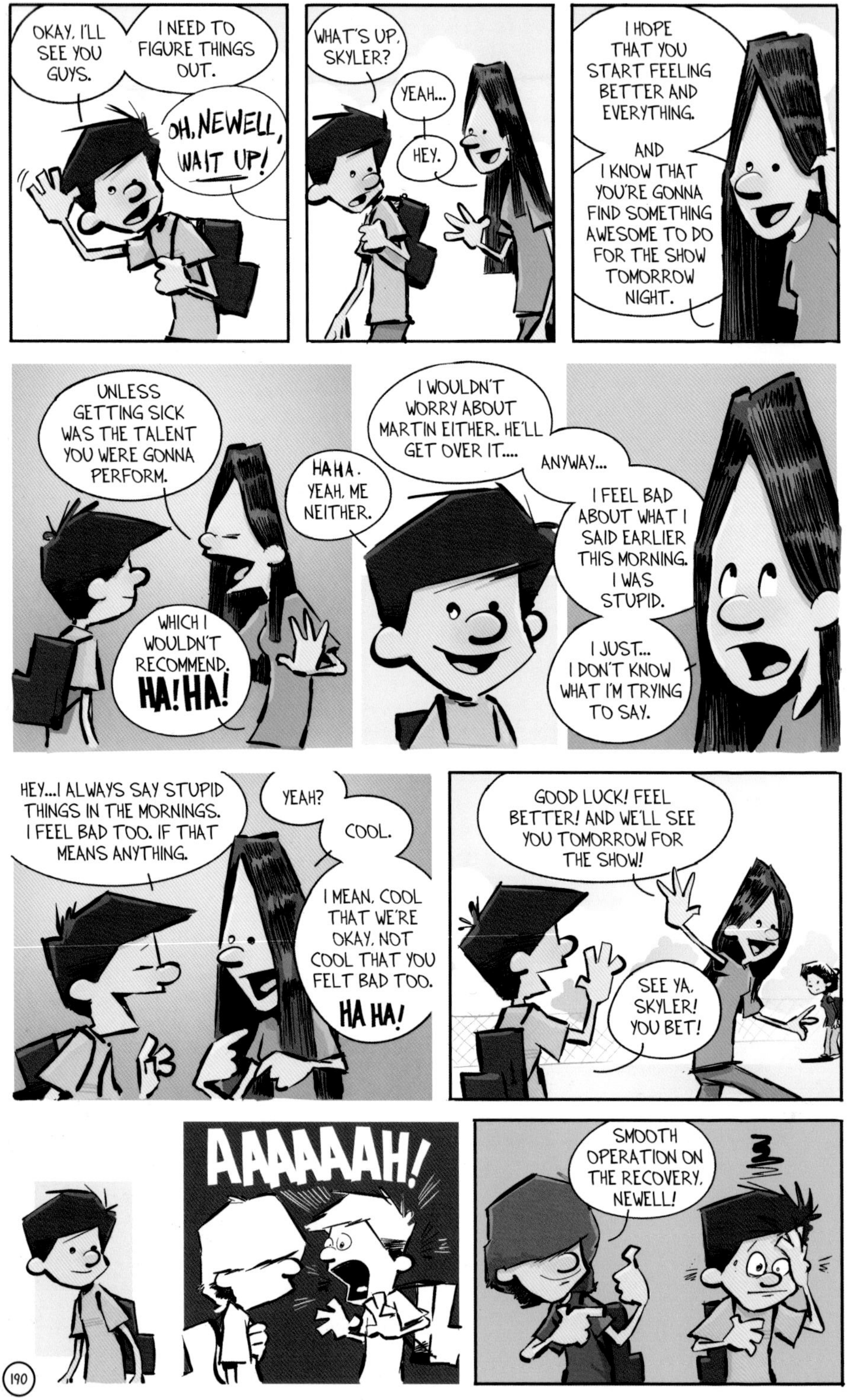
OKAY, I'LL SEE YOU GUYS.
I NEED TO FIGURE THINGS OUT.
OH, NEWELL, WAIT UP!
WHAT'S UP, SKYLER?
YEAH...
HEY.
I HOPE THAT YOU START FEELING BETTER AND EVERYTHING.
AND I KNOW THAT YOU'RE GONNA FIND SOMETHING AWESOME TO DO FOR THE SHOW TOMORROW NIGHT.
UNLESS GETTING SICK WAS THE TALENT YOU WERE GONNA PERFORM.
WHICH I WOULDN'T RECOMMEND. HA! HA!
HAHA. YEAH, ME NEITHER.
I WOULDN'T WORRY ABOUT MARTIN EITHER. HE'LL GET OVER IT....
ANYWAY...
I FEEL BAD ABOUT WHAT I SAID EARLIER THIS MORNING. I WAS STUPID.
I JUST... I DON'T KNOW WHAT I'M TRYING TO SAY.
HEY...I ALWAYS SAY STUPID THINGS IN THE MORNINGS. I FEEL BAD TOO. IF THAT MEANS ANYTHING.
YEAH?
COOL.
I MEAN, COOL THAT WE'RE OKAY, NOT COOL THAT YOU FELT BAD TOO.
HA HA!
GOOD LUCK! FEEL BETTER! AND WE'LL SEE YOU TOMORROW FOR THE SHOW!
SEE YA, SKYLER! YOU BET!
AAAAAAH!
SMOOTH OPERATION ON THE RECOVERY, NEWELL!

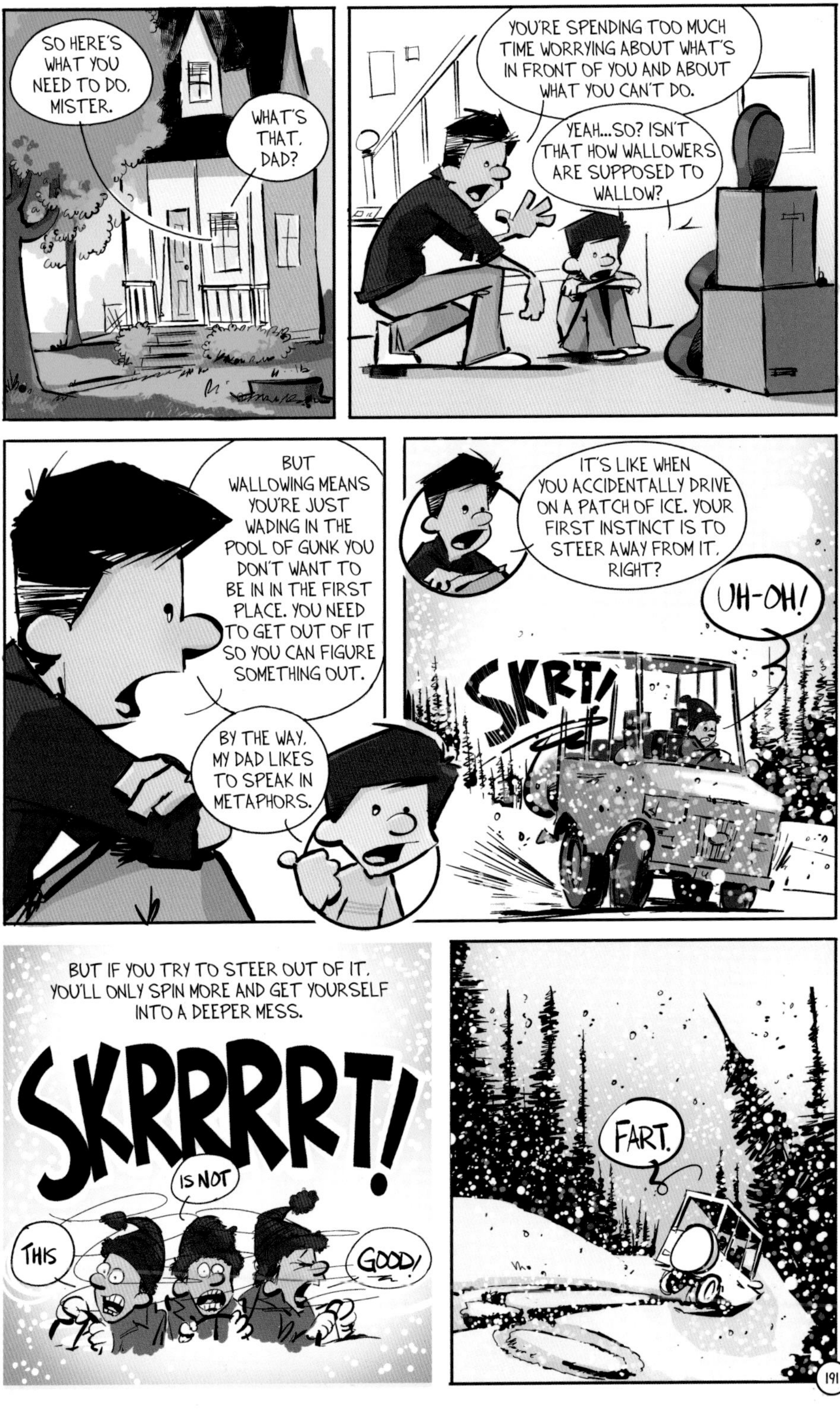
SO HERE'S WHAT YOU NEED TO DO, MISTER.
WHAT'S THAT, DAD?
YOU'RE SPENDING TOO MUCH TIME WORRYING ABOUT WHAT'S IN FRONT OF YOU AND ABOUT WHAT YOU CAN'T DO.
YEAH...SO? ISN'T THAT HOW WALLOWERS ARE SUPPOSED TO WALLOW?
BUT WALLOWING MEANS YOU'RE JUST WADING IN THE POOL OF GUNK YOU DON'T WANT TO BE IN IN THE FIRST PLACE. YOU NEED TO GET OUT OF IT SO YOU CAN FIGURE SOMETHING OUT.
BY THE WAY, MY DAD LIKES TO SPEAK IN METAPHORS.
IT'S LIKE WHEN YOU ACCIDENTALLY DRIVE ON A PATCH OF ICE. YOUR FIRST INSTINCT IS TO STEER AWAY FROM IT, RIGHT?
UH-OH!
SKRT!
BUT IF YOU TRY TO STEER OUT OF IT, YOU'LL ONLY SPIN MORE AND GET YOURSELF INTO A DEEPER MESS.
SKRRRRT!
THIS
IS NOT
GOOD!
FART.

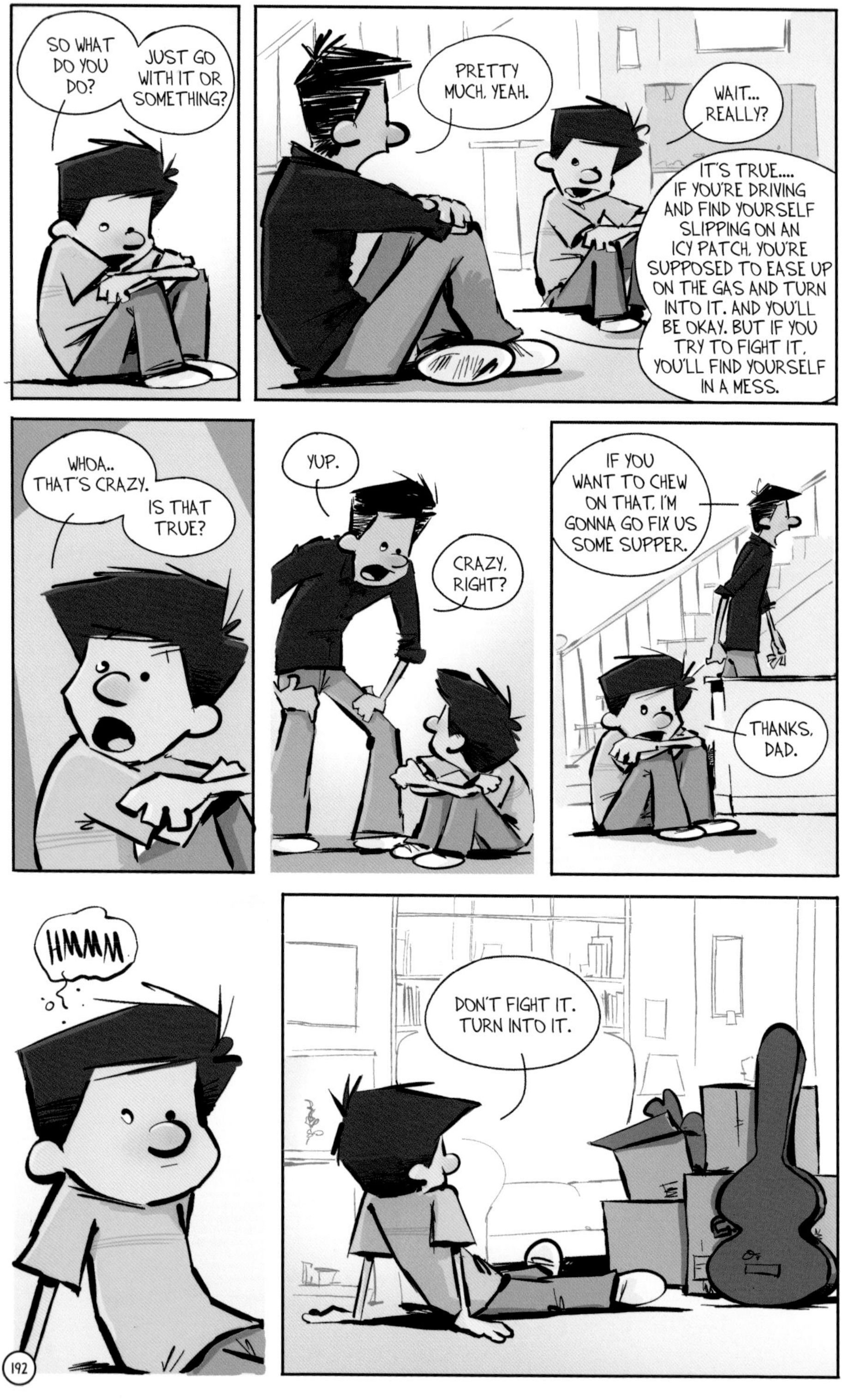
SO WHAT DO YOU DO?
JUST GO WITH IT OR SOMETHING?
PRETTY MUCH, YEAH.
WAIT... REALLY?
IT'S TRUE.... IF YOU'RE DRIVING AND FIND YOURSELF SLIPPING ON AN ICY PATCH, YOU'RE SUPPOSED TO EASE UP ON THE GAS AND TURN INTO IT. AND YOU'LL BE OKAY. BUT IF YOU TRY TO FIGHT IT, YOU'LL FIND YOURSELF IN A MESS.
WHOA.. THAT'S CRAZY.
IS THAT TRUE?
YUP.
CRAZY, RIGHT?
IF YOU WANT TO CHEW ON THAT, I'M GONNA GO FIX US SOME SUPPER.
THANKS, DAD.
HMMM.
DON'T FIGHT IT. TURN INTO IT.

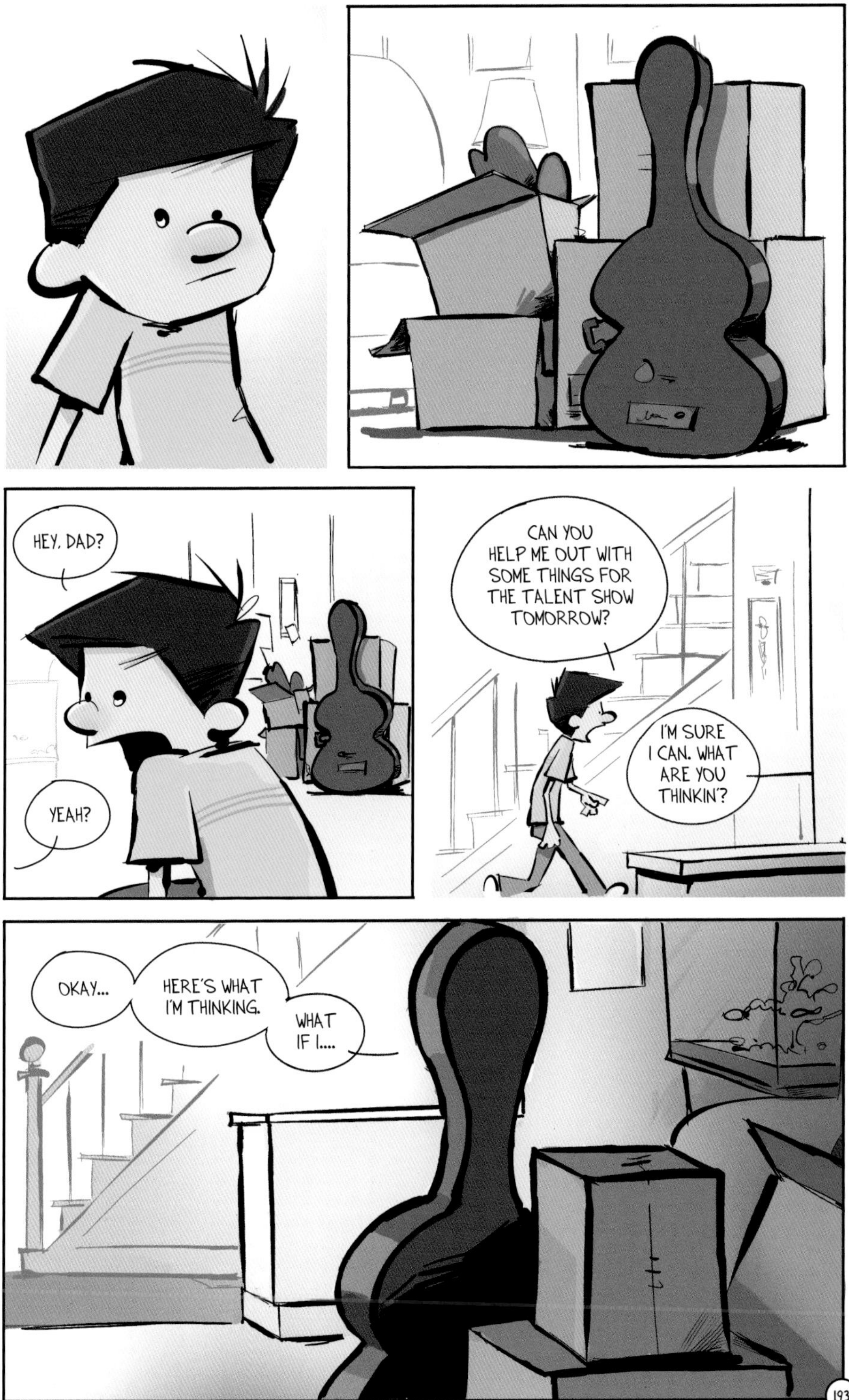
HEY, DAD?
YEAH?
CAN YOU HELP ME OUT WITH SOME THINGS FOR THE TALENT SHOW TOMORROW?
I'M SURE I CAN. WHAT ARE YOU THINKIN'?
OKAY...
HERE'S WHAT I'M THINKING.
WHAT IF I....

CHAPTER ELEVEN
THE TALENT SHOW

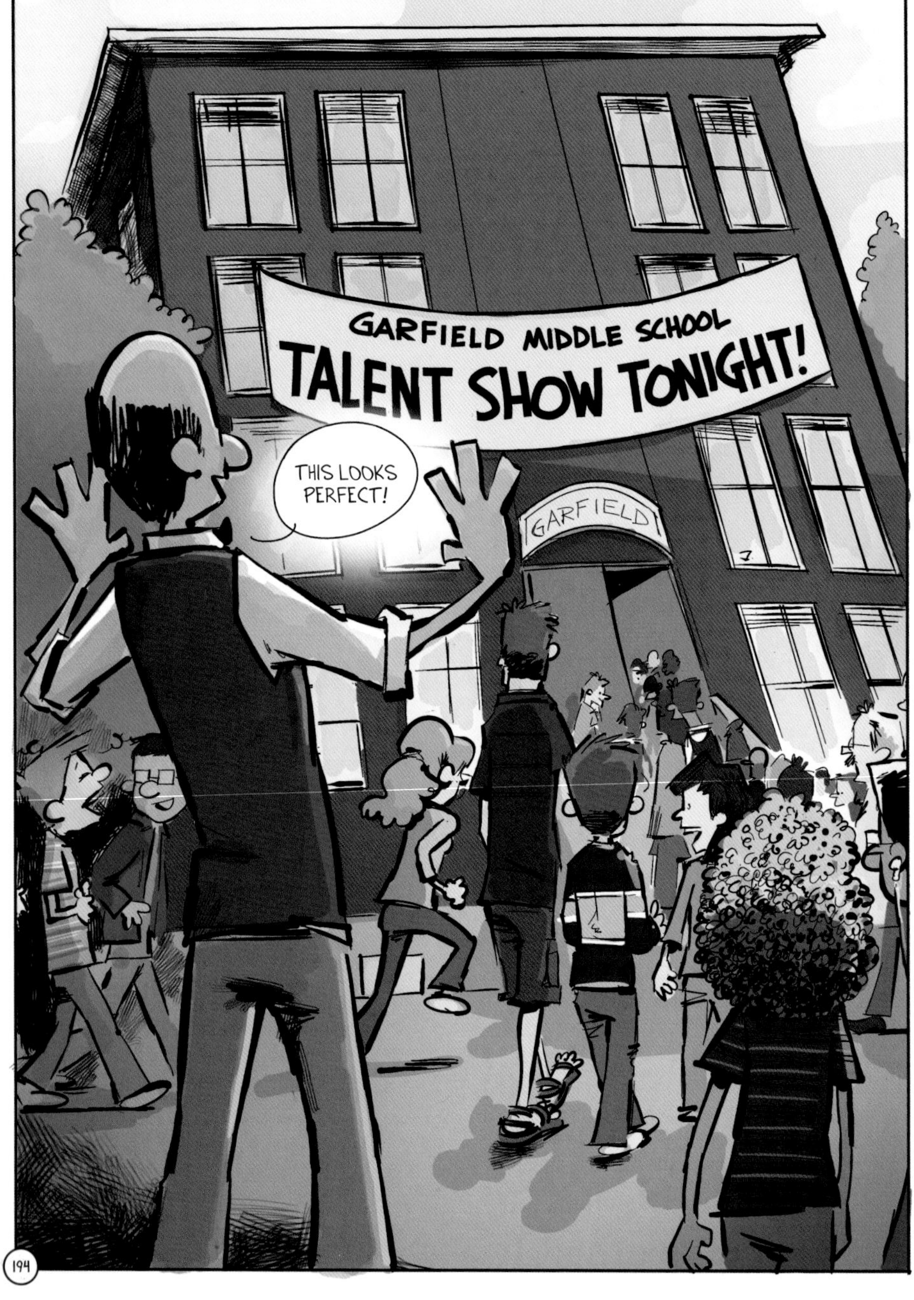
GARFIELD MIDDLE SCHOOL
TALENT SHOW TONIGHT!
THIS LOOKS PERFECT!
GARFIELD

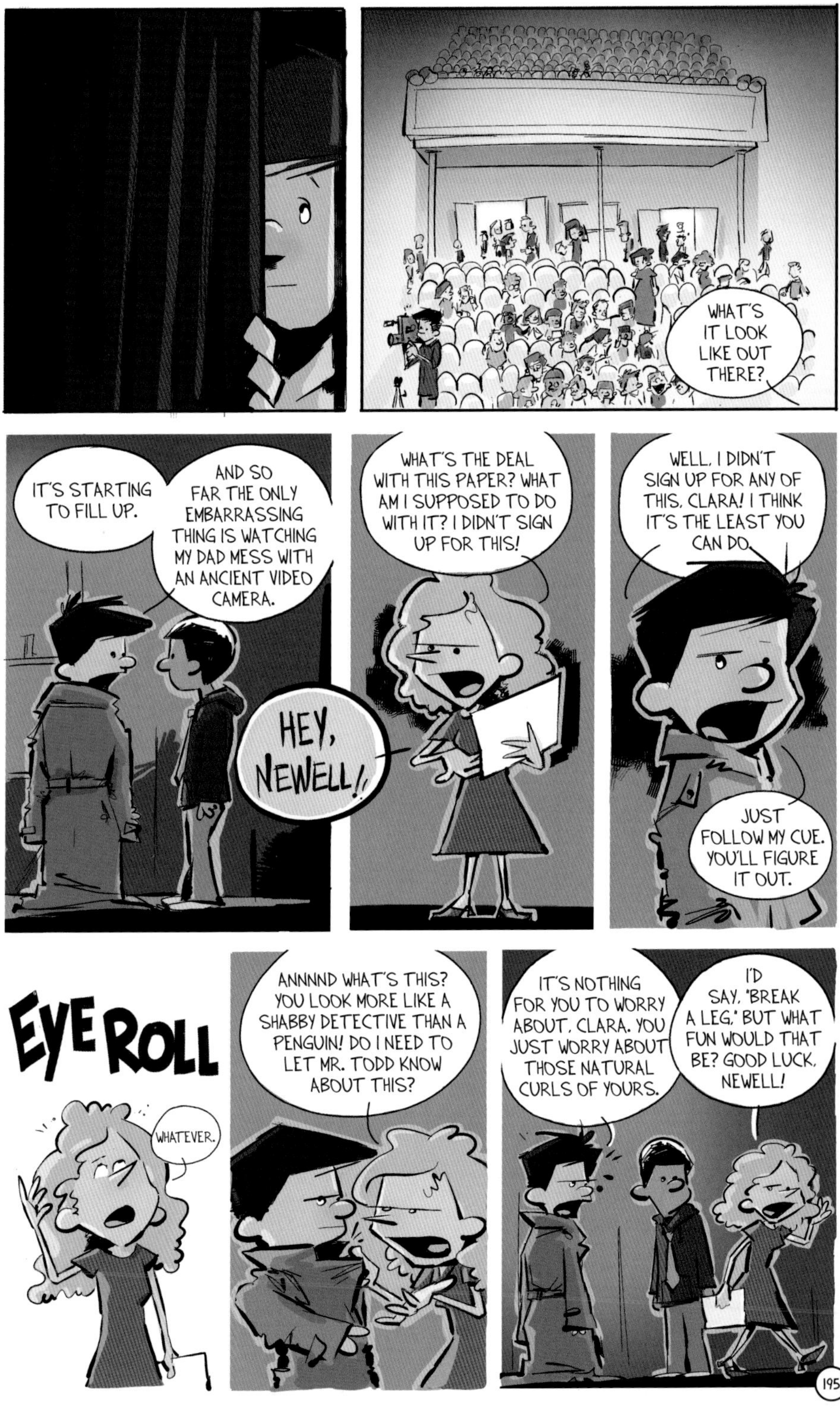
WHAT'S IT LOOK LIKE OUT THERE?
IT'S STARTING TO FILL UP.
AND SO FAR THE ONLY EMBARRASSING THING IS WATCHING MY DAD MESS WITH AN ANCIENT VIDEO CAMERA.
HEY, NEWELL!
WHAT'S THE DEAL WITH THIS PAPER? WHAT AM I SUPPOSED TO DO WITH IT? I DIDN'T SIGN UP FOR THIS!
WELL, I DIDN'T SIGN UP FOR ANY OF THIS, CLARA! I THINK IT'S THE LEAST YOU CAN DO.
JUST FOLLOW MY CUE. YOU'LL FIGURE IT OUT.
EYE ROLL
WHATEVER.
ANNNND WHAT'S THIS? YOU LOOK MORE LIKE A SHABBY DETECTIVE THAN A PENGUIN! DO I NEED TO LET MR. TODD KNOW ABOUT THIS?
IT'S NOTHING FOR YOU TO WORRY ABOUT, CLARA. YOU JUST WORRY ABOUT THOSE NATURAL CURLS OF YOURS.
I'D SAY, "BREAK A LEG," BUT WHAT FUN WOULD THAT BE? GOOD LUCK, NEWELL!

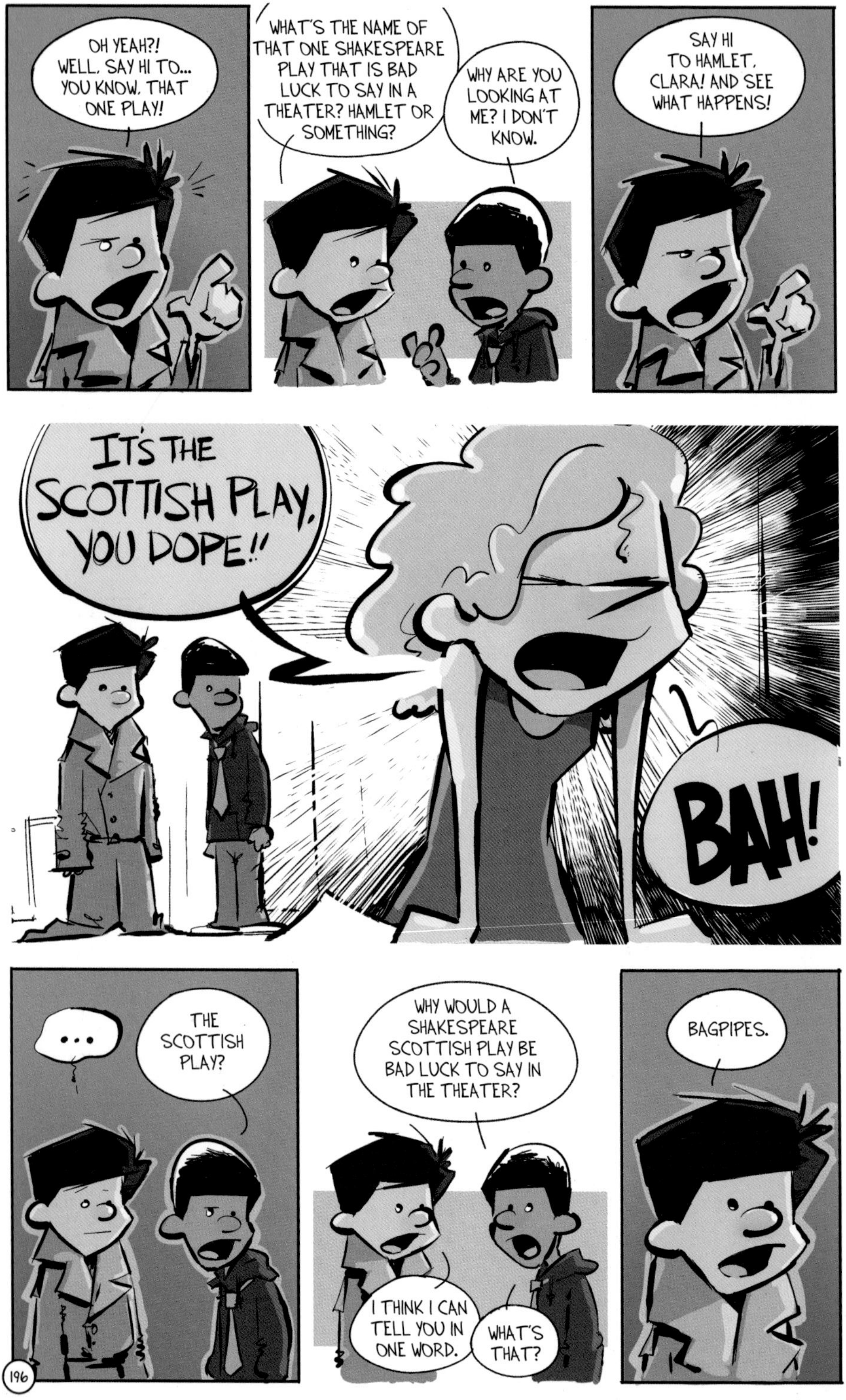
OH YEAH?! WELL, SAY HI TO... YOU KNOW, THAT ONE PLAY!
WHAT'S THE NAME OF THAT ONE SHAKESPEARE PLAY THAT IS BAD LUCK TO SAY IN A THEATER? HAMLET OR SOMETHING?
WHY ARE YOU LOOKING AT ME? I DON'T KNOW.
SAY HI TO HAMLET, CLARA! AND SEE WHAT HAPPENS!
IT'S THE SCOTTISH PLAY, YOU DOPE!!
BAH!
...
THE SCOTTISH PLAY?
WHY WOULD A SHAKESPEARE SCOTTISH PLAY BE BAD LUCK TO SAY IN THE THEATER?
I THINK I CAN TELL YOU IN ONE WORD.
WHAT'S THAT?
BAGPIPES.

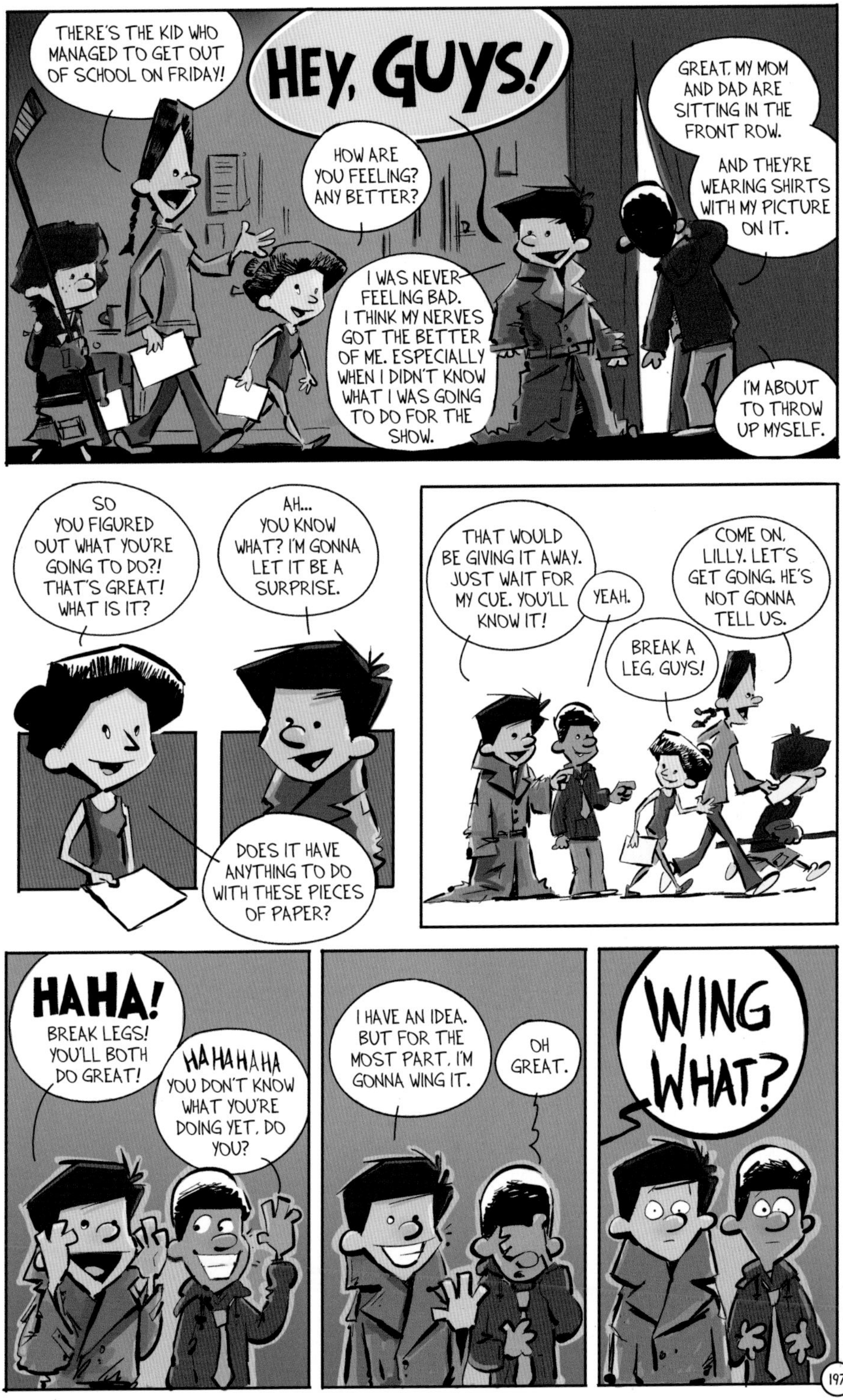
THERE'S THE KID WHO MANAGED TO GET OUT OF SCHOOL ON FRIDAY!
HEY, GUYS!
HOW ARE YOU FEELING? ANY BETTER?
I WAS NEVER FEELING BAD. I THINK MY NERVES GOT THE BETTER OF ME. ESPECIALLY WHEN I DIDN'T KNOW WHAT I WAS GOING TO DO FOR THE SHOW.
GREAT. MY MOM AND DAD ARE SITTING IN THE FRONT ROW.
AND THEY'RE WEARING SHIRTS WITH MY PICTURE ON IT.
I'M ABOUT TO THROW UP MYSELF.
SO YOU FIGURED OUT WHAT YOU'RE GOING TO DO?! THAT'S GREAT! WHAT IS IT?
AH... YOU KNOW WHAT? I'M GONNA LET IT BE A SURPRISE.
DOES IT HAVE ANYTHING TO DO WITH THESE PIECES OF PAPER?
THAT WOULD BE GIVING IT AWAY. JUST WAIT FOR MY CUE. YOU'LL KNOW IT!
YEAH.
COME ON, LILLY. LET'S GET GOING. HE'S NOT GONNA TELL US.
BREAK A LEG, GUYS!
HAHA! BREAK LEGS! YOU'LL BOTH DO GREAT!
HAHAHAHA YOU DON'T KNOW WHAT YOU'RE DOING YET, DO YOU?
I HAVE AN IDEA. BUT FOR THE MOST PART, I'M GONNA WING IT.
OH GREAT.
WING WHAT?

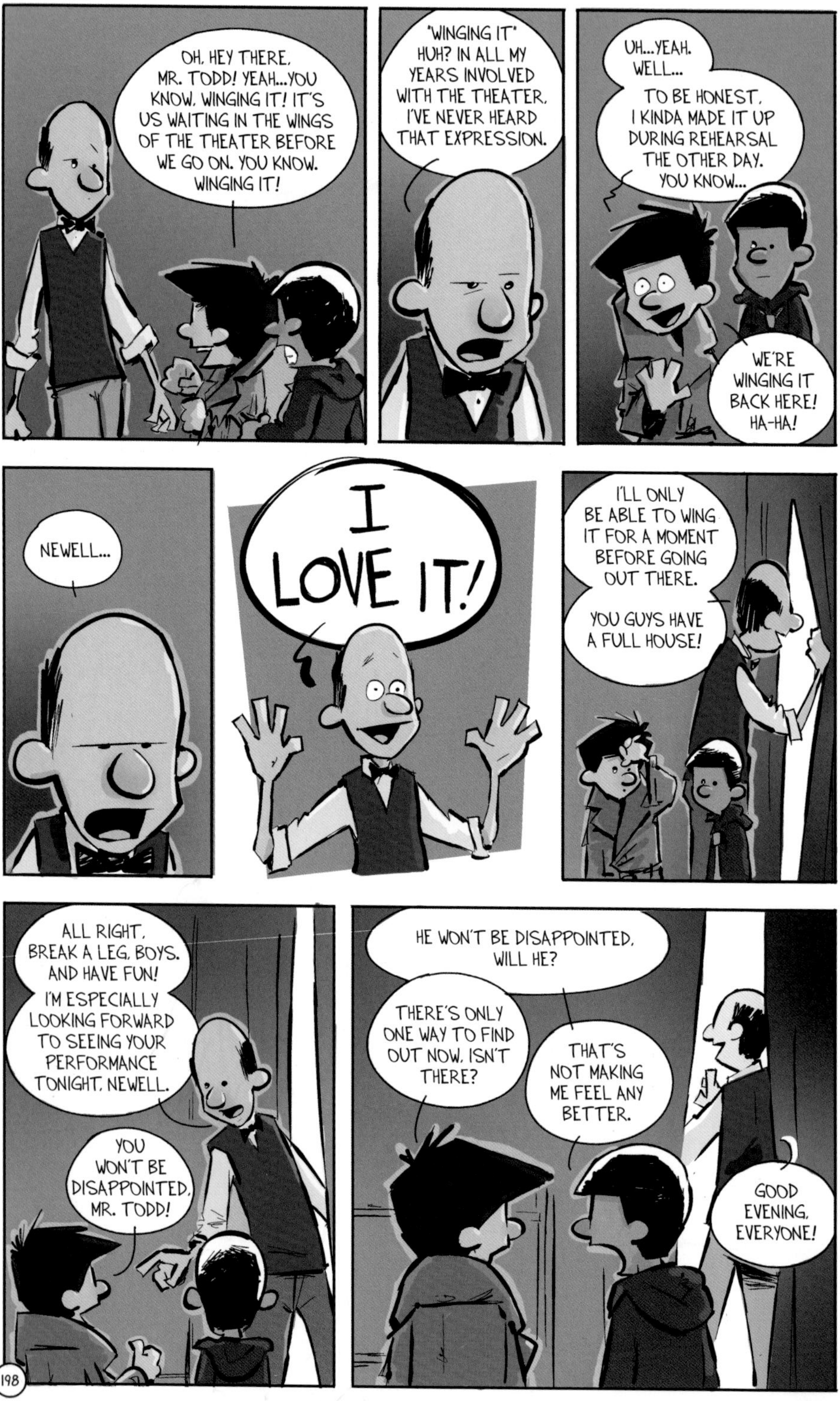
OH, HEY THERE, MR. TODD! YEAH...YOU KNOW, WINGING IT! IT'S US WAITING IN THE WINGS OF THE THEATER BEFORE WE GO ON. YOU KNOW. WINGING IT!
"WINGING IT" HUH? IN ALL MY YEARS INVOLVED WITH THE THEATER, I'VE NEVER HEARD THAT EXPRESSION.
UH...YEAH. WELL...
TO BE HONEST, I KINDA MADE IT UP DURING REHEARSAL THE OTHER DAY. YOU KNOW...
WE'RE WINGING IT BACK HERE! HA-HA!
NEWELL...
I LOVE IT!
I'LL ONLY BE ABLE TO WING IT FOR A MOMENT BEFORE GOING OUT THERE.
YOU GUYS HAVE A FULL HOUSE!
ALL RIGHT, BREAK A LEG, BOYS. AND HAVE FUN!
I'M ESPECIALLY LOOKING FORWARD TO SEEING YOUR PERFORMANCE TONIGHT, NEWELL.
YOU WON'T BE DISAPPOINTED, MR. TODD!
HE WON'T BE DISAPPOINTED, WILL HE?
THERE'S ONLY ONE WAY TO FIND OUT NOW, ISN'T THERE?
THAT'S NOT MAKING ME FEEL ANY BETTER.
GOOD EVENING, EVERYONE!

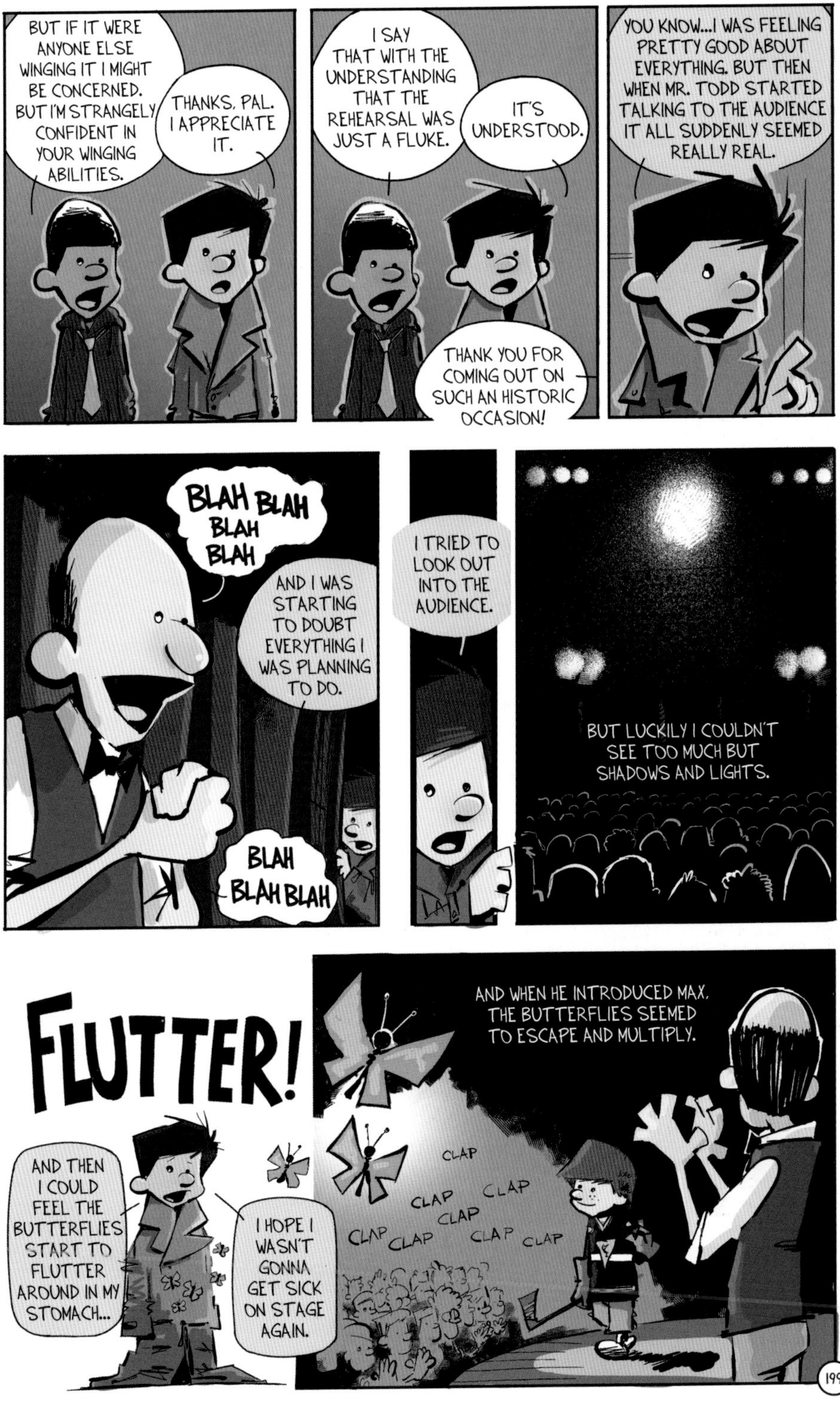

BUT IF IT WERE ANYONE ELSE WINGING IT I MIGHT BE CONCERNED. BUT I'M STRANGELY CONFIDENT IN YOUR WINGING ABILITIES.
THANKS, PAL. I APPRECIATE IT.
I SAY THAT WITH THE UNDERSTANDING THAT THE REHEARSAL WAS JUST A FLUKE.
IT'S UNDERSTOOD.
THANK YOU FOR COMING OUT ON SUCH AN HISTORIC OCCASION!
YOU KNOW...I WAS FEELING PRETTY GOOD ABOUT EVERYTHING. BUT THEN WHEN MR. TODD STARTED TALKING TO THE AUDIENCE IT ALL SUDDENLY SEEMED REALLY REAL.
BLAH BLAH BLAH BLAH
AND I WAS STARTING TO DOUBT EVERYTHING I WAS PLANNING TO DO.
BLAH BLAH BLAH
I TRIED TO LOOK OUT INTO THE AUDIENCE.
BUT LUCKILY I COULDN'T SEE TOO MUCH BUT SHADOWS AND LIGHTS.
FLUTTER!
AND THEN I COULD FEEL THE BUTTERFLIES START TO FLUTTER AROUND IN MY STOMACH...
I HOPE I WASN'T GONNA GET SICK ON STAGE AGAIN.
AND WHEN HE INTRODUCED MAX, THE BUTTERFLIES SEEMED TO ESCAPE AND MULTIPLY.
CLAP CLAP CLAP CLAP CLAP CLAP CLAP CLAP

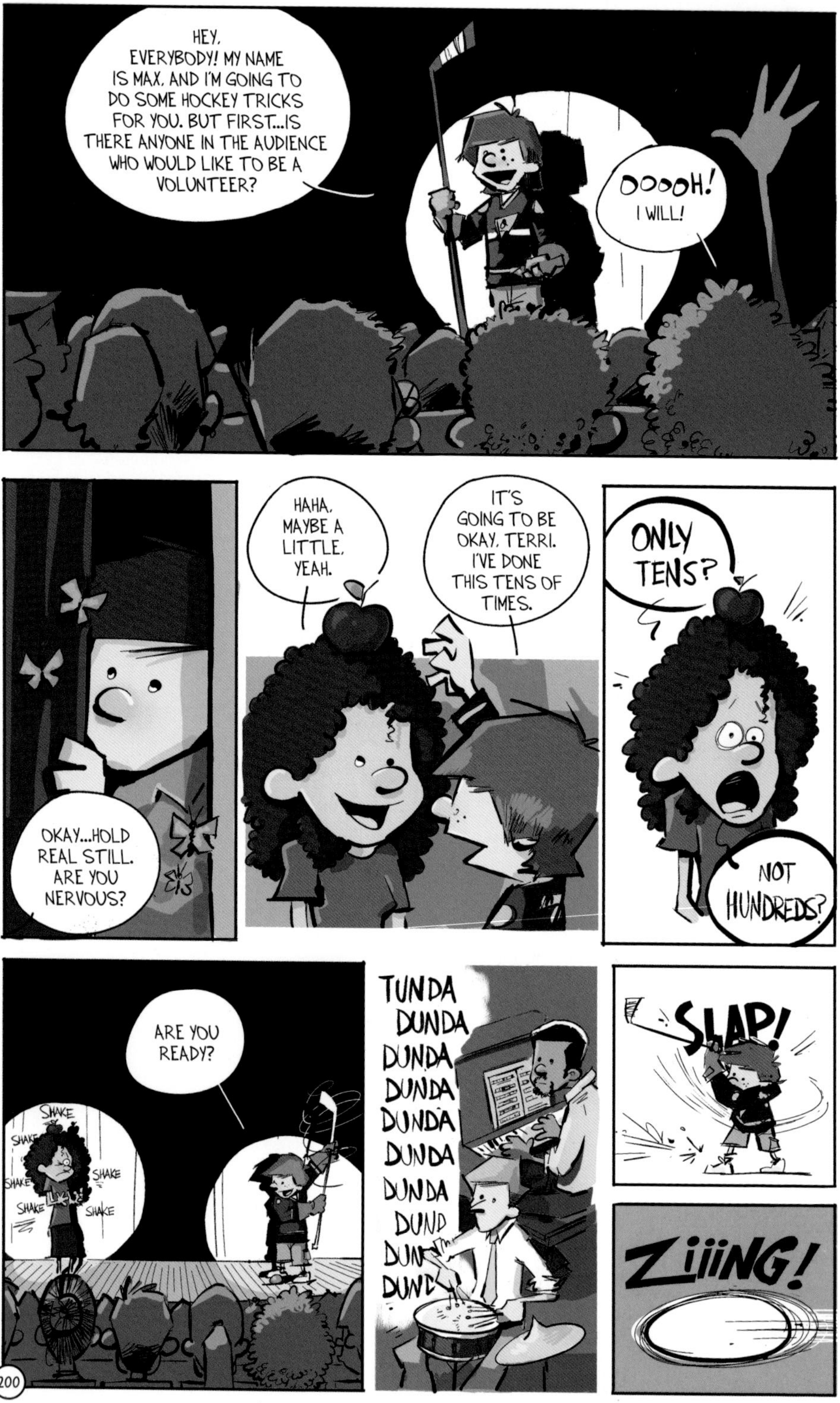
HEY, EVERYBODY! MY NAME IS MAX, AND I'M GOING TO DO SOME HOCKEY TRICKS FOR YOU. BUT FIRST...IS THERE ANYONE IN THE AUDIENCE WHO WOULD LIKE TO BE A VOLUNTEER?
OOOOH! I WILL!
OKAY...HOLD REAL STILL. ARE YOU NERVOUS?
HAHA, MAYBE A LITTLE, YEAH.
IT'S GOING TO BE OKAY, TERRI. I'VE DONE THIS TENS OF TIMES.
ONLY TENS?
NOT HUNDREDS?
ARE YOU READY?
SHAKE SHAKE SHAKE SHAKE SHAKE SHAKE
TUNDA DUNDA DUNDA DUNDA DUNDA DUNDA DUNDA DUND DUN DUND
SLAP!
ZiiiNG!

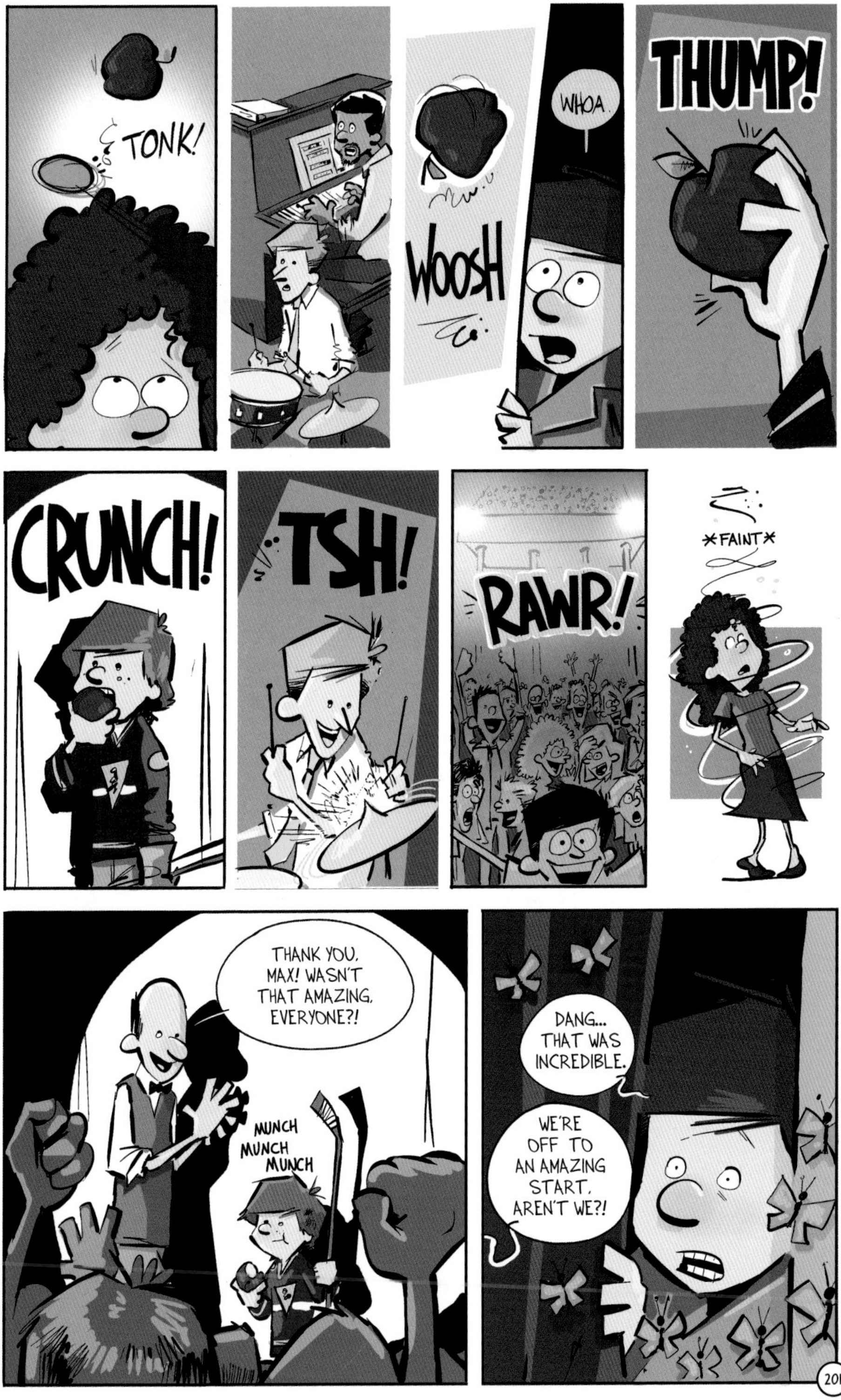
TONK!
WOOSH
WHOA.
THUMP!
CRUNCH!
TSH!
RAWR!
FAINT
THANK YOU, MAX! WASN'T THAT AMAZING, EVERYONE?!
MUNCH MUNCH MUNCH
DANG... THAT WAS INCREDIBLE.
WE'RE OFF TO AN AMAZING START, AREN'T WE?!

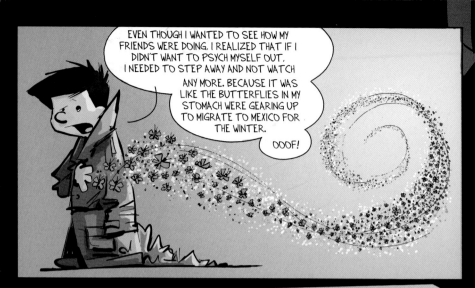

EVEN THOUGH I WANTED TO SEE HOW MY FRIENDS WERE DOING, I REALIZED THAT IF I DIDN'T WANT TO PSYCH MYSELF OUT, I NEEDED TO STEP AWAY AND NOT WATCH ANY MORE. BECAUSE IT WAS LIKE THE BUTTERFLIES IN MY STOMACH WERE GEARING UP TO MIGRATE TO MEXICO FOR THE WINTER.

OOOF!

I COULDN'T SEE ANYTHING THAT THEY WERE DOING, BUT I COULD STILL HEAR HOW AWESOME THE CROWD REACTED.

THEY LOVED LILLY'S GRACE. I MEAN, WHO WOULDN'T?

I COULD HEAR THEM LAUGHING AT SKYLER JUGGLING THE RUBBER CHICKENS.

THEY APPLAUDED CLARA'S MONOLOGUE FROM HENRY V.

MR. TODD CALLED WHAT'S-HER-NAME'S TAP DANCING PREAMBLE A SHOWSTOPPER. WHATEVER THAT IS.

TAP! TAP! TAP!

AND COLLIN KNOCKED IT OUT WITH HIS SONG. THEY ATE IT UP.

TICK TICK TICK TICK TICK TICK TICK

I WAS HAPPY FOR ALL OF THEM, BUT I KNEW THAT WITH EACH PERFORMANCE I WAS CLOSER TO MY TIME. IN FACT...

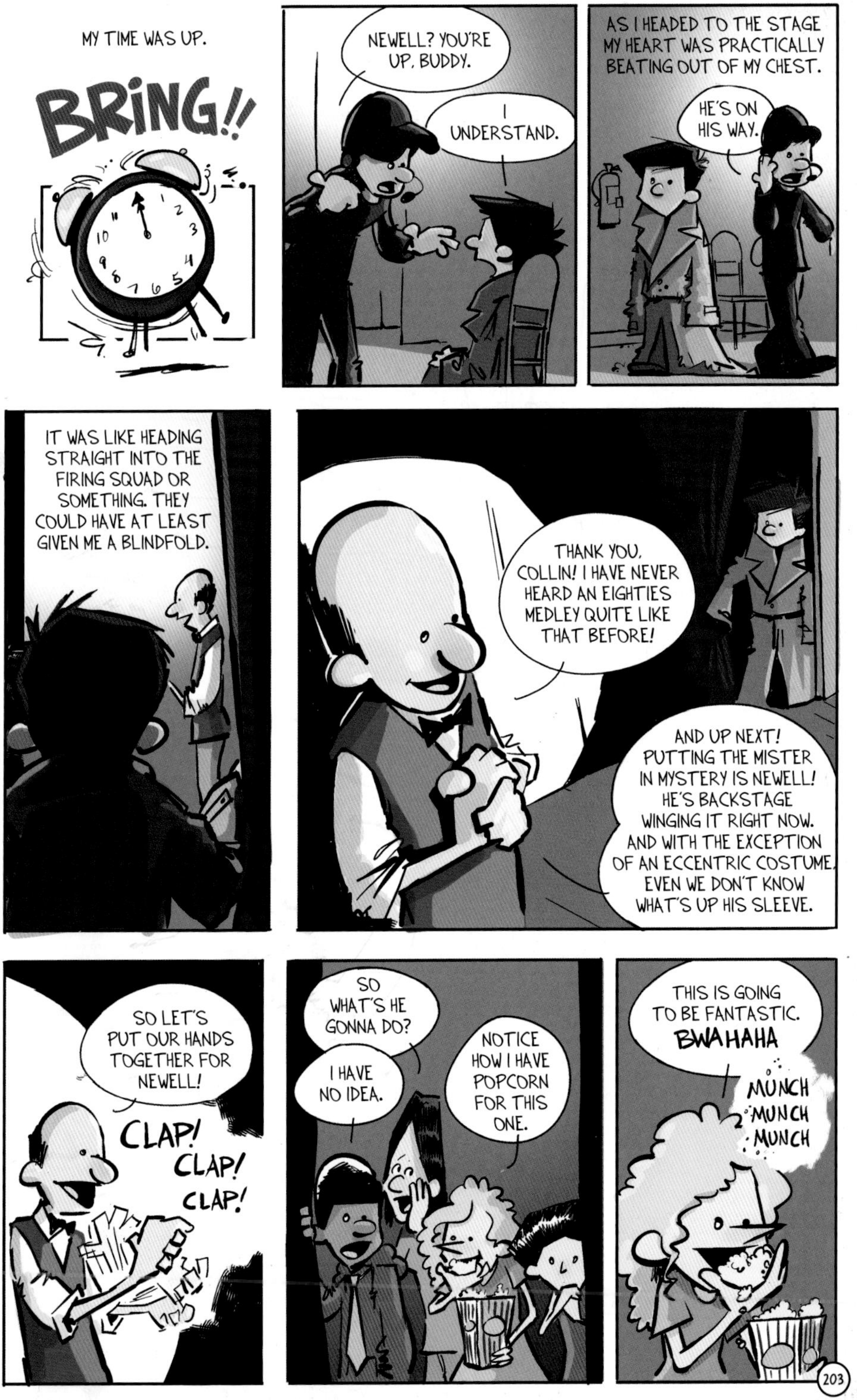
MY TIME WAS UP.
BRING!!
NEWELL? YOU'RE UP, BUDDY.
I UNDERSTAND.
AS I HEADED TO THE STAGE MY HEART WAS PRACTICALLY BEATING OUT OF MY CHEST.
HE'S ON HIS WAY.
IT WAS LIKE HEADING STRAIGHT INTO THE FIRING SQUAD OR SOMETHING. THEY COULD HAVE AT LEAST GIVEN ME A BLINDFOLD.
THANK YOU, COLLIN! I HAVE NEVER HEARD AN EIGHTIES MEDLEY QUITE LIKE THAT BEFORE!
AND UP NEXT! PUTTING THE MISTER IN MYSTERY IS NEWELL! HE'S BACKSTAGE WINGING IT RIGHT NOW. AND WITH THE EXCEPTION OF AN ECCENTRIC COSTUME, EVEN WE DON'T KNOW WHAT'S UP HIS SLEEVE.
SO LET'S PUT OUR HANDS TOGETHER FOR NEWELL!
CLAP! CLAP! CLAP!
SO WHAT'S HE GONNA DO?
I HAVE NO IDEA.
NOTICE HOW I HAVE POPCORN FOR THIS ONE.
THIS IS GOING TO BE FANTASTIC. BWAHAHA
MUNCH MUNCH MUNCH

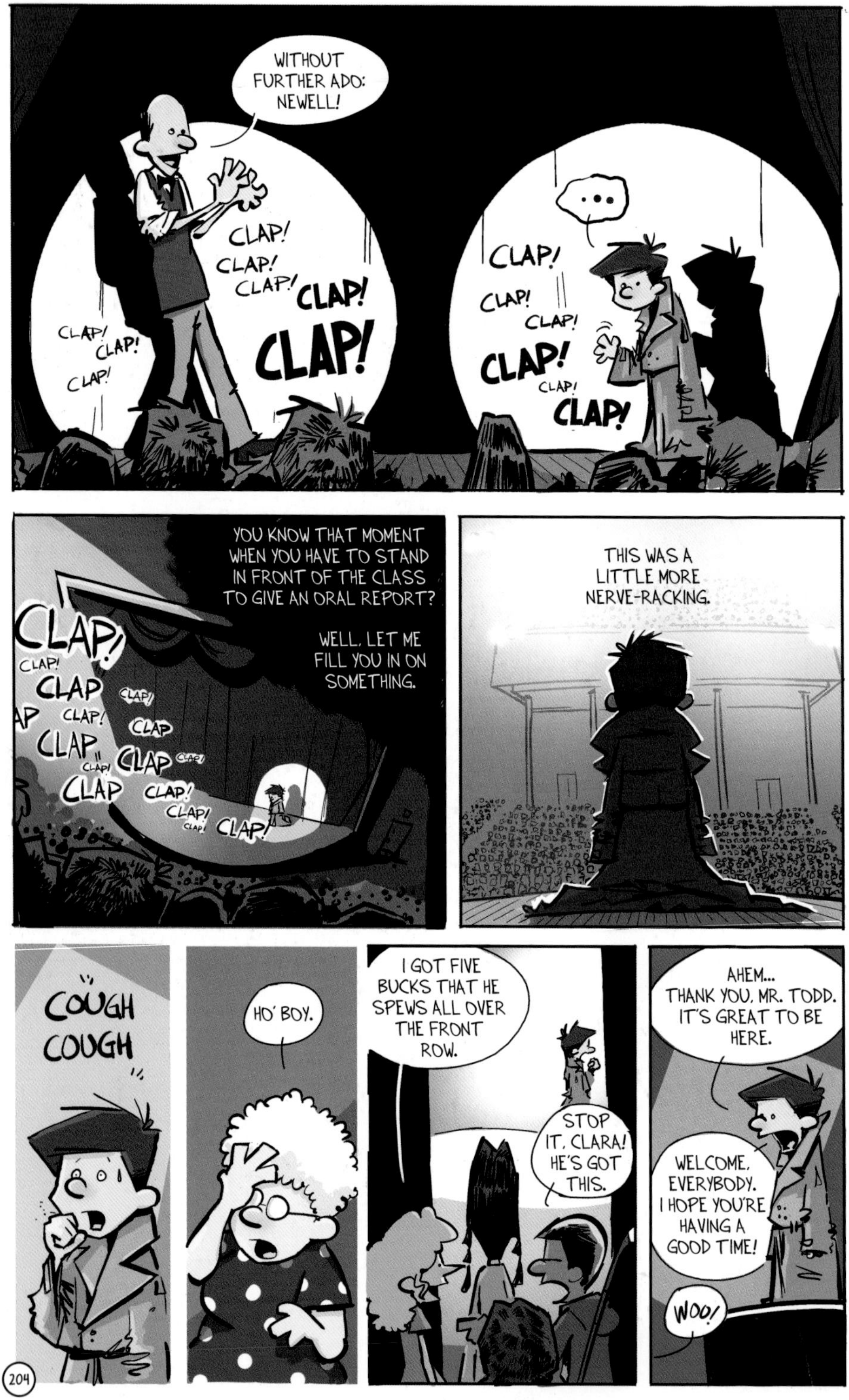
WITHOUT FURTHER ADO: NEWELL!
CLAP! CLAP! CLAP! CLAP! CLAP!
CLAP! CLAP! CLAP!
...
CLAP! CLAP! CLAP! CLAP! CLAP! CLAP!
YOU KNOW THAT MOMENT WHEN YOU HAVE TO STAND IN FRONT OF THE CLASS TO GIVE AN ORAL REPORT?
WELL, LET ME FILL YOU IN ON SOMETHING.
CLAP! CLAP! CLAP CLAP! CLAP! CLAP CLAP CLAP! CLAP CLAP! CLAP! CLAP! CLAP! CLAP!
THIS WAS A LITTLE MORE NERVE-RACKING.
COUGH COUGH
HO' BOY.
I GOT FIVE BUCKS THAT HE SPEWS ALL OVER THE FRONT ROW.
STOP IT, CLARA! HE'S GOT THIS.
AHEM... THANK YOU, MR. TODD. IT'S GREAT TO BE HERE.
WELCOME, EVERYBODY. I HOPE YOU'RE HAVING A GOOD TIME!
WOO!

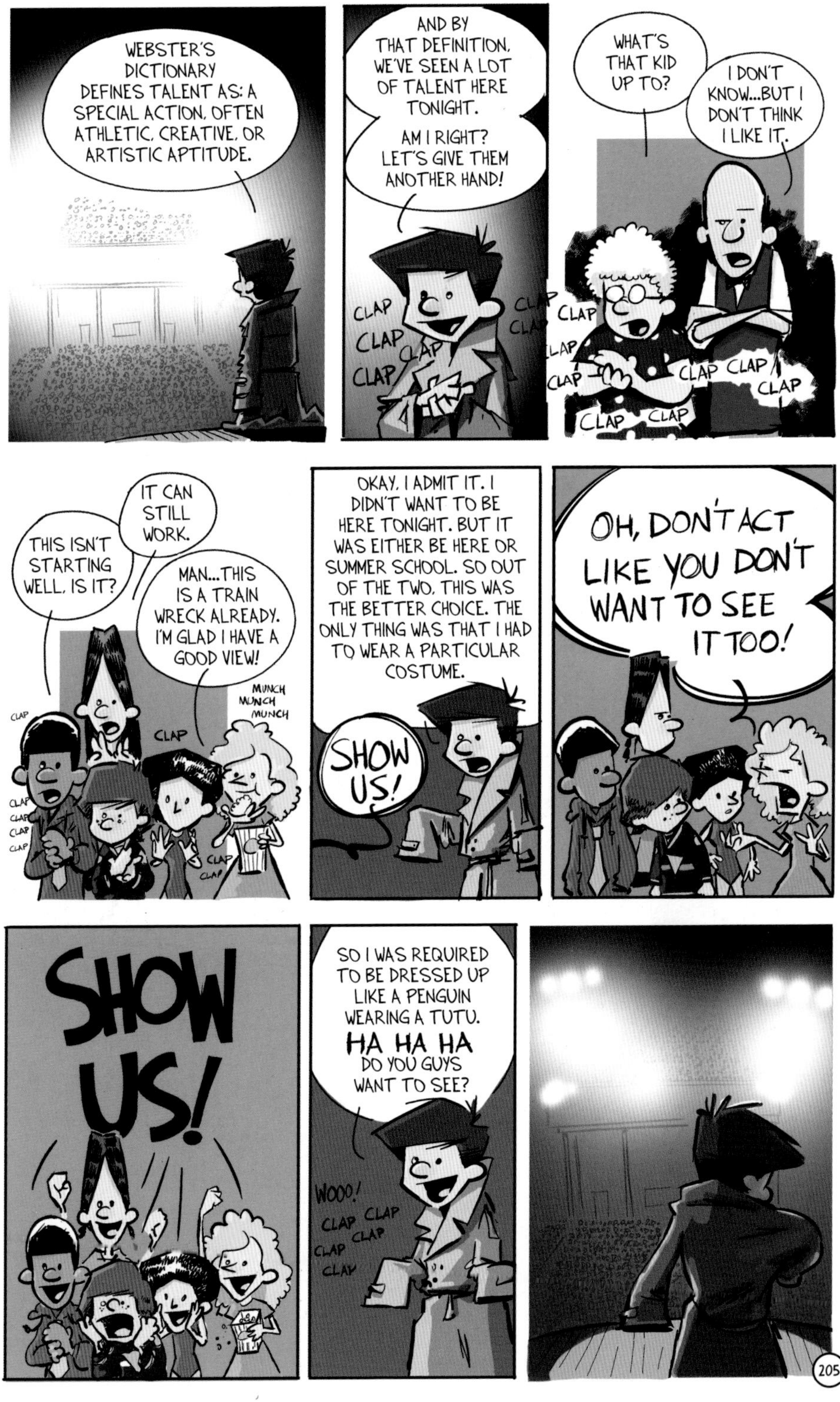
WEBSTER'S DICTIONARY DEFINES TALENT AS: A SPECIAL ACTION, OFTEN ATHLETIC, CREATIVE, OR ARTISTIC APTITUDE.
AND BY THAT DEFINITION, WE'VE SEEN A LOT OF TALENT HERE TONIGHT.
AM I RIGHT? LET'S GIVE THEM ANOTHER HAND!
CLAP CLAP CLAP CLAP
WHAT'S THAT KID UP TO?
I DON'T KNOW...BUT I DON'T THINK I LIKE IT.
CLAP CLAP CLAP CLAP CLAP CLAP CLAP CLAP CLAP
THIS ISN'T STARTING WELL, IS IT?
IT CAN STILL WORK.
MAN...THIS IS A TRAIN WRECK ALREADY. I'M GLAD I HAVE A GOOD VIEW!
MUNCH MUNCH MUNCH
CLAP
CLAP
CLAP CLAP CLAP CLAP
CLAP CLAP
OKAY, I ADMIT IT. I DIDN'T WANT TO BE HERE TONIGHT. BUT IT WAS EITHER BE HERE OR SUMMER SCHOOL. SO OUT OF THE TWO, THIS WAS THE BETTER CHOICE. THE ONLY THING WAS THAT I HAD TO WEAR A PARTICULAR COSTUME.
SHOW US!
OH, DON'T ACT LIKE YOU DON'T WANT TO SEE IT TOO!
SHOW US!
SO I WAS REQUIRED TO BE DRESSED UP LIKE A PENGUIN WEARING A TUTU.
HA HA HA
DO YOU GUYS WANT TO SEE?
WOOO!
CLAP CLAP CLAP CLAP CLAP

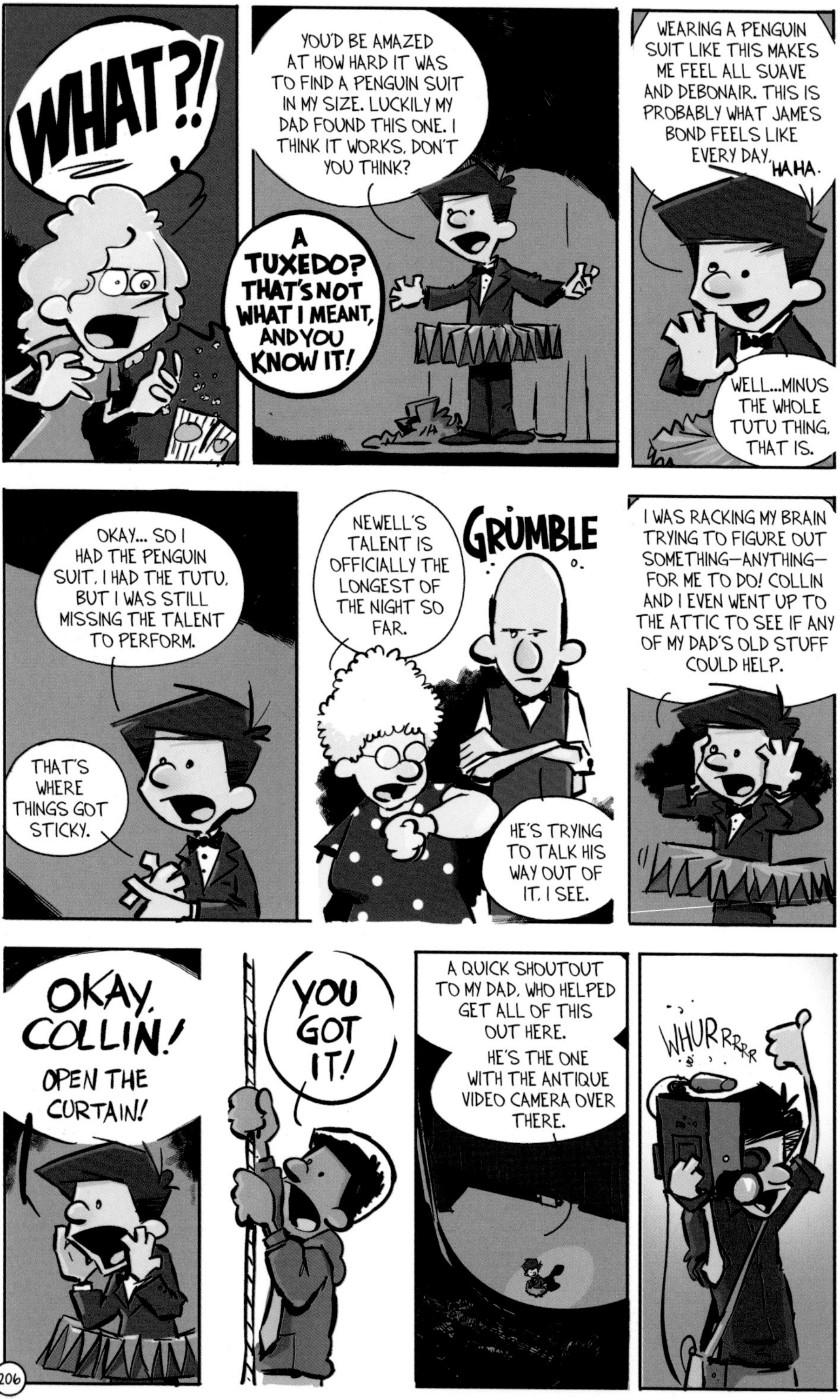
WHAT?!
YOU'D BE AMAZED AT HOW HARD IT WAS TO FIND A PENGUIN SUIT IN MY SIZE. LUCKILY MY DAD FOUND THIS ONE. I THINK IT WORKS, DON'T YOU THINK?
A TUXEDO? THAT'S NOT WHAT I MEANT, AND YOU KNOW IT!
WEARING A PENGUIN SUIT LIKE THIS MAKES ME FEEL ALL SUAVE AND DEBONAIR. THIS IS PROBABLY WHAT JAMES BOND FEELS LIKE EVERY DAY. HAHA.
WELL...MINUS THE WHOLE TUTU THING, THAT IS.
OKAY... SO I HAD THE PENGUIN SUIT, I HAD THE TUTU, BUT I WAS STILL MISSING THE TALENT TO PERFORM.
THAT'S WHERE THINGS GOT STICKY.
NEWELL'S TALENT IS OFFICIALLY THE LONGEST OF THE NIGHT SO FAR.
GRUMBLE
HE'S TRYING TO TALK HIS WAY OUT OF IT, I SEE.
I WAS RACKING MY BRAIN TRYING TO FIGURE OUT SOMETHING—ANYTHING—FOR ME TO DO! COLLIN AND I EVEN WENT UP TO THE ATTIC TO SEE IF ANY OF MY DAD'S OLD STUFF COULD HELP.
OKAY, COLLIN! OPEN THE CURTAIN!
YOU GOT IT!
A QUICK SHOUTOUT TO MY DAD, WHO HELPED GET ALL OF THIS OUT HERE.
HE'S THE ONE WITH THE ANTIQUE VIDEO CAMERA OVER THERE.
WHURRRRR

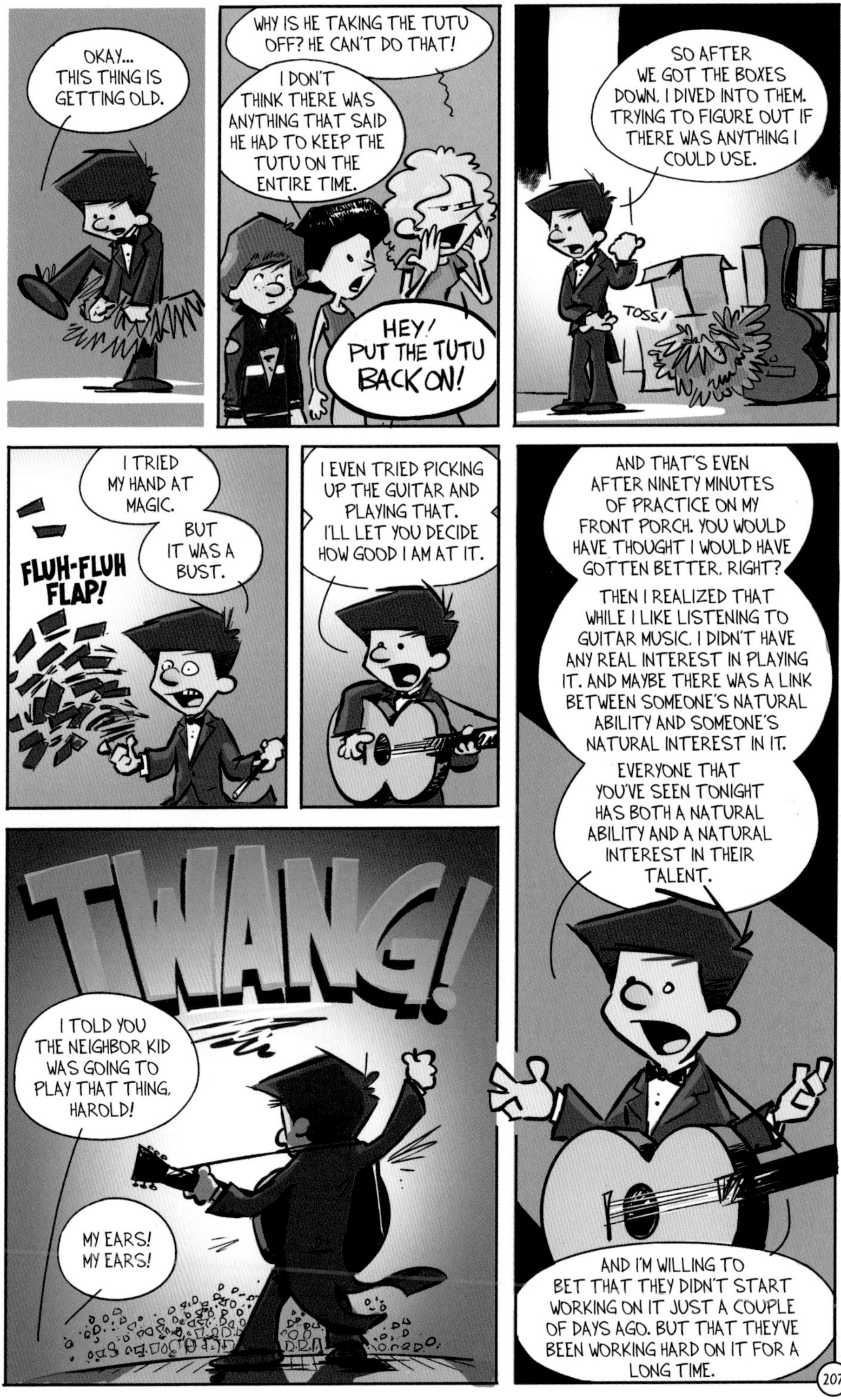
OKAY... THIS THING IS GETTING OLD.
WHY IS HE TAKING THE TUTU OFF? HE CAN'T DO THAT!
I DON'T THINK THERE WAS ANYTHING THAT SAID HE HAD TO KEEP THE TUTU ON THE ENTIRE TIME.
HEY! PUT THE TUTU BACK ON!
SO AFTER WE GOT THE BOXES DOWN, I DIVED INTO THEM. TRYING TO FIGURE OUT IF THERE WAS ANYTHING I COULD USE.
TOSS!
I TRIED MY HAND AT MAGIC.
BUT IT WAS A BUST.
FLUH-FLUH FLAP!
I EVEN TRIED PICKING UP THE GUITAR AND PLAYING THAT. I'LL LET YOU DECIDE HOW GOOD I AM AT IT.
AND THAT'S EVEN AFTER NINETY MINUTES OF PRACTICE ON MY FRONT PORCH. YOU WOULD HAVE THOUGHT I WOULD HAVE GOTTEN BETTER, RIGHT?
THEN I REALIZED THAT WHILE I LIKE LISTENING TO GUITAR MUSIC, I DIDN'T HAVE ANY REAL INTEREST IN PLAYING IT. AND MAYBE THERE WAS A LINK BETWEEN SOMEONE'S NATURAL ABILITY AND SOMEONE'S NATURAL INTEREST IN IT.
EVERYONE THAT YOU'VE SEEN TONIGHT HAS BOTH A NATURAL ABILITY AND A NATURAL INTEREST IN THEIR TALENT.
TWANG!
I TOLD YOU THE NEIGHBOR KID WAS GOING TO PLAY THAT THING, HAROLD!
MY EARS! MY EARS!
AND I'M WILLING TO BET THAT THEY DIDN'T START WORKING ON IT JUST A COUPLE OF DAYS AGO. BUT THAT THEY'VE BEEN WORKING HARD ON IT FOR A LONG TIME.

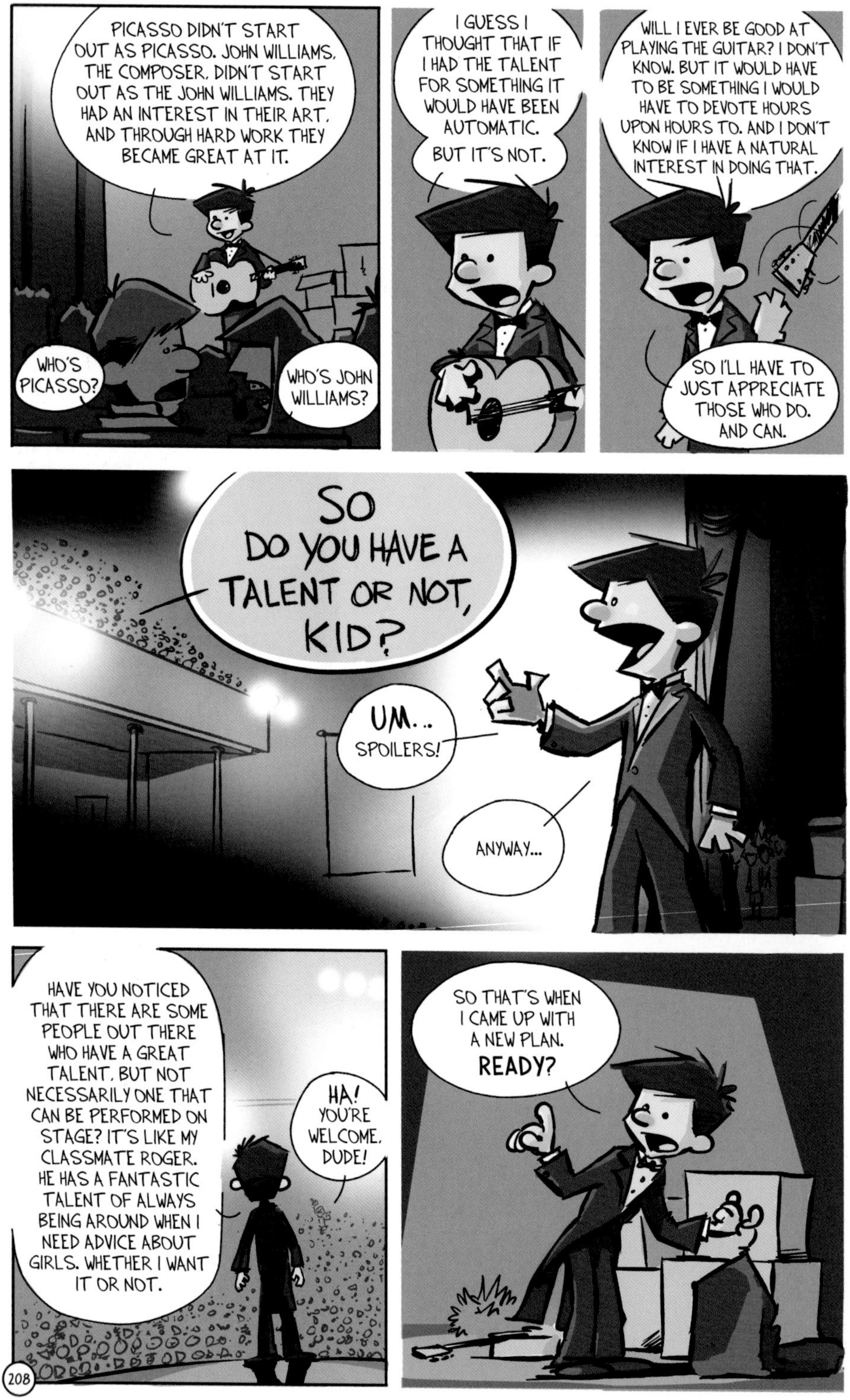
PICASSO DIDN'T START OUT AS PICASSO. JOHN WILLIAMS, THE COMPOSER, DIDN'T START OUT AS THE JOHN WILLIAMS. THEY HAD AN INTEREST IN THEIR ART, AND THROUGH HARD WORK THEY BECAME GREAT AT IT.
WHO'S PICASSO?
WHO'S JOHN WILLIAMS?
I GUESS I THOUGHT THAT IF I HAD THE TALENT FOR SOMETHING IT WOULD HAVE BEEN AUTOMATIC.
BUT IT'S NOT.
WILL I EVER BE GOOD AT PLAYING THE GUITAR? I DON'T KNOW. BUT IT WOULD HAVE TO BE SOMETHING I WOULD HAVE TO DEVOTE HOURS UPON HOURS TO. AND I DON'T KNOW IF I HAVE A NATURAL INTEREST IN DOING THAT.
SO I'LL HAVE TO JUST APPRECIATE THOSE WHO DO. AND CAN.
SO DO YOU HAVE A TALENT OR NOT, KID?
UM... SPOILERS!
ANYWAY...
HAVE YOU NOTICED THAT THERE ARE SOME PEOPLE OUT THERE WHO HAVE A GREAT TALENT, BUT NOT NECESSARILY ONE THAT CAN BE PERFORMED ON STAGE? IT'S LIKE MY CLASSMATE ROGER. HE HAS A FANTASTIC TALENT OF ALWAYS BEING AROUND WHEN I NEED ADVICE ABOUT GIRLS. WHETHER I WANT IT OR NOT.
HA! YOU'RE WELCOME, DUDE!
SO THAT'S WHEN I CAME UP WITH A NEW PLAN. READY?

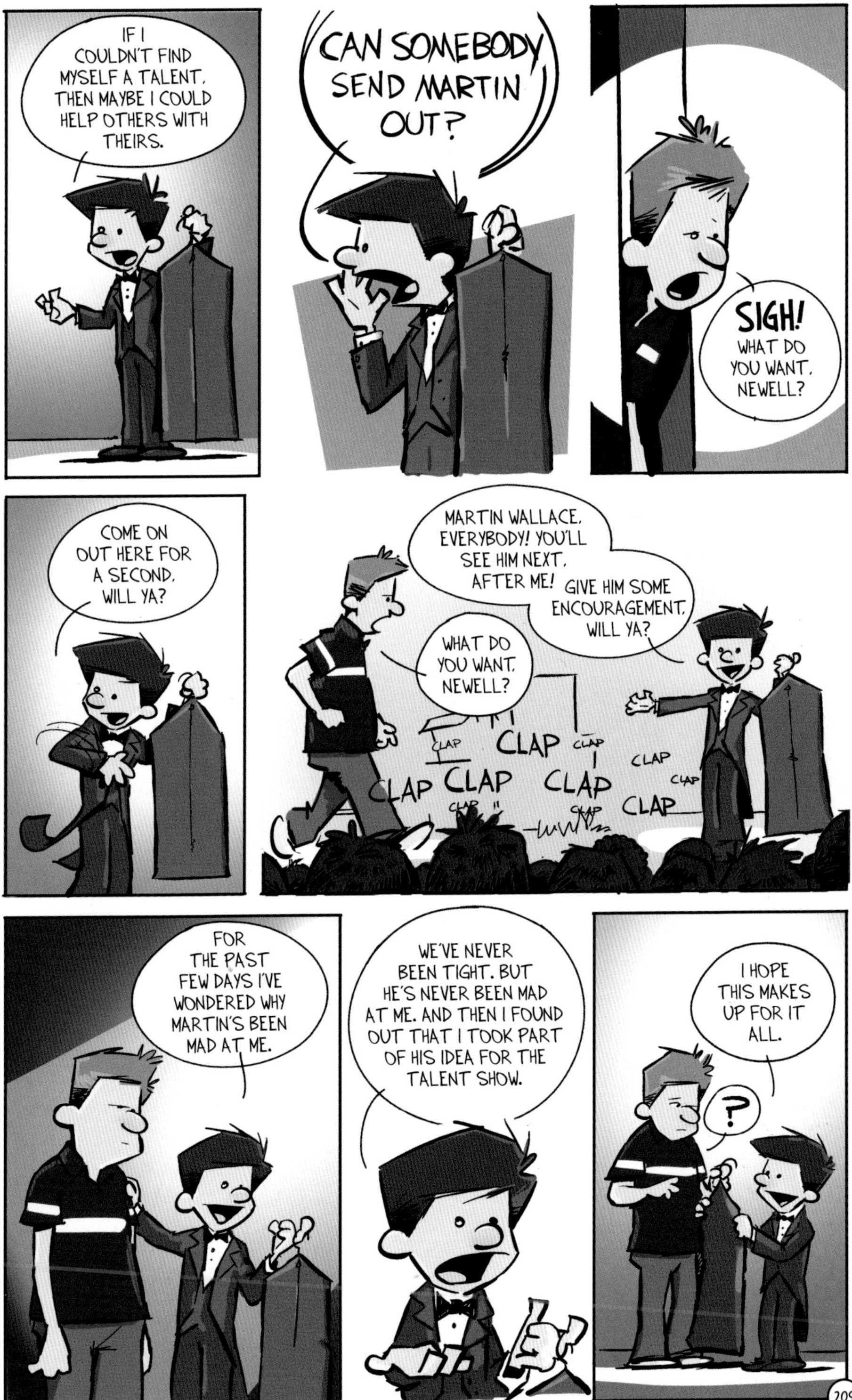
IF I COULDN'T FIND MYSELF A TALENT, THEN MAYBE I COULD HELP OTHERS WITH THEIRS.
CAN SOMEBODY SEND MARTIN OUT?
SIGH! WHAT DO YOU WANT, NEWELL?
COME ON OUT HERE FOR A SECOND, WILL YA?
MARTIN WALLACE, EVERYBODY! YOU'LL SEE HIM NEXT, AFTER ME!
GIVE HIM SOME ENCOURAGEMENT, WILL YA?
WHAT DO YOU WANT, NEWELL?
CLAP CLAP CLAP CLAP CLAP CLAP CLAP CLAP CLAP CLAP
FOR THE PAST FEW DAYS I'VE WONDERED WHY MARTIN'S BEEN MAD AT ME.
WE'VE NEVER BEEN TIGHT. BUT HE'S NEVER BEEN MAD AT ME. AND THEN I FOUND OUT THAT I TOOK PART OF HIS IDEA FOR THE TALENT SHOW.
I HOPE THIS MAKES UP FOR IT ALL.
?

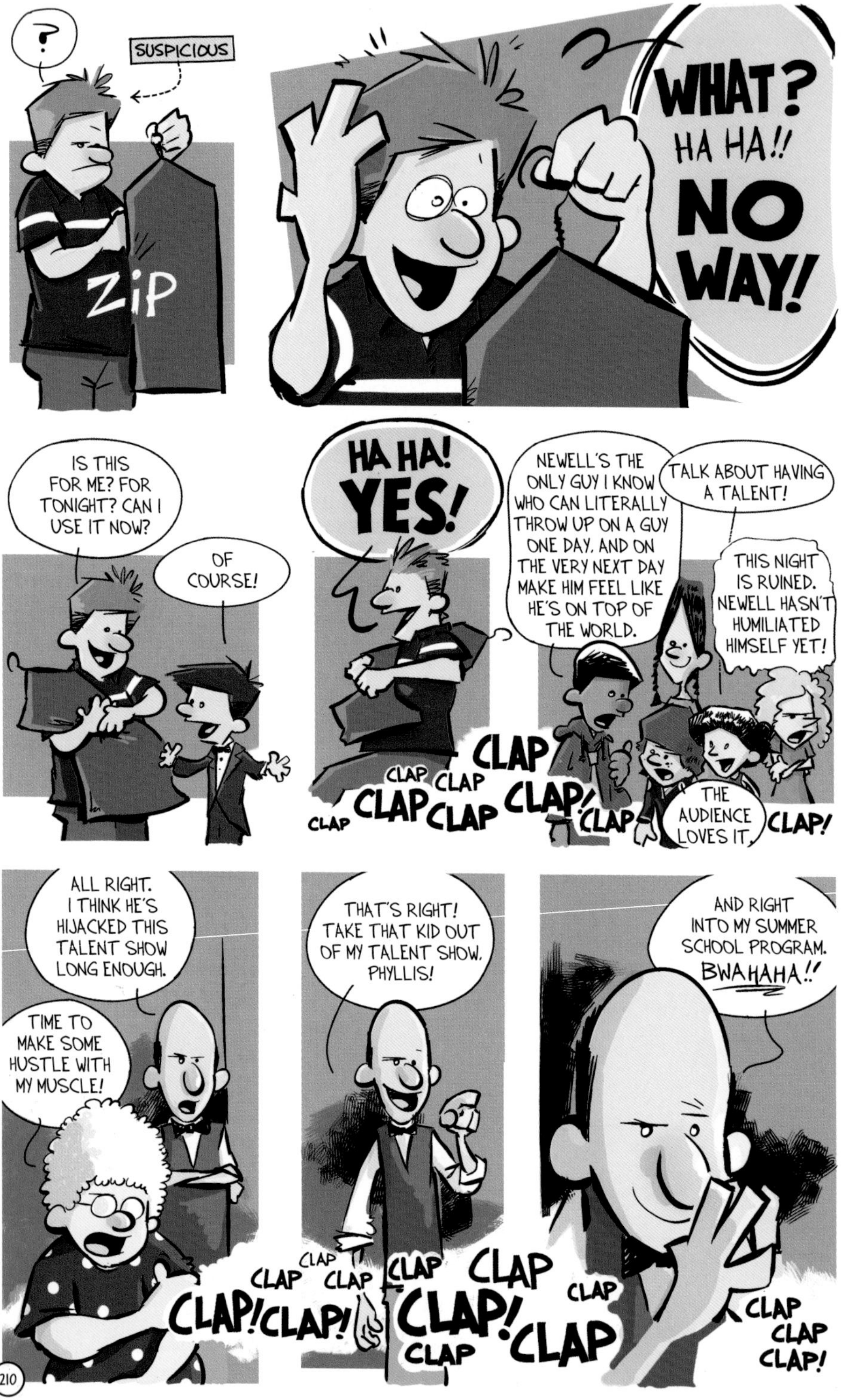
?
SUSPICIOUS
ZiP
WHAT? HA HA!! NO WAY!
IS THIS FOR ME? FOR TONIGHT? CAN I USE IT NOW?
OF COURSE!
HA HA! YES!
NEWELL'S THE ONLY GUY I KNOW WHO CAN LITERALLY THROW UP ON A GUY ONE DAY, AND ON THE VERY NEXT DAY MAKE HIM FEEL LIKE HE'S ON TOP OF THE WORLD.
TALK ABOUT HAVING A TALENT!
THIS NIGHT IS RUINED. NEWELL HASN'T HUMILIATED HIMSELF YET!
CLAP CLAP CLAP CLAP CLAP CLAP CLAP! CLAP
THE AUDIENCE LOVES IT.
CLAP!
ALL RIGHT. I THINK HE'S HIJACKED THIS TALENT SHOW LONG ENOUGH.
TIME TO MAKE SOME HUSTLE WITH MY MUSCLE!
THAT'S RIGHT! TAKE THAT KID OUT OF MY TALENT SHOW, PHYLLIS!
AND RIGHT INTO MY SUMMER SCHOOL PROGRAM. BWAHAHA!!
CLAP CLAP CLAP CLAP! CLAP! CLAP CLAP CLAP! CLAP CLAP CLAP CLAP CLAP CLAP CLAP!

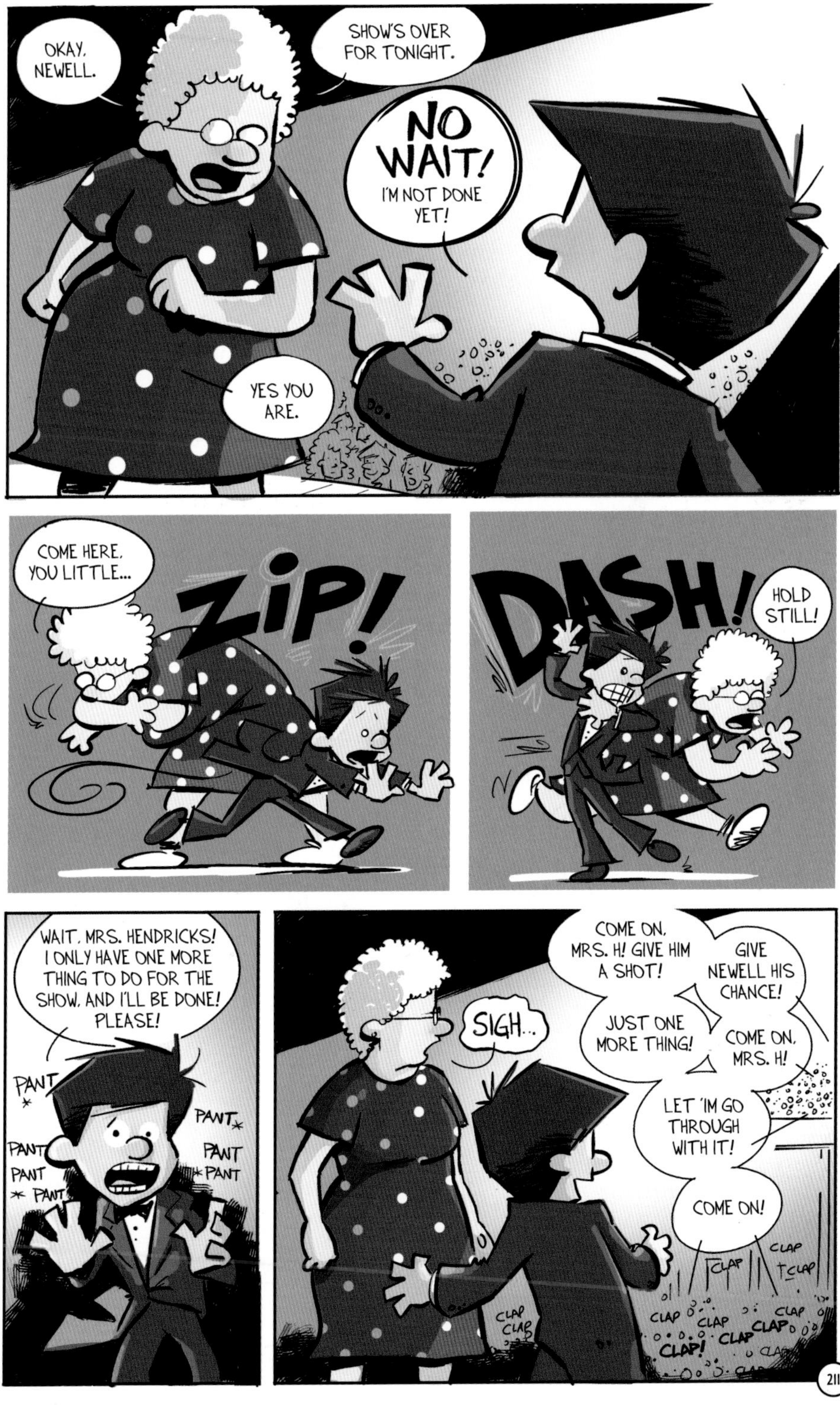
OKAY, NEWELL.
SHOW'S OVER FOR TONIGHT.
NO WAIT! I'M NOT DONE YET!
YES YOU ARE.
COME HERE, YOU LITTLE...
ZIP!
DASH!
HOLD STILL!
WAIT, MRS. HENDRICKS! I ONLY HAVE ONE MORE THING TO DO FOR THE SHOW, AND I'LL BE DONE! PLEASE!
PANT PANT PANT PANT PANT PANT PANT
SIGH...
COME ON, MRS. H! GIVE HIM A SHOT!
GIVE NEWELL HIS CHANCE!
JUST ONE MORE THING!
COME ON, MRS. H!
LET 'IM GO THROUGH WITH IT!
COME ON!
CLAP CLAP CLAP CLAP CLAP CLAP CLAP CLAP CLAP CLAP! CLAP

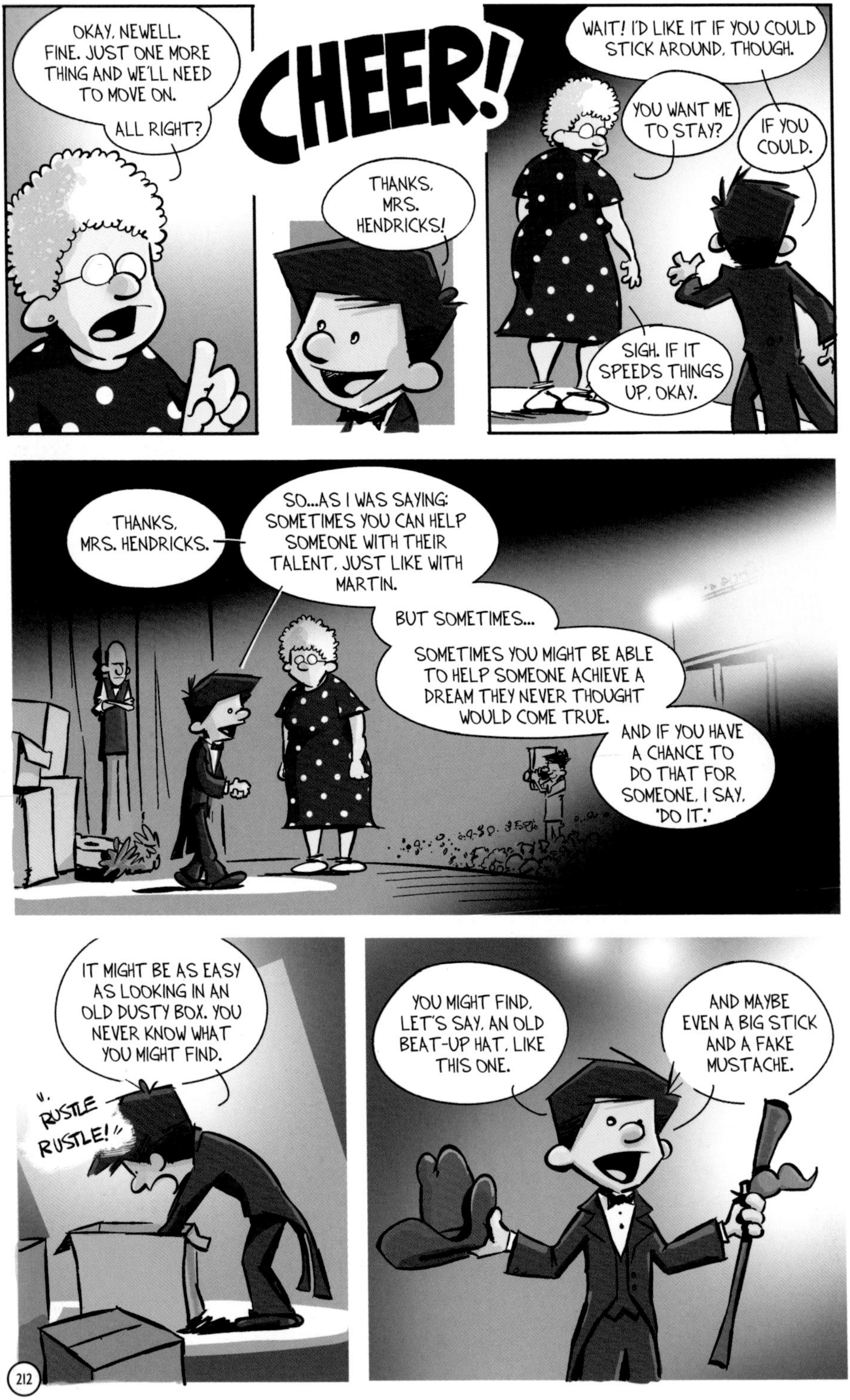
OKAY, NEWELL. FINE. JUST ONE MORE THING AND WE'LL NEED TO MOVE ON.
ALL RIGHT?
CHEER!
THANKS, MRS. HENDRICKS!
WAIT! I'D LIKE IT IF YOU COULD STICK AROUND, THOUGH.
YOU WANT ME TO STAY?
IF YOU COULD.
SIGH. IF IT SPEEDS THINGS UP, OKAY.
THANKS, MRS. HENDRICKS.
SO...AS I WAS SAYING: SOMETIMES YOU CAN HELP SOMEONE WITH THEIR TALENT, JUST LIKE WITH MARTIN.
BUT SOMETIMES...
SOMETIMES YOU MIGHT BE ABLE TO HELP SOMEONE ACHIEVE A DREAM THEY NEVER THOUGHT WOULD COME TRUE.
AND IF YOU HAVE A CHANCE TO DO THAT FOR SOMEONE, I SAY, "DO IT."
IT MIGHT BE AS EASY AS LOOKING IN AN OLD DUSTY BOX. YOU NEVER KNOW WHAT YOU MIGHT FIND.
RUSTLE RUSTLE!
YOU MIGHT FIND, LET'S SAY, AN OLD BEAT-UP HAT, LIKE THIS ONE.
AND MAYBE EVEN A BIG STICK AND A FAKE MUSTACHE.

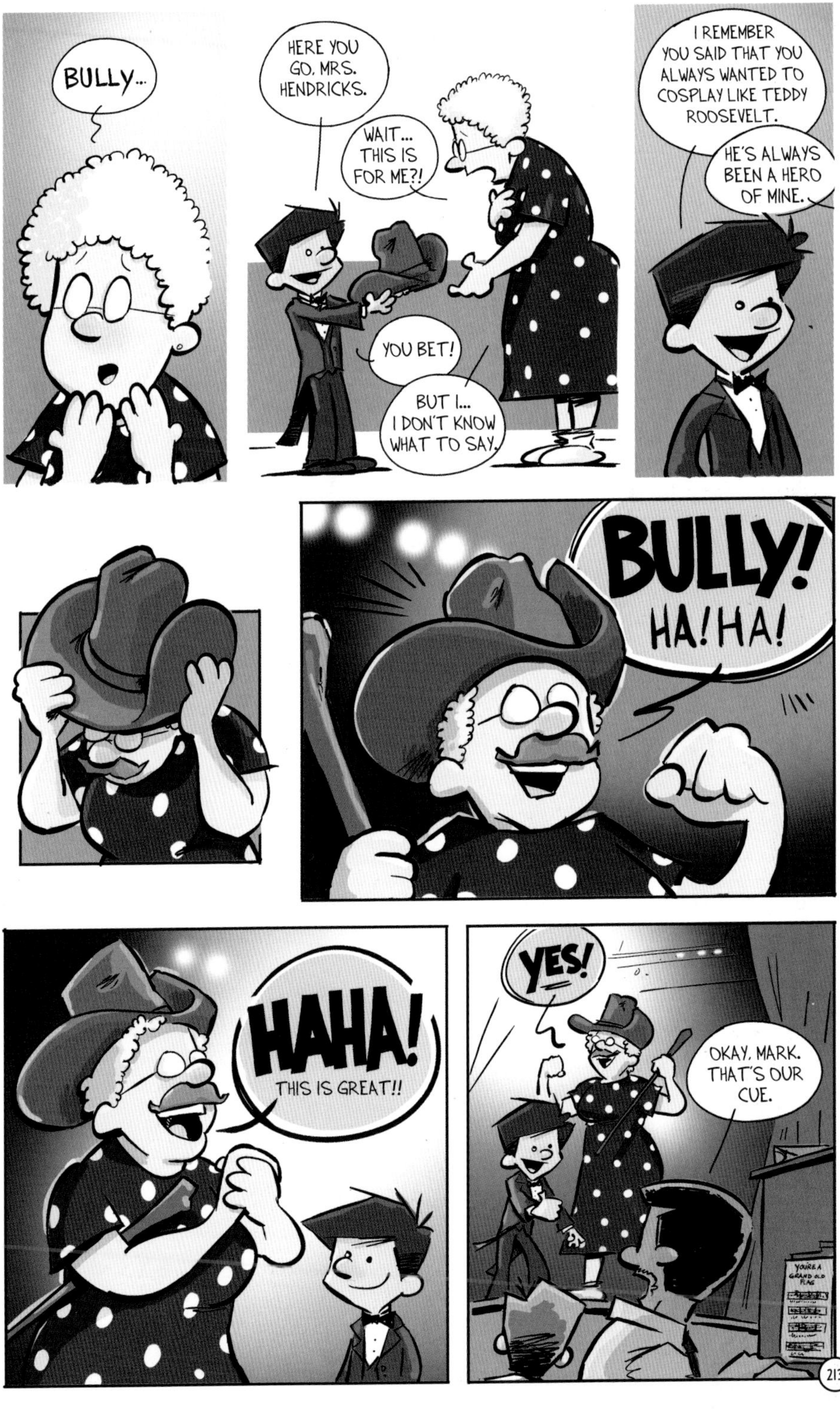
BULLY...
HERE YOU GO, MRS. HENDRICKS.
WAIT... THIS IS FOR ME?!
YOU BET!
BUT I... I DON'T KNOW WHAT TO SAY.
I REMEMBER YOU SAID THAT YOU ALWAYS WANTED TO COSPLAY LIKE TEDDY ROOSEVELT.
HE'S ALWAYS BEEN A HERO OF MINE.
BULLY! HA! HA!
HAHA! THIS IS GREAT!!
YES!
OKAY, MARK. THAT'S OUR CUE.
YOU'RE A GRAND OLD FLAG

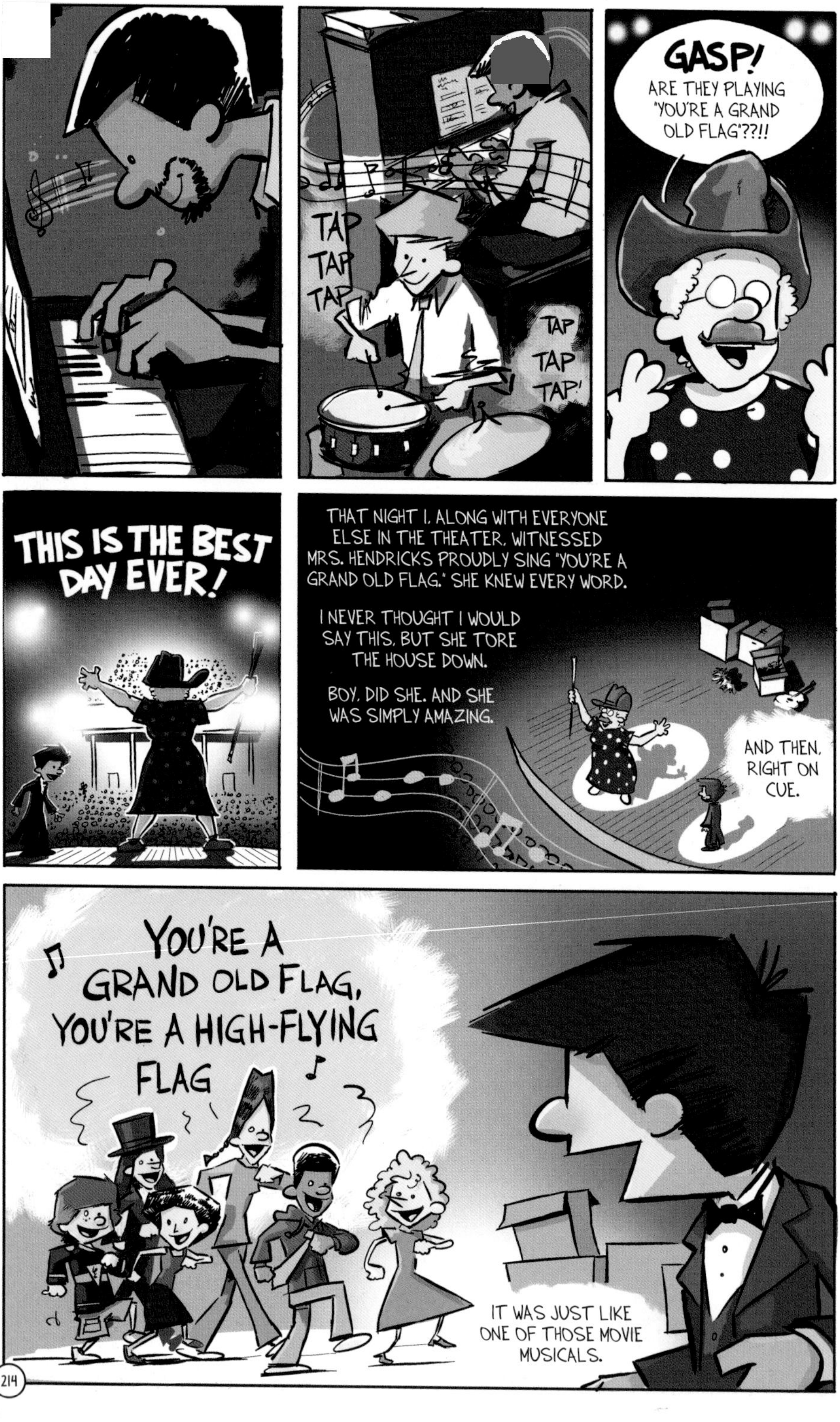
TAP
TAP
TAP
TAP
TAP
TAP!
GASP!
ARE THEY PLAYING "YOU'RE A GRAND OLD FLAG"??!!
THIS IS THE BEST DAY EVER!
THAT NIGHT I, ALONG WITH EVERYONE ELSE IN THE THEATER, WITNESSED MRS. HENDRICKS PROUDLY SING "YOU'RE A GRAND OLD FLAG." SHE KNEW EVERY WORD.
I NEVER THOUGHT I WOULD SAY THIS, BUT SHE TORE THE HOUSE DOWN.
BOY, DID SHE. AND SHE WAS SIMPLY AMAZING.
AND THEN, RIGHT ON CUE.
YOU'RE A GRAND OLD FLAG, YOU'RE A HIGH-FLYING FLAG
IT WAS JUST LIKE ONE OF THOSE MOVIE MUSICALS.

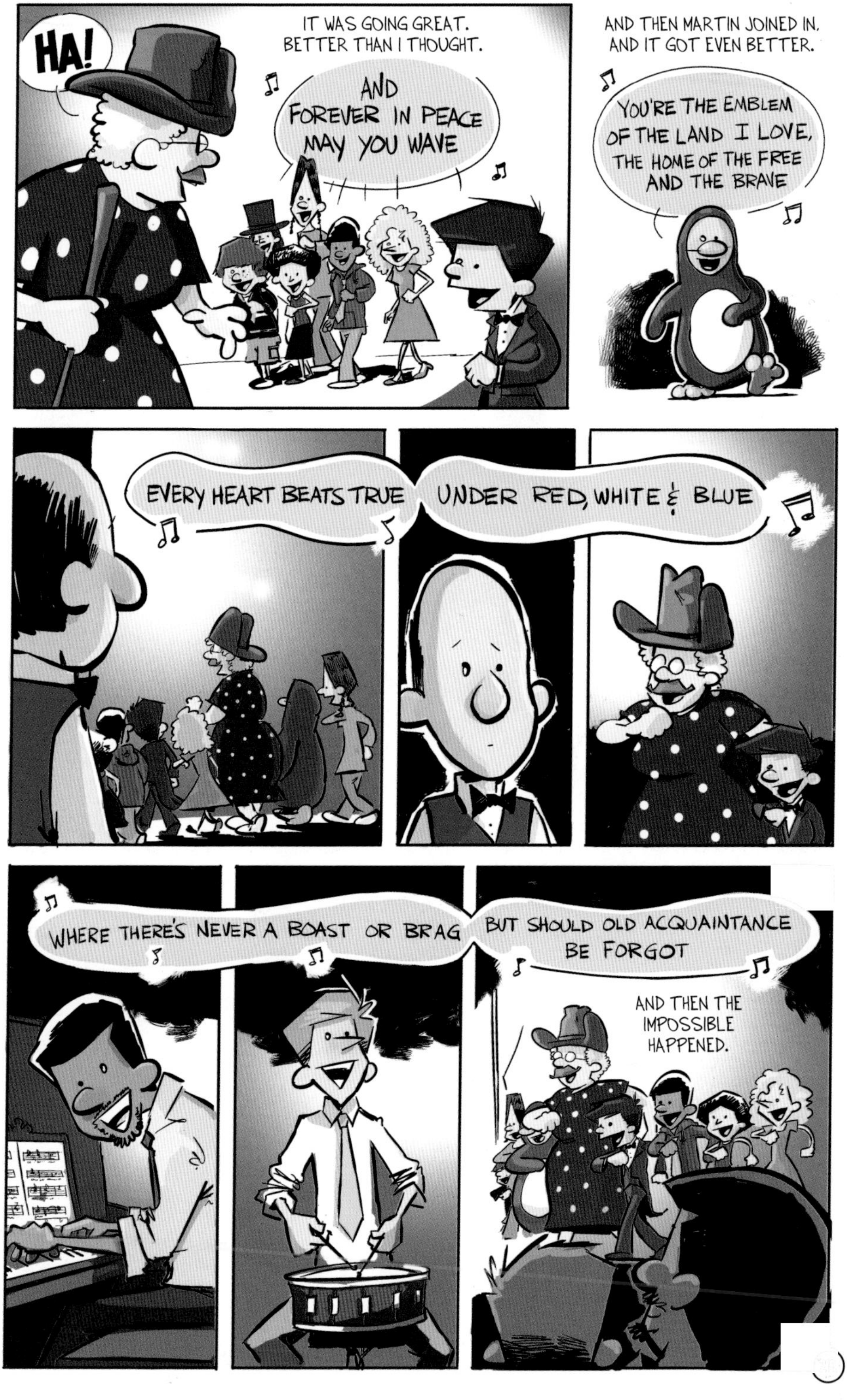
HA!
IT WAS GOING GREAT. BETTER THAN I THOUGHT.
AND FOREVER IN PEACE MAY YOU WAVE
AND THEN MARTIN JOINED IN, AND IT GOT EVEN BETTER.
YOU'RE THE EMBLEM OF THE LAND I LOVE, THE HOME OF THE FREE AND THE BRAVE
EVERY HEART BEATS TRUE
UNDER RED, WHITE & BLUE
WHERE THERE'S NEVER A BOAST OR BRAG
BUT SHOULD OLD ACQUAINTANCE BE FORGOT
AND THEN THE IMPOSSIBLE HAPPENED.

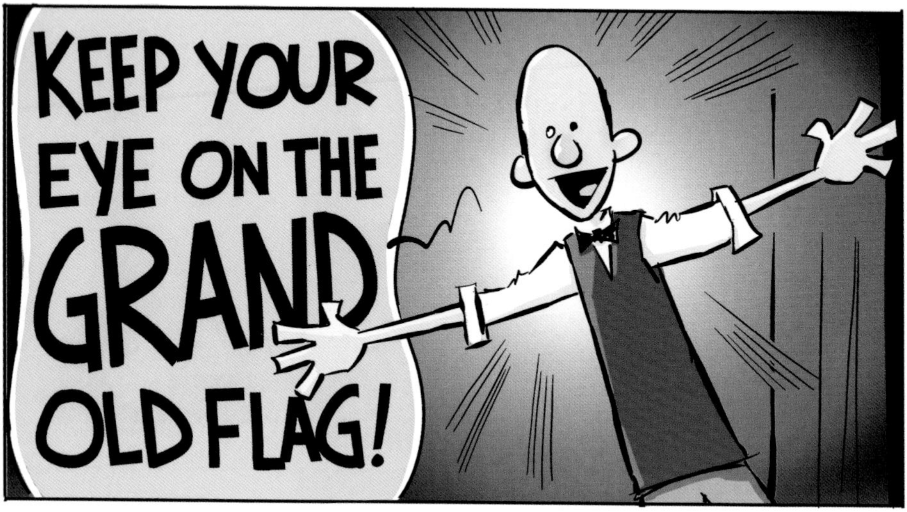
KEEP YOUR EYE ON THE GRAND OLD FLAG!

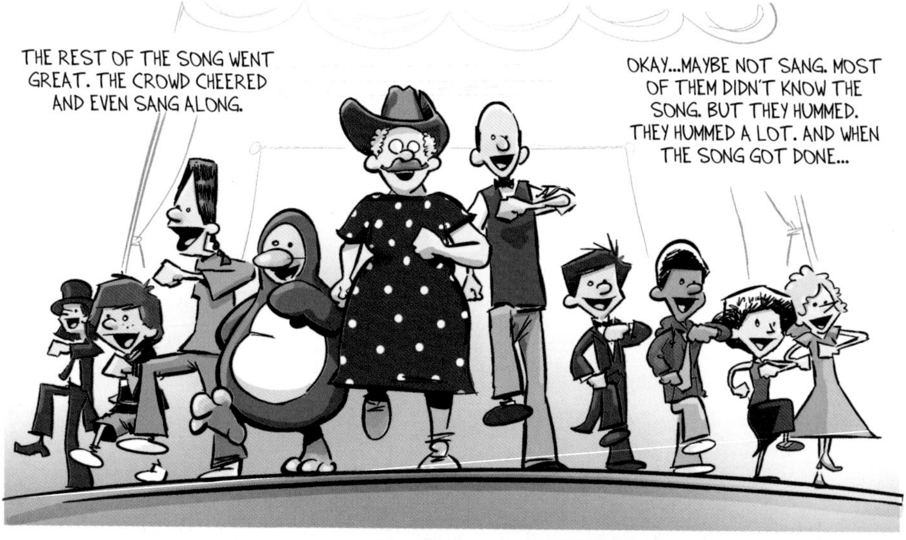
THE REST OF THE SONG WENT GREAT. THE CROWD CHEERED AND EVEN SANG ALONG.
OKAY...MAYBE NOT SANG. MOST OF THEM DIDN'T KNOW THE SONG. BUT THEY HUMMED. THEY HUMMED A LOT. AND WHEN THE SONG GOT DONE...

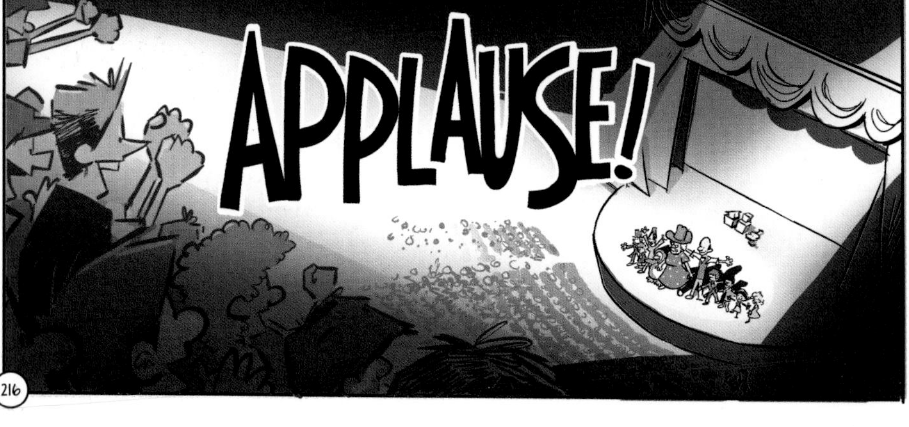
APPLAUSE!

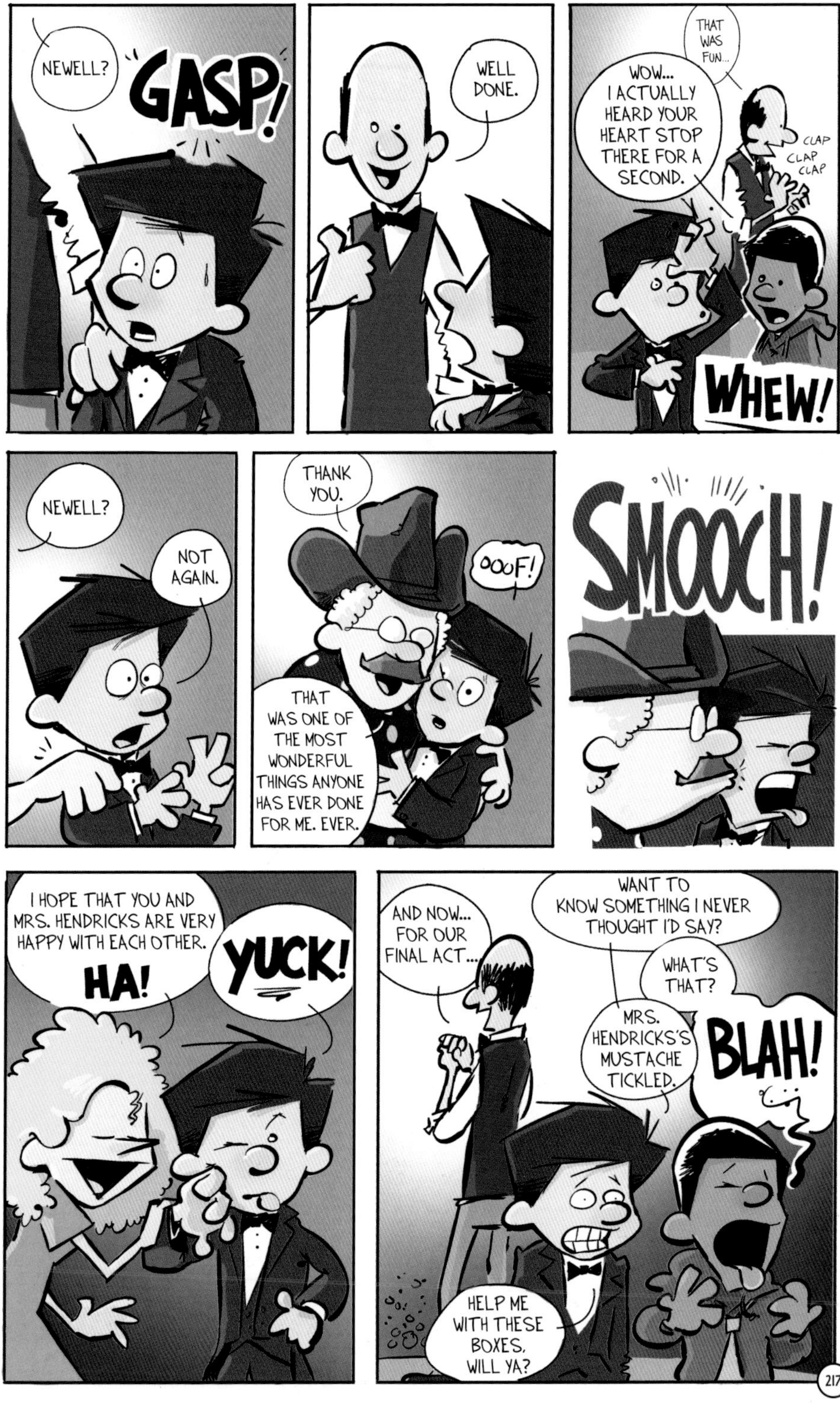
NEWELL?
GASP!
WELL DONE.
THAT WAS FUN...
WOW... I ACTUALLY HEARD YOUR HEART STOP THERE FOR A SECOND.
CLAP CLAP CLAP
WHEW!
NEWELL?
NOT AGAIN.
THANK YOU.
OOOF!
THAT WAS ONE OF THE MOST WONDERFUL THINGS ANYONE HAS EVER DONE FOR ME. EVER.
SMOOCH!
I HOPE THAT YOU AND MRS. HENDRICKS ARE VERY HAPPY WITH EACH OTHER.
HA!
YUCK!
AND NOW... FOR OUR FINAL ACT...
WANT TO KNOW SOMETHING I NEVER THOUGHT I'D SAY?
WHAT'S THAT?
MRS. HENDRICKS'S MUSTACHE TICKLED.
BLAH!
HELP ME WITH THESE BOXES, WILL YA?

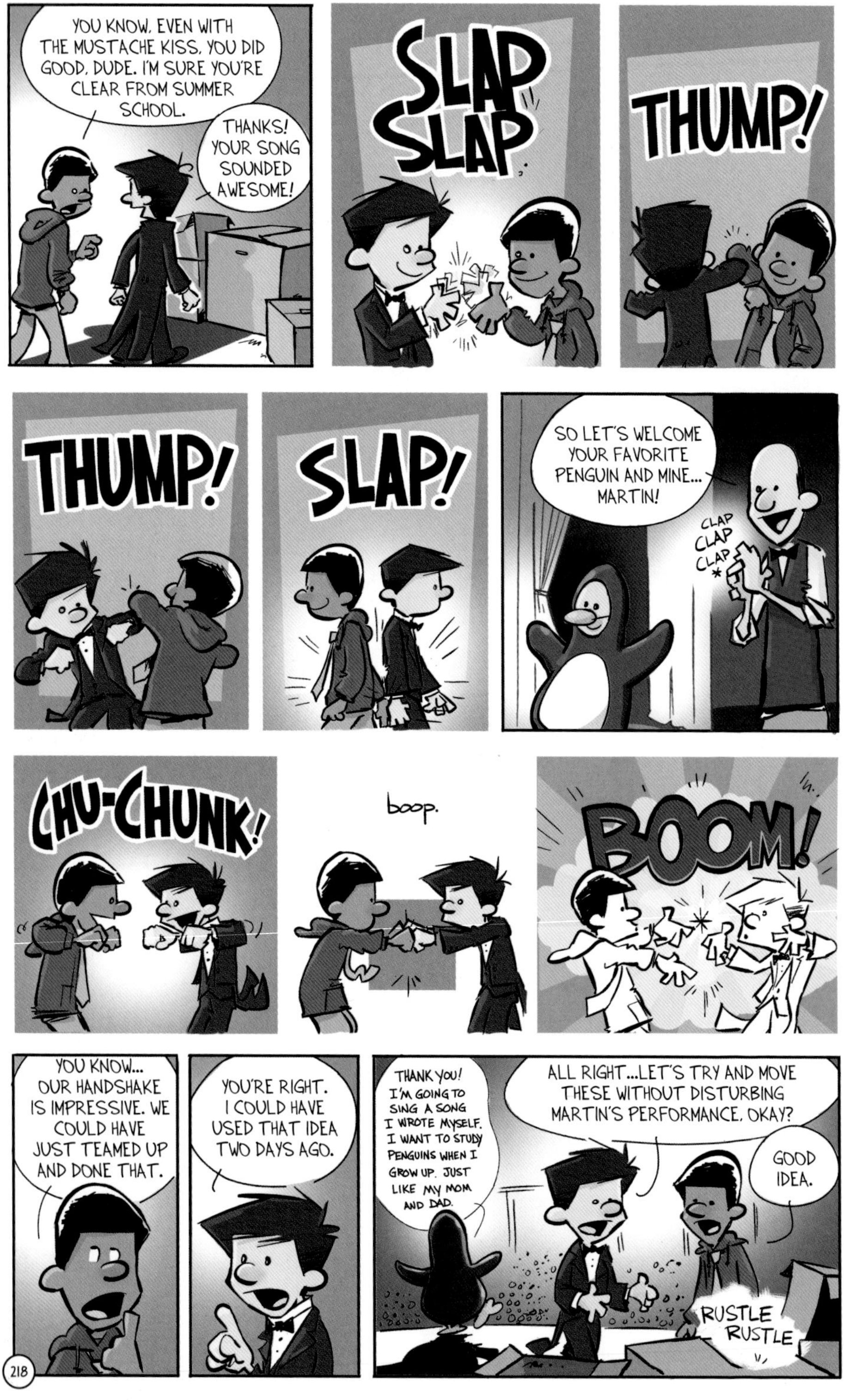
YOU KNOW, EVEN WITH THE MUSTACHE KISS, YOU DID GOOD, DUDE. I'M SURE YOU'RE CLEAR FROM SUMMER SCHOOL.
THANKS! YOUR SONG SOUNDED AWESOME!
SLAP SLAP
THUMP!
THUMP!
SLAP!
SO LET'S WELCOME YOUR FAVORITE PENGUIN AND MINE... MARTIN!
CLAP CLAP CLAP
CHU-CHUNK!
boop.
BOOM!
YOU KNOW... OUR HANDSHAKE IS IMPRESSIVE. WE COULD HAVE JUST TEAMED UP AND DONE THAT.
YOU'RE RIGHT. I COULD HAVE USED THAT IDEA TWO DAYS AGO.
THANK YOU! I'M GOING TO SING A SONG I WROTE MYSELF. I WANT TO STUDY PENGUINS WHEN I GROW UP. JUST LIKE MY MOM AND DAD.
ALL RIGHT...LET'S TRY AND MOVE THESE WITHOUT DISTURBING MARTIN'S PERFORMANCE, OKAY?
GOOD IDEA.
RUSTLE RUSTLE

RUSTLE
RUSTLE

POP!

AAARGH!

ZING!

NOT AGAIN!!

EVERYTHING WAS GOING IN SLOW MOTION.

BECAUSE PENGUINS ARE COOL ♪ PENGUINS ARE FINE ♫

OH NO...

DONK!

DINK!

TINK!

I KNEW WHAT WAS GOING TO HAPPEN.

BUT I FELT POWERLESS TO STOP IT.

MARTIN! NOOO!

GASP!

AAAAA AAAA AAAA AAAAAAAA AAAA

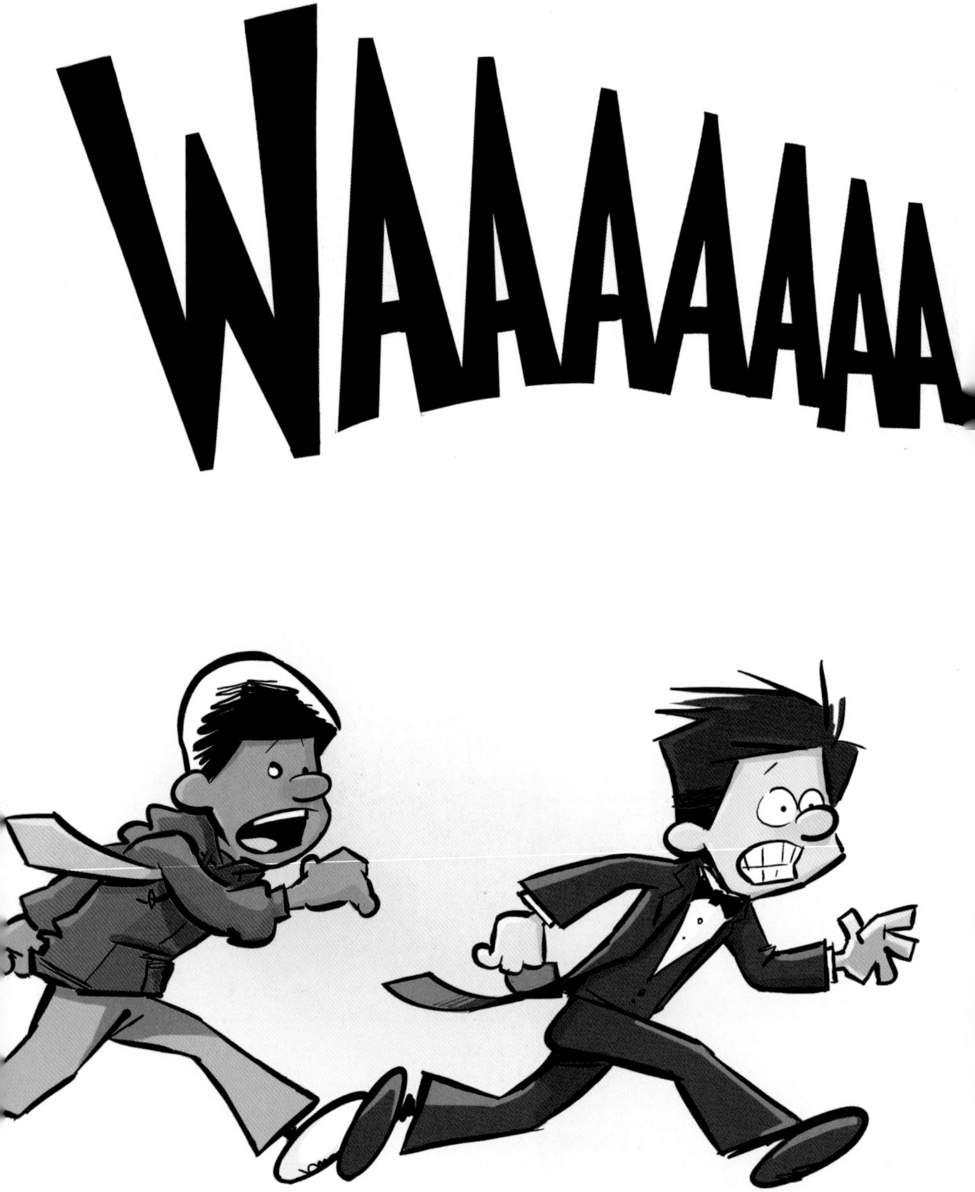
WAAAAAAA

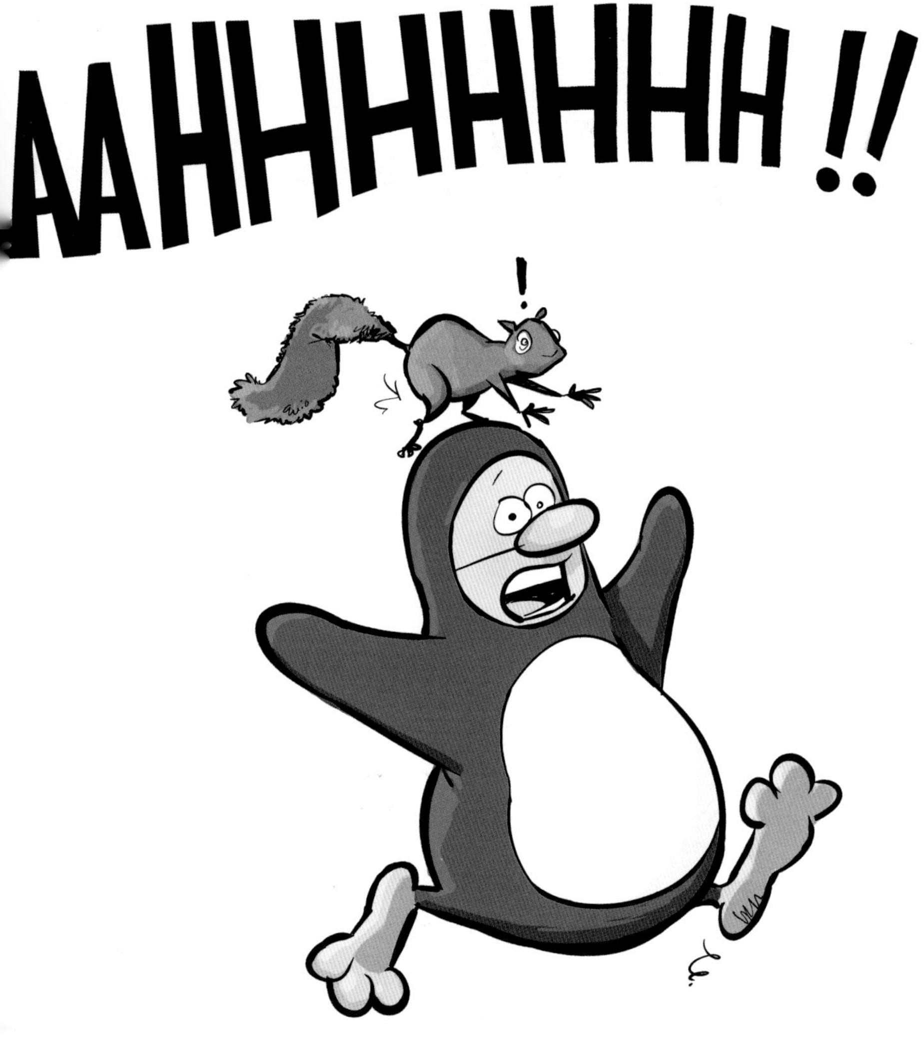
AAHHHHHHH!!
!

EPILOGUE

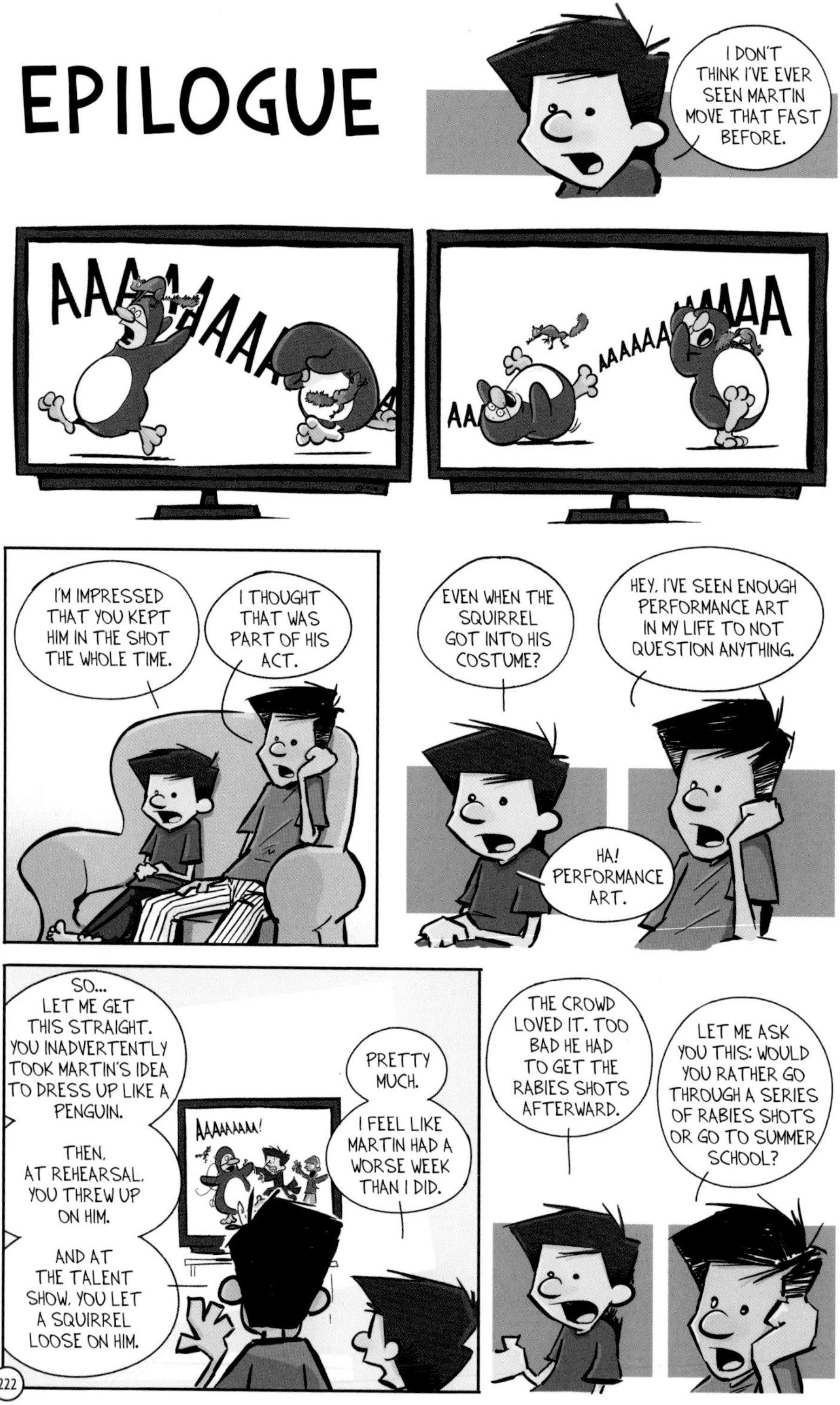

I DON'T THINK I'VE EVER SEEN MARTIN MOVE THAT FAST BEFORE.
AAAAAAAAA
AAAAAAAAAAAA
I'M IMPRESSED THAT YOU KEPT HIM IN THE SHOT THE WHOLE TIME.
I THOUGHT THAT WAS PART OF HIS ACT.
EVEN WHEN THE SQUIRREL GOT INTO HIS COSTUME?
HEY, I'VE SEEN ENOUGH PERFORMANCE ART IN MY LIFE TO NOT QUESTION ANYTHING.
HA! PERFORMANCE ART.
SO... LET ME GET THIS STRAIGHT. YOU INADVERTENTLY TOOK MARTIN'S IDEA TO DRESS UP LIKE A PENGUIN.
THEN, AT REHEARSAL, YOU THREW UP ON HIM.
AND AT THE TALENT SHOW, YOU LET A SQUIRREL LOOSE ON HIM.
AAAAAAAA!
PRETTY MUCH.
I FEEL LIKE MARTIN HAD A WORSE WEEK THAN I DID.
THE CROWD LOVED IT. TOO BAD HE HAD TO GET THE RABIES SHOTS AFTERWARD.
LET ME ASK YOU THIS: WOULD YOU RATHER GO THROUGH A SERIES OF RABIES SHOTS OR GO TO SUMMER SCHOOL?

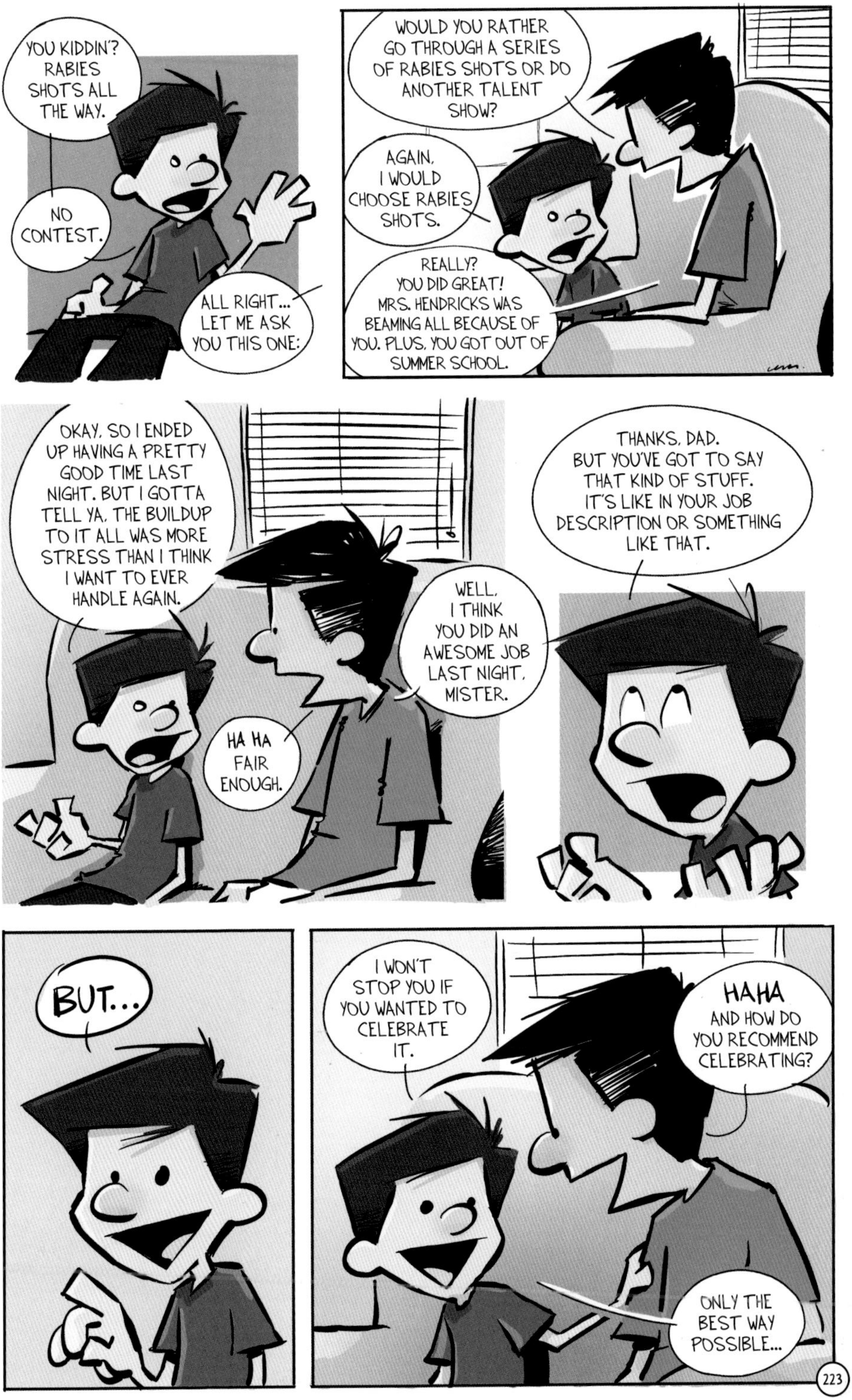
YOU KIDDIN'? RABIES SHOTS ALL THE WAY.
NO CONTEST.
ALL RIGHT... LET ME ASK YOU THIS ONE:
WOULD YOU RATHER GO THROUGH A SERIES OF RABIES SHOTS OR DO ANOTHER TALENT SHOW?
AGAIN, I WOULD CHOOSE RABIES SHOTS.
REALLY? YOU DID GREAT! MRS. HENDRICKS WAS BEAMING ALL BECAUSE OF YOU. PLUS, YOU GOT OUT OF SUMMER SCHOOL.
OKAY, SO I ENDED UP HAVING A PRETTY GOOD TIME LAST NIGHT. BUT I GOTTA TELL YA, THE BUILDUP TO IT ALL WAS MORE STRESS THAN I THINK I WANT TO EVER HANDLE AGAIN.
HA HA FAIR ENOUGH.
WELL, I THINK YOU DID AN AWESOME JOB LAST NIGHT, MISTER.
THANKS, DAD. BUT YOU'VE GOT TO SAY THAT KIND OF STUFF. IT'S LIKE IN YOUR JOB DESCRIPTION OR SOMETHING LIKE THAT.
BUT...
I WON'T STOP YOU IF YOU WANTED TO CELEBRATE IT.
HAHA AND HOW DO YOU RECOMMEND CELEBRATING?
ONLY THE BEST WAY POSSIBLE...

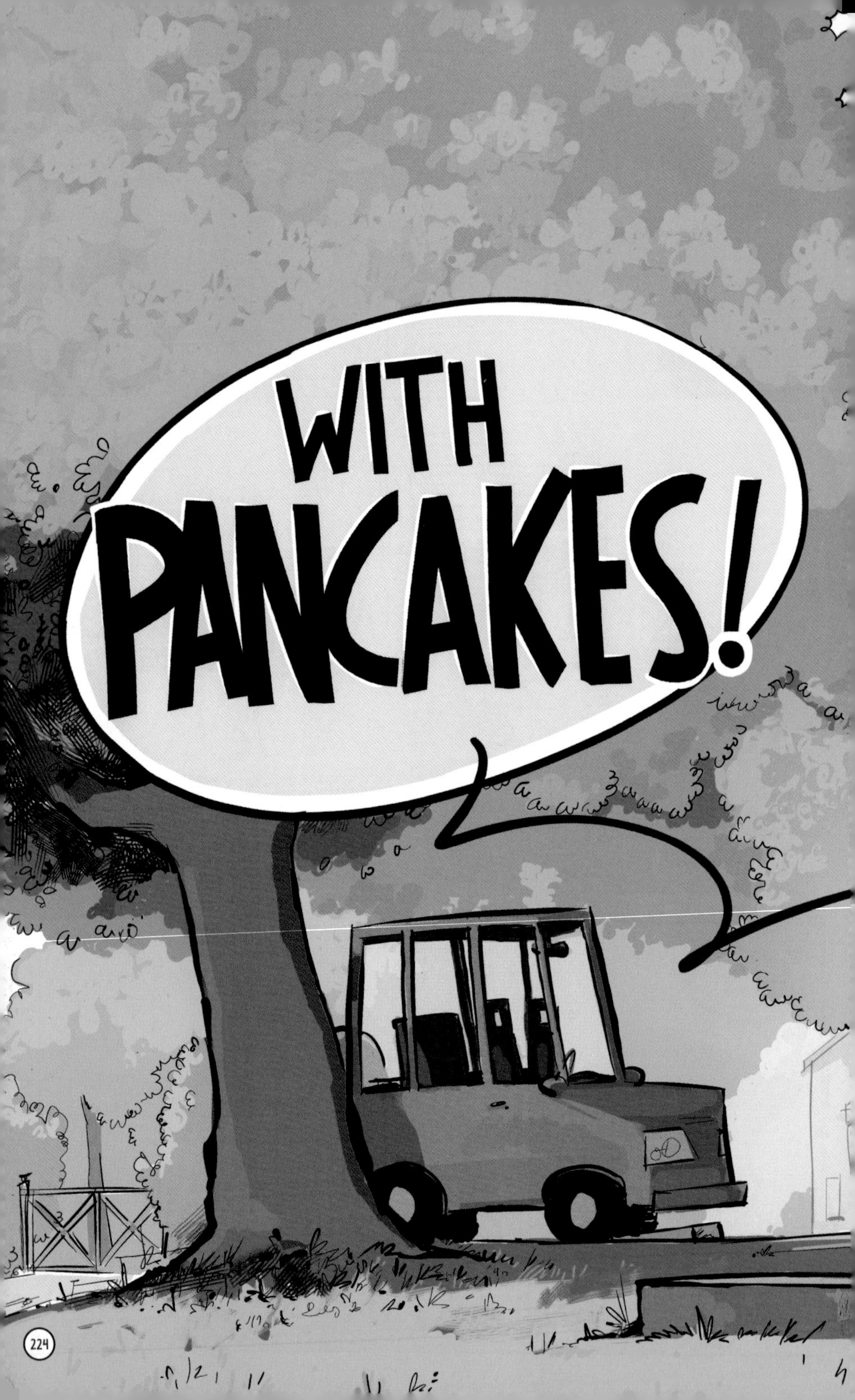
WITH PANCAKES!

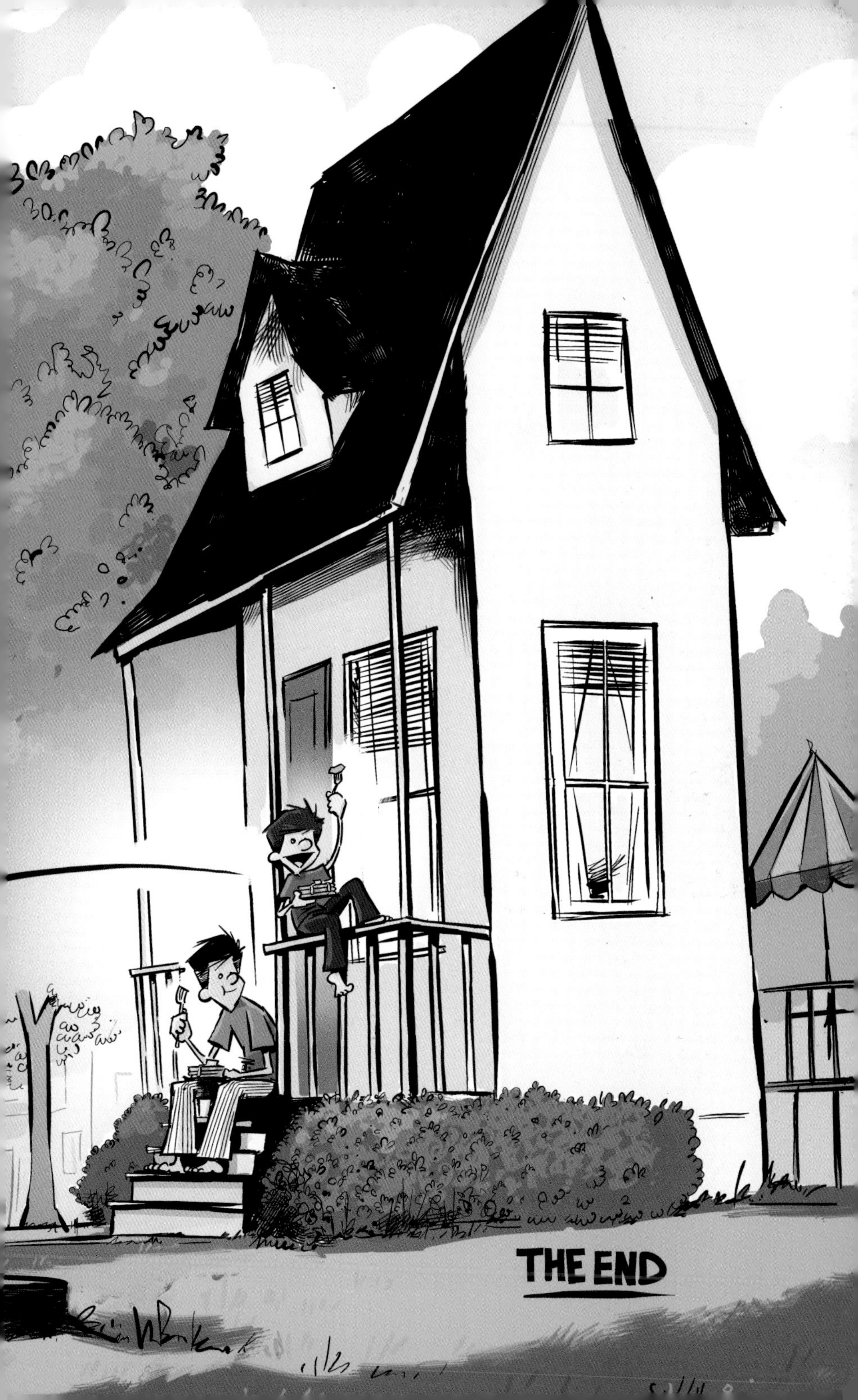
THE END

ACKNOWLEDGMENTS

* * *

I WILL ALWAYS BE GRATEFUL FOR THE THREE MAIN PEOPLE IN MY LIFE—WITHOUT THEM, THIS BOOK WOULD NOT BE POSSIBLE. THEIR LOVE, BELIEF, AND SACRIFICES DON'T GO UNNOTICED. MY MOM, KATHRYN, WHO WANTED TO LEARN HOW TO DRAW HERSELF, ALWAYS MADE SURE THAT I HAD PENCILS AND PAPER TO PRACTICE MY CARTOONING. MY WIFE, ERIN, WHO NEVER STOPPED BELIEVING IN ME, AND WHO SLEPT MANY NIGHTS ON THE COUCH NEAR MY STUDIO DESK WHILE I WORKED. AND, OF COURSE, TO MY SON, WYETH. THIS BOOK IS BUILT ON THE ADVENTURES, LOVE, AND LAUGHTER THAT HE AND I HAVE SHARED TOGETHER. BEING HIS DAD IS THE BEST PART OF WHO I AM. I'M A LUCKY MAN TO HAVE THESE THREE IN MY LIFE. THANK YOU.

THANKS TO ALL THE WONDERFUL PEOPLE AT LITTLE, BROWN BOOKS FOR YOUNG READERS WHO HELPED SHAPE THIS GRAPHIC NOVEL, ESPECIALLY TO MY TALENTED EDITOR, AND REALLY GREAT GUY, RUSS BUSSE. AND THANKS TO MY DESIGNER, CHRISTINA QUINTERO, WHO ORGANIZED ALL MY PAGES.

A BIG THANK YOU TO BOTH JODELL SADLER AND JILL CORCORAN. YOUR ENTHUSIASM FOR THIS STORY HELPED ME MORE THAN YOU KNOW. YOU'RE THE BEST AGENTS I COULD HAVE ASKED FOR.

AND, OF COURSE, TO ALL THE FANS OF MY WEBCOMIC, *MISTER & ME*. YOUR DEDICATION TO NEWELL AND HIS DAD HELPED THEM GET HERE. THANK YOU FOR ALL THE LAUGHS.

JASON PLATT IS A PROFESSIONAL CARTOONIST
AND MEMBER OF THE NATIONAL CARTOONISTS SOCIETY.
WHILE BORN IN THE MIDWEST, HE GREW UP IN DURHAM,
NORTH CAROLINA, AND LATER GRADUATED WITH
HONORS FROM THE SAVANNAH COLLEGE OF ART AND
DESIGN, IN SAVANNAH, GEORGIA. IN HIS FREE TIME,
JASON CAN BE FOUND PERFORMING OR WRITING FOR
THE THEATER. JASON LIVES IN DAVENPORT, IOWA,
WITH HIS WIFE, SON, AND CAT.